APOLLO

The Man Who
Loved Children

Christina Stead

△

APOLLO

Apollo Librarian | Michael Schmidt || Series Editor | Neil Belton
Text Design | Lindsay Nash || Artwork | Jessie Price

www.apollo-classics.com | www.headofzeus.com

First published in the United States of America in 1940 by Simon
& Schuster.

This paperback edition published in the United Kingdom in 2016
by Apollo, an imprint of Head of Zeus Ltd.

1 3 5 7 9 10 8 6 4 2

A CIP catalogue record for this book is available
from the British Library.

ISBN (PB) 9781784971489
      (E) 9781784971700

Typeset by Adrian McLaughlin
Printed and bound in Denmark by Nørhaven

Head of Zeus Ltd
Clerkenwell House
45–47 Clerkenwell Green
London EC1R 0HT

Introduction

Life can be cruel for a plain child. Christina Stead's Louie is plain. She is smart, too. So much the worse for her. And there are five younger half-siblings by her father's second wife, Henny, a stepmother who loathes her. Samuel Clemens Pollit, her father, the man who loves children, can't quite love her. He makes use of her, however, and her threadbare, joyless life is almost unbearable. Formed and warped by circumstance, Louie understands life without a jot of sentimentality. She learns to see her world by hearing it, its many self-disclosing, self-deceiving voices, her father's in particular.

There are few books in which the distance between what people say and intend on the one hand, and the reality they inhabit on the other, is so extreme. The result is high comedy in the language and potential tragedy in the plot. *The Man Who Loved Children* is, in part, about the paralysis that afflicts people who insistently express themselves in hyperboles. As the Pollits' circumstances deteriorate, their hyperboles increase in scale and frequency, until in their own eyes all of them (Louie excepted) become epic figures, fatally trammeled in self regard and self pity. Once disproportion sets in, nothing can restore a natural, rational and loving balance. Social existence becomes a matter of scoring and keeping score. In the tide of mounting grievances, the only way Louie can survive is by flight. 'They would look everywhere and conclude that she had gone for a walk. "So I have," she thought, smiling secretly. "I have gone for a walk round the world."'

In Louie, Christina Stead revisited her own childhood, though she transported it ('as if it were an emulsion or a streak of mist') from Australia, where she was born and lived until she was in her mid-twenties, to Washington and the Chesapeake, which she did not get to know until the 1930s. Like Louie she was a voracious reader: she deflected unhappiness by means of fiction. When the time came to write her own stories, she knew how to bring voices into the revealing cacophony of the Pollit family. *The Man Who Loved Children* is an exact revenge, hilarious and harrowing. Truth is a harsh judge. No formal verdict is required once the story brings the facts to life. Stead's portrait of the artist as a young woman is every bit as compelling as Joyce's male, Irish Stephen Dedalus, and every bit as readable as that other Samuel Clemens's Huckleberry Finn.

Christina Stead (1902–1983), among the first internationally acclaimed Australian writers, published *The Man Who Loved Children* in 1940. The timing was poor. The Second World War blunted the book's immediate reception and effect, though, in fact, it draws into its prophetic wake many of the political and ethical tensions that led to the war, and some issues – including environmental concerns and child abuse – which have an insistently contemporary resonance. The American poet Randall Jarrell re-introduced the novel to American readers a quarter of a century after it was first published. Again, the timing was poor: the United States was sliding into another set of crises and there was something remote about the Pollits, their Washington, and the rural realm in which they endured their exile from it. Again the book bobbed triumphantly to the surface, again it disappeared beneath the waves.

The Man Who Loved Children is the kind of book to which no moment will ever be entirely propitious: what it says and does are deliberately discomforting. The characters and circumstances it creates are timeless. In short, it is a classic that demands to be taken on its own terms. Doris Lessing identified Stead's 'most special gift: there has never been a writer who can take you so strongly into a room, or a house, or a street that you are immediately a part of it'. She takes us, with precision and ease, into a sunlit garden, a stale bedroom, a rabbit hutch, the intimate midnight of a resourceless and furious woman, the unreflecting optimism of an ineffectual pater familias, and the anguished life of a teenage girl. *The Man Who Loved Children* is 'a great novel, one that is always being rediscovered and then for some reason slips away out of sight, and then is found again.'

Samuel Clemens Pollit is an Emersonian idealist and a naturalist so detached from social reality that he is comic and monstrous in equal degrees. He cannot understand why he infuriates Henny, the second Mrs Pollit. In response to her husband's excess of character, she develops her own aggravated excesses and becomes almost sympathetic, a crusty snob unable to handle money or disappointment. When these characters reach a momentary reconciliation, after weeks of attrition culminating in violence, their make-up sex is intense and fruitful. The crop of children is clear proof of that.

The adults resemble Stead's father and step-mother, whose lives were similarly unstable and unhappy. Stead's lost world of *The Man Who Loved Children* is real without nostalgia: the author did not go back for pleasure. The world re-imagined is, however, palpably real, even if its reality, so beautifully achieved, holds no appeal for her. Had Stead set the novel in Sydney and its environs where her childhood actually took place, as she originally intended, it would have been hard to separate the story from the wounding particulars of her own life, the psychological abuse she suffered. The art of fiction is a way of telling common truths by means of particular incidents, and it may require fundamental adjustments in order to free the writer to recreate what has been survived.

And the publisher's editor can have a say. Stead's American editor insisted the book, her fifth of fifteen novels, should be relocated and set in the United States. The editor's considerations were commercial: American readers might have been distracted from the main themes by the exotic peculiarities of the Australian landscape. The translation of her book into an American story was a tall order. There was no precedent that she could build on. The altered setting had many artistic consequences. The American environment makes its political resonance stronger. Stead's Marxist politics, while not preached in this book, clearly inform her sense of a corrupt and self-serving establishment and of a system which wastes genuine talent as it pursues short-term ends.

The fact that the setting was not second nature to Stead meant that her powers of invention were continuously engaged. The world she creates is real, whatever its factual shortcomings. Family, not American life, is her subject; the treachery and cruelty of sentimentalism her theme. Her first novel, *Seven Poor Men of Sydney* (1934), had taught her how characters can be made to embody key, socially formative, and transformative, elements while remaining convincingly particular. Soon after *The Man Who Loved Children* was published, she was preaching what she practiced: in 1943 she ran a novel-writing workshop at New York University.

Mary McCarthy reviewed the book severely when it first appeared, tutting at what she saw as anachronisms and the author's tenuous sense of American life and language. McCarthy has a point, but in the end it is not a very important one. The translation of the story to America developed an originally unintended theme: the delicate connection between narrative intention and setting, how an environment can re-inflect what a writer sets out to do. The occasions for much of her social commentary have faded, but her characterization remains solid. Her satire does not resort to caricature or cod-psychology. There are fewer obstacles to our enjoyment of the book today than when Mary McCarthy read it: it is more true now than when reviewers, noting anachronisms and flaws, could not see the wood for the twigs.

Jonathan Franzen, another admirer of *The Man Who Loved*

Children, lists some of the hurdles modern readers encounter. The book is very long. Jarrell compares Stead to Tolstoy in this respect, and Stead herself invites comparison with *Huckleberry Finn*. But readers learn the language of the Samuel Clemens Pollit family and the dialects into which it is divided by the age, gender and relative independence of the parents and children. It is the right length: we have the anxious pleasure of watching and hearing the family fall apart, Sam Pollit justifying each step of its decline by high-principled – if entirely unrealistic – arguments. The Pollits (though not Henny) laugh at wrong things, for instance the old models of discipline, in which children and not parents were punished. 'The book intrudes on our better-regulated world like a bad dream from the grandparental past,' says Franzen. 'Its idea of a happy ending is like no other novel's, and probably not at all like yours.' Franzen has left Joyce's Stephen Dedalus out of this account.

Sam Pollit, a grinning tyrant of permissiveness, requires his children to acknowledge and love him day and night, in all their actions. They are lights he switches on and shines on himself. He is innocent: he abuses his children in the firm belief that he is liberating them. When an incident of literal child abuse occurs in the Pollits' neighbourhood, Sam cannot believe the rumours. This sort of thing simply can't happen. The apotheosis of new-world optimism, an American Pangloss, his naïve virtue undermines the moral world, his liberalism makes it impossible for the family to engage in social or economic life.

He does not love his wife nor she him. She has a different set of illusions and experiences disappointment on the quick. Mr and Mrs Pollit converse hardly at all with one another, except in battle. They speak quite different languages to the children, planting in them the confusions and polarities for which parents are generally responsible, and which provide the poison that has no antidote in the grown up child's constitution.

Stead set out to write a novel with the authority and broad perspectives of her great male predecessors. This book comes close – as Hemingway, Fitzgerald and Steinbeck do in their most compelling work – to life-writing. Narrator and author cannot quite be prized apart without damage to each. Louie gains strength, finds her feet, and slowly her point of view takes over the narrative. In 1940 it was possible to write with the nerves exposed, experimenting with voice, with laughter and without self-pity. On the contrary, the pity one ends up feeling is for the human and material waste that certain extreme forms of idealism give rise to.

Michael Schmidt, 2016

Chapter One

1 *Henny comes home.*

All the June Saturday afternoon Sam Pollit's children were on the lookout for him as they skated round the dirt sidewalks and seamed old asphalt of R Street and Reservoir Road that bounded the deep-grassed acres of Tohoga House, their home. They were not usually allowed to run helter-skelter about the streets, but Sam was out late with the naturalists looking for lizards and salamanders round the Potomac bluffs, Henrietta, their mother, was in town, Bonnie, their youthful aunt and general servant, had her afternoon off, and they were being minded by Louisa, their half sister, eleven and a half years old, the eldest of their brood. Strict and anxious when their parents were at home, Louisa when left in sole command was benevolent, liking to hear their shouts from a distance while she lay on her belly, reading, at the top of the orchard, or ambled, woolgathering, about the house.

The sun dropped between reefs of cloud into the Virginia woods: a rain frog rattled and the air grew damp. Mother coming home from the Wisconsin Avenue car, with parcels, was seen from various corners by the perspiring young ones, who rushed to meet her, chirring on their skates, and who convoyed her home, doing figures round her, weaving and blowing about her or holding to her skirt, and merry, in spite of her decorous irritations.

"I come home and find you tearing about the streets like mad things!"

They poured into the house, bringing in dirt, suppositions, questions, legends of other children, and plans for the next day, while Louie, suddenly remembering potatoes and string beans neglected, slunk in through the back door. Henrietta took a letter off the hall stand, a letter addressed to her, to "Mrs. Samuel Clemens Pollit," which she tore open, muttering, with a half-smile, "The fool!" She went into the long dining room to read it, while Saul, technically the elder of the seven-year-old twins, hung from the chair back, saying,

"Who's it from, Mother, who's it from?" and his twin, straw-headed Samuel, tried to wrest her handbag from her, meanwhile repeating, "Can I look in your bag, can I look in your bag, can I?"

When she heard him, at last, she relinquished the worn old cowhide bag and went on reading, without paying the least attention to their excited examination of her keys and cosmetics, nor to ten-year-old Ernest, her first-born, who, after counting her money and putting it into little piles, said sagely,

"Mother has two dollars and eighty-two cents: Mother, when you went out you had five dollars and sixteen cents and a stamp. What did you buy, Mother?"

They heard Louisa coming, chanting, "Hot tea, hot tea! Make way there!" and shifted a quarter of an inch on their hams. Louie picked her way carefully through their midst, carrying a large cup of tea which she put down in front of her stepmother.

"Did anyone come or telephone?"

"The paint came, Mother" Louie stopped in the doorway. "It's in the washhouse."

"Is he going to start painting and messing everything up tomorrow?" Henrietta asked.

Louie said nothing but moved slowly out.

"Mother, you spent two dollars and thirty-four cents. What did you buy?"

"What's in this parcel, Moth?" Evie asked.

"Oh, leave me alone; you're worse than your father."

Henrietta took off her gloves and began to sip her tea. This was her chair and also the one that all visitors sought. It was straight but comfortable, not too low, and set between the corner window and that cushioned bench which ran along the west wall. The children would line up on this bench and hang entranced on the visitor's life story. Visitors looked awkward there, arrayed in the accidents of life's put-together and rough-and-tumble, laughing uncouthly, unexpectedly at imbecile jokes, giving tongue to crackpot idioms; yet they thought themselves important, and it appeared that as they ran about the streets things happened to them. They had knots of relations with whom they argued and sweethearts to whom they cooed; they had false teeth, eyeglasses, and operations. The children would sit there staring with mouth open and gulping, till Henny snapped, "Are you catching flies?"

When Henny sat there, on the contrary, everything was in order and it was as if no one was in the house; it was like the presence of a somber, friendly old picture that has hung on a wall for generations. Whenever Sam was out, particularly in the afternoon, Henny would sit there, near the kitchen where she could get her cups of tea hot, and superintend the cooking. The children, rushing in from school or from the orchard, would find her there, quiet, thin, tired, with her veined, long olive hands clasped round the teacup for warmth, or gliding, skipping through wools and needles, as she knitted *her* pattern into bonnets and bootees for infants who were always appearing in the remote world. Then she would be cheerful and say to them in her elegant, girlish, spitfire way, "A fool for luck, a poor man for children, Eastern shore for hard crabs, and niggers for dogs"; and, "I have a little house and a mouse couldn't find it and all the men in our town couldn't count the windows in it: what is it?" When she had asked the riddle she would smile archly, although they all knew the answer, for Henny knew very few riddles. But these dear little rigmaroles would only come out when Daddy was out.

At other times they would find her, ugly, with her hair pushed back and her spectacles on, leaning over a coffee-soiled white linen tablecloth (she would have no others, thinking colored ones *common*), darning holes or fixing the lace on one of her lace covers inherited from Monocacy, her old Baltimore home. Then she would growl,

"If you stand there staring at me, I'll land you one to send you flying!" or, "Don't gabble to me about the blessed snakes: it's bad luck to have snakes, and he always keeps snakes for pets."

Now Henny sent little Evie running to get her hand lotion and nail buff while she discontentedly examined her great agate nails and complained about flecks in them and an injured half-moon,

"I don't know what I go to that woman in the arcade for; she hacks my cuticle too."

"You have money on your tea, Moth!" said Saul cheerfully.

"Yes, that's good," and she carefully lifted the circle of froth to her mouth in her teaspoon, but it broke, and at this she gave an irritated cry, "Oh, there, now I won't get any." The cup was a cup that their father had seen in a junk shop near P Street, old heavy china with the word "Mother" on it, between bunches of roses: and he had made them buy it for her for her last birthday.

Henny sat dreaming, with the letter in her lap. She was not nervous and lively like the Pollits, her husband's family, who, she said, "always behaved like chickens with their heads cut off," but would sit there still, so gracefully languid, except to run her fingers over the tablecloth, tracing the design in the damask, or to alter her pose and lean her face on her hand and stare into the distance, a commonplace habit which looked very theatrical in Henny, because of her large, bright eyeballs and thin, high-curved black eyebrows. She was like a tall crane in the reaches of the river, standing with one leg crooked and listening. She would look fixedly at her vision and suddenly close her eyes. The child watching (there was always one) would see nothing but the huge eyeball in its glove of flesh, deep-sunk in the wrinkled skullhole, the dark circle round it and the eyebrow far above, as it seemed, while all her skin, unrelieved by brilliant eye, came out in its real shade, burnt olive. She looked formidable in such moments, in her intemperate silence, the bitter set of her discolored mouth with her uneven slender gambler's nose and scornful nostrils, lengthening her sharp oval face, pulling the dry skin folds. Then when she opened her eyes, there would shoot out a look of hate, horror, passion, or contempt. The children (they were good children, as everyone said) would creep up, so as not to annoy her and say, at her elbow, "Moth, can Whitey come in?" or some such thing, and she would start and cry,

"What do you mean sneaking up on me like that, are you spying on me like your father?" or, "Get out of my sight before I land you one, you creeper!" or, "What do you mean trying to frighten me, is it supposed to be funny?"

And at other times, as now, she would sit with her glances hovering round the room, running from dusty molding to torn curtain frill, from a nail under the transom left over from the last Christmas to a worn patch on the oilcloth by the door, threadbare under so many thousand little footsteps, not worrying about them, but considering each well-known item, almost amiable from familiarity, almost interested, as if considering anew how to fix up these things when fatigue had gone and the tea and rest had put new energy into her.

Henny had never lived in an apartment. She was an old-fashioned woman. She had the calm of frequentation; she belonged to this house and it to her. Though she was a prisoner in it, she possessed it. She and it were her marriage. She was indwelling in every board and stone of it: every fold in the curtains had a meaning (perhaps they were so folded to hide a darn or stain); every room was a phial of revelation to be poured out some feverish night in the secret laboratories of her decisions, full of living cancers of insult, leprosies of disillusion, abscesses of grudge, gangrene of nevermore, quintan fevers of divorce, and all the proliferating miseries, the running sores and thick scabs, for which (and not for its heavenly joys) the flesh of marriage is so heavily veiled and conventually interned.

As Henny sat before her teacup and the steam rose from it and the treacherous foam gathered, uncollectible round its edge, the thousand storms of her confined life would rise up before her, thinner illusions on the steam. She did not laugh at the words "a storm in a teacup." Some raucous, cruel words about five cents misspent were as serious in a woman's life as a debate on war appropriations in Congress: all the civil war of ten years roared into their smoky words when they shrieked, maddened, at each other; all the snakes of hate hissed. Cells are covered with the rhymes of the condemned, so was this house with Henny's life sentence, invisible but thick as woven fabric. Here she sat to play solitaire, the late sun shining on the cards and on the green and red squares of the linoleum. When Sam was out, if Henny felt restless, she would take her double pack and shuffle them with a sound like a distant machine gun, and worry and reshuffle and begin to lay them out eagerly, by fours. All the children watched and showed her where to lay the cards, until she said good-humoredly,

"Oh, go and put your head in a bag!" and she taught Louie how to play, saying she must never touch them when her father was round, that was all.

Sam tried to impart everything he knew to the children and grumbled that the *mother* taught nothing at all: yet their influence on the boys and girls was equal. The children grabbed tricks and ideas according to the need of the day, without thinking at all of where they got them, without gratitude; and Henny saw this and so did not bother her head about her children. She herself belonged to a grabbing breed. Henny would also tell fortunes, by the cards, over her tea, though never for the children. While she was dealing to tell the fortune of Aunt Bonnie (Sam's twenty-five-year-old sister and their unpaid maid of all work), or Miss Spearing (Henny's old-maid friend from schooldays), she would always begin a wonderful yarn about how she went to town, "more dead than alive and with only ten cents in my purse and I wanted to crack a safe," and how, in the streetcar, was "a dirty shrimp of a man with a fishy expression who purposely leaned over me and pressed my bust, and a common vulgar woman beside him, an ogress, big as a hippopotamus, with her bottom sticking out, who grinned like a shark and tried to give him the eye," and how this wonderful adventure went on for hours, always with new characters of new horror. In it would invariably be a woman with a cow like expression, a girl looking frightened as a rabbit, a yellow-haired frump with hair like a haystack in a fit, some woman who bored Henny with her silly gassing, and impudent flighty young girls behind counters, and waitresses smelling like a tannery (or a fish market), who gave her lip, which caused her to "go to market and give them more than they bargained for." There were men and women, old acquaintances of hers, or friends of Sam who presumed to know her, to whom she would give the go-by, or the cold shoulder, or a distant bow, or a polite good day, or a black look, or a look black as thunder, and there were silly old roosters, creatures like a dying duck in a thunderstorm, filthy old pawers, and YMCA sick chickens, and women thin as a rail and men fat as a pork barrel, and women with blouses so puffed out that she wanted to stick pins in, and men like coalheavers, and women like boiled owls and women who had fallen into a flour barrel; and all these wonderful creatures, who swarmed in the streets, stores, and restaurants of Washington, ogling, leering, pulling, pushing, stinking, overscented, screaming and boasting, turning pale at a black look from Henny, ducking and diving, dodging and returning, were the only creatures that Henny ever saw.

What a dreary stodgy world of adults the children saw when they went out! And what a moral, high-minded world their father saw!

But for Henny there was a wonderful particular world, and when they went with her they saw it: they saw the fish eyes, the crocodile grins, the hair like a birch broom, the mean men crawling with maggots, and the children restless as an eel, that she saw. She did not often take them with her. She preferred to go out by herself and mooch to the bargain basements, and ask the young man in the library what was good to read, and take tea in some obscure restaurant, and wander desolately about, criticizing shop windows and wondering if, in this street or that, she would yet, "old as I am and looking like a black hag," meet her fate. Then she would come home, next to some girl "from a factory who looked like a lily and smelled like a skunk cabbage," flirting with all the men and the men grinning back, next to some coarse, dirty workman who pushed against her in the car and smelled of sweat, or some leering brute who tried to pay her fare.

Louie would sit there, on the end of the bench, lost in visions, wondering how she would survive if some leering brute shamefully tried to pay her fare in a public car, admiring Henny for her strength of mind in the midst of such scandals: and convinced of the dreary, insulting horror of the low-down world. For it was not Henny alone who went through this inferno, but every woman, especially, for example, Mrs. Wilson, the woman who came to wash every Monday. Mrs. Wilson, too, "big as she was, big as an ox," was insulted by great big brutes of workmen, with sweaty armpits, who gave her a leer, and Mrs. Wilson, too, had to tell grocers where they got off, and she too had to put little half-starved cats of girls, thin as toothpicks, in their places. Mrs. Wilson it was who saw the ravishing Charlotte Bolton (daughter of the lawyer, who lived in a lovely bungalow across the street), she saw "my lady, standing with her hands on her hips, waggling her bottom and laughing at a man like a common streetgirl," and he "black as the inside of a hat, with dark blood for sure." Louie and Evie, and the obliging little boys, tugging at the piles of greasy clothes on Mondays, puffing under piles of new-ironed linen on Tuesdays, would be silent for hours, observing this world of tragic faery in which all their adult friends lived. Sam, their father, had endless tales of friends, enemies, but most often they were good citizens, married to good wives, with good children (though untaught), but never did Sam meet anyone out of Henny's world, grotesque, foul, loud-voiced, rude, uneducated, and insinuating, full of scandal, slander, and filth, financially deplorable and physically revolting, dubiously born, and going awry to a desquamating end.

After Henny had talked her heart out to her sister, Aunt Hassie, or to Bonnie even (though she despised a Pollit), or to her bosom friend, Miss Spearing, she would sometimes go, and after a silence, there would steal through the listening house flights of notes, rounded as doves, wheeling over housetops in the sleeping afternoon, Chopin or Brahms, escaping from Henny's lingering, firm fingers. Sam could be vile but always as a joke. Henny was beautifully, wholeheartedly vile: she asked no quarter and gave none to the foul world, and when she told her children tales of the villainies they could understand, it was not to corrupt them, but because, for her, the world was really so. How could their father, said she, so fool them with his lies and nonsense?

The chair, and the slanting of the light, the endless insoluble game of solitaire, were as comfortable to Henny's ravaged nerves as an eiderdown. In the warmth of the late afternoon, some time before she expected to hear the rush of feet, she would sit there at her third or fourth game and third or fourth cup of tea. So sitting she would seem to herself to be bathing in the warm moisture of other summers. She would see the near rush or distant slow-moving glitter on the steeps of North Charles Street, see the half-dry fountain with a boat in Eutaw Place, which could be seen from the front windows of the brownstone house Hassie had there, and the hot-smelling, rose-colored stoops flowing down and up the gully: see the masts of little boats and the barges, the sole twinkle of a car on the bridge; see the hot, washed windows of dressmakers and the tasseled curtains of a club, the dormant steps of little night bars, the yellow and pink of some afternoon-tea place where she had gone with Hassie when she was a schoolgirl. Or if the wind was high and her headache had not yet come on, she could smell the brackish and weakly salt streams of the Chesapeake, scudding in her cousin's twelve-footer, or her father's motorboat; feel the sounds and scents of Saturdays long swept away on the long rollers of years, when she was a thin-blooded, coquettish girl, making herself bleed at the nose for excitement, throwing herself on the lawns of Monocacy in a tantrum, spitting fire at the servants, coaxing her father, waiting for the silly toys her father would buy her—engagement to a commercial fortune, marriage to a great name, some unexpected stroke of luck in blue-blooded romance, social fun, nursemaids, two fashionable children in pink and blue. These things surged out of the past, as she sat there, but faintly, no more distinct than a wind that is blowing ten miles off and sometimes sends a puff of air. If she became conscious of these streams on the rainbow fringe of memory, she would bite her lip and flush, perhaps angry at her indulgent father for getting her the man he had got, angry at herself for having been so weak.

"Sadie was a lady," she would suddenly say in the stillness, and, "Hrmph!" or, "If I had a ladida like that to deal with I'd drown her when a pup." Besides, she could not even now forget the humiliation of having her name five or six years in old social calendars among the "eligibles": nor of having married a man who was after all a mere jog-trot subaltern bureaucrat, dragged into the service in the lowest grades without a degree, from mere practical experience in the Maryland Conservation Commission, and who owed his jealousy-creating career to her father's influence in the lobbies of the capital.

Soon Ernie, her favorite, would rush in, saying breathlessly, "Did it come out, Moth?" This kept her sitting there. While she sat and played or did her microscopic darning, sometimes a small mouse would run past, or even boldly stand and inquisitively stare at her. Henny would look down at its monstrous pointed little face calmly and go on with her work, while it pretended to run off, and took another stand, still curious, behind another chair leg. The mice were well fed. They regularly set traps, but there was no coming to the end of the mice in that house. Henny accepted the sooty little beings as house guests and would only go on the warpath at night, when she woke up suddenly to smell in the great hall, or even in her own bedroom, the musky penetrating odor of their passage: or when she looked at her little spectator and saw that it was a pregnant mother. She would have accepted everything else, too, the winds, the rattlings and creaking of the old house, the toothaches and headaches, the insane anxieties about cancer and t.b., too, all house guests, if she could have, and somewhere between all these hustlers, made herself a little life. But she had the children, she had a stepdaughter, she had no money, and she had to live with a man who fancied himself a public character and a moralist of a very saintly type. The moralist said mice brought germs and so she was obliged to chase the mouse and all its fellow guests. Nevertheless, although she despised animals, she felt involuntarily that the little marauder was much like herself, trying to get by: she belonged to the great race of human beings who regard life as a series of piracies of all powers.

She would play on and on till her cheeks got hot and then call for another cup of tea, or else go and get herself some store cheese and Worcestershire sauce in a plate, pushing the cards aside.

"I wish your mother would stop playing patience, it makes her look like an old witch or an old vixen possum," Sam would say in a gently benevolent voice, in some offstage colloquy, if he ever came home and found her still at it. It did exhaust her in the end. She played feverishly, until her mind was a darkness, until all the memories and the ease had long since drained away. And then when the father came home, the children who had been battling and shuttling around her would all rush off like water down the sink, leaving her sitting there, with blackened eyes, a yellow skin, and straining wrinkles: and she would think of the sink, and mutter, as she did at this moment,

"A dirty cracked plate: that's just what I am!"

"What did you say, Mummy?" asked little Sam. She looked at him, the image of his father, and repeated, "I'm a greasy old soup plate," making them all laugh, laughing herself.

"Mother, you're so silly," Evie said.

Henny got up and moved into her room. It was a large room taking up a quarter of the original ground-floor plan, with two windows facing the east, and one window on the front lawn but screened from R Street by the double hedges. Although the room was furnished with the walnut suite that she had brought from home, and the double bed which she now used alone, there was plenty of room for their play.

Henny sat down at the dressing table to take off her hat. They clustered round the silver-littered table, picked up her rings.

"What did you buy, Mother?" someone persisted.

"Mother, can I have a nickel?"

Henny said, fluffing out the half-gray curls round her face, "I asked my mother for fifty cents to see the elephant jump the fence. Shoo, get out! You wretched limpets never give me a minute to myself."

"Mother, can I have a nickel, please?"

"Mother, what did you buy-uy?" chanted Henny's baby, Tommy, a dark four-year-old boy with shining almond eyes and a skullcap of curls. Meanwhile he climbed on the dressing table and, after studying her reflection for a long time in the mirror, kissed it.

"Look, Moth, Tommy kissed you in the glass!" They laughed at him, while he, much flattered, blushed and leaned over to kiss her, giving her a hearty smack-smack while he watched himself in the mirror.

"Oh, you kissing bug! It's unlucky for two to look in the same glass. Now get down and get out! Go and feed the darn animals and then come and wash your hands for dinner."

The flood receded, leaving Henny high and dry again. She sighed and got out the letter she had received that afternoon, reading it carefully.

At the end she folded it again, said with a sneer, "And a greasy finger mark from his greasy hypocritical mauler right in the middle: the sight of his long pious cheeks like suet and her fat red face across the table from each other—"

She looked at the letter thoughtfully for a while, turning it over, got out her fountain pen, and started a reply. But she tore her sheet of paper across, spat on the soiled letter, and, picking it up with a pair of curling tongs, burned it and her few scratchings in a little saucepan which had boiled dry on the radiator.

The letter was from her eldest brother, Norman Collyer. It refused to lend her money and said, somewhere near the offensive finger mark,

You should be able to manage. Your husband is making about $8,000 yearly and you always got lucky dips anyhow, being Father's pet. I can only give you some good advice, which doubtless you will not follow, knowing you as I do. That is, draw in your horns, retrench somehow, don't go running up accounts and don't borrow from moneylenders. I've seen my own family half starving. What do you think I can make out of the job Father gives me? You must get out of your own messes. The trouble is you never had to pay for your mistakes before.

Henny opened her windows to let the smoke out, and then began taking trinkets out of her silver jewel case and looking at them discontentedly. She threw open the double doors of her linen closet and rummaged amongst the sheets, pulling out first a library book and then two heavy silver soup ladles and six old silver teaspoons. She looked at them indifferently for a moment and then stuck them back in their hiding place.

She let Louie give the children their dinner, and ate hers on a tray in her bedroom, distractedly figuring on a bit of envelope. When she brought her tray out to the kitchen, Louie was slopping dishes about in the sink. Henny cried,

"Take your fat belly out of the sink! Look at your dress! Oh, my God! Now I've got to get you another one clean and dry for Monday. You'll marry a drunkard when you grow up, always wet in front. Ernie, help Louie with the washing-up, and you others make yourselves scarce. And turn off the darn radio. It's enough when Mr. Big-Me is at home blowing off steam."

They ran out cheerfully while Louie drooped her underlip and tied a towel round her waist. Henny sighed, picked up the cup of tea that Louie had just poured out for her, and went into her bedroom, next door to the kitchen. She called from there,

"Ernie, bring me your pants and I'll mend them."

"There's time," he shouted considerately, "you don't need to to-night. Tomorrow's Sunday-Funday, and we're painting the house— I'll wear my overalls."

"Did you hear what I said?"

"O.K." He shed his trousers at once and rushed in to her holding them out at arm's length. He stood beside her for a moment, watching her pinch the cloth together. "I bet I could do that easy, Mum: why don't you teach me?"

"Thank you, my son; but Mother will do it while she has the strength."

"Are you sick today, Mother?"

"Mother's always sick and tired," she said gloomily.

"Will I bring you my shawl, Mother?" This was his baby shawl that he always took to bed with him when he felt sick or weepy.

"No, Son." She looked at him straight, as if at a stranger, and then drew him to her, kissing him on the mouth.

"You're Mother's blessing; go and help Louie." He cavorted and dashed out, hooting. She heard him in half a minute, chattering away affectionately to his half sister.

"But I should have been better off if I'd never laid eyes on any of them," Henny grumbled to herself, as she put on her glasses and peered at the dark serge.

2 *Sam comes home.*

Stars drifted in chinks of the sky as Sam came home: the lamps were clouded in leaves in this little island of streets between river and parks. Georgetown's glut of children, issue of streets of separate little houses, went shouting, colliding downhill, while Sam came up whistling, seeing the pale faces, flying knees, lights and stars above, around him. Sam could have been home just after sunset when his harum-scarum brood were still looking for him, and he had meant to be there, for he never broke his word to them. He could have taken Shank's ponies, which, he was fond of saying, "take me everywhere, far afield and into the world of marvels which lies around us, into the highways and byways, into the homes of rich and poor alike, seeking the doorstep of him who loves his fellow man—and fellow woman, of course—seeking every rostrum where the servants of evil may be flagellated, and the root of all evil exposed."

On Shank's ponies he could have got home that afternoon in less than an hour, crossing the Key Bridge from Rosslyn, when the naturalists left the new bird sanctuary on Analostan Island. But today Sam was the hero of his Department and of the naturalists because he had got the long-desired appointment with the Anthro-pological Mission to the Pacific, and not only would he have his present salary plus traveling expenses, but his appointment was a bold step forward on his path of fame.

Sam looked, as he passed, at a ramshackle little house, something like the wretched slum he had once boarded in with his brother at Dundalk, out of Baltimore, and a smile bared his teeth.

"Going to glory," said Sam: "I've come a long way, a long, long way, Brother. Eight thousand a year and expenses—and even Tohoga House, in Georgetown, D.C., lovely suburb of the nation's capital; and the children of poor Sam Pollit, bricklayer's son, who left school at twelve, are going to university soon, under the flashing colonnades of America's greatest city, in the heart of the democratic Athens, much greater than any miserable Athens of the dirt grubbers of antiquity, yes—I feel sober, at rest. The old heart doesn't flutter: I must be careful not to rest on my laurels now—haste not, rest not! I feel free!" Sam began to wonder at himself; why did he feel free? He had always been free, a free man, a free mind, a freethinker. "By Gemini," he thought, taking a great breath, "this is how men feel who take advantage of their power."

Sam looked round him—just ahead was Volta Place, where Dribble Smith, his friend in the Treasury, lived. He chuckled, hearing Dribble practicing his scales inside, to his daughter's accompan-iment. Passing Smith's hedge, Sam said half aloud,

"What it must be, though, to taste supreme power!"

He thought of his long-dead mother, who came from the good old days when mothers dreamed of their sons' being President, *Poor woman, good woman: she little thought when she dropped a tear at my being sent to work in the fish market that in the fish market I would meet my fate.* Ahead of him, not far uphill, was his harbor and his fate.

"Another thing," said Sam to himself, "is that going away now, Madeleine and I will have time to use our heads, get things straight: the love that harms another is not love—but what desires beset a man! They are not written in the calendar of a man's duty; they are part of the secret life. Some time the secret life rises and overwhelms us—a tidal wave. We must not be carried away. We have each too much to lose." He strode on, "Forget, forget!" He struggled to remember something else, something cheerful. They had taken him to Dirty Jack's house to celebrate his appointment; there they had made merry, Sam being at the top of his form. There was a young creature there, timid, serious, big-eyed, with a black crop who turned out to be Dirty Jack's (that is, Old Roebuck's) only daughter, the one who did the charming flower painting. What an innocent, attentive face! It positively flamed with admiration; and the child-woman's name was Gillian. He had made up a poem on the spur of the moment:

Gillian, my Gillian,
He would be a villy-un,
Who would be dally-dillyin'
About a Lacertilian
When he could look at you!

"By Jiminy!" ejaculated Sam, who had strange oaths, since he could never swear foul ones, "genius burns: nothing succeeds like success! And did Dirty Jack jerk back his head and give me one of those looks of his with his slugs of eyes, to intimidate me; whereas, no one noticed him at all, at all, poor old Dirty Jack." He began to hum with his walking, "Oh, my darling Nelly Gray, they have taken you away."

"By Gee," he exclaimed half aloud, "I am excited! A pity to come home to a sleeping house, and what's not asleep is the devil incarnate; but we're a cheerful bunch, the Pollits are a cheerful bunch. But wait till my little gang hears that they're going to lose their dad for a nine-month! There'll be weeping and wailing and gnashing of teeth!" and Sam clapped his hands together. He loved this Thirty-fourth Street climb, by the quiet houses and under the trees. He had first come this way, exploring the neighborhood, a young father and widower, holding his year-old Louisa in his arms, with her fat bare legs wagging, and, by his side, elegant, glossy-eyed Miss Henrietta Collyer, a few months before their marriage; and that was ten years ago. Then afterwards, with each and all of the children, up and down and round about, taking them to the Observatory, the parks, the river, the woodland by the Chesapeake and Ohio Canal, or walking them out to Cabin John, teaching them birds, flowers, and all denizens of the woodland.

Now Old David Collyer's Tohoga House, Sam's Tohoga House, that he called his island in the sky, swam above him. A constellation hanging over that dark space midmost of the hill, which was Tohoga's two acres, was slowly swamped by cloud.

He came up slowly, not winded, but snuffing in the night of the hot streets, looking up at the great house, tree-clouded. Now he crossed P Street and faced the hummock. On one side the long galvanized-iron back fence of his property ran towards Thirty-fifth Street and its strip of brick terrace slums. Over this fence leaned the pruned boughs of giant maples and oaks. The old reservoir was away to the right. A faint radiance showed Sam that the light in the long dining room was on. He ran up the side steps and stole across the grass behind the house, brushing aside familiar plants, touching with his left hand the little Colorado blue spruce which he had planted for the children's "Wishing-Tree" and which was now five feet high.

He was just on six feet and therefore could peer into the long room. It ran through the house and had a window looking out at the front to R Street. A leaved oak table stood in the center and at the table, facing him, sitting in his carving chair, was his eldest child, Louisa, soon twelve years old, the only child of his dead first wife, Rachel. Louie was hunched over a book and sat so still that she seemed alone in the house. She did nothing while he looked at her but turn a page and twist one strand of her long yellow hair round and round her finger, a trick of her father's. Then without Sam having heard anything, she lifted her head and sat stock-still with her gray eyes open wide. She now rose stiffly and looked furtively at the window behind her. Sam heard nothing but the crepitations of arboreal night. Then he noticed that the window was sliding gently down. Louisa advanced jerkily to this magically moving window and watched it as it fitted itself into the sill. Then she shook her head and turning to the room as if it were a person she laughed soundlessly. It was nothing but the worn cords loosening. She opened the window and then shut it again softly, but leaned against the pane looking up into the drifting sky, seeking something in the street. She had been there, and Sam, whistling softly *Bringing Home the Sheaves,* was about to go inside, when a thin, dark scarecrow in an off-white wrapper—Henrietta, his wife—stood in the doorway. Through the loose window frame he heard her threadbare words,

"You're up poring over a book with lights flaring all over the house at this hour of the night. You look like a boiled owl! Isn't your father home yet?"

"No, Mother."

"Why is your knee bleeding? Have you been picking the scab again?"

Louie hung her head and looked at her knee, crossed with old scars and new abrasions and bruises: she flushed and the untidy hair fell over her face.

"Answer, answer, you sullen beast!"

"I bumped it."

"You lie all the time."

The child straightened with wide frowning eyes, pulled back her arms insolently. Henny rushed at her with hands outstretched and thrust her firm bony fingers round the girl's neck, squeezing and saying, "Ugh," twice. Louisa looked up into her stepmother's face, squirming, but not trying to get away, questioning her silently, needing to understand, in an affinity of misfortune. Henrietta dropped her arms quickly and gripped her own neck with an expression of disgust, then pushed the girl away with both hands; and as she flounced out of the room, cried,

"I ought to put us all out of our misery!"

Louisa moved back to her chair and stood beside it, looking down at the book. Then she sank into the chair and, putting her face on both hands, began to read again.

Sam turned his back to the house and looked south, over the dark, susurrous orchard, towards the faint lights of Rosslyn. A zephyr stole up the slope as quietly as a nocturnal animal and with it all the domestic scents, wrapping Sam's body in peace. Within, a torment raged, day and night, week, month, year, always the same, an endless conflict, with its truces and breathing spaces; out here were a dark peace and love.

"Mother Earth," whispered Sam, "I love you, I love men and women, I love little children and all innocent things, I love, I feel I am love itself—how could I pick out a woman who would hate me so much!"

Surefooted he moved way down to the animal cages, heard them stir uneasily, and spoke to the raccoon,

"Procyon! Procyon! Here's little Sam!" But the raccoon refused to come to the wire. He went up the slope again, thinking, *Fate puts brambles, hurdles in my path, she even gives me an Old Woman of the Sea, to try me, because I am destined for great things.*

When Sam came into the hall there was no light anywhere on the ground floor. The saffron dark through his sitting room at the head of the first flight of stairs showed that Louie was in her bedroom. She had heard his whistle and had rushed upstairs with her book.

"Why, why?" thought Sam. "She could have waited to hear what her daddy has been doing all day. She is so dogged—and she has her little burdens." He climbed softly upstairs and peeped into the bedroom. Louie's bed stood against the back or south wall and little Evelyn's against the front wall. A brown paper shade arranged by Louie cut off the light from the smaller girl's face. Louie in her petticoat, one sock on, one off, turned towards him guiltily.

"Why you up so late, Looloo?"

"I was reading."

"Been seein' things, Looloo?"

"What do you mean?" She looked suspicious.

"So you ain't been seein' things?" He began to chuckle.

She was silent, pondering.

"My mind says to me, it says, little glumpy Looloo been seein' things and Looloo's been unhappy too."

She hung her head.

"What you see in the darkness of night, Looloo?"

"Nothing!"

"That ain't much for tuh see. Air you tellin' your poor Sam de troof?"

"I never lie," she said angrily.

"No josts [ghosts], no sperrits, no invisible hands, no nuffin?"

"No," but she began to smile shamefacedly.

"All right, Looloo: bed! Early start tomorrow." He grinned at her, white-toothed, red-lipped, blue eyes bright.

"The paint came, Dad. Are you going to paint?" she asked excitedly.

"Sure thing. Fust thing you know! And Looloo—the big news, the big news has come! Shh! I'm going!"

"When?" She started towards him. He was very happy.

"You're going to be months and months without your poor little Sam."

"Who'll look after us?"

"Your mother and Auntie Bonnie: same as now. And you yourself, Loolook! You'll be in high school after the holidays!"

She reluctantly gave her book into his firm persuasive fingers. It was *The Legend of Roncesvalles*. He poked through it for a while and then handed it back, saying,

"Yes, you'll learn from that, Loolook, that where there are kings there will be wars; don't let it give you the idea, Loo, that there's romance in those old savages: but you know better than that. I know my girl."

So saying, he moved out and dropped downstairs, congratulating himself, "She said nothing about the little scene! Good girl! Nothing morbid there! Well, least said, soonest mended!"

He sat down to the covered tray that Henny had left for him as usual, and began to drink his milk and eat thinly cut sandwiches. He sat in the chair Louie had just vacated.

"To a certain extent," he continued ruminating, "to a child of mine, these negative early experiences are aids in the formation of character, will prove of great value in penetrating human nature and human motives later on: perhaps she will go far, like myself, on the path of human understanding. Self-control; and a penetration of the springs of human action. It's a pity she's not a good-looker," he finished hastily. He forgot Louie, and went on about Madeleine.

Madeleine was his secretary, Madeleine Vines, and he had only got her by a little gentle pressure, a little friendly smile in the right place, for she was the Helen of the Department of Commerce, and her admirers weekly predicted a siege by the Treasury, or State, War, and Navy, to get her. They made a splendid pair, handsome man and lovely woman; but months had gone by before Sam had suddenly seen the light pouring forth from her. On that day, a

Tuesday morning in late winter, she had said these simple words, "Mr. Pollit, I just love to hear you talk!"

"That did it," said Sam rapturously now, "yes, that did it. But what a slowpoke that same Samuel Pollit is!"

Suddenly there was a tapping at the back window and Sam started out of his delicious reverie. The shower had come; and it was very late.

Sam let the shower pass, but it came again. He, waking through the night, saw through the panes the tussle of cloud streak and sky spark, leaf blot and lamp flake, and smelled the damp cedar. Some marauder fluttered the nestlings. Sam looked out his window with "Hist, Hist!" and reduced the twig world to silence. Then, shutting the windows in his study, in the girls' room and the twins' room next to his and in the attic room, sometime towards morning, he woke some of his children and through their half-dreams they heard him say, Fine day, tomorrow, kids! I told it to stop raining by sunup! and tomorrow Sunday-Funday.

Louie, who had spent several hours already in an incommunicable world, woke to hear riding again the night rider in the street outside. For years now at night she had heard him riding his horse up and down, sometimes galloping faintly down the street but generally exercising around their very house, and for hours, as long as she could stay awake, Ker-porrop! Ker-porrop! Ker-porrop! he went. She had looked out before she went to bed, for the horseman, many nights, as tonight, and had not seen him. He only began to ride late after other folk were abed, Ker-porrop! Ker-porrop! on a thin-limbed, bay filly, as she imagined. Once she had asked, "Who is the horseman?" and been laughed at, "It's only a dream!" But it was no dream for she heard it only when awake, and sometimes faint and sometimes near, he rode tonight again, in the summer swelter. She could almost see him as he passed and repassed under the lamplight and the dapple of leaves. She got up and leaned out of the southward window, her plait tumbling over the window sill; but the sound had ceased, he must have turned the corner. Yes, when she went back to bed, there he was again. She liked to wake in the night and hear the friendly rider: so perhaps, she thought, went Paul Revere, tumbling through the night, alone, a man when all others lay like logs. Louie and the rider on the red mare were wakers.

3 *Sunday a Funday.*

On Sunday morning the sun bolted up brash and chipper from the salad beds of the Atlantic and with a red complexion came loping towards them over the big fishing hole of the Chesapeake. Before it was light the dooryard thrush began to drop his song, *quirt-quirt,* hesitant, fretful, inquiring, angelically solitary, from the old elm across the street. Sam whistled to him and then nestlings fluttered, a beast fell to the ground, the early birds got to work, and presently, by hearty creaking and concerted peeping, they and Sam made the sky pale and flagged the daystar. Sam was always anxious for morning. He was greedy for the daylight world, because the fevers of the dark, and the creatures real to man's sixth, inward, dark sense, which palpitates in such an agony about three o'clock in the morning, all disappeared at the dark's first fading. When the first ray came, he stood on feet of clay in a world of clay; the dread other worlds of dreams were gone beyond comparison. In these fresh summer mornings (it was fresh on the hill) when the earth perspired profusely, Sam would often get up before daybreak, patter downstairs in bare feet, just wearing bathing pants, and would go out on to the lawn, getting ready for some job, getting the animals up, or standing under the trees, whistling to the birds. But not today, because he had stayed awake most of the night.

It was six-thirty by the alarm clock. Sam began whistling softly through his teeth the tune of,

One evening in the month of May
(Johnny get your gun, get your gun!)—

and waited. There was a grunt next door in the twins' room. The twins were turning over, trying to dig shuteye out of their pillows, closing their ears. Upstairs, Ernie's voice joined in,

I met ole Satan by the way.

There was a slippery sound like a little fish flopping on the stairs: that was four-year-old Tommy hurrying down to his mother's room. Louisa, from her bed across the sitting room, said sleepily, "Shh! Shh! It's early!"

Sam waited a moment, thinking, Will I whistle up the Gemini or my Darkeyes? Of all these little affections, he was most sure of Evelyn, his pet, a queer little dove, who in her eight years had never been naughty and who bubbled with laughter when he grinned at her, hung her head, cried, when he scowled. He called her his little woman, *Little-Womey*. He began,

"Little-Womey, Little-Womey, git-up, git-up!"

"Sh, sh!" said Louie in whose room Evie slept. No answer.

"Is you awake, Little-Womey, or is you in the arms of Morpheus?"

No answer: but by almost imperceptible noises Sam could tell that everyone was awake now, listening. There was an exclamation in his wife's room downstairs. Henrietta had been awake for hours, as long as Sam himself, knitting, reading, waiting for her morning tea.

"Womey, Womey, c'mon, c'mon, giddap for your pore little Sam."

Evelyn giggled. He heard it all right and insisted, "C'mon, Womey: come on: do my head, come, scratch my head. Come, do m'head: do m'yed, do m'yed. Come on, Penthestes; co-ome on, Penthestes."

His voice had fallen to the lowest seductive note of yearning. Evie chuckled with doubt, pleasure. She had many petnames, any, in fact, that occurred to Sam, such as Penthestes (a chickadee) or Troglodytes (the house wren), names of engaging little dusky birds or animals. Saul, the more self-possessed of the twins, shouted to Evelyn, while the other, Little-Sam, who was his father's copy, shouted out that he was awake. Their mother, in her bed, grumbled again. Sam was enjoying himself and now began to whine,

"Womey won't come en scratch m'yed: Womey is mean to her pore little dad."

Evie jumped out of the covers and ran across Sam's sitting room. At his bedroom door she giggled, eyes flying, fat brown starfish hands together on the dark mouth.

"I heard you the first time, Taddy."

"C'mon," he begged, full of love for her. She jumped onto his bed and crouched on his pillow behind his head: there she began to massage his head and twist his thick silky hair. He closed his eyes in ease and asked in an undertone,

"Is Looloo up yet?"

"No, Taddy."

Sam whistled an ascending chromatic scale which was Louisa's whistle, and the same scale descending, which was Ernest's whistle. Evie, imitating her mother, protested,

"She is asleep, Taddy: let her sleep. She needs it." Sam took no notice but went on in an insinuating, teasing voice,

"Loobyloo! Loo-oobylool Loozy! Tea!"

Although Louisa did not answer she was at that moment crawling soundlessly out of bed. She heard him urging Evie, "Go on, Womey, call her Loozy."

"No, Taddy, she doesn't like it."

"Go on, when I tahzoo [tells you]."

"No, Taddy, she can hear."

"Loo-hoozy! Loozy! Tea-heehee!"

Out of the tail of her eye Evelyn saw Louisa flash across the landing to the stairs. "She went," she chanted soothingly, "she went."

"This Sunday-Funday has come a long way," said Sam softly: "it's been coming to us, all day yesterday, all night from the mid-Pacific, from Peking, the Himalayas, from the fishing grounds of the old Leni Lenapes and the deeps of the drowned Susquehanna, over the pond pine ragged in the peat and the lily swamps of Anacostia, by scaffolded marbles and time-bloodied weatherboard, northeast, northwest, Washington Circle, Truxton Circle, Sheridan Circle to Rock Creek and the blunt shoulders of our Georgetown. And what does he find there this morning as every morning, in the midst of the slope, but Tohoga House, the little shanty of Gulliver Sam's Lilliputian Pollitry—Gulliver Sam, Mrs. Gulliver Henny, Lugubrious Louisa, whose head is bloody but unbowed, Ernest the calculator, Little-Womey—" Evie laughed. "—Saul and Sam the boy-twins and Thomas-snowshoe-eye, all sun-tropes that he come galloping to see."

"He doesn't come to see us," deprecated Evie.

"No, he could live without us," Sam agreed. He opened his eyes, "Whar my red book?" His bedside table was littered with pamphlets from the Carnegie Peace Foundation, scientific journals, and folders from humanitarian leagues. On top lay three magazines. Sam picked out one which was folded back and laid his forefinger on the pretty, sober woman pictured above the title.

"Bin readin' fine stor-wy, Little Womey," he said, "'bout a fine woman en a fine little girl. Good sweet story—makes your pore little Sam bust into tears."

"Is it sad, Taddy?"

"It is sad and glad. It is just like our poor little silly, funny human life, but it comes to a good end because they are good people underneath all their poor willfulnesses and blindnesses. They really love each other, although they *do* show a tendency to scratch out each other's eyes at moments: en then they find they don't hate each other as much as they thought. People are like that, my *Troglodytes minor*. Love people, little Darkeyes, always be in love with human beings and you will be happy. And what is more, much more, you will do good."

"Taddy," she began, hesitating, "can Isabel come in today?"

"Mebbe," said Sam. "Oh, mwsk, mwsk!" He kissed a girl figured in a corset advertisement, "I'll marry her! Hello, beautiful! Look at the girl with da spaghett'—mwsk, mwsk, mwsk! I love her. I'll marry her too. Mwsk!

Oh, woman in our hours of ease
Uncertain, coy and hard to please:
But when the time comes round for chow
A ministering angel thou.

Look at this one with the mayonnaise. Mwsk! Here's a knockout. Mwsk!"

"You missed that one, Taddy."

"Not her! She's a fright: she's a holy terror. No ma'am: I like my girls often and I likes 'em pretty. En look at this one. Holy Methusalem! He must have had his mother-in-law staying with him. This one would frighten a screech owl at midnight on Bear Mountain. The question is, how bare? Mwsk! Oh, raccoons and rattlesnakes! This one knocks my eyes out! I only got one eye. I can't stand it. I must marry her at once and get back my eye."

Evie giggled, giggled, shivering with pleasure. The twin boys and Ernest had crowded into the room, and craned and gleamed round the bed, saying, "Oo, not that one, she's ugly."

"Here's a peach," said Ernest. Ernest was nearly ten.

"This one's a peacherino, though, she's mine," Sam said. He kissed the cocktail heroine several times, "young and juicy, a ripe tomato," he continued wickedly, grinning at the boys, while Evie pored over the picture. "Mwsk! Here's a little ducky, she looks naughty but she's a good girl really."

"How do you know?" Evie stared at the girl with thin legs in silk stockings and flying crayon billows.

Sam teased, "They don't write stories about really bad girls, Little-Womey, remember that. And they never make a really bad girl pretty, even if they do write about her for the sake of the truth. That's because they really want people to be happy and good, and want us to believe that the beautiful are the good and vice versa. Because, if we believe it, it will come true—"

"Here's one you can kiss, Dad," cried Saul, excitedly.

"Aren't we going to scrape and paint this morning, Pad?" Ernest wanted to know.

"When the tea comes—big news, big news," said Sam, raising himself in bed and looking round at them. They fawned round his bed, expectant.

"You're going to get a new car?" Saul hazarded; but Ernest knew it was no such thing.

From there they could hear the kettle lid hopping madly on the stove. Sam whistled Louie's whistle and shouted,

"Loozy! Water's a-bilin!"

This was followed by another shout from below, his wife's, and a third, a soprano hail came from the attic floor, where Sam's youngest sister, Bonnie, was still abed; she sang, "Hold everything! I'm coming down."

"In the sweet by-and-by," said Sam to the children and winked. The kettle stopped bobbling. Bonnie shouted,

"Ki-hids? Louie?"

"Stay in bed, Bon," Sam replied: "Looloo's making the tea." He explained to the children, "Bonniferous might as well snooze an hour longer da fornin [this morning]: Sunday a funday for all hands."

"But Looloo is working," objected Ernest.

"Looloo is asleep too, on her feet," grinned Sam. Now there was another shout from belowstairs,

"Tea up or down?"

"Up."

In a minute they heard the jingle of tea-things and Louie's grunting. She was a heavy girl, overgrown for her years. She came in with her large fat face pink, but glum. She put the tray down on the bed beside Sam's calves and poured out all round. When she came down from the attic, where she had carried Aunt Bonnie's, Sam sang out,

"Whar's yourn, Loogoobrious?"

"In the kitchen."

"Whyn't you bring it along? Ernest-Paine-Pippy! Go and get Louie's tea for her."

"I've got to make the porridge," she cried; and so got away. She tripped on the oilcloth at the head of the stairs.

"Johnny-head-in-air!" called Sam, "c'mere a minute: be here with your father when he tahzem [tells them] the great news! Kids, your Sam's going to Malaya with the Smithsonian Expedition, like I always told you I would."

"When?" asked Louie morosely.

"Don't know yet," he said: "will you be glad, Looloo, to see your poor little Sam go away to furrin parts?"

"No."

"Will you miss your poor little dad?"

"Yes," she lowered her eyes in confusion.

"Bring up your tea, Looloo-girl: I'm sick, hot head, nedache [headache], dot pagans in my stumjack [got pains in my stomach]: want my little fambly around me this morning. We'll have a corroboree afterwards when I get better. Mother will make the porridge." He was begging her, yearning after her.

"Mother told me to make it," she said obstinately.

He gave a sudden impatient glance,

"Go ahead then! I've never met anyone so cussed in all my born days!"

Lowering, she turned and trudged out. Halfway downstairs a smile flashed into her face—she was free! Upstairs her father was singing and chattering with her brothers and sister; her mother and aunt were in bed reading; the morning was beginning in slow time, and her book for which she had an unconquerable passion, the same *Legend of Roncesvalles* which she was now reading for the third time, was open on the washtub beside the stove. She could read it as she sifted in the oatmeal. It was a glorious hot morning; the birds were now in the full middle of their music. The shadows were diluted light; the air was hot and moist; sweet air from flowers and humus and pines drifted in. The old wood of the house smelled precious, and even the smell of oatmeal slowly coming to the boil was wholesome.

When the porridge was made, Louie took her book in to the showerhouse built at the end of the veranda, and propped it on a crossbeam while she took her cold shower. She stood under the water, stirring gently, and her wet fingers pulped the pages as she turned. Outside the house already resounded to their shouts.

Bonnie, with her silver-gilt hair in a pageboy bob, skipped round the kitchen getting breakfast and singing "*Deh, vieni, non tardar.*" Sam and the boys were in the washhouse, mixing the paint, and Evie was laying the table in the long dining room. A burst of song came from out of doors, the father and his fledglings starting up with "Mid pleasures and palaces"; and when they came to the chorus, Evie could be heard fluting away, "Home, home, sweet, sweet home!" The birds, cheered by all this, began to sing madly like a thousand little harmless brass devils under the leaves; hearing which, Louie at once put on the record that always made the birds begin to cheep, "Papageno, Papagena!" Henrietta sang out,

"He can't open an eye without having the whole tribe jigging and buzzing round him."

Coming from the shower, Louie saw through the door Tommy sitting in his mother's armchair, playing with her solitaire cards. A musky smell always came from Henrietta's room, a combination of dust, powder, scent, body odors that stirred the children's blood, deep, deep. It had as much attraction for them as Sam's jolly singing, and when they were allowed to, they gathered in Henrietta's room, making hay, dashing to the kitchen to get things for her, asking her if she wanted her knitting, her book, tumbling out into the hall and back, until it was as if she had twenty children, their different voices steaming, bubbling, and popping, like an irrepressible but inoffensive crater. Henrietta would not have them on the bed with her, though. She sat there by herself, in the center, propped on two or three pillows, in an old dressing gown, with her glasses on and her gray-speckled black hair drawn tightly back in a braid. Beside her would be some darning, or a library book sprawling halfway down the bed where she had thrown it in disgust, with a "Such rot!"

But she sometimes let them snuggle into the shawls, old gowns, dirty clothes ready for the wash, and blankets thrown over her great easy chair, hold their small parliament on the flowered green carpet, or look at all the things in her dressing table, and in what they called her *treasure drawers*. All Henny's drawers were treasure drawers. In them were spilled and tossed all sorts of laces, ribbons, gloves, flowers, jabots, belts, and collars, hairpins, powders, buttons, imitation jewels, shoelaces, and—wonder of wonders!—little pots of rouge, bits of mascara, anathema to Sam, but to them a joyous mystery. Often, as a treat, the children were allowed to *look in the drawers* and then would plunge their hands into this mess of textures and surfaces, with sparkling eyes and rapt faces, feeling, guessing, until their fingers struck something they did not recognize, when their faces would grow serious, surprised, and they would start pulling, until a whole bundle of oddments lay on the floor and their mother would cry,

"Oh, you pest!"

There were excitement, fun, joy, and even enchantment with both mother and father, and it was just a question of whether one wanted to sing, gallop about, and put on a performance ("showing off like all Pollitry," said Henny), or look for mysteries ("Henny's room is a chaos," said Sam). A child could question both father and mother and get answers: but Sam's answers were always to the point, full of facts; while the more one heard of Henny's answer, the more intriguing it was, the less was understood. Beyond Sam stood the physical world, and beyond Henny—what? A great mystery. There was even a difference in the rooms. Everyone knew everything that was in Sam's rooms, even where the life-insurance policy and the bankbook were, but no one (and least of all Sam, that know-all and see-all) knew for certain what was in even one of Henrietta's closets and tables. Their mother had locked cabinets with medicines and poisons, locked drawers with letters and ancient coins from Calabria and the south of France, a jewel case, and so on. The children could only fossick in them at intervals, and Sam was not even allowed into the room. Thus Henny had at times, even to Louie, the air of a refuge of delight, a cave of Aladdin, while Sam was more like a museum. Henrietta screamed and Samuel scolded: Henny daily revealed the hypocrisy of Sam, and Sam found it his painful duty to say that Henny was a born liar. Each of them struggled to keep the children, not to deliver them into the hands of the enemy: but the children were not taking it in at all. Their real feelings were made up of the sensations received in the respective singsongs and treasure hunts.

Louisa was Henny's stepchild, as everyone knew, and no one, least of all Louie, expected Henny to love this girl as she loved her own. But though Henny's charms had perceptibly diminished, Henny's treasures, physical and mental, the sensual, familiar house life she led, her kindness in sickness, her queer tags of folklore, boarding-school graces, and femininity had gained on Louie. Uncritical and without knowledge of other women, or of mother's love, she was able to like Henny's airs, the messes of her linen and clothes closets, her castoff hats and shoes, the strange beautiful things she got secondhand from rich cousins, her gifts, charities, and the fine lies to ladies come to afternoon tea. As for affection, Louie did not miss what she had never known. Henny, delicate and anemic, really disliked the powerful, clumsy, healthy child, and avoided contact with her as much as she could. It happened that this solitude was exactly what Louie most craved. Like all children she expected intrusion and impertinence: she very early became grateful to her stepmother for the occasions when Henny most markedly neglected her, refused to instruct her, refused to interpret her to visitors.

Henny, in the clouded perspectives of Louie's childish memory, had once been a beautiful, dark, thin young lady in a ruffled silk dressing gown, mother of a very large red infant in a ruffled bassinet, receiving in state a company of very beautiful young ladies, all in their best dresses. After this particular day, Louie's memory was blacked out, and only awoke some years later to another Henny. The dark lady of the ruffles had disappeared and in her place was a grubby, angry Henny, who, after screeching, and crying at them all, would fall in a faint on the floor. At first, Sam would run to get cushions; later, when they reached the epoch where Sam habitually said, "Don't take any notice, Looloo, she is foxing!" Louie still ran for the cushions, and would puff and struggle over the deathlike face, drawn and yellow under its full black hair; and would run to the kitchen to ask Hazel, the thin, bitter maid, for Henny's tea. When quite small, she had been trusted to go to the forbidden medicine chest, to get out Henny's medicine—phenacetin, aspirin, or the tabu pyramidon—or her smelling salts; and even once had brought the bottle of spirits hidden behind all those bottles at the back, which all the children knew was there, and which none of them would ever have revealed to their father. None of them thought there was cheating in this: their father was the tables of the law, but their mother was natural law; Sam was household czar by divine right, but Henny was the czar's everlasting adversary, household anarchist by divine right.

But here came Louie observing them both fitfully and with difficulty, since her last birthday. There did not seem to be any secrets in her parents' life. Henny was very free of comments on her husband, and Sam, in season, took each of his children aside, but most particularly the eldest, and told, in simple language, the true story of his disillusionment. In this light, Louie and clever Ernie, who observed and held his tongue, saw, in a strange Punch-and-Judy show, unrecognizable Sams and Hennys moving in a closet of time, with a little flapping curtain, up and down.

"The night of our marriage I knew I was doomed to unhappiness!"

"I never wanted to marry him: he went down on his knees!"

"She lied to me within three days of marriage!"

"The first week I wanted to go back home!"

"Oh, Louie, the hell, where there should have been heaven!"

"But he stuck me with his brats, to make sure I didn't get away from him."

The children tried to make head or tail of these fatal significant sentences, formed in the crucible of the dead past, and now come down on their heads, heavy, cold, dull. Why were these texts hurled at them from their parents' Olympus: Louie tried to piece the thing together; Ernie concluded that adults were irrational.

On her eleventh birthday in February, Henny had given Louisa the old silver mesh bag that her stepdaughter had desired for years. Love and gratitude welled up in Louie; the more so that Sam made an especially poor showing on the same occasion, giving an exercise book that Louie needed for school. Since then Louie had passed on to an entirely original train of thought which was, in part, that Henny was perhaps not completely guilty towards Sam, that perhaps there was something to say on Henny's side. Was she always a liar when she spoke of her pains and miseries, always trying to make a scene when she denounced Sam's frippery flirtations and domestic crimes? Henny was gradually becoming not a half-mad tyrant, whose fits and maladies must be cared for by a stern, muscular nurse; not all a hysteric, the worthless, degenerate society girl whom Sam had hoped to reform despite vitiated blood and bad habits of cardplaying, alcohol, and tobacco; but she was becoming a creature of flesh and blood, nearer to Louisa because, like the little girl, she was guilty, rebellious, and got chastised. Louie had actually once or twice had moments when she could listen to Henny's scoldings and (although she trembled and cried bitterly) could recognize that they came from some illness, her neuralgias, or cold hands and feet, or the accumulation of bills, or from Sam's noisy joys with the children, and perennial humanitarian orations.

Although Louisa was on the way to twelve and almost a woman, Sam had not suspected this veering. He went on confiding in her and laying the head of his trouble on her small breasts. But Henny, creature of wonderful instinct and old campaigner, had divined almost instantly. No, it was deeper. Henny was one of those women who secretly sympathize with all women against all men; life was a rotten deal, with men holding all the aces. The stepmother did nothing extraordinary to bring out Louisa's sympathy, because she had left too much behind her and gone too far along her road to care about the notions of even the flesh of her own flesh, but this irresistible call of sex seemed now to hang in the air of the house. It was like an invisible animal, which could be nosed, though, lying in wait in one of the corners of this house that was steeped in hidden as well as spoken drama. Sam adored Darwin but was no good at invisible animals. Against him, the intuitions of stepmother and stepdaughter came together and procreated, began to put on carnality, feel blood and form bone, and a heart and brain were coming to the offspring. This creature that was forming against the gay-hearted, generous, eloquent, goodfellow was bristly, foul, a hyena, hate of woman the house-jailed and child-chained against the keycarrier, childnamer, and riothaver. Sometimes now an involuntary sly smile would appear on Henny's face when she heard *that dull brute, Sam's pigheaded child,* oppose to his quicksilver her immovable obstinacy, a mulishness beyond rhyme and reason. Sam had his remedies, but Henny smiled in pity at his remedies. He would take Louie out, often in view of the street, in order to give his "lesson a social point" and say, in that splendid head tone of his,

"You see, I am not angry: I am not punishing you out of pique. I am just. You know why I am punishing you. Why is it?"

"For no reason."

He would give her a gentle flip, "Don't be obstinate! You know why!"

He would keep it up, till she began to bawl, yielded, "Yes, I know."

Then he would make her hold out her hands, and would beat her, "You will understand why I have to do this when you get a little older."

"I will never understand."

"You will understand and thank me!"—and in what a contented tone!

"I will never understand and never forgive you!"

"Looloo-girl!" this, yearning.

"I will never forgive you!"

He laughed. Henny, half indignant, half interested, behind the curtain, would think, "Wait, wait, wait: only wait, you devil!" Henny had begun to beat Louisa less; and Louie had not been wrong in seeing a distorted sympathy for her in Henny's pretense of strangling her the night before.

Chapter Two

1 *In the morning by the bright light.*

Louie, passing her mother's door on the way to the stairs, thought nothing at all of the night scene, but went in and dawdled awkwardly at the bedside.

"Mother, do you think my neck's getting too long?" Henny peered at her as if she had not seen her for months.

"Of course not."

"Mother, my dress is so old: in that dress my neck looks so long now."

"I have no money for new dresses. Perhaps next month."

"Sing it, Moth, sing it," whined Tommy. Henrietta looked at him, pulled her glasses down on her nose, and sang,

Like his father, like his father,
He has the cut of a kangaroo,
Bandy-legged and ginger too;
And his nose is very pecu-li-ar—
He winds it round the back of his neck
     Just like his pa!

"Sing it again, Moth!"

"Oh, go to Tokyo!"

Tommy was immensely flattered. Louie earnestly continued,

"Mother, when Miss Bundy makes my dresses next time could she make something distinguished?"

THE MAN WHO LOVED CHILDREN | 39

"Distinguished! Distinguished!" cried Henny, looking at her angrily.

"Sing, 'When Uncle John,'" urged Tommy.

"It has to be distinguished now, with the ten cents he gives me," cried Henny in indignation.

"Moth! Moth-er! Go on."

"Be quiet! Distinguished—some more of your Pollit swank and snobbery!"

Louie began to weep quietly and edged out.

"Mo-oth!"

"Oh, you pest!"

"Mo-o-th!"

When Uncle John came home from sea
He brought a parrot home to me,
And it could laugh and it could sing
And it could say like anything,
"Pretty Polly, Pretty Polly, Polly-wolly-doodle,"
all the day.

"Mother, I love that!"

"Well, I don't. Go and annoy your father now."

"Can I have a piece of sugar, Mother?"

"Go and bring in Mother's toast, baby."

"Then can I have a piece of your sugar?"

"My name's Jimmy: take all you gimme."

"Can I, Mother?"

"You can, my son."

"But Mother, may I?"

"Mother, may I go out to swim? Yes, my darling daughter."

"Mother!"

"Ask Louie: she'll give you a piece."

"No, she wo-on't, no she won't, Mother."

"Ask her."

"No, she won-on't, Mother."

"Tell her I said so."

"All right."

Tommy rushed out of the room, where he had been getting quite bored, with his usual small trophy. Tommy had brought one piece of wisdom from the womb, *Ask and ye shall receive*. His wide, crooked, irresistible grin and nodding curls did nothing to undeceive him.

But now Aunt Bonnie was heard crying,

"Hot pog, there! Hot pog, there! Make way," and Evie and Tommy, having raced to the gong, began to wrestle about who should *bong* it. Bonnie seized the stick and authoritatively sent the separate soft notes floating all round the neighborhood. There was a rush of overalled males from the washhouse, and Sam began whistling. Each one had a special whistle: there was also a signal for sitting-down and one for come-in-a-hurry.

They were standing in the hall, answering their whistles, the rule being that no one was to enter the dining room till the signal was given. Sam asked Ernest, *sotto voce*,

"Did you tell them?"

Ernest gave him a glance, rushed to the kitchen, shouting, "Dad's going to Malaya," then to the bottom of the stairs where he shouted, "Louisa, Dad's going to Malaya!"

Louie, who was standing at the top of the stairs ready to answer her whistle, started to come down, stumbled on the oilcloth, and sat down three steps below. She had hurt herself, but at the present time she was practicing to be a Spartan and so said nothing.

"Johnny-head-in-air!" said Ernie.

Louie came downstairs with dignity. The twins, who had answered their whistles from the animal cages, burst into the hall, and jostled each other at the bottom of the stairs,

"Looloo, Looloo! Dad's going to Manila [*Malaya, you dope! Manila and Malaya!*] Louie, Dad's going with the Expedition!"

"Of course, with the Expeditionary Force," confirmed Ernest.

"I know!" said Louie, loudly. "I knew before you."

"Tell Thomas-Woodrow to tell his mother," Sam begged Ernest, in a low voice. Since Sam and his wife were not on speaking terms, even this remarkable announcement had to be made by a go-between. Ernest had dealt with many difficult situations. He now took his stand in the northern, or front, door of the hall, nearest his mother's bedroom, and shouted officially.

"Tomkins, Daddy is going to the Pacific and Malaya with the Smithsonian Expedition."

Henny, of course, understood that this was for her. They heard her say to Evie, who arrived rather anxiously at her bedside, "Tell him to go to the big bonfire for all I care."

But Sam, ever true to his intention, had cornered Tommy, so that Henny's baby boy now appeared shyly beside her also, and repeated the news.

"All right, my son," she answered dryly.

But she was nervous. She sent Evie flying to the kitchen for fresh tea and toast. Today there was a big, unexpected painting job. She hated the noise of the blowtorch, and the smell of the paint, old or new, made her sick. Usually during painting jobs she managed to pay a visit to her sister Hassie in Baltimore, or to go down to the dressmaker's and discuss the little girls' clothes, or merely to gossip. But this had been sprung on her; and then, if Sam was really going away at last, she would have to get word to him, go over money matters, and discuss the care of the children. He was a fanatic about the children's education, having ideas all his own, and everything had to be done according to his notions, to the very last detail. Her children could be vaccinated, if she chose, but Louie must not be vaccinated; he would not obey rules about dental and medical inspection, and yet he made a spectacle of himself both at the school and at the Department, if the children could not go everywhere free, because they were not earning; and all the rest of it. She wished he would not always try to show himself superior to everyone.

Then, there was the care of the large, old-fashioned house, the neglected grounds; and not only Sam's small zoo, but his other possessions and constructions, a pond, a rockery, aquaria, his museum, and so on. What a world of things he had to have to keep himself amused! And as to clothing, food, provender, and household necessaries—they were as usual down to their last stitch, ounce, grain, and bar of soap. Sam would take a blue fit when he saw the length of the bills, and at that they were bills doctored by Henny or by a conniving petty tradesman for the sake of her father's estate. He would take a blue fit, probably try to divorce her, or separate, she thought, if he ever got to know the truth.

She bit her lip, got up, put on her red dressing gown and the drugstore slippers given to her by Tommy on her last birthday, and looked impatiently for her fountain pen. It was a beautiful and expensive one given to her by her father, but it was always hidden somewhere.

"I believe he takes it and hides it himself!" she declared irrationally. At last, she called Evie from the table and sent her to fetch school pen and ink; and she sat down to write a note to her husband on a sheet of white paper embossed with her initials HCP—Henrietta Collyer Pollit. The few lines finished, she called Louie, who was carrying in the oatmeal, and said to her,

"Put that on your father's desk where he can see it."

"Pog!" Sam shouted his cant word for food. Bonnie began to bring in the remaining plates of porridge.

"Tomkins was changing the stones on the path so they could see a new view," burst out Saul; and all the children shrieked with laughter while Tommy got very red.

Sam was served first, then a plate put in Louie's empty place, then in Ernest's, and so on in order of age. The ritual was that Saul and Little-Sam were to have their plates placed on the table at the same instant.

"Orb-epp," Sam said in a tone of reproof to Louie. This was one of his words for "serviette." She brought it to him. As soon as the plates were empty, all but Little-Sam's, Ernest nudged his father, who said,

"Go ahead, Looloo!"

Louisa then stood up in her place and repeated, stonily,

"The world stands aside to let the man pass who knows whither he is going.—David Starr Jordan."

"It's a little one," observed Ernest. Sam nodded quietly at Louisa, which meant she was to go on. She continued,

"Perhaps there is no more important component of character than steadfast resolution. The boy who is going to make a great man or is going to count in any way in after life—"

"Or the woman," Sam commented.

"That is not in it," she countered, and finished,

"—must make up his mind not merely to overcome a thousand obstacles, but to win in spite of a thousand repulses or defeats.—Theodore Roosevelt, The Strenuous Life."

Little-Sam was still struggling stolidly through his porridge which he found revolting. He flushed, now that the recitation was at an end. He was in line of Sam's eye (as who was not?). Sam did not fail him,

"Eat up, Little Samphire!"

The six-year-old plucked up courage to ask if he could leave the rest. He had the nerve for this at least once a week, always with the same result. Sam said solemnly,

"Waste not; want not."

Little-Sam gloomily fell to, picking up a lump of cold glue on the tip of his spoon. Sam, to cover his condition, continued cheerfully.

"Teddy was a great and good man, a good citizen, good President, naturalist, and father. He had some little wrong ideas, but he was a great American. And I can't say no handsomer than that, me lads!"

Ernest, with a malicious expression, but a modest tone, inquired, "How many sayings has Looloo learned this year?"

Sam fell in with his mood at once, "Oodles: but does she really underconstumble one of them? No: Looloo is obstinate. Loogoobrious does not appreciate her pore little dad."

Louisa went scarlet and flashed at him,

"I know more by heart than you."

Sam, with a glance of complicity round the table, giggled in an underhand style. Ernest promptly answered his own question,

"Looloo learned one hundred and sixty-five, only thirty in January because she didn't on New Year's and twenty-nine in February because it's leap year and this is June fourteenth, that is, sum total of one hundred and sixty-five sayings for 1936."

Sam smiled dazzlingly at Ernest, who continued with a comical grin, "How many balusters in the balustrade?"

They tried to guess, but of course Ernest knew.

"Feel better; hooray!" exclaimed Sam now. "Afore I had the collywobbles and pains in the lumbar region—by which I don't refer to Oregon none, lads. Here we are all reunited. You should have seen all Pollitry in the old days united round Grandpa Charlie's table, improvising their parts, singing the 'Anvil Chorus.' Now, I wish you kids would do that: your father's musical enough!

Bonniferous!" he shouted, "come on in out of the kitchen and we'll have a singsong before the job."

Bonnie came running in, her eyes shining. She sat down and bubbled over before she had even sat down, "Oh, I had the funniest dream: I dreamed I was a lumberjack, and we were hauling in the savannas: I had seven elephants—or was it nine?" She paused anxiously and looked round the table. "No, nine, because the ninth fell in the mud—a sort of morass—and we were hauling and pulling away for dear life to get it out. Can you imagine anything more ridiculous, me seated on an elephant's neck? Isn't it silly, what you dream?"

"I dreamed I was in a forest of snakes," said Sam: "bad sign! Snakes mean enemies. Whenever I dream snakes, I meet one or more enemies. It's a sign. Now last night I was walking through a mangrove swamp and from every tree hung snakes, hissing at me and swaying into my path. Got to look out. Woke this morning with a hot head and the collywobbles. But never mind. Here we all are united. Looloo," he said heartily, "go and tell Pet to come and sit down. I want the family united today. I want you round today, for I am going away," he sang.

"Across Manila Bay," chanted Little-Sam, relieved at having swallowed all the oatmeal. They all laughed in triumph at this rhyme.

Louisa could be heard in Henny's room delivering the message. They heard Henny, sharp as a rifle, "He has enough of an audience; I've eaten."

Louie came back looking foolish. "Henny!" shouted Sam indignantly.

They did not take much notice of this, but Bonnie pleaded, "If she doesn't feel well, Samuel."

"Henny!" shouted Sam.

"Tell your father to go and chase himself," shouted Henny from the kitchen.

"Samphire," said Sam, containing himself, "go and tell Mother, I order her to come and sit with us at this Sunday breakfast. I will not tolerate this everlasting schism," he finished with a shout of rage.

"Oh, I'm too tired to fight him," Henny said in the kitchen. She dawdled in, her color high and her eyes black, and sat down stiff as a poker in her armchair, which was always left vacant for her. She tossed her head in her old-fashioned style, giving him her famous *black look*.

"Let us be together, Henny," said Sam along the table, in a gentle voice. She gave him a glance more furious than before.

"Tell your father," she said to Evie, seated beside her, "that it's enough to be ordered like a dog: I don't want to listen to his mawkery." Evie turned her head toward her father and silently pleaded with him to consider this message transmitted. Sam had his eyes on his plate, trying to restrain himself, and getting redder every minute.

Ernest said at once, "Daddy, Mother says not to speak to her."

No one laughed. Bonnie said brightly, "Come on, kids, finish up your toast and your orange juice and scram! Lot to be done!"

The children obediently fell to. After a few minutes Henny got up to get herself some more tea. Sam could not prevent himself from admonishing her gently, "Henrietta, you really oughtn't to tan the inside of your stomach this way: it must be like leather."

She tossed her head and disappeared through the door. There was a brief silence of thanksgiving. Then Sam said very gently, "Singsong, boys and girls," and he gave the first notes, in which they immediately joined,

"Steal away, steal away, steal away to Jesus!"

2 *Monoman and the misfits.*

At this moment, a quavering little voice called from the street, "Samm-ee!"

The twins and Tommy scrambled from their places and rushed to the back veranda, where they were at once followed by their father.

From where they stood, they peered at Thirty-fourth Street going downhill, barely visible through the screen of trees and bushes. Diagonally across from the bottom fence were the houses of Reservoir Road, where some of their friends and neighbors lived. These were as wonderful a collection of people as were ever got together in one manhive. Sam, that quick and malicious observer, had got them by heart, and all without contact greater than "Good morning!" and "Good evening!" on the way to the Wisconsin Avenue car. "Many a good laugh the caravanserai had over their foibles and follies," said Bonnie. They were all eccentric, touched, ill-intentioned, ignorant, superstitious, avaricious, or full members of nitwitry. Their children, however, as Sam's children found, were commonplace and amiable little beings, and Sam himself did all he could to attract the very small boys and the girls of all ages to Tohoga House. Sam did not care for the girls of school age as much as for the baby girls.

He could often be seen spying out of the attic windows, up and down the streets, for some toddler from the neighbors' houses, who might be making for the Garden of Eden, Tohoga House, or peering up at its clifflike walls and the immense trees, full of birds and birds' nests, and at the man-high hedges and who might grin in a watery way or even wave its sea-anemone hand when it saw Sam's sunflower-colored head away up there amongst the birds and leaves. He beamed, he bloated with joy, to see how they feared and loved his great house. He had lately thought of calling it Tohoga Place, instead of Tohoga House. Through the eccentric neighbors (with smaller houses) and their worshiping children Sam loved his house more. For Sam was one of those careful, fearful men who well remember worse days, and are determined never to return to them. Once he had paid rent for the small sunless back room in his brother's jerry-built sham-Tudor ribbon dwelling in Dundalk, near the shipyards where his brother was then a painter; and even that was a step up from his father's house. Tohoga House, which this very day he purposed to call Tohoga Place, with a few scrawls of paint, and for which he paid only fifty dollars monthly, with taxes, to his father-in-law, was still all joy to Samuel, so much joy, in fact, that he could forget the black days of his marriage, Henny's early threats of infanticide, suicide, arson. For Sam was naturally lighthearted, pleasant, all generous effusion and responsive emotion. He was incapable of nursing an injustice which would cost him good living to repay, an evil thought which it would undo him to give back, or even sorrow in his bosom; and tragedy itself could not worm its way by any means into his heart. Such a thing would have made him ill or mad, and he was all for health, sanity, success, and human love.

Little-Sam was carrying on a conversation with the infant, Roger White, about the Pollits' soapbox truck, which Sam had made and had baptized *Leucosoma*. Sam called to the baby boy in his honeyed, teasing voice,

"Whitey! Whitey! C'mon in. C'mon in and yuh kin use me truck." Whitey giggled. "Hit's my kyar," wheedled Sam, "you got tuh aks me. Ain't dat de troof, boys?"

The comedy went on, rather feebly supported by the Pollit children. The truck transaction was a serious one, involving the White goat which ate the mayflower when imported into Tohoga's gardens, and their father was making a fool of himself; but they were high-minded about it, they let him amuse himself. Presently Whitey was induced to come up the steps to have some orange juice. They all sat on the homemade bench along the wall.

"Now I've got five sons," said Sam; "all I need is five more." His sons grinned with embarrassment.

"Oo, Taddy," murmured Evie, anxiously, "you'd have too many: there wouldn't be enough to eat."

"For ten sons, I'd make enough to eat. We'd grow it ourselves. We'd farm out all our land, one strip per lad, we'd grow all our own bread, veg, and everything. I'd get some more womenfolk and we'd make our own bread and everyfink. What do you fink, Whitey?"

"Sure, you could grow your own cows too and get milk too," declared Whitey excitedly. Sam was flattered.

"I wish I had a hundred sons and daughters," Sam rejoined with equal excitement, "then I wouldn't have a stroke of work to do, see. All you kids could work for me. I'd have a CCC camp for the boys and an SSS, spick-and-span settlement for the girls. No work for Mother, Dad, or Bonnie. Yes, the Mormings [Mormons] had the right idea altogether: fifty women and their children and no work for the old man." He grinned wickedly at Louisa who was staring out of the kitchen window.

"My father's going to Manila and Malaya," Little-Sam told the visitor.

Some discussion ensued as to whether he was going by bus, boat, or airplane. Sam let them spar for a while and then went into detail, dreamy-eyed, warmly describing the journey over land and sea, the peoples he would *come into contact with*. He carried them along with him, while they sat with dimmed glare of eyes and lips apart, telling that this—

"—came near to the heart of my dreams and will help me to fulfill one of my most ardent wishes—as Looloo knows and Ernie too—to know my fellow man to the utmost—as you will all, someday, and little Whitey here too, perhaps—to penetrate into the hearts of dark, yellow, red, tawny, and tattooed man. For I believe that they are all the same man at heart and that a good one; and they can be brought together sooner or later by their more advanced brothers into a world fellowship, in which all differences of nationality, creed, or education will be respected and gradually smoothed out, and eventually the religion of all men will be one and the same—world peace, world love, world understanding, based on science and the fit education of even the meanest, most wretched. Not the communism of today, which is a political doctrine—not of hate, I wouldn't say that—but of war, class war, hated sound—the doctrine of misguided but certainly well-meaning men, for I have met some of them and there are fine fellows in it, though not fitted to be leaders, because not understanding human love—but a doctrine of confusion, let us say, and confusion is not based on science. We are all, so important to ourselves, only members of a species. The species must be our concern. But we are not animals: species must not fight species for mutual extermination. We are men; we must get together for the good of the genus, indeed of the natural order, so to speak." He smiled a broad, public-meeting smile.

The children, after staring, as if at the movies, at his verbal pictures of all those colored men, had passed into a trance, but were now getting restless; and Sam stopped when he saw this.

Louisa was propping herself up against the railing. She was staring at her father absently. The morning was hot, and Sam had nothing on beneath his painting overalls. When he waved his golden-white muscular hairless arms, large damp tufts of yellow-red hair appeared. He kept on talking. The pores on his well-stretched skin were very large, his leathery skin was quite unlike the dull silk of the children's cheeks. He was not ashamed of his effluvia, thought it a gift that he sweated so freely; it was "natural." The scent that women used, he often remarked, was to cover lack of washing!

"My system," Sam continued, "which I invented myself, might be called *Monoman* or *Manunity!*"

Evie laughed timidly, not knowing whether it was right or not. Louisa said, "You mean Monomania."

3 *What should be man's morning work?*

The whole community worked. Louie was making the beds; Evie was doing the slops; Mother had decided to make some raspberry tarts, and Aunt Bonnie peeled the potatoes. It was a sizzling, pungent Sunday morning full of oven odors. Bonnie kept bursting into song, and upstairs Louie too could be heard crooning, "Bid me to live and I will live, thy protestant to be." A great chorus came from the washhouse. Henny was absorbed in her own ideas and hardly heard the jubilaum; besides which, she was so used to what she called the "Pollit buzzing" that she could bear it when the day was fine. She only opened her ears when Louie's song ceased. That usually meant that Louie was no longer working but was beginning to loiter or to read. In fact, Louie was staring out of the back attic window, southerly, where she could catch a glimpse of the stones of the capital widely tumbled through the river reek: and she was thinking—repeating rather, something from Thoreau, "Morning work! What should be man's morning work?" But she was not thinking that. She was glowing with pleasure and imagining a harlequinade of scenes in which she, Louie, was acting, declaiming (but not, not like the Pollits, nor like comic-opera Auntie Bonnie), to a vast, shadowy audience stretching away into an opera house as large as the world, with tiers of boxes as high as the Cathedral at least. She had a leading man, a shade of giant proportions, something like Mephisto, but he did not count, she only counted: she projected the shadow of her soul over this dream population, who applauded from time to time with a noise like leaves bowling over the path— as they were doing at this moment in the cement paths of Tohoga House and on the asphalt pavements outside, which she could see at intervals, through the moving shawls of leaves.

Now, at the same time that her stepmother downstairs, conscious of the silence above, was thinking, "I must remember to write Samuel a note to speak to his daughter about her dirt and laziness

Evie giggled and then lost all her color, became a stainless oliv appalled at her mistake.

Sam said coolly, "You look like a gutter rat, Looloo, with tha expression. Monoman would only be the condition of the worl after we had weeded out the misfits and degenerates." There was threat in the way he said it. "This would be done by means of th lethal chamber and people might even ask for the painless death, o *euthanasia,* of their own accord."

Louisa couldn't help laughing at the idea, and declared, "The wouldn't."

"People would be taught, and would be anxious to produce the new man and with him the new state of man's social perfection."

"Oh, murder me, please, I'm no good," squeaked Ernie suddenly Of course, he had instant success, and Sam chuckled. But nothing more happened nor was any more heard at the moment of Sam' ideal state, Manunity, or Monoman.

They heard a weird, distorted wheezing, "Phoe-bee! Phoe-bee! and looked round startled; for it was not the Phoebe, but rathe like the clanking ghost of a Phoebe, or even a very old man of Phoebe in his last sneeze at life. But then they saw their friend, th catbird, Mr. Dumetella, back on the little naked twig of elm, wher he swung all the summer: he was merely practicing the flycatcher' call for his own repertory. After a few such wheezes, the bird cease mocking and began to trill.

"How he sings, how he loves to be heard!" cried Sam with raptur and began to whistle to the bird. It stopped and listened attentivel For months they had been teaching him songs to put into hi medley. Sam and the boys were all excellent whistlers.

"And now," called Sam, "jobs, boys, jobs. Whitey can work up th putty." He lobbed off the veranda, leading them, and they all joine in his song, "I Know a Bank."

(only she is so darned callous, she doesn't listen even to him—),"
Louie muttered aloud to herself over the window sill, "If I did not
know I was a genius, I would die: why live?"

Evie appeared in the doorway of the boys' attic. "What did you
say, Louie?"

"Nothing; have you finished the slops?"

"Will you carry Auntie Bonnie's pail down?"

"All right," said Louie angrily.

Evie went back into the room, drooping, offended. "Mother said
you were always to carry it."

Louie turned on her and bellowed, "I know what Mother said."

Evie shrank back, startled, her eyes wide open, the pupils
enlarged with fear. She had seen an awful sight, Louie in one of
her passions. In such a moment, nothing would hold her back,
she knew nothing but herself, no one, and the worst thing, more
terrifying, was the way she villainously held back the animal in her,
while it waited to pounce. Once she had flown to Evie, started to
drag her by the hair: once she had burst a boil on Ernie's temple.
She went pale, her rather pale eyes on the contrary becoming dark,
and her hair seeming to stiffen.

Louie, for her part, felt her heart sink. She had never seen such
a look of terror on her sister's face: she felt she was a human beast
of some sort. She resolved never to let Evie see her anger again.
Evie might sink into a fit. One processional sunset, coming home
from Baltimore, they had had to get out of the car, carrying Evie
stiff and white, to a house on the roadside; and Louie might have
made this happen again. She was incapable of caressing her sister,
but she said gently,

"Never mind, never mind! I will."

Of course, the morning, every morning, was full of such
incidents. That was family life. They were all able to get through the
day without receiving any particular wounds; every such thing left

its tiny scar, but their infant skins healed with wonderful quickness.

A roaring broke out downstairs, the sound of the blowtorch with which their father was beginning on the porch handrail. The two girls hung out the window and observed a respectful group of little boys, the Pollit boys and Whitey, and Whitey's brother, Borden (who had been sent to bring him home).

Saul looked up at an airplane, saw his sisters, and yelled, "Daddy's using the blowtorch, come and see!"

Little-Sam yelled out above the blowing, "Is that Loolook? Soon time for alevena, Loolook!" *Alevena* was the eleven o'clock meal, with tea, sandwiches, and fruit, which all the children shared. They had either bananas cut up on bread or sirup-and-butter on bread. Louie hurried down to get it ready. Meantime a wonderful smell of roasting meat and cooking pastry streamed out of the kitchen, and there was in it the smell of slightly roasted linen. Bonnie was ironing blouses for her sister-in-law and herself for the afternoon. Just as Louie had got to the last three steps and had stopped to stare out at the wan, withered, and flourishing world, seen through the blue, yellow, and green panes of the pointed hall window, and at the fire-bellied newts in the aquarium, Henny's raucous shout came from the kitchen,

"Bonnie, look at you're doing!"

"Oh, heaven's sake!"

There was a rush of feet. Louie moved along too. When she got to the door, her mother turned to her at once and said, with concentrated exasperation,

"Look at your darnfool aunt's done! Look at it, my best blouse! I suppose I'm supposed to go out of this house naked; you'd think they'd put their heads together!" and she flung out of the kitchen into her bedroom. Sam was staring in the window, in consternation, his cheeks flecked with old paint, his mouth open. Bonnie, with her hair damp and tumbled, was holding helplessly in her hands, so that they could see, a blouse so badly burned that the burned piece flapped in and out like a shutter. It was a fine embroidered lawn blouse, which Henny had got from her cousin Laurie, the rich one in Roland Park.

"I just looked round for a second," Bonnie explained, frightened, looking first at her brother, then at Louie. "I looked out of the window because Pet told me she couldn't endure the smell of the blowtorch and I thought I'd say alevena—and then I seemed to smell something—I couldn't tell what, it seemed familiar. You know when there's a combination of smells, you find it hard to distinguish? When I looked back, there it was smoking up from the board. Such bad luck! I knew it. I knocked over that vase Mrs. Rowings gave me this morning. I'd better break a cup right away. And Pet's best blouse! Oh, I could cry." She was crying. "Poor Pet: you can't blame her," she pleaded with her brother. A row of little heads, like coconuts, was laid on the sill. Whitey's brother, Borden, had even come into the kitchen to stare. She was the guilty one, the cynosure of all eyes. Henny was exclaiming in her bedroom,

"Oh, God! What a pack! I'll shoot myself rather than live in the house with such fools! I must be mad!" Ernest, who had been staring solemnly, unexpectedly burst into a howl, a very comical howl, with his long black eyes shut and his mouth wide open and square: "Uh-huh, uh-huh," he sobbed.

Sam muttered, "You women are always doing such darned-fool things!" He drew his gang away from the window.

"A kitchen is a laboratory: what would anybody think of a laboratory assistant that did things like that? Women need more scientific training!" He suddenly looked away, hearing something, and lunged forward, giving Little-Sam a clip on the ear. The boy had been circling round the blowtorch, fascinated, and had picked it up, merely out of curiosity about its weight. Sam caught the torch out of his son's hands,

"You disobedient lout!" he shouted, in fear and distress. Little-Sam burst out into a faint yelping. The White boys ranged themselves side by side, entranced by the strange spectacle. Henny had not done exclaiming and now sallied into the kitchen where Bonnie was still fumbling and trying to explain everything,

"It was only a second—I don't understand myself!" Bonnie only received five dollars a month pocket money from her brother who was always in straits and she didn't see how she could get Henny such another blouse. Henny looked tragic in her long smudged dressing gown, with her hair hanging thin out of untidy braids, and she cried,

"Get upstairs and out of my sight, go on, I'm sick of putting up with you and your nonsense."

Bonnie, the survivor of many similar scenes, pleaded in a cowardly way, "Pet, I'll get you another (I don't know how) but you may be sure—"

"Don't call me Pet. I don't want you here. I only put up with you and your eternal gossiping and buzzing because you're too much of a fool to keep a job and your brother wants to keep you off the streets."

Bonnie flashed, "I work for it: I earn my keep and my—five dollars."

"Your five dollars, your five dollars, take your five dollars and ram it down your throat," cried Henny: "do I get even five dollars the months we're behind? Doesn't he punish me, the way he punishes the children and all of us? Why are you throwing it up at me? I'd give you more."

"I could bite my tongue out," said Bonnie.

"Do you think I get five dollars for slaving my head off for him and his breed, and never getting a decent bite, nor a rag to my back? Do you think I'd care about the silly, stupid thing if I had another rotten rag in my wardrobe to get on my back? You could have it and all the rest of your rot," she finished impatiently. "Get out of my sight: Louie will help me with the dinner, and then I'm going out, and let them lock me up for a lunatic if I ever set foot again in such a madhouse."

"What's the matter, Pet?" asked Bonnie, looking queer. "You're not yourself Pet: I know this is your offday."

"Go upstairs and pack," screamed Henny: "I don't want you and your filth round the house where my children can see it. Get upstairs and get out or I'll scream it out to the neighbors."

Bonnie crimsoned and huffily went into the hall while Sam, with a peculiar inquisitive and guilty air, was standing in the southern door of the hall. When Henny sped out of the kitchen, she saw him and gave him a black look. He said diffidently,

"Pet, don't make such a noise about it: you'll get another blouse: from your cousin Laurie, no doubt," he finished with a faint sneer. Henny went into action at once, glad of the provocation.

"I won't have your guttersnipe of a sister here, running after every cheap common man she meets in the gutter, staying out on the tiles till all hours, with her commercial travelers, going to their rooms and smoking. I smelled smoke in her room this morning."

Bonnie, pale with injured pride, was going upstairs without a word. Henny followed her intolerantly to the bottom of the stairs, conscious of Sam's standing there. Bonnie turned on the fifth or sixth step,

"Henny, how can you? I've always been your friend, you know that."

"Go up, go up at once, or I'll let them know what you put in the washhouse," said Henny with a spot of color under her rouge. She flung open the hall door, "I'll let that man Bannister, across the street, that you think's so fine, that you're always showing your legs to, know what I have to put up with."

Bonnie, pale, looked over the balustrade at her brother, who however said nothing, only looked foolish and helpless there in his overalls, half naked, with spots on his face. She started up the stairs again. Henny rapaciously cried out,

"You used your slip to wipe up a spilled pot; and not satisfied with that, you've brought home bedbugs from some dirty low dive you've been in, like a sloppy servant girl, and the mice go there to eat up all the greasy crumbs you've got in little bags in your dressing table. You were born in the slums and bring the slums with you into my house, you and your rotten, slave-driving brother. And the whole place looks like a slaughterhouse."

Bonnie began to bawl and they heard her tripping up the next pair of stairs. Behind her back Henny still cried out vile things, while Samuel with that intimidated but sordid expression moved away with his little tribe towards the back porch. He called out suddenly,

"Loozy! Alevena!"

He put out the blowtorch and gathered the children round him in the long dining room and looked out through the open northern window for a minute without speaking. They saw his wet eyelashes. Then he put one arm round Evie and one round the silent, mystified Tommy, drew them to him, and said,

"Let's be quiet together, kids. I wanted us to be so happy today, happy and rejoicing because your poor little Sam loves you and is doing what is best for everyone."

Looking at them all tenderly, he cut up the fruit himself and poured out the tea. On Sunday they were all allowed to have tea all day to be with him.

"Thick for the lads, thin for the girls," said Sam, suiting the action to the words as he handed out the slices of bread.

"Now masticate, denticate, chump, chew, and swallow." Then he fell silent again, and nothing was heard for a space but the mild breeze blowing through the hall and making the gong vibrate softly, *ton, ton!*

Gently Sam leaned over his baby, "Tomkins, here!" Tommy

reached his fat face to his father. To the boy's pouted lips he joined his own, siphoning the chewed sandwich into Tommy's mouth.

"Not only for the ptyalin," Sam communicated to them, "which is now already mixed with the food and helps Tommy to digest, but also for the communization of germs. Tommy will not, I think, suffer from the dyspepsia that all you other kids do. All you other kids are like your poor little Sam—your heads go whizz, and your digestion doesn't agree! Good digestion is for the bovine. But Tomkins, though not strictly bovine, will probably be a prize fighter, and so I'm helping him along. I used to do this to Looloo when she was a little girl and lost her mother." He stopped for a moment sadly, as always when harking back to Rachel and his short marriage with her. "I had to be mother and father too, to little Looloo. This is what parent birds sometimes do to their nestlings. We were very close then," he continued, looking Louie over intently, "and communicated by thought alone: she could hardly speak, but we each knew what the other was thinking, because she was the child of a great love!"

He passed a thin sandwich to Evie. He nodded all round the table at the exercising jaws, "Looloo still loves her father too, although she pretends to be so unfeeling and so cussed." He looked at her again and began to laugh. Very annoyed, with a stern face, Louie pretended not to hear. "Come here, my Looloo!" She got up and came to his side, rather shyly. "Right here!" Surprised, she came closer. Mottled with contained laughter, he stretched his mouth to hers, trying to force the banana into her mouth with his tongue, but she broke away, scattering the food on the floor and down the front of her much spotted smock, while everyone clamored and laughed. Sam himself let out a bellow of laughter, but managed to say,

"Get a floor cloth, Looloo-girl: you ought to do what I say!"

With a confused expression, the girl trudged to the kitchen and came back to clean the floor. When she got up she was scarlet with the exertion. She cleaned the cloth and then let herself out dreamily into the yard. Clouds were passing over, swiftly staining the garden, the stains soaking in and leaving only bright light again. Louie forgot the incident completely as a dream.

This messiness was only like all Louie's contacts with physical objects. She dropped, smashed, or bent them; she spilled food, cut her fingers instead of vegetables and the tablecloth instead of meat. She was always shamefaced and clumsy in the face of that nature which Sam admired so much, an outcast of nature. She slopped liquids all over the place, stumbled and fell when carrying buckets, could never stand straight to fold the sheets and tablecloths from the wash without giggling or dropping them in the dirt, fell over invisible creases in rugs, was unable to do her hair neatly, and was always leopard-spotted yellow and blue with old and new bruises. She shut drawers on her fingers and doors on her hands, bumped her nose on the wall, and many a time felt like banging her head against the wall in order to reach oblivion and get out of all this strange place in time where she was a square peg in a round hole.

There was a picture of a sweet, gay, shy little girl with curls all over her head, in an old frame in her father's room. She could hardly believe that she, the legend of the family, whom everyone had a right to correct, had been that little girl. She wondered vaguely, from time to time, if she would have been any different if her mother had lived. But she did not believe it, and the picture of a yearning, tragic, sickly young woman that Sam drew did not catch her fancy. She was not like that: she felt a growling, sullen power in herself which was merely darkness to the splendid sunrise that she felt certain would flash in her in a few years. She acknowledged her unwieldiness and unhandiness in this little world, but she had an utter contempt for everyone associated with her, father, stepmother, even brothers and sister, an innocent contempt which she had never thought out, but which those round her easily recognized. It enraged Henny beyond expression: "the Pollit snobbishness!" she would say ten times a day. But it fell on deaf ears. Louie knew she was the ugly duckling. But when a swan she would never come sailing back into their village pond; she would be somewhere away, unheard of, on the lily-rimmed oceans of the world. This was her secret. But she had many other intimations of destiny, like the night rider that no one heard but herself. With her secrets, she was able to go out from nearly every one of the thousand domestic clashes of the year and, as if going through a door into another world, forget about them entirely. They were the doings of beings of a weaker sort.

Henny was annoyed to see the tribe bow before herself in the role of virago; she had not been brought up to think that she would succeed because of a mean disposition. She had been nurtured in the idea that she was to be a great lady, like the old-time beauties of the South. So now she hurried to dress herself and get out of a house where all her hopes had been ruined and where she was forced by circumstances to slur and smut herself to herself. She was restless, full of spite, contempt, and unhappiness—what a spineless crowd, a Baltimore slum breed, the spawn of a man who had begun by taking the kicks and orders of some restaurant keeper or fish handler at the age of twelve and so had never learned independence! The worst was that they looked upon her as an heiress, and she hadn't a nickel in her purse and was forced to go into debt to keep the breed alive. She had no car she could use and was forced on a Sunday (Funday!) to rattle downtown in a streetcar, hungry and without a clean blouse. She supposed she could have forced some money out of him, but she hadn't the patience or the interest to carry on her victory. She was sunk for life. Old David Collyer would never take her back, and what other man seriously wanted a woman with five children even if the Collyer estate was free of debt? She did not care two ticks whether she won victories over such cowards or not: they had won the final victory over her.

She took a bit of cold meat, a hard-boiled egg, some currants, and an onion and made herself a one-man curry, which she ate hastily with some tea made for her by Louie. Then she swished upstairs to the attic, to find Bonnie. Bonnie was reading some old love letters and had only packed two vests in her trunk.

Henny said, with her head high, "I take back all I said: I let my temper run away with me. You can stay if you like, though I'm darned if I would! I'm going to town and I'll be late home."

"I know you didn't mean it, Pet."

"Oh, I'm a brute; but the way they drive me mad and I feel as weak as a cat through getting nothing to eat!"

"Let me make you a little bite, Pet!" Bonnie cried eagerly, rising and putting the letters back in her drawer.

"I've eaten a bit of curry," Henny unbent, and seemed pathetic and graceful to butter-hearted Bonnie. "I don't know why I jump on you."

Bonnie started to say something and bit her lip. Then, "I'll get the dinner, Pet. And I'll get you another blouse somehow."

Henny turned about and gave a hard laugh, "Don't be a fool! Where will you get the money to pay for one? Did I pay for it? I'm a mendicant from my rich relatives! Like an old washerwoman I get their out-of-date clothes, sweaty under the arms. Cheap servants like you and me can't buy decent clothes, or pay back debts. I'll wear any old thing. Who would look at an old hag like me?"

"Whatever you wear, you look so much the lady, Henny!"

She said roughly, "I look like what I am, a poor old wreck: if I'd done ten years of streetwalking I wouldn't look so weather-beaten! Well, will you look after feeding the kids and so on? I'd like to be out all day if I could."

Henny hurried downstairs again, but out of the flush of reconciliation, she thought, I have to smoodge her: I can't employ a girl here who would live in. I never could keep a servant. No one but a Pollit would stand me; not even an Uncle Tom. She laughed to herself and went in to finish her dressing.

Cheered by the news that Henny was going out before lunch, they all went back to work with vim.

"Little, Mother said to clean her shoes," dictated Evie to Little-Sam who was mooning on the path, on his haunches and drawing invisibly with one finger.

"Little is commooning with his thoughts and with Nature," said Sam-major in a low voice. "Leave him to it."

"Then Ernie must do them," said Evie strictly.

"You shut up!" snapped Ernest.

"What's Mothering want clean shoes for?" inquired Sam under his breath.

"She's going to meet Aunt Hassie."

"Why doesn't Hassie bring her car up and take Mother down?" continued Sam, painting with his practiced stroke.

"I don't know," Evie admitted sadly. When Hassie came she always brought something for Evie; but she did not come often.

"Why does everything have to be done in a hole-and-corner way?" said Sam without anger. "Pet simply loves deceit. It took me a long time to realize that that was part of the way she was brought up and I was rather harsh at first, I admit. I don't want deceitful ways round the home, kids! Now I know Henny doesn't look at it that way: that is the curse of the bringing-up of women to useless arts. They used to be brought up to catch men. Yes, that was the ultimate goal—to get a rich husband. Strange, in our republic! But it was so. Now, you know I'm always frank and honest myself. But women have been brought up much like slaves, that is, to lie. I don't want to teach you to criticize your mother."

Meanwhile, Evie and Ernest were whispering energetically and scowling at each other in reciprocating moods of admonition and Evie began to cry. As if a button had been pressed, Bonnie's pale head floated in the dark hall doorway and she recited,

"Dogs delight to bark and bite for 'tis their nature so!" while Louie looked out of the dining-room window where she was reading the *Legend*, and shouted,

"Stop it!"

Ernest grinned. "Who's cleaning my shoes?" called Henny.

Ernest made sham moves, while Evie, sniffling, began to trudge round to the kitchen steps.

"You do 'em," shouted Ernest after her, "I did them yesterday."

"Boy dear!" called Henny.

"Go on," said Sam, giving him a push.

"Yes, Mother!" shouted Ernest.

"Little Ernie boy," called Henny, "do Mother's shoes?"

"There's a darling, there's a good boy," crowed Bonnie: "there's a mother's boy; kiss its Bonnie. Who's a good boy? Don't use that rag, darlin'. Come, honey, give its Bonnie a big kiss."

Ernest nonchalantly brushed a kiss on her cheek, in between two rubs.

"There's a dear little man: someone's going to be a big hit with the girls, I know."

Ernest polished the shoes in an efficient style and rushed in with them, after putting away the polish and rags.

"Ten cents," he said: "that's what the shoeshine boys want, Mothering. That's all I charge."

"You go to Tokyo," said Henny: "you'll have to lend me your money box to go downtown."

"How much?" inquired he excitedly. "How much? Will you give me the usual commission, Mothering?"

"You bet your sweet life," said Henny. "Have you got a dollar, boy dear?"

"Five cents," bargained Ernest.

"Maybe ten cents, if Hassie gives me any money. And don't tell your father."

"Do you think Old David will give me five dollars for my birthday like last time?"

"Shh!" said Henny, shocked.

"Preparedness!" Ernie grinned at her. Ernie and Henny lived in an intimacy of their own, largely built up of calculations, loans, and commissions. Ernie understood her need of money; she understood why Ernie should make a profit out of her need. Twinkling at his mother, as he handed her the dollar in small change, and nodding his head carefully as he counted the residue back into the slot, Ernie concluded,

"Well, got to write it down," and he dashed upstairs to the attic to make the addition to his accounts notebook. He was a charming child, everyone's darling, he made no enemies, and he managed to remain above the domestic battle through concentration on his money matters. They ranted, but he had already defined all his relations to the world—Sam gave him a nickel every Saturday, Henny was good for at least twenty-five cents a month commissions: Louie, who loved him and knew his passion, gave him money on his birthday instead of a present, and so on. His passion interested all his relatives, and they liked to give him money to add fuel to the flames! Odd human race, thought Ernie. But he himself was no miser. At Christmas and for the various birthdays, he disbursed handsomely and strictly in order and percentage of age. He had a calculator in the back of his notebook, which now stood as follows:

New Year's Day, 1936.

Sam (father)	38, birthday on February 11–	25 cents
Mother	(I don't know) August 15–	25 cents
Louisa	11, birthday on Feb. 16–	15 cents
Myself	10, birthday on Nov. 16–	no present
Evie	8, birthday on Jan. 10–	10 cents
Saul and Sam (twins)	birthday on Jan. 1–	10 c. (5 ea.)
Tommy	4, birthday on Nov. 15–	5 cents
	Birthday presents (1936)	————
		90 cents

At Christmas Ernest divided his bank money by half and divided the half pro rata amongst his family. He always begged a gift for his rich grandfather from Henny, for Henny and he understood their duty.

Sam, issue of a poor family, ignored all such duties, and had chimeric views about money, the bright, the beautiful, the leveler, the just: he called it "the root of all evil." Henny raged and Ernie smiled at this. Henny was thinking already, "That boy will get me out of a mess later on: if only Father stays alive until he grows up! I wish one of my brothers had had the *nous!*" And even Samuel would wink and grin to the others,

"Nary a word! A chip off the old Collyer block!" but at other times he would see a great chemist or physicist in Ernie.

Ernie heard things humming out at the back and, as soon as business was done, rushed out.

"Lumpkin!" shouted Bonnie. "Sweet lumpkin?"

"As she walks, she wobbles," cried Sam provokingly from the porch, craning his head to discover Ernie; "as she walks she wobbles, boys!"

"Smithy is here!" Little-Sam told Ernie. Dribble Smith's ten-year-old son had, in fact, escaped during roasting hour and climbed the side steps to view wonderful Pollitry in action. When Gregg Smith laughed, he also dribbled, or blew bubbles, the habit which had won little tenor Smith ignoble fame amongst many bureaucrats.

"As she walks, she wobbles," chanted Sam, painting.

"Shh! That's Mrs. Bannister," said Saul from his perch on the handrail. "She'll hear you, Pad."

Bonnie rushed to the window of the kitchen, "So it is! Old Mother Slipperslopper."

"You hate her, don't you, Bonniferous?" teased Sam looking up.

"Sam, don't be ridiculous," said Bonnie, getting pink.

"Samsam, how will we paint the roof of the porch?" inquired Saul thoughtfully.

"Simplicissimus! Ex-cruciatingly simplicissimus," exclaimed Sam. "Put the board across on our two ladders. As she walks, she wobbles, boys," he continued, taking a dip of paint.

"As she walks, she wobbles," said Tommy.

"Old Mother Bannister, sat on her canister," said his father. Louie's face loomed in the open dining-room window, "Daddy, don't be so rude!"

The children were giggling, repeating Sam's crack, *sotto voce*, "Old Mother Bannister."

"You stop it; don't be so rude," cried Louie indignantly. Sam chuckled, "Toppid, Toppid, I god a gold id by dose!"

Old Mother White, oh, what a sight
In the middle of the night!

"Don't make them do it, Daddy!" Louie shrieked, this time from the hall doorway, where she stood book in hand.

"Don't get her mad," said Saul wickedly from above.

"Get her mad," winked Sam at Little-Sam; all the little faces turned toward Louie.

Sam obliged, "Old Mother Jewell is a durn foo-ell!"

The children shrieked in triumph. "Looloo's as mad as a hornet," confided Ernest.

"Make her mad, go on!"

Sam painted away merrily, "As she walks, she wobbles, all her skirts are hobbles, she tripped up on the cobbles, and oh, what a shine!" Ernest guffawed.

"You're disgusting," said Louie, lowering.

"Go on," urged Little-Sam, "Daddy, go on!" The children and

Smithy stood round with shining eyes. "Dirty Old Kydd has such greasy lapels! pooh," said Ernest.

Sam sang, "Old Man Goat and Angela Kydd stewed old cats, that's what they did: then they came to their last resource, they made potroast of a rocking horse."

Even Louie melted at this, though the Kydds, who lived in a tiny wooden house at the back, were her friends. The Kydds made toys for a living and led a cat-and-dog life. Louie laughed.

"Now she's not mad, oo-hoo," cried Little-Sam dancing; "Now she laughed. You laughed, Louie, you laughed." Louie began to giggle and bob about helplessly like a jelly.

"Say some more to make her laugh," Ernie jogged his father's elbow and whispered. Sam picked out the Boltons who lived in the expensive little brick bungalow across the road. They had one daughter, Charlotte, the seventeen-year-old brunette beauty whom Sam admired.

"Old Mother Bolton, couldn't get a holt on, old Dad Bolton, so he gave her a jolt on—the beezer."

The children writhed with joy. Ernie pulled his father's overalls, "Mareta, Mareta!" Mareta was the little Jewell girl.

"Nothing could be sweeter than Mareta when you beat her in the mo-orning!" sang Sam.

"Why do you beat her; is she an egg?" inquired Little-Sam wickedly, looking at his eldest brother.

"She's a good egg, mwsk!" said Sam throwing a kiss. "Oh, sweet Mareta, I'd like to meet her and then I'd heat her a cup of tea!"

"Ernest-Paine loves Mareta," Saul confided.

Ernie blushed but was flattered.

"John Coverdale Jewell is drunk as a roo-ell," sang Sam.

"Shut up, you fool," suddenly shouted Little-Sam to his father, with dancing eyes and an impudent lip.

"Oh, Daddy, he called you a fool!" Evie was very shocked.

"I'm tired of you," shouted Little-Sam, in a frenzy, "you make me sick!"

Sam giggled and winked at the children around him. "Say nothing," he murmured, "say nothing."

"You're an old gasbag," cried Little-Sam, a dervish.

Sam began to chant softly, a song about Little-Sam's school-teacher, "Ole Miss Jones, rattles her bones, over the stones: she's only a porpoise that nobody owns."

Little-Sam paused, eying his father.

"She has two glass eyes," contributed Ernie. "Two glass eyes and two real eyes."

"Saul is her pet," Evie said nastily.

"When Old Bebbo comes round, she certainly is scared stiff," said Ernie. "I saw her through the partition."

"Ooh, her hair, I hate it," cried Evie.

"When Old Bebbo comes in, she rushes round like a bat in hell," Ernie persevered.

"Hades," emended Sam.

"Hades."

"When Old Bebbo comes round, she falls on the ground in a fit," the father affirmed.

"But she loves Mr. McHenry," Evie chattered. "When she can she runs and talks to him and laughs and talks: she's in love with him."

"She wants to marry him," said the father coyly.

"But she can't," declared Ernie stoutly, "because she's an old maid. Oh, I hate her. She's so fat. And she's got two glass eyes."

Sam sang,

Two glass eyes, two glass eyes,
See how they run, see how they run,
Two glass eyes and a wooden leg,
She's too ugly to teach and she ought to beg,

And she cut off her nose with a carving knife
Through two glass eyes.

They all watched Saul softly. Saul unconcernedly began to whistle to himself, but Little-Sam scowled.

"What's her name?" whispered his father.

"Lil, Lillian," they cried at once: "Old Lil."

"She's a Red," said Ernie: "she's always talking about the union." Sam neatly finished his section of the wall, singing,

Jack and Bill
Wouldn't look at Lil;
It went to her head
And she saw red!

Saul began to climb down off the porch roof.

"Whar you a-goin', Saul?" inquired his father, much surprised. Saul said nothing, but continued down to the ground. He put his paintbrush in the turpentine and went round to the front lawn, where he stood silently for some time waiting till the song, sung for the second time, was finished, and poking his fingers through the privet hedge, looking for any insect that might turn up. Sam watched him carefully for a while, making signs to the others. Nothing happened. Then the father nodded to himself, nodded to the others, winked and said merrily, "Not bad, not bad! Self-control!' He nodded again; and sent Little-Sam up on to the porch roof to finish Saul's job.

"Taddy, can Isabel come in?" put in Evie.

"Isabel, wasabel-hasabel-possible," Sam answered.

"Taddy!"

Sam flung his brushes in the pot, "Tired-oo. Hot head. Spell till munchtime," said he. "Knock-off time, Littla-Sam!"

"Taddy, can Isabel go round the Wishing-Tree?"

"Powwow!" said Sam wearily. He squatted in the sun, drawing the children round him. "Got to tah youse kids 'bout my Wonderful Idea. It's about Pangea, the Earth United, or what happened in the year 3000. I was in the orfus doing nothing and it all came to me clear as could be: I really saw it, kids. Little-Sam, go and get the papers off my desk! That is what Louie and me and you others would make—if Looloo would ever be a dood dirl, with our heads, our hearts, and our hands:

"Heart and hands together, lads! Go on, Little-Sam! *Ah, love could you and I with Fate conspire....* But the beauty of it is, kids and Looloo," he continued wildly, "is that we can, we can do so: you and I and little Tomtom can build this Pangea of mine, this Eugea, we can make it come true! Perhaps even little Tomtom will see the time when the last wars are done and we see the Federal States of Europe, and man no longer hidden under a cloud of misunderstanding, hate-engendered, from his brother man."

Little-Sam came back, "I can't find it, Pad."

"The message to Garcia," said Sam, "the message to Garcia! Where there's a will there's a way. Run along, Little-Sam. You'll find it."

"I don't know which it is," cried Little-Sam desperately: "there are millions of papers. Gee!"

"I dunno vitch I vant, a vatch or a veskit," Sam ignored him, doing one of his favorite imitations, a vaudeville Jew. Little-Sam faded into the house, grumbling.

"I give you tree per cent," continued Sam. "Vot you vant vid a veskit? Vid a veskit I kip my visky [whiskers] from flyin' away in de vind!" The children screamed with laughter.

"Mr. Goldberg," said Sam, *sotto voce*, "Mr. Goldberg!"

"Do a Frenchman, Taddy," urged Evie.

"Oo, la-la! Vair is my corsets?" He pretended to tilt his hat over one eye (apparently wearing a stovepipe hat while looking for his corsets). "Vot ave you for little-breakfast zis mornin: I can only eat frogs!" The children capered.

Little-Sam came back rebellious: "I can't find it!"

"Good-by, children!" called Henny from the hall. There was a rush for the house. Sam lay back and closed his eyes. At that moment, a little voice no bigger than two twigs creaking together on a tree, said from the side steps, "Mr. Pollit! Mr. Pollit!"

He opened his eyes on the hazy blue world, said gently, "Yiss?"

Mareta Jewell, a little dark girl, came precipitately up the steps, and approached him with the little dancing hesitations of the shy, "Can I go round the Wishing-Tree?"

"Yes, love," he smiled.

"Will I get my wish, Mr. Pollit?"

"Maybe, if you wish hard, and are a good girl and it's a good wish, you will get it, I expect."

She gurgled joyously and ran round the little spruce.

Chapter Three

1 Beautiful and childlike was he.

In the after-dinner heat, when the dishes were dried and put away and the greasy sink was shining, Louie slipped down the orchard in her bare brown feet and, opening the unhinged back gate a trifle, looked out into the peaceful street. Just opposite were the little wooden houses of the only two neighbors who were Louie's friends—the Kydds and the Walkers. The Walkers were a middle-aged couple with a twelve-year-old boy called Mark Antony. Junius Walker, the dark, nervous father, worked in the Bureau of Engraving, and tried to teach his slow lad Latin at night. He inveigled Louisa into his parlor, from time to time, to read a Latin grammar with his boy. When the time came, blond, fat Mark Antony would go to a private school in England to learn to be a gentleman.

In between the Walkers' small lot and Middenways', the corner grocers, on a lot of the same size, was a similar wooden house, neglected and vine-grown, in which lived an old couple, John and Angela Kydd. John Kydd made toys and, to show it, had two rocking-horse heads on his gate. He left promptly at seven-thirty every morning and returned rotating on his fat legs at six every evening. In between these hours the lonely and scared old woman would often call in Louisa, who was such a big, brave girl, to keep her company. Louisa did not care for either place; they offered her nothing to eat and they reeked of eccentricity; but Junius Walker took pains to explain to her things that no one else had mentioned, ceramics, glazes, firing, and offered to teach her china painting, and as for the Kydds, no one in the neighborhood but herself had ever been invited into the frowsy, furniture-choked dwelling. Sam, always lampooning, found the Kydds and the Walkers inexhaustible sources of inspiration: every day he found new jokes about the two eccentrics. Though Louie knew them much better than he did, she saw them with his eyes, as ridiculous if not positively touched, filthy and mean-spirited to be so poor, vain to have airs and graces when so poor, superstitious to hold any religious beliefs, thickheaded to hold any political beliefs, hoity-toity to hold any esthetic beliefs, fustian to pretend to any education, when so poor. But Louie never said what was in her head and she had a kind heart; so she came down, with bare legs, and in her faded, dirty, outgrown dress, in torn underwear from her fine house on the hill, and listened for hours to the notions that these strange poor folk had about themselves. She felt at home with them. She was eccentric, ugly, and awkward, and they were quite evidently, in their lives, eccentric, ugly, and awkward. Sam had a voice, she had an ear, and these struggling, poor people, gasping just at the surface of the river, about to sink, had lives. They told her something about their lives, which were not cataclysmic, such as Pollitry lived, but lives lived in neat corpuscles, lives which only looked out, squinted-eyed, askance, dubious, through two fishy eyes. The Walkers and Kydds repelled Louie, but she was flattered that they chose her. Ernie knew all the men and women; Evie visited all the "ladies with babies," as she said, and Tommy was dangerously favored: only the two oddities wanted Louie.

Sam and the boys were resting in the deep coarse grass at the bottom of the orchard under the trees and Louie was about to join them. It was a fatty, dreamy hour. Sam's voice began behind Louie with a low insinuating humming that enchanted the sulky ear guards and got straight to their softened brains,

"Your Poor-Sam brought you up in Washington, the new Jerusalem, as I verily believe, because he wanted you to feel the blood beating through the heart of the nation. Think of the logcutters' children in Oregon and the little redskins on Indian reservations and the little tall-eared Missourians and the little frozen two-legged ears of Minnesota Swedish wheat whose only dream in life is to come and see the Great White Father—whoever he may happen to be: while my tadpoles can see not only him but me, every day that is."

"I'd like to go on an Indian reservation," said Saul, far away.

Sam began his humming again:

Most beloved by Hiawatha
Was the gentle Chibiabos,
He, the best of all musicians,
He, the sweetest of all singers.
Beautiful and childlike was he,
Brave as man is, soft as woman...
When he sang, the village listened:
All the warriors gathered round him:
All the women came to hear him:
Now he stirred their souls to passion,
Now he melted them to pity.

"The passion was the passion of nature, the passion for good, not selfish human passion," Sam commented.

Bare feet appeared now and again amongst the green blond spikelets, and now a summer-burnt head appeared in the same place. Saul said, "Where's Looloo? She went out the gate." The grass bottom bloomed with heads and eyes. "She's gone to Mrs. Kydd's." They giggled.

"I have many wonderful thoughts during those times when I am sauntering about by myself (and when perhaps to the foolish or mean eyes and heads that I seem to have round me I am just mooning about). Take the theory of the expanding universe—

I want to figure it out some day. It came to me by myself. The theory of wave motion came to me merely from looking at my mother's dishcloth hanging on the back veranda, when I was a little boy no bigger than Ernest-Paine here. And very often I have an idea and then find months, years later, that a man like our very great Woodrow Wilson or Lloyd George or Einstein has had it too. Of course, I believe in a transmission of ideas, on the same principle as radio, amongst a community of minds."

The children were silent, sunk back to the grass; but Little-Sam had sneaked off to the gate to look after Louie.

"It is a pity I had handicaps which you all know about," he said hastily, "or I should have been able to accomplish all the wonderful things in my heart." He sighed, "When you kids get bigger, and have your own life dreams, you will appreciate your Poor-Sam more."

Through all the soft wind sounds came the call of bobwhites in the White Field.

"Hear in the Buzzum of my famerly I am enjoyin' myself at peas with awl mankind an dthe wiminfolks likewise," Sam quoted dreamily.

"Little-Samuel, come'n lie down," called his father. But Little-Sam, after gaping at the Kydds' house, had slid on to the footpath to read the newest legends scrawled on the Pollit back fence. Opinions of the Pollits as well as of neighbors were written here every day by boys. Sam, used to being obeyed, did not know that Little-Sam was away still.

"Boys," said he, "boys, you soon won't have your little feyther with you. He is going away to Greenland's icy mountings and India's coral strand. You have to look after yourselves, your mother, and your sisters. I want all of you to stand together and look after the house for me, not only the female hanni-miles mentioned and aforesaid, but also the real honest-to-goodness hanni-miles, Procyon the raccoon, Gimlet the parrot, Didelpha the vixen opossum, Cocky-

Andy the sulphur-crested cockatoo, Big-Me the pygmy opossum, not to mention the birds and reptilians. That will be quite a job for even you smart boys. Now we'll have to work up a schedule. And fustest, you must write to your pore little Sam ebbly week and tell him how 'tis tuh hum; and second, you must keep a record of the birds and hanni-miles wot visit Tohoga House, Tohoga Place that is. No! Momento! Loogoobrious can do that. It will be a good thing for her, keep her mind off of her herself, on which on pleasant objeck," he continued (believing that Louie was there), "it is glued at time of speaking. But that is, no doubt, on account of her fai-hairy figuar and her bewchus face."

He waited for the boys to laugh, but they were all in a mood of indolence. Near them was only the warning chak-chak of the catbird.

"Yes, siree," continued Sam, "Loochus's eggspression at this yere moment eggspresses one idear, Give us Liberty or give us Death. But that is the age, that is the season; we must forgive Loochus her trespasses, or else bring in a verdick of arson in the third degree."

Little-Sam had been timidly flirting with a stray fox-terrier bitch, with a sore paw, but after a few pats from a safe distance, the dog showed such a sudden, desperate affection for the boy, that he got frightened and, darting to the gate, shut it in the fox's nose. In a surge of emotion he dashed up to his father with,

"Looloo's gone over to see Mrs. Kydd. Mrs. Kydd called her and took her inside."

"I hope Old Goat gives her a nice sardine tin to eat," said Sam.

The front gate to the Kydds' house was locked and fixed with barbed wire. The lock and hinges had rusted. The front path, unused for years, could barely be seen through the grass and weeds. Unpruned cedars lined this path. The only entrance was by the side gate, over a cinder path, covered by a trellis broken with the weight of untidy grapevines. Caterpillars dropped from this vine on to

Louie's hair, but she put her hands up and delicately removed them. The little old woman ran in front of her, turning every few steps to smile, nod, and beckon,

"Quick, come into my kitchen: I must show you something," and again a pretty nod of complicity. Louie hoped for something sweet, even though she had never eaten in this house before. They hurried down the side passage and onto a wooden veranda, very dark with vines. There were two rockers, with faded cushions and a rain-beaten table. Old Angela raised her finger warningly and pointed down at the broken plank just by the door. They went into the narrow hall littered with bits of furniture, indistinguishable in this sudden dark, but which Louie knew from other visits, and so into the old kitchen, where a wood-and-coal stove was set in a large fireplace. Old Angela, with her quaint bright mystery, beckoned Louie again to the fireplace and, when she got there, cautiously lifted the lid of a small black stew-pot.

"Look, look," she nodded with excitement. The little girl looked and saw nothing but a meat stew with vegetables from which steam was rising.

"And something else," cried the old woman in a fit of generosity, "look! Only wait!" She scurried to the dark larder and, after struggling for a while with something, returned with a half slice of bacon which she dangled before her. "There," she said, "you watch," and she dropped the bacon into the stew. "A better taste," nodded the old woman. "My, it will be wonderful tonight! Mr. Kydd loves stew and stew with a bit of bacon in it—mm-mm, he loves that. Mr. Kydd says to me, 'Angela, you're a good cook, and just put a bit of bacon in and you're a better cook!'" She nodded at the girl full of understanding. "Come, will we go into the front room? It's brighter, eh, more cheerful for a young lady! And you have such beautiful little feet," she continued, stopping in the hallway, "such beautiful, beautiful little brown feet, a little brown maid."

"Oh," said Louie, "I forgot—at home we go about barefoot because it is healthier—"

"Such beautiful little feet: you are quite right," said the old woman, "I am sure you are a wonderful girl at home to your mother, yes I am sure of it."

Louie would not be pushed into any admission, but followed her into the parlor. They passed one closed room which Louie had never seen, and reached the parlor where John Kydd had his organ. The sunlight poured through a triple window with dust-thick panes, and cast red, blue, and green stains on the thick dust of the floor. Three doors, beside the hall door, led out of this room, but it was impossible to reach two of them, and the third could be got at only by squirming around a large drop-leaf table extended, two chairs, and an old-fashioned glass table designed for showing a tea service under glass. Near the window was a dining table, a card table, and other odds and ends.

"We have so much furniture," said Angela, "so many things! Aren't people stupid, eh? You must think us so stupid! Now sit down and let me look at you. Your hair is so lovely, isn't it, such a nice shade, and what a trouble it must be to your dear mother to wash and fix and braid and all that!" Louie became conscious of the tatters of her hair.

"I am sure you play the organ," cried the old woman. "Do try it, do play me something? Mr. Kydd loves to play to me."

"No, no," protested Louie, "I can't."

"But you have such artistic hands," protested the old lady. She looked scarcely older, perhaps younger, than Louie as she sat there, or rather like a child face fitted into a bonnet of untidy white hair and stuck on an old wrinkled neck. Her dirty brown woolen dress had lost its belt, and its hem was undone. A black petticoat hung beneath, but revealed wrinkled stockings fallen round the ankles and turned black shoes. But the little heart-shaped face that nodded so eagerly at Louie had two large soft brown eyes, well set, and deep fringed, and a supplicating, kind smile blew in and expressions, begging for acquiescence, for information. Louie was used to her. Her dirt and the dirt of the old man were repulsive, but the old man beat her, so the story went, and Louie felt conscience-stricken. Often, Louie had seen her racing after him down the passage, as he strutted to the gate in the morning, crying,

"John, John! Don't leave me without a cent, John! What will happen to me? John, only a nickel! It's just to have. I spend nothing. What do I spend? I need nothing. But I must have money!"

Everyone knew of her and John. They sought no friends amongst the neighbors, despising them all. But everyone knew (for Angela had confided the truth from time to time, whispering into one ear and begging some little snatch of food from another) that this same John beat her, starved her, and insulted her and that she was abandoned by all her family, though old and frail, because John had systematically alienated them. The Walkers, on one side, Middenway, the grocer, on the other, had heard her cries and his storming late at night or in the peace of some holiday.

There was a strange vileness in them and in the house which fitted their solitary lives and their dirt perfectly. Louie had an ear that always lay in wait and after the honeyed greetings, the love, and the tender stories about John, the cruelty and coarseness of their lives would prick through oftener and oftener, until Angela would come to tell her about John's habits. What habits could anyone have in that house but the most hideous?

"I wanted to ask you something," said the old woman, "but you will perhaps be angry with me. But you are so good and big and brave and strong. It is something I can't do myself. I'm so little. Look at me! Look at my arm!" She bared a frightful faggot of sinews. "Like two threads! No, my dear, I cannot, by myself, and Mr. Kydd is so busy. But perhaps you will."

"Yes," said Louisa, "what is it?"

"You are so good, and you sit there with your lovely little bare feet—" the old woman paused, as if led astray by her own cunning irrelevance. She began again, "You know, nothing is worse than to hurt an animal, eh? Cruelty to animals is—" she shook her head. "You wouldn't be cruel to animals," she pounced on the child with her great eyes.

"No," said Louie, "but you have to trap some."

"Yes," cried the old one, "yes, harmful ones: yes, mice—even cats. Kittens are nice, so soft, they play and not even a little mew! But when they get to be big tomcats, ouf!" She shuddered. "You know last Friday I found my yard full of tin cans. Who put them there? I don't know." She peered at Louie, looking very old. Louie became confused and wondered if Angela suspected the Pollits of filling her yard with rubbish. "Who could do it?" inquired the old woman sharply.

"Who could do such a thing?" Louie asked angrily. "That is awfully mean."

The old woman sighed, "You see, I love animals. I have no food myself, but if an animal comes crying to my door, I must give it a scrap, mustn't I? What have I—spinach water, crusts, but what I have I give! (I give, I give)" she muttered angrily at the end. "I have a lovely pussycat, dear, you have seen it."

"Yes," said Louie dubiously, for now she saw daylight. The Kydds' cat was able to attract into the Kydds' back yard all the cats of the neighborhood; the cat club was there, and there they howled from moon to sun. The tin cans of Friday were the last, not the first.

"And John said," she continued, lowering her voice respectfully, "that we mustn't annoy the neighbors. Annoy!" She laughed suddenly and clearly. "Me annoy! I am so timid—like a little mouse. How can I get rid of the cat?" she demanded of Louie.

"Give it away."

"No, no!" She looked at the child for a long time, revolving something in her mind. "If someone would kill it for me—I must! I hate to. Kill a living creature! I can't kill a fly! And I haven't the strength, not to, not to get a fresh sheet out of the drawer. I tug and tug. It stays fast. What can I do? You are good, you are so strong, young, and healthy—" she paused.

"My father would kill it for you," offered Louie. The old woman refused at once: no, no, that would never do. No one must ever know she killed her cat, only someone she could trust, trust as she trusted no one. (Louie, for instance.)

"All right," said Louie.

The old woman stared, as if in astonishment, "You will."

"Yes."

The old woman began to cuddle herself, "Such a dear sweet little girl, with her little brown feet—" She paused and said in a businesslike tone, "Tom is out on the front porch." She immediately led the way to the rarely opened front door and showed the white cat sulking under a bench. Angela had tried to catch him herself. Louie said they had to have a box, and Angela at once produced a suitable box from under the kitchen table, and brought a hammer and nails, in a marvelously efficient way.

"You will have to give me a piece of your stew meat," said Louie. The little woman fetched her a piece without a murmur, like the smallest drummerboy to the largest general. And Louie managed, in a very short time, with savant caresses taught her by her animal-catching father, to get the cat and drop it in the box. They slammed down the lid. At once, the cat seemed to know its fate. It seemed to swell to twice the size, its hair stiffened, and its magnificent blue eyes shot rays of fire: its eyeballs turned to flames, and it began screaming in a horrid voice that neither had ever heard from a cat before. Louie felt a fear of the mad beast, and a wicked lust to down it and finish it, just because with all its shrieking it was helpless.

"In here," muttered the old woman. She led the way towards the locked door of the passage, unlocked it with difficulty, and put on the light by a string. There was a rusty old bath covered with dust.

"We'll fill the bath and drop the box in," said she. "You do it, my dear. You are so very kind: you do it. I can't see it," and she hurried out, leaving the girl with the cat. Louie turned the rusted tap and let the water run: the cat cowered and gleamed in the box. When the bath was full enough Louie got the box and pushed it under. The cat struggled with large floating gestures in its prison. At the first convulsion Louie felt a sort of sickness, then she pushed it hard under and, sitting on the edge of the bath, kept it under with her feet. The box heaved a little. The cat took a long time to drown. Presently she came out to the kitchen to find the old lady sitting there at the table, silent, with her great lamps glowing in her face.

"I did it," said Louie.

The old woman thanked her but rather perfunctorily. "I would give you a cake," she said, "but I have none, none at all. I will get you a little cake."

"Thank you," said Louie hungrily.

"Not now, not now. Perhaps your dear mother wants you, dear?"

"No, she's out."

"I don't like cream cakes," said the old lady politely. They had talked some fifteen minutes about cakes before Angela heard her husband's footsteps on the cinderpath. She bundled the little girl out the front door and directed her round,

"Come again, soon, soon, darling, little darling!" she whispered.

Louie was sorry that she had only been invited over for the cat, but she believed that the little woman loved her and that there was peace in her foul cottage.

2 *Intrepid passengers.*

It seemed at first as Louie edged in through the jammed gate that there was perfect quiet in the orchard. The sun shone, there was a flip-flop of leaves, and suddenly a silvery leap of a young boy's voice. The powwow was still going on! Little-Sam jumped up,

"There's Looloo! What did you do, Looloo?"

"Looloo went without her shoes," Ernie observed. Sam's head rose through the grass too.

"Loochus, why did you go without shoes?"

"You said it would be better if the whole population went without shoes, it would harden them."

Sam looked and suddenly popped with laughter, then cried, "You're a fathead!"

He dropped down in the grass again and waited. At last a voice came, "Go on, Pad!"

"There will be anagravitational ships, a word I made up myself," said Sam, "the ease with which gravitation could be cut off is so simple to us nowadays—of course we're in the year 3001, Loo-loo!— that it seems absurd—excruciating!—that twentieth-century brains which did show some signs of awakening out of the medieval torpor could have been so slow to grasp it—in fact, it was not even hinted at till 1994. Why? Their so-called minds were preoccupied with what might be truly described as self-destruction—pansewer-pipes or universal self-destruction. And a few are still seen, in museums, the cavorite ships of Wellsian cavorite, I mean, but in the main they had long been thrown into the discard even in the year of our Ford 2050, because of the simplicity with which gravitation could be cut off and taken in, to a major or minor extent at will, by a simple turn of a few levers or the pressing of buttons—the physical and practical application I will describe to you later, kids, or perhaps Ernest-Paine or Little-Sam themselves will be the ones to really work it out in some laboratory later on—and now I'm speaking of the year of our Ford 1936," he ended solemnly.

"Oh, gee, let's go and get on the job, Pad," said Saul.

"Directional Towers were then necessary for the stages of the cavorite ships," dictated Sam. "They were stationed here and there throughout the earth on high places, all done by our friends of the American Geographical Society and introducing the true Surplane Life, or Age of Surplaners. These Surplaners utilizing the Stratosphere Stations attained terrific speed—1200 mph was attained in 2050 as even little Tomtom learned in his kindergarten physics book. Our experimenters now reach 3800 mph, and we will soon supersede the need for vessels at all—it is fairly safe to predict that in ten years, say year of our Ford 3011, there will be *projection by dematerialization;* the cartridges in which the passengers will take their places will be sundered, smashed to smithereens, and so shot through space, as gas or lighter than gas, avoiding friction."

"But the passengers?" inquired Ernest, aghast.

"Also smashed to smithereens and reassembled," Sam expounded coolly.

"How?" asked Little-Sam in trepidation. His utter faith in his father made him believe that this would really take place.

"In tubes," said Sam airily. "Each passenger will be shot into a tube and decomposed."

"No one would travel," declared Ernest.

"That's what they said when the locomotive came in," Sam was contemptuous. "We are people of 3001. Each one has a formula and is reassembled according to that minutely correct formula. We haven't the freaks and neuroses of the Dark Ages. We were born according to formula: we are not a hazardous aggregation of mean genes. We approximate a mean, the mean of our intellectual class. When we are born, we are studied, and deviations, if noxious to the species, are suppressed; good deviations are preserved. And furthermore, we bear our formula on our arm band!"

"But the arm band would be decomposed in the tube," Louisa discovered triumphantly.

Sam grinned and bit his lip. "The formula for each passenger would be radiotelegraphed ahead with the notice of his having taken a ticket," said he. "Thus," he suddenly cried, "Looloo, you meant to be mean and clever, but actually you merely gave me another idea—thus, you could resurrect the dead from the residue of fires, after accidents—resurrection would be real, not a faded dream."

"That is wonderful," said Louie, much struck.

"Slightually," Sam smirked, "slightually, your poor little Sam is wonderful, but a prophet in his own mud puddle—"

After a silence of digestion, Saul said, "Let's do our job, Pad, go on." He started dragging Sam to a sitting position.

"O.K. Looloo, I been giving the boys their places in my Planned Economy. Ernest-Paine is my lieutenant while I'm away and Louie ain't a looie, she's going to run the women for me."

"I won't do what Ernie says," yelled Saul.

"You got to do what you're own legally elected chief says," gently said Sam. "And you're free to elect your own boss, you know, boys, as long as it's Ernie; and if there's complaints you kin throw him out en eleck another as long as it's Ernest-Paine, just like the Bolshies."

"I won't," said Little-Sam.

"I'll make ya," Ernest was calm.

"You shut up, you rat," Saul called lazily from the orchard path.

Sam softly admonished, "Don't call humans rats—rats are superior."

"I'll knock you into the middle of next week if you call me a rat," Ernest replied.

Sam chuckled and winked at Louie.

"You stink," drawled Saul, "you stink like Mr. Gardner, you stink like Mr. Kydd on ice; you stinkurate!"

"Go on," whispered Sam, letting out a kick at Ernest who was hopping over "the grave" (a depression in the orchard where seedling boxes had once been). "Go on, Ernest-Paine!"

"I'll murder you for that," yelled Ernie at once, "I'll push in your daylights."

Sam flattened the grass with both hands and squatted down in a flat place, saying gleefully, "Go on, Sawbones, give it to him; go on, Ernest-Paine, attaboy!"

Saul could never keep his temper and had flushed. Ernest came up to him coolly and said, "C'mon, c'mon, you coward!"

"Sawbones ain't no cowyard," said Sam gently. Saul rushed up from his position below Ernest, as if about to take flight, and rolled into Ernest with both fists going, landing both, though, on his chest.

"He's fightin' mad, Ernest-Paine," cried Sam, "you've got him! Keep your temper, Sawbones! You'll never down him, Ernest! They've gone into a clinch! They love each other! Break! Get him on the point, or you'll never do it. Sawbones, a foul!"

The two boys separated, Saul tottering aside in his misery. He was crimson, and tears of rage and humiliation were running down his cheeks. Ernest kept dancing at him, a thing that infuriated him. Saul had more solid muscles but always lost his temper, so that Ernest always beat him by first goading him into a paroxysm of resentment.

"Now," cried Sam, "Sawbones, go on, bust him wide open!" He laughed genially, more like his eldest sister Jo than himself.

"Daddy, don't let him," cried Tommy, frightened. Sam laughed, putting his great arm round Tommy,

"Men must fight, Tomahawk (but only for the right). Sawbones must learn to keep his temper. Ernest must learn to hold his own."

With a great effort, Saul had for the moment held back his temper and was going at Ernest like a windmill, his eyes wide open and glaring like jellies, his red lips pressed back over his teeth. Ernest, his conceit taken by surprise, was breathing hard, somewhat flustered.

"Go it, Sawsidge, you're getting there!" cried Saul's father. "You're getting Ernie down. He's getting woozy." He turned aside to Little-Sam and remarked very audibly,

"You see, if Sawbones keeps his temper, he's got Ernie beat a million, because Sawbones has a better fighting kit!"

Saul, with a deeper flush and half a smile, lunged at Ernest's cheek, missed, and himself received a painful blow on the upper arm which made tears of pain come into his eyes.

"Good hit!" recorded Sam.

Saul lowered his eyes and began rubbing his arm and stamping his feet and bellowing miserably.

"Daddy," said Little-Sam, "make them stop now."

"Take it like a man, you fathead," cried Sam to Saul. "Fight him: what are you bawling for?" He shoved him forward. Saul automatically sent a soft blow wide, and then suddenly, with a loud bellow, turned and ran up the orchard as fast as he could. But his legs were shaking, and he stumbled at every step. Sam shouted,

"Sawbones, Sawbones!" and impulsively, yanking Tommy to his feet, Sam crowed, "Come on, boys, after him. The boy who ran away! C'mon! Give him the fright of his life!" With shrieks, they started after the fugitive, Sam in front dragging along Little-Sam whose face was anxious. Saul gave a look behind, saw the pack after him, darted sideways through the grasses, and went sprawling behind a young pine tree. He lay there face downwards, sobbing into the earth. Sam came up, with the boys slightly astern, and stood there, for a moment, then poked his son with his toe,

"Get up, son!"

Quite broken, Saul began to pick himself up, dispersedly, as if his skeleton had become disarticulated and floated off in impossible directions. Sam got out his handkerchief and wiped Saul's eyes on it, then said,

"C'mon, kids: job! Work heals all sorrows!"

With an occasional sob, Saul tailed along, and in a quarter of an hour it seemed as if there had never been a cloud in the sky. When they were shifting their ladder so as to get on the roof itself, Sam sat down on the edge of the path and, drawing them round him into one of his powwows, said, with his arm along Saul's shoulder,

"Kidalonks! When there is bad blood in this family, I want you to get it out of your system by a man-to-man fight. Then we'll all be very happy and love one another. Nothing is worse than a nursed grudge. Our tempers are our worse natures and when they come along, we give 'em a good physical shakeup and hey, presto! we're wholesome and clean again, good citizens and good brothers." He looked round the little manhood with satisfaction. "My good boys," he said. And then began the difficult, exciting, and dangerous business of climbing on the roof. From it they saw the Cathedral and the capital city.

3 *Henny downtown.*

The capital city, always duller than hard-working, mercantile, familiar Baltimore, is detestable on Sundays, dull and Pharisaical, thought Henny. Nothing but an emergency would have induced her to go downtown on a Sunday: the department stores were shut, there was no obsessed crowd of women on Seventh and Eighth Streets in which she could hide her garments, shabby bag, untended hair, and old skin. Her poverty was naked on the empty streets, and if no one walked abroad she felt all the more ghastly, like a wretched sinner in the sight of God. For Washington is Heaven, and Henny, disfigured, burdened with shameful secrets, felt like a human being would feel on first entering the sight of the angels. She detested perennial Heaven, Sinai's thunder, the new Jerusalem's powerful hierarchy; she felt it was the Eden of fleshpot men and ugly women striving for God knows what ugly, unhewn, worthy ends, not for the salvation of miserable creatures like herself. When she had first come to Washington, she had come with no more sense of married life or of social life than a harem-reared woman, being then a gentle, neurotic creature, wearing silk next to the skin and expecting to have a good time at White House receptions. Here she was, Collyer's youngest spoiled daughter, haggard, threadbare, over-rouged, worrying about how to indebt herself, going to meet a coarse fellow who was her lover merely because she could not get him into trouble. She rarely cried now, but she felt her eyes smart.

Where, in all the self-righteous lying world, could she turn for a friend? She even thought angrily of her children—they were simply eating up her flesh as they had when they were at the breast, no less. Did they know or would they ever know what a torture cell her life had been for them, borrowing money to buy them clothes, to avoid quarrels with their father, the quarrels already too many and already making cowards and sneaks of them? What would have happened if I'd never been born? she thought; they would never have been born. That hypocrite would have got some other woman with his yellow hair and big smile, but I should not have been responsible for their calvary, nor had even this toothache!

She thought bitterly about all men, most of all about her brother-in-law, her beautiful sister Eleanor's husband. He had loved Henny first and then discovered that Eleanor was the favorite and would get a bonus as well as her share of the estate; or that was how Henny put it to herself.

How hot it was in Washington! It was a hundred degrees in the shade, at least, thought Henny, and she seemed already to smell herself; she was no better than the painted young girls who buzzed round the journalists in the cafes. She looked in open kitchen windows, at the suits worn by little boys, at their scuffed shoes. She swept along without looking at adults, thinking of her children and the mounting cost of keeping them. They were such fine big children (as everyone said constantly) that a suit of clothes lasted a boy about three months. She thought of her big house on the hill and snickered bitterly. Even Bert Anderson, who had known her for so long, would give a lot to get inside it, to be able to say,

"I was up at Sam Pollit's the other Sunday, you know he married the Collyer clam-and-oyster money, young Henrietta, she was a Baltimore belle at one time, and they certainly have a crowd of fine little kiddies—was kidding Sam telling him his Roosevelt, the Great Democrat, would soon be the forgotten man," etc. This little preview of Bert Anderson, her stand-by from the Department of Internal Revenue, made Henny smile a little. This red-cheeked, lusty, riotous giant was not a gentleman, but he treated her as a single girl, listened to every word she had to say, always seemed eager, gave her advice, and was fascinated by money matters. He called her jocosely "young Henrietta," too, tried to improve her appearance in his brutal style, behaved like a grizzly-bear cub, and had no morality, character, ambitions, or way of life that she need respect.

Henny went upstairs when she came to the bar and restaurant near Twelfth Street and was glad to see that it was after one already. Bert would be there promptly at one-fifteen. She fiddled with the table silver and the menu, wished she had dawdled longer, muttered, "But I feel too conspicuous parading up and down the streets smirking nicely at mothers with children: and I might run into one of the Commissioner's fine friends, too. Bert is never late."

She saw Bert, shining with health, bursting in through the door, his hat still on his head to hide his thinning hair. He looked young, presentable, with a tight red skin and a thick irrepressible black beard newly ground off to skin level, jutting nose and chin, bright black eyes, and a ready grin; the lips were too red, the teeth too white in this grin, one thought, at first meeting. He bustled down to her, holding out both hands, and hailing her,

"Well, I'm not late, I'm not late. I told you one-fifteen, didn't I?" He looked round for a hook for his hat, then pressed her mouth with his cushiony lips.

"You're good to me, Bert, to come running when I get a freak and ring you up."

"Bert Anderson, always on tap," he affirmed. "I'm your guy, aren't I? If not me, then who? Maybe you've got someone else." He chuckled. "Well, what are we eating? And drinking? Cigarette? Smoking? No oysters I guess for the daughter of Paty du Clam? You don't mind if I do? Hello, hello there! How's things, Mullarkey? What's new? That's fine, that's fine!" He gave their order and then, one hand washing another, leaned over the table to Henny,

"Now then, what's new? Want to hear the latest? Did you hear about the fellow who had a nag racing out at Bowie? He kind of liked the horse and took it out a few magazines to read in the stable. The horse just looked and turned back to eat its hay. The little dog burst out laughing, and said, 'Hey, you don't think a horse can read, do you?'"

"Where's the joke?" asked Henny.

"Ha, ha, ha—ha, ha, ha," roared Bert, "you don't see it! Did you hear about the two dickybirds who were sitting on a tree and one said, 'That's Hitler!' and the other said, 'What are you waiting for?'"

"What an idiot!" said Henny, laughing. "Oh, I'll admit one thing, I get a good laugh with you. That young miss at the telephone sounded snippety. I heard what she said!"

"I know," he howled cheerfully, "I told her to cover the goddam mouthpiece when she made a silly crack like that. 'Well, how old is she, anyhow?' the kid said. I said, 'Oh, about thirty-two, thirty-three,' I told her. 'Well, what did I say? I said an old lady,' the kid said; 'what is she beefing about?' I told her, 'That's a lady, something you don't know about.' I won't tell you what she said, since you are a real lady!"

"No, but you're dying to," said Henny with a grimace, "I should like a stiff drink. I wish the churches and the smug big shots with cellars of their own hadn't passed this law."

"Good old Sinai, good old Jenkins Hill," cried Bert, "got to make the nation's capital safe for the bug-eyed tourist. I guarantee Samuel the Righteous thinks it's fine."

Henny shrugged, "Of course, he thinks that if he could get in and have half an hour's talk with President Roosevelt, he would banish alcohol for his term from the White House. The reason he knew Woodrow Wilson was God Almighty was that prohibition came in in his presidency. I sometimes think I live in the White House—or I think Samuel thinks so—" she shrugged again. "I can't understand why he never went into politics, with his gift of the gab and greensward style!"

Bert laughed interrogatively.

"Biggity style, all in the higher regions. I wish to all creation he'd picked out another woman, for his own sake, too."

"Maybe he will," Bert consoled her.

Henny laughed bitterly. "You know his favorite quotation? 'Good name in man and woman is the immediate jewel of their souls.' The children, Dad's money, his fat job, his reputation with all the high and mighty people he knows!" She laughed in an embarrassed way, "And he believes men should be virgins when they marry!"

"Holy mackerel!"

"We had our first fight over that. I simply didn't believe him! Now I do. And all the rest goes with it—no cards, no dirty jokes, no drinks, no smokes, no lively books. When I married him he had

more than four thousand books and not one novel! He lectured
me so when he caught me with one of Hassie's library books that
I didn't dare read a novel for six months. But like all hypocrites
and sneaks, it's all right if it has another label. He lets that child
of his read stuff about hysteria—nuns having fits in convents and
dreaming the Old One has what he might have for all I know, and
animals breeding and old customs on European farms and all sorts
of rot he lets that child of eleven read, because it's science! She drives
me mad with her reading. She's that Big-Me all over again. Always
with her eyes glued to a book. I feel like snatching the rotten thing
from her and pushing it into her eyes, into her great lolling head: I'd
like to stew the rotten books in one of my jam pans and make them
both eat it. The feast of learning he's always talking about! I'd like to
see their great bellies swell with their dirty scientific books the way
he makes mine with wind and—" she stopped. Bert meekly ate his
oysters and drank his wine.

"Now the mistake you make, young Henrietta, is that you think
about these things all the time," said Bert, after a pause. "Now look
at me," he coaxed, "suppose I started to worry over the fact that my
old man never turned an honest cent in his life, but scrounged on
me, his kid, eh?"

"You know, Bert," she said, trembling slightly, "the impulse to
kill him becomes so strong sometimes, when I think of the way
he's taken my life and trampled all over it and then thinks it's
sufficient if he reads a few highbrow books, that I don't know how
to get over it. I clench my fists together to keep from rushing at his
greasy yellow head, or throwing something into that noisy mouth,
forever boasting and screaming. If I could kill him and that child,"
she said, "I'd gladly do time for it. But what would the kids do? Go
to an asylum? No one would stand it. No one could stand it. Hassie,
who only has one kid anyhow, says, 'Compromise, compromise!'
She wouldn't compromise; she has a meek little skinned rat of man

who runs out all over the streets anyhow and goes to bars with queer fish, while she stays at home and runs the business; what does she know about compromise? The very one who tells me to compromise wouldn't compromise for half a minute. He talks about human equality, the rights of man, nothing but that. How about the rights of woman, I'd like to scream at him. It's fine to be a great democrat when you've a slave to rub your boots on. I have to stuff mattresses because we haven't enough money to buy new ones! Look at my hands!"

She showed him her worn hands. The skin was darkened by dirt ground in and snowy in patches, where the coarse soap had bitten it.

"And I rub in hand lotion every day," she said bitterly. "They say in the magazines, look after yourself and your husband will love you. If love was got by a woman giving her last drop of blood to wash the clothes in and her last shred of skin to carpet the house with, I wouldn't get it, and he wouldn't notice it. He is injured, if you don't mind! He boasts and screams about how cheap he buys his clothes for a man in his position, and what he gives up for the kids! He writes poems to himself on the subject: and what about me? I'm the heiress: I'm the rich woman who can stop up all the holes and darn all the tatters in her underwear and borrow old coats from her sister and beg old-fashioned jackets from her cousins, and I don't sacrifice at all. It is all on account of me. The whole thing is due to my bad management." Bert raised his eyes quizzically and held up his pencil,

"Henny, why can't you make a go of it on eight thousand a year? You pay fifty dollars a month rent to your old man, that's all."

"What?" cried Henny indignantly, "Food alone costs me three thousand and more a year. Everything is budgeted to the minimum, and it never works out. You know how much I had to spend on the two girls last year? Thirty-two dollars. Hassie gave me a dress for Evie, but she detests Louisa and will never give me a thing for her. There isn't a person in the family her size, she's so enormous, and I can't get any hand-me-downs for her. And I waste money! So says the Professor. The house is falling to pieces: there are always repairs. That's why we got it so cheap. Dad couldn't sell it. And you know the taxes we have to pay on that white elephant."

Bert pocketed his pencil helplessly. "You're right. Isn't it funny: if you get seven hundred and fifty a year or eight thousand a year, it's never enough! But—" he looked at her, "Well, what's the use? You would have all those kiddies."

"Oh, don't let's talk about it," she cried feverishly. "I didn't come here to talk about him and my troubles."

"That's right, that's right, that's a good girl! Here, we'll have a drop more wine, just to celebrate the transwafting of Samuel the Righteous to parts unknown."

"If he gives the household money to me in a lump sum," she said more thoughtfully, "you see I can pay off some of my old debts. When I was so terribly strapped after Ernie came, I just borrowed right and left—I hadn't the faintest idea how to run a house, and I only had Hazel Moore five months before Samuel quarreled with her. I blush, even in my own room, when I think I never paid Connie O'Meara the hundred. She must think I'm a cheap chiseler! I'll pay her first." She laughed excitedly, "Here I am spending it all already. How much do you think I have in my purse?"

"A buck?" His manner was a little less jovial than it had been up to now. She noticed this and flashed a look of contempt at his great curly head, bent over the plate. He was stowing food away in his usual elephantine manner, seeming to have three or four hands which were all in operation, moving quickly in different directions, seizing bread, sugar, cream, and so on. She decided to punish him,

"Ten cents!"

"How come?"

"Ernie tore his pants. *She* had to have new stuff for a dress. I hope I'll be able to palm her off on Eleanor again this summer, if her own relatives at Harpers Ferry won't take her."

"Do they use any propaganda against the stepmother out there?"

"If they did, she wouldn't know it. I don't know what passes in that girl's head, it isn't anything normal. I just know that if she makes up her mind to do a thing, she'll do it: and it isn't just her damned obstinacy, although I yell at her that it is: it's that she's deaf."

"I didn't know."

"No, not deaf! She doesn't know there's anyone else alive walking this earth but herself. So if she wants to do it, she'll do it and if you cut her fingers off, she wouldn't know it, she'd just go and do it. She's terrible. She's a horrible sort of beast, it seems to me sometimes. She crawls, I can hardly touch her, she reeks with her slime and filth—she doesn't notice! I beat her until I can't stand—she doesn't notice! When I fall on the floor, she runs and gets a pillow and at that I suppose she's better than her murderer of a father who lets me lie there. And if she whimpers a bit or bellows, she'll go right off the next minute with a face like a stone and stare and moon away at some book and forget everything I've screamed at her. I show her the veins sticking out on my hands and ask her if she isn't ashamed. But I'm waiting a bit till she gets a bit older and punishes her father for all he's made me suffer: or she'll take it out on some other man. Someone will catch a beauty."

Bert laughed, "Revenge is a wild kind of justice! Not mine, Lord Bacon's: I had no idea you were such a vengeful tiger."

"I'd drink his blood but it would make me vomit," she said, with pain. "When I think that in a few months I'm going to be the stepmother not of a child but of a woman and a woman with his nature, I want to commit suicide. Why should I go through with it?"

"Say, would you like to take a stroll?" inquired Bert. "Or how about the movies? Then we can take a drink at home after, if you like."

"Yes, you're right, Bert. It's cool there and I can have some quiet. It's just that he's painting and scraping and singing and jigging from crack of dawn and he wants to take up my bedroom floor now, so for weeks I'll have to sleep with a bed full of sand and dirt and a floor covered with old sacks. It's insane."

"Thank God I'm not a handy man," said Bert sighing.

"Yes, you are, handy," she concluded, with a queer sideways glance. He laughed. When he got up to get his hat, she stood, pulling on her gloves, and looking up at his face which was turned from her. Suppose she lost him by yowling too much? For a moment she had a tinge of real love for the man. He was a queer sort. He would not marry anyone. He went out with, and no doubt lied to, girl after girl—nice romantic girls too; and though such a bounder, he looked like the ideal husband, stalwart, husky, bighearted, a good-time-Charlie, pretty sensible, and easy enough to handle, open to flattery, to pathos. There he was in a crisis, always helping her out in a friendly way. He even lent small amounts of money, showing her the amounts in his little vest-pocket book and saying, with a good-natured but meaningful slap, as she put it away, "It's there, it's mounting up: but you'll pay me off when the dividends come, won't you, young Henrietta?" She thought today she would get five dollars out of him.

Chapter Four

1 *Scandal in Pollitry.*

At three in the afternoon Aunt Josephine Pollit, tall, blue-eyed, with hail-fellow-well-met dental set came through the gate at a lively pace, though she was putting on a hearty middle age. She carried herself as if she were a yellow solid valise cheerfully borne by a successful commercial traveler. She carried other things with her, a light coat, an umbrella, a purse, a book, and a package. When the twins came flying down the path, she shifted the parcel to the other hand and patted them while kissing them heartily.

"Are you glad to see your Auntie, twinnies? Where's Mother? Is your mother inside?"

"Mother's out."

"Out! Didn't anyone tell her your Auntie Jo was coming? Oh, isn't that too bad! I must see her! I must see Samuel! Where is your father? Come inside, chickies, Auntie has something for you—later on."

"Ooch!" they shrieked dutifully, and "What?"

"In a minute, must wait for Auntie to get her things off. Where's Auntie Bonnie? Is she out too? Now, who's going to get their auntie a glass of water?"

"Me, Auntie!" said Little-Sam.

" 'I,' you mean, Sammy: 'I will, Auntie.'"

He grinned bashfully and started towards the house.

"Where's your father? ('I will, Auntie!') Now!"

"I will, Auntie," he shouted from the door as he fled into the house.

"On the roof painting the roof," said Saul.

"On the roof! On Sunday afternoon! Tell him I'm here! Sam! Samuel! Tell him I'm here!" She sniffed grandly and marched into the house. But Sam had spied her from the roof top and now he cringed and whined at Saul, over the guttering.

"Ask Josie did she bring me a little bit of choc? She always brings me sumpin."

"Oo Taddy!" said Evelyn, going scarlet.

"Go on, kids," whined Sam piteously, "ask Josie if she's got anyfink for pore little Sam; I won't come down unless. En I might fall on my head, I might get sunstroke, anyfink might happen to me up here!"

"Oo, Taddy, you said never to ask for anything," Evie said very gravely.

"Gwan, kids," squeaked Sam, "tell her she's got to bribe me. Oh, oh, I'm falling: vertigo's going to get me, my head's going round. All because of no choc. Got to have some!"

"Don't say it," Louie ordered them fiercely from the veranda, "don't you go and say that."

"Gwan, boys," urged Sam more miserably and shamefully than before, "want a little bit o' choc, even one little tablet, I'll even take a crumb. She's got to send me up a bit: or she's got to send out and buy a bit."

Louie rushed out and planted herself in view of her father. "I won't let them," she shouted. The children hung about, not knowing what to do.

Jo had gone inside and taken off her hat. She shook back the dazzling yellow furze of curls that could never be smoothed down and powdered her nose. She beamed at the discussion outside, but when they came to this impasse, she strode to the veranda and shouted,

"I've got some chocolate for you, Samuel; come down! I've got to talk to you!"

"You bring it up," whined and scraped Sam, perilously over the guttering; although he suffered from vertigo and vertigo's nausea, he could never resist a comedy.

"Come down and don't be a fool," trumpeted Jo. "I have to talk to you!"

Sam grinned and started to come down the ladder,

"Josie used to yell that from the back window in Lombard Street; when I used to drag home carcasses and fish bones to make fertilizer—you remember, Jo? Phew! What a stench! Josie would bang up the window and yell down the street, 'Father, speak to that boy! Sam, don't be a fool!' And bang went the window again."

"Come down to earth," cried Jo impatiently, "Samuel, stop acting the goat!" She started to frown, but a smile broke through. She went up to her youngest brother and kissed him, saying more gently than before,

"Come in and get your chocolate and Louie will make us some coffee. Louie dear, come here, come and kiss Auntie, dear!" She looked her up and down, ran her hand through Louie's helpless waterfall of hair and proclaimed, "Louie's getting to be a big girl now: she's going to be just like me. Only straight hair! I was something like you at your age, dear! You're going to be just like me. I hope!" she sniffed cheerfully and laughed aloud. "Run along, dear!" And now this Juno frowned and demanded, "Is Bonnie here?"

"I think Bonniferous is snoozing," Sam replied.

"A most disgraceful thing," said Joe, "absolutely preposterous. Sam you must insist, absolutely insist, that she stop seeing this wretched man, that card-trick horror: it's disgraceful! To think that a sister of mine should go out with a man like that, and a married man! You must stop it! I insist upon it, Samuel!"

Sam became very grave, laid his hand on his sister's arm, and led her away from the children into the sunroom, which ran south and north and was entered from the long dining room. This was a beautiful, quiet room, with a high conservatory window looking out on the orchard, lined with books and containing Henny's piano. The children stayed outside to play, for they were tired by the heavy painting job of the day. Louie made coffee. From time to time they heard the upright Jo and austere Sam in a passionate discussion somewhere in a corner of the house, or saw her stalking up and down in the sunroom, taking off her pince-nez, putting them on, tossing her head like a draft horse, sniffing, the sun shining through her loofah hair as she paused between the curtains, to give her nephews a good-natured look.

"Right is right, and wrong is wrong," she proclaimed through the window, "and any man, woman, or child with a sense of decency would refuse to speak to him. I won't hear any more about it; and there's an end of it. It must and will be stopped! He has a wife. If I had ever imagined that anyone in my family could so much as think of such a thing as attacking the holy bonds of matrimony—there's no excuse whatever. Be sure that sin will find you out! And if she persists, you must send her away. I am sure Henny agrees with me. I myself will speak to Henny. When I heard of it, to my face, I nearly died of shame. And it was Miss Critchmar who told me! Suppose they want to elect me to the chapter—and a rumor like that gets round? What will I say? How could I show my face?"

"It wouldn't be your fault, Jo," said Sam seriously, "but of course we will stop it."

"Such an abomination cannot go on. She must be stopped," Jo said. "It makes me sick. And just when I had discovered that one of our ancestors, Sam, fought in the American Revolution. This genealogist assured me that there were several of our name and one certainly is a relative. And just then this bombshell comes along and hits me amidships! I was so horrified, Sam, I didn't sleep for five nights! You can imagine the state I was in! Where is the stupid girl?"

"Upstairs. I'll send for her."

"I'll go myself! Don't move! I shall give her a talking-to she'll not forget in a hurry. Disgusting. Oh, it's disgusting! A sister of mine! How could she! What is the matter with her, Sam? Mother was such a splendid character and you and I have never committed a sin in our lives. I believe that. I am not a Pharisee! I wish that you would go to church, Sam, but I must say that for a nonbeliever you lead an exemplary life. But of course, Father's example—" she stopped, seeing Louie with the coffee, and then continued nobly, "Father could have been a better man."

"Well, that's not to the point now," Sam said quietly. "Perhaps you'd better leave it to me, Jo. I'll find out how things stand. Don't accuse without evidence. An evil tongue can do more harm than two foolish people—probably no more than foolish, remember! Make allowance for mere harmless folly, Jo."

"That's a lot of bosh and you know it! A married man! What must he be thinking about Bonnie, your sister, Sam? If you think I'm going to put up with it, you're much mistaken. I'm surprised at your being so weak-kneed, Sam, you so decent; you were always so decent. I always do my duty. Some people don't like me for it, but I know why."

Sam interjected, "Jo, you are not the avenging angel, you must be human in these matters. I have more experience than you."

"More? How more? You mean you're married. Rubbish! I have to deal with mothers and their problems all day long, too. They confide in me. I have a big following among the mothers. My opinion is objective just because I do not deal with compromise. Not that you do, Sam; I know you've always been good—the best; I don't say that. You're the best boy that ever was. You're too soft, that's all, so you can't handle this."

Sam motioned to her to sit down; and she did so, "You see, Jo, I used to be like you, I thought just the same way. I understand how you feel. But you are wrong, believe me; you cannot dragoon human beings even in the name of morality. It is kindness, human love, and patience with human weakness that is necessary. Remember this is your own sister, ten years my junior, and I know little enough how to run my own affairs! Be kind to her. Go and speak to her—I admit it's a woman's place: but be kind."

"I will never be kind to weak wickedness," cried Jo, bouncing up and tossing back her head; "be sure of that, Samuel."

"Run out, Looloo," said Sam, to the little girl who had just brought in the coffee tray.

"And another thing," cried Jo, more moderately, "I want to ask you about my income tax, Sam, about the deductions. A man came to ask me questions. I'm perfectly sure I'm overassessed; and I can't sleep at night with the pneumatic drilling in the streets; and I couldn't get half that price if I really tried to sell it. I'm going to get a loan to put in improvements—but what's the use really? I ought to lease it to a boardinghouse keeper who would give me my rents regularly and I shouldn't have to worry. It all keeps me awake and I can't afford to lose sleep over a lot of irresponsible people. That old woman with the rosary on her bed only comes once a fortnight to get her relief, or when she had a fight with her son-in-law. That nice German, such a decent fellow and a good tenant, is going to his homeland to see his parents. Such a studious man, nice and quiet; and those two awful Italians didn't work for four days. They went out on a beer party and got stinking drunk and didn't work. My house is simply going down, and I haven't time to do it up, put them out, and get decent tenants. That horrible little thing on the first floor is going to have *another* baby and the first one hardly with a tooth, she doesn't get through washing the dishes till eleven o'clock or twelve and then another bedraggled girl comes with her baby carriage and there they sit in the dark, in the damp, and chatter and cook a bit of spaghetti, and that shiftless tramp with a cigarette stuck between his lips when he hasn't enough to eat even and the rent not paid. It makes me sick, such shiftless horrible people in the world, and they are the ones the government supports! Can you understand it, Sam? I can't. And in the house next to mine is a woman with a piece of land in the country, who gets relief. Isn't it wicked, Sam? Oh, you don't know what's going on, Sam, because you're in a government department and you don't meet people as I do. I have to meet them face to face, I have to actually speak to these awful creatures, because they are my tenants, and I have to worry about the plumbing for them. Do you think they're pleased with anything? No, you don't know a lot yourself, Sam. That's what I say. Don't throw it up at me that I'm not married; for I could easily have been married, but I just said, 'No, no, I'm waiting for Mr. Right.' What do you think of that, Sam? Another baby, with one nine months old, it just makes me sick."

"Maybe they like children," said Sam, grinning.

"Tommyrot, it's sheer improvidence and shiftlessness!" said Jo, indignantly, staring at her brother. "They owe me three weeks' rent now! Stop being a giddy goat, Sam. Now, there, I've had my coffee and I'm going up to speak to that girl. I'll bring her to her senses."

Jo went upstairs boiling with self-respect. Henny referred to her agreeably as that "great blond beast, deaf, dumb, and blind to all but self, self, self"; and Sam said that "Jo was a very good woman, but not broadminded"; and Bonnie always said, with a laugh, "Jo's a good soul, poor thing!" Bonnie had been taking forty winks in her room, drunk with the heat, when Jo's irruption into the house had wakened her. She had at once applied her ear to the stairway well and heard most of what had been said to Sam by Jo. If she could have got out of the house, she would have, but it was impossible; the foot of the stair was at the dining-room door. Bonnie even considered climbing out of her window and trying to reach the porch and shin down the porch posts, a thing that she surely would have done ten years ago. But she could not do it here. With relief she had heard the voices of two little girls in the room opposite hers. Evie and Isabel were playing Mothers, Evie's favorite and perpetual game. Evie was a lady with a baby, and Isabel was her little girl going to school, a distribution of roles which had never varied. Isabel went to school (in the corner), put up her hand, scribbled on the floor, and after a surprisingly short morning came home for lunch. At lunch she was invariably rude to her mother and had to be slapped. After lunch she always refused to go back to school and had to be ordered out of the house in a cranky voice. While she was in afternoon school, the mother would change her baby's diaper, croon to it, smack it, teach it, and repeat infinitely the little attentions that Evie really had had to give to Tommy. Evie often asked her mother to have a new baby so that she could look after it, and in the meantime, she had become the occasional nursemaid for most of the mothers on the opposite side of the street. Evie was doing up Isabel's braid for the third time in the course of three fleeting days of motherhood, "and now you've got to go to school and I'll cook the dinner for my husband," said Evie, tying a rag round her waist.

"But you haven't got a husband," Isabel cried disconsolately; "you have two children but no husband. No lady has that. Let me be the mother."

The doe-eyed Evie showed a surprising forensic turn while she convinced Isabel that it was utterly unsuitable for her to be a mother; but she agreed, with a rather lost and disgruntled expression, to allow a phantom husband to share the honors of householding with her. Isabel insisted on a real husband, and Evie was obliged to hang out the back window and yell, "Little-Sam, I want you." Her brother argued. Evie yelled, "You must be my husband." "No," yelled Little-Sam. Evie turned hastily to Isabel and said sternly, "My husband is at the office; now you must go to school." Isabel vanquished, picked up her schoolbag, and went to school again while Evie, muttering happily to herself, busied herself over her doll and imaginary housework.

Jo, halted by the little scene, had let her face of stern rectitude crease grimly to release a smile for "the kiddies," and then she went in to the flabbergasted Bonnie. Jo stopped a few paces from Bonnie, who was sitting on her bed, and said sternly,

"Well, I heard a nice thing on Friday! What are you and that man Holloway doing going about together and in broad day all over Baltimore; and in a barroom too. I can't imagine you doing such a thing! You'll stop it at once, that's all. I'm not going to have my name ruined, if you don't care about yours."

"Mind your own business," said Bonnie flushing and springing up. On the bed were scattered collars, letters, and paper patterns.

Jo seemed surprised by this resistance. "What do you mean? It is my business. Do you know what you're doing? You're going out with a man with a legal wife; you know what that means?"

"Go and put your head in a bag," said Bonnie. "If I like to have an innocent friendship with a married man, it's none of your affair."

Jo burst out that there was no innocence with a married man and what was Bonnie coming to? Did she know where the primrose path was leading her and that being seen all over the place with a married man and drinking spirits in bars didn't look like innocence; and that she should think of her brothers and sisters if not of herself, and of what Henny's friends would think if they knew that that was Sam's sister running round the streets openly and brazenly with a married man? What did she think she looked like?

"A sight for sore eyes," said Bonnie.

"What?" shouted Jo. "Such brazenness!"

"*Honi soit qui mal y pense*," Bonnie told her, curling her lip. This was too much for Jo who rushed up and, shaking her by the shoulders, in a great passion, cried that she must write a letter at once, this very afternoon, in fact now ("Now, if not sooner," said Bonnie coolly) to the Horror and tell him that he would never see her again.

"His positively final appearance on all stages," said Bonnie, pettishly, which showed Jo that she was losing her temper (it never held very long).

"Stop acting the goat," cried Jo, therefore, "and think of the way he's treating you; what can he think of you?"

"He understands me," said Bonnie. "I'm naturally vivacious and though I love Sam's kiddies, I must have friends of my own: and he's a real gentleman besides."

"Fiddlesticks!" said Jo, "you behave like a child. Now sit down and write the man a letter and I'll post it myself. Sam agrees with me that it has got to stop."

"Anyone would think I was pickled in crime," Bonnie complained; "he's sweet on me and he's separated from his wife and he's going to get a divorce."

"I know for certain she won't divorce him," said Jo.

"He told me she would, she hates him and they're unhappy and they wanted to separate a long time ago, but he just jogged along till he met me, that's what he said."

But Jo told her to never mind, she knew all about it and she told Bonnie that far from hating his wife, he was now living with her again—everyone knew it; there had been a reconciliation, and so forth, and that the horrible man simply went, straight from giving Bonnie a good time, to his wife's table and that everyone was talking and that there would be a frightful scandal and she, Bonnie, might be the cause of another separation: "Whom God hath joined let no man put asunder," said Jo, solemnly.

Bonnie began to cry. "I didn't know, I can't believe it; he said to me, 'Why should we wait forever on a woman's whim?' That's what he said; can you blame me?"

"You let the cat out of the bag that time, didn't you?" asked Jo; and the end of it was that she forced Bonnie to write the letter then and there and, after reading it severely, she carried it downstairs with the intention of posting it.

Bonnie stayed upstairs sobbing, thinking she had a broken heart, until she heard soft things like the hands of ghosts rubbing her counterpane and soft ghostly feet unsteadily shifting on her rug; and looking up, she saw Evie and Isabel staring at her with immense rabbit eyes. In a little crockery voice, Isabel asked,

"What are you crying for?" and Evie at once piped up with the same question. Affectionate Bonnie threw her arms round the two little girls and dragged them to her, while she sobbed, "Auntie Jo came and took all the gilt off my gingerbread, that's why, darlings; there, you lump of sweetness!" (she kissed Evie). "Bless you, kittycat, bless its kind loving heart; there, darling" (she kissed Isabel), "you're a dear little girl too, never mind about poor Bonnie. I'm a poor lone, lorn crittur, that's why I'm crying; now don't you worry about the troubles of grownups, your little lives must be all sunshine, dear; you will have trouble enough when you grow up, because we all do; now, there, there, kiss poor Bonnie again, now, there there, look, look; Evie has a tear in her eye, there, my darling lump," she ravished Evie's head with kisses, parting her soft, glossy black hair in a fever of love, "there, let its Bonnie hug it for a minute to make me feel better!" Evie looked up lovingly at Bonnie's shining hair and periwinkle-blue eyes,

"You are pretty, Auntie," she said.

"Other people think so, too," said Bonnie nodding, with a faint smile; she was already beginning to see that "all was not lost," as she put it to herself. She got up and began to collect her bits of paper and lace, trying a collar on one little girl and the other and saying cheerfully, "Fear not: all will be well!" and "Never say die!" and "A merry heart goes all the way," and "Sticks and stones will break my bones but names will never hurt me!" and "Oh, don't you look perfectly, mm-mm! now, look in the glass, darlin'," until she was as chipper as a canary; and, bundling everything suddenly into the drawer, she pushed them out, "Now go and play, you two young puppies," and ran downstairs, humming a tune and determined to be "the gayest of the gay," to show them she "was not broken nor even badly bent."

When she got down Sam and Jo were talking confidentially about Jo's salary, retirement allowance, and an income-tax inquiry. There was some distribution of chocolate going on, and Ernie was hanging on to the bench, drinking in Auntie Jo with his eyes and ears. Jo was full of her summer holidays—she and Miss Critchmar, her other self, would go to Atlantic City, but not for long on account of her worries with her tenants in Lombard Street, Baltimore; and she went on to discuss these troubles again, the new bathroom, the new house she would like to take over on a five-years' lease, but always envisaging the difficulty of getting responsible people to live in it and a good furnace man. The children lounged or sat and stared at Auntie Jo with admiration. She was a marvel to be able to tell off a bank manager, a landlord, and to own two houses of her own. Auntie Jo was neither a married woman nor an old maid, nor a schoolma'am, she was a landlord.

"You were wrong, Samuel," said Jo, "to let that house go in P Street."

Sam put up his hand to silence her; he never talked about money or property before the children, thinking it a vile thing.

"What rot!" exclaimed Jo. "A man is none the worse for getting rent! You'd be better off today."

Louie spoke up, however, "It was my house and Daddy sold it to buy mother her ring and the dining-room suite."

"It was not your house," said Sam sadly to her.

"You said so," she answered timidly, "once, one time."

"Do you want to live there?"

"No, there are Negroes living in it. I went to look at it."

"You have a house to live in: of what use would it be to you?"

"I could sell it—if I had it," she said humbly.

"What for? What do you want to buy?"

She was silent: a rage of desire rushed through her, but she couldn't think of what she wanted to buy; she muttered, "I could buy a boat, I could go sailing."

"We must never think about money or of owning things," said Sam kindly, bending a rather dewy eye on her. "Greed, the desire to possess, money, the currency of greed, is the root of all evil, it is the means of devouring others, and the lives of others: you know how I feel about that." Silently Louie took her place beside Ernie, while Auntie Jo, with a beaming eye, smiled on them both, saying, "That is not for you little ones yet awhile: let us work and worry for you; you play and learn."

Ernie smiled faintly between his hands and looked at father and aunt with deep appreciation. His father earned $666 monthly, his aunt $200 monthly or more. His aunt got rent out of families in two houses, each with three stories and basement, and his father, though no longer a landlord, would make extra expenses going abroad on this expedition. His father was thirty-eight years old, though, while Auntie Jo was, as near as he could make out, at least forty-eight. But again, she was head of the kindergarten department, much in the same relative position as her brother, who was head of his department, and even a kind of superhead invented for himself alone. Auntie Jo had no car, but was saving the money to go to England and see the seat of the Calverts, even though they were Catholics, and the cathedrals of England. Who would manage her houses while she was away? he pondered. If she put it off long enough he would like to reside there and look after the tenants. On the other hand, his grandfather, Old David Collyer, would be more likely to give him a better job.

As soon as he could, Ernie wanted to open a bank account and put money into it. To put money into it, one had to make money by inducement of people who did not care so much for money or who needed it and would pay for it, or who were fools or who did not see the money in odd things, or who were simply like fruit trees growing wild to have the fruit picked off them. Ernie often thought of making money, but never by putting on a performance himself, say: only by manipulation of objects or of other persons. The idea of selling himself, which was, on the whole, Louie's idea, of selling her talents on a stage, seemed strange to Ernie. He sometimes figured that if Louie grew up to be an actress, he would sell photographs of her, or would take the money at the door. His father had stopped him from delivering groceries from the small, independent store at the corner. This did not worry him at all. He picked the eyes out of every conversation, for he knew there were hundreds of other ways of getting a living. Once for fun, Sam had let him black boots outside Tohoga House. To Sam it was an immense joke; but Henny, on this occasion, flew out of her muteness in a storm cloud and made such a bluster round Sam's ears that Sam had had to call off the joke. That time Henny had threatened to leave him and take the children home to Roland Park. People gave him money (though not Auntie Jo, who was very careful, even with chocolate); and people allowed him to earn money by services. He made money lending nickels to boys of good standing, charging them one penny, or interest in kind. He dealt fairly by them and did a good business. Only he himself knew (Henny had not guessed) how much money he had in his money box when, at Christmas, he left himself the half of his takings.

Ernie thought Louie lacked sagacity but calculated that after all she was putting her best foot forward, when she spoke of going on the stage. He himself also looked years ahead and saw himself making his way in the world, handling, changing money, cautiously getting the best of bargains, finding out how others made money. They had secrets, he thought, though no more intellect than himself. He watched and listened day by day for those secrets.

He knew he was a child and that children had no rights, but he did not fret since time would cure him. In the meantime he did business with children and relatives who were his natural guardians if not warders. He knew he could not go to law and win suits, nor go into business; he knew his word would not be taken against that of an adult, and that adults, if they so wished, could do him great harm, give him great insults and injuries and never be punished, nor even perhaps suspected; that was their power, the right they grew into, one of the privileges of manhood. He smiled at them, though, not as enemies, but as persons of privilege, and he really liked power and privilege, he had a zest for it. Ernie listened to all that everyone said about himself, finding it truly fascinating to know how each sucked a living from the earth. He rarely lost his head but had no criticism of the temperaments of others. Above all, he understood and was curious about the relations of people. Auntie Jo was Samuel's eldest sister and the head of the family as she often proclaimed. Samuel usually obeyed her in matters of relation, morality, for example, but she came to Samuel with her financial matters. Father and Mother fought because there was not enough money forthcoming. Mother wasted her money, and Sam was unable to understand how expenses could be so large. If there were only two children, himself and Louie, they would live in clover, but there were six. What if another ever came? That would be difficult. One morning, after thinking about this in bed, Ernie had gone to his Mother and said, "Mothering, don't have another baby!"

Henny had said, "You can bet your bottom dollar on that, old sweetness."

Ernie did not like this feverish phrase of Henny's, for the idea of his bottom dollar ever coming to light at all (from under the heap of other dollars) did not appeal to him.

"We must never think about money," said both Auntie Jo and Daddy. Ernie knew that this was one of the pious precepts handed down by people in power to smaller people in subjection, since both Auntie Jo and Samuel constantly thought about bills, salaries, and getting on, and always had money in their purses. Ernie knew that parents and guardians handed down many other wise saws for the same purpose, which was to prevent the young ones from getting into their game too soon. Get a piece of filet steak for your father— and don't eat the pie that's for your Aunt, and those almonds are for Mother; and don't quarrel—though we do; go to bed—though we stay up, going to the movies is not good for children—though I go; and don't talk whilst I talk; all commands enforced by power alone and obeyed by weakness alone—for as Louie grew up, she obeyed less and less, not letting things slip by inadvertence or sly disobedience, but refusing to do things in open revolt—"I will not because it is not right!" Now, Louie had her own right and wrong, she was already entering their world of power. Ernie studied their conflicts and made up his mind about things. Here was Auntie Jo always in conflicts, in which, by the way, she generally lost. She was deep into one of her favorite jeremiads,

"I didn't sleep a wink all night four nights in succession on account of the noise, the noise, their picks clinking all night. There ought to be some regard for taxpayers. Why can't they work in the daytime? I nearly fell asleep on the bus coming over." Jo sniffed and nodded her bright-colored head, "It's a scandal!"

"Why don't you get a little car?" inquired Sam greedily. "Then you could come and see us often—and bring me choc," he winked at the children, "and you could take us all out for a ride."

Jo smiled at him, "I would, Sam, only I'm putting by, you know, for my trip; I've got other relatives to visit besides you, Sam," she grinned at him. "You're not my only brother, you know!"

Auntie Jo sat in the chair bubbling and boiling, and Samuel, listening to her, rested from his labors until they heard Bonnie's brisk song on the stairs, *Voi che sapete!*"

Jo drew herself up and looked matronly at Bonnie, while Sam said reproachfully, "Jo has been telling me something, Bonniferous, that I never would have believed about you. We'll have a little talk afterwards."

Bonnie looked at her brother silently, while her blue eyes filled with tears. Sam said gently, "It's all right, Bonniferous, I know it's all right."

"Good heavens, I should think so!" cried Jo. Then she rose and strode to the sunroom and began to twirl downwards the piano stool, while Sam flung himself happily on the settee amongst the cushions and the children poured through the bars of sun and window shadows, nodding in the winds of jollity. Jo began to strum masterfully, *Marching through Georgia*. She stopped brusquely and asked over her shoulder with her hands poised,

"Another thing! Why didn't you go to Jinny's when you said you would? Besides you wrote to Jinny that you were looking for a job in Baltimore. I suppose on account of that man!"

"Play, Jo, play!" said Sam indolently. " 'Ta-ra, ta-ra, we bring the Jubilee!' Go on! Don't hector, Jo, go on!"

"Nonsense," cried Jo, swinging round and shaking indignant bright pince-nez at him, "hectoring indeed! Don't be silly! Here she stays writing letters all over the place and carrying on as she likes, and trying to get to Baltimore where she can be near that card-trick scoundrel. I know all about him. A fine thing for a sister of mine to be taken in by a—"

"Jo!" warned Sam, nodding and grinning at the fascinated children. "A sister of mine too!" He laughed, "Go on, Jojo, play: never mind the curtain lecture!"

"Curtain lecture," cried Jo. "Nonsense! I intend to speak my mind. I'm perfectly honest, and honest people need not be afraid to hear what I have to say. I always speak the truth!"

"A good principle," said Sam dryly, "but—"

"Let me play, Jo," broke in Bonnie heedlessly, "the kids love the musical monologues I give them, don't you, kids? How's abouts 'The Big Bad Wolf,' or the 'Gunny-Wolf,' or 'Mr. Possum and Mr. Dog'?"

The children began to clamor, while Bonnie blushed and explained to Jo, as if nothing had happened, "I make them up as I go along, the music I mean—listen! Jo! Let me have the piano a minute!"

"Who can't do it?" inquired Jo jealously.

"The 'Gunny-Wolf,'" cried the children.

"Listen, children," Jo said in her best kindergarten manner, "'The first Noel that the angels did say.'"

"No nims [hymns]," said Sam.

"You should be ashamed of yourself," cried Jo, "such prejudice!"

"No nims," said Sam firmly.

"You're not giving the children a chance to choose for themselves: is that impartiality?" inquired Jo. "You should at least allow them to hear about God."

"Why? When there ain't no sich animal?" said Sam comfortably.

"Sammy!" implored Bonnie. Jo burst out, though, "You'll regret it later on, if you don't: you distort their minds with fairy tales, absurdities: Hans Andersen but not the Bible! When they grow up they will have nothing to believe in."

Sam laughed very comfortably, "Now they believe in their poor little dad: and when they grow up they'll believe in Faraday, Clerk Maxwell, and Einstein; and snakes alive!" he cried indignantly, getting up into a sitting posture, "if my children can't distinguish between Grimm and Clerk Maxwell, let them go and jump in the lake, for sweet nuthatch's sake!"

"They are forced to go to school and they should be forced to go to church," cried Jo indignantly. "A nice set of citizens!"

Sam laughed, "It's not even right they should be forced to go to school when they have a father like me: I can teach my children. I don't need schoolma'ams!" And he grinned evilly at his sister.

THE MAN WHO LOVED CHILDREN | 117

"They need more women in the state legislature," said Jo, "and irresponsible fathers like you would be forced to: I know Henny thinks as I do."

"Yiss, but you ain't in it," said Sam, "and what's more you never will be. En if I had my way no crazy shemales would so much as git the vote! Becaze why? Becaze they is crazy! Becaze they know nuffin! Becaze if they ain't got childer, they need childer to keep 'em from goin' crazy; en if they have childer the childer drive em crazy."

Jo scorned him, "I'm as good as any man I ever met." She sniffed cheerfully, "Pollits for Politics, say I."

Sam turned to the children and said, "Did you notice the stones in this yere wall rock when Jo sniffed, kids? When Jo was a girl, Father used to say he wished he could have Jo's nose stuffed with silver dollars, he'd pay the year's rent."

"Don't be rude, Sam!" shouted Jo above her strumming. "Noses mean character: I've got a nobody nose!"

"Nobody knows the sniffles she got," sang Sam. Jo laughed. "You wish you had a nose like mine; only Father had one like mine and he looked like Charles Dickens. Sam and I are the only ones with the real Pollit nose."

"Jo's nose pickled in brine would make two sides of bacon for a week," said Sam. Bonnie, who had a tiptilted nose, by the way, laughed till she cried.

"Louie will beat you though," continued Sam. Louie smiled down her nose.

"Nonsense!" cried Jo gaily. "A big nose means a generous nature. Anyhow, don't you mind, Louie! Be like me! Let her have one."

"A big nose means a big cold," said Bonnie.

"A big nose means big lungs," declared Sam, vainly heaving his chest up and down, uff-puff. "Big lungs mean a big voice, big voice means reaching the hearts of your countrymen, even without the radio and with, my friends, with, you become a Roosevelt, than which is none whicher. I'm always glad I'm not a squib, like Crazy-Daisy down at the Department. He squeaks through lack of nose." Sam imitated the squeak of Craven Day, an old clerk down at the Bureau of Fisheries, politely called, by about one hundred intimates, Crazy-Daisy. He was a rusty, tall, round-backed permanent functionary, who became more eccentric as he approached the age of fifty. Sam went by the name of Softsoap-Sam. The children's eyes danced with excitement; they could never get enough of Crazy-Daisy, the accountant, or of Ratty-Atty (Mr. George Atson), another accountant, or of Skinny, or Finny, or Dirty Jack, or Dribble Smith, or Hohnenlinden, or Alphabetical Davies (Skinner, Finigan, John Roebuck, Bertrand Smith, Max Hohnen, and A. B. C. Davies), all Sam's inferiors by grades in the branches of the Department. Less interesting were the Moguls, the bosses, who, however, had respectable names, Mr. Virgen, Mr. J. Cappie Larbalestier, and Mr. Murphy, all Sam's superiors in the Department. Mr. Virgen had three beautiful daughters, all Virgens (said Sam), who moved through rose gardens, gave parties, and possessed three blue Persian kittens—Sam adored them all: he adored Iris, Penelope, and Maisie Virgen and had written a ditty to them one Saturday afternoon at tea, as follows:

What I most admire is—Iris:
But would have envelope me—the web
    of Penelope:
Though the one that drives me crazy—is Maisie.

Now the children had no need of a Punch-and-Judy show as their gifted and possessed father went through his antics, gibbering and hunching his shoulder, scolding and squawking, fawning and groveling, imitating Crazy-Daisy, talking to a Negro cleaner, talking to Sam. What a circus it was down at the Department! When the children, severally, taken down by Sam to the Department, chanced to see one of these grotesque and marvelous creatures, they at once burst out laughing or else devoured the fable with their eyes. This was Crazy-Daisy! This, Dirty Jack. The best thing was that Crazy-Daisy really hunched his shoulder and Dirty Jack really had grease on his coat and soup on his tie. Of Crazy-Daisy's goings-on, though, they could get no evidence—his stargazing, zodiac-fixed horse races at Bowie and his predictions about salary aspirations, lawsuits, and wills were all done in the secrecy of his own office, on his little office stool, or else in his faraway bungalow in Hyattsville. But here was something new.

Sam said, "The other day Crazy-Daisy was asking the Department of Agriculture for a bedbug."

There was a whoop of joy. Jo exclaimed, "Samuel!"

"But none was forthcoming, so he sent one of the messengers out to catch one, and the messenger had to go to Skinny's Hotel in Thirteenth Street and catch one and at first he got a black eye. Then the messenger brought it back, and Crazy-Daisy put it in a little Sen-Sen box with borated cotton. Then he took it home—"

"For a pet, oh, for a pet," gasped Bonnie, collapsing on a chair.

"No, he let it out of the shutter in the box and put it on his old coat. Then when the woman who has the bungalow saw it, she chased him out of his room without asking him for the rent. So he saved a week's rent!"

"Samuel!" said Jo, "you ought to be ashamed."

"I don't see you crying," said Sam, "I don't see you busting in two tears!"

Jo, grinning faintly, turned back to the piano, gave a sniff to settle her features, and struck a note.

Bonnie continued, "What did he do with the bedbug, oh, he-ha!"

"Ate it," suggested Ernie.

"Married it," said Sam, "got it a wife."

"It takes two bedbugs to make a world of trouble," said Jo from the piano, playing softly, "Ladybird, ladybird, fly away home."

"Quiet, kids," said Sam, "perpend, give ear: Jo will play us a toon, a little moozic." Sam lay back looking at the ceiling, while Bonnie tapped her foot and shifted uneasily, ready at any minute to point out the wrong notes. At last she burst out, when Jo struck out into the *Marche Hongroise*, "Jo, excuse me, but you're out of practice, I think! Your timing's wrong. You were never good at time. You ought to have had a metronome," she ended unhappily.

"What!" roared Jo. "What cheek! I play every day of the week at school and for my own pleasure on Saturdays. Mrs. Ogden always says she loves to hear the music drifting across the yard from my flat. How absurd!" She played louder and faster than ever. Bonnie persisted gloomily, "Let me show you how that bit goes, Jo: don't be so obstinate!"

"Obstinate! What?" cried Jo. "What nonsense. I'm never obstinate! You're itching to get at the piano. You know nothing about it! You never play. Oh, don't annoy me! I didn't get a wink of sleep last night. I shall get a headache. Don't irritate me." She turned to the keyboard and played with even more mistakes to the end. "You see, you put me out," she said indignantly to Bonnie.

"You should be above criticism," said Bonnie nastily.

"Kiddies, dance, round in a ring now," Jo cried, brightly ignoring her and determined to keep the piano at all costs.

Louie gravely came into the middle of the carpet, lifted her skirts slightly, and began to practice ballet steps, positions one to six.

Sam stared and burst into a roar of laughter. "Our fairy! Look at our fairy!"

Louie smiled slightly, thinking it a compliment, and began to skip about childishly. Jo chuckled; Bonnie took it all seriously and commanded, "Left foot, right foot, go on (there's no harm in improvisation—let me play for her, Jo!)."

The children began to skip around at will, and Bonnie, pulling up a chair to the piano, tried to play a little tune in the bass.

"You can't dance, Looloo, and don't try," said Sam nastily.

"Go on, darlin'," begged Bonnie, tapping away. Evie had stopped, looking from one to the other. Louie obstinately kept twirling farther off, in a corner of the carpet.

"Stop it, you fathead, you silly fathead," cried Sam wrathfully, "do you want to make an idiot of yourself? You don't know what you look like, you great fat lump. I don't want to see your legs: keep your dress down. And please tell Henny to lengthen it." With a sort of sacred horror he looked aghast at her fat thighs half revealed. Louie flushed and, moving down the room, towards the south window, did a few steps to herself, hesitating and quiet as a meditation.

"Stop it, you—mule!" cried Sam, half laughing, "or I'll give you a flip. I can't bear to see Looloo making a fool of herself," he explained to his sisters. "So cussed a child I've never seen." He looked at her sideways, taunting, charming, "You'll find your place in the world, Looloo, but whatever we eventually find in that mountain of fat, it isn't going to be a Pavlova!" Even Bonnie held her tongue. "Your head's big enough to hold a fair mess of brains, if they're not addled, always, of course," said Sam, in high good humor. He turned away from her altogether, frowning again, "I don't know where Looloo, though, gets the foolish, flighty notions she's been getting lately." He explained to every one present, "Bonniferous was an awful nitwit when she was a kid, always thinking she would be a stage or cinema star and darned if silly Looloo hasn't been bitten by the same bug." He began to laugh and there were some more silly jokes about the adventure of Crazy-Daisy.

Meanwhile, no one had noticed Henny return home and go into her room, leaving the door slightly ajar. Thus Henny heard that Sam, going into the men's room, had come into a discussion between

Craven Day and a messenger, from which he learned that Craven Day lent money secretly and at usurious rates to empty pockets, miseries, and follies in the Department. Samuel had been most irate and had reported this to the chief of Day's division, as was only his duty: "to think of an officer of the Department battening on the wretchedness or improvidence of his fellow being," said Sam, though less hotly than at that other time.

"Is he a Jew?" asked Jo.

"No more than you," Sam replied. "And it's just possible that you'll become one in time, Jo, collecting rents and grinding the noses of the poor."

"I keep my nose to the grindstone," said Jo bitterly.

"It doesn't do it much good," Bonnie hastened to say.

"Jo the Jew," said Ernie thoughtfully. Jo flashed a look at him by no means friendly. But this inspired Louie to remark that she had personally seen the stewed cats at the Kydds place today. Bonnie was all eyes and ears and wanted to know the details. Louie, giggling, informed them that she had dropped a piece of bacon in the stewed cats, and that she had escaped in the nick of time from Old Goat, who had returned early to beat Angela and eat his cats. Up till this minute she had forgotten the drowning; and suddenly she flushed and said no more. Sam was grinning at this improvement on his morning fancy and asked in a mean, driving tone what the stew smelled like. Immediately, Henny's door, which had been standing open, flew shut. Everyone started, "What was that?" The wind? No, no wind. Ernie drawled,

"It was Mothering: she's been home for ages!"

"Oh, I must see Henny," declared Jo in excitement and jumped up. No sooner had she quit the piano stool than Bonnie flew to it and began to sing and play in her best style, *"L'amour est un oiseau."*

The children, after knocking, rushed in ahead of their aunt and found Evie already there, asking,

"Do you want a cup of tea, Mother?"

"Would you care for—?"

"Would you care for a cup of tea?"

"Yes, I should be very glad of it." She rooted Tommy out of the armchair, saying, "You and your everlasting messing," and flopped into the chair sighing. She turned with a smile to the twins standing side by side and gave one of her queer little recitations that they all knew by heart but loved to hear:

"Have a cup of tea, sir? No, sir! Why, sir? Because I have a cold, sir! Let me hear you cough, sir! Hm, hm, hm!"

Louie, arriving at this moment, said with a silly smile, "Say, *Piccadilly*, Mother."

Henny obliged with "Offal baw the R.A. Show and yet a chappie has to go: the only thing in Piccadilleh I wegard as being silleh."

When they asked for *The Bath Bun*, her good temper evaporated, and she told them to clear out and shut the door.

"Aren't you coming out to see Auntie Jo?" inquired Tommy, who was new to life.

"I'd like to see her at the bottom of the sea," Henny replied genially (and Jo, on the other side of the door, hearing this, sniffed good-humoredly and prepared a smile); "and all the fool Pollits with her: now get out."

"We're Pollits, Moth," Ernest reminded her as usual.

"And I might screw your necks too," Henny agreed. They all laughed and scampered out, finding Auntie Jo at the door. She sniffed honorably to signal that she was there and called cheerfully,

"Henny, my dear, may I come in?" She carefully shut the door, and at this sound Bonnie stopped playing. After a moment, hearing Jo talking "nineteen to the dozen," she sighed and went on with her music, but with less verve. It was a mystery, thought Bonnie, that Jo was so wonderful with little kiddies and knew so little about all other kinds of people. As soon as children crossed the threshold of the elementary schoolroom they became forever incomprehensible and alien to Jo.

Evie, standing now between her mother and her aunt, fidgeting with her aunt's great arm round her, seemed to be looking up trustfully with her brown eyes, but those deceptive eyes were full of revolt, mistrust, and dislike. Evie saw only the peccary skin, long blond hair strewn on her aunt's slab cheeks, the powder and rouge (light as it was) caked with moisture, the loofah hair; she shrank from the long, plump, inhuman thigh, the glossy, sufficient skirt, from everything powerful, coarse, and proud about this great unmated mare. She shrank from her caresses and from the undulations of a voice intended to be full of honey: she understood that Jo was wooing her mother. The thin, dark mother seemed, as she grew more insolent, more polished, more ladylike, to be more enchanting to little dark Evie. "Oh," thought Evie to herself, "when I am a lady with a baby, I won't have all those bumps, I won't be so big and fat, I won't croak and shout, I will be a little woman, thin like I am now and not fat in front or in the skirt." She was very much ashamed of Auntie Jo's waggling; she feared that when her aunt went down the street, people would stop and begin to laugh, until the whole street would point at her aunt and shriek, "As she walks she wobbles." Evie gradually, politely, drew away from Auntie Jo and laid her thin brown arms over her mother's slender thighs.

"Run away and play, mother's pet," said Henny, now as elegant and sweet as she could possibly be. As Evie closed the door, she heard Aunt Jo say,

"Well, I found out all about that man! Bonnie has been carrying on with him as I thought. I can't get over it! A sister of mine! But then, I suppose I should realize that Bonnie lost her mother when very young," and Jo's voice, becoming sentimental and womanly, was lost to Evie, though she had closed the door as slowly as possible.

Presently Jo had to go, saying good-by all round, patting heads, waving very cheerfully and lovingly to Henny, even though once again she had to trample on her feelings and forbid the question that always came up in her mind, "Why won't Henny ask me just once to stay to a meal?" Henny, not even waiting till Jo had got safely out of earshot, ran out to the kitchen to get some more tea, exclaiming,

"Frowsy, blowsy old hen! I wonder I put up with her as much as I do! Why does she sit gabbling in my ear for an hour? Does she think I like her company? Why on earth doesn't she put a comb through that bristling ugly yellow haystack of hers. I can't stand it: it's like a birch broom in a fit. I wish she would stop pawing and mugging me. Ugh!" And the children pondered once more over this mystery; why was Jo's fine corn-silk hair so ugly?

Meanwhile, Sam, after a long and merry afternoon, at last declared that it was knock-off time and went upstairs to rest before dinner. He did close his eyes for half an hour before a bright idea unfolded itself to him and he got up to knock out a program for his Pacific trip on the portable. But during this half-hour he had been thinking about his little sister, Bonnie, for whom he had a great tenderness. She had always opened an eager ear to all his little-boy projects and schoolboy boastings and adolescent discoveries. When he was away, would she fall a prey to the card-trick man, the wolf Holloway? She knew nothing of the world, Sam thought, and he wished again that his mother had lived, if only for Bonnie's sake. This led him to think of Henny and her occupations during his absence. Although Henny was now old and leathery, scraggy and haggard, she had a large acquaintance in her old home town, Baltimore, amongst immoral and worthless men and women, who went in for alcohol and smoking.

Sam had discussed this intimate question at lunch yesterday with Saul Pilgrim, his oldest friend; Saul had given the world-old advice, had dug up the plan that had already served since antiquity.

For the tenth time, he told Saul Pilgrim about the second year of his marriage to Henny. He had brought a man to the house who had been the codlin-moth of marriage. He had told him never to darken his door again, but the mischief was done. A woman that Sam had loved, wooed, and given his name to, and had a child by, could in such a short space of time look at another man and perhaps worse! Only Henny's vicious upbringing, that of a rich wastrel, could explain it. Sam, like all men who have the traits of a man, had not failed to do, in the second year of marriage and ever since, what all real men do: he had confided his secret sorrow to a great many of his bosom friends, calling upon truth to witness that never was a more faithful, long-suffering husband than he, or a lighter-headed, vainer, more pernicious woman, than this that he, good soul, had innocently joined himself to. There were plenty of women, said Sam, yes, he knew it, with his views of loyalty; he believed in, loved the sex; but all the Collyers were corrupt.

Sam had told Saul about the delights of his first marriage. The first true joy he had known on earth, even greater than his first love, Louie's mother, was the education of his baby daughter Louisa. He had kept a journal from the first day, supervised her education from the first week. As a reward, he one day heard her say his name, "Tamma, Tamma!"

Thinking of the delight he had each time, to see the new inchoate mind burst from the womb, to see the clouds of larval imbecility disperse from the infant face, to watch that horrible throbbing patch close in the cranium and try to devise from its round forehead what its future would be, Sam got up with a sibylline smile and went to his desk to write out a prospectus of his Pacific trip. Though far away, he would carry his children with him in his heart and he would be with them too.

It was then that Sam found Henny's note, left since this morning, and till now covered by papers, for Little-Sam, looking for "The

Year 3000," had scrambled up everything. A minute later came the lusty shout,

"Henrietta! Come up here!"

Henny muttered in her room; it was like the rusty stirring of some weed-grown sea animal, bottom-prisoned by blindness.

"Henrietta! Henrietta!" shouted Sam. Henny muttered. Then, suddenly, she was in the door of the kitchen, tossing her head and rolling her eyes back so that her pale olive eyeballs glared—a bizarre trick of hers, saying loudly to Bonnie,

"Tell the children's father that he can come down to me if he wants to speak to me. I'm not a servant!" She then retreated as hastily to her bedroom. Bonnie looked discomfited at Louie and whispered,

"You go and tell Daddy he ought to go and talk to your mother when she wants him to; oh, dear," and she gave Louie a plaintive glance and nodded.

"Henrietta, speak to me, you devil," cried Sam.

Like a genie of smoke Henny again stood in the kitchen door; and said firmly, "Louisa, don't stand there like a stuck pig! Go and tell your father that if he wants to speak to me he can come downstairs to do it, even if he is the Great I Am." The little girl, hangdog, bowed under the guilt of both, stumped upstairs, as Sam continued to call and Henny continued to blackguard him. At the top of the stairs, in his sitting room, Sam was standing, holding a piece of paper in his hand and trembling with rage. He shouted at Louisa,

"Tell that accurst devil to come and say what she has to say, not to write letters!"

Louie mumbled, "She said to go to her, Daddy; she said she won't come up. She said she couldn't walk upstairs." Louie looked at his red face and whispered hastily, "Don't shout at her, Daddy, it makes her angry." Desperately she looked up into his face: but he was beyond her. However, he mastered himself and brushed past Louisa towards the stairs. At the head of the stairs, he turned towards her roughly and said,

"Go and look at yourself in the glass! You'd better clean up your face." While he was running downstairs, Louisa hastened to his shaving glass and saw that her nose was running with her crying, and she had brushed her face into smudges. She wept while she was rubbing her cheeks on his shaving towel. Everyone heard the birds outside.

Samuel found Henny standing, in her outdoor dress, waiting stiffly, and—as he admitted in a moment of surprise—attractive with her proud expression, high color, and curled hair. He handed her the note with a glance of contempt, and she mechanically read through what she had herself written:

Samuel Pollit: I have to talk to you about finances and about that child of yours. I cannot be left stranded with a houseful of children and no servant. I must have Hazel Moore back and be able to pay her. You must agree to this and also make regular payments. You can starve me but not your children.

HCP.

She threw it on the bed.

"What's the meaning of this, Henny?" he asked, pointing to the crushed bit of paper. "Don't send me notes. I ordered you not to do it."

Her voice rattled in her throat and she rolled her lids down over her large eyes and compressed her mouth, looking as ugly and bitter as she could,

"You take a jaunt whenever you like, and expect me to stay here when I'm sick with a great windy house gone to seed, full of little children. How am I to look after them? I do all the work and get all the blame while you streel off whenever it suits you and get your name in the papers. You cut a big figure with your friends, but I know what's behind it." She tossed her head, "I suppose you think I don't know how you tell everyone everything about me! What can you expect—?"

But Sam was taking hold of himself, and a surge of compassion, not only for himself, nor for Henny, but for the misery of all such souls wedded to bondage, rushed up,

"What do you want to see me about, Pet? As for the money, you'll get all I have: you'll get it regularly. I understand that it's not easy for you to be left alone here and you'd better make up your mind either to live amicably with Bonnie, or else to get a general servant. But I absolutely forbid you to have Hazel Moore in this house. She's a Bible thumper and hates me; she's a desiccated virgin and hates the children, and I won't have a cabal of women setting my children against me."

Henny threw her head back and laughed, the artificial, society laugh never heard in Tohoga House except in stresses, a gesture which showed all the cords and wrinkles in her early-aged neck and her saffron skin. She went on,

"I suppose you want me to bring up two little girls with a woman like your sister Bonnie in the house? Hazel is the only one who'll stand by me and she's the only one who would stand your insults and the poverty and dirt of this house, and the noise. I've got to have her. I won't, I can't undertake it by myself. You plant me in a charity house on the top of a windy hill and expect me to bring up six children without money, or heat, or proper clothes, or decent food, and in a town that's the most expensive in the country, where everyone has a car and servants. Why, I wonder you don't notice that everyone laughs in your face. Well, there's just one thing for it—either I have Hazel, and money to pay her, or I'll go home and take the children with me, and if you try to take them, I'll sue you and let out all the rotten bag of tricks you pull. I'll take the grin off your face and the flattering smile and the softsoaping handshake, and I'll wipe the great big, mealy words out of your mealy mouth."

He bent a little, baffled by her rowdiness, but replied, "I won't have Hazel, she puts my children against me. I haven't forgotten," he ended in a low voice, eying Henny accusingly. She gave a ringing laugh,

"She threw your stupid books on the floor and that's an injury for life; don't you think a woman gets sick of your jawing, and calling you to your meals, while she's got the dirty work to do?"

"Books are sacred to me," Sam said in a self-commiserating voice: "who would hurt them, would hurt a human being; it is more and worse, because they are the thoughts of people."

"And for one of your dirty books you would kill me," Henny cried, getting up. "Let's stop this. You have her or you don't have me, that's all. You can go now and make up your mind."

He softened his voice, "Pet, don't let's get into a conflict again: try to help me. This is for you and the children. Even if you hate me, you know this job is a good thing. I have a better position and better pay. You could have done much better and had social life if you had been willing. I can get a job anywhere after an appointment like this. If you are tired of Washington, we can go elsewhere perhaps."

She was silent for a while and relaxed slightly so that one could see that for him she had once had charm. At last she said,

"Don't be so pigheaded: you think of no one but yourself. You know I can't manage the children. I haven't the force of character of a Pollit. I won't let Hazel say anything against you. You ought to know that. As for her religious mumbo jumbo—do I go to church? You weaned me from that! You can rest assured."

He began to hector, "I won't have any negative talk round my children. I love my children: they are with me day and night." She cried, "Oh, Samuel, don't be such a fool. What humbug! Do you think I can't manage Hazel! She's been with me since I was a girl—and if I can't, Mother can. Let's talk about other things. Louisa's getting too big to beat. I don't know what to do with her. Her stupid great-aunt didn't ask her to her for the holidays today, and I'm darned if I'll have her round the house all the time. I want a little peace and to have my children to myself. She has your high-and-mighty ways. Another thing, she's over eleven and she's getting to be a woman already. It makes me sick to think that I have to tell her what's coming to her, what she has to go through. Why should I do it? Why should I go through the rigmarole with another woman's girl? I'm not going to speak to her. It's your place or the place of one of her aunts. I couldn't drag her into all the darn muck of existence myself."

Sam flushed, with an expression of excited curiosity,

"Why, already—?"

Henrietta tapped her foot with impatience, "You've got to talk to her and tell her how to behave. I'm not going to beat such a big girl any more. My veins swell and I nearly faint every time I have to face her. And you shouldn't beat her either. It's not right at her age. You don't know what you're doing, that think yourself so clever. Write to her mother's sister and tell her she has to take her and do the business too. I won't."

Sam lowered his head, "Henrietta, you must do that: you are her mother."

"Her mother!" cried Henrietta, looking scornful. "If you weren't what you are you'd see what a rotten beastly thing I am. If you weren't what you are you wouldn't drag her through this: but anything to suit your book. I detest the child but I'm sorry for her, which is more than you are. Take her away. I can't face it. Oh, God," she turned away from him, "when I think that whoever she is, she has to do what I have done, and know what I have known, and find out all the beastly lies." She looked up at him, "That's why I don't care what she hears or knows about our marriage. Let her know for herself what it is: then she won't look back to me as the one who tricked her. I beat her, but I don't lie to her."

Sam sighed; and, after a silence, he said, "Well, Pet, I'll, of course, speak to Louie and tell her to behave and help you all she can and to work at school and so on. But I'm no fit person and I'm afraid you have to act as mother to her. That is the duty you took on in the beginning and you must perform it. She is young yet anyhow. Let us hope—we'll let it go for a while!"

Henny shrieked with impatience, "Let it go! Why don't you send the miserable sulky wretch to boarding school, while you're away? What can I do with another woman's girl? Isn't it enough to have one of my own? When I think of the years ahead of her I want to drown myself."

Sam said in his deep, sympathetic tone, "Why don't you try mothering Louie a bit?"

Henny gave him a sulky look, "You try it!"

Sam bit his lip, "I've been hard on her, Pet, hoping you would soften. I taught her not to coax me or kiss me, or climb on my lap as the others do because in the beginning it made you so angry—but I hope she still looks to me for righteousness and justice! I thought she would turn to the woman for affection and love. It is natural. If I had been soft to her you would have turned against us both." His voice trembled.

"What's the use of going into that? How am I to get the household money? You know we need a new boiler."

He began to explain to her that she would get her money monthly, almost all his salary, and that he would exist on his expenses as much as he could and that he would get invitations from friends abroad which would stretch the money farther.

As soon as she understood the number of persons going, she sneered, "I suppose you fine scientists can't get along without secretaries; I suppose you're taking some of those eighteen-year-old high-class women along."

His face became stern, "Henrietta!"

"Well, are you?"

"I won't answer such insinuations."

She let out a howl of laughter, "I hear your answer. I know your breed; all your fine officials debauch the young girls who are afraid to lose their jobs: that's as old as Washington." He clenched his fist and brought it down on her dressing table; then, controlling himself, he turned to her, with a paling face and said quietly,

"Perhaps I have made a mistake, but Heaven knows I have been faithful to my marriage vows."

She chuckled, "The more fool you!"

He flushed and rushed to her, taking her by the shoulder and shaking her hard. She turned her face awkwardly to look up at him, "You know you're lying!"

He struck her hard on the shoulder, saying, "You are tempting me to do it!"

She at once let out a loud cry, "Don't you hit me, you devil; don't you dare strike your wife; I'll let everyone know!"

She struggled up from the chair and ran to the side window that looked out on Thirty-fourth Street and faced an empty paddock. There were no houses within hailing distance from this window since their house took up the side of that block, and she was gratified when she felt Sam's hand over her mouth. She spat and pushed it away, cried feebly,

"Help, help! Murder!"

Sam dropped behind her. She waited for him to speak, but he said nothing. She turned and walked to her chair. "Get me my smelling salts," she said to him. "You're killing me." She opened her purse and took out a bottle of pyramidon.

"Pet, don't take that dreadful thing!"

She laughed and pushed past him to the washstand from which she took a glass of water. Raising it, she asked him, "How do you know what's in this?" She looked at him through the water as she drank it and slowly closed her eyes. "Now get out," she said through the water.

Sam, turning away, saw Louie, a figure of condemnation, in the doorway. The look of concern she turned on her mother changed to rebuke when she looked at him. Sam put out his hand and said quietly, "Looloo," but she ducked ably by him and went to Henrietta, "Mother, can I get you anything?"

"Leave me alone," said Henrietta, "your father has done enough. Go out and close the door." Louie did so. Sam stood irresolute in the hall. When Louie came out, he said under his breath,

"Looloodirl!"

Louie looked at him, and turning, began to walk towards the kitchen.

"Looloodirl!"

She slowed up, but entered the kitchen at this pace. He called sharply, "Louie!"

She reappeared and footed the journey towards him unwillingly.

He demanded, "Why don't you come when your poor little Samuel calls?"

"I don't know."

"I know," he said with sudden bitterness, "because your mother's game is working after all. She is turning you against me."

"No," said Louie.

He looked at her pityingly, "No, I know you don't know it, Looloo."

"Why do you torment her?" Louie burst out blindly.

"Come into the sunroom," he said, "I want to talk to you; no, better you and I should go and have a little talky-walky. Comb your hair and put on your shoes, and we'll go and look at the dear old Plenty-Fish perhaps." Plenty-Fish was what he sometimes called the Potomac.

To make her farewells, Louie went back to the veranda where the children were sitting, waiting for her. Saul said,

"Go on, Louie, the story!"

"I can't, I've got to go for a walk."

"The story, oh, finish it first," said Evie.

Louie hesitated and then began in a husky voice, "When they came to the inn, he who had the pig's heart could not sit down to table, but went to snuffle in a dish in the corner."

She felt and heard without seeing the shudder of delight that went through them. Saul, who had been doing "Hrork, hrork!" like a pig, stopped, transfixed, looking ugly and comical, with a green velvet band tied round his head, holding up his short, stiff yellow hair. Ernie's brown face was merry and shining.

"Looloodirl!"

Ernie groaned, "Pad, let her finish, let her finish first!"

"Da seevo [this evening]!" Samuel sang out, "da seevo; now Loolabulloo and Sam-the-Bold have to have a little talky-walky." The children groaned but in a minute dashed off to other occupations. The sun was going down, and Sunday-Funday was coming to an end. They all felt it with a kind of misery: with such a fine long day and so many things to do, how could they have let it slip past like this? Tomorrow was schoolday, brief, snipped up into lessons, full of playground clashes, nasty, and without fun. There was no day going like Sunday-Funday with Sam at home.

2 *The meridian of murder.*

As they walked out, the sun went down in yellow pulp and Sam's New Jerusalem was dissolved in a milk soup, but there was a faint air on Georgetown Heights. The clouds were rising higher, but plenty of stars lay inanimate beyond the filmy sky.

"Judge not, Looloo," said Sam in an undertone: "who knows all forgives all. I knew before marriage to Henrietta Collyer that she and I should never have come together, but a young man's sense of honor, so often mistaken, misplaced as medieval chivalry, prevented me from making the break." He put his arm along her shoulders.

"But Mother said she didn't want to marry you," Louie remarked maliciously.

Sam ignored this.

"I say, frankly, Looloo, that I believed that I could remold her life and with my wife and children make a little nucleus of splendid men and women to work for the future. That was, is, my only dream, my life hope: for I am only a dreamer in realities. I want you to understand me, Looloo: she did not even try to."

Pale as a candle flame in the dusk, tallow-pale, he stalked along, holding her hand, and Louie looked up and beyond him at the enfeebled stars. Thus, for many years, she had seen her father's head, a ghostly earth flame against the heavens, from her little height. Sam looked down on the moon of her face; the day-shine was enough still to light the eyeballs swimming up to him.

"You will never understand, Looloo-dirl, what I suffered: but I have battled my way through. Fate puts stones in the path of those she wants to try; she found I had stuffing in me and is satisfied." He told her what he had suffered, tantrums, screams, fainting fits, lies, slander, the running to neighbors and family with tales, the planting in his household of an enemy and spy, Hazel Moore.

"One day she found some of my books on the table she wanted for luncheon, and she pushed them off on to the floor, hating me and them: this cut me to the heart, Looloo, because it showed me how both of them were in league against me and all that stands for man's progress and the freedom of his spirit. Don't think I was stiff-necked—I spoke to both of them gently, argued with the Devil—as the old Christians would say." He told her about the "tyranny of tears": "Men call it the tyranny of tears, it is an iron tyranny—no man could be so cruel, so devilish, as a woman with her weakness, recrimination, convenient ailments, nerves, and tears. We men are all weak as water before the primitive devices of Eve. I was patient at first, many years. You were too young then, Looloo: you did not see how kind I was, hoping for an improvement: constant dropping wears away a stone, and it was only much later that I found out hardness worked better than love. It broke my heart, nearly, to find it out. It would have broken my heart only that I had other interests. When you grow up, Looloo-dirl, you will understand what I mean, though you, Looloo, will never use those treacherous devices."

"No," said Louie, very good.

He pressed her hand, "You can never know the hell I have been through: you do not know what she did not only to me but to the little children. She has tortured them, turned them against me, lied to them, pretended I lied, I, who never told a lie in my life, Looloo: I want you to believe that and remember it always," he said sternly.

"Yes," Louie said solemnly.

"I do not know how I got through without breaking down, without my heart bursting from sorrow and shame. These heads and hearts I have come from that."

Louie became confidential, looking up trustingly into his shadowed face, "I saw things too, Daddy: I remember those things."

He said rather briskly, "Yes, you have seen things, too; but you cannot appreciate what I mean and will not for years to come, perhaps never. My sorrows, while all the time I was struggling upward, were more than man should bear."

"I had sorrows too," she piped up.

"I know, Looloo, I know," he said hastily, squeezing her hand. "We are close to each other: you are nearly of an age to begin to understand me. I wished to live only in the regions of thought and I was forced back, dragged down to earth—no, into the slime, by a woman who is—without knowing it, I believe, poor woman—as vicious as it is possible to be, without committing crimes. But there are crimes against the spirit of man." There was suppressed thunder in his voice. "Who tarnishes, assaults, threatens, hates the spirit of man is guilty of crime." After a pause he said gloomily, "Even at that I am not sure she did not want to commit actual crimes. Many is the time I have gone to the Department not knowing whether I would come home to find you butchered! Yes, Looloo, that is what she would say to me when I left for work, knowing it would torture me all through the day; she would ring me up at work to say it, knowing it would prevent me from working."

"I know," said Louie.

"She told me she would kill you and bury you in 'the grave' in the orchard, not to get rid of you, so much as to go to jail and get away from me: she said she would welcome hanging to get away from me. Can you imagine what my life was, Looloo?" he asked in a tone of horror, far away from his daughter, in the grisly past. "Murder! And she used to threaten to write insulting letters to the women I knew, noble-minded women—she said she would poison me and herself. She said she hated my children—her own children, Looloo-dirl, her own children!"

"She tried to choke me," said Louie sulkily.

Sam said, sharp as a whip, "What does this mean?"

"Last time when Tommy had convulsions, when I came in with the other blanket, I nearly fell into the bath of hot water, and Mother tried to choke me and then Tommy, and then she said she would drown us rather in the hot water and then she tried to choke herself."

After a short pause, Sam abruptly told her not to be melodramatic, that she could defend herself against a weak woman like Henny, and her brother too, "Your mother is not strong."

Louie sulked; then she said hotly, "You said it depends where it is whether it's murder."

"What are you talking about?"

"The Polynesians don't think it's murder: you said so. Old women collect money, then they get a young man to murder them and bury them. You said so. You said, it doesn't matter if the people in the country don't mind it."

His voice had cleared, "Oh! Yes, I did say that, Looloo, murder depends upon the meridian, so to speak: the thousand and one tables of morality (when we objectively consider the facts of ethnic mores), teach us not to be hidebound about our own particular little prejudices, even in law. Consider what is supposed to be a heinous offense, murder. Now, call it war, and it becomes a patriotic duty to urge other people to go and murder and be murdered. Foolish old Jo, who is a goodhearted woman, sent dozens of white feathers during the Late Unpleasantness or, in other words, desired young men to go and be murdered. En she could hev done with a young man herself: it was a combination of the sacred folly of race suicide, willful sterility, and murder. En ebblyone thought Jo was a big gun of patriotism: I bleeve your little foolish Aunt Jo will get herself 'lected to the D.A.R.'s yet—she's bin and discovered a Pollit what had no more sense than to go and fight long time ago: ten to one he was a redcoat—oh, what a joke on Jo!"

"Mother said to ask you for some money for a new dress, Dad," said Louie, after Sam had finished laughing. Sam chuckled again. "This one is all spots," said Louie.

"Now, wimmin is prone to murder," said Sam. "In wicked old Europe still, you get the village witch planning to murder husbings for them wives what is a bit tired of making coffee for the old man."

"Do they?" asked Louie, entranced.

"Yiss, and fum what I know of some wimminfolk what I know," continued Sam chuckling, "they would very much like to get to know them there witches. En some husbings too would like to know such witches." Louie giggled. "We could get rid of our old wives which is always mad at us and we could get sweet little beauts what is seventeen years old," said Sam. Louie giggled.

Louie and Sam chattered for a while on this interesting subject of countenanced murder, and then Sam told Louie that they must be serious, for murder was really a serious thing, because it meant hate, and hate produced all the wickedness of the world.

"If your own dear mother had lived, for example, my life would have been fulfilled and it would have been a paradise for me. I would not have minded if her mind had not developed, if she had just remained my own dear wife, for I should have been heartened to go on. Your dear mother understood my aims—or, let us say, she understood me and urged me on, in everything. She was anxious for me to study and get on, not for vulgar success, but because she was a true woman whose home was dear to her and because I was dear to her and you too, little Ducky she called you, and then because she knew of my high ambitions, through my so often having told them to her."

"What was your ambition?" asked Louie, full of interest. She too was very ambitious. She wished to be a Spartan, for example: if she could go to the dentist and never make a squeak, she felt she would make a great impression. Then she wished to become great. At present she only read about men of destiny.

"You know it, Looloo," he replied in a deep voice. "It is to be of those who spread the light, the children of light."

On the way back, he was soulfully happy. To amuse her he told her some more about permitted murder, for he could see it amused her. In some secret societies, it was understood that a traitor would be murdered by a member of the society: this was the understanding on which he entered the fraternity. Suicide ought to be recognized and permitted, for a person was captain of his own life. Murder of the unfit, incurable, and insane should be permitted. Children born mentally deficient or diseased should be murdered, and none of these murders would really be a crime, for the community was benefited, and the good of the whole was the aim of all, or should be.

"Murder might be beautiful, a self-sacrifice, a sacrifice of some-one near and dear, for the good of others—I can conceive of such a thing, Looloo! The extinction of one life, when many are threatened, or when future generations might suffer—wouldn't you, even you, think that a fine thing? Why, we might murder thousands—not indiscriminately as in war now—but picking out the unfit and putting them painlessly into the lethal chamber. This alone would benefit mankind by clearing the way for a eugenic race. I am glad to say that some of our states have already passed laws which seem to point to a really scientific view of these things, in the near future. But you are right, Looloo, the old savages went us one better—the Polynesians got there before us, in a way."

When they got home, Louie was full of excitement. She had never come so near to talking about her own ambitions, and Sam was in a comradely mood.

"You will be all right, Looloo," concluded Sam, kissing her good night. "You are myself; I know you cannot go astray."

"I won't be like you, Dad."

He laughed, "You can't help it: you are myself."

She sulked; she wanted to be like Eleanora Duse, not like Sam.

"I wish I had a Welsh grammar," she said swiftly.

"Don't be an idiot! What for?" He laughed.

"I'd like to learn Welsh or Egyptian grammar; I could read the poetry Borrow talks about, and I could read *The Book of the Dead*."

"Learn good American grammar," he said, good-humoredly, giving her a flip on the cheek.

"I know that," said Louie; "there's no one as good as me."

"And learn to hold your shoulders straight," he said, turning away from her and turning on the radio. "You know, Looloo, I'd like to get half an hour on a station and get direct contact with a broader audience: imagine talking to your fellow man from coast to coast!"

She went up to bed insulted again.

"I will repay," she said, on the stairs, halting and looking over the banisters, with a frown. "Vengeance is mine, saith the Lord, I will repay, no, vengeance is mine, I will repay."

She dreamed she had a large scythe, suspended in space, and in this dusky space was God, softly thundering with the rhythm of a pendulum, but the pendulum was the scythe. The scythe, which she was somehow operating, swung closer to the earth and began there to mow the grass. The heartbeats of God grew louder with long rollings, like the gong in the hall, and she thought, "It is the last day." She woke. The gong was being beaten in the hall as if to get them up for the morning, but it was dark still. Down in the hall Henny cried,

"I'll bring people in; help! Louie, your father's beating me!" Louie heard Bonnie rushing downstairs.

3 Conversation.

"He lives," said Henny to herself, in her bed, "in a golden cloud floating about over a lot of back alleys he never sees; and I'm a citizen of those back alleys, like a lot of other sick sheep. I'd like to pull the wool off his eyes, but I don't dare. He'd take the children away from me; I'd be branded, hounded—I know his Lordship. I'm steaming with this heat and the pain I'm in. I suppose he's too good to notice that, because he keeps making Dr. Doe itemize the bill, the tooth patchings are getting few and far between. Connie O'Meara thinks she's a modern woman; and I have a vote too. But the fact remains that a man can take my children from me if he gets something on me; and a lot of fat old maids and scrawny hags in their fifties stand back of every darn man-made law in this and any other state. I have to be pure and chaste before getting married and after—for whom please?—for Samuel Pollit; otherwise, I'm no good before and he can take my children after. He's dying to do it, too, and have them brought up by that monster Jo Pollit, I suppose, or his beautiful

Louisa, in memory of dear Rachel, the great love: anyone, as long as he grabs them away from me, because I'm no good."

Henny tossed and turned, trying to make some plans about her finances in Sam's absence. Would she get her own family together and arrange a kind of unofficial moratorium with her creditors so that either she could pay them off by economy and reform, or her father or Hassie could be eventually moved to pay them off? What would she do if Sam's stern nature or perfect morality should weaken or if, by any freak of scientific curiosity or middle-aged humanity, he might start looking into her life and asking himself what sort of a person he was married to? It would be all up with Henny and her children. Yet she daily trembled before the wild plunge of confessing herself to him and letting him know the worst; with rage, envy, malice, she thought of his ignorance of all her troubles. He thought she was a sort of ignorant servant, and so he paid her almost nothing. He hankered after women with degrees and time to run to committee meetings. "It is easy," thought Henny, "to worry about peace conferences when you have servants, a car, and new hats; yes, then you give teas and so forth at home, to show off your new Persian mat and cocktail table. I thought of doing the same: I understand. But it is easy to get a little flutter out of the latest anti-alien bill out of New Mexico and the fate of peons when a man hasn't the courage to get a mistress, or incur a debt, or take a drink of whisky!"

Henny got up and started to play patience on her dressing table, brushing aside the extensive toilet set and looking at herself occasionally in the mirror. She liked to do this: it refreshed and encouraged her. "Good God, what an old hag!" she said as she sat down; "really, that Bert is a good soul! I must do something, dye my hair or something—but I hate it! Especially with my wrinkles! A young wig on an old face—very convincing. Why with his prudery and chastity the wretch has used me up more than four husbands." She began to laugh, "But here he lives like a Mormon with women all round him, sister, wife so-called, servant at times, daughters to work for him, to say nothing of secretaries and public women to admire him and hold his hand, distant relations visiting him— and yet no one in his bed!" She slapped down the cards irritably, "Anything rather than lose my expectations! Poor wretches, poor miserable wretches! And to think the poor creature, his sister, that washes his floors for him can't even kiss her knave of hearts because it doesn't suit his name." She threw back her head and laughed fully but falsely to herself in the mirror. The pack was out. She lifted two or three cards and peeped, then abstracted a card and put it in its place. But after two or three more moves, she suddenly began to gather them in and shuffle them. As usual, she had cheated without the game's coming out. She began to lay the cards out again, then said, "Who the dickens cares if it comes out or not?" and, pulling her gown round her, went out to make herself some tea. First, she shut the door, because she had left the cards lying on the table. Louie and Sam both heard familiar noises in the kitchen. Louie dropped off at once again, but Sam had been restless and now lay awake thinking. Perhaps, now, in the middle of the night, he should go down and talk to her (or would she wake the children with her woman's hysterics?). He turned and tossed while the teamaking was in progress; he was afraid of her execrations, afraid of her hardness and misery. He called a spade the predecessor of modern agriculture, she called it a muck dig: they had no words between them intelligible. At last he rolled out of bed and stood dubiously on his bedside mat shuffling his toes into each other, and then at the head of the stairs, shilly-shallying. At last he padded downstairs. There was a curious rumpling noise in the kitchen. In the great hall below it was cooler. He stood just outside the fall of light trying to see what she was doing. He was startled to see her leaning backwards on a loose-jointed kitchen chair, fixing a roller blind. He waited until she had regained her balance and then cried,

"Pet, why couldn't it wait till the morning? Of all the fool things!"

"Oh, my God!" she cried, turning quickly with her hand on her chest; then furiously, "How you frightened me! Was that your idea? Why didn't you let me hear you coming instead of sneaking up on me, spying on me in the middle of the night? What do you want? Are you spying on me as usual?"

"Pet, why the deuce do you do these fool things? Half the accidents are caused by fool women in homes doing stupid things."

"If you think I care if I break my neck!" She laughed, all the deep smudges and lines in her face coming out. "A broken arm, and I'd have a holiday perhaps; a broken back, and I'd have a holiday forever."

"Henny, drink your tea. I came to talk to you quietly while the others are in bed—about my trip!"

"I should think so! But why at this unearthly hour? Are you afraid of their hearing what I have to say to you?"

"Let's talk, Pet, while we have the chance. We are bringing up a family and we haven't exchanged words for years."

"Whose fault is it, I'd like to know," she said tossing her head and her poor naked neck with its goose flesh. "Every word you say to me is an insult. I used to go out with you till you insulted me in public. I used to have friends here till you insulted them. I won't let my children hear their mother insulted. When they get sense what will they think of you treating their mother that way?"

"I'm not going into the black past—"

She interrupted him, turning her back, "If you have something to say, out with it and leave me alone."

"I am going away for six or eight months—that depends on funds and results," Sam said deliberately, "and during that time you are, of course, my lieutenant, and have to run the house and bring up the children. I hope you will try to do it on a proper budget and without unnecessary waste. The remuneration is good, and we can perhaps save something. We will need it, Henny. I have heard that your father, with all his obligations and his keeping of your weak-kneed brothers and their big families, is not doing well. It's pouring money into a quicksand to give it to your brothers. I wish there had been more like Hassie in the family. But let that pass. I want you to take thought to the future. And perhaps we can come to a better understanding. You know yourself that we can't go on like this."

"I wish to God we could not," said Henny desperately, "but we can, that's the devil of it—"

"It's on account of this language," Sam exclaimed impatiently, "that I have to come down like this in the middle of the night. My children ought not to hear such expressions. They hear nothing like that from their father. And I must insist on your controlling your language while I'm away. You know if I could I would take them from your influence—I cannot. The law keeps me in bondage and so I see them daily being filched from me, sneaked away by a hundred kinds of mean tricks and bitter expressions and my own home life run in the Collyer style—"

"The Collyer style," she repeated twice: "where would you be without the Collyer style? You Dr. Know-All! You don't know where your bread and butter comes from. You know everything but that!"

Sam gave her a hard look, "You know I cannot provide for two homes, or I would."

"You probably do as it is," Henny teased. "No, I know you; you haven't the guts for it. You just keep them tailing along." He kept his temper, "Well, I see you're not in a proper mood. I'll wait till the morning. Get some sleep. Don't stay up brooding and fixing your facial muscles into those hag lines: you look like a woman of forty-five!"

She gave him a fierce look, "Just as you please!" She turned to pour out another cup of tea, her hands trembling more and more. She realized that he was still standing there. Swiftly she turned to him, "I might as well tell you now; why should I drag through another sleepless night? It's beyond my endurance. It will kill me. Sam, let us separate! I can't stand it. You're not happy. I'll go back to Mother and take the children while you're away, and when you come back we can fix things up without anyone noticing particularly. Your going away makes just the right opportunity. We can close this damn-fool rackety old barn, and I'll live at Monocacy. I'll even take your stinking animals along and let the man look after them, if you want the kids to have them. And Father can let Tohoga House, if he's as hard up as he seems."

Anger and balking gleamed in Sam's eyes,

"You will never break up my home. I know that's been your object for years and the aim of all your secret maneuvers. I love my children as no man ever loved his before. I know men love their children, but mine are bound up in me, part of me—" he paused breathless for a moment. "In all my misery they are my great consolation; there could be no joy in the world like my home to me. Men wreck their lives, endure backbreaking toil for years for their children. Some women cannot even understand such love as man feels in his strength for those weak ones playing round him who—" He paused again, much moved. "The light of the years to come, to me; and the law would give them into your charge because you are their mother, no matter what kind of a woman you are."

"How dare you say that! How dare you—"

"Silence!" he said very sternly. "I'll say no more now. Get to bed. I see there are some things to be thrashed out. I might have known you had some such devilish scheme to work as soon as your chance came. You have no respect for my work; you only look meanly on this absence of mine as a chance to wreak all your spite and vengeance. When a woman hates, she will wreck a dozen lives to pay back what she conceives to be some injury. You only see in this a chance to further your own work of disintegration. You devil of rust and rot and boring. You will not smash my family life.

You will carry your bargain through to the end. You will look after my children—" his voice trembled, and he said very bitterly,— "ours!" He collected himself and turned towards the door. "Good night! I'll speak to you in the morning."

"I'll divorce you," cried Henny. "I'll find a way. There must be a way. And I'll take my children from you. The man who loves children! You can have your own. That's all you really care about, anyway. You and she can go and live together and think about your rotten fine thoughts and you can weep over that sweet woman that would have made your life a paradise. Poor wretch! She died."

Sam turned and shouted, "Don't try to smear my past happiness." The house no longer contained snores either fantastic, light, and querulous, or determined and snorty, but Louie still slept well.

Henny said, "When you come back there'll be no home. You'll have to find another way to provide for me and them."

"Shut up," shouted Sam, "shut up or I'll shut you up."

"You took me and maltreated me and starved me half to death because you couldn't make a living and sponged off my father and used his influence, hoisting yourself up on all my aches and miseries," Henny began chanting with fury, "boasting and blowing about your success when all the time it was me, my poor body that was what you took your success out of. You were breaking my bones and spirit and forcing your beastly love on me: a brute, a savage, a wild Indian wouldn't do what you did, slobbering round me and calling it love and filling me with children month after month and year after year while I hated and detested you and screamed in your ears to get away from me, but you wouldn't let me go. You were quite certain in your heart of hearts where your marvelous success came from, forcing me to stay here in this rotten old molar of a house to suit yourself, making me go down on my hands and knees to scrub floors and wash your filthy linen and your torn old bed sheets, your blankets, and even your suits—I've stuffed mattresses for you and your children and cooked dinners for the whole gang of filthy, rotten, ignorant, blowing Pollits that I hate. I've had the house stinking like a corpse cellar with your formalin that you're proud of and had to put up with your vile animals and idiotic collections and your blood-and-bone fertilizer in the garden and everlasting talk, talk, talk, talk, talk," she screamed in a hoarse voice, "boring me, filling my ears with talk, jaw, jaw, till I thought the only way was to kill myself to escape you and your world of big bluffs and big sticks, saving the whole rotten world with your talk. I've stood you and your rotten stinking little brat combing lice from her hair from the public school and her green teeth falling from the roots with dirt and your sweat and you know nothing all the time. It's ten years and it's too much, I'm through; you can pack your things and get out with your filthy brat. This is my house and you can go and find the tenement house you lived in, in Baltimore, before you slipped about in the slime in my father's fishshop, with the slum brats you were raised with; find the house and stay in it with your loud-mouth, dung-haired sister and take your whore sister with you."

Sam hit her, with his open hand, across the mouth. Looking back madly at him over her shoulder, she raced into the hall, groped and found the stick in the dark and struck the gong, shrieking for the children to come downstairs and saying she would rouse the neighbors, that the beast was at her again. When she heard Bonnie on the stairs, she ran into the kitchen, seized the bread knife, and rushed at him, slashing him backwards and forwards across the arm and shoulder, and began slashing at his face before he had the presence of mind to knock it out of her hand and push her away. She stumbled and fell to the floor, where she lay exhausted and trembling.

Bonnie and Louisa, who had been brought up short in the hall, petrified with horror, rushed into the kitchen, crying and begging the man and woman to come to their senses. Blind with her tears, and sobbing loudly, Louie, tripping over her nightdress, went to help her mother, who was resting on her elbow as she got up slowly, weeping dejectedly. Louie began tugging at her, but Henrietta pushed her away, saying, "Don't touch me, I've had enough of everything!" while Bonnie was wiping the blood off Sam's face and arm with a damp cloth, crying and saying, "What happened, Henny? Whatever happened, Sam? Oh, it wasn't because of me? What did you do to her, Sam? The children—!"

Sam was unable to articulate, full of rage, fear, and astonishment. He pushed Bonnie away and finished the wiping himself. Then as he watched Henny, leaning, like the dying gladiator, on her arm, and brushing her hand across her mouth, he said in a strange, distant voice, "Leave us; go to bed and leave us!"

Bonnie looked at him, terrified, but said nothing.

Henny looked up at him, "I don't want to be left with the likes of you; I'm afraid for my life." She began to move like a creature broken with pain, and sniffing, still feeling her mouth with a drooping wrist, she stood up and pushed back her hair.

Sam said automatically, "The gas is on full!" and Henny turned to it, and turned it down under the bubbling kettle.

"Go to bed," Sam admonished Louie in an undertone. Louie and Bonnie moved out, full of doubt, but not daring to intervene, realizing that this was a conflict on another plane. Bonnie, pausing on the stairs, sent the little girl to bed, whispering to her, "I'll just wait for a while, darlin'; don't you fret: Bonnie will watch."

"Henny!" Sam said.

"Oh, what do you want?" she murmured mournfully.

"Look at me!" He held out his arm and turned his face, showing the cuts which were still bleeding.

She gave a swift glance and picked up the damp dishcloth which she handed to him again, "Here, wipe yourself off: don't stand there with that blessed martyred air like a saint in church!" She looked at him awkwardly and with much difficulty wrenched her ashamed gaze away.

He dropped the rag in the sink, dried his hands, and, looking at her sideways from the towel, said evenly, "The worst part of it is, Pet, that you love me still in a way; everything you do—even this!—shows me that. I know it!"

Henny, after tightening all the taps on the stove, stood hunched, with her arms folded tightly gripping her forearms, her head bent towards her right shoulder; and in a moment she noticed the frosty glare of the wedding ring on her left fist. As she looked dully at the band of gold that was with her night, day, in her washings and cleanings, in the children's sickness and at their birthday parties, that went into the bath water, the dough bowl, and the folds of new cotton print running over the sewing machine, that went to the maternity ward with her and to the manicurist and fortuneteller's, that she saw when drinking cocktails with Bert and when signing away her every cent on some scrap of paper at the moneylender's, that stayed with her as stayed the man she had taken it from, she took a grip on herself. If this plain ugly link meant an eyeless eternity of work and poverty and an early old age, it also meant that to her alone this potent breadwinner owed his money, name, and fidelity, to her, his kitchen-maid and body servant. For a moment, after years of scamping, she felt the dread power of wifehood; they were locked in each other's grasp till the end—the end, a mouthful of sunless muckworms and grass roots stifling his blare of trumpets and her blasphemies against love. The timid, fame-loving wretch would never dare to shake her off; and that was how she had him still.

Sam was saying, "—I had long shuddering days, Henny, when it was as if the north wind was blowing all day, when I thought of our home here on the heights, exposed to all the winds of our anger and hate, those winds raging every hour of the day and night through our rooms and corridors. What would I find when I reached home?

You will never know—because you do not care in that way for me—what I suffered in the early days of our marriage. You talk of your own sufferings, Henny. I know, for instance, that that is why Hassie does not come here. But what about me? I loved you. Can you imagine the hours of horror I spent before I reached home, wondering if I would find my children slaughtered, as you promised, and yourself weltering in your own blood? One day I came home and looked everywhere for you. I called you. There was no answer. Nearly fainting, I rushed from room to room; and all the time, enjoying my exhaustion and horror, perhaps, you were hiding in the closet in the staircase. When I opened the door, I found you moaning and spent in the corner, worn out by your own dramatics! I never knew when you meant it, nor that you were always shamming so shamefully. I saw my entire life a waste, a desert of shame and unspeakable sorrow, and behind me, a suicided wife! I spent those years in fever and agony, those years that I would have gladly given to my country alone. The man with a peaceful nest to fly home to, has everything; there is no effort he will not make for his mate and offspring. A public office is a public trust; and yet above me I had this sword of Damocles. I could have gone farther, Henny. You could have been the wife of a bigger man, a better one. But I, the most natural and loving of husbands and fathers, have been denied this simple pleasure, the only reward, besides public esteem and the love of friends, that I ever wanted."

Henny, meanwhile, had been quietly busy at the stove and now pushed towards him, over the sink cover, a little white cup full of hot coffee.

"Take some coffee, Samuel; the sugar's on the dresser."

"I made long trips," said Sam, in a warmer voice. "I visited the hatcheries and the foreshores and even went with the investigation vessel so that you would have time to settle down."

Henny said nothing but sat with her back to him, taking gulps of tea. Her face flushed slightly, and her eyes brightened.

Sam broke the silence with a lamentable note, "And instead you flirted with Mark Colefax; I take your word it was no more."

Henny broke a biscuit and said nothing, though she slewed an impatient look in his direction. He missed it. "I have never forgiven him. It is against my nature. I love to forgive, let bygones be bygones, but a man who betrays his friend's most sacred trust and essays to foul his home is no ordinary man. I am sorry to say that I pass on the other side of the street and avoid the streets he takes. No man with the feelings of a man could forgive!"

These remarks brought up an expression of rage on Henny's face, but she was careful not to let Sam see it. Sam felt her silence and assured her that goodness knew he did not mean to bring up all the black past; perhaps they had weathered the storm now; perhaps this appointment would bring a change of life for them both. They were older, their children were growing up; in the joys and interests of an adolescent family, they might lose themselves and think of others, of young ones, the citizens of the future.

"I have done nothing in all these years to justify such dislike as you seem to show, or pretend to feel," continued Sam, "but perhaps we both understand whence such feelings spring; we are both poor human creatures, and in this understanding of ourselves may be, perhaps, the origin of a better life together."

"I don't know," Henny at last murmured, "exactly what you're driving at. What is the good of fooling ourselves? It has never worked—it never will. I don't know what you want to hang on to me for. You should have let me go at the beginning. Why did you beg me to marry you at Frederick that day? I would have got another man."

"Though I am not religious, marriage seems to me sanctified," Sam protested. "Even our marriage, Henny, is somehow above the tumult of life, if only because of our children. Could I see our children scattered, divided, with divided loyalties, trying to understand a sentence against father or mother! What a shocking thing!

It is impossible," and he shuddered. "No, home is the place for the fledglings till their wings are grown and they can flit to their own place in the world. I hope that you and I have turned out some splendid minds and souls among them, Pet; your father is a fine fellow. I hope there is at least one, perhaps another, great man of science amongst the boys, and the two girls will be fine women. I have shown them the way. If they be not as bright as I could wish, they can at least work in their country's service, in the government employ, working with me and after me, when they understand my ideals, towards that super state builded on ideals which are seeded in the oldest blood of our countrymen—scientists, socialists of a new socialism, leaders of men! Pet, you could not see our children divided. It has been my fondest hope that I would produce mighty children, a tribe of giants to come after me. And that is the sole reason, since you ask me, for my having dragged you through these years of discontent, yet years of ferment. I did it, ungrudgingly, despite my own sorrow, and without your love, you know that: no one who knows me could doubt my motives."

Henny preserved her silence and hung over her empty cup, her head on her hand.

"I hope that at last, Henny," said Sam gently, "you are beginning to understand me."

Silence brooded; the hot air stagnated.

"Pet," said Sam gently, after a long pause, "look at me; don't let me see only the back of your head."

Through the rest of the house was the breathing of sleep; Bonnie had long abandoned her post on the stairs. Henny, defenseless, in one of those absences of hatred, aimless lulls that all long wars must have, turned towards him, looking at him strangely with her great, brown eyes. These eyes, fringed with jet, long and well formed under the high, thin penciled brows, had always stirred Sam deeply; and even when he came on her in a mood he detested, when she was sitting staring into space, communing with her disillusion, his heart would be wrung by their unloving beauty.

"Pet," said Sam, reaching out his left hand, large and shapely, "come here; come to me. Don't sit there, forever a stranger, a stranger on my hearth."

She did not move but continued to look at him speculatively, her mouth moving uncertainly. Sam tempted her, "You will be alone here a long time; come to me now: you must want to."

In the end, he rose and came towards her; she put up her hands but kissed him when he bent over her.

"My dear girl," he said passionately, "let us have another child, the seal of all our sorrows. Let us start a new life with it! I feel so much before me: nothing can stop me now. If you knew how to take the strength in me and use it for our good. I want to be happy. Kiss me, my girl: let this be our fortress against the world. I will make you understand me. You see, Pet," he said very low, "I need a woman to understand me. That is my softness. I want you to understand me."

She started up, trembling; but his long fidelity to her, of which she felt sure, moved her beyond all her resolutions. She began to gather up the cups and saucers and, to justify herself, she thought,

"I'll wring every penny of my debts out of him some way, before he goes; I'll find a way, anyway. I won't suffer," and a small trickle of courage came back into her veins.

Chapter Five

1 *No more forsaken.*

In the first week of every summer vacation, Louie went quickly and mysteriously to her mother's people, who lived along the Shenandoah, some in the bloody stand of hills at Harpers Ferry and some along the slopes of the upper river, near Charlestown and Winchester, in mixed orchard farms. One, Reuben Baken, kept a needy store in Frederick; one kept a large store, ships' chandler's and general grocery, in the market place in Baltimore, opposite the fishmarket (and it was here that Sam Pollit had met Rachel Baken fourteen years before). They were Virginians and Marylanders but all of Maryland origin, the root strain having settled there soon after the Revolutionary War, coming from the West of England, the Welsh Marches, and all, since the Reformation, left-wing dissenters, independent, lovers of the Lamb of God, pale-skinned, black-bearded, tall, inbred people, the greater part apathetic or infirm with the antiquity of their race, small farmers, artisans, or shopkeepers, milky-natured, music-voiced, gentle but enduring, with the quiet natures and sweet intonations of Worcester and Shrewsbury still in them. The family was full of queer aberrations, but there were no ghosts in the cupboard, for everything was told with Biblical simplicity. The Pollits fiercely guarded with the red blood of children all manner of commonplace miseries; Henny was lying, hypocritical, and ashamed before "the other woman's child," but the Bakens never saw any reason to be more secret than Isaiah. The grandfather, Israel Baken, was a boy of seven on that doomsday of December in 1859 and had never forgotten it: the family had seen the history of the Union as a history of the curtailment and abolition of involuntary servitude, and Israel's father, fighting against the slaveholders, fell, in the taking of Winchester by the Union men, December, 1862, a week before the Emancipation. Israel, eldest of three boys, himself had eight boys and three girls: Reuben, Simeon, Judah, Beulah, Joseph, Benjamin, Leah, Rachel, Dan, Jacob, and Zachariah. Henny had a convention for her children that Louie had an aunt to whose house she went for the summer, and this aunt was Aunt Beulah, who came, once a year, for an afternoon tea of polite constraint with Henny, at the beginning of the school holidays, to take Louie away.

Rachel dying, when Louie was six months old, had whispered to her eldest sister, "Look after the little girl; he is a good man, Beulah, but he knows nothing about children," and Beulah had promised to watch out for the child. This maternal duty became more difficult each year. In those fat years, Beulah's boarding-house at the top of the rise at Harpers Ferry had been full all the summer, and on Sundays automobile parties from Washington had come out all through the day to eat Beulah's chicken dinners. Her husband, Charlie, had stayed all day in the closed-in back veranda, killing, cleaning, and preparing chickens, sometimes to the number of two hundred, for the car parties. But Harpers Ferry ceased to be fashionable, people took the skyride, the fashion changed; even Harper's Ferry people all started moving away to Charlestown and elsewhere, everyone's children got jobs in the Government, the river rose and drowned the lower town, and, long before the railroad yards had been shifted, Harpers Ferry was no longer the gateway to the South, the great strategic point for holidaymakers as for warmakers, and business died. Now Aunt Beulah no longer attempted to give Sunday dinners, and merely kept her large, clean, airy house open for occasional visitors. Her two sons were in government service, and her husband, crippled with arthritis, could do no more than a little gardening round the place, sometimes relieving at the garage, but not for cash. They owned a house in the street behind the house that led to the cemetery, but rarely rented it. Times had changed. But as times grew leaner, Louie grew larger and fatter and ate more and grew lazier. The rich Pollits (so they were to Aunt Beulah) had never paid a cent for Louie's vacation, nor for her trip back home at the end of two months, or three; and Aunt Beulah, irritated from time to time, would try to make the big girl help her in the house, but she was ashamed to do so: the child was yellow as light honey and yet she reminded her of the blue-black Rachel, long dead, but whose long eyelashes, rebellious little mouth, and high cheekbones survived in young Louie. Everyone knew that Louie had rather a thin time with that basket of young puppies and most of the time, no servant to help "the stepmother."

When Beulah's anemic, YMCA sons came home, they were kind to their little cousin, rigged up a hammock for her, showed her books to read, showed her how to make knots, to plant trees, and so on: and she would follow them naïvely, confidingly, and be sorry when they had gone.

At other times, Beulah would rouse her from her dreaming and eternal reading and repeating of verses or scenes to herself, in some sheltered corner of the garden, to go and visit the other Bakens. First, there was Uncle Dan, who lived in Charlestown and who would come to fetch them in his car. All the Baken men were tall (Grandfather Israel was six feet four, in stockings with heel holes, and straight as an iron stake), but most were spare, willowy, and hambacked. The only one of medium size was Dan. All the Baken men had busy, discontented wives (Grandfather Israel had one, Mary, who pleaded, begged, wooed him the one livelong day to get one bitter word from him), but Uncle Dan's wife, Rose, was a mitigated shrew. All the Baken men were religious (though Grandfather Israel was too proud in his cruel, revolutionary religion to join their holy-holies), and Uncle Joseph was shut up in an asylum where he recited to himself the livelong day, but none was as nauseatingly sweet in his Christianity as Uncle Dan. Uncle Dan had traveled in groceries for thirty years and believed in the family life of breakfast foods, but he was sweet as sugar, sweet beyond belief to the forsaken Louie, and was always the first (after the sensible Beulah) to welcome Louie to this Israel of the meeting of the waters. The first time she ever went, and wondered at the irritable kindness of Aunt Rose, she had supper with them. There was a large table, with Dan at the head and Rose at the foot; next to Dan, young Dan, two years Louie's senior, and next to Rose, young Rose, Louie's junior, and, in between them, young children, two boys. Beside Louie sat Aunt Beulah. When the soup was served, Uncle Dan stood up, and the children, now, Rose, Dan, little Nellie and David, began to kneel down round their chairs. Aunt Rose, meanwhile, was bustling out to the kitchen where a young woman was cooking. "Now, Rose," said Uncle Dan kindly, and Rose, angrily untying her apron, came back and sat in her place; and then Uncle Dan said, "You need not kneel, dear Louie, but if you like to, you can," and Louie at once knelt down, but with open eyes, looking round, and saw Rose and Dan smile and look expectantly at her. Now the unctuous, undulating voice of Uncle Dan began (as he stood with eyes closed, their long lashes on the cheeks, and his fine buttery oval of a face uplifted to the ceiling), "Psalm Twenty-eight, nine: 'Save thy people and bless thine inheritance: feed them also: and lift them up forever.' Amen." He then went on to pray, mentioning all their names, "But first our dear Beulah who is with us again and especially our dear little cousin Louisa whom we all love though we see her so seldom, daughter of my dear sister Rachel, and who will surely 'also be a crown of glory in the hand of the Lord.'"

He broke off, to say to the little girl who was peering through her fingers at her cousins (while they peered through their fingers at her), "Yes, dear Louisa, we are so, so glad to have you with us," and then to go on to pray for them and her, and then to sit down, with a joke, "Now we are in the soup," to the table, and eat heartily, while Aunts Beulah and Rose hurried out to the kitchen again, to begin to chatter at once, about "Eva getting up two days after the child was born and who ever heard of such a thing?" After supper, the little girl, Rose, went and climbed on her father's knee, and wreathed his neck with her arms, laughing and coaxing, asking to go to the movies on Saturday, and fourteen-year-old Dan came, with the same dulcet tones as his father, to invite Louie to go up the garden to see his pigeons; and the little boy, David, brought Louie a box, his peepshow, which he had made himself, which caused little blond Nellie to show Louie her doll. Meanwhile the women kept bustling, clearing away and chattering about family affairs: "And you know what I'd do if she was mine? I'd cut off those horrible yards of hair, and she would lose her headaches." Afterwards they both went and sat on the porch, rocked, and did crochet and darning, while Nellie hung around her mother's skirts, and Father Dan and Son Dan went for a walk with their arms round each other. Whenever Louie came in sight they called her "dear Louie," and when bedtime came, there was another prayer, which Aunt Rose read from the place marked by Dan, " 'Oh, that men would praise the Lord for his goodness and for his wonderful works to the children of men! For he satisfieth the longing soul, and filleth the hungry soul with goodness.' Amen"; then there was kissing good night all round, so that even Louie and young Dan kissed good night without giggling, and Louie got into bed in the girls' room, feeling a little self-conscious, because the two girls said prayers and she did not. But though she felt they were foolish, with their singing tones and sweetness, their climbing on knees and kissing, prayers and family love, weakminded and backward, the air of the low-ceilinged wooden bedroom, which flowed between four shuttered windows and which was filled with shadows from moonshine and trees, seemed pure as the water of a river over sandstone. She was again (as each summer) one of the children of Israel; she was unquestioned in the house of Jacob, no more called forsaken.

In the morning the sun shone, and breakfast began merrily with smiling Uncle Dan and fretful Aunt Rose coming to the table after the children, Uncle Dan fixing his tie and saying, "Good morning, dear Louie! (Did you say good morning to your little cousin Louie who came to us again?) Louisa, I always say at breakfast the first text that I think of when I get out of bed in the morning," and smiling, birdlike, on them all, he continued, "Children!" and when they had closed their eyes and folded their hands, he recited the text, "'And one cried unto another, and said Holy, holy, holy, is the Lord of hosts; the whole earth is full of his glory.'" Hereupon Dan had to recite the text he had learned before going to bed (his looking glass was stuck full of texts), which was from St. Matthew 5, and then they ate, though David first asked, impudently, "Can't Louie say a text?" at which Uncle Dan asked, forever singing, if she would say one, and she replied that she did not know texts. No sooner did she say this than the children laughed (having discussed the marvelous atheism of Louie overnight) and asked if she was not a sinner and whether God was not angry with her. Dan scolded them and they easily subsided. After this household, they went to Uncle Reuben's in Frederick. The young stout blond woman, plain and off-hand, whom Louie resented under the name of Aunt Jeannette, came in for a moment to see them and then retreated to the front of the store with Aunt Beulah, leaving Louie with Reuben.

Reuben was over six feet, bowed with his chest trouble, with a pale face planted with large dark eyes, wide set, and dark spare curling hair. He was the handsomest man that Louie had ever seen, and the gentlest. Aunt Jeannette came in two or three times, with a contemptuous cranky voice, asking questions to which Reuben replied with infinite patience and understanding, if not love. Then he would go back to showing the few books he had, *The Pilgrim's Progress, Paradise Lost,* and Redpath's 1860 edition of *The Public Life of Captain John Brown,* all with steel engravings. "His leg is hurting him today," Aunt Jeannette explained to Aunt Beulah in the passage after one of her sallies; Reuben did not show any suffering; he talked hesitatingly, telling her the story of *The Pilgrim's Progress* again, his face serious; and occasionally he would pause, the eyes would be fixed on her, and suddenly he would smile with his long dark lips; the face would no longer be the face of a man dying of consumption, with its burning eyes, but the ravishment of love incarnate, speaking through voiceless but not secret signs to the child's nature. He had no daughter of his own and loved the only child of his favorite sister. He thought that when he entered Heaven (if he was found worthy), he would first see his sister Rachel and give her the last news about the child she left in babyhood; so he now devoured the child with the eyes of death-to-be. Though the place was of the poorest, and the back room where the sick man sat, dark, untidy, and airless, and they could not even spare the broken biscuits from the dirty shop in the front, Louie did not want to go.

They completed the round of the four or five Baken men who had households (not counting the religious maniac and the poetic maniac) and, after six days, went back to the house in Harpers Ferry to find that Grandfather Israel had arrived with his soft, scuttling wife to stay two months. Israel was over eighty years old now. He had no money and lived on the circuit of his sons and daughters: and his arrival was always announced thus (in a whisper), "Father has come!" and his stay thus, "Father is still with me!" and the answer to this whisper was either a nod or an understanding glare of the eyes. Even at eleven or twenty-four miles' distance, "Father has come" was said in a whisper. Israel had never spoken to Louisa, for she was the seed of a disobedient daughter and an atheist. Mary, diligent, delicate, would bring her in each year (this year, Louie was as tall as the old grandmother and broader) and say, "Israel, here is Louie, Rachel's daughter," and the black panther of a man, always pacing, always pacing, would not even cease in his pacing, but would brush them aside (if they stood in his way) and say nothing, only lift his small-boned head higher.

This year, Grandmother Mary said, pushing the child forward, and a little querulous, "Israel, here is Louisa; Israel, remember, we are old, who knows if we will see her again!" The old man paused for a moment and looked down at the girl, and she, looking up, and not so alien from him as on the other days, saw his black-streaked hair, the long nose, firm, bitten, mouth and broad square chin, the unequal eyebrows over straight-staring gray eyes, the broad, filled, low forehead, with animal determination constricting the temples and the set of the head—villainously vain, yes, proud, disappointed but unyielding, on the wiry, stiff shoulders. She felt bashful with most adults, but when she looked at this old man who disliked her and thought her hideous, revolting, Louisa stared coolly, and saw no force in the gray eyes passionate for self. The old woman watched them both eagerly, saying not a word. After a minute, the old man threw back his shoulders and began his walking up and down again, ignoring the girl completely; then he said, fretfully, "Mary, what is all that noise?" which made his wife leap and run to the kitchen, taking the child with her. Those were the only words that Louisa ever heard from Israel of the cast-iron face.

He lived with his sons and daughters, commanded them from the fastnesses of spare bedrooms, but he was not of them, whether he lived with Beulah, a freethinker, or praise-God Dan, or stern Simeon (Reuben was too poor to have him). He would not sit down with them, or talk, or walk with them. He would do nothing but sit with one of his wife's shawls round him on the bed, dejected, staring at something, or pace up and down, looking intensely bitter, ready to bite, like a dog left in charge of some property. They knew his nature so well that they left him alone at all times, to preserve themselves, and so gave him no opportunity to rave, storm, and cry woe. He wanted to be angry, his mission was to be angry, and he had nothing to be angry about; the world would not let him rave, this was the great injustice he suffered from: he stalked up and down being angry, in futility; but this anger, little spent, had kept him young, black-haired, and strenuous for over eighty years. For the rest, they all secretly sighed for his death. They did not think of Scripture's injunctions in his regard, because to himself he was the Bible, the Bible was himself: what he willed was the Bible and so it had always been. He had built up an army against himself and liked hate and despised that army which was only his own children. He was a hearty despiser, hater, cynic, a surly, battling, sinewy creature. He lived a month in the house with his daughter Beulah while Louie was there and no one ever heard a living word out of him, though they heard Mary hastily mumbling to him at all hours of the day; no doubt, on his side, he conversed by signs and glances. Then, because Beulah could not keep them any more, with Louie too, Beulah wrote a letter which was answered, and there was a tearful scene in which Beulah explained that Rose would have them. The poor old woman, crying, said that they were tossed about like a ball and no one wanted them, no, not even the daughters she had brought out of her bowels; not the women who should know what she had to put up with, no one would have her. Then Beulah cried, and Louie, sitting at the head of the table, cried too; and the three women, after crying, felt united in a love. But this did not stop the grandmother from going. Beulah, ashamed but firm, went to pack the things and then there were heard sounds from the old man, who was at last angry with cause; but what was said, and if anything was said in human words, Louie never knew, for all this was behind closed doors. When the old people went, Louisa was given their room.

Dan's children, young Rose and young Dan, would come to Harpers Ferry, once a week or so, to visit Louisa. There was plenty of room for them in the tree-shaded upstairs rooms. Louie did not care for Rose, a brown-haired, restless, thin little spitfire, but hung round with Dan and, when Rose was out of the way, would go for a walk with him, sheltered at first from the radiant, moist heat when the clouds bowled over, or the clear heat of midsummer, by the old trees of the back road, and then would come out into the old graveyard, all grass and long sights, like the house of the Lord on the mountaintops, like the mountain where Dan's Lord of hosts would make unto all people a feast of fat things. Then they would either go down by the little path behind the Jefferson Rock, overhanging the river road, to sit down and stare across the water gap, or up the Shenandoah, or, sliding down by the other side of the weather-stained caretaker's cottage, find a path looking out over the Potomac, that goes down from the heights by solemn shades and rusted gates, by the steps to the bottom of the hill, the street of little poplars and the flood-ruined houses, with jagged rents and sagging beams, by lush worthless gardens and back yards with fat, sun-struck pigs to the old armory emplacement and the rowboat ferry. Sometimes they went on from there, under the Jefferson Rock, whence they would climb perilously up and back to their starting point. Dan said little, but he liked what she liked; he was merry-hearted and would bubble out confidences, in his double-stopped voice. Aunt Beulah laughed, and Uncle Charlie called them Black and White, "Well, I see Black and White have been for another walk to look for the Cutpaper Tree." He would pretend that no one could find the cut-paper tree, and then would tell them one of his tales.

One day, when they were building one of the houses on the hill, an old wooden house with carved wooden posts (it happened to be Christmas Eve), a man drove up in a carriage with two horses and said that if they would take the carriage and horses and take him in with them, he would help them build the house. He had no money and no home. They took him in. He carved for them the four posts of the veranda, and lived with the family a year, and on the Christmas morning of the following year, he took his hat, said good-by and went his way, saying that each had fulfilled his contract. There stands the house, dilapidated, but with its four posts: and that is the story. Uncle Charlie would ask them to tell him the names of the trees in his garden, English walnut, Japanese plumage cedar, and two Colorado blue spruces, one flour-powdered blue and one plain green, a catalpa, a persimmon; and then they would walk up slowly through the deeply green streets to the Negro college, with its splendid trees, and look far out into blue, chalky, smoky valleys. Dan sometimes put his arm round Louie's waist, sometimes held her hand behind her waist, and what with the Baken strictness of speech (they were without circumlocutions), their directness of gospeling villagers, all to her, in this land, all, with the meeting of the waters, and the Southern sun pouring over the hills and their burning silky heads, John Brown's Fort, the starry nights, skirlings downhill on skates from this haunted and embattled siege rock, the quiet, deserted streets, the frank worries about the death of the town and its real estate, made the Harpers Ferry of her summers a retort of revelation to Louie: the placid, high-minded heavens of Pollitry were rolled up and there was a landscape to the far end of the sky—an antique, fertile, yeoman's country, where, in the shelter of other customs and tribal gods, people believing themselves to be the children of God stuck to their occupations, gave praise, and accompanied their humblest deeds with the thunder of mystic song.

The day came when Louie had to go home. Grandmother was there, separated from tyrannical Israel for a day or two, and there was much huffy muttering in the kitchen while Aunt Beulah and Grandmother wondered why Louie's father and mother did not send the money for her fare, nor anything more than a letter asking for her. But Louie was fat and spoiled by two months of ease, she floated in a cloud, wreathed in smiles; and not noticing their complaints which were made, in fact, in a low tone of voice, she also begged them for money so that she could take home presents to all the children. She now looked forward eagerly to seeing the children and their excitement when they undid the wrapping papers: she never went home in her life without taking them something. The two women made grim faces, but said sharply, "You'll get your money," and then went on conversing low and crankily; but Louie wondered how much money she would get. She had no pocket money, except at these times.

Then the little journey through the bluffs to Point of Rocks, leaving Reuben, and Dan, and all Israel in the hills, and sulky Aunt Beulah mastering her feelings to greet a Henny all honey, and the children tumbling in; Louie rushing to her valise, the children pawing the ground, and Tommy asking, "Where did she go, Mother?" and hearing the traditional reply, "To her aunt's in the country." In the house of Pollit the people of the house of Baken remained unnamed.

2 *Monocacy.*

The trees were turning in the gullies beyond, the day they came up by hired car along Cold Spring Lane, and, turning slowly into the rising drive, jumped out at the glassed-in porch of Monocacy. Henny's family home was named not after the village but after Frederick's serpentine stream. The two little girls, in new coats, were joyous: they loved the old home with its trees, lawns, wildernesses, old barnyards, old cow and horse paddocks, and dependencies; they loved the autumn, with its blotched valleys, the rivers of warm and cold temperature flowing in the air, the smell of burning leaves, the half-raked lawns, and the stilling brooks. A creek ran through the bottom of Monocacy's grounds, and out along the railway. Opposite was an old mansion on a hill, surrounded by noble trees and a weather-beaten fence, existing from the early days of the district; and on farther hills, hidden from the road, were other old family places, dating from Henny's childhood when this had been a distant plantation of wealthy Baltimore homes; now apartment houses and new dark-brick, gabled bungalows stepped down hill towards the creek, two-family houses opened gaping plackets on the unbuilt greens, and overdone artistic modern houses were stringing along the Lane.

In Monocacy's gardens the standard roses were too heavy with flowers, the ornamental shrubs were untrimmed, the grass grew thick on the lawns, one door of the hothouse swung open, and the sun dropping spidery into the arboretum showed a jungle of weeds. "There's no gardener," cried Louie, shocked. The wind hissing in the tall grass sang abandonment; the sun smudged on unpolished windows placarded the big house with rooms vacant, dusty, and shut up. Henny, in her big fur coat, lent to her by Hassie, paid the taxi and turned into the house, biting her lips. *Everywhere money needed*, was what this spelled to her. She knew that since Hazel Moore had left Monocacy in July, to come to help her, during Sam's absence, there had been no work done in the old house, except by a little reformatory schoolgirl from a Baltimore slum, "some love child of some horrible other Bert," thought Henny, disgusted with everything, as she came into the dusty hall, "oh, what is the world all about?"

They found Old Ellen Collyer in the housekeeper's room, buttoned to the full, sagging throat, in black, stout and placid, doing coarse crochet. The little girls ran forward and kissed her, "Hello, Old Ellen," and "Hello, Old Ellen" (for, she said, with all her grandchildren, she would think she was grandma of the whole world, if she let them say, *Grandma*); and Henny, pouting, "Hello, Mother, isn't it a beastly day?" threw her coat on the sideboard and sank into a chair, after pulling the old-fashioned bellpull.

The little girls at once ran out, while Old Ellen was saying, "Oh, only this same old shell stitch," and Henny fretted, "I hate it, it looks like an old Irish Biddy's petticoat," and asked for tea, and an aspirin, and damned the world and said, Yes, she had letters and money from Sam; when he was away she could stand him, and the farther he was away the more she could stand him! Now, the little girls were allowed to roam freely over the house, into the round room, the nursery, all the shut family bedrooms, no longer used, the billiard room, and even the dark trunk room in which was the foot of the winding stair which led to the roof and the lookout. They went into the kitchens, the closets; Evie ended up in the drawing room full of closed cabinets of china dolls, with china lace petticoats: and Louie ended in the empty stables, still sweet with hay and clean flagstones, where the sun explored the cracks of old greased halters hanging from the beams. Blowsy, tall, dusk cherry in complexion with the long summer's sun was Louie, fresh from running up and down the rock at Harpers Ferry and getting herself confused with Christian meandering upwards Beulah, she and Dan with Christian and Hopeful freed from Doubting Castle, seeing somewhere in the air (over the greens of West Virginia), the Celestial City, freed by the golden key Promise—but what promise? The promise of reaching the grass uplands of youth and understanding the world. No one asked her any questions about her summer any year, and so this world was her own secret Mesopotamia and angel-guarded pleasure, the valley of rocs and the land shadowing with wings, all strange countries, skies, spheres, and songs rolled into one small rock of the earth, known to others as Bolivar Heights, but to her as Louie's dreams which have put on flesh. For nine months of the year were trivial miseries, self-doubts, indecisions, and all those disgusts of preadolescence, when the body is dirty, the world a misfit, the moral sense qualmish, and the mind a sump of doubt: but three months of the year she lived in trust, confidence, and love.

With some dim idea of the golden stair, Louie climbed up the dusty wooden staircase between stable and barn to the lofts above the stables. There were two doorways without doors. In the right-hand loft was an army bed, and on this Uncle Barry lay on his back, with his mouth open and a yellow beam on his tired cheek. He was slender, dark, like Henny, thirty-five, one year her junior, and Old Ellen's last child. Within reach of his dangling hand were two empty whisky bottles, the like of those bottles which Louie at various times and years in her explorations of Monocacy had discovered in Barry's room, the billiard room, the round room, on the lookout, in the dung heap, in the tree guards of the cow paddock, and in the groom's toilet, which was situated behind the potting shed. The gardener and groom had gone: and here in the sweet-smelling dusty loft Barry had established his new playground, an inebriate's holy of holies, where he lay in pleasure, king of solitude. Louie pored over the snoring man. He was tall and had been handsome, but was putting on a little paunch. Louie liked Barry. He was usually out, as they said: even Louie sensed somehow that he had *a woman in Baltimore, like the old man, a chip off the old block.* Who had heard it said? But the children knew it, without wonder. He liked the drink. He had large, absorbed eyes, he lurched slightly, he would smile in his dark mustache, with meaningless satire, and would murmur and mutter, in his sweet Baltimore inaudibility, something or other to Louie. He did not detest her; he even took an interest in her, faintly, as if from a great distance; and occasionally would show her things. Once, in some webby past, he had studied the dyeing of textiles with the idea of going into a hat factory downtown; and then he had collaborated with a Johns Hopkins man in a little idea—the printing of obscene books after hours, on a little press, and they made a bit of money, and then he had given up the effort altogether and devoted himself to drink, which was now his only occupation. He had charm, he could not be affronted: Louie liked him. After watching him for a while, Louie got bored, because nothing happened, he did not shriek, or see snakes, or get up. She wandered back over the saddling paddock, through the now-empty kitchens, to the housekeeper's room.

"—and said she was going to take permanganate," said Old Ellen, "because Barry wouldn't marry her to get her out of trouble. I had enough trouble with them."

"Remember that poor unfortunate—what was her name, you know, the Sleighs'—Delia!—they found her on the floor in a terrible state and she had taken Lysol?"

"They found that woman last year under a bush, you remember, who had taken about two hundred aspirins—Heavenly Father!"

Henny said impatiently, "There are so many ways to kill yourself, they're just old-fashioned with their permanganate: do you think I'd take permanganate? I wouldn't want to burn my insides out and live to tell the tale as well; idiots! It's simple. I'd drown myself. Why not put your head in a gas oven? They say it doesn't smell so bad. I don't know. I thought of asking my dentist, Give me some of that stuff, you know, nitrate, no, nitrous oxide, too much and you go out sweetly, or too much ether, eh? Permanganate, or carbolic acid, or arsenic, who would take it? There are so many things. Why, Sam has cyanide in the house any time: that's what they kill vermin with, you blow it in the holes. Why? Barry could get me some: anyone can get the easy things. Catch me eating two hundred aspirins—my heart would kill me; I couldn't stand that. I don't think much of drowning. I've thought of opening a vein in a warm bath, I heard of a woman who did that, but I think I'd feel too weak. Why be in misery at the last? There must be plenty of things. I've thought of getting too friendly with a doctor, you know, and getting him to give me something. Get in with him, and let him get too friendly with you, then he gets sick of you, you begin to bother him, tell him you're pregnant or something, or ask him for drugs, and he'll give you something quick enough. Or you go to his consulting rooms, and he trusts you and leaves you alone—or he leaves the stuff unlocked purposely—foo, I've thought of a hundred ways. It's only a stupid servant girl would do that carbolic-acid trick. And rat poison is too nasty and they can always trace it. I couldn't touch a revolver—your hand would shake! I'm sure I'd be a poor shot, and then you wouldn't know where to do it. Oh, in labor pains, it's different: you want to die, but you want to see the kid too. I don't have such a bad time, and just about the time I start to tell them to take me and drown me and it too, it comes, and then you begin to wonder about it. And apart from that, I can't get sick enough. Anyone would think a thin stick like me, weak and miserable, would go down with everything: do you think I get more than my old cough every winter? I bet I live till ninety, with all my aches and pains. To think that's fifty more years of the Great I-Am. No wonder I want to make away with myself. Who wouldn't? You grumble, but at least Dad left you alone, he didn't try to talk you to death."

"Eleanor had none, Hassie had only one miserable shrimp, and you had all those," said the old woman, "and look at you—you were never any different! Just a cornstalk. You were a nice-looking girl, though! I thought you'd marry that Albert!"

"Oh, shut up!"

"Look at Wally," said the old woman, laughing: "what's the matter with you? Why don't you get another? You're slow, that's all. You can pick up a king yet at your age."

"I have a fine king, a god. One king is enough. Next time I pick an I.W.W.; better than the Professor at any rate. I'd rather wash for a drunk than let a high-and-mighty work for me. At least I'd have a lively time. Yes, you know I was sure of it. I'm gone. Think of it.

Isn't it a disgrace? What am I to do with another one and I owe what I owe already? I've been feeling wretched and I got sick on the taxi over. God, what we women have to put up with; and I'm not even allowed to complain."

"You know the story of the doctor who found the man walking up and down in the lobby of the hospital and said, 'What's the matter?' 'My wife's having a baby upstairs,' said the man. 'Well, why don't you go upstairs?' asked the doctor. 'No,' the man said, 'we're not speaking, I don't want to show interest, we haven't spoken for two years.' 'But, well,' the doctor said, 'explain to me, will you?' 'Oh,' said the husband, 'I'm not as mad at her as that.' Reminds me of the woman with six children who told the census taker she was an old maid but not the fussy sort. Did you hear about the woman who kept going to Dr. Uno for operations and he asked her, 'Who's the father?' and she kept on saying, 'Mr. Whosthis,' until the doctor said, 'Why don't you marry the man?' and she said, 'I don't like him, doctor.' That's like you, Henny, that's just like you!" She slapped her crochet down on her knee, laughing, "Oh, you're a case, you take the cake. What for? You can't blame the man for—"

"All men are dogs," said Henny.

"Stop eating bread and sauce now, if you love me," said Old Ellen, "is that the proper thing to eat? No wonder you feel bad. You always did it when you were growing up too, and that's what made you such a namby-pamby girl. If you'd had a bit of flesh on you you could have got that—"

"Oh, do stop harping on Albert every time I come," Henny said impatiently. "When's Archie coming? I think I'll go and lie down. Where's Hassie? I hope she'll drive me back, I can't afford taxi fares, and I can't afford a new tire, so here I am."

"Will you stop flouncing round?" asked Old Ellen.

"I'm getting sick of this pattern," grumbled Henny. "But everyone admires it. I made three bonnets last month."

"You were always soaping and sighing," said Old Ellen, "and making cow eyes at the boys, you had no reserve. Remember the time Dunne Legge kissed you and you told me you were going to get married. Oh, ha-ha!"

"If you think that was a joke," said Henny; "I was wild about Dunne—all the crushes I had."

"Well—well—well, it's all over now."

"That time Dunne was in the hospital and I sent him a pair of bed socks and he said he wanted girls to have fun with, he wasn't after a sick nurse! The sneak! That's the second stitch I've dropped; I'm all to pieces. Father was in a hurry. A fisheries inspector!"

At this moment there was a rush in the hall, Evie tearing in to announce Aunt Hassle's arrival in the car. Henny and her mother went out to see Harriet, and Hassie came in saying cheerfully, "Guess who I ran into? Of all people—Dunne! You know what he told me? Poor Connie died at last. It's a good thing. I heard she kept asking the doctor to put her out."

"What was it, I didn't hear that?" Old Ellen asked.

"Cancer, intestinal cancer—"

"Oh, why didn't he give her an overdose and put her out of her misery? You'd do it for an animal, but we have to suffer!" Henny shivered. "It makes me sick. I'd do it for one of mine, I don't mind telling you. Poor girl!"

"She wasn't a girl any more—she was a great big bouncing woman, like me, with shoulders broader than me," said Hassie: "and she wasted away, she looked like a ghost. I couldn't have borne to have seen it. I've had bad luck myself! That boy of mine in the shop ran a bone into his finger and got blood poisoning, and just five weeks after Pete got his finger into the sausage machine."

"Nothing but trouble," declared Old Ellen; "there have been a lot of accidents round here lately, isn't it funny? It goes in seasons."

"Connie was thirty-six, I think," said Henny slowly, "and she was a beauty when she was a girl: she never got married—I can't understand why. She was stuck on that Senator fellow. Well, if she'd married she'd be leaving some man and children miserable at this minute. Did she linger long? How long was it? I hope not." After a silence she added, "I didn't want to earn $100 that way—I owed her that and she went to her grave thinking I was a cheat, I don't doubt."

"She was such a big jolly girl," said Hassie: "she was on the hockey team. Then she went to Washington to get a job, and there was that man in the Post Office, and then this friend of her father's, the Senator, a married man even then, but—there was something—I never heard—"

"It was her lookout," said Henny angrily, "a woman who tries to take a man away has it coming to her: but I didn't think Connie was that sort, to take another woman's man—you can never tell, when they get the itch, but mind, I liked her: she was a decent sort; and perhaps he went after her—"

The talk fell into murmurs, although the women had no idea that anyone was listening, but soon rose again with Henny retailing her part of it, "She got into trouble, money troubles, I heard every word about it, from—a man I know, I saw her going into a moneylender's, to tell the honest truth though I never let her see, and he wouldn't leave her at home, she had to travel round with him as Mrs. if you like! Then the wife got to hear of it and tore down the house; and she went round with him. Then they used to throw them out of hotels in the country, for brawling at night. I saw her once in Washington in my younger days, at a *conversazione:* she had a breath like a salt mine and a great belly like a foaling mare, floating and bloating and talking about her medicine and when she went to the toilet. Then she died, and what does he do? Turns round and writes a book of poetry about his angel and I don't know what not, the greasy hypocrite, crying and tearing his hair and pretending: and of course he couldn't marry Connie then. Some other excuse. It was her own fault, but in a way I pitied her. And see now! Isn't it rotten luck? Isn't every rotten thing in life rotten luck? When I see what happens to girls I'd like to throttle my two, or send them out on the streets and get it over with."

"Don't be a fool," said Hassie, "don't let anyone hear you talk like that, people would misunderstand."

"What?" asked Henny with a short laugh. "Where the devil is that custard pie, Archie? I'm going mad with my debts, and he stays away, higgles and haggles and pulls a parson's nose and looks through his spectacles. I don't wonder Eleanor is sick of him."

"Shh," said Hassie, "you don't know that!"

Old Ellen laughed. "And did you hear the latest about My Lord? Barry saw me burrowing into the dirty-clothes basket and thought it was the washerwoman and started to feel my sitdown! Did I turn round like a fury and give him something to think about!"

"Mother," said Hassie.

"Mother, Mother, Mother. Stick up for your brother Barry."

"I'm not sticking up for him, Mother."

"He'll end by hanging," said Henny coolly: "he would have been fruit on a peculiar tree before this if he'd lived in a decent country, the Casanova; is he still with that woman? I've no patience with men and their tricks."

"Is it true that when men hang they give a last kick?" asked Old Ellen. "I often thought I'd like to go to a hanging to see."

"You know that Jenny fell down the cellar stairs and nearly brought it on?" Hassie said severely.

"I know a man that went to see an electrocution," Henny said, through half-closed mouth, "I don't know what he went to see. You broke your glasses, Mother?"

"Yes, Barry's friend, that old eye man, was on a bend since last Thursday and I wouldn't let anyone but him fix them, drunk or sober: someone saw him lying on the sidewalk dead to the world, in Aliceanna Street, poor old coot. Last time, he went down to Mahogany Hall, and when he came to his senses there he was with a nice one, 'a sweet little bit,' he called her to me, shameless, and he says, 'Where am I? I got to get to work.' She put her arms round him and said, 'Don't you go, you're my man.' 'Oh, I'm sorry, but I've got to go.' But she still kept holding on to him and hollering, 'You're my man!'"

"If I thought that child was spying round and eavesdropping with her ear at the door," said Henny.

"For the love of Mike," cried Hassie, "where is she then?"

"I haven't the strength to keep her in order," said Henny.

At this Louie retreated quietly, step by step, corner by door ajar, until she reached the back veranda which lay between the housekeeper's room and the upper kitchen; just at this minute, the bell rang in the kitchen and the little new maid dragged her chair. Louie hopped into the pantry, up one step, and pretended to be studying the preserves. When the maid returned and began to fuss at the stove, Louie tiptoed back to her post and heard the end of a discussion about varicose veins, girls in factories with unwanted babies, and clots in the brain and the heart, and then suddenly they were back to the romantic Barry again, and the two young women scolded their mother for spoiling him.

"I know he's a ne'er-do-well. But if I don't look after him, who will?" says the old woman; and the two others began to laugh, especially Hassie.

"Why, what's the matter with you, Hassie? I've never seen you so gay!" said Henny laughing too, "You're always messing in politics and too good to laugh at people's jokes."

"Didn't you know she fell down the cellar steps?" said Old Ellen in an uproar. "She cracked open her head."

Hassie began to tell it rapidly, "Pete was up all night with a toothache and he was taking forty winks when he heard me scream.

He never heard me scream before; he jumped out of bed with only his pajama coat on and appeared at the head of the cellar steps…"

"She knew she was seeing stars!" said Old Ellen.

"I thought it was an angel," said Hassie, laughing coyly.

"Perhaps it was worth it," remarked Old Ellen.

"Don't be two such fools," Henny said angrily.

"She was so surprised," said Old Ellen, holding her sides, "oh, a great experience."

"And then he yelled at me, instead of helping me up, and he went out to give the man a clip on the jaw for leaving the trap door open."

"And left you lying there," said Henny roughly.

Old Ellen was still laughing. "What harm did it do her? Perhaps she needed it all along. She's been laughing ever since."

"You ought to go to a doctor, Hassie," Henny said earnestly, "perhaps it's serious. The way I worry about the kids' heads when they fall down, I know it's no joke. I never hit them on the head. Samuel wouldn't allow it. I used to flip his marvelous offspring on the head and maybe I turned her stupid, who knows?"

"I don't understand what he keeps her there for," said Hassie.

"Why do you worry about her; she'll grow up like the rest of us," said Old Ellen.

"She's so pigheaded she drives me crazy. Her father should keep her with her own family. She always comes back from them like a stuffed pig, fat as butter. She took the car out of the garage the other day. I'd rather something happened to one of mine than to her. Her father would never let me hear the end of it." Henny choked on something.

"Much ado about nothing," said the old woman. "What do you care now?"

"I care and so would you. The child's father nags me morning, noon, and night about her looks, her future, her skirts, her fat, her yellow rattails, her filth, and her lessons."

"Henny, don't eat all that sauce," said Hassie, "in your condition, you know, you'll be ill."

"All her life she's lived on gherkins and chilies and Worcestershire sauce; it won't kill her. She preferred pickled walnuts at school to candy. Ugh! I kicked myself on the leg of this darn table. Why don't you take it, Henny? I've got no use for it. I eat my breakfast in the upper kitchen. It's sunny. You take it, Henny. You know what I'd like to do? Give all the furniture away before next time He comes! Ha-ha! Some joke! I'll bet my bottom dollar it's mortgaged. Will you take it, Hassie, then?"

"I'll probably need it," said Henny dryly, "she doesn't. Pete eats in the garage as far as I can make out. He never ate in the house that I saw."

"He's always in the refrigeration plant; it's his mania," Hassie exploded. "I don't mind: when he's at home, he gabs so much my jaws ache."

Old Ellen began to laugh healthily, "It's dangerous not to talk to your husband. Now Samuel didn't talk to Henny for four years and more—"

"I didn't talk to him; do you think anything on earth would stop the Great Mouthpiece from talking?"

"—and your Dad didn't talk to me for twenty-two years, and I had fourteen youngsters as a result."

"It isn't necessary to talk," said Henny bitterly. "Can't we get some more to eat? This is old and cold."

Louie heard the bell ringing. The young maid Nellie, sloppy and cheerful, came in suddenly from the kitchen. She went to the room and got their order for new toast, but on the way back she swerved into the pantry room and said in a fresh, childish voice to Louie,

"Why don't you come out into the kitchen? I'll give you a bit of cake."

"All right." Flustered, grinning, the child followed her. The windows were open on the lawns. Tea roses grew unpruned outside and sometimes dropped in to see them. While waiting for the kettle to boil, the new little maid sat down again in her chair by the window and took up a sock on which she was turning the heel. She pointed to a chair at the table and said to Louie, "Pull it over by me."

Louie hurried to obey and sat opposite the blond, lank-haired girl, much pleased.

"Can you knit?"

"No." Louie writhed.

"Can you talk French?"

"No." Louie looked blank.

"Say, parlayvoo fraongsay."

"What did you say?"

"That's French. Parlayvoo fraongsay. Say it." The little girl blurted it out, with blind eyes: *povvloo frossay*. Very severely, the little maid repeated her French and made Louie repeat it.

"That means, can you speak French. Then you say, wee, wee. Go on."

"Uh?"

"Wee wee."

With much giggling and blushing they got it right; and then the toast was burning.

Putting on a new slice, Nellie continued, "Voozett jolly."

Louie stared meekly at her, blushing to ear lobes.

"Say, voozett jolly."

"What does it mean?" asked Louie cautiously, for there had been a rash of dirty sayings lately; e.g., *Polly, polish it in the corner.*

"You are pretty."

Louie turned scarlet and gaped at the girl, eyes popping from their sockets.

"That's what it means," said the girl in a practical tone, after cocking half an eye at her. To cover her embarrassment, Louie got out quickly, "Fazette jolly!"

"Very good, very good: you could speak good French," the girl approved her. Louie was much encouraged. The girl went away, stayed some time, and when she came back Louie was fumbling with the needles trying to work out the how of a stitch.

"I'll show you," offered the obliging creature, "then you can knit your own tennis socks; wouldn't that be nice?"

"Yes."

"See, come and sit by me."

A long interval followed during which Louie learned to make one clumsy great hole of a plain stitch.

"And now I must undo it and do it myself," said the girl. "See, this is for Mr. Barry. He will only wear handmade socks."

"Uncle Barry will?"

"Yes, they're the best. He isn't your Uncle Barry, you know."

"Yes, he is," Louie assured her, thinking she was a stranger to the place.

"No; he's your little brothers' uncle and Evie's uncle, but not your uncle."

"No," confessed Louie.

"Well, don't say he's your uncle."

Louie was irritated and said nothing.

"That's a lie," said the girl, "because your mother is dead."

Louie studied her with a puzzled expression.

"If you lie you are a bastard," said the girl.

"I'm not a bastard."

"Yes, you are. A bastard has no father or mother."

"I have a father," said Louie angrily.

"He's gone away and left you," the girl said calmly, "and you're a norphan. A bastard is a norphan."

"You're not telling the truth."

"Yes, I am; you ask Miss Hassie. You ask Old Mrs. Collyer. That ain't your mother, that's your stepmother. You've got a stepmother. So that proves you're a bastard."

Louie was silent.

"And no one likes you," said the girl, without malice, "that's because you're a norphan. Nobody likes you."

"Yes, they do," said Louie.

"Who?"

"Everyone; a lot of people."

"Who?" continued the maid, calm in her demonstration.

Louie hesitated. "My father and my mother."

"Your brothers and Evie have a mother, but you are a norphan. And your father doesn't like you because he beats you. I know. I heard. A little bird told me. I know. You're a bastard. You get beaten."

Louie was perplexed and ashamed.

"Your father doesn't want you; he sends you to your uncle's at Harpers Ferry. They're poor. Someone told me," the young girl said with conviction. "I know; you can't fool me. You're just a norphan. They send you away. You're no good. They're going to send you to work soon."

"I'm going to high school this month," Louie said.

"You're going to the reform school for children," Nellie said sharply. "That's where they send bastards. You see. Someone told me. You stole a cooky at the grocer's."

"I'm not, I'm not," Louie said, very stormy. "That's not true."

"You stole some cookies. The grocer sent a note to your mother and she told that other maid, Hazel, and she told Mrs. Collyer. You're a thief." Louie was silent. The girl pounced, "You're a thief; you stole."

"I had a right to," said Louie angrily, "he gave it to me: I had a right to."

"You're a liar," said the girl happily. "He wrote to your step-mother. And you stole flowers from Mrs. Bolton's."

Louie was thunderstruck. One day she had picked some flowers through the fence, in fact, and then taken them inside and offered them to Mrs. Bolton to conciliate her. But how did anyone know it?

"You steal everything and they'll send you to reform school. I'm a norphan and I know all about it," said the little maid calmly. "You're a norphan too: they're going to make you go out and work like me."

Louie stared at her glumly and rebelliously. The little maid ran on cheerfully,

"Near where my folks live there's a family with two pianos. When they moved, I seen two pianos in the street. And the girls moved them out themselves. They're strong. They've got big iron muscles like men. They moved everything out themselves."

Narrowing her eyes, Louie watched her with distrust.

"You don't believe me?" said the girl sharply.

"No."

"That's calling me a liar. You called me a liar; I'll tell your step-mother on you."

"No, I believe you," said Louie hastily. The girl rattled on at once, "And they don't wear any stockings, or anything under their dresses, just bare skin, pink. One time I thought they had on pink pants, then I saw they had nothing. And they were doing high kicking on the front porch."

Louie was silent, disbelieving her.

"You heard what I said? They wore nothing on under their skirts. Nothing."

"What about it?" said Louie with contempt. At home the children ran about naked, or with only overalls on.

"It ain't right. It's wrong. You take it from me. They're fast," said the girl solemnly to Louie. "They go dancing naked with boys, you know that."

Louie was silent.

"Eh?" the girl nudged her. "Eh? What do you say to that?"

"Let them if they want to," said Louie, embarrassed.

"They go for a swim and take off their things as soon as they get in," said the young girl, very mysteriously. "What do you think of that? Is that right? I bet that makes you blush."

"No," said Louie, "why shouldn't they? If no one sees them."

"But people do see them," said Nellie. "Of course, I've never seen them; but I know people," she nodded at Louie. "I know plenty of things, plenty of things. And what I don't know won't hurt me." She laughed her infantine brittle laugh. "What do you know?"

"What do you mean?"

"Don't you know anything?"

Louie hesitated, "I know—

Rebellious subjects, enemies to peace,
Profaners of this neighbor-stained steel,—
Will they not hear? What ho! you men, you beasts—"

Nellie began to smile, "That's nice. Can you recite?"

"Yes," said Louie. "*That quench the fire of your pernicious rage*; but it's a long one. Do you want to hear it? Besides I don't know much more."

"What else do you know, kid?"

"*Lars Porsena of Clusium by the nine gods he swore.*"

"You say that at school?"

"Yes," said Louie.

"But you're a norphan," said the girl, shaking her head. "You got to go to work."

Neither of them had heard wistful Evie come pussy-footing into the kitchen. She now stood at the door, staring at them, in their wonderful intercourse. But espied, she came up and proffered herself, "I can dance."

"You run away, little Evie," said Nellie.

"I better go," Louie said hastily. The company of the norphan-obsessed young person was palling and she felt uneasy about the thefts. "Don't go," said Nellie quickly, "stay here. I got no one to talk to here from one day's end to another."

"You didn't tell me the truth," said Louie getting up courage.

"I did so; and they wear pink socks when they go to bed too," Nellie gabbled, with a sneer. "They do all sorts of things; but I couldn't tell them to little girls like you."

With a severe expression, Louie left the kitchen, drawing Evie after her. Louie was deeply puzzled and sin-filled. But at once she began inventing, in the cockles of her heart, a hocus-pocus of denial, and explanation, about the cookies and the flowers. But how, in the name of everything under the sun, did anyone find out about them? She began to feel that the Boltons and Middenways were little better than creeping spies and callous slanderers trying to gnaw away her reputation. She had a right to the cookies and flowers, she calculated; whatever she did for herself, on her own initiative, was right and she would defy the world: but what about the miserable insect souls and minds of adults who spied on children and tattled? Louie was full of righteous indignation, and ready to battle her way through anything. But (mystery added to mystery) no one ever mentioned the strange thefts to her: and in due time she began to think that little Nellie, the norphan, had lied, too.

3 *Does Fate avenge Louie?*

The two little girls sat side by side on the third step, Evie impatient to get back to her stuffed birds and musical box, but Louie, afraid of her footsteps, and selfishly sinking into a daydream, while her hair mingled with Evie's chestnut mane.

"Where are those girls, I wonder?"

"They can't come to any harm here. Give yourself some rest."

Hassie said, "You know Molly's poor boy spoke the other day? She heard him calling and couldn't believe her ears: she flew like the wind. He had his eyes open and seemed to be trying to lift his poor great lolling head. When he saw her, he said, 'Mother, Mother!' Then in the night she heard him again and she woke Albert and Albert heard him too. Then he said no more. After twelve years of punishment, poor Molly heard her boy speak to her. I'm sorry for poor Molly."

"It's going to die," Old Ellen declared; "that's a sign."

"Better it should die! Only the poor wretch would have nothing in her life. If it died, she would die. Imagine twelve years tied to an idiot lying oil its back." Henny sighed.

"She's had her punishment on this earth," said Hassie.

"It's her own fault," cried Henny, "leaving a baby on a table while she goes to the door."

"Only a minute," sighed Hassie, "just one minute."

"One minute! I'll guarantee she was gabbing fifteen minutes."

"They will never forget that one minute all their lives. I think it's tragic," sighed Hassie. "He's very good to her."

"Men are always good to fools and perfect idiots," cried Henny impatiently. "A man will run ten miles from a woman with sense. I wonder where those kids are now. I'll have to go and look for them."

"Oh, you're like a hen with chickens," said Hassie.

"To think," said Henny, after a pause, referring to something else, "that a woman like that will probably get a slice of the estate, and the law allows it. Oh, life is too vile. If it happens, I'll go and see that woman and show her the six kids I have to feed and clothe and show her my rags. Even if she throws me downstairs, I'll give her something to think about; I'd rather scream her house down than let her get away with it. She may be a mistress, but she's the lowest of the low if she sees my six children starve because of her frills and flounces."

"I won't have her discussed in this house," Old Ellen said violently.

"And she's taking the bread out of your mouth! Don't be a fool, Mother; make a scandal. Tell Father you'll write to his club."

"I won't," said Old Ellen. "I'm through with fighting, I'm through with scolding and shouting, I'm through with thinking I'll get my rights. I'm through with your father, I'm through with the estate. If they give me a little corner to go and live with Barry when he's dead, that's all I ask. Let her get it and enjoy it: she's got life before her. Let her enjoy life over my old stringy carcass."

"But can you imagine Archie standing for it?"

"He told me he fought the old man bitterly on that," said Hassie in a low voice, "but—you know—" she stopped.

"I know," said Old Ellen suddenly.

"You can't let a kid starve even if it's beyond the pale," grumbled Henny.

"I'm too old for argy-bargying after all these years of not speaking," said Old Ellen.

"I'd fight for money to my last drop of blood," said Henny indignantly. "Can you live on air? Father comes smiling at my children, and all with that beau-of-the-nineties air, and smelling of lotion, and I know he's come from and going to his love nest."

"And your little tin Jesus," said Old Ellen suddenly, "what is he doing when your back's turned. Ha-ha! Your little tin Jesus."

"Shut up, Mother," said Henny, "don't be stupid. I wish to God you were right. I'd get a divorce. No such luck. You know who I saw the other day as large as life? Dunne Legge and his wife. She was hurrying into Woodward, Lothrop's, and he was meekly sitting there at the wheel. She's not fat, but beefier than ever in the hips, you know how she was, well ten times more so and great big shoulders lolloping, but well corseted, and there he sat grinning calfishly like a lap dog after her. She always heckled him and hackled him and that's what he wanted. I didn't know that! I took his word for what he wanted. But when I saw her the first time, I knew I'd been a fool to take his word! She bossed him and he took it in big gobs: it got him. It would have been a bad mistake. It's enough to wave the big stick over the kids without a great big bear of a man. He saw me and I bowed to him very quietly, but he got out of the car and came over to me and stood talking, and I don't mind telling you he made a sort of gentlemanly pass at me, but I wasn't having any. I know the fine monsieur. If he thinks I have no memory! It gave me a sort of satisfaction, I tell you, to be so distant with him. Then she bustled up and just ran over, sirupy and saccharine and I skedaddled: I can't stand such falsity! The last thing I saw her struggling to get that great body of her into the car door. But there she sits, a ton of beef, and has cars and servants and everything. Oh, it all makes me sick. It all makes me sick: what's the use of struggling? You fall madly in love with one man and nearly break your heart because he throws you over and years later you find out you would have been miserable with him; and you go to a man you don't care for and it's just the same with him too. Life is nothing but rags and tags and filthy rags at that. Why was I ever born?"

"It's too late to ask me that," said Old Ellen. "But you mightn't have been." She began to laugh, "Your old man sent me anonymous letters himself to make me divorce him." She rippled with he-hes. "I hung on to spite him. I didn't want him. It's my only pleasure left." She laughed. "All I've got left is to sit in the sun and watch Barry booze and sometimes give him a kick in the pants. Sit in the sun and watch barflies, huh?"

"I'll bet that child is hanging around somewhere spying and listening," Henny worried.

At that Louie got up and pulled Evie silently up after her. The two of them started to tiptoe into the long dining room, but Evie, who didn't know the reason for this maneuver, broke away and ran to the door of the breakfast room calling,

"Mother, where's Uncle Barry?"

"Evie, Evie," Louie called.

"Just as I thought, I was sure," said Henny.

"Send the child away," Hassie said.

"Let her stay," Old Ellen commanded comfortably. "She's a big girl now, and Evie's too little a girl, eh, my dears? What do you fret yourself so much for?" she asked Henny. "Wait till you've had as many as I've had. They know more or less, it makes no difference in the end of the book. Sure, let her stay, you want to stay, don't you, Louie?"

"Yes—no," Louie looked from one to the other. Henny laughed with irritation, "Let her stay, let her hear the dirt." Old Ellen laughed, "You want to hear the dirt?"

"She's got her ears stuffed with dirt," said Henny. They all laughed good-naturedly. Old Ellen affected to disregard the child's blush and cried,

"Well, I've got a head full of dirt. You could comb it out. These windy days I don't wash it for a sixmonth. Life's dirty, isn't it, Louie, eh? Don't you worry what they say to you, we're all dirty."

Louie lifted her head, her eyes opened gladly, and she began to laugh while Evie moved slowly into Hassie's skirts. Old Ellen said loudly,

"Only it's all over now; I'm clean now. The worst was when they were all at school and running to the stables and dirtying up the house and worrying about women with that hang-dog, up-and-down-day, blue-Monday look, tramping through the house, dirtying it all up with cigars and cigarettes and stealing your father's keys and getting at his lordship's decanters." She laughed uproariously, "Oh, I used to listen at night for Barry creeping down, the way you listen for a mouse to squeak. There I would find him tasting and nipping with an electric torch! What a lad!" She laughed. "Now, it's different. I'm a decent body, fit to talk to my washerwoman. No more milk on my bodices, mud on my skirts, only snuff on my mustache."

With utter repugnance, the two little girls looked at the well-filled old parchment face with its corrugated lips.

"Mother! Louie, run out onto the lawn. Mother, I wish you wouldn't talk that way before the children. Evie, run and play in the drawing room! Will you stop it, Mother! You're disgusting."

The old woman laughed, "Oh, let her stay. One day she'll get married, won't you, Louie?"

Louie looked shyly at her, filled with gratitude.

"And I'll have a baby," said Evie.

"You'll have a man in your skirts soon enough," said Old Ellen.

"Mother, for shame! You ought to blush!" cried the two women. "Before babies!"

"Baby me no babies!" cried Old Ellen. "They're grown women. When I was Evie's age I was looking after cows and horses and listening to the bellowing, with the cows a-bulling in the great big yellow summer moons. Kids grow up in the country. You keep them in bibs, you're child spoilers. Louie's a big sensible girl. Teach your grandmother to suck eggs, eh, Louie?"

Louie simpered vaguely.

"Mother, be quiet!"

Old Ellen had the devil in her. "Do you know that old joke that you brought home from school, and did I give you a smack-bottom then, though I remember the day with a laugh this many years gone. Mrs. Jones had a black baby. Mr. Jones died of fright when he had to explain it."

"Mother! Louie, leave the room. Mother, she'd do better to go and talk to that poor miserable creature from Highlandtown in your kitchen than to you. Go at once, Louie!"

The old woman gabbled on, ignoring her daughters' frowns, and Louie lingered. "Then the baby died and they buried it in one coffin and everyone saw that the little thing was black. Haugh!"

Hassie flushed and bounced up. But Henny sat in her place and merely commanded harshly, "Leave the room at once, or I'll make you."

Louie, struggling for a foothold, said quickly, with a whine, "Mother, Nellie says I am a bastard."

They all thoroughly enjoyed the cries and questions that followed. But Old Ellen herself bounced in her seat, saying, "I'll put salt on my lady's tail," while Hassie cried that she must get rid of the wicked little faggot and Henny told her this was what came of letting Barry choose the kitchenmaids. At that moment, there was a sound of a car honking plaintively, and they saw Archie's big sedan behind Hassie's car on the gravel drive. At the same time, Henny violently tugged at the bellpull and there came Nellie's running footsteps.

Archibald Lessinum came up the drive with a fretful expression which changed to polite pleasure when he saw the ladies. Mother and Hassie and Henny were all greeted and kissed, and he already noted their trouble and anger—three matrons with tumbled laps and Henny still carrying her serviette and wiping her lips.

"Did I alarm you, ladies?"

Archie was a short, neat, small-boned blond of a family of decayed officials whose money had gone during the war. Old David Collyer, self-made man who loved struggling talent, picked out Archie Lessinum and made him his clerk, then lawyer, then son-in-law, just as he had picked out Samuel Pollit and made him son-in-law and advanced him. Archie, thin and weak, had first liked a little the sprightly, spoiled young Henny with her dark great eyes; but after a few months of feeding, he felt the power rise up in him to cope with noble fleshly Eleanor, her father's pet, who fell romantically in love with him. This passion held for seven years when they were married.

Hassie, who expected to be named executrix of her father's will, treated Archie very seriously and confidentially as man to man; Henny saw him with a twinge of pain even now. Eleanor had no children. As for Old Ellen, she could hardly distinguish him from the rest of the world or her sons; having produced so many after pregnancies of identical length and after so many identical childhood illnesses, she could hardly tell one man from another. She was as glad to see young Archie as anyone else.

"Here you come as usual in the nick of time, young Archie," said she. "A young puss I have here has been giving lip again. I want you to speak to her. She must be sick of listening to women's jaw."

"Certainly, Mother," he said, taking it to heart, and fixing his little round glasses at the girl who was retreating through the back hall.

"Nellie! Come here at once."

The women looked very serious. He planted himself a little to the side of the three women, all taller than he. "What is it?" he muttered to Hassie. Hassie told him the offense.

"What did you say, Nellie?" he asked. "Repeat the word. You told Louie something." When he said "Louie," he winced slightly, for he detested the child as well as her father. It pained him to have to be compared with this other hand-picked son-in-law. The harum-scarum little creature looked worried; but she was frightened and told all. Archie said,

"You will go up to your room and pack, Nellie."

Immediately there was a movement amongst the women, Henny saying, "Quite right; I'd do the same," but Hassie looking doubtful and Old Ellen taking the apron from Nellie's hands,

"Well, if she's going, I have to get the supper."

"She can have her notice, but she must wait till tomorrow," said Hassie, "Mother can't be left alone and Barry is out."

Louie started forward to help, "No, Uncle Barry is in the stables."

"How do you know?" cried Henny.

"I saw him; he's asleep on the bed up there." There was another cat's-paw of emotion, Henny declaring, "You had no right to go sneaking up there, haven't I told you not to," and, Hassie fervently ejaculating that Henny should look after a young girl better, both tweaked hold of poor Louie's dress and urged her out on to the veranda, "Now go and play and don't cause any more trouble." Too much was going on, however, for them to notice her, and Evie, who remained sitting all the time on the bottom shelf of the big hall stand, saw everything unrebuked.

In the end Nellie went up to pack, Hassie driving her before her like a heifer to market, through the kitchens and to the enclosed stairs. Old Ellen going up the front stairs, arrived heavily and flatfooted in her room at the same time, going through the billiard room to say,

"Stop blubbering, my girl, and get your things together unless you want us to pack for you, and it mighn't be a bad idea. I'm sorry to see you go: you were a good girl in your way."

Meanwhile, in the breakfast room, where Archie sat with Henny and Hassie had returned, a violent conversation had arisen about Nellie's bags. All servant girls stole, said Archie; and Hassie said that where they didn't it was the exception that proved the rule.

"I'd steal if I had only her threadbare rags, and rich rotters swanked their things under my nose," said Henny viciously, irritated by Archie's pious look and cautionary notions. Archie did not deign to answer this; but he gave Henny a secret glance which seemed to mean that he wouldn't put it past her; and she replied with a black look.

"But I feel embarrassed," confessed Hassie, "when I look through and find nothing. It is like a slap in the face."

"You must not think of yourself," Archie assured her severely, "it has a demoralizing effect on the girls if they think they can get away with anything. If they don't steal this time, then they will next, provided they fancy they will not be searched."

The upshot of it was that Archie's male authority won. No sooner had Nellie brought down her old-fashioned trunk and valise than they had to be set down in the great hall and opened again. Henny poh-pohed and declared she would not stay there poking her nose into any slovenly, filthy Highlandtown rags, and went out of the hall, while Archie held up his small white hand, trying to frown down Henny of whom he now violently disapproved, and sternly told the girl not to touch the things but to let her mistress go through them.

"Then she must get the potstick or the copper stick," said Henny, from the door. "If she touches the mess, she's a fool; I'd rather be boiled in oil than put a finger to it; who knows what dirt is there— bugs or some disease, who knows what dirt? Here," said she, and stuck out between Hassie and Old Ellen towards Archie a pair of brass-handled tongs that she had seized from the fireplace in the breakfast room, "here, Archie, lift her things out with these!" But it was an insult to Archie, not the girl. He turned away and said,

"Mother, will you look through, please."

Henny shrugged and gave the tongs to Evie to put back. "Of all the dam foolery," said Henny.

Meanwhile Old Ellen was puffing over the trunk and pushing her fingers under old stockings and the remains of a dark apricot outfit bought for Nellie's last Easter, and presently hauled out a photograph of Barry, from Barry's room.

"What is this, my lady?" she asked, as she held out her hands.

"You are a thief," said Hassie, horrified.

"You know what we could do to you for this?" inquired Archie, solemnly.

She looked around at them, frowning. It ended by her having to unpack everything before their eyes and then repacking and trudging out with both packets to Hassie's car where she had to sit. Hassie would take her downtown when she went. Meanwhile, Henny was very angry with them all, because this meant that Louie or she would have to stay overnight and get their own food, and that Hassie would have to engage a new servant by tomorrow; and Henny was more angry still because now it could not be put off any longer and they would have to sit down at once and discuss Henny's financial position. The family was to make Henny a loan, in order to pay off bills she had run up for the children's clothes and dentistry, unknown to Sam, and she was to pay Archie back each time she received money from Sam. At her own urgent, exasperated request, after many threats of suicide and tears, Archie had agreed not to tell Sam about these debts.

"He would make it an excuse for taking my children away from me," said Henny, and related how Samuel struck her when he found out about the $102 owing at Middenway's, the corner grocer's. There was some talk about speaking to Samuel about striking his wife, but secretly they all felt that it would not do their spoiled sister any harm. Old David had paid Henny's bills so long after they each had had to struggle for every cent they used.

4 *Shoes.*

The clear autumn weather was with them, fresh as spring; and for the children it was always spring anyway: shriveling summer was spring, the blight of the leaves was spring, the frozen gutter was spring, and spring waiting for the buds to glisten and the birds to break eggshells was early spring too, spring so young and foolish that no poems yet applied to it, spring just born, spring with throbbing head, spring babbling and spilling, spring with jelly backbone.

Louie, going to the eastern veranda, to hang out the dishcloths and dish mop after washing up, saw the strange girl, Olive Burchardt, going down beside the fence, between the thinning lower branches of the trees.

Olive, who was fourteen already, looked at her and smirked, "You wash the dishes."

Louie grinned and blushed, but the rictus of embarrassment pleased Olive.

"You wash up; I seen you hanging out the dishcloth," Olive elaborated.

"Yes, I know."

"You do the work," Olive continued, sidling along up the street, towards the back steps, her dark, famished face never to be fed, looking backwards over the paling tops. Louie watched her intently. Olive laughed.

"Mr. Middenway said you passed lowest in all the school."

"How does he know?"

"He went down to ask why his kids didn't pass and he found out everything."

Olive sidled down the street again and, without another word, but with a few backward grins and grimaces, made towards the Middenway store. Louie stared after her as painfully as if Olive was dragging some piece of her living flesh and blood over the fence tops with her. She knew Olive was going to chat about her and her mother with the Middenways and that everyone knew they owed a huge bill to the Middenways: she knew that to owe a huge bill was both a distinction and a disgrace. Then there was the hushed-up theft mystery. Olive bought from cheap Murchison, the butcher. Although the Burchardts lived just down the block, Mrs. Pollit knew nothing of them.

Hazel Moore, the maid from Monocacy, looked between the curtains of Henny's room and called, "Your mother wants you."

"Yes, Hazel."

She went reluctantly indoors, giving a last stretch after Olive, now out of sight. Henny was continuing to Hazel,

"Lord, I hate to go and get the kids shoes: I can't keep them in shoes the way they scuff and kick and shuffle along. In summer they play football and skate, and in winter they tramp in the wet till the leather is sodden and rotten."

Louie called from the staircase, "What dress will I put on, Mother?"

"Don't ask silly questions. I hate her to go into Washington, in that old thing: she looks like a sack of potatoes. Tell Toddy [Ernest] to clean my shoes. A-ah, deuce take it. I burned my neck again; where's the cold cream? Don't I look foul? I look like a half-breed."

Hazel, the tall-boned, blue-tinged Catholic maid, called from the bedroom,

"Toddy, Toddy: clean Mother's shoes."

Evie called, "Ernest is feeding the animals."

Hazel went to the south hall door calling, "Toddy, Toddy."

"Yippills?" Ernest answered.

"Clean Mother's shoes, darling."

"Momento, zecond; Little-Sam has the snake out."

"What do you say? What is that you said?" Yes, this was followed by a shriek of horror, "Henny, that boy has the snake out of the cage."

"Momento," shouted Ernest soothingly. "Smart's the word and cool's the action: snako, go back."

Little-Sam said nothing during this excitement, but picked up the cold, sulky snake by the head behind the ears, and as it began to wreathe itself slowly round his arm, he offered it the cage door. The snake put out its forked tongue tentatively, hesitated, and began to penetrate the cage, moving slowly over the dried grass. Meanwhile Henny had burned herself again, under the ear, an ugly burn that she could not afford, for her hair scarcely fell there. But the slot door fell to, and the snake was home again, sitting in the eleven o'clock sun, grudgingly awake on this cold day.

"Hurry up," shouted Henny.

"Ya'm: come nup," Ernest answered, bolting into view over the steep lawn, now rough with grass and weeds of all summer. He appeared breathless, under the back veranda, cheerfully anxious and conciliatory.

"Naughty boy," cried Hazel, "to let the snake out."

"I was cleaning the box," said Ernest. "Dad-pad told me to clean it. Gee, I didn't know Mothering was going already. O.K."

Louie loomed on the second floor south and leaned over, "Ernie, hay! Toddy, Ernesto!"

Ernest craned upwards, "Whappills?"

"How's the possum?"

"Mean, she hissed at me."

"Are any of the snakes asleep yet?"

"Sure, one and there's another shutting her eyes. Gee, they are torpid, gee are they sleepy!" He jubilated. He ran back into the kitchen to finish the half-blacked shoes. Louie went slowly into her father's room, which she now occupied alone, and finished dressing at a snail's pace, pondering over the possum's meanness and the snake's hibernation. On her father's open roll-top desk was a book on parthenogenesis, a fertile and beautiful book of metaphysics, as it seemed to Louie, a lens on Life and its transparent secrets. Spreading glass but subtle wings, wide as the world, Louie, meandering through flowery mazes of metaphysics, was walking out with beauty and destiny. This made the process of dressing very slow, and Henny was powdered, curled, pressed, and had her hat on before Louie had buttoned her dress down the back.

"Louie, Louie!"

She fastened on her sailor and went downstairs. Her shoes were old and down at heel, but it was a happy day today, for they were going to get new ones. Henny and Hazel stood in the hall with a tinge of acrimony in their remarks to each other; something had been blowing up for days past. Hazel, twelve years older than Henny, strict, sober, and religious, made no bones about lecturing her on her wasteful ways; and Mr. Middenway, the grocer, had made some tart remarks around the district about the Pollit bills, which Hazel had picked up coming out of Mass the Sunday before. Another Sunday loomed, and Hazel wished to pay the bill in time.

"I have you and the children to look after," said Hazel, standing very stiff.

"Go to Tokyo!" Henny answered, continuing to Louie humorously, "Can't you shift your great haunches faster than that? The great fat lump drives me crazy. I suppose you were mooning over some book?"

Coming downstairs, Louie was wondering whether Olive Burchardt was still running round the streets doing the errands, for if so, she might see her. She began to run downstairs headlong and tumbled over the last three steps, falling straight on her nose and finishing in a heap at the bottom. She picked herself up, crying. Henny said,

"Oh, she's black and blue: I'm ashamed to be seen out with her—they'll think I beat her: everyone knows I'm the kid's stepmother"; and to Hazel, tossing her head, "I'll give the order to Mr. Hankin myself, and pay him; and I'll pay Middenway on the way back. Please stop bothering about it."

"I should if I were you," Hazel remarked stiffly.

Although the day was mild, Henny was wearing the heavy fur coat lent to her by Hassie, and fur-rimmed boots.

"That's so pretty, Mother," Louie said.

"Help your mother and see she doesn't slip on the snow," Hazel warned her.

Ernie whooped and dashed out to help Henny down the steps, which he had just swept, and to the gate. The flurry of children's good-bys set in again, and left them in a drift across the path and veranda.

"Good-by, Motherbunch," shouted Ernest, at her ear. The twins were struggling together in an upstairs window, squeaking urgently, "Mothering, Mothering!"

"What is it?" She turned back. Louie was hopping from one foot to another, craning her neck to see if Olive was anywhere in the neighborhood.

"Good-by, Mothering," the twins cried.

"Good-by," said Evie, on the verge of tears.

"Oh, good-by, for the love of Mike," but she waved and smiled at them. Evie rushed down the path unexpectedly, sweeping Tommy and Ernie out of her way in her passion, and her breaking voice was lifted,

"You didn't kiss me!" Henny blew her a kiss, saying between her teeth, immediately,

"The whole caboosh busting into tears because I don't go round mugging them. I'll go to Hankin's first and pay him and he can send the order. You can get the sugar, six pounds of granulated, on the way back, and tell him I'll be over to pay him this afternoon without fail."

Louie's heart gave a painful throb. Olive Burchardt had just dawdled round the corner of R Street, from the Avenue. She saw Louie and her mother at once and made the same smirk and gesture as before; she meant to say,

You do work, you wash up.

"Can I talk to Olive, Mother, while you go to the butcher's?"

"What on earth for?"

"I want to ask her, tell her—something."

When Henny said yes, she ran across the street and yet she knew it was all aimless; she did not really like Olive. Olive waited for her. Louie was much taller this year, tall for twelve, but Olive was weedy, and what Henny called a skinny gutter rat.

"What did you come over for?" asked Olive. "Your mother's gone into the butcher's."

"I know."

"I just seen Middenway: I was talkin' to him. He said you passed lowest in the school."

"I didn't."

"You did."

"How does he know?"

"He went and asked at the school about Dorothy, his silly kid. And they told him you were the worst."

"They wouldn't tell him about me."

"They would."

There was a pause, during which Louie with flustered face picked at the curb with her shabby shoes.

"Haven't you got any other shoes?" inquired Olive.

"I'm going to get some today," she waved vaguely in the direction of the butcher's.

"You're a liar," said Olive enviously, anxious to be contradicted, greedily contemplating Louie's face; but Louie was absorbed. After a pause, Louie said, "Perhaps I can walk home from school with you on Monday; I'm in the same school with you."

Olive waited a moment and then said evilly, "I'm not goin' to school on Monday and no day. I'm leavin'."

Something seemed to hit Louie. A new sort of pain, sharp and quick as lightning, tore out of its swaddling clothes of flesh, inside Louie. For a moment, she was conscious only of her wrung bowels and the cause of misery beside her, the dark spindly creature. I can't bear this, something said very audibly inside her. It was like the first stab of an abscess; the sufferer knew it would come back. I can't bear it. She looked at Olive, "Oh, Olive, don't go."

Olive could not have known anything about this little girl. Louie had never walked home from school with her, had never been allowed to play with her, and, being clumsy where Olive was spry, had never got into Olive's athletic, knowing circle in the playground. Louie knew nothing about Olive, had only seen her from a distance, and once, a few mornings ago, in the light falling from a classroom window, a queer light making her complexion greenish. But Olive had the instinctive strike of the cat,

"I'm going away, you'll never see me again."

"Oh! Where? Don't go."

"I'm goin to work: I'm sick of school."

"Oh, where, Olive?"

"You couldn't go there. In Baltimore."

"I could go to Baltimore."

"What for?" drawled the wretch, eying her oddly.

"I don't know."

They began to cross the street, towards the butcher's, Olive enlarging on her new life and Louie drearily trying to take an interest in it. Outside the butcher's they paused,

"Well, so long, got to shove off," said Olive, but not going.

"So long."

Louie took one step towards the door and stopped, "Perhaps you could leave on Tuesday?"

"I'm going on Monday to get my books; otherwise I wouldn't go. You'll be in school," said Olive.

"All right."

"So long."

Olive dawdled off, while Louie, standing in the butcher's door, gaped after her miserably. It was a relief that Olive had moved away: but ideas began to pour frantically through Louie's brain; perhaps something would happen and Olive wouldn't go, her parents would not move till the end of the week, or at least Tuesday, or they would decide to make her go back to school, or Olive would call by to say good-by, or even give Louie one of her books. But a minute later, Louie, looking down the street at Olive's pleated blue back and ankle socks, knew that that was the last she would see of her.

"Come inside and help me, Louie," called Henny in a sweet voice. She was on excellent terms again with the butcher, who, even when the debt fell deepest, still respected her father's business reputation. Henny was not rude, sharp, and overbearing with storekeepers or their assistants, although most women of her sort think they are obliged to be so; but never failed to "butter them up," as she put it, and was always recounting the compliments paid to her by them.

Two women standing inside, with red specks of sawdust on their suede shoes, and wearing respectable felt hats, one mustard and one red, were beaming like two bowls of peaches and cream at Henny, and then turned faces like two bowls of prunes and prisms at Louie. One said the expected thing,

"I'm sure she is a great help to you, Mrs. Pollit," while the other nodded sagely at Louie, "I'm sure you love children, dear: you must be a great help."

Louie stood stony before these old lines.

"Is she fond of the children?" inquired the second lady turning to Henny with a twitch, for like all ladies she prided herself on getting on well with the little ones. The wide-eyed Louie gave no answer. Henny shifted impatiently,

"I don't know, I'm sure; I don't know what she likes. She's a secretive child."

"But I hope you can trust her with the little ones," said the first severely, "such a big girl!"

"Oh, you could trust her if she didn't always have her nose stuck in a book," Henny exclaimed, getting out of patience with the women who were worrying one of their favorite subjects.

"Too much poring over books is bad for the eyes," confided the mustard-hatted woman demurely.

"Oh, we take great care of the children's eyes," Henny assured her with sudden insolence. "Come along, Louie," and with two dignified nods and a sweet "thank you" to the butcher, she swept out of the shop, saying, "Let's hurry along: I've no time to waste." A few steps away she cried, "Silly old gobblers with their dirty hair like a haystack in a fit. Imagine a woman that age with a yellow hat perched on her bun. Making up to me and making eyes, Mrs. Pollit this and that. I don't want their sticky beaks prying into my children. And it makes me mad I have to drag a monster girl like you round with me in that outfit because your father won't let me dress you properly. Now they're probably cackling behind my back and calling me a stepmother. It makes me sick. What were you doing all that time with that skinny gutter rat?"

"Can we look in the animal shop, Mother?"

"As if you didn't have enough stinking beasts at home. This afternoon."

The river gleamed at the bottom, as they walked down the avenue to the next car stop; at the foot of the street was a bare tree. They saw the blue-painted pet shop from across the street, because Henny wanted to see what was on at the cinema, and, yielding to the child's fever, Henny crossed the street and allowed her to pore over the animals until the car came in sight. Getting into the car, Louie slipped on her turned heel and went sprawling "in full sight of the whole car, covering me with embarrassment," as Henny put it; and a pleasant-faced, middle-aged gentleman came to the rescue, taking off his hat to Henny. In the car Henny met a neighbor, whom she detested and called an old upholstered frump, Mrs. Bolton, in fact; but each woman at once became tenderly confidential with the other, and a long discussion ensued about the awkwardness of young girls, and yet the impossibility of sending "young girls" about the city alone. This was but a prelude to Mrs. Bolton's searching questions about Mr. Pollit in his absence; and Henny, with a great degree of wifely pride and modesty, retailed all Sam's political opinions and described his work with the Anthropological Mission in the Pacific.

"You must be very proud of your husband," the woman remarked with affectation.

"Oh, I am," Henny answered, with perfect good grace, "I think he is a remarkable man, he works so hard, and no one can shake him from his opinions. He would not change his opinion for anyone, once he had one. Samuel does not really care for success, but for science and getting at the truth of things. I think he is a really remarkable man; but I suppose that's foolish of me."

Mrs. Bolton's cheerfulness shriveled perceptibly, but they went on "la-di-da-ing," as Henny called it, until Henny unexpectedly got out at the White House. This enchanted Louie, who at once started looking for the squirrels.

"I could have slapped her face," cried Henny, "old upholstered busybody, prying and poking, 'What is Mr. Pollit doing now?'" she mimicked. "She had better find out what her daughter is doing now, running round with other women's husbands: I wonder she dares to look me in the face, or any woman. If my daughter did that, I'd stay at home. A woman with a daughter like that pawing my daughter. I was simply fuming and it was all I could do to be decent to her."

The morning was full of excitement, with its infinite and mysteriously varied encounters, Henny giving battle on great provocation and invariably coming off victorious. This glorious, mettlesome morning was capped by Henny's being very charming and disarming to a shoe salesman and getting Louie a new pair of scuffless shoes. In her new shoes, Louie was allowed to go to the Museum to study the exhibit of local fauna and flora, in order to get up a satisfactory nature report to send to the greedy Sam, far off in foreign jungles.

After assiduous scribbling in a new five-cent notebook, a deadly horror overcame her, the nausea of museums, and the "nature record" had to stop there, where she was taken by sickness. But after that, in obedience to Sam's further desires, she dropped in at the Bureau of Fisheries to see Dr. Philibert, her father's other self, in the well-known cave of aquaria, where she ran across various characters of the legend; for instance, Crazy-Daisy, who stared at her very hard but did not acknowledge her, and Dear Old Ratty, who rushed up to her babbling, to pump her hand and ask after "my old friend Sam." His thin neck wobbled in its loose halter, just as Sam showed them in mimicry. Then, having "come into contact with people," according to Sam's orders, and "having begun her little life journey through the highways and byways," as he put it, having borne Sam's messages of high good will and cheer to various officers in his Department (while thoroughly convinced of the absurdity of these verbiages), Louie went home satisfied, walking to the old Rock Creek double bridge, along Pennsylvania Avenue, thick strewn with leaves. At home she was in command until six, when Hazel came home in a good temper.

Hazel, though forty-eight, had a young man; though a vixen (in Louie's opinion), she had been loved by this young man for nearly twenty years and had been engaged to him for fifteen years. But, as it was explained carefully to everyone who came to the house, Hazel was obliged to wait until she could not have children before she could marry Mr. Gray, because Mr. Gray was a Protestant and Hazel's priest would not let her children be Protestants.

When Henny came home, she and Hazel discussed the whole thing again; and Hazel, flushed, announced that she had agreed to marry Mr. Gray this year. They would go back to Charlestown, whence Hazel had come many, many years ago, to be the Collyer kitchenmaid, and live on Mr. Gray's apple orchard. The evening buzzed with visions of Hazel's future happiness and old evening of life as Mrs. Gray amidst fat apple trees.

"Perhaps you will be sorry you waited so long," Henny said rather mournfully to her old crony.

"No," Hazel shook her still black head. "When I see what you've been through with that man and his parcel of children, Henny, I think I'm better off. It's no deprivation."

"You won't always think so," said Henny, "you wait and see."

"With Mr. Gray I will have everything I want," said Hazel firmly.

"And what about me? I'll have to wrestle with these children alone again," said Henny, "and me half gone to another one. Hazel, you must wait at least till I'm up and about. What difference does it make to you? You've waited so long."

Hazel colored a little and it looked as though a tiff were blowing up, but Hazel cooled down again and told Henny she was a selfish girl, but that she would wait until Pollit came home.

"But Pollit and his Pollit relations I can't abide," declared Hazel with a spot on her cheeks, "and if I'm obliged to live in the house with that man, I'll say something we'll all be sorry for. He's ruined your life."

Between Hazel and Henny, though, the stream ran deep and still: Henny only felt a little aggrieved that Hazel looked forward so eagerly to leaving her.

Chapter Six

1 *Letters to Malaya.*

It was a cold and windy March night. Four of the children sat round a wood fire in the long dining room on stools and hassocks, with Henny who had again queerly become a large woman, though her hands, feet, and face remained small and narrow. Ernest sat at the oak dining table bent over his schoolbooks, very industrious, and Louisa, excused from drying the dishes, was copying the last of her "Georgetown Record" of birds, insects, and plants, which was supposed to be a daybook of observations, closed each month and sent on, but which she had again got from the Museum. The house was cold away from the fire and the children's bodies made a fire screen; they were toasted in front while chills ran down their spines. Louie had on her now shabby coat as she worked. Henny, sitting at the end of the table nearest the fire, had before her a child's mattress newly covered with ticking which she was tacking and tufting with a great steel needle. As she worked she execrated the work still to do, the coldness of the house, her poverty, her fatigue, and the infinite household tasks that lay before her. The children used to this running commentary, pegged away at the letters they were writing to their father. Henny groaned and cursed Sam's orders from afar, the squeaking pens, and cried, "Darn it!" whenever she stabbed her finger by mistake.

"Will you put my letter in with yours, Moth?" asked Evie.

"I'm afraid to write to your father: he criticizes my spelling," sneered Henny. "And it appears I know nothing about geography. Hang his stuck-up conceit."

Louisa restlessly rose again from her writing to go and look through the grimy curtains of her mother's bedroom at the every-night scene which was wild and brilliant now—the trees of the heath round the Naval Observatory, the lamplight falling over the wired, lichened fence of the old reservoir, the mysterious, long, dim house that she yearned for, the strange house opposite, and below, the vapor-blue city of Washington, pale, dim-lamped, under multitudinous stars, like a winter city of Africa, she thought, on this night at this hour. After a little while, she came back and began to drag her pen over the sheet of paper again.

"Darn it!" cried Henny again. "For the love of Mike, tell Hazel to give me some tea and an aspirin, my eyes are burning out my skull."

The dishes stopped rattling in the kitchen. They heard Hazel hang the big washbowl on its high nail; and then Evie came running in, holding the silver tight in two hands. She thrust it into the drawers of the old scratched sideboard and came bursting into the semicircle round the fire, saying,

"Oo, gee whiz, is it cold; jiminy, I'm freezing. Moth, when are we going to get the coal?"

"Your father thinks I can heat it over here from the lurid tales he puts in his letters," Henny chattered. "I'll get the coal, don't worry. Oh, that's enough for tonight."

"I wish you'd let me do it," said Louie; "let me try."

"You're not strong enough, my girl: you need my tough old arms to do this," Henny exclaimed. "Wait till you've washed and scrubbed for a man for ten or twelve years. Until that time, I won't let you turn into a drudge. You do the darn birds, that's all you're asked to do. Ernie, boy, go and get Mother's tea, I hear it being poured out."

Henny edged in close to the fire and placed her bony hands to warm them on the hot, silky heads of the twins. They turned towards her, inwards, two similar red and yellow apples, and Saul began to sing falsetto,

I would not marry a butcher, I'll tell you the reason why;
He'd chop me up for mincemeat and put me in a pie.

"Let Mother sing it," they clamored.

"Let Mother alone," said Henny.

Hazel sat in the kitchen in the cold, wrapped in a black, crocheted shawl brooding. During the last month or two she and Henny had quarreled much, and it was always over money. Henny ignored her maid's sulking in the kitchen and, to show her indifference, consented to sing, very low for them, "I wouldn't marry a butcher," a song she had dug up for the Düsseldorf scandal.

"Have you finished your father's letter, Louie?"

"Nearly."

"It's about time; you've been all night at it, and you haven't touched your homework. I don't know why you leave it to the last moment. You know he looks for it and you know if your father doesn't get it, he blames me. You don't want me forever to be the scapegoat, do you? And if you don't get through this rotten homework they pile on you, at your age, he'll blame me too. I'll write to the principal."

Louie was silent, in dread; but passed over the two-page letter she had written. Henny read it with distaste, jerked it back to her, and said, "Get the letters together and let's post them tonight; then I'll have no more of this trash round the dining room."

Hazel, looking bitter and neglected, stalked in from the kitchen, untying her dark blue apron, emphatically, from her waist. In a sergeant's voice, she demanded, "Has Louie written to her father?"

"Yes," Louie answered dryly.

"Have the others written?"

"Yes, they've written. Thank God, there's another mail off. I simply dread mailing days; I can never get the kids to write to their father."

Ernest, great favorite of Hazel, lifted his soft, wide-eyed face and shot at her, "All the 'varmints' start out with, 'Dear Dad, I hope you are well, I am well, Mother is well,' and then they get stuck."

"Evie put 'Dead Dad,'" Saul informed them.

Tattletale tit, your tongue will be split,
And all the little puppy dogs will get a little bit,

Hazel recited. She stroked down Evie's hair, "There, my kittycat is Hazel's baby; never mind what they say: it's all right."

"That child can't spell a word, and her father blames it on me," said Henny irritably.

The little dark girl mourned amongst them, looking abashed and melancholy from one to the other.

The letters were piled on the table, each addressed in the awkward writing of the author. Each envelope had been long and proudly fingered, and tears and smuts were strewn over them.

Just when they had all forgotten Ernie's cleverness, Evie bleated, "Ernie hasn't got any homework tonight: his class didn't have homework; I heard Miss Morrin say."

"I have, too," Ernie declared.

Louie looked at his book for a minute and decided, "It's made-up homework."

"I can do it," Ernie said angrily.

"You're screwing up your eyes there and you don't have to do it?" Henny demanded, much put out. "I've been letting you sit there half an hour longer because I thought you had to do it: you told me that, you wretched little fibber."

"It's some problems the teacher told us to do."

"Told you you could do," corrected Louie. Ernie stuck out his lower lip rebelliously.

"Ernie's nuts," said Little-Sam, "he's always studyin'; he's a fairy."

"What did you say?" cried Henny. Little-Sam grinned foolishly while the other boys (except Ernie) looked pleased. After a devious discussion which revealed that Little-Sam used the word for anyone but a football hero, Henny suddenly cried,

"Now pack up, kids, and go to bed. I've never seen such pests," while Ernie's voice was suddenly heard, contemptuous,

"Is there a law sayin' I can't do homework?"

Tommy whimpered, "Oo, my itti-gutties [itchy-scratchies]" and started to scratch at the large pink welts appearing on his legs.

"Don't scratch, and get away from the fire," Hazel commanded. Tommy jerked up his head, said, "I go bed," and scrambled off his stool. Then he burst into tears.

It was hard to get away from the hot fire and plunge into the icy air that waited for them just outside the hearth and that got colder and colder as they went to their rooms upstairs. The central heating had been off for some days, since the coal and some remains of wood blocks had given out. Little-Sam stopped at the door, whined,

"Willya tell's a story, Louie?"

"No, I've got my homework."

"Oh, go on, Louie," both the twins whined disagreeably, and Evie got up expectantly, "I'll get into Saul's bed."

Hazel's voice came over the stairhead, "Children!"

"Louie!"

"Oh, all right."

They scampered upstairs like iron nuts and bolts falling downstairs. Suddenly the noise halted. They started to come down again, "Mothering, Mothering!"

"I wish they wouldn't call me that idiotic name," Henny said, over the white wool she had begun to knit.

"Mothering, you will come up and say good night, Ernie says," Evie's figure reappeared in the doorway.

"No, I will not. Go upstairs before I chase you."

"It's so co-old," said Little-Sam, reappearing. "It's so mizz [miserable]." He shuddered.

"You go upstairs before I fan your pants," said Henny. They whinnied with fun and scampered for the stairs again. Ernie came and stood before his mother in his winter bunnyhug pyjamas, round, rosy, eager, to begin their private ritual, made up accidentally, in Ernie's second year of life, by them both,

Good night, Mother.
Good night, my son.
Will I see you in the morning?
You will if you've got any luck.
Well, I've got heaps of luck and loads of luck, so will I?
You will, my son.
Good night, Mother.
Do you love me, Son?
Yes, Mother.
How much do you love me?
Lots and lots of love.
But how much is lots?
More than all the money in all the world in all the years and all
     there is.
That's good. Well, good night now.
Good night, Mother.

It was Ernie who first insisted on repeating this, each night before going to sleep, to his mother, and on having her solemn assurance that she would be there when he woke up; and even sometimes he had insisted, "But you will be there when I wake up?" Nor had he gone to bed one night without saying it with her except when, as she said, she took a busman's holiday and went for two weeks to the maternity ward.

Ernie dashed a kiss off on his mother's cheek and sprinted for the stairs, crowing, "I wonder what story Looloo's going to tell us? I hope a story about Malaya."

There was a dive and scramble for the beds. When they had all snuggled in, sheets and blankets up to their ears, whimpering and giggling at the heat and cold, Louie, sitting in an armchair, in her winter overcoat, between the two doors, after waiting for silence and hearing all the hisses and gigglings die down, said solemnly,

"I'll tell you a story about Daddy, Sam-the-Bold. When he was just outside of Kuala Tokang, in Kelantan, he met a Korinchi-man."

There was a speechless silence.

"Although it was midafternoon, they noticed when they came near to the village on struts, in a clearing in the jungle—"

"Who noticed?" asked Ernie.

"Daddy and his men. They noticed that all the doors and windows were shut. They have no windows, only shutters in wood. The only thing they could see was a small kid tied in a rough cage."

"A kid in a cage?"

"Goat kid," explained Ernie dreamily, "like Whitey's."

"The cage was made of rough stripped saplings with its door held open by a long sapling. The kid was tied to a notched stick in the inside of the cage. 'Tiger expected,' said Wan Hoe."

"Who's Hoe?" asked Evie.

"Daddy's secretary, dumfie," said Little-Sam, while the others said "shh!"

"The Malays began to shin up trees," said Louie. "Daddy and Wan Hoe went and knocked at one of the cabins, and Wan Hoe and one of the Malays talked to them. 'They will not answer,' said the Malay. 'Ask them what it is all about, friend,' said Daddy."

"Why did he say 'friend'?" asked Evie. Solemn as a church, Louie replied,

"Because Daddy wishes all men white and black to be his

friends. And he tells people when he says that that it is because he is American and he came from the great white city of brotherhood, Washington."

"And he says he is with the American Smithsonian Field Expedition," said Ernie.

"Yes. Eventually, however, there was a babble from inside the hut which burst out like a packet of crackers and then stopped. The Malay, although he was a Mohammedan and had been to Mecca, a traveled man, and was called Awang Haji, seemed afraid and kept looking everywhere over his shoulders, into the trees and undergrowth, and he kept looking at his companions, too, who were scattered around. 'Korinchi-man about here,' Wan Hoe explained to Daddy." Louie waited. The children waited. Then Little-Sam said slowly,

"What is a Korinchi-man?"

"The Korinchi-men are a wandering breed of Malays who are supposed to be weretigers, that is, they are men by day and turn into tigers at night."

"Oo-hoo-hoo-oo!" they shuddered.

"When night falls, they come and knock at a door. People open the door and ask them what they want. Then the Korinchi-man says, 'Please let me stay for the night, because tigers are prowling round. Who is so cruel as to shut out a naked man without a gun?' So the Korinchi-man asks and gains admittance to the household and when they are asleep he turns into a tiger and eats them all."

"Wheese!" Little-Sam exclaimed.

"But is it true? Do they turn into tigers?"

"Of course not," said Louie. "That is just what they think."

"Who think?"

"The other natives who live in the cabins."

"But haven't the Korinchi-men got cabins?"

"No. They are too poor."

"Why can't they chop down trees," Tommy wanted to know.

"I don't know," said Louie, "they are just a kind of gypsy; but people hate them because they have no cabins."

"If—" said Ernie, but Louie promptly jumped into the breach, "If the natives think he is a Korinchi-man they won't let him in, but make him stay out in the jungle all night. When morning comes, very often they find a tiger's tracks and no man at all; and no man comes back the next night."

They waited. Louie waited.

"Or," said Louie, "they see by the marks on the ground that the tiger has dragged a body off into the jungle."

Evie and Little-Sam shivered and hid their faces for a moment.

"So they think it is the best thing to kill Korinchi-men if they can, if they catch one alone in the daylight," said Louie, "at least some think that. Because it happened amongst Daddy's Malays there was a Korinchi-man, no one would let them in, and they were obliged to pitch tents in the open. The others, I tell you, did not like sleeping with the Korinchi, but Daddy said they would have a fire all night, and watches kept."

"Go on," said Little-Sam, "go on!"

Louie waited cunningly.

"Go on," said Ernie to oblige her. They had all heard the story several times before and yet their interest was more passionate now than at first.

"In the night Sam-the-Bold heard a giant harsh breathing just outside the tent, near his bed. He heard soft movements, and later the kid screamed. In the morning, though, the kid had gone and the bad Malay, the Korinchi-man, too. The trap had fallen, but this was one of those cunning tigers that eat up natives for years and are too smart to be caught. They were going back to their launch anyhow and they could not wait to look for Tong—"

"—the bad Malay," said Saul.

"—and no one wanted them because people thought they had brought along a weretiger with them. So they had to get back without Tong who had gone back to the jungle, perhaps to his death, for if he had the mark of the Korinchi-man he was wanted nowhere and had to go straight to the tiger's claws."

"Oo-hoo-hoo-hoo," cried Evie in a little emotional convulsion.

"Tell another story, not creepy," said Saul promptly, "so Evie won't get a dream."

They all laughed and, more sleepily, more relaxed, slid into the bedclothes.

"The golden box with the glass key," Louie announced. "Oh, goodness! Oh, I've got to go. Go to bed. I forgot to give Mother the letter. There's a registered letter from Malaya."

She rushed to her schoolbag with Ernie at her heels and drew out from a slot between books a long, much-stamped, blue-penciled letter addressed to Mrs. Samual C. Pollit. With this she ran downstairs, with Henny calling out,

"What's happened now: is the house on fire? At least we'd get warm," while Hazel continued her yarn, "And because Barry wouldn't marry her she drank iodine and they gave her white of eggs, but she was in a state—what have you got there, Louisa?"

"A letter from Daddy, Mother!" called Ernie.

"Give that to me! Where did you get it?" Henny rose from her seat, sliding her work onto the floor. "Where did you get it? Why did you hide it from me?"

"The postman brought it and I put it in my bag to keep it safe and forgot it—"

The children had tumbled downstairs again and were gathering like soft-footed, eel-haired ghosts round the fire.

"Go upstairs and get into bed," called Henny harshly. "You'll hear what you have to hear in the morning." The children trailed back again regretfully, calling questions down to her all the way up.

"This is a most important letter, this is the letter I have been sitting up for to put me out of all my misery," said Henny stormily to Louie, "and you go and hide it; what did you do it for? Are you a devil or a girl? Here I have been suffering and pricking my fingers and going through agony for hours waiting for this letter and wondering what on earth had happened. Do you like to see me suffer? Do you do it purposely? You great, woodenheaded idiot: oh, go up to bed and take that great moon-face out of my sight, and stop your sniveling."

"Is it from Daddy, Mother?" Louie could not resist asking.

"Of course, don't be an idiot. Go up to bed quickly before I hit you. When I think of the hours of agony I put in because you were too lazy and stupid to give me my letter, I want to beat you till I fall down. Oh, stop that bawling. Good night, good night."

Louie, on the stairs, heard her say, "He sent money: look—five hundred dollars. Now, thank God, the children can eat."

"You'd better give it to me," Hazel said grimly. "I don't understand how you get into such a hole."

"There's a lot you don't understand!"

Louie flushed with joy. The twins were reciting,

I went up one pair of stairs (Just like me!)
I went up two pair of stairs (Just like me!)
I opened the door (Just like me!)
And looked out the window (Just like me!)
And there I saw a donkey (Just like me!)

Louie smiled to herself and went to stand in their doorway. Said she,

Will you kindly stop your hollers?
Daddy sent five hundred dollars!

Pandemonium broke out of bed and the anvil chorus standing at the head of the stairs shrieked, "Mummy, did Daddy send five hundred dollars?"

Henny rushed to the foot of the stairs, her old red dressing gown flying from her in the black of the hallway.

"Louisa, mind your own business! Kids, go to bed, and if one of you mentions it, I'll beat you till I can't stand up! What will I do with that child?" she moaned, going back into the warm room.

"Now we can get the new tubes for the radio," Ernie whispered to Louie.

"Hooray, hooray, hooray!" Evie capered in a slipper dance. But Louie succeeded in getting them all to bed in a few minutes. It was not long before Tommy was steaming away in sleep, and the twins, with their moon complexions, were glimmering quietly on their pillows, and Evie, with hair wild and clenched dark face, was tossing in sleep too; but Ernie was awake, calculating what they could get tomorrow; and as for Louie, in a few minutes she had entirely forgotten the five hundred dollars and, lying on her back, was halfway to sleep, thinking dizzily,

"I thought it was a horseman and it's only the blood beating through my temples when I lie down: it was a horseman, riding up and down and—wampum, purple strings of shells, fimbriate horsemane shell and the ctenidium deep, deep down in this dusty— red—" She woke up with a start, trying to remember the beautiful thoughts she had been having; and tried to thread back, but could not. She fell asleep really and woke up shrieking, dreaming another old nightmare that she often tried to describe to them, "Hard-soft, hard-soft," a dream without sight or name, which her hands dreamed by themselves, swelling and shriveling, hard-soft. She turned on her side, and the friendly horseman (she still thought of him riding, though he was now only a phantom) lulled her to sleep with his *ker-porrop!*

2 *Sam in Malaya.*

It was not raining, but it should have rained. No fresh breeze had cleared away the exhalations since the evening before, and the air stuck to them like a wet rag. There were bucketfuls of water hanging in the air over their heads. Sam, towhead bare, panama in hand, all in crumpled white, with his Indian secretary, a Madrasi Kerani, trotting, walking hurriedly a step in the rear, went pushing his way along the busy five o'clock street. The immense open gutters, pitfalls, were spanned every few feet by large flagstones, and Sam and Naden had to keep dodging over these into the open street to avoid crushes and social affairs on the pavement—a family with its mattresses and rags preparing to sleep out during the steaming night, a wedding feast, with its tables and benches and hundred guests taking up several frontages, the thirteen-year-old bridegroom bedizened and bedaubed, in white cap, posing with father and uncles for his photograph. All the traffic of the pavement as well as Sam and Naden had to serpentine around these knots. Chinese lanterns and naked bulbs were strung across the pavement, and open flares lighted the tables. A Chinese peddler with a small basket was selling noise-makers, a whirring whistle very loud and highly painted, and red, white, and blue trumpets, but he could hardly make himself heard, even though Sam and Naden were thrusting along right beside him. A peddler somewhere in the throng was shouting "choklets-choklets," but all they saw were two sandaled feet sticking out of a globular swarm of market baskets of all sorts—no head was visible, nor a body, but through the rattan and pandanus solar system came the voice.

Sam was head and shoulders above most of the people. Not so Naden, his clerk, the Indian. Here and there a giant Sikh policeman, with bearded face and turban on his uncut hair, dominated the throng of torn, patched, ragged, turbaned, and capped heads. Many of these heads had no business whatever, but had so lounged and mournfully, vacantly gazed from morning to night for many months, unemployed and disorganized, hopeless and without any shelter save those of a few charities, sleeping in filth and eating garbage. The employed were scarcely better off; the smallest frontages, back rooms, passageways, holes in the wall, served for shops, businesses, and schools; and a good many businessmen kept their merchandise in their cap, pocket, lap, in the sole of their shoe or the palm of their hand. Some used the pavement, with ready-cooked food spread out before them; there were public scribes and pavement shoemakers. It was a raving, wild, thirsting, vain, money-loving, patriotic city, its own pride, the gateway of the East to the West, and the West to the East, the key of the Golden Chersonese.

"And all of these," shouted Sam, "squashed flat as pancakes under the well-oiled, deep-wrinkled, naked-naveled bellies of yellow Greed: running on the futile messages of Greed and his two secretaries of the Treasury, British Government and the Chinese Chamber of Commerce!"

"I beg pardon, sah," shouted Naden.

"Mammon," shouted Sam, "Mammon, Naden, Greed, Briton and the Yellow Peril on top of the heap!"

"Yessah."

"That's a bit of irony," yelled Sam, putting his hand between his mouth and his secretary's ear: "he can't make himself heard to sell his noisemakers."

Naden looked swiftly at the merchant, "Those are trash, tuan: I should not buy them."

"I told you not to call me 'tuan,' Naden."

"Yessah." Naden smiled and bowed slightly, "You see, I can't help myself, and I assure you, sah, it is the regular thing. My wife, sah, would be very, very much ashamed if she did not hear that: she would be afraid I should lose my job."

Sam laughed, "You have a very young wife, you must teach her differently. Tell her there is no difference between you and me, or you and the moneylenders, or you and the men of money."

Naden, not hearing very well, bowed slightly again, "Yessah! Only two streets more, please," he pointed. "You will not mind if my friends are there," he asked in the tone of one repeating a question.

"Your friends are my friends, only they probably like you better," said Sam.

The thick, moist Singapore night closed round them. In many parts it seemed to Sam that he alone could be seen amongst those dark myriads, thick as migrant birds twittering and jostling on a cornice, struggling for a foothold in this notch of the universe. Here and there the gleams of eyes and teeth could be seen, lemon faces, hadji caps, laundered coats, pale garments. As they turned out of the thoroughfare, they jostled some stretcher-bearers who were jog-trotting along with a corpse announced by bells. Merchants of live birds and lizards, merchants of fishballs and sweetmeats they left behind them, as well as the ordinary foot passengers, and a little surge of trouble that was merely a native policeman arresting someone suspected of murder.

"Good heavens, Naden," exclaimed Sam indignantly, "how can they tell one dark face from another in this light?"

"Ofttimes they can't," said Naden, "but they arrest someone. Someone they know. It is fair enough. It is certain he has already committed a murder. They would all murder if they got a chance."

"They're your people!" cried Sam.

"No, tuan, they are not," said Naden, "we have passed through a lot of scum. I am a government servant, however humble."

But Sam misunderstood the ambitious fellow entirely and considered him abject. "If that is the justice of Government," said Sam, "would you not be better without it?"

"No, tuan."

"Do you believe in masters' justice, imperialist justice?"

"You have great experience, sah: you have seen more than me."

"No, Naden, do not overrate me. I am nobody. If I seem strange to you, it is because I am not a socialist, as Colonel Willets, my boss, was once (though now, you may be sure, he is for millionaires and not the millions), nor a Laborite, nor a Democrat, nor any party man, but I look forward to the Union of Democratic Republics of the World, the United States of Mankind. Look at this poor old world as we see it today—you may look at home, Abishegenaden, for all Europe, Asia; and the Pacific World is no better nor wiser; the men of money, the bankers, the evil ones have been coming together and torturing this poor old world for a long time now, Naden. We must get rid of them, by wisdom, by spreading the light amongst these dark, dark masses. You are dark, Naden, but you are light: you are an educated man. You, too, though you are poor, must think you are rich, because you have millions—behind you! Millions of poor men who would be your brothers."

"You are a very good man," said Naden. They had now turned into the quiet streets of dwelling houses, with trees, and an occasional car, where the better-paid government servants and junior clerks lived. It was a brilliant, black tropical night, swimming with powerful scents landwards and with vapors skywards. There was still a restlessness of birds in all the trees, and insects flew round the lamps.

"Look at my poor Lai Wan Hoe in shackles because he owes money to a Sikh moneylender," mourned Sam. "That is terrible, Naden. I am afraid some harm will come to my wonderful Wan Hoe, all because of extravagance, and the awful power of money, like a great hairy foul spider with a million eyes, as this night, sucking the blood of us poor humans. Yes, it sucks the life from the rich too, but they can stand it." He laughed heartily into Naden's eyes.

Naden laughed, but could not help remarking, "He is a ne'er-do-well, I fear, sah, speaking privately, sah."

"And that wedding feast, Naden," Sam caught him up warmly, "in the open tumult, with its gay little bridegroom sitting on his father's shoulders, and the admiring relations, the cheerful drinks—little as I approve of them!—the cakes and candies, Naden; that was a fine sight, a human sight, wasn't it?"

"Yes it was, sah!"

"It was for that that Wan Hoe got himself indebted, friend: because his brother is away in China, and he must marry his brothers and sisters and keep his old father and bury his mother. It was for pure goodness of heart and kindness and duty that he got himself indebted; perhaps they will throw him into prison—all for being profuse with the milk of human kindness. Is that bad?"

"One is obliged to consider ways and means," said Naden, unshaken. "Who goes to the moneylender, indebts his grandchildren."

Naden had been melting and glinting through his glasses, smiling, and now bowed Sam to a little house behind a lush garden. There were lights in the house which glowed through glassless windows. In that climate windows would collect mildew.

"This way," said Naden, bursting with pride and joy; and with great dignity, he stepped into the square sitting room, where a number of people were sitting and standing, and he said,

"Here is Special Field Commissioner Samuel Pollit, my most honored chief."

Sam swam up to the surface of the river of moisture that was drowning, suffocating him, and looking at all these happy or inquisitive dark faces, flashed smiles at them, talked to them all, felt the great urge of love of man rise up in his throat. What a gift he had been given, he thought, to love and understand so many races of man!—and why? His secret was simple. They were all alike: they all longed for love and understanding.

In a bed near the window hole was the timorous black girl, Naden's young wife, whose new firstborn was a son. The sick woman tried to rise, out of respect and fright, but Sam waved her back to the pillow and bent over the bed, shook the tiny hand of the baby, and kissed its head; and then put into its hand the little necklace of silver shells he had got at a friendly curio dealer's that day. The mother nearly fainted with emotion. Then Sam, smiling graciously once more, withdrew. He could not speak one word of any of their languages, and he had to go home, change, address a Y.M.C.A. meeting, and then go to an evening at a friend's house. He suffered without respite from the tropical heat, and his principles prevented him from ever taking the solace or strength of alcoholic drinks. The room of the weatherboard house smelled of mildew and sweat; snakes coiled under the floor, bats lived in the attic, and swallows squeaked in the air or in the eaves, all this without mentioning the thousand kinds of insects, all new and unpleasant, even for a naturalist, to live with.

As he stepped into the street, Sam wiped his neck with his handkerchief already wringing wet, "You have a sweet wife and child, Naden."

"No, indeed, sah, I am ashamed: they are not worthy of your kind visit. You are so kind, sah."

Naden, naturally severe, became wet-eyed and soft with emotion. Sam told Naden how lucky he was, again. He himself, Sam, had had the pleasure of being a father, five times already, and imagine the joy when he found that at one birth he had twins! He could never have it enough. Each time, he explained to Naden, he felt an immense pride, a belief in a limitless future, in an unfolding universe, a hope for the proliferating human race in that shadow of dust, and infinitesimal corner of dimensionless space, even so.

"We were monkeys, we were men: what will be men in the time to come, Naden?"

"Gods perhaps, tuan. Who knows?"

"You are right: men like gods. A great white writer wrote a book about that once. But you see, you have the same idea. Ideas unite us,

Naden. I am so tired, Naden. I wish I was at home with a new little baby to cheer me up. Soon I will have a seventh child. I myself am a seventh child. You know, Naden, though, I wish I had a black baby too. A tan one, a Chinese one—every kind of baby. I am sorry that the kind of father I can be is limited." He laughed in a tired way and ran his finger round inside the collar. "Men have thought of schemes for fathering many children," he continued faintly, still laboring to bring the ideas of the west to the cultured Indian, "for preserving man's seed in tubes and fertilizing selected mothers."

"And there would be a marriage ceremony?" inquired Naden politely.

Sam smiled, "I don't think so! But that is a detail. But now we are very backward. A man who knows he is a good father of good stock may still only have one wife."

"It is a pity, sah?" inquired Naden politely.

"I am not so sure it is a good thing," said Sam, shaking his head, but very dubious about his own idea, "either for man or woman, especially for women. Many fine women would make good mothers—" he shook his head.

Naden nodded but he said merely, "Will you work late tonight, sah, when you get back?"

Sam said briefly, "No." After a moment he laughed generously, "If I had the money, do you know what I should do, Naden? You remember that orphan asylum I addressed the other day? I should adopt them all—well, not all. I should have a little Chinese baby, an Indian one, out of the asylum and take them home with me."

"And your wife, too, she likes that too, tuan?"

"The women have to wash the diapers: they are not quite so generous as ourselves, it is not mankind, but little Sam and little Naden," said Sam. "But if one could have many wives, wives too would get the idea of the community perhaps. That would be splendid—godlike, eh, Naden?"

Naden laughed, "You are joking, I know, tuan."

"Then you do not think that I could manage all those wives?"

"Any man can," said Naden calmly. "Sah, if you will permit me: you take a great risk going down all those streets at night alone."

"I was not alone: I was with my fellow men."

"No, no, Tuan Pollit, you must never do that again. When I saw you last night, my throat jumped into my mouth, my heart, I mean."

"Man must never be afraid of man, friend."

Naden looked up at him soberly, "You are very full of ideals, sah: you are a good man. God protects goodness."

"But I keep my feet on earth, Naden."

Naden smiled at this. Sam, looking keenly at him, because there was no reply, saw the smile and asked, "Do you think I have feet of clay?"

"That is the only safe thing to have, sah. But, pardon me, you really should not go down so far into the streets at night. Every one sees you. You are so very much the white man with your fine, white hair, too, sah. There are men from the west, dark, with dark hair, but you are everything that is the white man. It is not done, I assure you, sah. Pardon me a thousand times."

"Ah," said Sam, "my natural love, Naden, my friend, of the study of mankind, man's proper study, and my real longing—it is a prodigious yearning, a passion beyond all other passions in me, Naden, for the time of the One Great Nation to come, when we will all be joined, man to man, regardless of color and creed, has given me a prodigious disregard for what is *not done*. What is not done, man can do."

"I beg your pardon," said Naden.

"And a wonderful regard for what is done, by the people."

Naden said nothing.

"And particularly by your own people or peoples, Naden, whom I love, respect, and wish to understand. How otherwise can we teach them the few things we ourselves know in human progress?

And we have something to learn from the ancient civilization you represent, the antique cultures of India."

"We are children, tuan. Thank you very much; we do not know very much; what we had we have forgotten. We are not modern."

"I wish you could come to my country and visit it: I should like you as my guest," Sam sighed. "You would see my children, and you would bring your little fellow."

"You are good, sah: you are as a god."

"No, Naden: just a man looking for the right and for the happiness of others."

"Sah, you are as the gods."

"I do not believe in gods, only in good," said Sam. "Gods demand sacrifices: good gives to all."

Naden smiled a little to himself, in his small, dark mustache and felt kindly towards the pale man wrapped in his dreams. He became a little more serious.

"I believe in God. I am sure God is coming soon, and if you are here, you will see him: then you will believe. And he will see you."

Sam said fretfully, "You know, my friend, I would rather be at home, with my children, and hear the elms and sycamores and the cedars rustle, and hear dear little Mareta, with her thin voice, asking if she will get her wish, and keeping my record of Georgetown birds, than even be near the throne of a God. And if I had to choose between such a Him, and them, I would choose them at once. And so would you, Naden. There never was a father would sacrifice his son to God, as the wicked old story has it: there never was."

Naden was silent, astonished by this idea. Sam felt he might have been rude to his believing secretary, so he added, wearily, but whimsically,

"Perhaps there is a black god and a white one." They were now crossing the little Cavanagh Bridge and under the sky, paling before moonrise, could see the flotilla of barges tied up in the river at the left hand. Sam halted to get the thin currents of coolness which were heavily moving through tons of wet air, like trickles pushing and nosing against a leviathan and gradually persuading the sleepy bulk to move an inch or so.

"I have not thought about the color of God," came the Indian's tricky, two-toned voice out of the dark.

"Abishegenaden, you are very black!"

"Yessah," he said firmly.

"Wouldn't you like to be light-colored like me?"

"No, tuan: I am not Heaven-born as you are."

"You must not say that to a poor mortal like me," said Sam.

Again Sam misunderstood the Indian clerk but was happy in his error, "You know the white man, the stupid white man feels superior to those of other colors. How do you feel about that?"

"They feel, sah, that the darkest races are the oldest; it is not so long since the white man became powerful. He thinks what he thinks because he is young in the world, as a child, as my child will feel when he is a two-year-old and will be butting me with his head. That cannot last very long. The Kings of Egypt were dark; all the world was dark until a very little while ago. Then the white man came from some little crack in the earth. He does not know about the times before he came. That is how we feel, sah; he is an accident."

This surprising answer quieted Sam for a space; at length he answered (they were walking through a garden, planted with old trees, and beside high white walls),

"This is a wrong idea you have, Abishegenaden; the Egyptians were pale (coppery at best); even the very darkest among you are descended long ago from whitish or pale people like the ancient Persians. The Chinese are almost white, too, for the most part. The black man is rather rare. Do you really think, Naden," he asked, "that primitive man was black? Do you think he was black and got white?"

"Perhaps there were two or three primitive men," said Naden.

Singapore is all native quarter, with the exception of small parts given over almost entirely to Europeans. The dark and mustard skins are of many races from the mainland of Malaya, from India and China, from Tanah Bugis (Celebes), Negeri Jawa, and Malays from the Menangkabau districts of Sumatra and natives from Burma, Siam, Cochin China and even dark-eyed men from Turkey, Armenia, Portugal, with a few sons of Nippon. The British direct, with the aid of white British Empire and American overseers and bosses, but the Chinese are bosses, too, and are the machinery of the place: Malaya is strung together by the Chinese chambers of commerce. Sam's heart seemed to expand at the contact of so many alien peoples and the generous feeling that he called love of man and worship of mankind had grown up like a puffball in Singapore. He tried to learn the greetings of each race, to distinguish them and their accents, if not their languages. Very different was Abishegenaden the clerk, who, on a precarious footing in the government service, like all bureaucrats, moreover, despised not only all other races, but all grades inferior to himself. His affection for Sam was temporary and had something patronizing in it— Sam had come from outside the service and by no means could understand the niceties, strict taboos of the service. There were flabby men from outside the service, a strange sort of Yahoo, and the white man of the East, who was on the inside: Naden smiled in his sleeve,—what can a white man in a country of white men know about anything of that sort? Naden forbore to make further remarks to his superior about dark skins in America, but he thought to himself—this also is a man who—Washington or no Washington—knows nothing about how his own country is run. As they mounted the steps of the boardinghouse where Sam was staying and where his Chinese secretary was still working over his notes, Sam said with good intent,

"You are but an ebonized Aryan, Naden, and I am the bleached one that is fashionable at present."

Naden pretended not to hear this.

* * *

Lai Wan Hoe, a Baba Chinese (Singapore-born Chinese), his polyglot secretary, was still transcribing out of a notebook of beautiful, endlessly flowing shorthand. He was Sam's right-hand man and, in fact, did most of the work for him; without him Sam could never have done anything at all in the fainting climate. Sam sank into a chair, laughing ruefully,

"Wan Hoe, I wonder why the white man is so screwy as to worry about what is in the tropics, man, beast, or mildew! We should leave it to you and your wonderful people."

"And so you will, sir, one day," said Wan Hoe affectionately, knowing that this was one of Sam's favorite ideas, for he had become wholly enamored of all things Chinese, Chinese manners, intellects, polish, capacity for work and for living in the heat.

Naden, after seeing his white man back, had gone home again. He did not wish to work after hours, and he left the two outcasts talking together. If Sam was not a government man, Wan Hoe, who was, was just the same riding for a fall. Naden knew all about his money affairs, which every minute went from bad to worse. In fact, Wan Hoe, after drawing ahead on his salary, had got himself into debt to the moneylenders to the extent of nearly one thousand Straits dollars. Everyone in the service knew about it and whispered that Wan Hoe had stolen government money. It was a question not of who would peach first (for they had told on him long ago) but of how long the Pathan moneylender would wait for his money.

This money waste was to Sam, the only bad spot in his noble Wan Hoe.

"Sweet little woman, Naden's wife, and sweet little tar baby too," murmured Sam. He laughed, "I asked him if he liked being very black and he said, 'Yes.'"

"Yes, sir, very likely." Wan Hoe smiled. "Should you like some tea, sir? You look all in."

"Dead to the world, Wan Hoe, dead to the world," said Sam. "Any telephone calls?"

"Colonel Willets rang up, sir, and wished you to come to his hotel immediately," he said as if it were of no account.

"Good heavens! Now I'm a messenger boy to run to his hotel when he gets petulant. The white man in the tropics degenerates every day," grumbled Sam.

Wan Hoe was sympathetically silent.

"Did he say anything else?"

"He asked when you were going to address the meeting; and seemed quite angry, sir: he said they should have asked him, and further, he thinks it is a compromising subject."

"Trade-unionism is taboo, I suppose."

"He thought it improper for an American, sir."

"The old billy goat's jealous, that's all," declared Sam. "They asked me because I'm a good speaker." After a while he relented and said coaxingly to Wan Hoe, "Colonel Willets is only interested in making up to the English official set and attending the Governor's Sunday service with special italic-script invitations, and taking stengahs at the Raffles or Lady Modore's. How could anyone suspect that he would be interested in the Y.M.C.A.? He sits there making Hitlerist jokes: it is time the melting pot melted, and I wish it wouldn't melt on me. He's been here four months and he has learned to treat the syces in just the right British way. Could the Y.M.C.A. guess he was interested in spreading human knowledge?"

"He is not interested in that; he said he is the head of the Expedition."

Sam flared up, "He arrogates it to himself: we are all here on an equal footing. Dictators amongst scientists and men of mind! About the orphanage, too—and because I wrote a little thing for *The Straits Times* and because he thought I was trying to get out of paying my seat in the automobile, the time I flew to Kuala Lumpur, and, in short, friend, because he is against me. I represent the young service, and he represents the gerontocracy that is on its last legs. Shame on the old intriguer! He sent a letter about me back to Washington by the last mail. Oh, Wan Hoe, how tired I am! I don't like to complain, but I am in pain most of the day; and I have terrible insomnia. I don't know how the others get through, because, after all, I take no drink, I have no poison in my system."

"Will I now telephone Colonel Willets, sir, or will I leave it till the morning?"

Sam was thinking about the night ahead of him. He would sink on his fresh pillow and at once sweat would start from him, a Niagara of sweat, and drown the pillow and the bedding and his pajamas. Shutters, cool floors, open verandas, baths, and changes of clothes twice daily did nothing against the exhausting sweating and the heat. He would drowse and wake up any moment, any hour, with fear in him, his heart yawing and plunging into some small but bottomless pit, his head full of lead. All he could do, if it was near morning, would be to call to the boy, "Syce, tea," and swing slowly up and out, balancing himself and his head carefully. The tea would help him for a while, making him sweat profusely, and he would have half an hour in which to hope that one of his heat headaches was not going to arrive and stay with him till the four-o'clock breeze or the next nightfall.

Wan Hoe, seeing that Sam did not answer, left him to reverie and went on transcribing in his clear handwriting. His face was dark and, though fleshy, drooped with fatigue. He paused several times and laid down his pen, looked at Sam Pollit as if about to broach a new and personal subject to him; but on observing Sam's drained, drooping cheeks and his mouth loose from the long day, he quietly took up his pen again and went on writing.

When Sam had come first to British Malaya a few months ago he had been shocked by the white man of the tropics and had made up his mind not to go the way others went. He would take exercise every day, walk wherever he could, to find out how the people lived and what they were; he would speak to the dark skin and strange nether garment as a brother, and he would never fall under the sodden spell of alcohol. He struggled unaided except by iced water, through the drowsiness of the siesta hours, trying to write his impressions and articles for papers back home (he very much admired the profession of the journalist, thinking him a good retail purveyor of enlightenment); and about five or six would go home to take a shower and would sit with a bath towel round his loins, or with nothing on at all but a clout, while he wrote up his diary or his mail for the day. But in this climate everything had become a weariness of the flesh, even writing and speaking. He, a man capable of doing walks of twenty miles on Sundays, at home, here could hardly make ten paces without feeling weak. Still he kept it up, walking round Singapore, or the other towns, or struggling through the jungle without a moan, avoiding the European streets and shops, finding the poorest, immigrant and native-born people, the ones with no home, the ones that walked the streets all night, even after nightfall and against all warnings roaming the congested streets, through dark throngs whose faces he could not see but only suspect in the flashing of an eyeball, tooth, or trinket, in the light of a shop lamp, or electric sign hanging downwards, or the frosted bleary sparkle of some miserable shopwindow, perhaps mildew-grown.

Both Naden and Wan Hoe were worried about this habit of Sam's and warned him often, but he walked on, tall amongst the small people, protected by his humane folly. He walked bareheaded; he believed that his wonderful white-gold hair, rarely seen except in

Friesland or Norway, protected him, that these childhearted people took him for something next to a god. When Naden told him he was like a god, he saw no humor in it. He thought that to the poor Indian clerk he must seem something like a god; he knew their superstition (he said to others) and how easily reverence and love passed into worship. Quietly, he would explain, "I believe in myself, because I know I love the good, and as that old sinner Thoreau said, 'I will never let the vestal fire go out in my innermost recesses': people feel that vestal fire and they feel that its possessor is sacred: they will not harm him. He walks unharmed amongst people reputed savage because they honor what is most good in man."

To whatever argument they made against this strange talk, he merely replied that he did come back unharmed and that he had ventured, on the upper parts of wild rivers in innermost Malaya where no white man had been before, and had never been harmed or hated. Only once a wicked little urchin in far Trengganu had hooted him, a boy with a mean rat face. But at Kemaman and elsewhere they had all been his friends and followed him around, the women first laughing and much embarrassed and then praising him, admiring his white hair and white bare narrow feet, or so he heard. The streets of some of these towns were almost like the back streets of a quiet Southern town where the Negroes live, the houses standing side by side, cabins and huts with occasional weatherboard houses, a hard dirt road, and, instead of telegraph posts, the tall palms clashing in the breeze, partly shutting out the blasting blue sky and the dazzling shadows and furnace lights on the road. But the Southern Negroes would never have made friends with Sam as these people did. His heart was flooded with a blue sea of hope; it was his own experience with the cheerful, good-natured people that made him hope that the progress of friendship between nations would be as easy—it merely required a little good will, such as he had and the thing would be done in half a day.

In a short time he had fallen madly in love with Malaya and saw her as a great country, unplundered, untouched, undreamed of, brimming with natural wealth, which would make all of its soft-skinned people rich and happy. All that was needed was understanding and the eviction of the People of Greed. He himself was helping mightily the people, he believed, by getting to know them and finding out their different types and entirely addled strains. He could tell the indigenous Malays from the new imports from India, Hailam from Canton, Hohkien from Teochiew, and he tried to have a friend in each of these and many other strains. He felt like a kind of Livingstone going into the heart of the darkest unknown, as he put it, the heart of man. Some day, with the help of believers like himself, the pure souls of the earth would get together, the good and energetic who understood men, like, say, Woodrow Wilson, Franklin D. Roosevelt, and Ramsay MacDonald, Upton Sinclair, Nicholas Murray Butler, H. G. Wells, and even himself, Samuel Pollit, and it would not be too soon for Eden, "the time of the internation," to arrive. If such a concourse of great souls could have been got together five hundred years back, Sam believed, the world would have been saved from its sorrows, wars, hate, misunderstanding, class wars, Hitler, and moneylenders; and the Golden Age, permeated by simple jokes and ginger-ale horseplay, tuneful evenings, open-air theaters and innumerable daisy chains of naturalists threading the earth and looking, looking, would have already produced a good-hearted, mild human race. Were not his own children happy, healthy and growing like weeds, truth-loving and inventive, merely through having him to look up to and through knowing that he was always righteous, faithful, understanding?

"Have you heard from your children, sir?" asked Wan Hoe, pausing.

"That is wonderful," cried Sam, "telepathy, Wan Hoe; that was telepathy," and he proceeded to tell him the chain of thought which at that moment had caused him to think of his children. He told his Chinese friend about them once more, "I suffer from the heat, the humidity, and the strangeness—not of black, but of white men— but I suffer most because when I wake, under the pressure of the heavy waves of moisture in the foredawn, before the stabbing light can get to my eyeballs I cannot call to them as I do at home, to my little dark-eyed, smudge-eyed Evie, my Little-Womey. You know what I do, Wan Hoe? I call, 'Sedgewing, Sedgewing, Sedgewing!' (Sedgewing is a made-up word that reminds me of her.) 'Sedgewing, come en do me yed.' Then she rolls out of bed grumbling gently, a thing I love to hear, and trots in in her long pink cotton nightdress, pouting gently, saying, 'Daddy, lemme lone, I wanna sleep!' But when I put out my hand, she trudges over and then hops onto my pillow and thrusts her soft finger into my hair to stroke the scalp; then my headache goes away, if I have one. Then I call up my eldest girl, Louie, a girl with a great head, perhaps too many troubles, but it makes her wiser in time to come, and she makes the morning tea, and then I get the boys out, Ernie and the Gemini, to go whistling round the place with me, sizing up carpentering jobs and bits of stonemasonry required. That is the happy life, Wan Hoe. Little-Sam sits there thinking on the path, thinking the strange, long thoughts of childhood, pondering over things which he will fashion into thoughts of science one day: and Saul, sensible and cool, goes his way poking and deducing; while Ernie, my little wonder-boy, who will certainly be a great mathematician, or (I hope not quite a dryasdust, not altogether a blue stocking) a physicist."

Sam suddenly cried, with a smile, "Bless you, Wan Hoe, you're such a good friend to me! I never had better friends than the Chinese friends I have met here in half a year, and you principally. No one understands friendship like the wise, the good and ancient People of the Middle Kingdom."

Wan Hoe's sensitive face, a soft boy's face thinning into sorrowful manhood, changed several times and his eyes smiled at Sam, "I am glad you like us very much."

"In the Chinese are great treasures of wisdom and good subtlety, craftsmanship and labor that we could do with in our country," said Sam stoutly. "I think you are the most wonderful people in the world."

Wan Hoe listened intently; and after a moment he said almost cautiously, "If you had no children, sir, I would think that you were coming to live amongst us."

"How happy that would make me! But I couldn't stand the climate and I could not bring all my children up here, Wan Hoe. No, you will have to contrive to come and visit me."

Wan Hoe shook his head, smiling pitifully. Just as Sam, guessing his troubles partly, began to speak to him about his great debts, the telephone rang again and there was Colonel Willets, irate, asking where was the s.o.b. and did he think he was going to sit round there twiddling his thumbs, and telephoning forty times in that heat. Wan Hoe said that Sam would soon be back and would no doubt go over to Willets' hotel at once. He put it down and looked regretful again that he had not spoken to Pollit about his own affairs. But Sam had quite forgotten about it.

Wan Hoe looked round cautiously. Sam's temper was wasting. Sam confirmed Wan Hoe in his view that people born and living outside the Asiatic world were children in the world. Other men were indiscreet through temper, brutality, or contempt of their subordinates; Sam was indiscreet through trust of his subordinates. Wan Hoe speculated on the American government service and wondered for a moment if Sam had been sent to Malaya to get him out of the way. But now Sam had to swallow another mouthful of gall and trot off to Colonel Willets' room. Who was he, he asked Wan Hoe, but a vain old man who had cast his Socialist skin twenty years ago, after he had made money in real estate? All had gone by the board for Mammon, and now he thought everyone admired his boots of gold: he wanted to be cock of the walk everywhere. "May I never be an old man!" said Sam.

"Our old age is perhaps life's decision about us," said Wan Hoe, "but I hope there is no living god we may blame for the invention. Everyone remembers himself as a child and cannot recognize himself in the tatters and wrinkled, dirty flesh, in the stench and hairy moles he is forced to inhabit. He wants to cry out, 'Look, I am not like this, I am a fairy little child with peach skin and sky-blue eyes, I am like a sun gem, I sing, dance, skip; I am not this old relic of the ragbag, cadging, cheating, scolding, whining, faking, dying.' The Chinese are a knowing people; and I daresay that is why they once made a religious odor about old age; to prevent their sons seeing their own future. They sealed their eyes. You see when a man knows he will be old, he is afraid: when he becomes old, he cares for nothing—love does not count, only comfort; honor does not count, only cheating for a niche."

"How queer," said Sam smiling, "I am not Chinese, but I honor old age: I hope I will have a happy one. My sons will be grown up, men of science, my daughters married with grandchildren: my hair will be silver, not much different from now. You are rather morbid, aren't you, Wan Hoe? I hope to have a long and happy life."

"Do you think that is possible nowadays?" asked the secretary.

Sam looked at him but said nothing. He had gathered from some vague hints that this native-born Singapore Chinese was a revolutionary, belonged to the Kuomintang frowned upon equally by the British and the rich Chinese. He could not be sent back to China, however, as immigrants could. Sam knew that Wan Hoe was on the verge of disgrace. However, he made it a rule not to inquire into a man's political actions, especially into his dangers; and he got up quickly to go out and see his colleague. He had first to strip off his soaking clothes, bathe, and get fresh ones. One of his coats put away damp, by accident, was hanging in the closet spotted with mildew. The smell of mildew could not be got out of the closet.

* * *

Sam had a quarrel with Colonel Willard Willets at the Raffles, but it ended as all their quarrels had to date in a sort of querulous capitulation on the part of the old man. He said Sam had engaged a seat in an automobile with him to visit a village of pygmies. Pygmies usually wander about in search of their food, but these pygmies, about forty in number, had been in this spot for a number of years. In the meantime, Sam had been taken up by the Governor and his wife, and it was arranged by them that he was to go with a visiting British scientist on the same expedition, but in a private car for which he would not pay. Now Colonel Willets thought Sam had let him down again and that he would have the whole expense of the trip himself.

Sam, who could ill afford it, however, said he would pay his share of the trip, but he would go with the English visitor as arranged: this was an anthropologist from Cambridge, and Sam cherished the opportunity of meeting him. While the Colonel was somewhat mollified at hearing that Sam would pay, Sam had got under his skin by refusing to ride with him.

But Sam had no sooner got back to the house than Colonel Willets was on the wire again, and began pulling his ears like an office boy, "And besides I don't like the catalogue of the Photographic Exhibition," he screamed.

"That's not my business," said Sam, "ring them up yourself."

"But you're in it, your name," said Willets. "Here it says: 'Anak Melayu, Menangkabau punya—Samuel K. Pollit—Smithsonian Expedition! You are not the leader of the Smithsonian Expedition: I am. What do you mean by that?"

Sam flushed, "You refused them any photographs: you wanted

to keep them for your own book. They applied to me, and I gave them some. It's a very successful photograph. I gave it on my own account. I didn't tell them to put in the Smithsonian, and it doesn't say I'm the chief."

"I won't have it," said Willets' little screaming voice made moist by tears of wrath. "Tell them to take it out. You won't get away with it: you're always the same, taking glory to yourself. They'll hear about it. Don't think I'll keep quiet about it. No sooner do you get with the British, than you start with their airs. Damn you all." He raved on, in that thin, hissing trickle of a tenor that Sam's ears could barely stand. Sam put down the telephone. He plunged his hands in his pockets and took two or three impetuous steps, to work off his rage. He felt his head begin to swell and ache again, and the thick fumes of sweat rose—he must take a bath at once. Then—a lemon drink and then dinner, and then he would be drenched again.

While he was drying himself he noticed that his hands had grown to be just like his dead mother's, the same long fingers, square tips, and veins. He thought of her with love again. Until he had married Louie's mother, Rachel, he had known no woman, because of the promise to his mother, dying.

He went into his room to dress; and, dressing in fresh linen, felt with pleasure a cool, wet wind blow; relief was rain and the eternal wet blanket of the night air, but it was a relief. He let it blow away his thoughts of the distant past. He did not think of it very often now, for he did not want to be sentimental; but sometimes, the last few weeks, these thoughts rushed in on him and fastened in his flesh, devoured him, as an invisible but rapacious creature. He had once prayed (to himself, the powers of darkness, to the unknown) to see Rachel's ghost; he had tried to see her. Now he felt as if the ghost of his own mastered desires, potency that had sunk into the earth, had grown up, a genie that was surrounding him, seizing him, thrusting him out of his honest path into the flame-leafed tropic jungle of desire. He thought of Rachel, and then suddenly his tender thoughts transformed themselves into the love of woman: he stood appalled, for a minute, feeling his heart beating fast, mad with the love of woman.

He suddenly knew himself—he had seen at least half a dozen women since he came to Malay that he wanted to kiss, embrace and even that he could conceive becoming more intimate with.

"What is this," he asked himself, with dismay, "middle age?"

But to become obscenely middle-aged in one's thirty-eighth year, he instantly realized, is not common.

"Therefore," he reasoned with himself, "it is love coming to claim me: I have been so long without love, hated at home, living in terror of my children's lives: it is pure, tender, normal love."

He began to think of other things, his daughter Louie, who would soon be a woman and who would be able to create new life, to have her own children.

"Poor, motherless girl," he sighed.

Certainly Louie would grow up to be like her own sweet, womanly mother, a blessing to some man. Thus he dismissed Louie and went to dinner thinking of the divinely good, charming expression which made him want to kiss Lady Modore. He was such a good fellow, although he knew nothing about women. One evening, for instance, after dinner, he thought it appropriate to lecture her about superfluous hair. Hair under the arms, for example, he said, should never be removed, for nature had put it there, and evidently it had some use. She had suddenly said, "You have too many children, Mr. Pollit."

"I could never have too many," he cried earnestly and began to tell her how he would like to have a Malay wife, a beauty like he had seen with her baby this day, a Chinese wife, and an Indian wife— "there are so many little lovely dears—" even a strange pygmy wife with her immense bust, belly, and buttocks—he laughed, "and the most beautiful women in the world, for example, are the Cingalese...."

"You wouldn't go native, suddenly?" she teased him.

"I would indeed," he said seriously and began again to outline his ideas, return to nature, phalanstery, peace, industry, love, law-abiding.

"Darling, call the boy."

Sam, of course, took only ginger ale. He would leave in a few days for a trip to Kuala Lumpur again, a place he loved despite his sufferings there, from heat and humidity. During the rest of the evening, he told her about his native land, its democracy, its liberty, its possibility of rebirth from generation to generation: a Thomas Jefferson, whom he was always quoting, had said, it seemed,

"There should be a revolution every twenty years."

She said coldly, "How uncomfortable! I think if I were an American I would live in the British West Indies."

Wonderful how these women could seem so disdainful!

He said playfully, "Why don't you come and visit our wonderful country? Washington is a paradise. It is all flashing walls and long avenues of trees such as would keep off the sun of Seville (only I don't want to drag in the dogs of Seville), and the people there are really interested in international affairs."

"What are the women in Washington like, tell me?"

"Oh, that's what I like about it; it is full of high-minded public women."

She looked astounded, "Really! Oh, I see what you mean," she laughed.

"And does your wife like the people there?" she asked with curiosity, having found out before that his wife was a Baltimore heiress.

He looked grave. "No, I am sorry to say. But let us not talk about that. In our early days she went with me to the eugenics meetings, but that period soon ended."

She gave him an inquisitive sidelong glance and returned to her stengah. She was glad he was going to Kuala Lumpur tomorrow. He was presentable and even handsome. He knew how to ingratiate himself, quite unconsciously, with only the best people; but how serious! Never a blink of humor and always relating how he had had a serious talk with a priest or a minister or a missionary, and how he had told the press that they were venal, and how he had addressed this and that body of high-minded public women. Dull; but for the moment, one of their class, and so to be borne.

When he returned from the meeting there were waiting for him at the house letters delivered from the office by Lai Wan Hoe on his way home. Lai had come out of his way. There was a budget—for a wonder, everyone had written—and even a letter from his wife which read:

> *Tohoga Place,*
> *Georgetown, D.C.*
> *March 15, 1937*

To Samuel Pollit:

I acknolledge receipt of five one-hundred dollar bills for household expenses.

Henrietta Pollit

Then there were big envelopes with letters from all the little ones, covered by a long letter from his eldest, Louie.

Sam hungrily seized on this letter.

In her painful handwriting, Louie had written,

> *Our Place.*
> *Georgetown, D.C.*
> *15ᵗʰ March, 1937*

Dear Father,

I am enclosing the children's letters and also my Georgetown Record, which I hope you will like. Everyone is all right. The children miss you. Mother is not very well. It has been cold, but tonight is a night of high moonshine over all the knolls and trees that I can forget the cold, at least. However, the little ones feel it and no doubt would like some of your Malayan heat. I hope your headaches are better. Tom said today, "Where is my little brother?" I said, "Which little brother?" and he answered, "My little brother Evie." Of course, we laughed and said, "Evie is your little sister; Saul and Sam are your little brothers." Just then Evie called him to get his face washed for lunch and he shouted, "All right, little sister." Isn't that pretty? But there was a sequel. This afternoon Tomkins said, "Saul and Sam and Ernie are my little brothers, aren't they?" I said, "Yes, Limpopo, they are." He said gravely, "I have other little brothers." I said, "What little brothers?" thinking he meant the boys across the street. Then he said very quickly, "Hutzler Brothers," and suddenly held his stomach with both hands and rolled all round on his legs the way he does, you know, screaming with laughter. Oh, they are full of tricks, and they are not naughty, even though it is some job getting them all clean for school, etc.

I have some homework to do, English composition, "get goyn lazybone."

Looloo

Sam read this three times and put it to one side while he read the others.

Ernie's said:

Dear Sam-The-Bold,

I hope I am not disrespectfull. I hope you have many boys, syces, and secretaries to wait on you all the time, like you said in your last letter. We went down last Saturday and saw the new Treasury building under construction. Also I like going down along the

Reflecting Pool, and I found out how it mirrors. We are all going to see the expieriments in the Academy of Sciences, I mean with the teacher, Mr. Blake. I have homework to do. I swan I best be getting on: giddy-ap, Napolyun, it looks like rain.

Lovingly,

Your stupid son,

ERNEST-PAYNIM-PIGSNEY-PRINCEPS

Next in proper order of age came Evelyn's in large, clear, round writing like her Mother's:

Home.

16.3.37

DEAD DAD,

I hope you are well, Everyone is well except Mother. I am glad you are staying with a nice lady. I am glad you are going soon to Kuala. Will there be tigers in that part of the jungle? I am afraid a tiger will get you. I hope you have someone to shot the tiger. Can you shoot? I am well.

Your loving dauhter EVIE

(kisses) xxxxxxxxxxxxxxxxxxxxx

"Dead Dad," he muttered and then shouted it with laughter. Then miserably he said, "Dead Dad, it's almost telepathic: I bet little Smudge knows how her poor Dad really feels."

The twins had two sheets of paper pinned together and written in straggling, broken-backed letters:

From Saul (said the first).

Homealome.

Tha sixteenth.

DEAR DAD,

I hope you are well. We are well. Mother is not well. She has a cold.

Samulam and me have good games. The shaits are waking up and are hungry. We gave them some meat. I found a young spug. It died. This is all now.

> *Your loving son,*
> SAWBONES
> XXXXXXXXXXXXXXXXXX

From Sam (said the second).

> *Homealome.*
> *Tha siteenth.*

DEAR DAD,

I hope you are well. We are well. Mother is not well. She is sick. Sawbones found a little sparrow that could not fly. Looloo put it in the stove. But it died. We are tired because the Hams and the Eggs played this afternoon and the Hams one.

> *Your loving son,*
> SAMOLUS
> XXXXXXXXXXXXXXXXXX

The letter of Tom, the four-year-old, Sam looked at without interest. It was written in a surprisingly clear, round hand—his mother's, just a little shaky, to show where the infant hand had stumbled under her fist.

> Home.
> *16th March*

DEAR DAD,

I hope you are well. I am well. We are all well. It is cold. We have a fire. I am sorry you are so hot. When will you be home. The snakes are awake.

> *Your loving son,*
> TOM

The letter he opened last was from Dirty Jack's daughter, Gillian Roebuck. Gillian had started to write Sam letters about their naturalist's interests and, suddenly getting fed up with her home, had taken a position as governess with a senator's family in Washington. The typed page said,

DEAR MR. POLLIT:

Sorry not to have answered before this—the explanation is that the Wellbeens have been staying in St. Augustine, Fla., and I with them of course. It was nice; the beach is wonderful and I like the strong sea air better than the inland air. We motored to the beach every day and all over the place. You would like the place. Of course the mental atmosphere could be better: but that is partly me, I know. The weather has improved somewhat since our return: most days have been bright and sunny, but unfortunately lack any warmth yet. We came back too soon for me. I go riding once a week as before, tho found the country interesting now. As you suggested, I am taking one tree and studying it: mine is the yellow poplar, that lovely tree *Liriodendron tulipifera*. I suppose I chose that because it is so beautiful—or else because it is our oldest Liberty Tree. Daffodils and hyacinths are beginning to come up from the South. I know you don't like the South because of the racial situation, but it is part of our lovely country just the same and so lovely. There were flocks of *Bombycilla cedrorum* and of course jays and robins by the *million* (that isn't scientific) and so many throngs of birds on their way north. They take it so easily. How I should love to have a pet; I should not feel so lonely. I envy you your wonderful collection of pets at Tohoga House and of course wish I could see them; but when I feel too blue I go to the Zoo just as you recommended and you are quite right! It's a pickmeup. I was thrilled at finding a *Rana sylvatica* the other day, heard the typical clucking-of-chickens call and there he was, leaf-brown to gray. Spring is here. I have rather a handful at present: one of the children is sick—but that didn't make me lose any weight. I am still a bit on the pudgy side and am afraid it augurs ill for the future. However, hard work—as you say, clean living and high thinking—and I may slim down. Yes, I am serious about Wild Life: it gives me a wonderful feeling for nature and has expanded my interests: I really *love nature* now, thanks to your teaching: I mean real love. It was just something to do before. It is wonderful to realize how much there is in the world.

> *Yours sincerely,*
> GILLIAN ROEBUCK

The letter shocked him in a strange way. He had a kind of awakening and saw how interesting was this youthful freshness turning to him from its dark old home, moldy with prejudice and tobacco smoke and this frank belief in his ideals. He believed he could be of some help to the girl who had started out on life's journey on her own account.

Sam read them all two or three times, but presently the leaden air pressed him down, and he put out the light, crept under the mosquito nets, and lay on his pillow. In a little while it was sweat-drenched: his blood beat feverishly and his head ached, ached. Meanwhile the birds outside the window, perched on the trees, fences, and the telephone wire outside the gate, twittered and squabbled for places. Every night they took up their footing there to sleep and not an inch of wire would be left. Some even slept perching on the backs of others. Every new wire that was put up was likewise utilized by the metropolitan and therefore homeless myriads. The night was not quiet at any time. Outside in the streets, too, even in this pleasant district, there would sometimes pass one of Singapore's giant population of waifs and hungry, strayed out from the steaming chowder of the streets, to the small European settlement.

* * *

He woke up in an hour or two, eyes burning, head throbbing, ready to weep with the continual pain and fever of the heat. If he could only have got to high ground it would have been better. He did not want to disturb anyone and went himself to get some iced water. He found the kitchen, which had a refrigerator, and opening the door, he leaned his head into the cold air for a while. It refreshed him a little, and then he came back to bed. But the reeking pillow, already drenched with sweat and steaming, and the moist sheets did not invite him. He opened his wardrobe to find a sarong that he usually wore when he was writing, a long strip of red, black, and yellow linen which he tucked in round his waist. The stench of clothes which could never be got dry and of the endemic mildew greeted him. Destroying and breeding nature reached in everywhere here, could not be banished, made man ridiculous.

He sat down, naked except for the linen cloth, sanguine, broad, muscular, and hairless, and after fanning himself for a few minutes and leaning his head on his hand, sighed and pulled the little portable typewriter towards him. His busy small click did not make any appreciable difference in the noises of the night.

"Singapore," he wrote, "and twelve o'clock of a night decocted in Hades."

Dear Looloo-dirl,

Lai Wan Hoe brought my budget of mail home to me tonight and so I have all your un-news.

Well, I don't mean the Georgetown Record and the story about the shaits [snakes] waking up—that is news. Anything to do with old Mother Nature, the mother of us all, is news; and I know you kids know it. So that's one good thing.

Now here is something for you, Loobeck, fir you always did love blood and thunder and here it is. I went into a Buddhist temple just outside Singapore and though I was an infidel they were glad to see me because I paid the right amount for propitiation at the entrance to the temple, also took some of their holy water. It was a wondrous temple and in it, besides a lot of heathen gods engaged in horrid activities, truly human activities and truly god-like too, if it is true that we humans are so poor as to be copies of the gods—for example, cheating, fighting, and making the most awful grimaces when not pleased. There was one appalling wall painting showing the sufferings of the damned and the resources of hell, and it was no slouch, I can tell you. It was certainly done by a male painter (but there aren't any others here in this land of domesticated woman-animals), and to placate a male god. There were two women who wouldn't do what their husbands told them. They were tied down on a bench and two demons (men-demons of course) were hacking their heads off. In fact, one is off already and is hanging up on the wall and the other is nearly off. It is just a Buddhist Bluebeard tale. And the expressions on the heads! I saw one poor Chinese woman looking and she had turned very pale—pale ivory, but not natural ivory—so I guess her husband, who was with her and had perhaps brought her just there, for his own reasons, will have no trouble with her for a while.

Then there is a man who wouldn't contribute to the gods; what a rascal! He is very neatly tied up inside a frame of wood, in an erect position and two demons with the most horrible grins on their faces are sawing him down from the top of his head to his toes. They are sawing him across so that his back is being separated from his front. Judging by the man's expression, he doesn't like it, but the demons do, judging from *their* expressions. They have just got down as far as his stomach. A great jagged crosscut saw with teeth about two inches long and wide.

There is a man being thrown into a great fire off a high place, a man who looks very worried, being boiled in a pan. As only a bit of him can be boiled at a time, the attendant demons are getting much pleasure out of turning him round and over so that all parts will get a fair, democratic boiling. Then one is being boiled in a deep pot of boiling oil—I don't know *what* for—but the Buddhists seem to take an interest in cooking. The one in the deep pot is a woman, perhaps she is in a deep one for more decency. As she squirms about and tries to get out of the pot the demons laugh at her and push her back again. It is a case of the clam who wouldn't be chowder. Then, in the same chowder department is a woman being held upside down in a very deep pot, almost a bottle—of boiling oil. She is held firmly by two demons, one to a leg. There is also more activity in the same department. A man is being sawn across the middle this time and right next door, in the hook-and-eye division, a man is having his stomach pulled out with great hooks and some (petty offenders, I suppose) are having their tongues yanked out, red-hot irons pushed into their eyes, which are sizzling, and there are others, quite venial, with hands and ears being lopped off with large and apparently specialized lopping knives. But these folks are specialized in knives, as you will see when I get home, with my collection of swords and scimitars and the like. So much art into such wicked weapons! And perhaps, says I, we should suspect all art capable of being applied to such a use. Think of that, Looloo-dirl, when you are reading your *Styles of Ornament* and all those funny, dopey things you read, godfather knows why!

Well, back to the joyful scene, for I know you: I bet you are enjoying it in your solemn, poker-face way. There is a particularly joyful little act—for the demons, I mean. Three men are chained to a tall metal funnel (there must be modernism), and a great fire is raging inside and being kept up by a demon stoker. The victims are being frizzled and grilled against the heated funnel, and turned round at the right time, so that they will be the right shade all round.

There are quite a lot impaled on spears put close together, and there is a man being flattened between two stone slabs; his blood and innards are oozing through in a very natural fashion. There are many other inventions—all in natural colors and blood, blood everywhere. This is all for Chinese Buddhists: I don't know whether they are tougher than other people and like this, or whether they are weaker than other people and have to have more awful warnings.

The whole thing is quite a nice little business and the priests being successful businessmen look no different from the chetties and the big fat Chinese butchers and bankers, perhaps better-humored because of the pictures they have on their walls. At the entrance to their little place of business, there are big figures of the Chinese Buddha and his pink-white marble wives and all sorts of demon gods, some of them crushing little demons under their feet, just like the advertisement for backache pills. There must be at least fifty little gods of different sorts: you can choose your god, as your pills, in the druggist's—it is rather a good, comforting idea, for surely the gods go in for competition and try to do a little better than the next god.

There is a sacred snake in a cage that attracted me. You can worship it too, if you are scared enough. Of course I went and hissed at him, but he took no notice; he knew he had no power over the rational, I suppose.

There is much burning of joss sticks and firing-off of crackers; that is the great way of worshiping because you get something for your money. I gave the priest one Straits dollar which he put in a bowl as an offering to the Lord Buddha, though I wondered how the high and mighty, suave and grand Lord Buddha should want one Straits dollar. Then the priest gave me a packet of crackers which I let off in front of the Lord Buddha, and the great god looked down on me and seemed to grin at me through the curls of smoke. It seems that now the demons of the sea and forest will let me pass—all on account of the packet of crackers, and the silver dollar. So tell my little foolish dark-eyed Smudge-Sedgewing that the tigers can't get me now, for the great Lord Buddha is watching me.

Am tired-tired with the heat and my head. Will write later. Meanwhile keep-up your Georgetown Record, Looloo, and work at your schoolwork. I expect great things of you later on, even if you do seem a little dopey now.

Your loving father,
SAMUEL POLLIT

P.S. I am not sending these notes from the ordinary tourist's love of the sensational: but because one might say truly that these are the—horrors of superstition, from which, Looloo, may you ever stay free!

DAD

P.P.S. Ask your cousin Leslie to put off getting hitched till I get back so I can join the jubilaum. I'll bring her some peachblow Chinese silk if they let me.

DAD

Sam went back to bed and slept soundly, and it was not till the next evening that, borrowing Wan Hoe's typewriter at the office, he wrote to Gillian Roebuck.

The Holy Lion City.
15th April, 1937

DEAR MISS ROEBUCK,
(Because I may only call you My Little Gillian before a host of witnesses, because you are a young lady now):

I am very, very glad you got away at last to such a wonderful place. Yes, it is wonderful to have something to love, something that will last a lifetime, or many lifetimes, and if it's nature and man in nature, that is the best thing of all.

It isn't such fun seeing things here. You have an ever-present and all-pervading conscious and subconscious sensation that it—is—HOT. You see a lovely vista of palms and wonderful trees: it is too hot to walk down to them. You see a wonderful mountain clear in air, floating in crystal and it is too hot to even attempt to go even a hundred yards towards it on foot; I'm not thinking of the dense jungle which you would have to cut your way through. You see the glorious foreshores, with their four tiers of trees, the fifty feet, the hundred, the hundred and fifty, and the two hundred, all shades of green, all fronds and foliages laced together; and it is too hot to take a boat to go there. (There is such a lovely stretch behind Singapore in the Strait.) Then you see a lovely sheet of water; but it is too hot to so much as go down to it. You are invited to tea by a lovely lady, and it is too hot to go. You try to keep your temper with a foolish, vain gnat of a human being, and it is too hot to do so. Because it is TOO HOT everywhere. The heat wilts you like a soft leaf, just like the pumpkin leaf goes in our place on a very hot day at Tohoga. You put on nice clean clothes and they wilt when you touch them and they are full of perspiration before you finish dressing. You sweat at breakfast, you sweat at tiffin, and you sweat at eight o'clock dinner.

You don't want to go anywhere; you don't want to see anything; you don't want to know anybody. You just have one paramount thought, again conscious and subconscious, "Let's strip Jack naked!" You refuse invitations to afternoon tea because politeness prevents you from taking your clothes off in your host's house; and your tea's no sooner in than it's out quicker than in, through your skin. You can't go out to tiffin or dinner unless you sit under a punkah and then you get a chill in your back. You go for a walk in the evening to study the many interesting types of humans and their funny ways—for they live, boil, stew quite cheerfully in their infernal temperature—and you sweat and sweat and sweat and all you study is THE HEAT.

And your clothes reek and everything goes moldy in one day—hats fuzzy, boots furry, bag leprous, spectacle cases blanched, books diseased, coats blotched. Your bed reeks with the sweat of ages (an age is a week here), and the pillow at about midnight is just a sponge.

And just think, my little Gillian (yes, I will say it and call up a host of invisible witnesses as I have none visible), all that would be unnecessary if we wore shorts or a sarong like sensible people do and didn't try to be gents: you don't mind sweat pouring out of you when you've no clothes on; and the great Chinese rich men go about happily in their automobiles naked to the waist with great shining free bellies, ready to catch any breeze that kindly blows to our relief.

And now, Miss Roebuck and Miss Gillian, good-by to both of you; and I'll be seeing my dear naturalists soon in dear old Washington, our new Jerusalem, the one sane, great city, built on a definite plan for a definite purpose and not by the worst cases in a madhouse. (And with the naturalists, my little naturalist!)

Yours sincerely,

SAMUEL C. POLLIT

When they got back at last and the work was about done, Sam set to work to get his notes in order and present his section of the report. He was at first too ill and too overworked to notice that Lai Wan Hoe, his senior clerk, was more harassed than usual; and when he did notice it, he thought that it was because of the pile of work to be got through in a short time. Colonel Willets had decided to close the mission at once, being sick and tired of the Malayan heat, habits, and company. Sam had a pile of notes without end but would have been unable to get up his report without the lifetime knowledge of his Chinese secretary.

"I'll get you an assistant," said Sam, though he was cutting expenses as much as possible himself in order to take as much money home as possible to clean up accounts at home and pay for the new baby that was coming. Sam himself had urged Willets as subtly as he could to get through the work and sail for home, for he wanted above all to be there when the baby came. He also felt himself on the verge of a physical breakdown. Wan Hoe merely asked for a holiday of one day, "Only one day, sir, please!"

Sam sighed, "All right, Wan Hoe, though I can't really spare you."

But Wan Hoe took two days and on the day following, Sam found a note that had been left mysteriously on his desk;

DEAR SIR,
Please find it in your kind heart to forgive me. I had to run away. I am in trouble. Do not be angry with me. I could not help it. You were right about the moneylenders; but I was unable to take your advice. When we came back from Port Swettenham I found everything had come out into the open; and for several days I have been trying to avoid this shameful expedient. A disgraced man in hiding.

It was in Wan Hoe's fluent handwriting but not signed. The same day the police called to apprehend Wan Hoe who was wanted for immense sums owed to moneylenders and for a relatively small sum embezzled through someone in the treasurer's office. Sam, who usually hid nothing and who regarded the police as his friends, good, stout fellows with a difficult job, acted on impulse, gave terse replies, and concealed the note. The loss of Wan Hoe struck him down. There were thousands of notes scattered about the office in good order which Wan Hoe had read, but not Sam: it would be torture for Sam, with his headaches and bloodshot eyes, to try to get through them here. He was obliged to go to Colonel Willets and say that his section of the report would be turned in later, either on board ship or in Washington. This default pleased the Colonel greatly.

When Sam took his walks at night, he kept seeing Wan Hoe, it seemed to him. Whenever he saw the police taking up a man, he was afraid it was he. He saw many a Chinese with Wan Hoe's pleasant, sensual face and even spoke to one, but in error. Where was he hiding? Was he rotting in some shameful cell, without help? Sam tossed far into the night, thinking of Wan Hoe and discreetly made inquiries about him in the daytime, but nothing came to his ears. He was questioned by several seniors about Wan Hoe's behavior and political ideas and also was politely interviewed by the chief of police, but he replied that he knew Wan Hoe was a Chinese patriot, nothing more; he assumed every man was for his country as he, Pollit, was for his. Wan Hoe was the best secretary that ever lived since the world began. And when they suggested that Wan Hoe had gone off on the spree, Sam's hackles rose; it was a personal insult.

Just as Sam was packing up the last of his folios and manuscripts, he received anonymously a small, scented, and carved chest, seven inches by five by four, containing six teacups not much larger than eggcups. Each cup was of six segments of carved chocolate wood and was lined with pure Straits silver, so soft that it was easily dented with the fingernail. The box opened out as a cabinet, and the cups stood on two shelves. The following day he received an invitation to take an assistant professorship of ichthyology at Hangkow University. He then understood that both these things came from Wan Hoe's brother, a professor in Hangkow and also a

Chinese patriot, and that Wan Hoe was safe. Sam was as joyful as if the message had come from heaven on silver wings. But he wrote back to the University a characteristic letter in his fat civil-service phrases:

DEAR SIRS,

I am deeply honored and gratified by your letter of the 20th ultimo and your very kind offer. I wish to assure you that nothing would please me better than to be able to accept it and that it is with very deep regret indeed that I find myself obliged to send you a refusal. If I were able to proceed to the post, I should be gratifying a lifelong wish of mine to study at close quarters a people I have much admired, whose philosophy I find so much more exalted than our own in many ways. I would willingly be one more of the too few links between your people and our own and try to advance in my minor way the Pan-Pacific Comity of Nations. Your great country liberated, Malaya enlightened, the United States more Pacific-minded and a great Empire more deeply aware of its responsibilities in the Pacific—this is what I have worked for all my life and this is what I still hope to see in my lifetime.

What feasible excuse can I offer? One that you will, I trust, understand. I am the father of six small children, whom I love deeply and whose health I am afraid would suffer in these latitudes. If they were older I could move them here, but at present I could not dare to do so. Nor do I want them brought up in a distant land, much as I hope they will be citizens of the world, for I wish them to be American patriots in exactly the same degree as your own fervent, admirable patriotic young men of the new China. This is my only reason for refusing your kind offer.

> *Believe me to be, Sirs,*
> *Respectfully yours,*
> SAMUEL C. POLLIT

After sending off this letter, Sam had little more to do but to pack his things, get the curios he had had his eye on for months and have them shipped, soothe old man Willets and fight with him every day, help him with his packing, say farewell to Bargong, his "gunner" from the launch, Naden, his Indian secretary, Teo Mah Seong, a self-taught naturalist, Teochiew Chinese, in whose workshop he had spent many hours, and get to the boat at the last minute.

"God damn it, I thought you had decided to stay behind with those darkies," said Willets. "I've been sending messages to you for an hour. Lady Modore was here, did you see her? Well, she only drove down to give me a message for a friend. She didn't ask after you, Pollit."

"And I didn't ask after her," Sam said, nettled. "It took me a long time to say good-by to all my friends and leave my presents for them, and get my presents *from* them." He grinned wickedly at Colonel Willets who replied, "You'd better put the presents in your report!"

Sam turned away to take a lingering look at Singapore, hoping never to forget this eleven-o'clock view, the hills with Government House beyond the city, the long bund, the crowded native craft and the steamers and warships sharing the famous crescent. Beyond were brilliant green islets and jetties with water in every direction, the long, low shoulders sloping towards the town and huts on piers standing in the water. The ship was gorgeous as ships can be in the tropics, with decks, walls, and every object radiating heat and light, the women in colored dresses of semi-transparent stuff or white tropical weaves, handkerchiefs on their heads and waists, and everyone bustling and gay, glad to be going, excited by the Singapore stop.

"I loved the place," said Sam to Branders, one of the artists of the Expedition, "but never again. She is the Queen of Sheba, but she is too much for me."

"Here we are between the Gulf of Siam and the Bay of Bengal, with everything to see, and we have to go back to the Potomac: it's pretty flat, isn't it? Well, life's long. We'll all come back perhaps. How about a shandy?"

"I'll take a lemonade," said Sam.

Chapter Seven

1 Family corroboree.

Jo got to Tohoga Place late. The Pollits were scattered all over the house and grounds. For five minutes the sunroom was the scene of straw-colored fireworks. Jo threw down her flowers, chocolates, her hat, while the others started to pour in around her, through doors and long, open French windows, and exclaimed, "Where's Sam? I want to give him a big hug! Where's my baby brother? Where is he, where is he, where is he? Tell him I'm here! Tell him Jo is here! Tell him Jo the Jolly Sailor has brought him his chocs! Where is he?"

With a rhinoceros bound, she burst out of the circle, looking for Sam, shouting for Sam. She bounded all over the place. She was a Golden Horde by herself. When she found Sam beside the snakes' cage, she fell on his neck,

"Old boy! Samivel! It's himself! If I could have got to the train I would have, Sam! What have you been doing to yourself? You lost weight! I cut out your picture in the paper and put it up in the kindergarten! You should have seen their little faces when I told them it was my brother! I'm proud of you, I say it who shouldn't. Father, tell that boy to stop it! Stop it, Sam, stop it! You're putting us all in the shade! Hooray, hooray: he's famous. He's a great man. How are you, Samivel?"

"Easy, easy, old girl!" said Sam, weeping a little, "don't be a fool, Jo! Easy, old girl! Dry those tears. There were others there besides myself, strange as that may seem to a big sister! I ain't the only white-haired boy in the days of the sun! Hooray yourself! Hooray for Jo!"

"You lummocks, you dumbbell," said Jo, wiping her eyes.

"Nary a lummocks," said Sam, "nary a lummocks! Where is the rest of the reception committee? How many more is a-goin' to fall weepin bitterly on my neck! Oh, these are too much! This is some doin's! Femaile, sez I, go home to your wife and chilluns, ef you hev sich! Weep not, fair made, it is but a slight contree-temps!"

"Fool!" cried Jo sniffing.

"So you went and missed me?" inquired Sam.

"Why not?" demanded Jo.

"There's a law saying no big yaller-haired cornstalks kin miss their little brothers," said Sam.

"You know Brownell's brother is Inspector now?" cried Jo. "That man you detest in the Department? He's forged ahead. He's a nice man. He came round last week and that Gray woman made up to him shamefully, to try and get that position. She sat up all night making a picture of Rumpelstiltskin and she signed it! 'Rembrandt'! She signs her charts too! A Leonardo in the kindergarten. Myrtle Gray! Hff! The Catholics help each other; it's a state within the state. It's a disgrace. Everyone is furious. A teacher wrote God with a small g, and she reported her! Not that I'm for atheists, but we don't want any Rome-controlled delators! Spying and snooping, with the priests behind her back. He complimented me and said, 'I enjoyed the lesson very much, Miss Pollit.' I could see he was favorably impressed. In the playground he came up to me and started making vague remarks—I could see he was hinting. So I up and told him what I thought about the Gray woman. Someone has to speak out! I said to him bluntly, 'I don't like sectarianism in the schools. I never did, I never shall. It's against my principles and it's against the Constitution. It's against the law. But there are some' (I said) 'that have a law higher than the law. Anyone whose political or religious capital is outside the U.S.A.'"

Sam had meantime sat down on the grass bank and was laughing languidly and pulling away at the rank weeds, "All right, Jo, all right: O.K., old girl, cool off!"

"Cool off," cried Jo, tossing her head. "What for?"

"Dear old Jo, on the same old warpath," said Sam.

"I prefer a hot head to cold feet," said Jo. She went on with her story. In the meantime, sounds of cheer came from the house where everyone was helping Jinny, Sam's sister-in-law, and Louie and Hazel decorate the place and get ready for the banquet to which they would sit down at six o'clock. Bonnie was there, not herself, a little sad and quiet, with a thin face. She was staying with Jinny in Baltimore and helping in the house. But Bonnie, after quietly embracing and weeping over Sam, had gone back to work for his party, just the same, and she was at present tasting her Badminton Cup, her own secret specialty, for which dear Lennie, her brother, had brought three bottles of claret and one of curaçao. As all Sam's parties hitherto had been nonalcoholic, this was to be the great surprise of the day; for certainly, everyone argued, since Sam went abroad, he had learned to be more a man of the world, and he, at least, would never object.

Everyone noticed that Sam had changed greatly. He was more restrained: he did not complain and patted his children on the head with a wise, sad smile, more like an ordinary father than the eccentric he had been. He had been eight months amongst people of his own age and had conversed only with them, although he had made a few casual friends of eight to twelve, Chinese and Malays, schoolboys, sons of his Teochiew friend, the naturalist and of the curio dealer and all the boys of the villages. But his relation to these, since he did not speak to them freely, was that of a tribal uncle, something of the older generation.

The children were gamboling all around their father, and as Jo's story went on, rising and falling with the urgencies of the storm, he beckoned his Ernest (who had grown more thoughtful and distant and had fewer smiles than Ali Mahmoud, Sam's friend in City Road, Singapore) and his twins, melancholy Little-Sam and thoughtful Saul, towards him. It had been a great day, this day of welcome, and they were glad to sink on the grassy bank and swell his humming,

> And thar we see a swampin gun
> Large as a log of maple
> Upon a dandy little cart
> A load for feyther's caytle...

Jo waited till they paused and sniffed good-humoredly, "Well, you're too glad to see your Daddy back to think of me: it's Father's Day."

She left them there, a handsome buttercup garland sprawled along the lawn. After a short silence, Sam raised his eyes from the depths of the orchard, where he had plunged them, drinking in through them the green and the blue, and he said wearily,

"You kids didn't lose any dorsal vertebrae weeding the gardens while Dad-the-Bold was in furrin parts, did you?"

Ernie defended himself, "The varmints wouldn't work."

They defended themselves, "He never told us to."

Their father said miserably, as if to himself, "And the boiler wasn't fixed up; and there's no new boiler; and the possum died and a snake died. Nobuddy did nuffin. When Sam went away everybody just plain forgot him. 'Near can I forgit the surblime speckticul which met my gase as I alited from the Staige with my umbreller and verlise.' [Artemus Ward: The Atlantic Cable.] Weeds, springing up everywhere, the paths cracked and our hanni-miles dead." He did not even laugh; just went on sadly recounting to himself the default. The boys sat round with him, as miserable as himself. In all the wild, vacant months that had passed, like a stupid, shouting, windy holiday, they had never given one thought to their father's schemes and ideas. It had been nothing but Little-Sam's and Saul's and Ernie's ideas, a great savanna of opportunity in which they stumbled, ranged, hallooed, occasionally catching sight of each other, at intervals dreaming about a personage, genie of the swamp, who called himself Sam-the-Bold, their father, and was away, his wand broken.

All the joyful Pollits were still running up-and downstairs, and the clink of plates, silver, and glasses could be heard, as well as Bonnie's gay call, "Nearly ready, folks, nearly ready: get ready! Who's going to strike up?" and Lennie's wild bagpipes (made by vibrating his long lean cheek), *The Campbells Are Coming, Hooray, Hooray!* Then the strains of the wedding march started up under Jo's tough fingers as Leslie Benbow, *née* Pollit, new-married, arrived with her short, half-bald husband, rather more flustered than is common in a twenty-six-year-old bride and plump in the waist. Leslie had not stayed her marriage for Sam. Many things had gone on without him.

But they all stayed in the house or on the porch, leaving Sam to his children at the top of the orchard, and to his thoughts which, it was evident, were not of the sweetest, not the sort a man might be expected to have on returning to the bosom of his family from a glorious trip to the Far East. Sam felt it keenly that Leslie, his favorite niece, did not come to see him, and that no one seemed to bother about him. He went on talking tiredly to the boys, with a joke from time to time, trying to regain his old style: " 'The people gave me a cordyal recepshun. The press was loud in her prazes,'" but Artemus Ward fell off his tongue without a rebound.

Now the noises had quietened a little and the Pollits seemed to be conferring about something. In another minute, Bonnie sang out, "Come on, now, Samuel: we want you in the sun-room!"

Sam got up holding out his long fingers to his boys, and trailed them with him to the house. He stopped a minute, without thinking, before the back porch, staring at it, and then said mildly, "Needs a couple of coats!"

Inside they were avid for him, waiting to pounce on him.

"Here's our Sam! Samuel! Sammy, my boy! Sam!" Bonnie rushed forward and pecked him on the cheek. Her skin had yellowed through the winter; she was overrouged, and her beautiful hair new washed, full of blue lights, made her look sicklier.

"You're not the only one in the paper," cried Jinny affectionately, buxom and pretty in a blue dress, her red hair in more of a fuss than ever. "Jo was in the papers. Jo sent one of her poems to the *Sun* and they published it."

"Did you see our poetess?" asked Bonnie. "Jo's poems? Did you send it to him, Jo?"

"It's pretty," said Leslie, in a retiring way.

"You're flattering me," said Jo, "it's not so wonderful as you make out."

"It's very good, Jo," Bonnie declared reproachfully.

"Did you write a poem, Jo?" Sam asked with interest.

"In the Baltimore *Sun*," said Ernie breathlessly; "she got paid for it."

"Josephine M. Pollit!" affirmed Jinny Pollit good-naturedly. Because it was Sam's welcome-home, she tried to cover up the quarrel between herself and Jo; but Jo did no such thing. She turned her back on Jinny in a grand manner.

"Have you got it, Jo?" Sam asked.

"I have it," said Bonnie, rushing to the settee and rummaging in her purse. She at length produced a dirty, browned scrap of paper which she unfolded and handed with pride to Sam. Jo said with bonhomie, "I just thought I'd send it in; and they accepted it at once."

"You could make money that way," said Lennie to Jo.

"Isn't it wonderful, Sam, a poetess in the family?" demanded Bonnie. "Being published? You ought to publish some of your letters, Sam. They went all round the family; we could never get enough of them. We read them aloud. Henny sent us all your letters. Henny was such a dear and so good to the little ones: but then she is a wonderful mother to the little ones, she really is."

During Bonnie's enthusiastic rattle, an uneasy silence had begun to gather over assembled Pollitry, but it was not till it was well advanced that Bonnie saw it and stopped. Henny was not present. Faintly Bonnie repeated, "Read it, Sam; it's wonderful."

"Don't be absurd," commanded Jo, frowning, "such a silly fuss!"

The children clustered round Sam, looking at Jo, this combination of Minerva and Juno.

"Read it, Deddy," said Tommy in his pretty, chipping accent.

Sam laughed ruefully, "Don't call me Deddy. And my Sedgewing who wrote to me, 'Dead Dad.'"

They all shrieked with laughter. Evie looked greatly mortified. Sam continued tenderly, "And who asked me if I could shot a tiger?"

There was wild hilarity, kind Bonnie and Jinny stuffing their hands into their mouths, kind Lennie and Peter Pollit, uncles, turning side on, because anyone could see that Evie was nearly in tears. Sam's old father, seventy-year-old Charles, sitting behind the throng on the settee, laughed consumedly, laughing at them all, delighted to have them together for once. He no more noticed little Evie than some puppy hiding in a corner. Sam held up his hand for the merriment to cease, saying,

"Listen, kids and kinfolk, Josie wrote this and it's very beautiful."

("Listen, listen," whispered the relatives on all sides. Old Charles Pollit leaned forward, laughing still. He could write poetry better than the lot of them.)

Sam read,

In Peggy's eyes
Is the blue of the skies
And innocent looks
That are more than wise.
In a garden plot
Of forgetmenot,

And water brooks
Beneath blue skies
A duplicate lies
Of Peggy's eyes.

Evie stared at her Aunt Jo in the delicious, timid, vacant admiration of the inept. Ernie slewed a look at Louie, standing behind two visitors, and saw her flash a look of contempt at Sam and Jo too. Sam raised his head and saw her too. He said pleasantly, "Isn't that pretty, Looloo?"

"It's nice."

Sam was pleased, "It's very nice, Looloo. Why don't you try to write something like that too, Looloo? All of us Pollits are a good hand at jingle: we can all turn out a rhyme. I think you could, and they might publish it too."

Louie became speechless with resentment, but none saw this but the watchful Ernie. Jo bounced and cried, "Oh, she's very like me: I know she's got a talent: Louie's all right. I bet she could do one nearly as good as that right now."

In a choking voice, Louie said quickly, "Oh, I don't think I would write one like that."

"Well, perhaps not right now: but soon, some day! And now, Father, Father! Come on and do your stunt!"

They began to clear back, leaving a wide circle into which old Charlie advanced with accomplished hesitations, pretending to be broken down with age and rheumatism. They began to clap and back farther away to leave him room for his dance. Louie, choking with rage, slipped out of the door without being noticed, and went into the quiet upstairs. Henny had retired for the day to the girls' room. She was sitting in a big, easy chair looking very bitter and pale, with the brown, mottled skin of pregnancy's end, her neck corrugated. Louie came slowly towards her,

"Everyone's here now, Mother."

Henny grunted, in contempt. "They were reading Auntie Jo's poem in the *Sun*."

Henny grunted.

"I think it's rot," pouted Louie.

"Oh, the Pollits are all so conceited," Henny said impatiently, "that if they write two lines, everyone has to take three fits and a faint. Don't you be like them, that's all I ask."

"Will I tidy the room?" asked Louie.

"No, leave me alone. No one's coming up here; I gave orders about that. I wish to God I could take a taxi and get away from their idiot party and all that buzzing and jigging that they think's so clever and funny."

The grandfather's cracked baritone chirped away to the audience below,

Slap, dash, slap, with a whitewash brush—
Talk about a county ball!
In and out the corners, round the Johnny Homers;
We were a gay old pair of gorners—

"Wouldn't you go down for a little while, Mother?"

"No, I'd rather go to the big bonfire! I suppose now the word will go round that I am sabotaging. Oh, darn everything. Go on down and help. Don't stand there fidgeting and staring at me."

"Would you like some tea, Mother?"

"Oh, I suppose I've got to take something. I'm so empty, I feel like a big barrel floating out to sea."

Louie, delighted, ran downstairs. Whenever her irritations got too deep, she mooched in to see her mother. Here, she had learned, without knowing she had learned it, was a brackish well of hate to drink from, and a great passion of gall which could run deep and still, or send up waterspouts, that could fret and boil, or seem silky as young afternoon, something that put iron in her soul and made her strong to resist the depraved healthiness and idle jollity of the Pollit clan.

It was a strange affection. It could never express itself by embraces or kisses, nothing more than a rare, cool, dutiful kiss on the withering cheek of Henny. It came from their physical differences, because their paths could never meet, and from the natural outlawry of womankind. Downstairs came Louie, for the tea, cheerfully muttering,

> Moonbeam, leave the shadowy vale,
> *To bathe this burning brow.*
> (Shelley: "To the Moonbeam")

The indefatigable Jinny was stretching and puffing on the stepladder on the front porch, fixing a forgotten string of Chinese lanterns. In the dining room and the hall stood the wooden cases Sam had brought back from Malaya. None had been opened, though many a curious finger had poked them since early this afternoon. As soon as Sam knew that they were giving a surprise party, he had announced that, despite his fatigue, he would open them all and that everyone would see the Eastern treasures and carry off a present.

Grandfather Charlie, in high feather, spied Louie and called excitedly,

"The Old Gaffer's going to give another show! Come on, Granddaughter! The Old One's about to present 'Mr. Wemmick and the Aged Parent.' Come along, come along, roll up, roll up, come right in, the show's just about to begin! All star performance: manager, Charles Pollit; business manager, Charlie Pollit; stage manager, Chas. Pollit, and barker, Old Charlie. Mr. Wemmick, played by

Charles Pollit, and The Aged, played by Charles Pollit. You must excuse, not stare at, the redundancy of that beautiful name, Pollit, in the caste, ladies and gentlemen, if there be any of that name here, for it's all in the family. And the play written by Charles—Dickens, the greatest Charlie!"

"Oh, Father, you're a perfect scream," declared Bonnie. "The old gaffer's all right," she assured the rest.

"Shut up, girl," said her father, "no talking in the free seats. Curtain! Lights! Action!" He gave three taps as he said the last three words. In a profound silence, he began the act that he had worked up himself from *Great Expectations*.

"'Massive? I think so. And his watch is a gold repeater, and worth a hundred pound.'"

The little ones sat round like idols in front of the throng or on their relatives' laps, with carved smiles on their faces and round, floating eyes. The old man, with nothing but a red bandanna, which he ordinarily used to brush off his snuff, became alternately Mr. Wemmick and The Aged, Old Grandfather Charlie, through some trap door of the imagination, disappeared until the act was over; when he suddenly popped up again with a here-we-are-again, crowing, and stumbling into his little buck-and-wing dance. At last they dragged him off the center of the stage. He sank into a rattan armchair near the door and drew Louie towards him,

"How did you like it, granddaughter?"

"Oh, you were very good," she exclaimed.

He twined a strand of her hair round his fingers gently, repeating with great affection,

Blue were her eyes as the fairy flax,
Her cheeks like the dawn of day,
Her bosom white as the hawthorn buds
That ope in the month of May.

She blushed to the roots of her hair and the flush crept downwards to stain the hawthorn. Her grandfather patted her and turned away, pulling Evie towards him instead, to hide her embarrassment. Then there was a bellying of the crowd at the southern end and something black dropped in through the window; and this black thing hopped into the middle of the room, grinning and rolling white eyes, Cousin Sid doing his Yacht Club Boys, Mammy-Minstrel Act. Then Uncle Leonard sang *The Two Grenadiers;* and this was followed by a hush. Ernie had stolen out, and there came the expected notes of the gong, liquid gold, bommm-bommm scarcely a sound, that rippled, spun, and spread itself through all the air.

The old man arose with a knowing air and came into the center of the carpet again, tramping, stamping, pawing.

"Snake dance," cried Saul excitedly.

All the Pollits lined up behind the old man in order of age, the children last in a long skeletal tail; and after stamping thunderously, they began to sway and weave out the long south window, singing at the top of their voices, "Oh sound a blast for freedom, boys, and send it far and wide!" They circled the animal cages and the rock garden and, circumnavigating the house, came in again by the front door, the old chief entering the long dining room where the banquet was spread, just as they came to the chorus of the second verse: "Hurrah, Hurrah, we bring the Jubilee!" roared the Pollits, and the rafters rang. Sam and the old man were weeping tears of emotion, and there were other damp eyes in the crowd. Then there was a great rumbling of chairs and scurrying of women, all wedging and hedging in, fitting of elbows and knees, groans and giggles until the great tribe was set to table. They had fitted into the table the two dust-stained, extra leaves from the attic, and yet it was hardly big enough. At one end of the table stood a broad-bottomed armchair empty. Old Charles, after one glance at it, wriggled out of his seat again (he was at the other end, next to Sam), saying, "Wait and see, wait and see: the Old Gaffer's going to get our Henny." Sam's head and lower lip drooped at this, but the others urged him on, saying with honest enthusiasm, "Yes, beg her to come, Father," and explaining to each other, "You see, poor thing, she's miserable in her condition," and "She hates to be seen—it's very natural: I don't blame poor Pet," and so on. There was indeed no malice in all Pollitry, for Henny. From time to time, one or other of them was inspired by the awful idol they worshiped, their Bounding Health, to go On the Warpath against one of their own; and when On the Warpath, a Pollit was a strange, frightful being, a being of brawn and no human understanding, armed with a moral club; but they had no malice against them who hated them; they loved and pitied the intractable, malicious Henny.

After a little while, they heard Old Charlie's voice on the stairs descending slowly and in a moment he appeared, gallantly bending and bringing in Henny by the hand. Henny had waited to fix a bit of lace round her throat with a pearl brooch and to brush up her hair, so that as she came in swaying slowly on her hips under her new rosepink flowered smock, with a touch of rouge on her cheeks, she looked impressive. Her eyes were set into her skull and her face drawn, but her reluctance and pride gave her a matronly dignity. The men all rose except Sam who was sunk in a brown study and who anyhow despised such courtesy as "a foreign mannerism." When his father jogged him on the arm, as much as to say, "You get up too, Sammy," he merely looked round indifferently; and he refused to rise. At this, his brothers, Leonard, Peter and Saul, busied themselves, pulling out the chair for Henny, inquiring after her health, speaking sharply to one of the children in order to cover Sam's clumsiness. At the same moment there was a bustling and twitteration amongst the women to prevent remark and to make Henny feel that she was wanted. Sam sat silent till Henny was seated. From her seat she sent a look of thunder bowling along to the other end, to her morose spouse; then tossing her head slightly, affected to ignore him and began a society clatter with Lennie, her brother-in-law, a leaner edition of Sam, but a goodfellow, a Masonic brother, a cocktail mixer.

Henny had not gone to the train or been on the porch to greet Sam when he came from it, surrounded by all his children. Her sickness, the explanations she had to give about the money, and the scoldings she feared about the untidiness of the place drowned her in a nausea so deep that when Sam had come to the door of her bedroom where she sat she had only given him a look of hollow melancholy; and he, after a long look moist with angry, pitiful tears, had said, "Hullo, Henny," and looked away. There was so much to untangle, and Henny felt her hands nerveless. She would never again try to knit even one stitch in the long chain of their married life. She hated all that was to come. She was glad that the Pollits had surrounded him and put off the dark hour; and yet she resented their joy at him, when to her, he meant the day of reckoning. Lennie Pollit was handsome, a successful traveling salesman in men's shirts, and an angel to his wife, Jinny. Lennie and Jinny gave parties, liked a good time, and had a little money. Why did I have to pick the only Pollit mad and silly with ambition? Henny had often thought. But now she had swum beyond all Pollitry and their considerations: she was on the edge of the maelstrom and was about to sink down, down, circling. She put her hand on the edge of the table and looked round her for a glass of water, which Lennie hastened to pour for her. Henny said, "I felt faint, but it's all right now." Jinny asked her if she would like to lie down, but she refused, "I'm here now; I might as well stay."

There was a two-tiered iced cake made by Jinny; potato-and-egg salad with homemade mayonnaise, also made by Jinny; delicatessen and lemonade, little iced cakes with chocolate tears upon them, made by Henny; raspberry wheels, made by Henny;

popovers made by Bonnie and a large box of chocolates given by Jo; contributions from the whole family in the shape of edibles; and down the table, three large pitchers, one transparent, one blue, and one pink, containing a rose-colored liquor with fruit floating in it. This mysterious drink intrigued the children beyond expression. They kept swallowing and looking at the glassware. Before the children were only lemonade glasses, but before the adults were wineglasses. The children suspected that even on this occasion the sherbet of paradise was to be drunk under their dry lips by the loudmouthed, money-pocketed monsters who had them in thrall. Why didn't these giants ravish the table, send the food flying besides, gobble, guff, grab, and gourmandize? To be bestial giants with the power of sherbet and also to exhibit such mean-spirited stinginess towards their own appetites was a conundrum the children could never solve. Let them once be such giants, let them even have the privilege of Louie, and they would not leave a crumb on a plate nor a drop in a bottle. The children sighed internally and ate as hard as they could hoping by their hunger, to soften the miserliness of their elders.

"What's that?" exclaimed Ernie, overcome by desire, pointing to the fascinating pitcher, "What's this, Auntie?" The cruelty of tyrants must be broken down somehow.

"Not for you, Tommy Tucker," said Bonnie hastily, hushing him with a grimace.

Lennie got up and, seizing the pitcher at a signal from Jinny, then went round pouring out the Badminton Cup into the wineglasses.

"What is this?" inquired Sam abstractedly.

"Badminton Cup," Lennie said. Sam said nothing, never having heard of such a thing. When the glass pitcher was empty, Lennie started on the other. No one had touched it. When Lennie got back to his place and all were provided for, he picked up his glass and said in his best Freemasons'-toastmaster voice,

"Old Oddfellow, Brothers and Sisters, Sons and Daughters, before we swallow a drop, let us drink a health to the man we celebrate—to SAM, our wanderer returned!"

All stood up but Henny, but Henny took hold of her glass out of politeness. Sam looked round at them smiling in a grave style, saying almost *sotto voce*, "No, no; you're wonderful people—no, no!"

Lennie repeated, "To Sam!" and the whole family intoned it, in a beautiful response, "To Sam!" They took mouthfuls of the claret cup and a few of the younger ones choked. Old Charles said by himself, "To my youngest son, Samuel Clemens Pollit!" and drank his at a draught. "Not a bad cup!" he nodded to Bonnie. Sam's bloodshot eyes moistened again and he fingered his own glass thoughtfully, as does a man accustomed to speeches, smiling faintly at several of them in turn. Jo, of course, shouted, "Speech, speech," stamped on the floor, beat on the table till the tableware rang again, and the little ones took it up foolishly, crying like a lot of young crows, "Speech, speech!"

"All right, boys and girls," said Sam, at which they all fell silent and sat down irregularly. Then he got up and told them how very, very glad he was to be home again, home again, jiggity-jig; gladder than they ever would know, although they might try to guess, knowing him and how much he loved them all and particularly how much he had always loved his native land and his splendid, flashing Washington, and his own Tohoga House and his tribe, flesh of his flesh, most particularly; and the work nearest to his hand. He did not object, he said, to wandering in the highways and byways of the world, as a student of men and manners, to receive enlightenment, and spread it again; and when Fate held out her hand, he made it a rule to take that hand with whatever it held, for Fate always had a lesson for him, just as every book that fell on its face open, and every scrap of muddy newsprint blowing in the wind and even every shop sign might hold a message for him, because the Word was sacred to him; and whatever that message might be, he was not one to turn his face away, but he smiled at Fate, for he believed Fate was on his side.

Then he lifted his glass and said quietly, "To you all, my friends, friends of my own tribe!" and put the glass to his lips, tasting it mildly, afraid it was one of those saccharine women's drinks. But he, as soon, put it down, looking round, affronted, and he said to Bonnie accusingly, "Bonniferous, what is in this? There is alcohol in this?"

She flushed and acknowledged petulantly, "It's claret cup, Sam; it won't do you any harm—it wouldn't do Tommy any harm, only on account of your views we didn't give it to the children. There's so little, just enough to give it a taste on this festive occasion; you can't be so ultrazealous—it's a fruit drink really!"

Sternly he said to her, "Bonnie, you know I never touch alcohol, nor allow it in my house!"

Henny's face twitched with a sarcastic smile.

"Your brothers and sisters like it!" cried Bonnie.

"I am sorry it is on my table," he told her coldly and sat down. He sulkily picked up his spoon and fork and messed up a piece of cake; but in a minute he thrust it aside, saying in a spoiled way to his father, "This has quite taken away my appetite: why can't I be obeyed? I thought this occasion was to give me pleasure?"

"A little tolerance hurts no one," Old Charlie said, with embarrassment, since his son had often rowed him about his own nipping and tasting.

"I refuse to discuss it here," Sam told him harshly.

Old Charles looked at him for a moment; but his face softened again and, with a roll of gay abandon, noticing that the others hesitated to sip their claret cup, he cried,

"Bonnie, my girl, more of the cup that cheers but not inebriates. The Good Book says, 'Let us eat and drink, for tomorrow we shall die!'" and in his best glee-club voice he began to troll,

A boat, a boat, haste to the ferry!
Let us go over and make merry!
To laugh and quaff and drink good sherry!

Sam began to pick at his food again, refusing to be drawn. The family took up the round and rang the changes round the table, Lennie singing seconds, Old Charles' voice growing young again as they sang. Even Sam could not resist the charm of the family singsong, oldest Pollit custom, and when his turn came, he took up the song, "A boat, a boat, haste to the ferry!" while Bonnie, at his left, was singing soprano, "Let us go over and make merry!" This removed the dampener that Sam's strong principles had put on the cheer; in any case, they knew Sam's fortes and foibles of old and easily forgave him.

Then Jinny and Bonnie started to discuss the recipe for the Badminton Cup, and jolly Lennie said, "Well, if my little brother won't drink it, Bon, I will drink it for him!" and in the general good humor even Sam recognized that he was swamped. Brother Ebby busied himself now with food and drink seeing that "one and all were in a mood to rejoice," and when Sam, seeing Henny take some of the Cup, said sternly, "Henny, don't drink that, especially in your condition!" and Henny, merely smirking, tossed off a whole glass, almost no one took any notice, for the same pebble cannot ripple the millpond twice.

Henny smirked even more, seeing this wildcat, hedgerow, wild-weed, slum-artisan, cheap-Baltimore family grow more jolly; seeing Ebby, poor ship's carpenter, who had an imbecile for a wife and one doddle-headed child, and gaptoothed Benbow, with that strumpet girl, Leslie (as Henny put it), and two dumb boys, and old soak Charles, and garage-owner Peter (who had actually begun with a junk cart and three cowbells collecting old bedsprings and fat women's bulging corsets!), and Bonnie (obviously sleeping with some man who was doing her dirt) and Jinny (whose pert daughter Essie needed her face slapped) and Jo (whose hair was like a haystack in a fit) and all their weedy, rank children getting merrier and merrier on the dungheap that was their life. Born in the muck, thriving in the muck, and proud of the muck, thought Henrietta! Well, it's well to be some people and not know how badly off you are! Let them rot, for all I care. How she had fretted at these people who didn't care if they had an old automobile, and didn't care if they lived cheap, and didn't care if their daughters went to work in hat factories, and didn't care if their cousins married when they were two months pregnant, as long as they lived and crawled fatly over the earth! Despising them, she despised herself, who had been married to them, because she had been useless as a belle, too hysterical and featherbrained to be married as a possible financial catch in Baltimore. Poor Henrietta, thought the Pollits, who never doubted a moment that she felt degraded by them, after her fine upbringing. Ebby gravely brought round the jug to her shoulder while Lennie encouraged her by pushing across to her a plate of true-lovers'-knots in pastry, made by Ebby's wife, Emma, "Eat and drink, Henrietta," and he gave her a bright blue look.

"Sam," said Old Charlie, at the other end of the table, "live and let live; we don't know why we're here, and it's a good rule to let live, till we find out!" He took another swig of the claret cup, which was beginning to blush his ancient mind.

Sam was unhappy and irritable, "Father, you know what my principles are. Fermented and spirituous liquors dethrone reason, deform morals, and disgrace social gatherings. You know I stick to my principles through thick and thin. You know, you all know, I have never faltered in what I believe to be the right. Why do you cross me? Today of all days! In Singapore I saw what alcohol can do to the best of men; the white man in the East is soaked in alcohol.

There isn't a decent liver goes out there but becomes a slave of his liver; as for its effect on women—our ministering angel becomes a harridan and—worse! You must forgive me."

Henny scrutinized him closely during this speech and at the end laughed shortly and put the second glass to her lips.

"Henny, put down that glass or leave the room: my children are here!"

"Samuel!" cried Bonnie, horrified. "Pet!" she pleaded, and Jinny said, "Sam, Sam, Sam, don't break up the party!"

"You heard me, Henny," Sam said with flushed face, "you all heard me."

Henny laughed on a high, artificial note. Her voice cracked as she said, "I heard! You wouldn't hear me bellowing that way across the table insulting my own guests—you and your Singapore society manners!"

She shut her eyes, rolling her head back in that ugly, incredibly theatrical way of hers, then snapped open the heavy lids, again giving them all a smoking look.

"He writes letters home about the fine ladies who befriended him while he was away, Lady Battersby, Lady Modore, Lady Muckymuck, and Sir William Pat my back and I'll scratch yours, with all his fine friends in fine feathers, and this is the real way he is at home, the great I-Am. Trying to boss me about when you've only just got off the boat. Probably you think I'm that nigger secretary you had or his nigger wife!" She laughed insolently and took another sip of the glass, "I'd be ashamed to insult my guests at my own parties, especially when it all came out of their purses—but that doesn't bother him, he can't drink your wine, he's too pure. He's so pure that he just came back from the sluts of Singapore, who have the staggers from gin-slings, and he wants to order me round the way he orders those wretched beggars, Chinks, and niggers the government gives him. The family carpet-bagger."

Sam sprang up, sending his chair sprawling, "Henny, quit the room!" The brothers and sisters jumped up too, to restrain Sam, pacify Henny, and send out the children. The old father got up with his bent knees and laid his knotted, veined hand on his son's arm. Samuel did not notice him, thought it was some child. Henny, laughing, stood up slowly, brushing the crumbs from her knees,

"Look at me! My back's bent in two with the fruit of my womb; aren't you sorry to see what happened to me because of his lust? I go about with a body like a football, fit to be kicked about by a bohunk halfback, an All-America football, because of his lust, the fine, pure man that won't look at women. Don't you regret my condition because of his lust? Didn't he fix me up, pin me down, make sure no man would look at me while he was gallivanting with his fine ladies? I guarantee, Samuel, that no man looked at me while you were away. Oh, what do I care?" she said, weeping to Jinny, who was talking to her, pleading with her, "What do I care, Jinny? You're a mother yourself. Haven't you done the horrible thing three times yourself for a man? What do you care when the time comes? What does any woman care for the man who got her that way? I am such a God-forgotten imbecile as to be going through the bloody mess again for a man like that, that's been slinking through the slime of Singapore with his high-society whores for eight months, and left me in this misery. I hope I never come back; I hope this is the last you see of such a rotten, helpless, stupid thing as I am, falling into his trap every time; I hope I die. I am sure I'll die. I pray to God I'll die. I can't fight any more. I'm not one of his tigers to fight all my life. I'm not a grenadier like a rotten old schoolma'am to squabble all my life. Look how he insults me! He no sooner gets back than he insults me before the whole swarm of them! Let me go; why do you hang on to me, all of you? What have I done? How did I get here? I know, through his sniveling, whining, get-rich-quick tricks. To you he's something wonderful; if you knew what he is to me, something filthy crawling in the sleeve of my dressing gown; something dirty, a splotch of blood or washing-up water on my skirts. That's what he is, with his fine airs and don't-touch-me and I'm-too-good-to-drink. The little, tin Jesus! Oh, let me go, Jinny! What do you know about him? Oh, let me go, I'm a damned fool to give way this way."

The old man said, "Son, son, go and speak to her: you ought to remember the condition she's in; a woman is not a man," and Bonnie whispered to her father, "Sam's dreadfully tired, let him alone too," while the gaping, frightened children stood stockstill in their places. Only Essie, Jinny's daughter, was grinning, a naughty girl who sneered at everyone, Jinny's pride. To Louie she said, poking her, "I always knew they fought like cats and dogs in your family: Aunt Henny gives Uncle Sam hell!" and Essie laughed. At this moment Jinny, red as a May Day flag, arrived behind her pride, and boxed her ears, which sent her howling and kicking into the passage, although Essie was twelve years old. Henny's attention was attracted that way, and Henny, feeling a deep shame for the scene she had brought on, cried out, to Louie, "What are you doing, you fat pig, slopping over the table like that? Take your fat belly off the tablecloth and stop looking like your greasy father!" and laughed desperately.

"Henny," said Jinny. "Henny, dear, come and lie down. I'll get you an ice bag for your headache; come and lie down, dear!" and Bonnie was frowning and crying at Sam, "Samuel, how could you, today of all days?"

"This is the home I come home to," said Sam and sank into his chair.

Soon Henny was lying down on Louie's bed upstairs and Louie came up with tea for her, to calm her and an aspirin, and the party, in Henny's absence, had made a shift to reorganize itself, and gather in the children to get them into a better state of mind and make them forget. They were now singing the "Hallelujah" Chorus, in a moderated style, round Henny's grand piano, with quick-witted

Bonnie at the keyboard. Sam had wandered away from them, beside himself, ill and out of his usual mind, to look at the rock garden, wind-picked and weed-covered, and the cement fishpond, green with rags of moss, with sick-looking fish—the whole place had been given a lick and a promise in preparation for his coming, no sooner than yesterday. He took with him Ebby's boys, kindhearted, fox-snouted Cousin Sid, and Little-Sam. Of all the boys, he had thought most of Little-Sam throughout his exile from home, the strawheaded, tempestuous, stubborn little boy of unpredictable reactions, with his shouts of mirth and shouts of rage, the boy who looked most like himself and who, Sam told himself, was a young genius, sure to be a great scientist and carry on his own work.

To him, kicking his heels round the rock garden, came Evie scurrying with a telegram in her hand, "It's for Mother; but Auntie Jinny says for you to open it."

Sam tore the paper and read:

FATHER COLLYER DIED SUDDENLY THIS MORNING CAN YOU COME TO YOUR MOTHER ARCHIBALD LESSINUM

"I will go after the opening of the boxes," said Sam. "Don't take it to your mother. Old David is dead. Dear old David is dead."

2 *Brought to light.*

Now Ernest and Tommy came in deputation to him, running and out of breath but with hope and embarrassment.

"Daddy, everyone wants to know if you're going to open the boxes now?"

"Deddy, are you going to show us the things you brought?"

Sam smiled, "Sure-LY," and started up the slope. They skipped round him, rushing toward the house and back towards him.

Suddenly Ernie spurted off to carry the news. A movement began again, breathless and happy among all the Pollits; they had been straying, and now they began circulating slowly but regularly in groups like creatures swimming round an aquarium.

"Sam is going to open the cases; Sam is going to show us the Chinese things. Oh, isn't that grand!"

"Wow!" "Gee!" "Gee, I'm excited, aren't you?" "What has Uncle Sam got in there, Mumsy?" "Shh, you'll see."

Sam went to the tool house and came in with a hammer and a cold chisel. Presently all the boys and men were lugging, tugging the boxes, but as gently as they were able so as not to break the flimsy and precious things inside.

Sam was rather reluctant to open the cases because, although he was generous, he had brought many things that he intended for the adornment of his own bare house with its great rooms. He was unaware of the sensuality of his own nature and of the joy he took in these porcelains, silks, and embroideries, the longing, the lust he had for them. He had always been poor and modern, and suddenly in the East he had found the treasures of the past. He had always despised the past, hated history, believed only in man today and in a sober, future commonweal; and now for the first time, through his love of the Chinese he loved the workmanship, treasures, theories, men of the past; and through his new acquaintance with white men in the East in positions of power. He had gone, stupidly, for the pomp and spreadeagle of scientific societies and human uplift associations, now for the first time, he had seen the exquisite beauty, sensibility and sensuality of the things treasured by those who put others in bondage. Poor good man, he thought that he had discovered a new principle, which was, as he told Saul Pilgrim, that the rich and powerful are human beings too. Talk to them of some innocent thing, like natural history and human advancement and they were as human, more human, tender, than the wages-obsessed workman:

they had seen much and understood much. But he bore a little grudge to his raw, sensual, penurious family, at this moment, for standing there, adoring his success and his possessions so openly; there they stood, good-natured vultures, his own blood, ready to fall on his stuffs and snatch them, saying oh, and ah, and slavering for them; but he would not give them much, his own children came first. For them he would make a nest, a haven, a palace, a university, all in his own plot of ground and this phalanstery of a house: he would now be the East to his children as well as the West.

They first opened the box of ceramics and found two twenty-inch vases smashed; but there were left a dozen or so cloisonné and lacquer vases of various sizes. Everyone helped to put the things on the table, the mantelpiece and the piano. It was like a village fire brigade passing buckets. The expensive chips were shoveled out into the ash can. The second case had on its very top a mandarin gown of celestial blue with gold metallic threads, which was for Louie. Louie, who expected nothing of the shortsighted world, was baffled by this gift.

Her father raised his tired eyes upon her, "I bought that for you, Louie; it was sold by a real Chinese prince, a refugee, and my friend gave it to me for almost nothing, for my eldest daughter."

With a sullen, downcast face, but with a faint flush, she took it. As she went past the ranks of Pollits, they looked curiously, grudgingly at her, or fingered it. She laid it out on the sofa in the long dining room. When alone with it, triumph surged up—mine, she thought, mine; and grasped one of the stiff folds, mine—and she laid the other hand flat on it. She went self-consciously and stolidly back, but no one noticed her. Two ordinary Chinese silk dressing gowns, one pink and one yellow, with heavy embroidery and gold threads, lay on the chair, and Auntie Bonnie said fussily, "Those are for your Mother: why don't you ask her to come down, dear?"

"I'll take them up to her," said Louie.

Henny had already regretted her act of tempest, and she looked with melancholy softness at the dressing gowns, "Put them there and thank your father."

"They say, won't you come down, Mother?"

"No, I only want to be left alone." Louie withdrew.

Sam had emptied one box, all packed with silk suits of pajamas and gowns, scarves, and a long, feast-day banner of red, showing a woman in a multicolored gown. He broke open another case which chanced to contain small jade ornaments, in dark, pale, and white jade, snuffboxes and little pots and napkin rings. The furniture and fixtures could no longer be seen, overwhelmed with the china, bronze, brass, lacquer, and silks he had brought and with two cork pictures and some bits of embroidery. Sam made the boys bring in a light pine table from the veranda and on this he set out for show all the little *objets d'art*.

"Now," he said, clearing his throat, "there is something for everyone. Let us clear the chairs and put all the stuff in the other room: everyone will sit down and everyone will choose what he likes from the pine table."

Ernie, quickly looking round, saw the discomfiture amongst his relatives. They, the poor, were only to get the little things. They were not experts, and they loved the polished vases, the red lacquer, the silks and banners. The small things seemed of little value to them.

Sam, too, no slower than anyone, had seen the disappointment and embarrassment of his brothers, sisters, and their families. He looked embarrassed and gave a little grin. He hurried his boys with their bundles of stuffs. Bonnie, good girl, seeing how things were, immediately became very cheerful and rattled away, "While you're all getting seated, I'll give you a song," and she took a flying leap into *Funiculi, Funicula*.

The distribution began. Sam made himself a dispenser of bric-a-brac, with a pin pot here, a matchbox there, a napkin ring beside, and a snuffbox neighboring, and again a pin pot, according to the choice of the men and women. He had a wonderful set of actor dolls, with a demon, a prince, a princess, and several minor fiends, and a little stage, but these were for his own children. He had Chinese instruments which he played for them in between times, to give a saving touch of grotesquerie to the whole thing. Perhaps soon they would forget the parsimony and disperse and not come together again until the memory of the pin pots was half gone.

There were seven cases to unpack. Sam, once started and sunk to his waist in a lake of treasures, with his tools and his relatives around him, worked without stopping, except once to say to Bonnie, "Bon, cawf [coffee]." Now Sam had reached the seventh case, which contained metals, knives with chased, inlaid, and beaten blades, and with carved and inlaid handles of ebony, ivory, and brass-inlaid silver and so on, a Chinese two-edged broadsword, a creese, a mace. At the bottom was something that he unwrapped with surprise and dragged out with difficulty, a Chinese bronze gong two feet in diameter, with raised figures. Struck once, it gave out a long, distant mellow roll, a sound which was never a single note, always a whole meditation of sound.

Sam said, "I see now why he packed it himself; it is a present from my friend Abdul Jamid ben Ali. Yes, now I remember, Abdul Jamid said, 'I hope nothing breaks,' and I am sure there is something that will not break. This is his gift. What friends in the east!"

Louie said,

A yellow plum was given me and in return a topaz fair I gave,
No mere return for courtesy but that our friendship might outlast the grave.

"Eh? What is that?"

"That is a poem after Confucius!"

Sam was careful to show no surprise, "I am glad you have got to Confucius and beyond Confusion. Abdul's little boy, Mahmoud," he continued, turning to his father, "I met every day going to school; he was intelligent and quick and spoke good English and had a ready smile for everyone."

Meanwhile there was a subdued chatter all over the rooms, where the Pollits were exclaiming over the stuffs and curios. Louie stood abstracted, with the peach-bloom silk, brought for Leslie, at her feet; and unexpectedly, she took a step forward, over the bolt of silk and declaimed,

A simple peach was given me, and in return a ruby gem I gave,
No mere return for courtesy, but that our friendship might outlast the grave!

Her cousin Essie, who was playing with the little wooden toys, models of water carriers and buffalo carts and sawyers' blocks, gave a sidelong glance and turned back intently to her game. No one else took the least notice, except Little-Sam, sitting near her, who kept looking up into her face questioningly. Big Sam took no notice. Encouraged by this, Louie declared,

A loquat branch was given me and in return an emerald I gave,
No mere return for courtesy, but that our friendship might outlast the grave!

Sam paused and leaned back on his heels at the beginning of the stanza, and with long lank cheek he studied Louie, who seemed to have grown out of recognition in the eight months of his absence; or else his imagination had twinkled and transformed her memory in that hot climate. Was this tall, powerful girl with stern, hangdog face really Louie, the child of love? But now the face

290 | CHRISTINA STEAD

twitched with a clownish pleasure and grave conceit; the face was both ludicrous and lachrymose: Sam wanted to strike her across the face to obliterate that execrably bizarre tragicomic mask which disgraced him. Sam stared her into silence so that the mask settled, sad, too old by years, between the waterfall hair, and then abruptly, his mouth opened and he laughed hard,

"Ha-ha-ha-ha-ha, he-he-he; Ha-ha! A booby trap was given me and in return, a herring trail I gave; no mere return for courtesy but that our friendship might outlast the grave."

The Pollits were flocking back, grinning from ear to ear, not knowing what the joke was but glad to see Sam at last in high spirits. They saw Louie and Little-Sam, Essie and the others, and had no idea how the thing had started,

"Ha-ha-ha," shouted Sam, rocking on his haunches and pointing at Louie (at whom the newcomers looked in surprise), "an old black boot was given me and in return a herring head I gave, no mere return for courtesy but that our friendship might outlast the grave! A chamber pot was given me and in return a toilet bowl I gave, no mere return for courtesy but that our friendship might outlast the grave!"

The astonished Pollits crowded in, grinning confusedly and peering from one to the other, while Auntie Jo ignorantly, cried, "A wedding cake was given me and in return a petticoat I gave, no mere return for courtesy but that our friendship might outlast the grave!"

Ernie, very knowing, with a narrow-eyed leer, capered and delivered himself, "A dusty pup was given me and in return an old tin can I gave, no mere return for dusty pup but that our friendship might outlast the grave!"

"Louie said it," declared Essie to everyone. "That was what Louie was reciting!"

But Sam recaptured the floor saying angrily, "If that's Confucius, I'll eat my hat."

"It is," cried Louie, "it is. You don't know. Listen:

Let me be reverent, be reverent,
Even as the way of Heaven is evident,
And its appointment easy is to mar."

Bonnie ignored all this, calling out, "Now let's have a little song before we break up, not too loud, but not too soft."

"Yes," said the old man eagerly, "yes." He picked the snuffbox out of his knitted waistcoat with the cat's-eye buttons that he had got once when strolling round the world on a sailing vessel, from New Zealand, and offered it to his eldest son, Ebby, who was the only son to share what the girls called "father's disgusting habit."

"Yes," he repeated, "for he's a jolly good fellow, and so say all of us. What's the matter with Sammy? He's all right!"

"He's a chip off the old block," cried Bonnie beaming; and Old Charles tee-heed under his yellowed mustache.

"Samivel's all right," said he, raising the snuffbox to the level of his eyes and scrutinizing the design, vaguely scandalous, which consisted of two mermaids sitting on a beach. He raised the snuffbox higher and motioned round the family with it, beginning with a laugh, "Samivel is wery satisfactory to the old codger; 'wery' spelt with a 'wee.'"

"Father!" cried Jo indignantly, as the little ones started to giggle, "Wee, wee."

He slid the snuffbox into his pocket, "Shall I do All-of-a-Twist?"

"Oh, no, Father," said Jo. "Not now."

Old Charles appealed to the children, abstractedly picking his own pocket of the bandanna meanwhile, " 'I won't abase myself by descending to hold no conversation with him.' replied the Dodger."

"For he's a jolly good fellow," sang out Bonnie, touching the piano.

"For he's a jolly good fellow," Ebby sang.

"And so say all of us," shouted Jo.

"Don't," said Sam, "don't, boys and girls," but his eyes were moist and to the children's surprise he seemed older. His eyes had new crow's-feet, and the tired upper part of the face, with sunken temples, for the hour resembled the weathered mahogany face of Old Charles.

"And why not?" shouted Jo jovially. "Aren't you our very own Smithsonian? Our family genius? No, or yes?"

"Yes, yes!"

"Our only genius," Jo continued.

Louie's face lowered. By a curious chance Jo looked straight at Louie, grinning evilly, Louie thought.

"And you, Jo, aren't you our genius too?" inquired Bonnie innocently. "Well, I guess we're all small pertaters, only we don't know it, all except Sam." She spun on the stool.

"Tune up," cried Grandfather in his trembling voice, and he began, in a furry voice full of little hidden screams or scratches, *The Gang's All Here.*

"Let Father give us a tune," said Ebby delightedly, his good gray eyes caressing his father. "What'll it be, Father?"

The old man ran to the center of the carpet, bagging his trousers, fussing his bushy gray hair, and pinching his cheeks to make them pink; so that they all answered that they wanted to hear *The Bold Fisherman.* Out of his coat pocket came the red bandanna which he tied in the open V of his blue shirt. The little boys were a bit ashamed, too, of the way his trouser band bulged, of the wrinkles in the legs, of the snuff spots on the handkerchief and the coat, and, in particular, of his eagerness to sing to them. But he was used to giving performances wherever he could, and he had far too many spawn, and spawn's spawn, to notice the greensickness of little boys in seven-inch pants. He threw himself into the song, and the shocking perpetual youth of Grandfather ceased shocking them for a while,

> Oh, there was a bold fisherman and he set sail from Billingsgate
> To chase the mild bloater and the gay mackeeray;
> But when he arrove off Pimlico, the stormy wynds they began
> to blow, and the little boat wibble-wobbled so,
> That smack overboard he fell!

This was followed by an adorable *parlando* with improvisations during which Grandfather performed on his accordion, "my I. W. W. pianner," as he called it, "music on the hoof." Grandfather was generous with his shows, and he went through three stanzas. They had hardly stopped laughing and got through wild, prolonged applause (during which Henny was seen bleakly rotating past the doorway into the kitchen), when Grandfather ran to a corner of the room and seemed to fall behind the settee. They were just wondering whether they should go and help him when he reappeared jubilant, holding his old banjo between his legs and hands. When they saw it, they all shouted. Old Charles positively gave a goatlike leap at this shout and himself cried, "A seat, a chair for the wandering minstrel!"

Well, there was no stopping him; the children were delighted, and only the distrait noticed Henny, during the next song, moving with elephantine grace in the dining room, carrying a silver sugar basin. Then Ebby took the banjo and played *One Evening in the Month of May*, and during this Bonnie saw Henny, with a scowl, heaving herself to the bottom of the staircase and then heard her moving slowly up.

More refreshments were served, and during the bustle Henny came downstairs again, this time in the new pink Chinese dressing gown.

"I feel full as a tick," said Henny, discouraged, "but I must take something; I know I'm empty," and she sat down to the kitchen table with Jinny, not saying much, but gulping down hot tea hungrily. Then she restlessly went upstairs again.

"We'll all be going soon," said Jinny kindly. "I'll pack them off, Pet!"

"Oh, it doesn't matter; I'm so darned restless, I don't care what they do: I hardly hear them," said Henny. "Ugh! I'm going upstairs to rest; now I have indigestion! I'm a fool to mix my drinks. Tell Louie to bring me the bicarbonate."

She labored upstairs. The Pollits below sang madly, "The flowers that bloom in the spring, tra-la, have nothing to do with the case."

"I suppose Collyer left this house to Henny and you?" inquired Lennie of Sam.

"Oh, he promised it," said Sam. "Don't talk about it, Len; I was very fond of the old boy and he of me."

"And that's what I mean when I say and I sing," sang the Pollits, leaning on each other's shoulders round the piano.

"Have you told Henrietta yet?"

"No, she's probably very tired. I telephoned the house and explained I'd tell her in the morning. I'll go to the funeral; it will be the first I ever went to. I don't like funerals, but dear Old David was different: I'm sorry I didn't see him; I bitterly regret it. I loved Old David."

They moved to the hall door.

"Pet will be very upset."

"Of course! Her father!"

Louie came downstairs quickly, "Daddy, Mother's sick, she says to call the doctor."

"Ugh, ouf!" said Henny loudly.

"She shouldn't have taken that wine," said Sam, "and overexcited herself. You see, I can't tell her tonight."

"Oh, damn it," said Henny loudly above.

Sam frowned.

"Louie!" called Henny, "Louisa! Bonnie!"

"I'll go," said Sam.

"Let Auntie Bonnie go," Louie advised. "Auntie!" The Pollits were roaring, "The music goes round and round!"

"Auntie!" called Louie, looking through the rooms. Bonnie came running, flustered but cheerful, from the bathroom, holding a newspaper in her hand and saying, "Oh, Sam, what are they saying about Wally in Singapore; I forgot to ask? What does the British Empire say about the American Beauty?"

"And it comes out here!" they shouted, groaned, whined, and squeaked at the piano, bellowing with laughter.

Louie said quickly, "Auntie, Mother says will you go up!"

"Louie!" screamed Henny, unseen, seething with exasperation. "Louie, tell that mad crowd to stop it!"

Leonard turned back, "Shh! Shh! Henny's sick!"

"I'll pack them off," cried Jinny, hurrying up to them.

Suddenly Henny screamed, "Samuel! Tell the damnfools to go," and they heard her begin to moan. Jinny rushed in and turned herself into a dozen Jinnys, patting and pulling, packing them off, telling them where their coats were, apologizing, explaining— Henny was overtired with the excitement and must be left alone with her family.

Henny shouted, hoarse with anger, "Samuel! Samuel!"

Louie rushed downstairs again, making a noise enough for a cavalry horse, "Daddy, Mother says she's too sick to stand it!"

"Nerves," said Sam, in a tired way, "but I suppose it's natural. Poor Pet is waiting; it's the waiting at the end."

Grandfather hurried up to Samuel, "What is it? The—"

"No," said Sam, "it's a fortnight too soon. Just hysteria."

Old Charles said hurriedly, with a shamed, begging face, "Samuel, they never called any of the little ones after me—when it comes, if it's a boy, will you call it Charles? I'll ask Henny myself, dear boy, when the time comes. I haven't got long to go; I'd like to see a little rogue of a Charlie called after his worthless old gaffer."

"All right, Father," Sam laughed a little; "he's staking out his claim."

"Here's your coat, Lennie," said Jinny bustling up, already dressed for going out. "Will you go out and start the car? and I'll get the children."

Bonnie came running down, "I can't quite understand it, unless it's—" she looked worried from one to the other. "Send for the doctor, Samuel."

"Has she Doctor Rock still?" asked Sam frowning.

"Of course!"

"All right!"

Bonnie went to the telephone.

They heard Henny above.

The Pollits went scurrying, flying out by the open long windows and doors, shaking hands, backing into their coats, settling their hats, shouting, "Good-by! So long! See you in the comic supplement!" being whispered to, by their fathers and mothers, falling over people's feet, tangling up their own and streaming out to their automobiles and along the street to the streetcar. Neighbors facing Tohoga House, in the semidetached brick cottages, came out on the porches to watch them go.

No one went to say good-by to Henny, who was reported sick. Upstairs Henny heard them go, racing and tramping. She sat in a chair beside Louie's bed, with a stricken look, and when Louie reappeared after saying good-by, Henny said quietly,

"Tell your father to come up and see me!"

Samuel went upstairs reluctantly, and Louie, waiting at the foot of the staircase, heard his expostulations and Henny's angry answers,

"How could I arrange for it? I had no money. It's going to be here!"

"No money? What happened to all I sent? I denied myself for you and the children."

"Don't fight about money now, with the state I'm in! Get Doctor Rock."

"I told you not to have Doctor Rock; he has a reputation."

"I don't give a damn what reputation he has: he suits me. He's a good family doctor. Do I have to scream at you to get something! No sooner do you come home than it becomes a bedlam. Do I have to scream at you? Get him! Bonnie! Louie! Tell this idiot, tell this blockhead, tell him, Bonnie! Get him, you ugly beast! A woman in my condition has to beg and pray and explain!"

Louie rushed to the telephone and telephoned Doctor Rock again. The doctor's calm voice, insolently calm, it seemed, said, "What is it? What did she say?"

"She says to come quickly."

"I'll send the nurse."

The quarrel upstairs was being carried on in subdued tones. Sam presently came downstairs looking grave and quiet. He murmured impersonally to Louie, "Keep the children quiet: Mother's ill."

"I know," said Louie rudely.

He looked coldly at her, "If you know, keep them quiet. I'm sick myself, Looloo," he said breaking down suddenly. "I can't go much further myself."

He stumbled into the riotously littered dining room and across it, skirting every manner of grotesque and outlandish thing to the sunroom, where he threw himself on the settee.

"Looloo-dirl," he called piteously, "come and talk to me." She went in.

Upstairs they heard Henny groan with impatience.

"We have a long night ahead," said Sam. "I want you to arrange the children's beds downstairs. Mother wants to sleep upstairs."

"Is she very sick?" asked Louie, much frightened.

"All that," said Sam, "is a child trying to be born. I guess that by sunrise tomorrow we will have another child in the family."

Louie looked as if she could not believe her ears. She faltered, "Another child?"

"The groans you hear are the beginning of the greatest drama on earth, the act of birth." He looked at her with luminous eyes; his voice had taken on a tone of incantation. "With the coming of morning, Samuel Pollit will have a new son or daughter."

Louie blushed from head to foot.

"And I myself am so ill, Looloo-girl, that I can hardly rejoice as I always do at the birth of a child. The great glory of man, the great glory of the flaming forth of new stars, the glory of the expanding universe, which are all expressed in our lives by the mystery, wonder, and tragedy of birth have always thrilled me beyond expression. And here I lie, with bones of jelly. It did for me, Looloo. The last nights in Singapore I was so tired that when I shut my eyes, I saw blue and yellow flames, I saw things as clear as photographs, not ordinary visions; I dreamed there was a dragon on my bed. Don't tell anyone that, Looloo, and not Henrietta either, now. I don't want her to be worried."

Louie stared at him uncomfortably. Sam laughed, "a giant in his weakness."

Louie said,

The desolator desolate,
The tyrant overthrown;
The arbiter of other's fate,
A suppliant for his own!

Sam looked at her with a puzzled expression, "Why did you say that?"

She melted into a grin, "I just thought of it."

"Leave me to sleep; go and see if your mother wants anything."

When Louie got upstairs she found that Doctor Rock had been admitted by Bonnie.

"Get some clean towels for me, Louie," said Henny gasping.

The doctor turned to her with an angry expression.

"Go on, my dear," said poor Henny, quite kindly.

Bonnie was making Louie's bed.

"You will have to sleep downstairs tonight," said Henny grimly.

The doctor kept staring at her angrily.

"The water is beginning to drip, Doctor."

The doctor glared at Louie, "Go away, run away!"

3 *Morning rise.*

Sanguine and sun-haired Sam Pollit, waiting for the birth of his seventh child, had not slept all night. Louie, after some attendance at the door of the birth room, had slept well, downstairs, in Henny's big bed, with Evie. Kind Bonnie had stayed all night. The four boys, used to wind cries and human cries, had slept very well on mattresses on the floor in the sunroom, exactly as they had on the day of the great gale in 1933 when Sam feared the chimney pots would blow down. One or two of them woke once or twice and, hearing their mother cry out, saw nothing in it at all but an ordinary connubial quarrel between her and Sam, and turned and slept again. There were torments in the Himalayas, windspouts in the Grand Canyon, and Judges of the Supreme Court got into sacred rages. What could little boys do, too, about differences between their hearthstones, Mother and Father? They listened for a while, turned, and slept again.

At four o'clock the sky grew lighter and, one by one, the birds began to creak, some like rusty winches, some like door hinges, and some like fishing lines unreeled at a great rate. There was one that sang joyously like the water burbling down a choked drain. At any rate, to Sam's ear, all of these were singing hymns of praise to the rising dawn, and congratulating themselves on their broods and him on his new child. "All Nature is awake," thought Sam, prowling amongst the chance-sown seedlings of pine at the bottom of the orchard, "and my latest young one, in a new suit of flesh, is trying to greet the dawn, too." At five-thirty the flame-red sun, so heralded, was kicked out of the horizon's waist and visibly jerked upwards. Not even a breeze stirred the hundred-year-old elms on the south-facing bluff of Tohoga Place. Overhead stretched an immense, tender spring sky. The budding trees, already root-hid in weeds, ran up the hill on all sides. The surrounding streets, their hollows, the lesser heights, and dome bubbles of reeking Washington were visible; the world was a milky cameo at sunup. The neglected garden thronged upwards with all its plants into the new sun, with its guava trees, peach trees, magnolia trees, apple trees, seedling pines and forsythia, and the wild double narcissus that grew so rank and green on the possums' graves.

From the girls' bedroom that looked due south into Virginia, carried on the sloping airs to Sam, his wife's screams began coming louder and closer together. No doubt their neighbors with the small, pinched brick faces, feverishly avoiding the sunspots on their spoiled sheets in bedrooms on Reservoir Street, and the encroachers on old Tohoga House Estate, slums of Thirty-fifth Street, back-bedroom dwellers, who rested their hot eyes on green Tohoga's wilderness, if they were awake, heard the sound too. The air was still and lazy. Sam plied fast his long legs and reached the house in a minute.

"It's the end," said Sam. Both leaves of the tall south door stood open letting in the moist air, and he raced from the porch through them and along the hall to Henny's bedroom where the two girls were fast asleep. Brick-colored light fell through the shutters of the French windows on to the ceiling, and moved quickly in bars farther and farther into the room. The air breathed heat and nightlong sweat mixed with the dewy morning coming through the shutter slits. The windows were open. Louie's long hair was spread out in a fan on the pillow, and the rumpled sheet was kicked to the bottom of the bed on her side, though it still half embraced Evie. Sam, standing at the foot of the bed, whistled Louie's whistle. When she opened her eyes, he said quickly, "Get the kids up and dressed, Looloo: I want 'em to hear the new baby come."

"Is it here?" asked the girl, half awake. He pointed in the direction of the noises, "Coming, coming; hurry. That means the end. I'll get the boys."

His daughter jumped out of bed, after shaking Evie.

"Little-Womey, hurry, hurry," said Sam, stooping to the level of her vague, surprised eyes, on the bed. "New bimbo, new bambino!"

Evie sat up suddenly, her face pulled into a grotesque and comical grin, "Have we got a new bimbo?"

"Not yet; coming, coming!" He bent and kissed her, "Bimbo's in a hurry; wants to see Little-Sam and Little-Womey."

Evie looked round everywhere, "Where, Taddy?"

"With Mother yet," Sam said tenderly.

He went to get up the boys. Ernie was out of bed like a shot and pulling his pajama pants off his feet. He looked interested and serious. He stopped with his day shirt half over his head, his two big eyes out like Brer Rabbit's from the mudhole, questioning Big Sam, at a noise from upstairs. But Big Sam did nothing, only put himself everywhere at once, on all sides of the mattresses. "Git-up, git-up," pulling and tugging at arms and legs, while the twins, not yet aware, groaned and muttered, "You get out, Erno, or I'll hit yer," and then at one moment shuttered up their eyes finally and gladly stared at Sam, back from Malaya and Manila.

"Daddy!" they both cried.

"Git-up, git-up!" he whispered joyously, mysteriously. They shot up and began prancing on their mattresses. The sun shone, but there was trouble above-stairs. Sam, however, instead of pulling a long face and slewing towards them woebegone eyes, was all merriment and gratulation, his eyes a playground for scores of dancing little twitching elvish smiles, here and there, come and gone; his tired, yellow, and flabby cheeks, flushed a little; his ugly bloodshot eyes, which had gone creased, half shut and Indian, in the tropical sun, squinting at them, leering at them, with every token of a good time to come.

"New bimbo," half whispered Sam, "new bimbo; get ready, get ready."

To Louie who appeared, hastily dressed, he said, laughing, "Get 'em dressed, Looloo."

Little-Sam stood up straight, his eyes and ears straining towards the stairs, as Louie knelt to fasten his sandals. The sun blushed on them all, banana yellow on the blonds and ginger on the brunets. They were all amazed and sober, examining the faces of Louie and Sam attentively. Sam was unconcerned. He smiled and, bending to kiss Evie, crooned, "Ming! Sedgewing! Smudgewing! Wat oo so sober fower? Wat oo ready to bust in two tears fower? Mummy get a new urchin, Daddy get a new shrimp, Evie get a new cradle kid, Tommo get a new brudder, Louie get a new somebuddy to make *wawa!*"

Evie raised her pansy kitten-face and pored over his lineaments, trying to make sense out of it all, trying to suck information out of him. He looked at her adoringly, and suddenly swung her up into his arms.

"My Little-Womey! Should have come to Malay with Poor-Sam to see all the—little brown, little bronze, little copper, little sulphur, little corn-cake, little waffle babbies; should have come to nurse all the little brown babbies; shouldn't have stayed so far away from her poor little Sam."

She threw back her head like Henny, and laughed provokingly, "But you wouldn't take me, you wouldn't take me!"

Three ringing cries came from the room upstairs, above the ceiling of the sunroom. Evie looked frightened. Sam's face changed. He plumped her on to the floor.

"Quick, quick, all hands on deck!"

He ran amongst them, behind them, marshaling them, like a sheep dog, to the bottom of the stairs, where they stood with charmed expectant faces raised towards the landing.

Sam began to chant rather low, bending over them, with his hands on shoulders, bunching them together,

Mother's got a lot, but she bought a new cot!
Daddy's got Sedgewing, but he's got a new Thing!
Louie's got another little Creaker to her string!

All the children laughed, a babble of little chuckles and crows, like a summer wave rearing on the shingle; but stopped, with their mouths open to listen, as Henrietta screamed wildly, hoarsely, such a cry as they never thought she could make: Louie turned startled eyes to Samuel, believing that she had gone mad. Evie started to cry. Sam grew solemn and held up his hand,

"Kids, I want you to listen: she's been crying all night; this is the end; soon you'll hear a new kind of cry. That will be the new baby. Listen, listen!"

The children strained their faces upwards listening. Sam said softly, "This is the first sunrise and the first day on earth for one of our family. See what time it is, Looloo."

It was six-thirty. When the baby's cry came, they could not pick it out, and Sam, eagerly thrusting his face amongst their ears, said, "Listen, there, there, that's the new baby." He was red with delight and success. They heard voices, and their mother groaning still, and then, quite free and separate, the long thin wailing, and the voices again.

"Six-forty-five," called Louie.

"Did you hear, Ming," he asked, "did you hear?"

"Yes, Taddy, I heard."

"What is it?" asked Tommy.

"The new baby, listen, the new baby."

"We heard," Saul announced, for the twins.

They were still there puzzled, but believing in him, so that they were convinced that a baby had in some miraculous way arrived by the roof; when, in the soft stir upstairs, they heard their mother's speaking voice and a man answering her.

"Who is there, Taddy?" Tommy asked.

"Go tell Bonnie," Sam commanded with a little satiric grin; for Bonnie, in tears and full of objections, had refused to be with them in their waiting and had gone off to the back porch to cool her feelings.

The next moment the door opened upstairs, and a strange, severe man came to the top of the stairs, surveyed them all with distaste and choler, and unkindly said to Sam, "Mrs. Pollit wishes to see you."

Sam instantly swarmed through his children, putting them aside with his hands, disengaged his long legs from the mass of little legs, and bounded up the stairs. The doctor disappeared. At the top of the flight, Sam stopped and, turning round to them, gave them a wide grin, a chuckle, and said softly,

"Wait and see, kids: wait and see!"

The door closed. They heard their parents' voices.

"Is it a baby?" inquired Little-Sam again, much surprised.

"Of course, silly; Daddy said," Evie corrected him. They had understood nothing at all, except that Mother had been angry and miserable and now she was still; this was a blessed relief. They began to scatter through the hall after Louie had forbidden them to follow

Sam upstairs. Suddenly Sam was at the bottom of the stairs again, flustered with a new love. He grabbed the twins by the shoulders and said excitedly, "Tribe, you have a new brother."

The children looked at each other. "What's his name?" inquired the twin Sam.

"He has no name," said big Sam comically, knowing how odd that seemed to them. "We got to give him a name. What'll we call him, kids?"

"Sam," said twin Saul promptly.

The rest of them, all but the twin Sam, laughed. They began to suggest names, calling the baby after friends at school and street friends; and then a strange, unpleasant woman who had flown in, in the night, came halfway down the stairs and said agreeably, "Mrs. Pollit wants to see Tommy."

The frightened Tommy made a step and hung back.

"Can I go? Can I go?" they all babbled.

"She said me," Tommy objected and made a slow progress to the stairs. But he refused the nurse's hand and looked sullen when she remarked with professional unction that he was a big boy now and had a little brother to look after.

"Charles Franklin," said big Sam, "that's what we'll call him probably, after Grandpa and after the President, the greatest man of our time, the Daniel of our days. May little Charles-Franklin grow up to be like him."

"And like Grandpa," Ernie remarked.

"Grandpa is all right, but Grandpa is Grandpa; Grandpa had a hard row to hoe when he was a young man; but you kids have advantages. Grandpa came to this country with nothing but a tin box with his clothes in, but Charles-Franklin is going to have a better chance, and this is a better age. Things have changed since your grandpa's day. Grandpa specially asked for the baby to be called after him; it's just a little sentimental matter, you see, kids: Grandpa's old; we can't refuse him." He nodded his head over them and sent them outside to play till Bonnie and Hazel got breakfast ready.

"What's your name?" asked Evie, playing "mothers" with the twins.

"Ippa-pa-tixit!" declared Saul. "Mr. Ippa-pa-tixit!"

"Mrs. Ippa-pa-tixit," corrected Evie. "You're Sam's mother. What's your name, Ernie?"

"Oh, shut up," said Ernie, measuring himself against pencil marks on the veranda post.

"You're a lady, too, no," said Evie, ignoring the obstreperous Ernie, her usual antagonist and claiming Little-Sam. "You're his new baby. Mother has a new baby, and the lady in there has a new baby. Her name's Mrs. Arkus.

"Who's Mrs. Arkus?"

"Mrs. Ahss," said Ernie. The boys laughed, Evie frowned.

"The lady in there with the white dress, the nurse," explained Evie. "I have a new baby; and Mother's name is Mrs.—I don't know."

"Ahss," said Ernie.

"Mrs. Curling Tongs," Saul suggested.

"Mrs. Garbage," said Ernie.

"Mrs. Curling Tongs: and Aunt Bonnie is Mrs.—what, Saul?"

"Mrs. Garbage," said Little-Sam.

"Mrs. Cabbage!" said Evie.

"Mrs. Cabbage is making a cup of tea for Mrs. Curling Tongs; and she will go up and see her new baby. And Mrs. Curling Tongs says, 'How is your new little baby, Mrs. Cabbage?'"

They went on playing quietly and waiting for Sam (who had gone back to the bedroom to seek Tommy) and for their turns to see Mother. Bonnie meanwhile, with a rueful expression, was leaning out the front window, and presently she could not help interrupting them, "Why is my name Mrs. Cabbage, why not Mrs. Garlic or Mrs. Horse Manure?" They did not hear her, so intent were they, visiting each other and inquiring after the health of their respective new babies. They did not hear her complaining to Louie that, instead of being Mrs. Grand Piano or Mrs. Stair Carpet, they called her Garbage, "Greta Garbage, Toni Toilet," said she, laughing sadly, "because they always see me out there with the garbage can and the wet mop; association in children's naive innocent minds, you see!"

"Oh, no, it isn't that," protested Louie, "Garbage is just a funny word: they associate you with singing and dancing and all those costumes you have in your trunk!"

"Do you think so?" Bonnie was tempted to believe. "Mrs. Strip Tease?"

Suddenly there was Sam racing madly up the slope and shouting,

"Gas, gas, I smell gas; Looloo, Bonniferous, GAS! Hazel! Ernie tell those dad-blamed women, GAS. All down the slope."

A breeze had arisen and trailed faintly through the house like a sick woman in a long dressing gown, and with it the odor of a blown-out jet, under the oatmeal. The sky was faintly greenish. The children had left their game and were wandering about over the buffalo-grass lawn, under the impression that, with Daddy's return and the now baby's advent, there would be no school. Breakfast would be in the back grass so that the house would be kept quiet. Meantime, the twins had gone up to see mother, but had been refused at the bedroom door; Mother was too tired to see anyone now; and back they came again, hand in hand, disconsolate because the new baby was invisible.

"Ma mither ca'd it God's pockit breeze," said Sam, for the thousandth time in their lives, in his imitation of a Scottish accent. "Ma graunmither useta caw me, Wee Saumy, coom ben the hoose; en she tawd me, 'Your mither, ma bonnie dochter Mary, hes muckle childer, but she hes ae ween ah luv en that's ma wee Saumy!'"

Thus Sam, in a sickly voice, reclining on the grass under the back porch, and he went on to other reminiscences of his babyhood, all in his idiom that he had from his grandmother, as he assured them, his grandmother being a stout and bonny woman afraid of no man, and his mother a stout, braw woman, though a bit bony, and very good and religious, but "no unco guid, but wi' a human hert." This morning reminded Sam of the dawn of life when, with the house full of monstrous brothers and sisters, he, the Benjamin, with an ailing mother, skipped about, peered, pondered on the mysteries of Nature, thinking the long, long thoughts of youth and discovering, by his lonesome, Nature's secrets; and he told how then and there, when his eyes were scarcely unsealed from babyhood's blissful ignorance, he fell in love with Nature and made up his mind never to leave her. So he hoped would they all, so little Charles-Franklin (that was to be) when he could toddle.

"It is never too soon to maunder and ponder," said Sam whimsically, "and there are few adults who give children, thoughtful children, that is, credit for the ideas they have. What is more promising than a wondering child? Preserve your wonder, kids! Lavoisier was a child once; Newton was once a child in arms; Joseph Henry once was no older than Charles-Franklin; Thomas A. Edison, that great man, once lay in his cradle and puked."

A few white clouds appeared in the sky, "It might be the childhood of a new Agassiz," said Sam.

"A gas, or a Gassy?" asked Ernie.

"Going to have a light westerly," said Sam.

The children began to skip, exhilarated by the new light and new air. Inside was a clacking of pot lids and cups. A flock of starlings flew overhead.

"Orchard oriole," shouted Ernie from the breast of the orchard slope, "Samulum, Sam-the-Bold!"

"Oh," cried Sam, with a great sigh, "boys, boys, I'm home: oh, what that means to me. You know how I love the great world; but how glad I am to be home with ma ain folk, no one will ever know."

He threw himself full length on the ground and grasped handfuls of new spring soft grass. "To Singapura to see many fat pigs; home again, home again, jiggity-jigs."

Suddenly he turned over sniffing the air loudly, "Gas, gas," he exploded, "Ernest-Paine, gas! Sawsam, run tell Looloo, gas!"

Ernest started to run towards the kitchen shouting, "Looloo, gas, Daddy says Agassiz." The smell of gas streamed out stronger. Sam started up and himself came to the kitchen window trying to crane in, "Gas, gas in the kitchen, tell Bonnie, Gas. Kids, tell them shemailes, gas." The four streamed after him, helter-skelter, laughing, shouting, "Gas, gas!" Suddenly Louisa put her head out of the kitchen window "Tea's ready."

"Gas," said Sam. "Hitting up the bills, eh? Friend of the gas company, eh? Here, Incorporated Friends and Allies of the Gas Co."

Louisa laughed, "It was too low under the oatmeal; it kept blowing out."

"Waste not, want not," said Sam. "Tea's ready, kids; Little-Womey (Big-Womey now), Mornin' tea! Syce, syce, tea!" He squirmed about looking for a nonexistent syce; then imitated, "Yes, tuan!" He called again to his syce, "Syce, *teh pagi-pagi!* [early morning tea]. "Ya, tuan!" He grinned at the children, who were just getting used to having their big comrade and shock brigader back with them, and he chattered suddenly at them, *"Hantar-kau barang barang saya ka-Raffles Hotel* [Send my things to the Raffles Hotel]." But as they could not understand him, they looked bored.

"Whenever I went into a little village, I rattled off a few phrases to get the boys and girls friendly," explained Sam. "No master, no white man bothers with their lingo, so they loved me for trying. When I saw a little puddle, I would say, 'Are there any crocodiles in there?' Then I would say, 'Panas-nya sangat terek' [The heat is terrible]. All the kids ran after me. Wait till I go through my bags. It will take Sam-the-Bold nine months to tell you all that happened to him; no, I can't tell you the tithe; but no matter, here you all are with open eyes, mouths, and ears and I can talk to you, thank God (who isn't), thank goodness and thank goo."

Then he began himself to hand out the tea to them, counting in Malay, *satu, dua, tiga, ampat*…and taught them to count the same.

"Now I am home again with my Malay little friends and home again in Tohoga," he said with a broad smile. Everything had to have its Malay name; and already he was beginning to slop over, drown them with his new knowledge, bubbling, gurgling as he poured into them as quickly as possible all he had learned. When the tea was finished, he got them to their feet, marshaled them in order of age, to walk round the garden and survey the animals with him, saying,

"Ermy-Paine [Ernie], Mouse-deer [Evie], Gemini-Seltsam [the twins], Bullhead [Tommy], all follow Tuan Pollit to the hanni-miles, left-right, left-right! Hayfoot, strawfoot!"

Then when he had them swaying in different directions, he serpentined them across the backyard patch towards the animal cages, singing, "In de mornin', in de foren'n, by de brightlight, you can hear dose darkies singing, in de foren'n." Then he gave their several whistles, making them answer; and he murmured in a weeping tone, "I used to whistle your whistles, kids, many mornings way back on the backwaters of Malaya, but you never answered; didn't you hear your poor Sam whistling to you across the waste of waters?"

He grinned and gave a jig, "Now I got to get a new whistle, one for Charles-Franklin (maybe)," and after a moment's thought, he began flutings until suddenly he heard the orchard oriole at the bottom of the slope warbling on its own; when he cried, "That's for me; the bird sends me its song and that will be Charles-Franklin's whistle," and he went through the whole range of whistles, adding last six sweet warbling notes which he now called "Charles-Franklin's whistle."

As they stood in front of the snake cage, he said anxiously, "Kids, last night I was dozing on Bonniferous's bed when Bonniferous was helping Mother, and I had my snake dream. Great snakes alive were crawling around da kitch [the kitchen] and out of one of my boxes jumped two beautiful young spotted cats, ocelots, *Felis pardalis*, which relieved me considduble, because they began to fight with the naiks [snakes], and then an ocelot with a snake curled round him and hissing at me tried to break through the netted back door here at me and I pushed with all my strength against them, crying out, but they gradually opened it, when I saw the door opened right on the city of Washington! There it was, with all its marbles like bones gleaming under me, and I hung on the edge of a precipice—it was the snake, or the bone yard!"

He laughed tiredly, "So, kidalonks, Fate is giving Poor-Sam yet another nest of enemies, for snakes mean enemies for Pollit. Fate loves me, kids, *or* she wouldn't give me so many hurdles to jump. Fate wants to put fight into me. Only I wish she wasn't quite such a worrying, devouring mother, sometimes."

Lowering his voice and looking towards the house, he said, "Kids, don't tell Mother, any time, or Bonniferous, but on the boat coming over I was so worried by silly Wiliets that at night I saw dragons round my bed," and he looked anxiously at the mansards of the house as it expected to see a Chinese dragon flying through the robin's-egg blue sky at him any minute.

Then, mildly, he told them that poor Old David was dead at this minute, lying, waiting for his funeral, but it meant nothing, no more than when poor Vulpecula, the Australian opossum, died; and soon Old David would be in the fermenting, jolly ground. Daffy-downdillies [daffodils] would spring from the soil, the fresh winds would blow through the daffodils that were Old David and spread all that was mortal of Old David through the airs: "And there wasn't nuffin that was immortal in Old David," said Sam kindly, "only the love you have for him in your little beating hearts, for that's the only immortality we can have, loves; just as I have a little immortality already way over there in Singapore, in the heart of Law Chew Teng, my wonderful Chinese friend, the curio dealer—he gave me a queer present all right, a Chinese coffin, all carved—it's considered a treasure; and it's coming on after me; and then I have immortality in the breast of Mohammed bin Hassan, a Malay friend and his little boy, Ali, and in the breast of Lai Wan Hoe and others; and poor little Sam has achieved this little speck of immortality because he loves his fellow man. You do the same, kids. Now you see until the day you die, Old David is living in your hearts and memories; and perhaps longer, for you will tell your children, when you have them, about dear Old David."

Then he got them to sing a little song for dear Old David, the little ditty that their grandfather would always sing to them, *Always Merry and Bright!* Thus old David Collyer's painful and, for them, disastrous death passed over in a minute, like the death of a gnat or bee, less than the miserable, straggle-feathered death of some poor little bird in the long grasses of the White Field.

Sam worked hard, but he could not conceal from them that the distant and authoritarian Sam who had come home was not quite the lighthearted Sam that had gone away; he was harsher, and a European, he had the germ power, in his brain. At breakfast they had the nurse, Miss Putnam, with them; she was a bony-faced, bright-eyed woman, with long, irregular brows that jigged questioningly. She asked, with a sort of grace, "Mr. Pollit, will you pour me some more coffee, please?" too unctuous perhaps, for Sam, rising and pushing the electric coffeepot in her direction, turned his back and said rudely, "Pour for yourself, Nurse Putnam!" Everyone felt most uneasy. But not Sam. He went out into the hall and grumbled to Bonnie,

"I don't want any maternity nurse vamping me; let her try her

charms on Dr. Rock. If I'd had my way, Louie would have helped
Pet this time, as I intended. How better can a woman-child get her
apprenticeship than helping an older woman?"

"Samuel," cried Bonnie, "you are joking."

"In Malaya, full of little bouncing healthy brown babies, the
adolescent girls help their mothers in the villages: I don't want a soft,
effete generation of women. If it hadn't been for Pet's darnfool belief
in doctors and all the other civilized superstition, I shouldn't have
had a doctor at all. Pet herself knows better than any doctor when it is
coming; and her girls are little women. It's all tomfoolery, this idea of
a medicine man with a degree. I detest all degrees. It's antidemocratic:
a way of separating the monastic, university type from everyday
life. I want my girls to be like those sweet brown women of the East.
Their girls are beauties, better than mine because they are women."

Bonnie, carrying in another serving of toast, after having studied
him for a minute, said briefly, "You don't know what you're talking
about," and sprang into the long dining room with a high color. She
bent officiously over the flustered nurse, saying, "My brother has all
his own ideas; don't take any notice, Nurse."

But the nurse, a good-natured, foal-faced girl who always put
her foot in it (as Bonnie later explained), after some mild laughing,
said, "But I do know a man who made his eldest daughter do that;
and she married very young; she had a son at eighteen years old. It
didn't stop her at all. Isn't that funny?"

Bonnie sat biting her lip and trying to nod the careless nurse
towards the listening children; finally she said stiffly, "Well, please
don't tell my brother; or he'll take your word for it. That kid knows
enough already; she had enough trouble," and she motioned
towards Louisa, who was just returning flushed from viewing the
new baby. She burst out without noticing anybody,

"The new baby's going to be called Albert-Charles, Mother says."

They all turned to her.

"Charles-Franklin," cried Sam appearing, where he had been lurking, at the southern door of the long dining room. "My Benjamin will be called Franklin, and I should put in Phoebus Apollo if I wanted to imitate those silly old Dagos what thought our beloved old Sol was a young man, a good-looker too; he was born at morning-rise, and I have just been giving him a serenade outside his window, not that he hears it yet. Morning is sacred; all great ideas are born in the morning or at midnight's starry clang. I have thoughts in the morning, in the new-time, in the dewtime, that I don't have the rest of the day. Most poicks [poets] write poems about sunset and that's jes why I don't read no poickry; poicks don't love nature enough to get up early. In the morning everyone is the same age, father and child, Ming-Sedgewing and Bullhead and Loogoobrious Looloo and Dad-the-Bold-Tuan-Pollit too are all the same age; yes, even Looloo here what has the burdens of the world on her shoulders, which is only right because she makes the poor old world heavier herself, and even Nurse Putnam and Bonniferous are all the same age in the morning."

"Then we're all just born," cried Evie, astonished.

"Charles-Franklin didn't get up yet, so he's old," declared Little-Sam grinning.

"Looloo never gets up early in the morning," piped Saul maddeningly, thinking thereby to earn approval.

Sam said wearily, "Kids, no sarcasm please; sarcasm is akin to hate. More coffee, Sedgewing! Get your little Paternal *subbor cawf* [some more coffee]. *Kop kopi, syce.*"

He surveyed them all, but refrained from criticizing them for various disorders he saw in them, bad manners, grins, wasteful habits. He could not conceal for a moment that he was grown a more serious man; his jokes and comic names rolled rustily off his tongue.

"I want you to listen to an idea I had today while your little brother was being born. The laws of nature are few, and she follows them inevitably; she obeys her own laws. She can't help it. The law of nature which the plant, the family, and the universe follows is expansion, growth, sometimes growth by transmutation, sometimes by acquisition."

"What about death?" asked Louie.

"Death is only transmutation. Now I believe that the universe, our universe is the same. I believe in the expanding universe, and you will find as time goes on, that great men will prove that it is so. I pick these ideas out of the air, and yet, I have proof too for all things go by analogy. That's the Mark Twain new-world spirit; horse sense and close analogy.

"Perhaps as Looloo says, it sometimes expands and sometimes contracts, for death is only recession, just as our minds do, the tide does, metals do and our fortunes do, going from richness to richness and understanding to understanding, just as the life of man does, following the law of progress.

"These things are not mystic, they follow an inexorable law. Remember my words!"

"How do you know?" asked Louie.

"When you get older and wiser," he said, "you will know your dad was always right. I make it rain, don't I, kids?"

"Yes," they said eagerly.

"When I say, 'Sun, you can shine!' doesn't it shine?"

"Yes, yes," they chorused joyfully.

"And when I say, 'Rain, you kin rain half an hour and then stop,' don't it obey me?"

"Yes."

"But Looloo thinks I don't know nuffin; Looloo only thinks of hummilatin [humiliating] her wise father."

"You don't make it rain," said Louie. The children, much interested, looked from one to the other. Sam, looking to them, saw the hesitation.

"Kids?" he inquired reproachfully.

"No, you don't," cried Ernie at once.

"Don't I, Little-Womey?"

Puzzled, she looked at the three older faces, "I dunno!"

Sam went to the window, studied the sky carefully for a while, then went out into the back yard. After feeling the air, he came in solemnly and said, "Because I have a lot of mean kids around, I just went out and told it it could rain tomorrow morning or this evening at the earliest."

Little-Womey looked scared, thinking about her own incredulity. Louie laughed, "You're just faking. You know it's going to rain, perhaps."

"The sun draws up the water, the water makes clouds and when they reach an icy layer the water is precipitated," Ernie explained. "The teacher told us, the teacher told us."

"How could you have the rainfall chart behind the door, if you could make it rain any time?" Louie said. Sam grinned self-consciously at this; but he would not give in, and to crush the influence of his two older children who had reached the age of dissent, he wickedly seized a large blowfly which he had been watching on the tablecloth for some time and putting it between finger and thumb flipped it at his elder daughter. It hit her on the nose. The children turned red with laughter. Louie gave him a glance of scorn and saying nothing, dug her nose into her glass of milk. Her father was now laughing, and singing, "Longnose Bluebeak, bluebeak Loobeck: why don't you laugh, Looloo: bluestocking Looloo got hit by a blowbloo!" Little-Sam, holding his belly, rolled backwards and forwards on the grass, yelling with laughter. Louie sat quite still, and this new sort of behavior calmed the children sooner than Sam expected.

Sam became solemn at once, "By smiling, we turn devils into angels, enemies into friends; the cup of poison becomes the loving cup."

"I have no enemies," declared Louie sternly.

"One day you will get to know the world better," said Sam, still unable to forgive the skeptic of his blood.

"I know something," said Louie, "I know there are people not like us, not muddleheaded like us, better than us."

"What do you mean?"

"But I know something else: if it is chaos, it will not be chaos forever: 'out of chaos ye shall give birth to a dancing star!' Nietzsche said that."

Sam blushed, and he said gently, "You mean, out of confusion we will bring order."

"No," cried Louie, "no, no; you understand nothing. People like us understand nothing. I know people at school better than us, better in their minds than—" she stopped in deep embarrassment. The children were following her intently, trying to understand what she had found out, something they were dimly groping for.

"All right, Looloo," said Sam gently, "all right. All right."

Five minutes later he was singing them some more of his saga, as he fixed a red silk Chinese pajama suit on Evie and wound a sarong over her head and shoulders.

"Little *perempuan Melayu, Singapura punya*, sitting under an umbrella selling Eastern candies, black eyes moist as the antelope, oval copper face, full wide lips, my Little-Womey, Little Malay beauty!" and he sang to each of them as he busied himself with them, dressing them up in all the wonderful scarves, sarongs, a Kelantan shawl of woven silk with body of royal yellow and ends of Malay red and orange; a sarong batek made in Java of dyed cotton, blue with center bister and white; a handkerchief of Malay-red silk interwoven with gold thread, the center brocaded in heliotrope and yellow; a blue and gold silk sarong from Trengganu; and beautiful strange clothing that he had picked up wherever he went, for his women at home, for Henrietta, Louisa and Evelyn, getting to be a woman lover in the land of wealth, beauty, and color, promising himself, who had despised all sensual things, a future madness of material beauties.

Short of the old family plate he had acquired on his marriage with Henny and the wedding presents, he had had none of this world's goods and despised them with puritan alarm and scoffing; but the moment he set foot on the age-old shores of the East, where no one respected his new Western morality, he easily let slip this hardness and came out for every glorious profusion of art in artisanship that was possible to his purse or persuasive powers. He had learned to smile, beg, and collect, largely take the largesse of his friends. "My smile brings it to me," he would say contentedly, and, "They know I love them."

Mrs. Smith, from Volta Place, came to the open front door to inquire about Henrietta. Sam, who thought her a fine, upstanding woman, was delighted to bring her in and show her his treasures, which still lay in profusion in several rooms. Then the White boys came shyly ("How big you've got to be!" called Sam), with a message from their mother about Henrietta. What with the new baby and the splendors from Malaya, it was a morning of satisfactions. Sam could see, himself, that his return was considered a great event in the neighborhood. Resting on the settee, on a billow of silks and cottons, with his head on his clasped hands, he dropped a tear over the passing of Old David Collyer and began to imagine his own future now. Tohoga House would be his own, and there might be a quarterly allowance for Henrietta, or one or other of the children, from the estate.

"These are sordid considerations," he said to himself; but with the sun and fresh wind and the kindness of the climate, so different from all his Malayan mornings, he could not help being cheerful. Soon the nurse came down, smiling, and said Sam was to go up to see Mrs. Pollit, and carrying in his hand a pair of tiny red silk pajamas that he had brought specially for the baby and an exquisite little wreath of artificial orange flowers (he had hoped for a baby girl) that he now intended for Henny's dark hair, the happy father went upstairs. The new baby had hair of an almost invisible blond.

"Seventh child of a seventh child," said Sam, grinning at the nurse.

"Born with a caul," said the nurse, grinning at Sam.

When Sam went down, he telephoned his little prig of a brother-in-law, Archie Lessinum, to announce the birth to the family and to make arrangements about the funeral.

4 *The wheel turns.*

David Collyber was no better than other millionaires: when he died, his estate was scandalously less than anyone had supposed; and in fact, since Old David loved children too much, and had too many, and treated them too well, when he found out that their characters were weak all, he left even less than anyone could have predicted by any skimping of a mean imagination. Rather he left something very great—a great hole in his credit that it would take his executors a number of years to fill in. Monocacy, Tohoga House, a great stretch of still unsettled land along Cold Spring Lane, a row of white-stepped houses in South Baltimore, a house of dubious reputation (that is, certain reputation for evil) in Highlandtown, and all his shares and bonds were to be sold; and a certain amount of money was to be put back into the business. This part of the business alone would remain to pay small quarterly dividends to the sick, sallow, and financially suffering members of the great Collyer brood. Old Ellen received nothing but a small cottage in which to spend her last days with Barry.

Sam Pollit came home from the reading of the will with drooping shoulders. Nothing else since the death of his first wife

Rachel had been able to affect his long-legged gay walk and the straightness of his backbone. It seemed to him, at moments, that this was nothing but a dream, that Old David could not have died so inconsequentially as to leave his youngest, spendthrift daughter penniless in a cold world, without a shoe or shell to house her children. This house, now named Tohoga Place, that he had painted and carpentered, where he had built his rockeries and all his dreams of the future, had to go under the hammer. It was not marketable as it was; would, at last, be cut up for a row of unhealthy, elbowing houses like those already spawned along one side of it. Sam did not know where they would go. He supposed he would have to join the great number of commuters who came in from Virginia every day, and settle in some ugly new bureaucrats' suburb without trees, with new-turned clay and garages lumbering along the landscape; live in some modern bungalow with a Dirty Jack on one side, and a Ratty-Matty on the other, himself indistinguishable from the crowd of public servants and their newfangled offspring. He felt bruised. He had always believed that he was the favorite son-in-law of Old David and that Old David liked him better than his own boys, because of his struggles.

Henny was still in bed, looking wasted, her eyes were red. Her hair was pulled back and plaited in two tails.

"I was there," said Sam.

Henny's black eyes searched his face bitterly, but it was not bitterness because of him, but because of all the blows she could feel were coming, from the family and from the world. She had been through the pains of death, and she felt that she did not care whether she ever saw outer air again or not. Many times that day she wished she had been buried with her poor "beau of the nineties," her gay, kindhearted father who had ruined her life by spoiling her so.

"Well," she said, after a sigh, "well, I suppose it's bad news, or you'd tell it to me. He was broke, of course."

"Yes. I'm afraid Old David was in deeper than we dreamed. Your mother is to have the cottage." He stopped, knowing that she would understand a great deal from this. But she flashed an angry look at him and cried,

"What? He didn't leave me the house? What are we to do with all those children? He came at a nice time," and she nodded at the new boy, "A caul and he brings nice luck to us. Poor Old David, poor Dad: with his fine air, and his flighting and floating, and his keeping fifteen homes going, I might have known. I *did* know! But everyone's too much of a darn coward to look out for himself. I knew! Why didn't I go and see him oftener before he took so ill?" She gave Sam a blue look. "I did go: but he was too ill. Before he lived with his woman. He put me off. Archie wouldn't tell me. He knew! Why didn't he tell me?"

Sam sat with his hands hanging loosely between his legs. "It's a blow, and no mistake. We've got two months to get out."

"I'd like to be able to do something to that man," said Henny, referring to Archie Lessinum. " 'The law is a divinity above justice even'! Dad was just bewitched by him. He gave him his own way in everything. He gave him Eleanor, made him executor. And he used to go round making great calf eyes at me and saying he was a mystic and the law was almost a mystic idea. I said, 'How interesting!' And here I sit now with seven children in rags, while there he sits with the mystic idea of Dad's estate in his hands."

"What's the good of this?" asked Sam pathetically. "This is sordid. Don't think about it now, Henny: wait till you're up. Meanwhile I'll look about for a house." On the mantelpiece stood the little wreath of orange flowers. He took it up absent-mindedly and said, after fingering it for a while, sighing, "I'll try this on Little-Womey's hair. It was for a little bride of fourteen; but I got the man to give it to me." He had forgotten that he had taken it as a childbed present to Henny. She watched him depart with it, with a bitter look, but said nothing.

Sam told Louie first, trailing out his misery, then Ernie, and then took the three little boys away down to the snake cages and told them they had to leave those slopes and gardens bursting up into a new spring. They were to be sold: other children would have the right to be there. One by one, the children became subdued, all except Little-Womey, who, with the orange wreath in her hair, was running to all her friends, the neighbors, showing off her beauty, with her soft deer eyes running over with mirth and excitement, while she told them they were all going away from Tohoga House and going to live in Virginia. By ten o'clock the next morning everyone knew it who knew Sam, and the Department was full of excitement. So he got nothing out of the old man at the last: so he had sold out for the fleshpots of Egypt and in the pots was nothing but dandelion salad. So Old Softsoap wasn't going from triumph to triumph; and one evil young man got up a story that it was very queer, Sam had been away from home ten months and yet he arrived home to the birth of a new son, oh, entirely in order, the result of a queer gynecological condition. Although it was a lie, everyone was delighted and by nightfall, instead of its being a joke and a tall story, it had become a bit of truthful scandal, the low-down on the private life of a social and service climber, a grinning Pharisee and rich man's pet. Twenty-four hours before, Sam had been the rising star of the service and now people skipped from desk to desk laughing about him and saying that he was a sneak, milksop, and goody-goody. Sam, for all his credo of the firm handclasp and frank smile, had made a sufficiency of enemies for all sorts of reasons—little enemies, people beneath him in grade and fortune, people he had never troubled to conciliate because they were mean. He had refused to consider religious partisanship or join any fraternities, "no phratries," he said contemptuously, and he had joined gaily, frequently, and with the naïvest faith in his luck, in all sorts of foolish campaigns against minor bureaucrats, sprinkling his talk with their insulting nicknames.

Then, when he was absent in Malaya, his rivals and enemies had a chance to work against him, and it could have been argued (it was argued) that Sam had deserted his official post for a floating, indefinable job and that he had excellent prospects anyhow, anywhere, so why need he get back his old job in the Department? To cap it all came the shoals of complaints from Colonel Willets in Singapore. He sat in the Raffles Hotel, or in some bungalow where he was a guest, and wrote or dictated journals and letters, full of complaints about everyone but chiefly about that snake charmer and departmental meteor, Mr. Samuel Clemens Pollit. "He arrogated every honor to himself, he went out of his way to push into official circles, he sucked up to English officialdom, he was always holding an umbrella for some lady; he did what he could to oust Colonel Willets and ingratiate himself with foreign governments, he applied for jobs in foreign (Chinese) universities, he ran round with members of the Kuomintang and abetted absconding clerks." There was nothing that Colonel Willets did not know, in his spite: his correspondence with Washington made a wonderful Eastern romance of intrigue and hate. But Colonel Willets did not despise influence, nor lobbyists, nor Senators: he had a few of them in his sleeve, as he occasionally remarked to a select audience. When, by good luck, the great pillar of Sam's career, David Collyer, brother of the railroad millionaire, Bradford Collyer, died in debt, Colonel Willets decided to get rid of the irritating young man. He had no very good reason for it; Psalm-singing Sam (he called him this very unfairly) simply got under his skin. Sam ridiculed him. Sam offered him the hand of friendship when Colonel Willets would have been glad of a punch in the nose; he smiled at him when Colonel Willets wanted a row; he defied him pleasantly but firmly to ever put an obstacle in his brilliant career. Sam could go back to the strange yellow and brown men that he seemed to like the smell of so much, said Willets.

Washington papers were full of the return of the Expedition and the report being presented by Colonel Willard Willets. Other members of the Expedition were mentioned, including Samuel Pollit, originally of the Bureau of Fisheries and organizer and now head of the Conservation Bureau; and it was hinted (much to Sam's surprise) that Sam now might move to another sphere of activities. As the Conservation Bureau was Sam's beloved child, and yet coveted by numerous others who considered themselves better qualified than he, this unexpected paragraph in the *Post* gave him a sinking feeling; and he began harking back to the dreams of snakes he had had since his return home. "Shoals ahead," said Sam in a midday conference with his old friend Saul Pilgrim, "but I am on deck, they won't torpedo me. This is Crabby Willets' doing. Residents of Virginia and Maryland are allowed to crab in the Potomac, not in the Bureau."

But the local papers, being hungry at that moment for some juicy departmental scandal, seized on the romantic story of Sam, and with a show of spicy amiability told all, with that display of intuition and penetration of character told tersely, which is common in the world's journalist capital, that city from which (it is the proud boast) half a million words are telegraphed daily. Everyone kicked Sam about, had his opinion about Sam, including the respectable breakfasters in the S. & W. cafeteria, star-spangled visitors to the Occidental and eaters beneath its senator-ribanded walls, fish devourers in O'Donnell's, perpetual peaceful roomers of Franklin Square, and such lions as got to the zoo. Sam was daily accused of inefficiency, of bureaucracy, of pusillanimity; even malversation was hinted at. Sam's fair face became clouded, became scarlet, became pale: he ran from friend to chief, and ran into those he knew to be his enemies as often as possible, going up to them in corridors, holding out his hand, asking them why they pursued him, speaking to them of government service and charity, humanity, the service of the people: "A public office is a public trust." To a certain extent these tactics succeeded in that he embarrassed his enemies dreadfully, and they ran away from him, hiding their faces under hat brims and their necks under coat collars. They crossed the street from him and changed their routes to the office. But nothing stopped the log that was rolling towards his neck. As soon as Sam saw how badly it all was going and that those he called "the people of evil, the enemies of the commonweal, those in whom the devil, that wicked idea of our ancestors, was in a sort incarnate," were getting the upper hand for the moment, and heard with great wrath but great helplessness, that his suspension was hinted at, pending inquiry, he went to his brother-in-law and asked him to arrange to postpone the sale of Tohoga House for a few months till things were decided. Archie Lessinum, gravely kindhearted, now that handsome Sam Pollit was rolling in the mud, agreed to do this; and Sam, instead of looking for a house in Virginia, began to think of his prospects in his natal soil of Baltimore. Solicitous friends in the Department, amongst whom was the malicious, gleeful, but somewhat paternal J. Cappie Larbalestier, were warning Sam that his days were numbered.

"I am innocent," cried Sam, "my record is spotless; I am an exemplary officer. I defy them to pin any scandal of any sort on me."

"They will ease you out if they can," said the younger Brownell, who had become very friendly with this man under a cloud. But Sam saw in the younger Brownell an agent of evil and the spokesman of his enemies. Now nobody hesitated to take Sam aside and, with a frank pat on the back, tell him the sober truth; his faults had been such and such; so and so was a worm digging into his back, and since poor old David Collyer died, of course he was without his best support. Sam came nearer to knocking a confrere down than ever before whenever this last remark was made, for it was Sam's boast that he had had no support in all his life but had hewn his way through the granite of official indifference and public ignorance.

"Alone I did it," would he say. "God helps those who help themselves," and, "All things work together for the good of them who love the Lord," but by "the Lord" he only meant an obscure creature of his imagination, possibly "the Public Good," or even just his own will.

Things were blacker for Sam every day and, with his heart sounding hourly in bitter, secret oceans of misery, Sam faced something he had never conceived of in all his life—the triumph of calumny. He would go about repeating to his friends and children, "Truth crushed to earth shall rise again, the eternal years of God are hers," but the traitor thought crept in every day, as a mouse through a rotting door, that he had not before him the eternal years of God, but only a few of human fame. He suppressed these thoughts and resolved never to blacken his hands with the pitch being poured around him, and to try to tread the path of goodness, smile at his enemies, and proceed exactly as if nothing had happened. He would not seek partisans, not enter at the head of a flock of witnesses, only tell the plain truth: plain truth would shine through in beauty, more dazzling for the black or bedizened lies that "the evil ones" brought in. Sam gave one or two sober interviews, and refused to write to the papers to answer indignant letters from persons both official and private who seemed deeply stirred over his ways and personality.

"You are doomed with this air of Christian martyrdom," cried Saul Pilgrim wrathfully and humorously. His square-set, big-nosed face, a clownish variant on Sam's own, had long, lugubrious, creased cheeks, which came from his having been an intimate acquaintance of defeat since his boyhood. But Sam would just as wrathfully, and not at all humorously, reply that he had no churchly reek, he was merely acting for the right, and that the good would win, it must win.

"Suppose it does not win?" asked Saul. "You see, Sam, you call me a cynic; but I am a creator, I am a God myself. Here is a little world I have made up and in it beings: for years I have struggled to make the good triumph, but it is still a drawn battle."

In this way Saul referred to his serial story, *When the Day Comes,* which appeared in a little Alexandria advertising paper Saul had published himself, for the last seventeen years. *When the Day Comes* had begun, Chapter One, of Part One, in the very first edition of the paper seventeen years back, and this serial, the only serial at all competitive with the serial of the sun, was not yet finished, for the simple reason that the paper was still running. Saul had never been able to bring himself to botch up a happy, but improbable ending, yet could not resign himself to unpopularity with a sad ending, and hence had gone on adding incident to incident, hoping the problem would solve itself accidentally.

"It is just like life," Saul would think to himself, in surprise, as he considered the latest chapter of *When the Day Comes.* So he was in a position to look at Sam's fix in a resigned and human way. He admired Sam for his glorious, messianic belief in himself, the world, and other people, and wished he had this temperament; but he now felt impelled to tell Sam some of the truths of life, just as if Sam had been one of his characters.

"Saul," said Sam, "what I am telling you may sound weak and willful, but it is not so: it is the innermost heart of my belief in myself and human nature. My silly Louie has written a motto on a piece of paper and stuck it on the side of her bookcase, 'By my faith and hope I conjure thee, throw not away the hero in thy soul.' In that, at least, she shows the power, the strength, and the glory of her poor Sam. She is beginning to see the light. But that is not what I wanted to say, my dear old Saul. There is a faith men live by; I have it in me. I cannot sully it by entering the forum of public debate, much as I believe that all things in the republic should be aired in the public eye. Yes, Saul, even aliens, people of a strange culture, feel this entity in me. Naden bin Tahir, my Indian secretary, asked me if I believed in my white God. 'No,' said I, 'friend; I do not need a God for I believe in ultimate good.' 'Tuan,' he said (though I told him many times I was no master but the servant of the people), 'I am surprised at this, for you are one of the Heaven-born.' 'No, brother,' I replied, 'I am a humble man who loves his fellow man.' 'I am sure, sir,' said my faithful black friend, 'that you will go to heaven. God is coming to earth soon,' said Naden, 'everyone can see it by the troubles that are going on. When he comes, wherever you are, sir,' he said, 'he will take you up in the hollow of his hand and place you on a celestial carpet near his own.' 'Oh, Naden,' said I, 'I would ask the Lord at Judgment Day to leave a little bit of my own earth and make me forever mortal on it; then under a great green-headed native elm I would sit and watch the little mortal birds. I do not want to go to heaven; I want my children, forever children, and other children, stalwart adults, and a good, happy wife, that is all I ask, but not paradise; earth is enough for me: it is because I believe earth is heaven, Naden, that I can overcome all my troubles and face down my enemies.' That is what I said to him, Saul: and to this poor black civil servant with nothing but a mean ambition and a superstitious belief in the immediate coming of some cruel Jehovah, I told what I really believe. This is God's footstool, my dear good mother used to say: and if it were really so, I should be glad to live forever by the little toe of God."

"Sam," said Saul fervently, "when you talk, you know you create a world. I live in a wonderful illusion: especially when we take walks at night, I can hardly believe in the workaday world! I can even hardly believe it is you talking: you have such wonderful faith."

"Faith," said Sam, "yes, I have faith: that is the great gift my dear good mother gave me: faith in the good."

"But why does faith prevent you from answering the charges made against you?" asked Saul.

"Who touches pitch is defiled," said Sam.

"You will lose everything, Sam: position, salary, pension. What about your children?"

"I'll never answer such wicked charges," Sam declared, scarlet with indignation, "and if my children have to live in utmost poverty, let them do what I have done. 'Sweet are the uses of adversity, which like a toad ugly and venomous, still has a precious jewel in its head,' said silly old Broadway Willy Shakespeare. I don't go much by what poets say, but he was a man, he had his reverses, as his verses sometimes show."

Saul laughed heartily, cast a sidelong glance at his intimate, but said nothing on this head.

Chapter Eight

1 *Tohoga to Spa.*

Strangers began to drive white surveyors' pegs into the children's own gardens at Tohoga House, and everyone was glad to go. Sam had been scouting round the district for weeks, looking for a suitable nest for his young ones. He could not bring himself (considering his dubious prospects, too) to rent or buy a house in the ugly new dormitory districts used by Washingtonians, expensive and inconvenient, and now that the Collyer glory had faded, he yearned to go home, back to the old-fashioned, heterogeneous views at the head of the Chesapeake tidewater country. Baltimore has many exiles, as near as Washington, as far as Heidelberg, who never cease reviling their native town with soft-tongued, exquisite scurrility, whose hunger to be away from Baltimore and obsession with the town create an appetite for Baltimore in the stranger. Baltimore is multifarious; has the attractive dirt of a fishing town, the nightmare horizons of a great industrial town; it is very old, sordid, traditional, and proud. It despises no sort of traffic that can be conceived of; it is not fanatical; it has a self-sufficiency as towns of old Europe, even in the hideous yellow waste bays full of abandoned shacks, the mazy sameness of its mean, white-stepped streets, its traffic in pleasures both respectable and disreputable. It is at the head of an inland sea and stands between natural sea-level parks and thick-wooded hills. It does not imprison. Nature has no states' rights in Maryland. Baltimore sees the meeting of two cultures of man, Northern and Southern. There mingle from the south-eastern sands to the Appalachian crests two regions of trees and plants, and two of birds and fish. Sam loved his state with passion. Released from what he dimly saw had been a bondage to the Collyer idea of financial success, Sam with love and longing had hurried round the residentials of Baltimore during the past few weeks, until he found a real home for his children. For him no apartments, no town slums and modern jerry-builts. He had resolved that even if he went back to his own old position as a Deputy Commissioner of the Conservation Bureau (and he was sick of it), he would motor to Washington every day, a matter of fifty minutes perhaps, and bring his children up on this waterside, where he had fished for gudgeon as a child.

Henny refused to take any interest in the house-hunting, only saying bitterly that she hoped he wasn't going to plank her down in rotten old Baltimore right next to some flossy friend of her schooldays who had done a million times better than she had. Henny still had some belief in Sam's abilities and his way of getting away with it, as she put it, but she saw bursting out in him a hothouse flower of idealism that he had kept in bud during Collyer's lifetime. He had conceived, since his Pacific trip, a gigantic plan. He had every hope of being appointed one of the American members of the International Pacific Salmon Fisheries Commission in a few months and he had views which he much regretted not being able to put before the whaling conference in London in June. Beyond that was the four-day September meeting of the North American Council, and conferences of other bodies to follow.

Sam, a great partisan of the Roosevelt works plans because of the work done in fish and forestry conservation by the W.P.A. and C.C.C. workers (hatcheries in North Carolina, Massachusetts, West Virginia, Pennsylvania, Indiana, Texas, and elsewhere), and seeing with pleasure new works being acquired from several states and placed under the surveillance or control of Federal bureaus, saw in President Roosevelt the first great socialist ruler, greater and more answerable than any European chief because serving so short a term. He favored a bureaucratic state socialism with the widest possible powers and a permanent staff, a bureaucracy intricately engineered, which would gradually engulf all the powers great and small of what Sam called, with a tinge of elegance, "govam'nt." But states having rights, the relations of states and the Federal Government must be negotiated by Interstate Commissions with their Commissioners, both full and deputy, attached. Sam had in his head this plan for the knitting together of all the state and Federal conservation services, eventually to be made into an immense North American Conference, which would foreshadow the All-American Republic; and on top of this an International Conservation League of Nations which, by regulating supplies and conserving instead of wasting, would prevent wars and feed all people.

This plan, with an infinity of councils, subcouncils, and town meetings, Sam had got down on paper before he left. He hoped it would have borne fruit in his absence; and within a year or two he hoped to be named, with others, to this Supreme Conservation Council. Roosevelt, loved of "the people," could do all. Sam believed that it was opposition to this grand socialist plan which was fermenting in the Department; and to his proposition that a quarter of a million dollars should be the petty cash at first allocated to the new branch of Federal Government therein proposed. In his mind's eye he saw internations within internations; and overnations over nations, all separate functions of Federal Government rising to one crest of supreme judgment, sitting in a room; all glass, no doubt, with windows on the world; each power of government to be independent, though interdependent. Sam had numerous codicils to add to his great scheme, after his taste of Imperial Government, not that he admired it—he thought the American system far more modern—but he liked the word *farflung*, the farflung bournes of conservation, and *public necessity's eminent domain*. Sam was a vague eclectic socialist, and some of the things he wrote were far more horrifying to his friends than he understood; not to mention that he went about proclaiming fair play in opinion and saying that there was some good, no doubt, in the U.S.S.R.'s system as well as holiness in the ideas of Confucius.

"I wish I could go to jail for my ideas," he said more than once, in a burst of fervor, "and then scoffers—there are scoffers even at my patent sincerity—would see how deeply I feel these ideas."

Sam with all this behind him, then, did not feel as anxious as his friends about the present attack on him: it was the rotten fabric woven by evil, the overnight sham bulwarks of enemies of the people; it would burn to ash at the match of truth. Besides Sam had powerful friends who loved the truth.

Some of this, indeed, all of this, he was able to tell the children while the old Pollit sedan was passing out of Washington and into the wooded areas on the road to Annapolis. But when they reached the richer part of the wooded road, he broke off and began to talk to them about the Free State of Maryland which would from now on be their home, how it was the first, finest, richest of the states and that with the most vision, how its foreshores had remained untouched because the pikes had had to go far inland to avoid the marshes and watercourses. No sight on earth was like the moonlight on the Choptank, and he made a great many other remarks which proved that it was only after a strict examination of all the other states in the Union, he had impartially chosen the Free State to be born in. Then he sang them a song of the trees of his home state, the oaks, red oak, scarlet oak, black oak, white oak, water oak and willow oak, shingle oak and post oak, mosscup oak and overcup oak, rock oak and swamp oak and all the others, elms, maples, hickories, dogwoods, persimmons, and pines, from Rising Sun to Snow Hill, Port Tobacco to Port Deposit, Liberty Town to Bohemia Manor, Fox

Hill Levels to Deep Creek Lake, Spaniard's Neck to Indian Head, Love Point to West Friendship, Cole to The Bunker, Governor's Run to Cover, Humphrey to Pumphrey and Beaver Dam to Bivalve and a great many more which he had worked up into a recitative for them months and years ago, showing them the map and teaching them the counties. When they came into Anne Arundel county, he began to show them the soils and trees of the county that would be their future home and expressed a hope that in a very short time they would beat him at distinguishing every natural feature, because they were boys at liberty to roam and he was their busy father, earning bread and lemonade for them all.

To all of this Henny, her weary face a little softened by the fresh summer air, said nothing, but held the baby in her lap and sometimes hushed one of the boys who shrieked too loudly.

But as they went along, nothing could bottle up their effervescence, and every half minute one of them asked, "Are we nearly there?" "What's the house like?" "When will the animals get there?" and "Is the first van of furniture there yet?" Sam meanwhile being very happy to answer each and all of the questions and not even once rebuking or frowning at any of his little citizens. The sun sizzled, the birds sang, they saw two baby rabbits foolishly sitting on the roadside and startled a pheasant. It was the finest holiday imaginable. They had all left school before the end of the term and would go no more till the summer was over.

Henny thought of this as she scudded along and worried about two things: how she could get help to set the house in order, and how, without Louie's help, she would manage through the summer (for she had determined to send Louisa to Harpers Ferry again). Sam was still going into the Department but himself confessed in her hearing (they were not speaking) that there was talk of his immediate suspension until the Civil Service Commission could inquire into the whole confusing business. It had all blown up out of nothing at all, out of those vague "enemies" and "evil ones" whom Sam had mentioned for many years.

Then they began to pass indications of summer camps and new houses, half finished in new clearings, and came into the older cottages settled behind Annapolis. At length, wild with excitement, experiencing disappointment, after the grandeur of Washington, they drove round State Circle, were unable to admire what Sam admired, the colonial charm of the State House, the pleasant retirement of St. John's College (though they saw quickly enough the little black kitten hiding in its bushes). But when Sam drove them slowly down College Avenue to King George Street, and they could see the Academy, they were excited, though the boys declared nothing would induce them to associate with such flossies, yet they would be glad enough to get in to see the Orioles v. Navy when they could; and suddenly thinking of this, Annapolis appeared to them a great and glorious place; it burst forth in the most brilliant colors. Having achieved his effect, Sam smiled and drove them back by cobbled Randall Street to the Market Space and saw the Dock, and so with them asking frenziedly, all the time, "Where is it, our House, Pad?" "But where do we live?" by Compromise Street to the Eastport Bridge. Until this moment, Henny had not had too many qualms about the place where she would have to bring up her brood. She had visited Annapolis so very often when a girl that she liked it, and yet because it was old and isolated, she knew she could avoid her old friends there or meet them there, as she pleased. She knew they were to have a house with two acres and a water frontage, and she had imagined one of the old, pretentious houses some distance up Spa Creek, or one of the primly coquettish little brick affairs standing in rows down to the boat basin. The view was exquisite there, at nightfall rivaling in stillness and sheen some little foreign lake of postcard fame. But they were to cross the Eastport Bridge. Eastport is a pleasant, little, hopeless, poor mudbank, level with the broad and shallow Chesapeake. The Chesapeake at this point is not picturesque and scarcely salt. The Eastport Bridge, low, awkward, and makeshift, looks as if it had been thrown across by an army in a hurry and forgotten there. Spa Creek is rimmed with modern and even expensive houses on the Annapolis side, but on the Eastport side to which they were now crossing, it is rimmed by a couple of slipways, boatsheds, dilapidated family houses with crumbling loamy banks and long grass down to the thick water. On the Bay side are jetties, gardens, yachts, and powerboats for bay and sea fishing. It is the sort of place for a fisherman, a mudstalker and hookbaiter, but seems pretty messy, wet, and penurious to any other person. Sam belonged to the first sort and Henny to the majority.

The children craned from the car like geese at Thanksgiving from their crates, gabbling about the yachts, jetties, and shrieking "Which house is it, Dad?" for they knew it was near the bridge and on the water. They fixed on a tidy house with a private jetty on the left hand but Ernie picked out a large tumble-down place, two stories with an attic, on the right hand, right on the shallow reach above the bridge.

"Yes," said Sam excitedly, "Yes, Ermy, Ermy right as per usual: it is, it is, the cannon's opening roar."

"Is it ours, Ded?" inquired Evie, viewing it with alarm because it was so different from Tohoga House, and she had pictured an identical place. Henny stared at the ugly old castle comedown, with its rooms upon rooms and unkempt grounds, and looked as if she would cry, but not a word came out of her until Charles-Franklin whimpered. Then she muttered, "No wonder!" Meanwhile the twins were shouting, "Can we sleep upstairs on the balcony?" and Ernie shrieked, "Wait till you get there, you dopes!"

"'It is indeed a momentious event,'" said Sam softly, in the verbal tatters of Artemus Ward. "Kids, there's a marvolious old orchard full of apples, a manure heap, seedling frames, and all: we'll really have a garding here."

Evie repeated in her dolly voice, "I beg your parding, Mrs. Harding, but there's a blowfly in your garding."

Ernie looked at her with contempt, "You kill me!"

Evie looked quickly at her father for protection, but Sam was too anxious to know Henny's unexpressed feelings about the new house to bother about squabbles in Lilliput.

Sam had wheeled them quickly round by Severn Avenue, hoping they would not take too much notice of the weatherboard cottages. The house could be entered in two ways, by boat, from Spa Creek, or from the back by way of a long serpentine dirt drive, edged on one side by the creek and on the other by the orchard. Along this drive stood very tall old trees, all kinds of maples and an elm. The drive turned round to the left (they had now made a hairpin bend), and they stopped on ragged grass beside the glassed-in and viny side door. Towards the water was a pleasant half-moon of lawn with shrubs; beyond the shrubs was the fall of the bank on which grew large trees and rushes, and under that was a small sand beach. A rotted row-boat lay sunk in the beach. The children discovered all this in a minute, poured out of the car, and dashed about with cries.

"The house, kids," cried Sam, "here we are, here we are home again, home again. Spa House. We'll put up a board tomollo [tomorrow] saying 'Spa House' and 'No admittens.'"

"Are we going to live here?" inquired Evie somewhat dubiously, after surveying the porch and balcony, the old withering walls and the broken planks.

"Yes, Love, *e pluribus unum in proprietor persony!*" exclaimed Sam, more heartily than he felt, for as he unlocked the side door, he saw Henny sniffing angrily at the decaying timber and dirty panes. The house had been abandoned for a year, and Sam had got it cheaper than he expected, at a price of a little over $5000, with a mortgage, because he asked for no patching-up (he and the boys would do it, aided by Uncles Lennie and Ebby), and because, with a great many new building schemes and threats of condemnation, the despised Eastport was considered to be altogether unmarketable. All that part of town was now sniffed at by progressive residents: the town was progressing towards the west where the high school stands, with modern bungalows and new highways. The officers at the Naval Academy were soon to be taken out of their apartments in private houses in the town and housed in special buildings, and government and state officials from Baltimore were to be moved down here into special new buildings. The old town round the Academy was dying. People were dubious about the fate of St. John's College, and the old part of the town could look for nothing but visitors in June Week, visitors for the August fishing festival, and a possible revival in wartime. At all events, not a householder in Annapolis but considered Eastport a civic disgrace of deep dye, and would see it cleaned out and rebuilt. On the farther side of the East-port flat, beside huge old houses built on neglected estates (it was once thought that Eastport would become fashionable) lived Negro families in a desperate situation and poor-white families, and in the little cove there are the most abandoned, hopeless old rat-eaten and rotten tubs in the whole of the watery world.

The first van of furniture was turning into the drive before they had explored even the second story, so the children were turned out to grass and Henny went to sit on a weather-beaten rocking chair with the seat out that had been left on the veranda. She faced Annapolis. Only a few hundred yards from her was the sheeny basin, a tiny Como. She had cast one glance into the Spa House kitchen and seen its old stoves (one iron oven built in and one old gas range), leprous sink, and wormy floor, and then gone silently to the rocking chair. For the past half hour she had felt a curious, dull, but new sensation and as she sat there she found out what it was. Across the water was a houseboat, a cabin on a raft, about which climbed two or three young plump girls in skin-tight satin bathing things and a couple of lanky boys in trunks. Cars were parked beyond in Shipwrights' Street. Casual mosquitoes buzzed in the damp silent rafters of the veranda but did not annoy her in the mild sunlight. All the children but Louie had already disappeared to the fringe of beach, and she heard their voices through the reeds. A girl took a plunge from the houseboat; a middle-aged man with a sandy fringe of hair round a bald spot rowed languidly past in a suicidal rowboat; two naval cadets had come into the Creek and were clutching at a flapping sail. Henny heard the men moving in some heavy thing, and heard her husband say wearily, "Looloo-dirl, make some cawf!" The reek of weeds forever damp and of the brackish water came up to her and the smell of the ground under the veranda. It had rained slightly in the night. Louie, who pretended not to hear Sam's call, came in a dawdle round the house and leaned against the veranda post behind the vines, chewing a grass stalk. She was droning to herself and presently she droned clearly, "Oh, the waterskin crawls shore-wards; and the leprous sky scales earthwards, from the musical moaning channel, to the dirty margin." It was halfwater; the surface was dull, and the sky was windy.

At that particular moment, Henny awoke from a sort of sullen absence and knew what was happening; her heart was breaking. That moment, it broke for good and all.

"Stop that rot," she cried madly to Louie, startling her out of her wits, "I never heard such damnfool tommyrot. Go and get the coffee. A big lumbering sheep, and on a day like this, she holds up the veranda post." Louie, with tactful soft-footing, disappeared from behind the vines, and presently Henny heard her saying,

"I say, Dad, this gas won't turn on; it's jammed."

The men trundled backwards and forwards and puffed. Louie soon came to the veranda with a cup of tea for her mother (Henny's heart would not stand coffee), "Mother, Daddy says, 'Where do you want things put?'"

"What the devil do I care? Put them in the orchard and make a bonfire of them. Put them where you like," she ended, less ungraciously. "Is it my home? It's your father's idea. Do what you like; all I want is a place to lie down, and get me a bed for Baby. Tell him I am not going to lift a finger to fix up his stinking tenement: the animals have better cages. Go on now, don't stand there staring."

Louie, not at all offended, and now observing more closely the many defects of the old house, the hanging window cords, unlatchable latches, and sunken floors, went in to say, "Mother says put everything where you like."

Sam, only too pleased, at once hallooed and whistled for the gang of children and consulted their tastes. It was not hard to suit most of them.

2 *Sam suspended.*

For the next month, until the middle of July, in deep middle of the bee season, old Spa House rang from six in the morning till nightfall with the boys' shouting and Sam's whistling, hammering, ripping of timbers, and falling of plaster. Sam, with the boys, was taking the house apart and putting it together again on a different plan. He himself would renew the furnace system, take down the chimneys, pull out the bathroom, install a shower room, make new steps, put in timbers in the decrepit veranda, put in glass where it was broken, patch the plaster, calcimine, paint, and otherwise repair. The great project filled him with joy. "With my own labor union," said he to them, "I need nobody; no strikes, no trouble, only the work going up fast."

"You don't pay anything," Ernie said disagreeably. He felt first, after Henny, the pinched circumstances in which they were now living. His perquisites had ceased, and because (after a first visit during which Henny had remained in her room) one and all of the relatives in Baltimore had become timid or distant, he received no nickels or dimes in presents. His rich grandfather was dead, and Henny, more ferocious than ever, had absolutely forbidden him ("whatever your father says") to run errands for the grocer, black boots, or do any of the other things that his imagination suggested to him. Henny kept completely to herself, refusing to speak to any of the poor neighbors. Since the breakdown of her hopes, many things had come home to her. She was ashamed of everything, especially ashamed of her laboring husband who could be seen at any hour of the day crawling about the house and acting like a common workman. Why wasn't he at work? the neighbors might be asking. Henny, too, had suddenly become ashamed of having so many children; for now that Collyer was dead and the estate dissipated, people asked her ordinary questions.

"It's all bets off, and they think I'm one of themselves," Henny told her friend, old maid Miss Orkney. "I'm ashamed to go out of the house with that string, I'm like a common Irish Biddy." She was glad to hide behind the wild growths of Spa House.

Sam was being treated ignominiously in the Department. He had been suspended without pay after receiving pay for three months, at first; and though his case was up before the Civil Service Commission, friends warned him that he was likely to find himself out on his ear, in the street, penniless and cheated of his pension.

"It is impossible," said Sam stoutly, "I am guiltless, and I will not fight them with their own weapons. I will not excite opposition—for I do excite opposition. When they see how unselfish I am, it somehow arouses the madness of anger, and jealousy in my enemies. My absence serves me better than any number of petitions and any logrolling. I have been accused of receiving support from Old David's political friends: may that never be said about a Pollit!

I will only go to Washington to see my friends. Their machinations are beneath the very contempt of a man like me."

Henny, never speaking to him, heard him with fright; but she had given herself up entirely to despair; she said nothing, and it seemed to her that (now that the clouds had rolled away) she saw her husband for the first time: she had married a child whose only talent was an air of engaging helplessness by which he got the protection of certain goodhearted people—Saul Pilgrim, who was penniless, various old Socialists, of small property, and in the dim past, by the same means, her own father.

"Why don't I tie a stone round my neck and drown myself in his idiotic creek?" she asked Louie with quiet sadness, when she heard these declarations from Sam in the intervals of hammering. Money was slow coming from his pockets, and Henny's allowance (which had never been more than $10 to $20 monthly from Sam, on account of her father's generosity to her) ceased altogether. When Henny sent Louie with indignant messages to her father about this, Sam coolly sent back his answer, that, "Soon she would get her quarterly allowance from the estate, and in the meantime, they must all pull in their belts." Henny would reply (by the same telegraph) that "he ought to be ashamed to live off a dead man," to which Sam, with a stern expression, would answer nothing at all, or merely mutter that if it had not been for her devilish extravagance of a spoilt fool raised for the marriage market, they would have been well enough off on his savings. This was a constant source of quarreling (always by telegraph) and, because of it, the children knew almost all the ins and outs of their family society.

Louie, who was much involved in all this, was a hotheaded person easily getting indignant over the injustices of one to the other; and about her own share of injustice storing up a wealth of vengeful feeling, a tempest on a chain which she intended to let loose at some vague season in the future. But, to her great surprise, the rest of the family who were, after all, own sons and own daughter of Henny, seemed to take not the slightest interest in the obscene drama played daily in their eyes and ears, but, like little fish scuttling before the disturbing oar, would disappear mentally and physically into the open air or into odd corners of the house. When a quarrel started (Henny and Sam did speak at the height of their most violent quarrels) and elementary truths were spoken, a quiet, a lull would fall over the house. One would hear, while Henny was gasping for indignant breath and while Sam was biting his lip in stern scorn, the sparrows chipping, or the startling rattle of the kingfisher, or even an oar sedately dipping past the beach, or even the ferry's hoot. Exquisite were these moments. Then the tornado would break loose again. What a strange life it was for them, those quiet children, in this shaded house, in a bower of trees, with the sunny orchard shining, the calm sky and silky creek, with sunshine outside and shrieks of madness inside. For Sam, in his rages, had long ago forgotten all kindness and said to his wife the vilest insults, throwing up at her all that could possibly be called her life; and she retaliated, but losing, losing all the time. From the moment they came to Spa House Henny had begun to lose ground in the war. Back she went, step by step; and it seemed that Sam, as poverty closed round them, gained stride by stride. Poverty was a beautiful thing to him, something he was born to and could handle: to her it was something worse than death, degradation, and suicide. She envied every creature she saw if she did not immediately think with bitterness, "Little the poor wretch knows what is coming to it," or, "The poor dumb fool is too stupid to see what a life it leads." Of these remarks she was free to her children and to Louie. She often said to her stepdaughter, "Your father broke my heart, then he broke my body with housework, now he is breaking my children: I have no money—what do you think there is for me? How can he criticize me? The great ignorant howling fool! Let me die."

It was a beautiful summer. Sam hoped still that "truth crushed to earth would rise again" (he meant his case would succeed). He found a thousand theories to justify his changing the children's food from butter to margarine, and from meat, to beans, spaghetti, and fish. He superintended the cooking himself, reproaching his Little-Woman with her clumsy attempts at cooking and himself instructing her because her mother would not. He knew a noble woman, it appeared, in the Conservation Department, who put out pamphlets on cooking, and Sam was always chatting about her recipes and always trying them out. He imported gallons of oil, of all kinds, himself making experiments in the kitchen, peanut oil, corn oil, fish oil, and every kind of oil, which filled the wooden house with a roof-lifting stench and made Sam very gay indeed. He raged against Henny's odors, but for himself, in his own universe, concocted such powerful, world-conquering odors as could be smelled across Spa Creek and up and down the foreshores. Waiting for his case to be decided, he was able to forget the world and be happy.

"What a pity," he said a thousand times, grinning at his children, "that the Law forces you to go to school. Children with a father like you have need no school. See what I would do! You would learn everything by projects: you would learn to build houses, plaster, repair—you all do know that now—you would be bricklayers, carpenters; the womenfolk would be good cooks, seamstresses; we would get the best, most modern machines, have every household process done by modern machinery, and we would have none of the archaic, anachronistic, dirt, filth, and untidiness which Henny strews about because she comes from the stupid old world. Baltimore, my native heath, used to be famous in the world, for commerce, yes, even for banking (though you know what I think of the Greedy, the Money-Powerful)—Brown Brothers had a great reputation as far away as wicked old London, that capital of evil. But there is a secondary strain in dirty old Baltimore, and that is a shameful love of vice. Not only did all these silk-skirted 'great ladies' (as they liked to call themselves, though they were silly little chits) breed slaves and sell them down to horror and hell, but they were themselves bred for marriage to wealthy men from abroad and from home too, I am sorry to say. Baltimore loves other things much worse, a real underworld of vice, which is, strange to say (you kids will understand this later), considered the upper world, society—a wicked convention which has imposed itself on a silly world, full of drinking, cardplaying, and racing. Baltimore has beauties, but what corruption does the ugly old girl hide under her parasol too? But let us leave this. Baltimore is sweet because she is between the great pothole of Nature and the wonderful Blue Ridge. That saves her."

The children listened to every word he said, having been trained to him from the cradle. Only Louie, who had much to think about (nothing to do with Sam at home), would always seep away from the group, linger deceptively for a moment round the door, and a few seconds later would be seen shining on the brink of the slope, or would have completely disappeared, and be mooning and humming on the beach. Henny thought that she had sneaked off to avoid work (they had no servant now). Sam suspected her thoughts—if they were not thoughts she could share with him, what sort of ideas could they well be; something unpleasant and even depraved. He feared, with the shrinking of the holily clean, the turpitudes of adolescence, and although boys might go through it, he heartily wished that bright pure womanhood could leap straight from Little-Womey's innocence to the gentle sobriety of Gillian Roebuck's nineteen or twenty years. The swelling thighs and broad hips and stout breasts and fat cheeks of Louisa's years (she was getting on past thirteen and having lived entirely in the open air and been fed on Henny's rich meats, she looked fifteen, yet with uncouth childish manner) were repugnant to Sam: he wanted a slim, recessive girl whose sex was ashamed.

Louisa was his first adolescent, too: he was full of the mystery of female adolescence of which, in his prim boyhood, he had been ignorant. He poked and pried into her life, always with a scientific, moral purpose, stealing into her room when she was absent, noting her mottoes on the wall,

By my hope and faith, I conjure ye,
throw not away the hero in your soul—Nietzsche

and investigating her linen, shivering with shame when suggestive words came into her mouth. Her speech, according to his genteel ideas, was too wild, too passionate, too suggestive. He told her not to use the words "quick and the dead," because "quick" meant the unborn; and not to use the words "passionate" or "passional," which she was fond of, and not to recite certain of her favorite passages because she did not know the meaning of them; and all with a shrinking niceness, a qualmish sensibility which surprised and repelled her. His nice Louisa, brought up on sawdust excerpts from potted philosophers, intended for the holy life of science, he could see (much as he closed his eyes), was a burning star, new-torn from the smoking flesh of a mother sun, a creature of passion. This was what her years of sullenness had concealed, not a quiet and patient nature, like her mother's, but a stern, selfish, vain nature like her grandfather's, wicked Israel's angry seed.

Sam tried all the recipes. He gave her her mother's photograph to hang above her bed.

"What is a photograph to me?" asked Louie insolently, "Mother is my mother" (meaning Henny). He gave her a photograph of himself taken when he was twenty-three, just before marriage, an incredibly mild, beaming angelic face, blond as the sun, dreamy and self-doubting. He carefully went through her books, her notebooks, and scraps of paper in order to guide her, set her right: his palpitating heart could not bear to think of her coming to shipwreck on the hidden reefs of youth: and, for her sake, he went through all the literature on adolescence, becoming more horrified every day as Satan's invisible world was revealed to him, who had been a bloodless youth living on greens and tap water. Youth was one of the beasts of Revelations, the worst, and more insolent than the Sun. He writhed within himself to think that his high-souled, sober-minded Louie had to go through all that. Why? With the proper training and abstracted from all bad companions, and carefully watched, he felt, and kept in touch with pure adult minds, she would pull through without scar or blot. He would be her constant companion: they would communicate thoughts, and she would be drawn to his side.

With mental lip-licking, he followed her in her most secret moments. She had papers and all sorts of rubbish to burn (she was always "clearing up her drawers"); she would build a fire by the side of the orchard and stand by, in a dream, smelling the smoke, differentiating the odors of burnt grass, paper, rag, and printed cardboard and so on, with the intoxication of an old drug fiend, adding things to the fire to get the smell: and then he would come creeping behind her, stealing up on her to discover what she was doing, what was in the fire, and what in heaven caused this strange drifting nebula to spin.

He did the same to the other children, particularly to Ernie, who had become withdrawn and gloomy, and Little-Sam, always an absorbed and uncannily tempestuous child, full of wild, formless agonies. He sensed that there was something going on, like an incantation perhaps, about which he knew nothing. He tried to think back to his youth, but could remember very little but quickly repressed shames and moral thoughts. He pried and pried, hoping to discover, in the love of science and youth, the mysteries about him. Suddenly, overcome with an inexplicable feeling of embarrassment, he would laugh aloud, run up to the child under observation and poke fun, or poke the boy with his toe, or poke Louie's fire with an inebriated, quizzical expression. Louie would flush, rake out the fire, and turn her back, without a word: Ernie would fling away from the intruding toe; Little-Sam would hang his head, flush dark red and sometimes hit out clumsily. This amused and intrigued the innocent father; and it became a sort of game with him to come upon his children in their silences. Once he had thought their silences full of long, lofty thoughts, but now they were too old, he knew they might be thinking dangerous, filthy thoughts. From all that, he was there, their shield, to protect them.

So now when Louie stole away, with what tricks and speed she could, she was pretty certain to find Sam at her back in a short time, or to hear one of the children calling her from the slope or the orchard lanes (if she was in one of her cubbyholes at the far end of the orchard). Very often she would take there with her one of the younger children: Saul, who remained in fair equilibrium through all the storms, or Tommy, the handsome child with the rosy cheeks and thick curls, who was very dear to her and whom she would nurse, between her loins and her breasts, feeling his sweet weight maternally. Tommy always yielded himself entirely, sinking back into her warm hard flesh, a boy to love and never to question womankind. Sam, seeing two of them there, would roam near and rove away again satisfied: or would ask in a quiet, paternal voice, "What donin, kids?" and would wait for the reply and depart.

Louie was not to go away this summer. Her own relatives at Harpers Ferry were tired of keeping her without any payment at all from the wealthy Pollits. They themselves had become poorer as the health of the various heads of families declined, and the male youths were still looking about for wives and careers. Bradford Collyer had a magnificent place in Montgomery County, half cultivated, with ancient trees and thousands of wild birds and a farm and livestock in little, prize porkers, cattle, a barnyard, blood horses, fodder crops, and fruit. Completely neglected, but fed and befriended, Louie had spent several summers here without seeing another child or even any adults in the daytime. The family was old: one daughter was in a sanitarium and one married in Baltimore. Bradford Collyer divided his time between Baltimore and Washington and the South, and Mrs. Bradford, a superannuated beauty, once an overwhelming society matron, cooled her rattled brains comfortably in retirement.

Mrs. Bradford, Henny's Aunt Phoebe, had agreed once more to take the child off Henny's hands, for the summer of 1937, when David Collyer's death occurred; but after that, sentiment languished and withered between them, and Henny's family became too scrubby for charity even. Besides this, if Louie had gone, the house would have been left to Sam's raving gang of boys and to Little-Womey's cooking! Hazel had married, and was now Mrs. Gray of Charlestown, West Virginia; and the irreplaceable Bonnie had dropped from human ken—no Pollit had heard from her for some time, and Pollits now lowered their voices and looked anxious in speaking of her. Sam had no money for a servant, and servants would rob him of the freedom of his own house where he ran about in shorts and the children ran about naked. No; all was for the best, and his two women, Louie and Little-Womey, would replace Henny, who was in her worst mood of bitterness, languor, and weakness. Try as she would, Henny could not do the work, make the children's clothes, repair mattresses, beat carpets, launder Sam's summer suits, and mend stockings. Sam never ceased to repine about his slovenly housekeepers and the bright beauty of homes of high-class public women who were friends of his in Washington. All went merry as a marriage bell; ringing the old changes. The children were happy and free. Louie was happy and as solitary as she could be—she had a real genius for solitude and could manage to have the solace of loneliness even in this community. She was lazy, said Henny: she was secretive, said Sam; but Louie, dragging herself by main force out of those frightful sloughs of despondency and doubt and uncleanness which seemed to be sucking her down, with amorous, muddy lips, saw hours of lightnings, when the universe split from heaven to hell and in the chasm writhed the delirium of glory, the saturnalia of which explained her world to her: she would stand on the beach watching the tall dry grass which stood in the moistest part of the shore and suddenly she would think,

Who can see aught good in thee
Soul-destroying Misery?

and in this flash of intelligence she understood that her life and their lives were wasted in this contest and that the quarrel between Henny and Sam was ruining their moral natures. Sam, once pathetically modest in his speech, now could hardly speak of Henny without using the word "devil; the foul devil, the miserable devil," said Sam, in his pain, over and over; and even in fun he had come to call the obstinate Louie "you mean devil, you pigheaded devil," though for her he had this dancing, inebriated look of the bad boy who teases the village idiot, and yet the two of them roamed about the village of Eastport together, following the motor roads and getting round to the small flat horseshoe inlets by rowing boat, like the closest of friends. There was nothing Sam had to say that Louie did not already understand.

In this new intimacy with his children and while patching up his new house, Sam was able to forget his troubles in Washington. He ceased to read the newspapers, except when some friend sent him a marked copy showing some attack upon him, or some indignant letter from a friend. If Sam thought about it at all, his heart beat so hard and his head ached so much that he could neither sleep, eat, nor work: therefore the only alternative was not to think about it at all.

Henny saw with alarm that Sam did not intend to fight: he was drifting, and no one seemed to know where their money was coming from. Sam referred vaguely to "your mother's quarterly checks," and remarked that "Henrietta must now expect to help with the household expenses." The children, who had heard so often from Henny that "these few miserable dollars were her very own," thought Sam very unjust, greedy, and even thieving. They did indeed see their mother in rags, and could not understand why their father did not go to work any more.

When the mail came in, in the morning, Sam at the breakfast table, with a bedraggled expression, would show Ernie and Louie the articles which attacked him and say, "See, see there; see how base mankind can be—but you must learn not to hate, but to understand: who understands all, forgives all." But Louie and Ernie would cry desperately, "Answer the letters: why don't you answer the letters?" Then Sam would enter into a long defense, point by point, showing them everything that was wrong in the attack, and naming the interest which inspired each separate enemy.

"Oh, why don't you write, Dad? Why don't you put it all down and send it in?" cried Louie, wringing her hands, with long, drooping cheeks, "Why do you let them say it?"

And Ernie, desperate too, anxious, fretted by his calculations (where did their money come from?), would say, "Write in, Dad! Please write in; why don't you tell them? If it's so easy to show them that they're all liars; why don't you do it? Please write in, Dad, why don't you?"

But Sam would shake his head, more mournful and pale than ever, and look at them both, and then at them all, with his big frank blue eyes, wet with tears, "At present the evil ones are in the ascendant: we must wait till they are on the run, but we will get them on the run."

"But how? But how?"

"Everything comes to him who waits," Sam would smile painfully. "Looloo, don't be impatient: we must not fight the enemy with his own weapons."

"You are not fighting at all, Dad," cried Louie. "You tell us all this: you can write it in. Look, it is in all the papers: everyone will believe them. I can't understand why you don't."

All the children, though, believed that Sam was utterly innocent, which in fact he was, innocent too, of all knowledge of men, business, and politics, a confiding and sheltered child strayed into public affairs.

The children felt more worried every day, those too old to be diverted into jobs and projects. Where was their food coming from? There were to be repairs and some new building in the Collyer Seafood business in Aliceanna Street, and Henny would get no dividends for two years at the earliest. Mother could no longer get them clothes on credit at Old David's store, for the account was closed. Already Sam had formed a complete, new project, whereby Louie was to leave school and be his secretary (attending business courses at night), and Little-Womey was to leave school as soon as she could, after attending cookery and housekeeping courses, and would look after the kitchen.

"Even if the worst comes to the worst," said Sam, rather cheerfully, "you will see, Sam-the-Bold will manage: never say die! Sam-the-Bold cannot be conquered by circumstances. The evil ones may fly, but when the sky is clear, Sam-the-Bold has a kite to fly after them."

Through the long holidays, Henny, tight-mouthed and determined, went at her work. In her poor clothes, she would take trips, be away for hours, going to Baltimore, to see her sister Hassie, or Uncle Archie. Once or twice Uncle Archie advanced her money upon her expectations, and on these days Sam would find a little pile of money on his desk, with a note beside it:

Sam Pollit: "Use this for household expenses," or *Sam Pollit:* "Get yourself a new shirt."

No one knew how they rubbed along; but when schooltime came, Louie was allowed to go to the Annapolis High School in a new flannel blouse and seedy old serge skirt which Hassie had sent her, and a cinnamon brown overcoat given her by Auntie Jo. She felt pretty wretched till she got to the school when she saw before her a flock of girls, half of them looking like a litter of puppies tied inside a sack, tumbling and rolling; and, adding herself quietly to the homely and ill-dressed section and subtracting herself, without even a twinge, from the pretty and smart section, she began to bounce about in her new sphere with stolid self-confidence.

3 Miss Aiden.

There were several new teachers in school, two fresh from the university. Of these two, one was a staggering beauty, black-haired, blue-eyed, and with a high fresh color; and the other, tall, limber, with deep gold hair and a fresh, sonorous voice, always wore a red swagger coat. There was a third, also new, though not glamorous, who had drab hair, a worried expression, who wore brown and gray eternally, was timid and cried when the girls made a noise. The susceptible girls at once divided into two camps—those who went for the beauty (Miss Bellmore) and those who went for the redcoat (Miss Aiden). Everyone but a few timid, uninteresting souls did her best to make the drab one (Miss Paramore) lead a life of misery. Louisa, who had done badly in elementary and seventh and eighth grades, discovered dazzling aptitudes within a few days in the new school. Several girls announced that they were Louisa Pollit's friends and insisted on her company. No sooner had Louisa opened her mouth than Miss Aiden gave her a smile of nonpareil sweetness and understanding, and no sooner did Miss Aiden or

Miss Paramore or Miss Bellmore appear, moving kaleidoscopically through the leaves and paths, than all the girls fell to laughing, and thousands of suggestions, skits, and quotations reared their heads. All the girls had grown out of their clothes in a few days, or at least they looked like it, and associations formed naturally of friendly thinkers: girls who spoke freely but eschewed vileness, girls who giggled over dirty jokes and thought about men, girls who went frantic over what was in the newspapers, featherheaded girls who thought about clothes, sad grinds who thought about homework. It was wonderful and new; it was Arcadia. No sooner did Louie see Miss Aiden, with her painted red mouth and goodhumored smile than she began sneering and inventing stories about her, and then the first time she sat in this redcoat's class, she felt obliged not to listen to the lesson but to get down on paper all the comicality in her heart; and this was what came out:

"There was a wedding at the circus! The hermaphrodite married the bearded, the giant the dwarf, the fat lady the hungry wonder, the clown in bags the lady in tights, the flea the elephant, the tiger a lily, the tent a Pole, the wind a Russian, the Hairless Mexican a hairtonic, the barfly a pony, the dollar a bill, the prophet a punched nickel, the instep a stepin, the punch a free pass, the judy a free-show, the cough a little hoarse, the neck a noose, the papal bull a chinashop, the pope's nose a tailfeather, the grille a sideburn, the kink a Jew, the fly a trapeze. Who told all this? The belle tolled. Who knelt? The bell knelled. Who opened the door? A jar. Who had a flower? The doughnut. Who baked the cake? Beg and borrow a pound. What size? Two sighs, seven tears. When was it ready? Tomorrow. What was the fruit? Henfruit, cockscombs, larkspurs, chickpeas, crabapple, passion-fruit, breadfruit, deadseafruit. What came in on two legs? A breadbasket. Who drew the carriage? Shanks' ponies. Who paid the money? Pneumonia. Who was there? You-all. When was it? When time was a pup."

This production, which left Louie astounded (for she had no idea how she had written it, nor why with such ease), followed the tracks of all the other notes and scraps of paper which were passing round the class, and caused such gales of idiot laughter, beginning with chuckles, sniggers, and ending in uncontrollable spasms, that within a few minutes Miss Pollit found herself on the floor, the cynosure of neighboring eyes, while Miss Aiden, frowning, and then grinning, read it through.

"Did you write this, Louisa?"

"Yes, Miss Aiden." (Giggles.)

"When?"

"Just now." (Whispering.)

"Is that what you come to class for?"

"No, Miss Aiden."

("No, Miss Aiden," confirmed the class in varying tones, groans, and flutes.)

"Go back to your seat," said the mistress firmly. Louie expected the worst: she would be late home again, but to her intense surprise, she was not punished, and she sat there blushing badly, thinking of the handsome and agreeable creature in possession of her paper and able to see to the vacuous center of her silliness.

"I'll never do it again," thought Louisa a thousand times, more miserable than she had ever been before, as if one of those dreams had come true, those dreams where she found herself walking down the street in a hat and a bodice without any skirt or shoes. She did not dare to look at Miss Aiden, but sulked and blushed till the end of the lesson, when Miss Aiden with divine pity gave it back to her.

At home the domestic agony was intense. Everything that happened, a nail forgotten and left to tear the children's bare feet, set Henny screaming at them. The short entente between Louie and her stepmother was at an end. Now "the mere sight of the great flopping monster" made Henny want to tear her own eyes out, and the "mere sight" of Ernie going around with "his lumps of lead" made her want to jump in the creek, and the "mere sound of the boys snarling at Evie for their breakfast" made their mother want to pack up her traps and leave them all forever. It was not easy at home, and being kept in was a pleasure to Louie. It gave her a chance to dawdle along the road home instead of going by the bus and to chat with one or other of her friends. She had been adopted by two girls, Leana and Edie: and in the meantime, her appetites were excited by a classmate named Clare who described herself as a "Kind of Wobbly" (whatever that was), a tall, vigorous, yellow-haired girl with boy's curls and a splendid medallion face. Clare was dressed like a ragpicker's girl, and slouched and scuffled along, partly out of good-humor and partly because she wore ragpicker's shoes, from which either the toe, the heel, the upper, or the sole was always missing. Her lisle stockings of a washed-out dung color were wrinkled, dirty, and in holes; her blouse would be on inside-out, rough-dry, her skirt spotted and with hem hanging. Her shapely artisan's hands would be dirty, and even her face, if she cried (she cried sometimes, frankly), would show clean traces. For lunch she would have a sandwich or some dry bread, and she never had any money for school contributions.

"You ought to know Clare Meredith," girls would say, watching her, in a disinterested tone. Clare forever wasted time, was always chatting with her large shapely curly head laid just above the top of the desk, next to some other head, always making up skits and sending them round the class, little bits of paper written in an exquisite, fantastic small hand. She had never done her homework, nor was ever ready for a question, but would laugh up at the teacher with a gay, good-natured sloven's laugh.

One day, Louie received a note in class, sent by desk express,

"I'll kiss thy foot; I'll swear myself thy subject," and there was Clare, giggling and grinning at the far end of the room like a curly mooncalf, bobbing and hawhawing, showing all her strong white teeth, a blue-eyed female Caliban. Louie at once seized her pen and, with a most serious look, wrote back, by the same post,

"By this good light, this is a very shallow monster. I am afeard of him! a very weak monster."

Clare's yell of laughter brought down the house, and even the mistress, on this occasion the Bellmore, laughed, and said in her distant silvery voice, "Gals, gals!"

Louie became chief flatterer of Miss Aiden. As soon as Louie got home (she went slower and slower as she neared the gate of Spa House and stayed a long time in the shadowed drive, for now the storms were more than could be borne), and had done the vegetables, she would pretend she had homework and, rushing upstairs, shut herself in her room, where she would go on with her poem, or scene, for the next day. She made a point of never going to school without a poem or scene (in a play) in Miss Aiden's honor. Leana, Edie, and (soon) even Clare, laughing but loyal, would wait for her at the gate and ask, "Have you got a sonnet today?" Louie had formed a magnificent project, the Aiden Cycle. The Aiden Cycle would consist of a poem of every conceivable form and also every conceivable meter in the English language, each and every one, of course, in honor of Miss Aiden. Part of the Aiden Cycle was to be *The Sonnets,* dedicated to The Onlie Begetter, a little thing which would occupy but a brief time in that life which was entirely for Aiden. The high school contained only one such fanatic, and thus Louie became chief of all the Aiden men. Clare inclined towards Bellmore, and even wrote one sonnet (a comic one) in her favor, but she bowed before the enraptured Louie, and this intensity of feeling brought her to Louie. In a short time, though, she would chat with her old friend or lie down on a bench with her torn straw hat over her head, taking the sun. She was mostly to be seen with Louie holding long and earnest discussions. She tried to get Louie to be a socialist and to read *Progress and Poverty,* but all other passions, at this moment, meant nothing to Louie. At school, when she saw the red coat come weaving up the path, she was joyful, all triumphant love; at home, she had her hands full, using up all the spare hours to learn her plays and write her Cycle. She recognized that the Cycle was a lot of work, and she never dropped it. She began to learn *Paradise Lost* by heart. Why? She did not know really: it was a spectacular way of celebrating Aiden.

Sam and Henny complained bitterly of the amount of homework given to a growing girl and thought the teachers must be mad; they were always threatening to write to the school; and then Sam decided that all Louie's homework must be done in the family dining room, under the eye of one and all—it would prevent dawdling, and enable her to learn to concentrate—for if one can work when bedlam is loose, then one can work anywhere at all. This was Sam's theory. Furthermore, when the others had gone to bed, Sam was full of little speculations and homilies, trying to draw her out, trying to get in touch with her. Following her bad example, Ernest too was drawing away from Sam, and Sam felt that he must fight it out with Louie; it was now or never in the struggle for power.

The children soon knew all about Miss Aiden, and tried to tease their eldest about her love, but she was too serious, and too enthusiastic, and she would recite to them for hours on end, while they sat with rosy, greedy faces upturned, listening. Then Louie would act, and tell them how it would be done on the stage, thus and thus; and she would try to get them to act with her. Sometimes, Sam would creep in, unexpected, in this verdant theater at the orchard's end, and would stand quietly at the back, rather surprised at his daughter. On these occasions only did a kind of humility creep into him; and Louie, seeing it, would strike at him verbally, or flash a look which said, plainer than speaking, "I am triumphant, I am king."

4 *Clare.*

If Miss Rosalind Aiden was the heavenly love, Clare was the alter ego. Everyone knew about her: the older ones thought her a crazy kid, while the younger ones wondered who was that dirty, ragged girl full of shouts and horseplay. When she came in through the school gate, without a hat (her hat had at last fallen to pieces), she would rip off the ragged overcoat and, showing its ripped lining and hanging seams, she would begin to sell it, ducking and grinning solicitously, smoothing down its burst seams and expatiating on its beauty, and she would offer it at auction for a dollar, fifty cents, ten cents. One day a youngster offered her ten cents for it, and she sold it, took the ten cents, and refused to take the coat back; no, it had gone under the hammer and been parted with fair and square, said this tragic muse. She trudged home to her home in a yard in Compromise Street, in Annapolis, without a coat, although it was a gray November day, with a sneaking, damp breeze and snow threatening, and the next day came in a man's coat that a neighbor, an old man, had lent her. She herself had gone in and borrowed the coat till he should ask for it. She turned out the pockets before half the school, finding string, tickets, and a mucus-streaked handkerchief which she flung away from her with a magnificent gesture of loathing, and all the time, unselfconscious, amused at herself,

"Look at this now—a bit of string to hang myself with: but my neck's too thick—he didn't think of that! And the pocket's—where's the pocket? Ouch! I can feel my knee—my knee's in the pocket. But who said anything about pockets? Look, just air—it's lined with air: but that's a swell style, the latest thing: there are more wearing pockets of air and linings of air at this minute than linings of silk. Who cares for the naval dears with their plackets and braid? The best part of mankind wears overcoats entirely of air. First a suit of skin, then a decoration of hair, then an overcoat of air!"

Then deciding that she was dissatisfied with her overcoat, air or no air, she would shuffle off a few steps, and Louie, who would have been standing, grinning but dissatisfied, sometimes rather stern, at the edge of the crowd, would take her arm and say, "Clare, Clare!"

"What, Louie?"

"Clare—" Louie knew that Clare only behaved like this when her poverty rankled worst; Clare's poverty was no secret to anyone— she came of a brilliant family that after the death of father and mother had come into the hands of a poor, stiffnecked maiden aunt. One eldest sister was even now at work, helping to keep the two younger sisters and small brother. As soon as Clare graduated, she would take up the burden. Half the weeks in the year it was a question whether Clare would have a roof over her head at all. What was there to say? Clare would smile at her ruefully and grip her hand.

"Ah, Louie, what do I care? When I get through I'll earn; but where will I be still? There's my sister and brother and two mortgages— the only thing that worries me is the boys: the brutes won't look at a poverty like me! What does it matter what I am?"

Louie was silent. Then stupidly she would say,

"Well, you're only fourteen, Clare—" Clare would open her arms wide, spreading the loose garments that fell about her, with a gesture that somehow recalled the surf beating on a coast, the surf of time or of sorrows,

"Look at me? Will I ever be any different?" Clare resolutely refused to visit Louie at her home and would never even cross the bridge to Eastport for fear of meeting Louie with her family; she would always refuse, hanging her head and smiling to herself, though at what, Louie could never make out.

"You don't want me, Louie: I'll see you at school."

One day, just before Christmas, she came, without galoshes, but dragging, on a stockinged foot, a completely ruined shoe.

Her toes peeped through holes in the stockings. Some of the girls who were hanging about exclaimed, pointed, and others running up commenced to make a great hullabaloo. Clare stopped in her tracks and, laughing at the great fun, picked up the shoe out of the muddy snow and began swinging it round and round her head: suddenly it flew loose and seemed to fly into the sky, but it landed on the roof instead and while they all stood laughing hysterically, holding their bellies and going into shrieks of laughter, Clare rushed into the janitor's room, took a ladder, scrambled up to the roof, and began mounting it towards the shoe, making a fall of snow, but still going up carefully on hands and knees. Her patched and tired underwear could be seen all over the grounds. An old teacher (Clare was her protégée) came running and, in a stern high voice, cried out to Clare to come down quickly, while the janitor with a long pole began to poke after the shoe. Clare, looking round, and greeting her audience with a flustered laugh, began to back down again—the shoe slid towards her, she tweaked it off the roof and sent it flying down to the ground. She happened to be looking at her friend, the old teacher, and so the shoe struck the woman in the face. She started back but said nothing, only blushed and rubbed her face; and then she stooped and picked up the miserable object, and stood with it dangling in her hand until Clare had reached the ground again. The children, much struck, had fallen silent, and as Clare sheepishly came up to the woman and said, "I'm sorry, I'm sorry," and they looked from one to the other, they saw that Miss Harney (the mistress) was crying. She took Clare under the arm, upstairs and into her own room. Louie trailed after her, and because Miss Harney also liked her, she was allowed to remain there.

"Have you no other shoes?"

"No, ma'am," said Clare brightly.

"Why not?"

"No money, ma'am!"

"Don't call me 'ma'am,' Clare."

"No, ma'am—Miss—ma'am—Miss…"

Miss Harney shrugged, "I am going to send to get you a pair of shoes."

"No need, ma'am: no need at all, thankee kindly."

"Stop acting the fool, Clare."

"No'm, yes'm thankee'm."

Miss Harney, very tall, spare, spectacled, with iron-gray hair, struggled with a smile, "Clare, you don't have to go through this, surely? I'll write to your aunt. You have friends here: we'll gladly help you."

"Don't want any help: no'm," Clare said.

Soon the school was talking about it and saying the teachers had got together and bought Clare a blouse, skirt, and so forth, and that the very next day, out of pride, no doubt, Clare had come back in the former sordid outfit—but this protest did not last. She wore the better clothes, and during the winter Miss Harney looked after her constantly, for Clare had developed a bad cough. She parodied the cough too, of course: it was a great source of inspiration to her. Just before they broke up for Christmas, Clare tied the draw cord of the Venetian blind round her neck and accidentally fell out of the window.

When examination results were posted, Clare appeared in most lists at the top or as runner-up. Most often she would be "sick" the day before a test, or her aunt would be sick the week before a term examination. On the morning of the examination, Clare would turn up, ragged, but with a clean blouse and cheerful as ever. She would throw balls of paper about the room, write hard, begin early, and end late. Louie, meanwhile, spent so much time pouring out her energies for the love of Miss Aiden that though she worked like everyone else, her results were mediocre. But in Aiden's subjects, naturally, she was unequaled. The class went into examination on all literary subjects with great *sang-froid*, and it never entered anyone's head to try to compete with the great lover. The staff room made serious complaints: Louie worked only for one teacher, and her example set up little frenzies in the rest of the school amongst the younger girls: there were numerous cults now, and some of them had developed into secret societies. At first Louie had founded, with Leana, a secret society, wearing white ribbons with gold letters, SSAA (Secret Society for the Adoration of Aiden), but the inactive members eventually fell away. Parents complained about the plague of secrecy and suspected their children of dark schemes and evil thoughts. In a few weeks, all secret societies were suppressed, by the principal's order: one or two of them rebelliously stuck it out for a day or two, but these withered away under public ridicule and suspicion. When the story of Louie's Aiden Cycle became public, there then began a fashion in original poetry so that pathetic pallid serious-eyed girls would be seen sitting in classrooms and corners of the ground scribbling; and some would timidly send their efforts to Louie for criticism. Needless to say, the ferment round Miss Aiden irritated all the rest of the staff. Miss Aiden was admonished by all the older teachers and told that she must discourage her admirers. But who could? What teacher can discourage popularity? It was asking too much of her.

Sam (after the secret societies were beaten) displayed the greatest interest in Louie's friends and in Miss Aiden. In the noisy morning of some Sunday-Funday, he would always send one of the children flying inside to ask Louie,

"How are Aidoneus' bunions this morning?" or, "Daddy said to ask you does she Miss Aidin' Franco?" or, "Daddy said, Do you love him better than Miss Aiden?" and he begged Louie every day to bring home to Spa House, Claribella, or Clarior-e-tenebris, as he variously called her. Clare would meet Louie at the joining of Compromise and Duke of Gloucester Streets, and they would walk all round Annapolis; Clare would then cross the bridge with her again, even to the Eastport side, and from the middle of the bridge they would stand and look at Spa House while Louie pointed out its parts and named the Pollits who happened to be in sight. But beyond that, Clare would never go. Sam knew this was only a little girl's timidity, and sent loving messages to Clare, "Tell Clarigold from Little Sam-the-Bold that she gotta come the next Saturnday that is and paint the porch," and, "Tell Clarior-e-tenebris to come en wun woun [run round] the Wishing Tree." (Sam had planted a new Wishing Tree on the lawn in front of the house to attract the small fry of Eastport Village.)

All through the winter months, on any bright day after school, or after dinner, Sam and one of his children would be seen patrolling the dirt roads of Eastport, rowing up and down the creek, or taking long walks around Annapolis. On Saturday and Sunday afternoons, when the jobs round the house were done, they would sometimes take the train to Severnside, or even as far as Jones and beat around the hills, studying the birds, insects, and trees, if the roads and tracks were passable, getting up great roses in the children's cheeks and freezing their fingers and toes. Every Sunday, though, Sam and Louie alone walked out to free Louie from the house and to walk off her fat. She was by this time a mere barrel of lard, as everyone said; and nothing was more clownish on earth than Louisa with her "spiny gray eyes, long ass's face, lip of a motherless foal, mountainous body, sullen scowl, and silly smile" (as Henny remarked), going into ecstasies over Miss Aiden and forever scribbling about love.

"What is going on in your head, all this time, besides this foolishness?" Sam would often ask, in kind gravity. "You must be thinking about things too?" Louie would be silent, trying to recall anything she thought about besides Miss Aiden.

"You do think about things, as I have taught and shown you, Looloo-dirl?"

"Yes, of course," she would mutter, flustered.

"When you are ready, you will show me your thoughts," Sam would conclude, not wishing to annoy her. When he got away from the children where his weakness for playground leadership forced him to cavort and fool, he was as kind as he could possibly be; and he would explain this to Louisa,

"Naturally, I am thinking much about you, Looloo, but I am not saying anything; I know this is a phase and it will pass over; it belongs to your age and a little later on you will get out of it and you will laugh at yourself, I suppose—we all do." (How darkly the girl flushed! Certainly things passed in her mind that he was unaware of: he had himself well in hand, though, and left her to her own devices.) After a pause he would say, dubiously, "I can trust you, Looloo: I know I can trust my own girl; you will soon be a woman, and I know you will be very close to me; for although you tend to be mean now, you will improve—you have some of your dear mother's traits."

One Saturday in early April they went for a quiet walk along the back grass-grown streets and bays of rotting hulls, Sam hailing everyone they met (he knew most of Eastport by name), jollying the pickaninnies when they came to the daylight-pierced, damp-rotted shacks where the Negroes live—shells of verminous woods, with shrunken seams, afloat on the marsh and horrider than Coleridge's death ship, A. Gordon Pym's carrion hulk. These places, as all Eastport, are repugnant to the refined citizens of Annapolis, sure enough; but with the houses they condemn the population. Sam, burning with shame, had already sent in three memorials and was preparing a pamphlet, "Eastport Squalor: A Backwater of the Chesapeake," which his friend Saul Pilgrim would publish on his little press and sell. (If he was kicked feloniously out of the Department of Commerce, said Sam, it would be but one of Fate's little tricks, for the country at large would gain in other ways: his energies no longer being at the service of official business, he would seize the crying question of the moment, publicize it and regiment men's minds and the sympathies of the public-spirited. "I begin at home," said Sam, referring to his pamphlet.

Presently they came back from the mud-sunk cove, after interchanging a few words with the Ryatt boys, who were patching up and painting an old fore-and-aft coffin with a motor, which they had renamed "Our Dimes," and after saying hullo to the shopkeepers at the three corners and to "Coffin" (James) Lomasne, they turned to the Eastport Bridge, laughing at his scurrility. Jim Lomasne was a derelict of the Florida boom, native of Connecticut, who, working his way north after the collapse, had never got farther than Eastport. He had sold coffins and rowboats on all the dead-and-alive waterways and in all the bankrupt resorts of the coast. The coffins were for Negro and poor-white funerals; they were worth ten dollars at the outside, while Lomasne (as he shamelessly told all and sundry) sold them for seventy dollars and had laid up a nice piece of change for himself. His boat business was slow, and he was now offering to sell the land on which his rickety boat shed stood, as well as his coffin-*cum*-boat business to the first comer. He also tried to interest speculators in the lucrative or coffin side; but, as Sam peaceably observed, not even a Johns Hopkins fanatic collecting peculiarly loathsome antediluvian growths, or a syphilographer, would touch "Coffin" Lomasne with a forty-foot pole. He had two legs, but clearly he crawled on them; he had a backbone, but it was pliant as a willow wand; he had clothes and they were as clean as any boat-builder's on the shore, but these clothes were looser than grave-clothes, had a moral not a corporeal stench quite sensible to the nose, and though "Coffin" Lomasne did not lack flesh, through his long immersion in marshy places and abandoned, despised sumps, it clung to his bones like grave wax. You looked at Lomasne and saw an obsequious, fifty-year-old dead beat and, as soon as your back was turned, you felt certain that there stood a loathsome ghoul. But it amused Sam to chat with this mud turtle, and, still chanting and improvising on the immoral perfection of "Coffin," they crossed the bridge.

The afternoon had clouded after a still, warm blue day; the water was halfway down, and contained jellyfish. They paused and looked down to count them.

"They are early," said Sam. "What is it, Looloo? See if you know."

She hesitated and flushed, then said, "*Dactylometra?*"

"*Dactylometra quinquecirrha,* in the Chrysaora stage, thirty-two marginal lappets; you only get the forty-eight lappets and forty tentacles in the regions of greater salinity. You know, Looloo, I think we should begin to keep a salinity record of our poor little crick! Why shouldn't you turn out the Spa House Journal, or Natural History of Spa House, like Selborne, and you can put in the human beasts, too, what inhabit the area, or human ecology." He laughed into her face, with his sorcery: "Loo, you and me is going places, but good places. Now, take this: as far as I know, this yer form hasn't been recorded at this time of year: and in my humble opinion it presages an abnormal run in the bay. We will see. The daughter of a friend of mine has a job measuring the height of water in the Shenandoah—heow would you like a jeob like that, Lazybone?"

"All right!"

Sam laughed. The water was almost smooth, with long splinter-shaped ripples, and the long, delicate shells of rowboats stood obliquely along the near jetties, which were mere sticks and runways. Two handsome steam yachts were anchored in close, and a small two-master with a schooner prow. Over the low houses and bare trees rose the bell dome of Bancroft Hall. Everything was ships, shipping, and the sea. On the left hand were the shore houses (of which Spa House was one), grassy dead ends, and tree-topped bluffs around the little pooling creek.

"Lovely," said Sam sniffing, "lovely; came the northeast monsoon perhaps—but it blew this little Malay into a quiet harbor. Despite the troubles that, you know so well, Looloo, have cast shadows on a life that was meant to be all sunshine, we will do well here."

They went along towards the Market Space and then Sam swerved left.

"Why are you going here?" asked Louie suddenly.

Sam smiled, "Hesk no kvastions en I tal no lies."

"You're going to Clare's place," she said in fright. Sam smiled,

"I am a-follerin' my nose, and you is a-follerin' your poor little Sam."

Louie wrenched his hand, "No, Dad, don't go there: she doesn't want us to, they're too poor. She doesn't want us to go."

"Poverty isn't a disgrace," Sam remonstrated, "I'm surprised atcha, Looloo-dirl. I hope Clare isn't as stupid as that."

She dragged at his arm in a frenzy, "Dad, please don't go." She had gone scarlet, "Please don't."

He flew into a temper and grumbled, "Of all the stoopids I ever met; now her father can't see her best friend. I want to get to know your Claribella. I'm sure she's a good girl, and when you told me she was orphaned twice, and was such a good kid, she's the right girl for Looloo to know and git some foolish notions out of her head."

Louisa sulked. When they came to the weather-gray cabin, Sam went in the little picket gate and knocked at the side of the open door. Louie, waiting on the street, saw Clare's shape in the dark hallway and then Clare, standing oafishly in the doorway, taking in the scene. She was barefooted, and wore only a ragged sweater and skirt: her arms, bare to the shoulder, were covered with suds.

"I'm Louie's father," explained Sam, pleasantly, "and Louie talked my two ears flat about you, so I thought I'd come along and take you out for an ice-cream soda." Clare seemed pleased, stood considering, gave Louie a glance, and then with a bound, declared that she would come with them, but they must wait till she got into her bonnet and shawl. It was hideous, thought Louie. She did not wish to share Clare with her father. Sam, on the other hand, glowed with paternity; here he was, not only hands, ears, eyes, wisdom, and virtue for his little daughter (being buffeted too hard by the northeast monsoon), but he was friends and friendship too, ice-cream sodas and Saturday afternoons. There was nothing he would not do for Louie to bring their two worlds together.

"I like your Clare," said Sam. Louie perseveringly skinned her shoe on the curb.

They went up Main Street and into an Italian ice-cream parlor and restaurant. Sam was very jolly, calling the waiter "yon devious devil-may-care Dago," *sotto voce*, and saying all he could to make Clare giggle. When the ice creams came and they were sucking at them, he became serious and asked Clare what she would do for a living. "My living will be paying the rent," said Clare. Sam said that he did not know what Looloo (at this name Clare opened her eyes and then smiled secretly) would do, "because she was at time of writin' a heap of muddleheadedness, but it would parse over, no doubt." The two girls looked at each other over their sodas and giggled. Sam smiled, too, at their bent heads and was encouraged to say that "at the momuent Looloo thought of nothin' but eating of all the dickshunaries she could find and went around chock-full of big words aspewin' em out and destroyin' the peas of mind of the famerlee." Clare stuck to her soda but began to gulp dangerously. Sam approved of this enthusiasm and declared that Louie "went in for Christian martyrdom on a much larger scale than them aneshunt Dagos (by which I mean no more nor less than the Roman-arounds), and I really believe thet thet Jo Bunyan what made Uncle Dan wear shoes two sighs too big was the maggit what had got into Louie's brain." At this Louie left off laughing and looked thunder at the happy Sam. Clare went on tee-heeing to herself over the soda.

"I'm telling you, Clare," said Sam, genteelly, leaving off his Artemus Ward imitation for a moment, "because I know you're Looloo's best friend and maybe you can talk some reason into her skull: though I doubt it." He grinned and slewed his bright blue eyes towards Louisa, expecting her to be full of his fun. He was surprised to see she was not. He began a sprightly inquisition, looking quickly from one to the other, asking, How was Aidoneus, and, Did Clare adore old Aiden the way Looloo did, and, Did Clare think Old Aido was a good woman as well as an allfired beauty, "for beauty lives with kindness," and it was impossible to get anything out of the lyrical Loo but moonlight and roses.

"Do you like her, Clarior-e-tenebris?" he inquired, solicitously, "because I'll take your word for it: I can see you're as quick on the trigger as I am myself."

"She's a good scout," said Clare.

"She's a good scout, that's fine: that's wery satisfactory, wery with a wee: though who is she scoutin' for, that's the question?"

The conversation lapsed. Sam, after a hesitation, invited Clare to have another soda, which she eventually accepted and then Louie too had another. This uncommon blowout delighted Louie; she loved her father at present: and when he began to speak again, in that low, humming, cello voice and with that tender, loving face he had when beginning one of his paeans or dirges, she listened as well as Clare.

"If I had my way—if I were a Stalin or Hitler, Clarigold—I would abolish school altogether for children like you and Looloo, and would form them into communities with a leader, something like I am myself, a natural leader, for man only learns in communities, he is a social animal. I love children and what I should like best, what I should love, Claribella, would be to form the Eastport, or Annapolis, Junior Community and introduce a totally new curriculum. In it the children would wander by the forests and fields and get close to their denizens, the fauna and flora of stream, thicket, and plain—they would be nature lovers, bird lovers. (For don't think I don't understand this foolish little passion of Looloo's: it is good in itself, it needs only direction: I am not unsympathetic as she thinks in her poor big silly obstinate skull!) The system we have now is good at best for making ditchdiggers, clerks, and schoolmarms—not that I am one to laugh at schoolmarms—they are in the noblest profession in the world! But we must follow the curriculum of Nature herself. They must be bird lovers, nature lovers, water lovers, fish lovers, those schoolmarms and dominies: they must not teach formally, but Nature herself must teach *them* to love her and to fossick in her treasury until they find out, slowly but oh, with how much wonder! the inexpressible beauties and glories of her secrets—though they are open secrets to who can see. We unconsciously understand many of her laws—the thing is to bring them to consciousness, to know her, to follow her. Then we should have a different generation, the free air for our arts and sciences, the free use of natural gifts, free speech, few laws, free government freely elected and changing frequently, and phalansteries here, and law in the heart of nature where naturalists and poets of nature develop. It will come. In the meantime I have thought much over Looloo and will put her among the aristocrats of the human mind. I can show her the light and many like her. What terrible losses do we endure in our foolish, cut-and-dried system, when upon natural genius they wish to put a government stamp with a number. I am only speaking of government schools—I am utterly indifferent to institutions run for class, greed, and snobbery. You and I and Looloo, Clarigold, could make the world over: it would be a glorious world then, the world of men and women of good will. We want it; others want it. Why cannot we have it? Yes, we will have it, perhaps in our own lifetime. Only we must get away from this dry-as-dust system which crushes the inspiration, the faith, dreams, hopes, aspirations of youth."

Gravely Clare burbled through her straw in the bottom of her empty soda glass.

"Looloo, for all her gloom and obstinacy," said Sam, in a yearning voice, "is beginning to understand me, whether she will or not—though why she fights against me, I can't make out—though I daresay she has told you a little since you are her best friend and playmate, Clare, about the little troubles we have both had—little troubles, scarcely worth mentioning, in a lifetime, just a little stone Fate put in the path of both of us because we are one nature. But she thinks the way I do, or is beginning to: and that is all I ask. I want you to understand, Clare," he continued, pleading, "because I see Louie has not gone astray, she has chosen aright: you are the right friend for her, and I hope you and Looloo and I will have many intimate talks and walks together. For all education is outside, not inside, the schoolroom."

Clare sat very gravely tracing designs in the wet on the table. Once she raised her eyes and looked at Louie curiously, but Louie was not looking at her. Sam sighed with pleasure.

"Well," he said, stirring, "I suppose we better be stretching our legs, as well as our minds: what say, girls? Shall we walk a little?" He did not release them for a moment but walked them jollily round State Circle and through the retired green grounds of St. John's College, discoursing on everything that met his eye—a stray dog, and the inroads of worthless dogs on planted deer, bred bobwhites, and all wild life of their state and how all dogs should be abolished or at most held on a leash (dogs had many other vices: they carried hydatids, bred lice, bit men, howled at night, made the fair countryside hideous with their wolvish brigandage in the guise of house protection, were vilely lubricous in decent streets, fouled footways, ate their own vomit, smelled to high heaven, and fawned and crawled on man as no decent-spirited beast could!). Then he saw the great liberty oak and sang, in their ears, an ode to that; and so on, for an hour or two, during which Clare mumbled and sometimes grinned and Louie looked stonily ahead or desperately aside.

Soon Clare had to go home, but Sam took Louie's arm and they walked slowly home together, Louie in utmost silence, and Sam talking, pleading, holding her ear, trying to rouse her to sympathy and enthusiasm.

"You will soon understand many things, Looloo-girl."

She smiled sourly.

"You will be like me!"

She grinned, "How do you know I will be like you?" They had paused on the Eastport Bridge to look over to Spa House. Ernie and the twins were splashing about in the water, rushing out on the beach to shiver, flinging their arms about and rushing back into the warmish water again. At the same moment, Henny appeared running, and began beckoning with her arms and calling them out of the water.

"I don't want you to be like me," cried Sam, annoyed; "don't be such a dope. I only want you to think the way I do: and not even that if you have good reasons for your convictions."

Louie grinned sarcastically, "You say so: but you're always trying to make me think like you; I can't."

He became silent and walked along, dropping her hand, in a dignified stride. She felt terribly ashamed of herself: why couldn't she be civil, after the four ice-cream sodas for her and Clare? But as sure as he opened his mouth, she knew, she would begin to groan and writhe like any Prometheus; she smiled apologetically, "It's the nature of the beast."

Sam softened and looked down at her, "Why must you always be such an obstinate cuss?"

"I don't know."

"I have such dreams for you, Looloo. Don't always oppose me.

I have enough opposition. Why aren't you frank with your dad? Why don't you tell me what you are always mooning about? You can come to me with everything. I thought at one moment that the demon had done her work, and that the forces of sin, crime, and evil had torn my daughter from me; and that even the onset of womanhood was making you more bitter. But the love you show for your teacher tells me that you are not like that: it is just a passing phase, a storm—let us say cat's-paw of the pubescent period. I know you have little troubles general to your age and sex, that no doubt upset you. And then there is the situation at home."

Louie's lip trembled, "When I begin to get near home, I begin to tremble all over—I don't know why. I never told any one what it is like at home."

"That is right, Looloo: a merry heart goes all the way; there is nothing we cannot forget if we have a high ideal fixed before us."

She said in a rebellious tone, "That is not the reason: I do not say it because no one would believe me!"

5 What will shut you up?

Spring was coming and Sam was very restless. For weeks he would love Gillian Roebuck; then he would go to see Saul Pilgrim's sister, Mrs. Virginia Prescott, a widow, in Francis Street, near Druid Hill Park. She sat amongst the rich and plentiful furniture left to her by the extinct Prescott and "planned" little meals for friends and let rooms. At times she gave music lessons. Sam thought her a wonderful little woman, and she obviously admired him, but in a respectable, respectful style. She was a round-faced, dark-eyed, dark-haired woman (like all Sam's women), with nice false teeth, a short thick neck, short, thick bosom and little waist, much corseted: she was of medium height and very light on her feet. Sam did not love her, but when his feeling for the nature-spelled girl, Gillian, became too strong, he went and talked to Virginia. He was unable to see Gillian because they both felt they were too conspicuous in either Baltimore or Washington, and Sam despised hole-in-the-corner meetings: it was not worthy of them.

But this spring Saturday that he walked out with the two young girls, the need for Gillian rushed back into his veins like a relapse into fever. Only by talking, diverting his own attention all the time, could he forget her, smile and save himself from despair; and so when he reached home, sure enough, he gathered all his little ones round him, stealing them from whatever occupation he found them in, setting them round the long table in the square dining room that looked up Spa Creek, and he began to tell them all that had happened that afternoon—the walk, the wicked dilapidation of the Negro houses, the charming little wooden village that a Negro woodworker had there (birds, dolls, Mary-quite-Contraries, houses, picket-fences all in miniature and painted, in a little Swiss village), the *Scyphomedusae,* and Clare, and all he had said to Clare and Louie, with new variations. Meanwhile Louie got supper, and Henny, nearly mad with toothache and neuralgia, was crying in her room, her head tied up in an old flannel nightgown that once belonged to Tommy. Filled with love, with his eye on Louie, who was running backwards and forwards with the supper dishes, and who was wearing the pretty flowered blue dress that she had got new for school, he said to the children,

"When Bluebeak [Louie] was very tiny and could hardly speak, she and I often communicated by human radio, telepathy: one day she was playing in a little blue dress, just the same blue as that blue dress she has now—it was made from the dress her mother, my dear Rachel, wore when she was married—we came out to Annapolis—isn't that queer, kids!—the day before and she wore it then, too (for we were very, very poor). Bluebeak (I called her 'Ducky' then), Ducky was playing with her blocks—and she was wonderful at building with them, so serious, stopping for nothing, nothing could disturb her, shrieks, the milkman coming, the streetcar, nothing—I was standing there, thinking about poor Uncle Ebby (he didn't look so old and worn then, though he had his troubles, he had bad troubles)—and my Ducky suddenly looked up and said, 'Wassamattr wi' Uncle Ebby, Daddy?' Later on, I tried experiments with Bluebeak and they always worked. I always knew when you were sick, Bluebeak" (he broke off, addressing Louie who had just come into the room with a glass of water in her hand), "and the strange thing, is, kids, I always know what Bluebeak is thinking."

The children giggled at the new name, Bluebeak.

"Her nose isn't blue," said Little-Sam thoughtfully.

Louie laughed. Sam thought she laughed at the new name, "Whop you tee-heein' at, Bluebeak?" he asked.

"You always know what I think!" she said and shouted with laughter.

"You think Sam-the-Bold can't fathom your great thoughts?"

"No."

"Then whop you larfin at poor Sam fower?"

"You don't always know what I think." She became even more hilarious.

"Don't be a goat, Bluebeak."

She kept on laughing.

"The way you think you're so clever," she managed to get out between explosions.

He frowned, "Stop that hysterical teeheeing, Looloo."

She began to calm down, only giving an occasional giggle; the children were all giggling, all their little bellies and shoulders shaking. He said solemnly, "I will always know what Bluebeak thinks all her life."

Ernie burst out, "I betcha you don't know what she's got written in her diary."

Sam's face cleared in a second. He looked at Ernie with surprise and delight, "A diary? Looloo, you bin keepin' a diary, after all. Why, I told you to, but I didn't know you did."

Louie protested that she did not but Ernie, only wishing to be of service, rushed into her bedroom and, though Louie rushed after him, he was back in a moment, ducking past her, evading her grabbing arm, and showing Sam the five-cent notebook which he had just taken from under her pillow. Sam began laughing like a jackass, and all the children began bobbing about, like targets in a shooting gallery, laughing and shouting. Ernie thrust it into Sam's hand, but he was serious: he did not laugh:

"You can't read it," he told his father.

Louie stood like a stone image at the door, looking stupidly at them all.

"What is it, Looloo?" asked Sam gently, pushing Ernest away from him.

"A notebook."

"I see that!" He had not opened it. "What's in it? Notes on nature?" He was very kind.

"No."

"What then?"

She flushed purple. "It's in code; in code—I make up my own code: so that no one can read."

"You can show your poor little dad," he cadged, and winked at the children who sat round simmering, waiting for the excitement. He insinuated, "It isn't something you're ashamed to show me, is it? You see, Looloo, though you think I'm too dopey to see through you, I know more'n you think."

It certainly was a pleasure to tease Louisa, for she fell into every trap.

"I never said you were a dope."

"Well, if I ain't a dope, I can see your own brilliant *aphorisms*," and he winked at the children, in a circle of winks—for the past few weeks Louie had been solemnly stuffing them with the aphorisms of La Rochefoucauld, results of French books she had got from the library. After a short struggle, she burst into tears and gave in, unexpectedly. He then opened the rolled, dogeared little book (he was honorable, he had not looked at it without her permission!). On the first page were only a few lines.

(i)   *8 2800 h3f34 5300 q 083*

(ii) *ejsy s dytsmhr yjomh yjsy ejrm s, omodyrt pt s v;rtl pt s kidyovr pg yjr 1/2rsvr 1/2tpmpimvrd s fre eptfd pbrt s ,sm smf ep,sm s vr;; nrhomd yp frbr;p1/2—*

(iii) *jdjayfvy jpcjatjqzj sntzn tl etljay fjhafjl ej—*

(iv) *Ii7i-7i5iii5iii-Ii7i-3i7ii-8iiIiii7i-4iii3iii3l3ii7ii   3i-6iiiIi5ii-7ii5iii-4iii5iii5iii4ii-2iii-5iiiRiii-7ii3i2ii-8ii2ii4iii4iii-Ii5ii2i-7ii3ii2ii-7i6i3iii2i2ii6iii-and the high barn, only yesterday found out they were dreams.*

The code expert had apparently got tired of this slow way of writing, and the fifth entry was merely in her French: "*Dans les moyen âges les parents envoyaient les enfants à les etrangers.*"

"What does this say?" asked Sam, after studying all these items and pointing to the fourth entry. The children crowded round in great curiosity, while Ernie, who worked codes in school with a friend of his, pretended to ignore it. But Louie could not read her own entries and had first to go into her bedroom whence she came again with several scraps of paper, which she held away from Sam. Then she slowly read, "As soon as it was light I ran to look for the well and the spider and the high barn, only yesterday found out they were dreams."

He was very puzzled, "What is it? What does it mean? Is it a dream?"

No: she explained that long ago before she could talk, she had dreamed about a well in the yard and never been able to understand why it was not there; she had tried to ask, but they had not understood her. So with other things. This treasure hunt fascinated Sam, who insisted on the translation of the other codes (the numbering referred to codes, one to four, not to the entries). After work that made her sweat, she finally read to him,

"*i*: I will never tell a lie."

"Well, that's a change, that's something good," said Sam, grinning and winking, his smiles reflected on all the little mirrors round him.

"*ii*: What a strange thing that when a minister or a clerk or a justice of the peace pronounces a few words over a man and a woman a cell begins to develop."

This caused Sam much consternation and merriment when he finally understood it, for though he had given Louie a book, and Henny had given her a talk about marriage, Louie now imagined that marriage was essential to conception and that, provided no powders were administered to the bride and groom (she had made cautious inquiries on this subject—did they eat anything special on their wedding day?), a miraculous or magical event took place during the marriage ceremony. This was confirmed by her reading of various sentimental stories in which, after a hasty wedding, the bridegroom departed leaving the bride at the altar, and yet some months later a baby appeared on the scene. She explained this, with embarrassment, but honestly enough, to Sam who guffawed into his hand, and worked himself up into a paroxysm of fun. But after the first few minutes, the children sat round sad and mystified, for in fact they saw nothing comical in Louie's theory. Heaving with laughter, Sam insisted on Louie's going on with the next item, even though she refused, with a very red face, and so she went on,

"*iii*: Everyday experience which is misery degrades me."

At this he pulled a long face; and then there was nothing more but the ungrammatical French sentence which meant, "In the Middle Ages parents sent (their) children to (into the care of) strangers."

However, this all struck Sam as very bizarre, and he thought over the whole thing during supper. When Louie wanted to go to her room "to do her homework," he made her come to work in the common room, as he called it, saying that he hoped she was not intending to do anything that she would be ashamed of in front of her little sister and brothers and himself; so that she stamped around the house in a great temper, and Henny opened her upstairs bedroom door and screamed out that she'd come down and strangle the great ox that thought it was funny to make so much noise.

When the children went to bed, Louie went up with them to tell them their story, leaving Sam sitting alone, down in the common room, and when she came back to gather up her books, he was still sitting there with misty eyes and a thoughtful expression. She said very sulkily, "Good night."

"Doin' beddybye so soon, Bluebeak?" Sam asked kindly.

"Yes."

"Sit down, Bluebeak, Sam-the-Bold wants to talk to you. What do you mean by saying misery degrades you? What can you know about misery?"

"The misery here at home." She knew it was cruel, and she would have said it a thousand times to make it sharper a thousand times. After a silence, he said sullenly, "Sit down!"

She sank into a chair, frowning at him. Presently he raised his eyes from the table where he was jumping a table knife,

"Well, Louie, since you're beginning to understand some things and since you're occasionally getting a thought into that fat head of yours" (but after this insulting beginning, which she knew was only to cover timidity, he went on to tell her about his boyhood; and how in poverty and ignorant youth, with a gay, licentious father and a dying mother, he had begun his experiments in science and fought upwards, ever since).

"Your mother loved me dearly and short as was her life," said Sam in a weeping tone, "she sacrificed every deed, every thought to you and me: she was a most beautiful soul and I hope you will grow like her; in love we must sacrifice—love is sacrifice, and that is why for love of the people, I have sacrificed my whole life, and would again, had I a thousand lives. I love, all my life has been love, love to me is the whole world—love of nature, man and mankind's good, I mean. Man is naturally good, not wicked, though wicked men, more beasts than men, transformed by greed, have led him into evil. When the time for man comes, though, he will see and rise to the light—there is no need of revolution, but only of guidance, and through evolution and good laws by wise men administered, we will reach the good world, the new age of gold. I heard you speak the other day of the Augustan Age, Looloo: now, that was a wicked age. I wish they would not teach you history, for the pages of history are blotted with crime—only in the good around us, and in our own lives, can we do good. And even we are stained."

Louie had laid her sheets of paper down on the table and was idly scribbling on them. Sam paused for a moment, to attract her attention, but since she said nothing, he went on in a softer, more insinuating tone, "And you later on will lead others to understand: first you must come to understanding yourself. It is not study but the penetration of human motive, you see, Looloo. I think you can do that."

Outside was the plashing of the creeping tide, and the shrieks of young people on the little lighted houseboat, at the end of Shipwrights Street. They both listened to it, and to the breeze, still brittle, not fully leaved.

"The year is young, gawky," thought Sam to himself, "like poor Looloo, so ignorant of herself and me." He said in a low voice, "What are you thinking of, Looloo?"

She replied, with a rush, "*It is night: now do all gushing fountains speak louder, and my heart also is a gushing fountain.*"

"What is that?" She did not reply.

After a silence, he went on, "You know I call myself an agnostic; and perhaps you will be too, Looloo. But we both believe that good is paramount and will spread through the nations, perhaps through the help of the radio. I always said that a second Christ could arise with the radio, speaking to all mankind—though for that we need the universal tongue and not cranky Frongsay and guttural Deutsch: yes, I believe it will spread even to the mean-spirited Frogs and the savage Rossian Tartars, though they may be the cream of Tartars, since Lenin's little tricks—"

He waited for the laugh, but it did not come. Louie was scribbling at the other end of the table.

"I am not personally concerned in what anyone believes as long as he believes in those main principles which you have so often heard me set forth, so often that you know them by heart, Looloo, Looloo, Looloo!"

She raised a drained, martyred face.

"What are you writing, Looloo? Are you making notes of what your dad is telling you?"

She said nothing: her shoulders writhed slightly. He could see that all of two sheets were covered with her little scrawl.

He went on, "And in you I see sure signs of the love of man— Looloo, look at me: what are you writing?"

She sat with her head sunk between her shoulders. Amazed, he got up and came up to the other end of the table. She sat there without a movement. He bent over her shoulder and read,

Shut up, shut up, shut up, shut up, shut up, I can't stand your gassing, oh, what a windbag, what will shut you up, shut up, shut up. And so ad infinitum.

He was terribly hurt. He could hardly believe his eyes. He flung at her, thrusting her shoulder back so that he could look into her face,

"What is the matter with you? You're mean and full of hate. You love hate. I think of love and you are all hate. Sitting there you look like some mean cur in the street, whining and sniveling; you look like a mean gutter rat: your devil of a stepmother has done for you. What can I do with a girl like you? You have no looks, and instead of trying to light up your sullen face with a smile, and beaming on people as I always do, you sit there scowling with a hangdog expression. Get out of my sight: go to bed. I don't understand you."

Half smiling, bursting with confusion, the hulking child rose, gathered together her papers, and went into her bedroom.

Sam flung himself into his armchair and then got up and went out. Louie heard the screen door close and felt a pain in her heart. She sat down on her bed when she had put her papers on the table. Then she rose mechanically and got out her pen and journal preparatory to writing her sonnet to Miss Aiden; but she sat staring at the blank page. She put her head in her hands and, not even crying, groaned, "What can I do? What will be the end of me?"

When Sam came back from a long pacing back and forth under the old maples and elms of the avenue, Louisa was sitting patiently at the common-room table waiting for him.

"Do you want some coffee, Dad?"

"Yiss, Looloo," he cast a pathetic look upon her.

When she set it before him, she sat down, folded her hands, and said, "I'm no good to you: why don't you let me go and live with the Bakens at Harpers Ferry? I could go to school there. What is the good of my staying here? You and mother are always fighting about me."

"Good heavens, I'm trying to bring you closer to me, and the first thing you think of is to go off to Harpers Ferry. It must never be, Louie—a woman must not leave her father's home till she goes to her husband: that is what I am here for, to look after you."

"But all these quarrels—we don't understand each other," Louie said sadly.

"Yes we do, Looloo girl," he answered gently, "yes we do: these are just little storms in a teacup that will pass over."

"No, I must go: you must let me be on my own," persisted Louie quietly. "What is the good—what is the good?"

Sam flushed, "If you were to go, Looloo-girl, I would blame your mother as I've never blamed her for anything. I would put all the blame on her shoulders for driving you from home. It has been her lifelong object to break up my home. I have always fought for the sanctity of my home. Do you want me to blame *her*?"

"No."

"Then there is nothing more to be said."

Chapter Nine

1 *Sunday a Funday.*

It was May, fullest spring, and all the week Henny had been
whimsical and cheerful: she was dressing a doll for the eighteenth
birthday of Cathleen, Hassie's only child. Cathy had dark gold hair,
a thick, creamy skin, and pretty, vacant, tender blue eyes under
auburn brows. Her face was oval and empty of all but a little child's
experience. By ill luck her squarish shoulders concealed her wide-set
breasts, round as cups. Her frailty expressed itself in an eighteen-
inch waist and thin legs and arms. She wound a bath towel round
her waist before dressing and wore skirts as long as possible and
long sleeves. The style of costume no longer favored eighteen-inch
waists, and her powerful fat mother kept drumming in her ears that
men no longer wished to embrace a matchstick middle. She was
deeply ashamed of her figure, stooped to hide it, and clung fervently
to her mother's side. Cathleen had been one of those rare children
who love dolls passionately: her entire uncompanioned childhood
had been spent nursing dolls and dreaming of them. An expensive
doll had always come to her on every anniversary—birthday,
Christmas, New Year's Day (which was the great Collyer reunion
day at Monocacy), and at odd times during the year. Not only
Hassie gave Cathleen dolls, but also all the relatives. Now that she
was eighteen she had a doll collection and with factitious ardor still
prattled about it, her only interest in life. Hassie, madly loving and
maliciously depreciating her, accompanied her everywhere still. A
young girl, brought up in traditions of the sweet-minded middle
South, must go nowhere alone. (David Collyer had come first from

Gloucester, Massachusetts, and his people from Biddeford, Maine, of old Devonshire people.) Henny and Hassie were great friends and for this eighteenth birthday had worked up a great surprise—Cathleen was to get six differently dressed dolls.

"I think it is so nice," said Hassie to all her friends, "it keeps Cathy's mind on the dolls and on looking after them, it gives her something to do: if she marries, the dolls will come in handy for her own nursery and if she doesn't—and you can never tell, men don't like wasp-waisted women any more, they think it means they have no stamina—if she doesn't marry, she always has the collection, hasn't she? It will be worth something. Every stitch in the dolls' clothing has been put in by hand. It's nice for girls, that's what I always say."

Henny sometimes said fretfully to Louie, "A lot of tomfoolery giving dolls to a great big woman who ought to be looking for a husband—does she think she'll keep her a child forever?"

But Henny got on well with Hassie, had a lot of fun with her, and collaborated with her. Of the three, Henny did the best sewing. Her long, strong, firm-tipped fingers gave her power and delicacy: she did beautiful Madeira embroidery, made darns fit for an old-fashioned ladies' workbook, and, when she could, sewed seams by hand with tiny stitches. She prided herself on it still and had even in the last few years taught Louie to sew and embroider. Every one in the immense double family praised "Henny's exquisite work." Now Henny had put out her best effort for the dressing of a dark-eyed, bisque-complexioned china doll (she still preferred the china dolls to the new composition and cloth ones, with their quaint upturned modern eyes). Henny and Hassie were full of wonderful lore and morality, all concerning dolls. Dolls should be expensive and daintily dressed; girls of eleven and so on should have baby dolls with real diapers; little children should have rag dolls (Henny had made a plenty of rag dolls for her family, running them up on the machine); boys and girls alike should have dolls till about the age of eight; paper dolls taught them to do nice handwork, and so forth. They could discuss the doll question for hours and all most solemnly, laying down the law, and discussing the moral deformity that came from too-late or the wrong use of dolls. Henny's doll was dressed in the secrecy of her room. She said, a dozen times a week, "I have no home—they only allow me a room here, but it is my room." The little girls were allowed to come in after knocking, and would tiptoe forward, holding their breath, fascinated by Henny's magic. At other times she would be sniffing her smelling salts, or taking aspirin, or mending linen, or reading, always using her eyes which grew darker and more tired every day, always doing things that were private to herself. She was a charming, slatternly witch, their household witch; everything that she did was right, right, her right: she claimed this right to do what she wished because of all her sufferings, and all the children believed in her rights.

The entire house was a dark cavern of horrors and winds perpetually moving and howling. When Sam was in all day, now, Henny would send a message that she would be out all day: and, no more complaining of her untidy loose clothes and stray graying hairs and ugly old black hat, she would skip out of the house as soon as she could "to escape the damn hammering and whistling," and go up to town "to meet Hassie." She looked much older than she had in Washington; she was viler, she had lost even the seeming of respect for Sam, but she was merrier. For months she had not spoken to any one of the "mud rats" of Eastport, but after school opened and Tommy went to school, for the first time, she went over to "ladida" with his teacher, a nice little old maid called Miss Lake, and soon got to know "the parents." She had given up all pretensions to middle-class elegance. She was one of the Collyers of Baltimore, the bankrupt Collyers, she sneered and laughed at herself and, pointing to her old clothes, her grease spots, would say she was an old joke and life was an old joke.

The children were happier with this Henny than with the other. She would always insult Sam when she mentioned him, but now with a laugh as if he was of no more consequence than the butcher or than dirty old "Coffin" Lomasne. Henny soon knew all the personalities of the place and as she used to jeer at the neighbors of Georgetown, now mocked at them instead. The children, too, became very friendly with the "mud rats," and Henny did not even try to keep them away from fishermen's and boatbuilders' children. "We're all mud rats," she would say to the children as they crowded about her bent shoulders, peering at her satin stitch or Madeira work, "my kids too: I'm not proud; well, I don't care what happens to you kids, I've done my best and if that's not satisfactory, you must try another shop." Then she would lift her head and laugh at them. She was turning into a dried-up, skinny, funny old woman, "I'm an old woman, your mother's an old woman, so I'll be an old woman, and I'll do what I please."

Sometimes Hassie would drive down to Annapolis, but it took her forty-five minutes and she could rarely leave the sea-food shop for the day: so, generally, Henny had to take the little rackety train which passed through hated woodland and straggly little suburbs (as Henny said) before at last teetering into Camden Station where Hassie would meet her. These days (the dividends coming much sooner and faster than anyone had expected, and Henny being able to get money irregularly from the not unkind Lessinum), Hassie and Henny went in for shopping sprees, following all the "opportunity" and "budget" sales and "throwouts below cost." Henny always came home exhausted but happy with bundles in her arms, or bundles to follow by express, while the children danced about or waited impatiently for the carrier and post. True, Sam had at last decided to ask for a job as biologist with the Maryland Conservation Commission, although he resolutely refused to work for "the prostituted press" or for "private greed," but their money had run out and now they were living entirely on credit, on Henny's promises, lies, and tricks, and on Henny's dividends. Sometimes when Henny was broke, Hassie would lend her money "until her check came in," and once more, then, Henny would come home, smiling, lovingly, to her brood, with her arms full and clothes for them all, and even something for Sam whose wardrobe was worn out, and even sometimes toys and rare delicacies that she craved for—crystallized violets, preserved ginger, pickled walnuts, and little lengths of cloth and little bits of confectioners' ingredients that she could use for school and church bazaars. For though Henny never went to parents' meetings and church services, she loved to donate things made by herself to their festivals, bazaars, and sales of work. A lot of the local women, especially the mothers, came to like her and respect her because (coming of such a fine family) she put on no airs, because the poor thing managed so well on nothing with so many dear, well-behaved children, and because she was so generous. She was a genius at making both ends meet indeed, for they managed to live and when she could, Henry disobeyed Sam's orders about substitute foods (margarine for butter, maize oil for olive oil, pork and beans for red meat), because, she said, her children should not live on trash, her children had to fight for their livings, having such a silly, puffed-up ignoramus of a father, her girls were not going to be underfed "mud rats." Sam ignored all her darts, and even pretended to ignore where the household money came from (he would find it lying on his desk, in this time of distress, with the usual note: "Samuel C. Pollit: Use this for your expenses,"), though he often spoke of their poverty and his sartorial misery, saying, "And I'm a good-looker too, the cheapest suits look like eighty-dollar suits on me, and I can't even get twenty-five dollars for a suit because of the wickedness of men." About their money, as about everything, he was vague and sentimental. But in a few months he would be earning, and in the meantime, he said,

"It was only right that the mother too should fend for her offspring." Henny, hearing this, would merely say, "Hrmph!" or, "The damn fool!" or, "Well, I'm doing it, aren't I?"

How thrilling were the days, for the children, when Henny was heard stirring early, before breakfast, and when they would see her already dressed for town, not in her wrapper! They would crowd round her shrilling, "Are you going to town, Mothering? Mothering, am I going to get my new suit today? Mothering, you ought to see the big hole in my shoe!" and Henny would push them away with her hands, laughing a bit, "Yes, yes, yes, now keep quiet and don't shout so loud or the Great I-Am will be asking questions and preaching about extravagance." At this the children would flush happily, giggle, and break up into atoms of humanity, but still ask softly, If they could have a belt, and, Whether Mothering was going to get Saul a baseball mitt or not. "Wait and see," Henny would say, "wait and see." Then off she would rush, leaving a sweet quiet in the house, the sun falling on unswept floors and undusted furniture. Charming was this slatternliness: this dirt was a heaven to the harassed children, and they loved Henny for leaving it so.

Meanwhile, Sam, whistling and singing operas and popular hits, would be leaving his trail of sawdust and brickdust, cement pellets and putty crumbs, and never an experiment in chemistry or physics did he perform nor ever work with them over a book, but only talked with tender abstraction of "great lives" and "great chemists" and of his own beautiful soul and sympathetic life story. He would reform the state, even the world, because through love he knew more than all the politicians, and yet the queer thing was that the children were always having to help him, tell him what Tommy and Evie and Louie were doing in the secrecy of their rooms or the nooks they had made their own. With what surprise and joy he would seize on all this information of his loving spies, showing them traits of character, drawing a moral conclusion from everything! Yes, he and the children were very close: they were leading an ideal life, and Sam felt very sorry, as he often told them, that he had to leave them soon and go back into the struggle, for his great fitness was to be leader of children. He hoped, he said, that all of his children would enter the service of the people and perhaps some of them would be schoolteachers, because to lead youth was beautiful, and then it was a safe job, and respected. Now, this appealed to the children who had been worrying about his job and their future jobs; especially to Ernie who studied the bills that came into the house and always asked his father how much money he earned every month, and tried to calculate, even, his mother's dividend earnings, a thing impossible because of the irregularity of her drawings.

This Sunday in mid-May, Henny was to go to town for Cathleen's birthday, and the house buzzed joyously from early morning, because a "new deal" was to be had by all members of the household—Henny was to have Sundays off, this being the first Sunday; Sam was to superintend the housework and show them all how easily it could be managed by "system" and "scientific management." The girls were to cook, the boys were to do the ordinary jobs of house upkeep such as hoeing, weeding, washing verandas, and moving heavy objects. Henny left early and as soon as she went, they all rushed in, clustered round their father, while he "started the machine going."

"Man must work and women must sweep," declared Sam, first of all. "Little-Womey, subbor cawf! Now, I'll show you all how to wash the dishes." Commanding from his honorable position behind the coffee cup, he made Little-Womey and Looloo scrape and stack the dishes in the wash-basin, get the dish towels, dishcloth, dish mop, and soap saver, while he entertained them with his philosophy and schemes for the world.

"The Philosopher at the Breakfast Table," he announced complacently, "we have risen superior to the raw struggle for supremacy, the tooth-and-nail stage; it is now a struggle of types, brains and philosophies. With a council of scientists running the world—" and so forth, and then, "If I were autocrat of all nations," with "supreme power, the lives of all, the life of the world in my hands," he told them what he would do. For example, he might arrange the killing off of nine tenths of mankind in order to make room for the fit. "This would be done by gas attacks on people living ignorant of their fate in selected areas, a type of eugenic concentration-camp; they would never know, but be hurled painlessly into eternity, or they would pass into the lethal chamber of time and never feel a pang."

"But you would keep yourself alive," said Louie unpleasantly.

"The great point in washing dishes," said Sam, "is to have the water bilin' and the dishes scraped and rinsed first under the tap: all extra grease should be removed and the plates can then be dipped and stacked without extra work. A little scientific method would eliminate all work from the household, so to speak: now, if me and not Henny was runnin' this institution, you would see: because all the improvements in household technique have been made by men, becaze women got no brains. Now, Looloo-Meany, is the water a-bilin'?"

"Yes."

"Then Sam-the-Bold es a-comin'," he sang, "quick's the word and smart's the action: watch me—we'll be through in two shakes of a dead lamb's tale. Ermy?" He gave all their whistles and marshaled them in order of age with the dish towels. "I hain't had time to make that there dish rack, but I got cheap labor well organized."

With a great deal of shouting and bumping they got through most of the dishes, and then Sam slid under the sink the oatmeal saucepan, coffeepot, and skillet, remarking that "the women could do the dirties next time." Sam then retired from scientific management and went out into the sun, "Can't miss great Sol's benefits," said he, "for a lot of women's messin'," and when they all hastened to jump on him and point out that he did no work, he only laughed and stretched himself on the grass. "I work with myed [my head], I got lieutenants to do the rest of the work," said he, and expatiated on the work he did with his head during the times he had his eyes closed. This foolery annoyed and amused the children; but while he rested, they scattered off to their innumerable occupations. Tommy had a gift for carving boats out of bits of wood: he imitated the skiffs, powerboats, and even the *Reina Mercedes*. The fish-and boatmen round the shore gave him bits of wood and showed him how to shape the hulls and prows and where to put the masts. On one of his productions, a sort of marlin-bellied yacht, they had shown him how to fix a fin keel. He had a lifeboat round which Louie had looped a cord. Sam at once predicted great things for him as a boat designer: "Perhaps you can design special observation vessels for the Bureau of Fisheries, or the Government Chesapeake Fisheries which I envisage for the future"; then when Tommy had run out again to chat with his dearly beloved longshoremen and boat owners and Chesapeake sailors, Sam would shake his head at the others, "Tommy great lad, great lad, but no bean, no upperworks, a fine hull but no captain on the bridge: that's all, but no matter, no matter, we cain't all be philosophers and scientists: there be they what must hew water and draw wood."

It was jolly, though, with Henny away: the morning flowed away like a clear running tide. Sam schemed with them; they listened to the birds and wondered where the mourning dove was nesting. They had birdbaths and seedboxes in their grounds and the thick trees invited many birds. They had left a wilderness patch at the far end of the orchard where old ivy, clematis, and honeysuckle mantled the tottering fence; for the hedge dwellers and the low-flying, insect hunters who loved to dart and sway on the slender sappy masts, goldfinches and flycatchers. Along the side porch, inside the beams, were five nests, two of house wrens and three untidy ones of sparrows:

they had thrown out the sparrows' nests in order to leave the house wrens in peace. It was a thriving, thickly inhabited wilderness, and merely lazing and looking, amateur naturalists, they could have spent the day. No urgent calls for help—to beat eggs, string beans, peel potatoes, empty slops, came from the unwomaned house. "Peace, perfect peace," sighed Sam a dozen times in the morning.

When he felt cheerfully warm, they began to talk about the neighbors, about whom they had just as many comical legends as about the Georgetown neighbors; and the kingpin, of course, was the atrocious "Coffin" Lomasne. Fearful tales were told of him— he was a vile spider of usury spinning foolish, weak, necessitous flies into his web. Sam told them all about poor Lai Wan Hoe and his troubles with the usurers, how he had to embezzle and fly, all because of Usurious Greed; and how they should not say such a man was an octopus, because an octopus was a sweet, clean beast whose rose-pink flesh they had eaten, but who would want to eat ghoulish Lomasne? An octopus was swift as shadow, a subtle chameleon, brave, clever, a battler—who could say so of "Coffin" Lomasne? And then they invented wilder tales about "Coffin"—dead marines rose out of his cheap coffins at night; one night the sucking marsh would open underneath him and try to digest him into the black mud where his poor corpses, oozing from their cheap coffins, lay, but being too vile and indigestible, he would be spewed up again. He was so mean, said Sam (inventing freely), that he kept his own excrement in a pit and doled it out to his own vegetables. The children shrieked, gasped with laughter, and got red in the face; for in general such jokes were not allowed at Spa House. Sam averred that "Coffin" was slowly turning diarrhea color, his clothes were stolen "from the swaddling clothes they wraps corps [corpses] in," and his cap was a candle extinguisher stolen from a wake. He made his wife eat candles stolen from wakes, said Sam, and they ate dandelion salad. What were the rats and cats that hung round "Coffin" Lomasne's, asked Sam, especially at night? Where did "Coffin" put his money, Sam speculated. He pictured the money put away in one of the coffins, and then he pictured "Coffin's" end: one night at one o'clock when all slept and the mud bubbled round his place, the mud that could not digest him, three poor blacks, invisible in the black night, would come and take "Coffin," place him in one of his own coffin-rowboats and row him out and across the deeps of the Chesapeake; and when they came to the Happy Hunting Grounds of the dead Susquehannocks, the shady braves would skin him alive and skin him dead and burn him at the stake and chop him up to feed the ghosts of sharks upon, and those ghostly sharks expiring in a shady way would become devil sharks and feed upon the others, and so on to a great Armageddon in the shadow world, all because no one could stand the poison of "Coffin's" shade.

The children breathed peacefully before this wonderful story of "Coffin" Lomasne and were half believing it; but at the end, to bring their father back and make him start another of his tales of marvels, they pricked him on a sore point—why was the local postal delivery at present being done by a relieving man, given into the hands of Popeye Banks? Popeye Banks was a revolting being of seventeen years old, with an exophthalmic goiter excruciating to see. Generally he wore eyeshades, but sometimes he did not. Sam declared he was feeble-minded as well, and gosh only knew what else he did and had! He probably stole and spied: he certainly leered and limped. Like many a handsome body, Sam was not only revolted by deformity and plainness but actually saw essential evil in it: and essential evil, most particularly, was what robbed him, Sam Pollit.

Join the Navee and see the world!
And what'd we see? We saw the sea,

sang Ernie.

The boys flew into an excited discussion of the Naval Academy's spring sports schedule, baseball and plebe baseball (here Sam stuck in his nose, and said on no account to use that British import, "plebe"), and crew and track—they despised "the sissies," but Naval Academy made up half their talk, and the boys all now had an interest in living: they did not miss the nation's capital for a moment, but felt that they were now living in the heart of the United States. Here they ("the sissies," that is) were visited by Dartmouth, Harvard, Princeton, Cornell, Columbia, University of Virginia, Pittsburgh, and, of course, their own Georgetown. Their life was full of passionate discussions. They blessed Sam for bringing them to this little creek which was a whirlwind of boy life, and Ermy had even begun to weaken—with his mathematical talents he might even go to the Academy: how the little boys would admire him then! Many of their schoolmates, and Louie's too, were children of the Academy staff, and the boys brought home plenty of gossip: So-and-so was a stinker ("say a stench," emended Sam), and they were sissies, they had to arrange and sew their own clothes and sweep their own rooms like girls, and Navy could of course win this year—no Baltimore college had a ghost of a chance (for their patriotism was limited to Spa Creek, and the United States Naval Academy was a Spa Creek affair). Sam was very happy, for he saw his gang (he now called them "his plebes") very happy. The "little women" were discontented, but, after all, he was a man too: this was a man's world. All girls were discontented till they married and had men and babies.

Both Sam and Henny now speculated openly (though separately) about the sort of man Louisa would marry. Henny went to Hassie's fortune teller who told her her stepdaughter would marry an officer at the Annapolis Naval Academy. "It's wonderful," said Henny in great surprise, to all her friends and even to Louisa, "I am certain she never saw me before yesterday." She immediately began to believe that Louisa would marry a naval officer and she looked on Louisa with more respect, began at last to listen to Louie's pleas about getting a permanent and a dancing frock. "If you're going to begin going about," said Henny optimistically, "your father will simply have to give up his stupid ideas about dancing and all his insane puritanical ideas. A great big girl your age who has never had a dancing lesson!" and she went so far as to write a note to Sam on this subject: "Samuel C. Pollit: You must arrange for your daughter to get dancing lessons and a suitable dress." This note enraged Sam beyond belief; in it he saw only another vicious attempt of "women brought up in the Baltimore white-slave tradition," to debauch his daughter. He refused once for all to allow Louisa to take part in such orgies or even to think about them. Henny, with grim, bitten lip looking ugly as sin (for her lips were purplish now and her skin dry saffron), had gone out with Hassie on a shopping expedition and bought what she conceived to be a young girl's dress, a thing that might have suited her well enough in her young days, a peach-colored, silky, filmy cotton, made with three frills round the shoulders and a trail of roses hanging from the waist.

It ended in Louie's not going to any dances, however, and in "mooning and moping" over Miss Aiden till the entire family of Pollits thought the child was queer, while Hassie told Henny she must early look out for a husband for her, or else some accident would happen to the great overgrown child. Henny, though she felt old-fashioned now, began to look round Baltimore, surreptitiously, for a husband for her stepdaughter—there was time, of course; Louie was only fourteen, but she looked like seventeen at least, and, thought Henny, "I've got to save her before he makes her a bluestocking that no man will want!"

They lived in a strange world. Sam did not yet go to work (although now a job as biologist was assured); Henny picked money out of the wind; Louie had left this earth completely and was floating about somewhere between Elysium and Inferno; Ernie had become "a crank," and the little children were inextricable from some mazy world of birds, flowers, winds, and tides. Sam was as near happy as he could be, and his chief worry now was Ernie and his "miserliness." The greatest family joke now going was that Ernie was growing up to be a miser, both a reproach and a great joke. Sam, too, not long ago, deciding to take the bull by the horns and to be as scientific as possible, much perturbed because Louisa had an "unscientific" view of procreation, had come to her where she stood washing her long waterfall of hair in the bathroom, and after poking his nose this way and that round all the corners to be sure that "the childer" were not within earshot, had given her three books—Shelley's *Poems* (to help her poetry, said he), Frazer's *Golden Bough* (for the anthropological side of the question, said he), and James Bryce's book on Belgian atrocities (to explain our entry into the war and the need for America's policing the world, said he). Louie now read stern proofs of stranger fairy tales acted in reality, more gruesome than any Grimms have recorded, though the Grimms are fearful enough, with their tales of forest cannibalism and murders. From the two latter books Louie was able to fill her daydreams and night thoughts with the mysteries of men's violence—women crucified (so it was set forth with judicial severity) and unborn children torn from their bellies, young girls sent into barns with detachments of soldiers and "the ripening grain," soldiers winding the hair of women round their sabers and thus dragging them to the floor to satisfy their bestial desires.

There was plenty of this, and during the warm advancing spring Louie became more and more thoughtful and round-eyed. Sam might rave at her woodenheadedness as he liked, she had too much to dream about. Now, "so that you can tell the good from the bad, and avoid what your own conscience tells you is the wrong thing," Sam had revealed to her in a few weeks, and without a word of his, the unspeakable madness of sensuality in past ages and concealed imaginations; nations had done this, armies, great names and glorious artists, and her father had told her to study the books carefully with the following strange words: "It is the father who should be the key to the adult world, for his daughters, for boys can find it out for themselves." After this, Sam turned shy and avoided saying one word more to her on all these subjects, even avoided her, and when she turned her darkened, staring eye on him by accident, he would glance away as if ashamed. But the more she read of these works, the more she felt guilty of power of her own, and she began suddenly to despise and loathe Sam with an adult passion.

A very unpleasant thing had been discovered in an outlying part of the district in recent weeks. A girl child having been found pregnant, her father, a jobless roustabout, had been accused of incest; the girl went to a state home, but the father, only accused by hearsay and on the confused testimony of the child, still remained at home. The papers contained accounts and mysterious charges which the children read eagerly but did not understand. Sam's hair rose on the first evening and, suddenly flaming with temper, shouting with rage, he seized a stick and declared that there and then he would head a posse of respectable fathers and citizens and go to chastise the editor of the paper. "I am a man of peace," cried Sam shouting with rage, "but this is a case where vigilante law comes into being and has its function. The miserable cowardly yellow devil who dares attack a father in his own home, on top of the sorrow he must be feeling at finding his daughter in trouble, a little girl with a baby to come—think of that, Looloo, a girl two years younger than you, poor baby!—has to suffer undefended an unspeakable charge like this. He is to be brought up on this charge," shouted Sam, grasping his walking stick, "and because he is poor, and has only one of those windblows of shacks to live in, they can attack him with impunity. Every decent-thinking man and decent-living man in this community will be roused by this: I am a man of peace but I would go myself and horsewhip the dirty cur," and a frightening typhoon raged for a long time, a storm with a high yellow glare and copper-colored waves hissing, licking, and rising round them.

But Sam did not go: he only cursed the editor and declaimed every day until the subject died down. The daughter had accused her own father, "poor miserable wretch," said Sam sternly, "baby taught to say something to help the cause of a wicked lawyer. No doubt, Loo and Ernie," he continued, "you will find behind this story some dreadful corruption: a landlord trying to evict the man—doubtless he is a good man who has tried, in the past, to show up the forces of evil, and this is their stenchful revenge. My boys and girls, mark this; and notice other things that I bring to your notice. Your father does not get angry about things for nothing. This world is full of corruption, and when the foul press, the sink of greed, the gutter of moneybags spewing its filth back to the gutter whence it came, the harlot of the world, begins to get its back up and get moral about something, be sure that things are not what they seem and that they are trying to cover up, not *expose*, a scandal. When a man is poor," said Sam solemnly, turning to Ernie and pouring his white heat into Ernie's serious, round eyes, "the world hates him: you must be prepared for that, Ermo: you might fight it as I have. The entire gamut of scandal, hate, and lying is prepared for a poor man in this world who dares to work for the truth. That is why they got rid of me too: they feared me, for wickedness fears Truth."

Ernie stared at him for a moment longer and, getting slowly off the porch where they were all sitting now, looking at Sam's blond flame, walked off by himself. They saw his round brown head disappearing amongst the bushes, down towards the beach. Sam winked at them all, and, nudging Looloo, said *sotto voce*, "Thinking! A thoughtful head! Not a big head but a brain with many corrugations, I'll be bound!" He smiled and nodded at them all, "A good boy!"

It was a queer thing, that though Louie had been brought up on *The Origin of Species* and *The Animal Kingdom* (of Cuvier) and numerous works in biology and psychology, not to mention the works Sam had just given her, she scarcely comprehended at all the actions meant by "sexual commerce." But after this horrific happening which had taken place in one of these hideous far suburbs built on yellow sumps and dominated by the Gargantuan black pipes of Bethlehem Steel, with nothing but tracks over the mud and colorless dry grass, she got the idea that she had run up against one of the wickednesses of the universe, an infernal middle kingdom of horror that she alone could stand. For Sam could rave and the little children could look at her queerly when she blurted out the half-formed thoughts in her mind, but she felt sure that she only *felt* what was going on under the ribs of the visible world. Under the eternal belching black organ pipes of Bethlehem Steel was the vile lake that covered an agony of fire, a lake that hid something like Grendel, or the pained bowels of an Aetna, or the cancer of a Prometheus, and in this lake too was this hideous father with his lying child half smothered by the swelling fruit of her womb.

Louie's brain boiled by day and by night, and every joke of Sam's, every silly crack and harmless tease made her flame with a murderous revenge. Whenever she and he were at home, she would mutter at him (from a silent distance), "Vengeance is mine, I will repay." Against this went her terrible passion for Miss Aiden, childish in its ignorance, adult in its turbulency. At school she was in heaven, at home she was in a torture chamber. The children would often study her attentively and seem to know that she was now in a very strange world, but to Sam she only seemed "more muddleheaded than ever, instead of brighter as I had hoped." To escape Sam she would always run away from the house with her book, usually Shelley (she wanted to marry a man like Shelley, only Shelley), and read and learn. *The Cenci,* a famous piece, she had avoided for weeks because the subject seemed forbidding, but when she at last began to read it, she began marveling again, for it seemed that (eliminating the gloomy and gorgeous scene) Beatrice was in a case like hers. The Saturday afternoon before Henny went to town, then, with the doll for poor Cathleen, she had learned,

...I, alas!
Have lived but on this earth a few sad years,
And so my lot was ordered, that a father
First turned the moments of awakening life
To drops, each poisoning youth's sweet hope;....
(Shelley: The Cenci, Act V, Scene 2)

It was mid-afternoon when they saw Louie coming up from the beach again: the blood-gold sun rimmed grass, leaves, and Louie's new-washed hair.

"See where Looloo walked by herself, thinking her thoughts," said Sam to the twins, who were stretched beside him on the grass at the western side of the house. "Always thinking, always mooning, it's a pity she didn't have her own mother for a few years, and she would have been better. You see, I think I made a mistake letting her talk to Bonniferous so much, when poor Bonniferous was here, for Bonniferous had silly ideas about going on the stage and now Looloo does nothing but talk to herself," and cheerily he hailed her, "Bluebeak? Is you talkin' to yousef or is you recitin' poetry?"

Louie stopped and looked at them and said very proudly, "Reciting poetry, if you must know."

"Come, recite it to us, Looloo," said Sam stretching himself. Louie did not wait a moment but stepped over to them and declaimed Cenci's speech,

God!

Hear me! If this most specious mass of flesh,

Which Thou hast made my daughter; this my blood...this devil

Which sprung from me as from a hell, was meant

To aught good use...

Sam stared and his eyes narrowed, but he was reassured by the book in her hand, the very one he had given her; Louie continued,

...if her bright loveliness

Was kindled to illumine this dark world...

Sam repeated softly, "If her bright loveliness was kindled to illumine this dark world," and waited patiently for Louie to continue, always with the gentle smile playing on his long, well-formed lips. Louie stopped and said proudly again, "You're making fun of me!" She started to leave them.

"Stay, Looloo," begged Sam. "No, not to be made fun of." "Stupid Looloo," cried Sam, in surprise. "Looloo, afternoon tea in the common room."

When she brought in the jingling tray and set it down at the western end of the long table, Sam and the boys had a lighted candle before them, and Ernie, who was very keen on physics, was explaining to them that in the center of the flame was nothing but a cool spot: if you put a match there, said Ernie, it would not light. The children, giggling with excitement, began brushing their fingers through the flame, to feel the cool spot. Ernie held his finger there for a moment and pulled it away with a comical shriek, and then Sam put out his big yellow forefinger and put it into the flame and drew it away, blowing and making a great travesty of his sufferings. Looloo stood watching the candle's pale ear of light floating beside the dusty sunbeam streaming through the window.

"And Looloo try," said Ernie, appealing to her, "you try too, Looloo," for Ernest was always anxious that everyone should be convinced of his proofs. The children meanwhile were dashing their fingers back and forth in a silly way, giggling and licking their hands. Louie, with a slight smile, stuck out the little finger of her right hand and held it in the flame. The children's faces stilled with surprise, their eyes opened, and Sam, whose face had held as always a merry jeer, looked questioningly at her, and he suddenly cried, "Looloo, don't be a fool!" while Tommy said, "Ooh, Ooh, you'll hurt yourself," and Ernie said, "Looloo, don't." There was a nasty smell of frying flesh in the room. Louie withdrew her finger and showed it to them for an instant, charred, and then coolly walked out of the room to go and wrap it in oil. Evie and Little-Sam were bawling, and the others were pale with fright, while Sam repeated several times angrily, "Looloo is a cussed, mulish donkey: Looloo has not an ounce of sense in her bonnet." He even got up and came to the door of the kitchen and asked angrily, "Looloo, isn't it hurting you?"

"It is not hurting me," she said stiffly.

"It must be."

"Nothing hurts me if I don't want it to," she told him. He lumbered away, shrugging his shoulders and utterly at a loss. The child was beyond him. He made up his mind that he would never let Ernie get out of hand like that. As for Evie, she was not going to go to high school. He had made up his mind that it was the higher education that had "knocked spots off Looloo's common sense," as he now told his little family in a soft grumble, and he would eat his hat if they ever caught him making a cantankerous wretch out of Little-Womey.

But Ernie pussyfooted out to the kitchen and asked, "Doesn't it hurt, Louie?" to which Louie replied with a smile, "Yes, of course it hurts, but it doesn't matter." With the children she felt cool; all her passions flowed far above their unharmed heads. This evening

Sam left her alone in the cool of her room upstairs; and it was this evening, looking at the sky bloom darkly and the pendent globe of Jupiter, that she had a splendid idea. In June would be Sam's birthday, and for it she would write a play which the children could act. She got out her pen and paper and, instead of writing for Miss Aiden, wrote for herself, not for the children, a strange little play. When it was written (there were scarcely twenty lines in it), she turned it into a secret language that she began to make up there on the spot. This was a good idea, she thought: so that she could write what she wished, she would invent an extensive language to express every shade of her ideas. "Everyone has a different sphere to express, and it goes without saying that language as it stands can never contain every private thought." But she was only a weakling and a mental dwarf now as before, and the new vocabulary did not ever exceed a few hundred words, nor was there ever more than one play written in it! She was called from this by a bump and Chappy's (Charles-Franklin's) scream, and as she plunged to the rescue, she heard again Sam's plaintive, bashful question to Little-Womey, "Why is Mothering out all day? Why is the Henny-penny always away from the chicken-lickens now? Don't she want to take her responsibilities any mower? Why, Little-Womey, soon you got to be my wife, I speck."

"Yes, Taddy," Evie answered, from the porch door, seeing that Chappy was already in Louie's arms. She rushed up, too, seeing that he still sobbed, "Wassamatter, Chappy? Hurt ooself?" Sam came running, snatched the little butter-blond boy away and started tossing him to the ceiling and at last ran off with him, hallooing and doing the round of the orchard. They heard Chappy's loud crowing laughs.

"Daddy said I could be his wife," Evie told Louie, looking up at her confidentially and not sure whether she would laugh and approve. Louie turned her back, and Evie's face fell.

2 *Miss Aiden to dinner.*

Since May the little boys with real fishing tackle had been fishing the streams that feed the Severn, and the local coves, with Sam. Sam predicted a roaring summer. Saul Pilgrim, who did a fishing column for one of the Washington papers and who wrote fishing poetry which he syndicated, was to come down to Spa House, just about Sam's birthday, June twenty-third, on his way to Ocean City, for the big-game season. The boys had caught plenty of poor sport, gudgeons, minnows, even pike and sunfish, but they nagged Sam to be allowed to go with one or other of the fishermen and boatowners down to the Winter Quarter Shoals or the Tide Rips, for catching the game king, the marlin, who in midsummer here strikes his most northerly point. Sam refused, and the boys found to their sorrow that even the fishermen were joking; the marlin is no minnow, will fight from four to fifteen hours, and kills his fishers when he can. The season was now the talk of the bay, for many men idle during the year are in good work from May to November. About three hundred thousand persons go to the Chesapeake for the summer fishing, six hundred and thirty odd boats are employed at a rental of nearly three hundred thousand dollars yearly, a giant revenue for the tidewater section of Maryland; meantime, the bait for trout, spot, and croakers, chiefly peeler crabs in all stages, sold at from fifty cents to two dollars a dozen has increased the income of the crabber, and, in addition to the big boats, are all sorts of rowboats, sailing boats, canoes, and lighter craft. The boys looked forward to a raging summer. Sam and other fishermen predicted from certain signs (early swarming, strange electric weather) a great catch. The air was alive with fish stories, the points of a good fisherman, and Sam was full of indignations and moral points—depletion of the crab supply, use of beardless hooks, the democratization of game fishing, and the commercial utilization of the immense supply of big game fish taken in at this season and wasted. "The marlin is a singularly oily fish"; said Sam, "no doubt the flesh is inedible, though it may possibly be treated, but surely we ought to use this valuable supply of animal oil, thrashing about in the ocean under our noses. The fishing is done for us, at great expense by wealthy fishermen," and he proposed schemes for receiving the marlin as soon as it was caught after verification of size and poundage, and to try out the oil and use the offal for fertilizer perhaps. "We are now slowly awakening to the need for reforestation," said Sam, "and why should we lay waste the great treasuries of the sea?"

The house rang with all this great lore, for now Sam was in his fishy element; and, from long hearing and training, his sons and daughters were as expert with the hook, line, and sinker, as they were with the brace-and-bit and plumb-and-level. The boys were only at home half the day, being out with the men of the bay, getting information and swapping eagerness. Although friends had long since ceased to come to Sam's house, Saul Pilgrim, the author of the interminable serial, had patience and pity and, without false pride, he would sneak in and out of Spa House, without meeting its lady and without asking for a meal. He would come into the dark narrow hall (very different from the broad thoroughfare of Tohoga House) and, while Louie took his hat, would begin poems and conundrums,

Oh, do not bring the catfish here,
The catfish is a beast I fear,
Don't bring him here at all!

and,

If I were born a Pelican,
I'd do my best to be a Man;
If I were born a Man, I'd wish

I might associate with Fish;
If I were born a Fish—but then
What use to wish? Men must be men.

and very solemnly to Louie he would ask, "Do you know Latin?
Well, translate this:

Isa belli haeres ago
Fortibuses in aro
An be sidem forte trux:
Si voticinem! Pes an dux."

When Henny would come gloomily downstairs, he would
murmur politely and make himself scarce till she had passed. Then
he and Sam would sit down over some tea or coffee and biscuits, and
it would be nothing but flannel bait, white-line peelers, green bait,
beach casting, mine bilge pollution, Conowingo Dam shad, rainbow
trout, and *Tetrapturus albitus*. In the days just gone Saul Pilgrim had
got information for his columns from Sam, and Sam still could put
him right on the technical and formal side, for Pilgrim had but a
messy, literary mind and scattered experience. The children would
sit around for a while, casting in questions and hearing strange
things—how, sure as the calendar, the blue tuna turned up in the
Bahamas on May fifteenth each year and then worked north, arriving
in Nova Scotia on July fifteenth, and then disappeared entirely from
view for nearly a year, though they were sighted cruising round the
Atlantic end of the Mediterranean, and then, sure as the calendar,
would turn up again in the Bahamas on May fifteenth; how they
were hunting him by boat and by plane; of the great deeps off the
Bahamas, when the sea, suddenly shelving from four hundred to
four thousand fathoms, looks like a low-lying island and fatefully
attracts unwary planes at nightfall; the mystery of what happens in

those abysses, and all the mysteries of the sea; what is bred in the Sargasso Sea? They spun each other old true yarns, known to the children from their cradles, but which they listened to again, about the conger eel, born a thousand miles from shore in the Sargasso Sea, transparent as glass, which, working slowly shoreward, turns into the elver, and at last near the coast he begins to feed and turn dark.

"Now," said Sam, turning to the wide-eyed children, "millions of those elvers are approaching our shores, entering our tidal basins and estuaries, here and all along the coast from Gulf to Gulf. In from five to twenty years, until they are older than you, much older than Looloo, they stay up streams and creeks and feed, and then the females begin to drop downstream again, sleeping in the daytime, traveling by night; then they change from that olive green to black, they meet the males, and males and females move out to sea. When they leave our shores they disappear, like so many migratory pelagic beings; no one knows how they go—whether in a great swarm like the great migrations of men in the Asiatic continent, or singly, on a tremendous love journey. Their offspring are found out over the watery abysses, beyond Florida and the Bahamas. Then it seems they die. Out there in mid-ocean, they meet the European eels, but they do not go back with the Frog eels and the Spik eels and the Arab eels—no sirree, their children all know where they come from, and they come back to America when they are born, ribboning transparently through the heavy, dark sea water."

The children grinned from ear to ear, and Saul (who only in fishing found peace from his termagant wife) would grin too, and then would earnestly turn to Sam again and ask, Did he think the migratory schools of tuna and marlin traveled all the year in the Gulf Stream, as they were always to be found in the Stream; but even so, how they knew the time of year was a mystery.

"Do they come on May fifteenth in leap year too?" asked Ernie with his mouth open, for the answer to pop in. Oh, they spent long hours together, and then the children saw a different sort of man, a thoroughly democratic sort of man who had no thought of grades and length of service, or of mortgages and of his sons' being great scientists—they saw the Fisherman Sam; and Sam would say that though crops and livestock were privately owned, and birds and freshwater fish might be claimed by the land-grabber, the sea was socialist, the fish of the sea was for all, and it was wrong and a shame that anyone should presume to get separate fishing licenses and go fishing for private interest in the free and democratic sea: the fish should belong to all, the whole nation, the entire world could live off the sea, if it were properly used. But look how rash we are! When Captain John Smith came to the Chesapeake, he could ladle fish out of the bay with a frying pan—to fish with a line was not necessary. In Hiawatha's time, the Great Lakes were stirring with fish, but we know so little that if the law did not arm inspectors and wardens, we would empty the whole giant Chesapeake system of fish, crustaceans, and bivalves, all that were edible, and kill what was left with the hideous effluvia of capitalism! "We are all the sons of old David Collyer," said Sam, not troubling to drop his voice, "cramming our mouths, satisfying every taste, and wrecking his fortune and even grubbing into the ground under the house he built for odd pieces of good fortune that might be left. We are nothing but the locust; and the Department of Agriculture should send out planes to destroy with gas bombs those locusts of our foreshores and fishing waters who decimate the commissariat of our great and good mother Nature." (Then, as a footnote, Sam mentioned his idea, that man himself should be decimated, and, with the good tithes left, a new race, especially interested in fish conservation, might be propagated.)

"Would you kill off everybody?" inquired Little-Sam thoughtfully. The children were much intrigued by this idea of universal destruction. But Saul Pilgrim was not interested in social ideas, and he would proceed with some idea of his in fish cookery. He wanted with Sam to work out a fish-cookery column "to interest the ordinary greedy and the housewife, who can be touched only through their stomachs," said Sam, "in the conservation of some of our wondrous wild life."

Then Tommy took him off secretly to the washhouse where, from behind the copper, he drew out the brace of boats he was making for Sam's birthday, June twenty-third, a whaleboat and a buckeye. The whaleboat was little different from his rowboats and dinghies, but Louie would put cord round it in loops and make it all right; and on the buckeye Louie would put three sails, and they would fill it with little shells to look like a heavy load of oysters. Little-Sam had been scouting round the district for weeks and now had a marble bag full of wire and flooring nails, brads, tacks, and staples that he had found—most of them new or only slightly weather-stained. Saul had been selling newspapers, running round with his pleasant rosy face and straw hair, in a pair of gaiters against the mud, to get money to buy his father a new brace-and-bit, but now he had only enough money for a putty knife or two hinges for the new gate they were making for the driveway from driftwood. Saul hoped that this tale would draw a nickel or two from Mr. Pilgrim's tender pocket, but it did not. Meanwhile, Ernie, with the same idea, was hanging impatiently in the background. Ernie was in the worst stew of the lot. (Ernie's morale had, as Sam frequently said, "disimproved," and he was showing a sad strain of Collyer sullenness and a tendency to weep when jeered at; so, to cure him of it, Sam had taken to calling him "Glossy-eyes.") Glossy-eyes had meant to buy for his father a new steel square, but money had been short for a long time. He would never empty his money box if he could; but Henny had been borrowing from him for her trips to town and other little things, and not only could not afford any interest any more, but hardly ever paid him back. Even when she got her checks, she usually spent nearly all the money in a day or two, and what was left had to be sent to butcher or grocer to keep him in a good temper. Henny would not allow her eldest son to do jobs round the neighborhood; but Ernie had collected a great store of empty bottles, old iron, old springs, and old lead which he cheerfully begged and collectedly "found" in every rotting corner of the creek and cove. When would he have money? Ernie wondered. When would they let him go and get a job? Old David was dead. Old Ellen lived in a tiny cottage with Barry, who was pressed for money to buy drink and had had to let his mistress go (everyone knew it, and Ernie had seen the cottage and been frightened to notice that Old Ellen sat in the kitchen calmly, with her plump parchment hands on her knees, and her old black dress stretched to her hanging throat, and her large old eyes clear of any determination). The estate was nearly all sold and the business loaded with debts. Uncle Norman Collyer had quarreled with the whole family, the whole family was in debt and mostly without jobs (for now Old David was dead, the business could not keep them), and Uncle Philip had shot himself.

Ernie thought about it all during long hours. He harried Henny many days with his questions and calculations. He alone knew, of all the children, that Daddy had realized on his life insurance, that there was no fire insurance, and that there was a second mortgage on the house. He knew there was some delay about Daddy's getting his new job, and he had already asked Sam to sell the strip of viny wilderness at Spa House alongside the dead end or at least build two garages there and rent them. With his money so low, Ernie found it next to impossible to sell his lead in dribs and drabs to get a few cents, but wanted to accumulate it, in order to get a fat sum at the end. If only his mother had allowed him to sell papers, he would have been happier. Meanwhile, Ernie's lead was a standing joke, and even Henny grumbled perpetually about his "damnfool lead collection collecting dust and making rust marks on the cement floor, under his bed." Sam wisely kept away from the washhouse while the children were showing their presents to Saul Pilgrim and, having nothing better to do, went into the boys' room to smile to himself and also to step off the dimensions of a darkroom for photography that he proposed to build in one corner of it, near the kitchen sink, until such time as he could build in a bench and sink for the darkroom. He moved Ernie's bed, and an astonishing sight met his eyes, five or six large lumps of lead, irregularly formed, and several small ones that seemed to have been hammered out of shape. He had not looked for several weeks and had no idea how Ernie had got so much. Beside the lead were the bottles and several pieces of iron. In moving the bed, he had upset a chamber pot, and the urine, with the sight of the lead and the rust marks on the floor, caused him to begin hallooing and howling for the children, in a great state of excitement, fun, and horror. Saul Pilgrim had to come in and see how his house was kept at eleven in the morning; and then Sam flung out of the room with him, until the mess was cleaned up, and then once outside he began to poh! and pooh! and fooey! and fwow! at the smells and sights, while the little boys stamped around giggling, and Ernie, the cause of all this, stood aside mournfully, until Sam called him "Glossy-eyes," when he turned the corner, even more mournfully, and went down to poke a stick in the sand and write his name, "Ernest Paine Pollit." On the beach their shouts still reached him, "Oh, fwow! What a pigsty!" and then commandment, "Goyls, clean up the stinking shop! It's a pigsty! It's a sump! It's a garbage tip! Chicago is a violet farm by comparison," then the boys giggling again, and a remark by Saul Pilgrim, and Henny shrieking out of a top window, "What's the matter?" and Sam, actually replying to her, "Tell the dirty girls to clean up this pigsty of a house for once," and Henny answering (all in the tops of the trees), "Ten maids couldn't clean up after the filth you slop over the house every minute," and Sam shouting, in a towering passion, "You look after my house and children, or I'll get a separation," and Henny yelling, "I couldn't look after your child if I had ten hands and twenty eyes. Why don't you stop her picking her nose?" (For Henny had had a row with Louie ten minutes ago.) After this came a calm, during which the girls, both bawling, cleaned up the room and stripped the beds to air, while Sam, in a low, sad voice, lectured the boys outside on female sluttishness, and told them the sort of wives they must pick. "When I saw my first baby was a girl," continued Sam, pathetically, "I gave a whoop of joy, I wanted a little girl—"

"Roll yourself into a hoop and roll away," cried Little-Sam boldly, and was immediately terrified. After months of silence and even savage mutism, he would come out with something queer and insolent, and could not stop it. Sam was used to him and merely gave him a mild kick in the pants. But Sam was quick enough to catch a little smile on his friend's face, so he led him round to look at the new aquaria, and then into the boys' room to ask his advice about the darkroom. Saul was an old hand and he knew better than to expect lunch; so about eleven-thirty he took himself off, after promising to send Sam a marlin for a birthday present, "the very next Tuesday as ever is," said he. The children saw him go without regret; they felt he was a silly man enough to be writing poems in newspapers about "Goin' Fishin'"; he had not handed out any nickels; he was in trouble with an old vixen (as Sam told them a thousand times), and his name, amongst his colleagues was "Baits" Pilgrim—even Sam often called him "Baits" or "Peelers."

When he had gone, "Now," said Sam, "tell Glossy-eyes to come and hump himself, too. I want to see that lead in the wash-house before lunch."

"Ernie's got lead, under his bed," sang Little-Sam, and danced. "And Ernie's got old iron; there's the ferry siren."

"It don't Mattapeake," said Sam.

Ernie rose slowly above the front rise (which Sam called the Butte) with a martyred expression.

"Lead out, Ermineus," shouted Sam.

Ernie smiled with constraint, "I'm collecting it."

"Collect it in the washus."

"I'm collecting it."

"It's gotta go to the washus, Ermineus," wheedled Sam; "lotsa room there; no one will run off with your coupla tonsa lead. Two centsa ton, oh, boy what fun, but when de war come, it will go into a gun—" He stopped and said gravely, "That's true: no Ermy, we cain't colleck lead. Ain't it enough to have the planes dropping bombs on ducks? We gotta get rid of it."

> Ernie will knock them dead,
> With his lead,

said Little-Sam.

"I'll get rid of it when I can sell it," said Ernie. "You kids leave me alone: you all suck round Pad."

"Now don't say that, Ermy," Sam reproached him: "they love their father. Do you think the Gemini like a mountain of lead in their room?"

"You leave me alone," said Ernie.

"Now, Ermineus, now, now!"

"Well, you leave me alone," remarked Ernie sulkily.

Sam looked handsome, spiritual, when he reproved Ernie, "I don't want you to lose your temper, Erno; you're all right, you're a good sort, but sometimes you get that Collyer expression and then I want to kick your pants."

Ernie tried not to look like a Collyer. When lunch was finished, though, Sam felt intrigued by the lead, and he said nicely, to Ernie, patting his shoulder, "Well, kids, a little yob before readin' and

writin' and 'rithmetic; we'll jes heft that lead out to the tool house."
The twins gamboled ahead to their room, which was at the back,
looking over the orchard, and when they got in, they began to shriek
and tug. "There it is, there it is!" Little-Sam lugged forth a huge,
misshapen gray lump. Ernie went for him, gave him a whack, and
said, "You leave that lead alone or I'll murderya." Sam was bending
over looking at the lead, and Ernie cried angrily, "You leave that lead
alone, I collected it," and he gave Sam a push.

"What?" cried Sam, astonished. He pulled out the lead with
assiduity after bestowing a bear cuff on Ernie. Ernie kicked him in
the pants. Sam was so surprised as to be almost pleased. "Imagine
doing that to your poor little Dad! Ermineus! Kids, Ermy akshooly
went and kicked his poor little dad." Ernie grinned shamefacedly,
"You leave my lead alone, and I won't."

"You won't anyhow," said Sam, giving him a good whack. Ernie
turned angry. Sam had managed to drag all the heavy stuff out
now and, bothered by the exertion, he said angrily to his eldest son,
"Ernest, if you're going to sell it, why the juice don't you sell it?"

The children tattled, "And he went past on Thursday, and Ermy
wouldn't."

"He's keeping it: he can't bear to part with it," the twins said.

"He's in love with it," said Evie, giggling and putting her fat
brown hand over her mouth.

"He loves it," said Sam, smiling to himself.

"Oh, I love you, lead," said Saul falsetto. "Oh, I'm going to marry
you, lead."

Ernie grinned faintly. Sam smiled, and commanded, "Now,
ebblebody ep cawwy yout diss yer leadulead." (Everybody help carry
out this lead.) The children buckled down and with much puffing
and groaning heaved it all out, along the side porch across the lawn
(which would some day be a tennis lawn), to the tool house which
stood over near the dead-end street. Ernie stood by, not lifting a

finger, disobeying Sam, grim until the last piece was stowed away. Sam surveyed him and then, with sundry comical kicks, told the children to start their homework. Ernie stood, self-contained, at the end of the porch. Sam went down the orchard, watching him from moment to moment, interested to see what he would do, ready to rush in and give a final nick, like a fisherman playing a game fish and ready for the plunge and tussle. As soon as they had dropped the last piece, grunting, and had made themselves scarce for fear of further jobs, Ernie rushed forward and began to drag and tug it all the way back. Sam let him take back two pieces before he fell upon him.

"Take that back!"

"It's my lead!" Ernie doggedly dragged out another lump.

"Do what you're told!" Sam dragged it from him and sent it loudly clopping across the yard towards the washhouse door. Ernie began to cry, at first, miserably and then bellowing, but obstinate, and rushed at his father like a bull calf,

"It's mine, don't touch it: it's mine, I collected it; it's mine!" He banged Sam with his two fists blindly. Sam caught him roughly by the arm and swung him round to look in his face. Ernie kept his face lowered and tried to punch Sam again.

Sam said sternly, giving him a mild kick, "Sam-the-Bold said, 'The washhouse'!"

"It's mine."

"Then you've got to sell it. What are you keeping it for?" The family was again timidly collecting, in various stages of beach attire, at the far edge of the scene, peering through the trellis from the western porch. "What are you keeping it for?"

Saul shouted helpfully, "It's for your birthday, Pad!" Sam dropped Ernie's arm at once and said gently, "Is it for Sam-the-Bold that you're doing this?"

"I'm saving it!"

"Is it for me, Ermineus?"

"I'm saving it!"

Sam was beginning to smile to himself again, "It's nothing to be ashamed of."

"I'm saving it!"

Sam, suddenly tiring of the struggle, began to stretch his long legs across the grass. At the porch, Little-Sam whispered wonderingly, "Pad, he's taking it back again." Sam nodded, "Sure nuf! Sure's you're alive! Ermy's got some will power! Yessuh! And is it for me, really?"

"Yes," they all confirmed eagerly.

Sam was delighted. He wheeled the twins round cheerfully and began to march them. "Now then," he said, "To market, to market to buy a fat pig, home again, home again, jiggity-jig!"

When Louie started to bring out the lunch, she paused with a dish in her hand, and asked, smiling sillily, "Dad, can I ask Miss Aiden to lunch soon?"

"Old Aido," shouted Sam, in appreciation: "the bewchus dame shall grace our board. What say next Choosday, my burf-day? Ask Old Aido to dinner next Choosday evo [evening]." Louie blushed and almost crumpled to the floor with pleasure. The children jeered a little, but they were anxious to see the famous and beloved beauty themselves. Henny, who was in the kitchen, grumbled a great deal, but gave in easily, only saying, "She must take potluck: I'm not making anything special for any hoity-toity schoolteacher."

"She's isn't hoity-toity, Mother: she's a wonderful woman, she's so kind and understanding, she's so nice, she's a wonderful woman."

"I don't doubt it," said Henny; "well, when she comes here she'll understand a few things too, if she's so wonderful." Louie never doubted for a moment that Henny would exert herself to make a good dinner for Miss Aiden, especially as it was Sam's birthday too; but Ernie worried like a major-domo, running five times on Sunday and twice daily on Monday and Tuesday to ask, "Mother, what will we give Miss Aiden? Mother, are we going to have roast meat? Mother, what are we going to have for dessert? Mother, will there be a clean napkin for Miss Aiden? Mother, will you have some of my snapdragons on the table or some of Saul's wallflowers? Mother, the oilcloth on each doorstep is worn right out, you can't see the pattern."

At each excursion, Henny would grumble and mutter things like, "Let her see! Who is she, the wonderful woman? What do I care? Don't drive me crazy! Oh, you kids will have me in the bathouse! Stop bothering! I don't care if we eat off the floor!" Though Louie was too blind to see it (after ringing up Miss Aiden in Baltimore and getting her consent, being in a delirium of expectant love), Henny made no special preparations even for Sam's birthday. "Let his kids amuse him," said she, to Louie who, however, took no more notice of this ominous remark than of anything else. Henny secretly believed that Miss Aiden could not be such a bad creature "if she took an interest in such a slummicker as Louisa," and she made up her mind to let Miss Aiden see how the little girl really lived and how the grand Pollits really lived and how she, "the mother of so many children," really lived.

Sam's birthday began in a lovely morning, and everyone got up early. There was dew on everything, the cedar-waxwings were eating the mulberries, and there was the sound of a bombardment from the corrugated iron roof of the new shed, where the wasteful little wretches, in their hundreds, threw down scarcely tasted berries. There was haze over everything, dew on the anthills, and the determined, brilliant wasps were at work, scratching wood fiber off the old wooden bench with a light rasping sound, zooming dizzily and plastering with a do-or-die air. It was so steamy-soft that the birds were relatively silent, except the bobbing, stripping cedar-waxwings and the black "devils of the sky," far off with a soft cah-cah. The sky was gray with humidity, the sun could be looked at with the naked eye, a pan full of liquid, like a dish of snapdragon, and against this sky the leaves were sharp and austere as in a steel engraving. Henny, running about early to get the tea "so that the kids could prance around their father," declared that she felt nervous as a cat. Louie looked at the silky sulky reflections of sepia and dun in the creek and thought they were like the shades of a woman's unsunned breasts; there was a still, breeding, inward-looking moist atmosphere, so that it seemed beans would begin to push out of the earth suddenly; it was like a bride, heavy with child, dull and potent. Louie could hardly lift her heavy stumps, even when Henny called sharply, but she did arrive in the kitchen in time, and there Henny was kind to her, asked her if the children had all a present for their father, and what she had got for him; and furtively, and with a shamed face, Henny gave Louie a little parcel in tissue paper for him; it was a pair of hand-knitted socks (which he preferred and which were easier to reheel and retoe). "And your present?" whispered Henny. Louisa said, "I wrote a play." Henny looked at her curiously, wondering at her cheapness, but at length said, "Well, I suppose your father will like it, at any rate," and sent her off upstairs with the tea, where a great jamboree was in progress.

"Is this a present for Sambo-the-Great?" inquired Sam, lifting the tissue paper parcel off the tray.

"From Mother," said Louie.

Sam squinted comically at them all, opened it, and, after inspecting the knitting, said, "Well, I don't say no, boys and girls: socks is socks; but I love hinges and nayrers [nails] en doyleys, even ef the stitches which is there are a bit spidery, en doyleys Little-Womey, enwhaleboats en bugeyes what is on the way, en I will go fishin for eisters en whales disarvo [this afternoon], en I like the shavin' brush what Charles-Franklin guv me—" and he looked at Louie.

"And Louie wrote you a play," said Ernie, dancing with excitement. Louie marked time shamefacedly, "It's a tragedy, and it's only in one scene."

"Hit's doubtless a tragedy," remarked Sam, "en once seen, is seen pretty often: bit whar is hit?"

"In my room," Louie said unwillingly, "but the varmints" (she waved her hand towards Ernie and Evie, who for once dropped their squabble and glanced with meek conceit at each other), "the varmints know it; they are going to recite it."

"We learned it," burst out Evie, and looked all round the room, red with excitement. "And you can't understand it." Sam stared at them all, grinning and pleased as punch at the great secret, which he had known was simmering for the past week.

"We don't know what it means," said Ernie.

"Ernie is the father, and Evie is the little girl," Saul told them; "it is about a father and a little girl."

They were all mystified and excited. Sam said, "What's all this? Now, Little-Sam, you bring in the prog, en after prog we see the play."

The two actors scooped up the oatmeal with the greatest speed, but Sam insisted on everyone polishing his plate with his tongue, before the play. Then, when the coffee was put round, Louie came and put a piece of paper in front of Sam and herself recited the prologue, which was nothing but a quotation from Longfellow (*The Masque of Pandora*):

Every guilty deed
Holds in itself the seed
Of retribution and undying pain.

Sam, with open mouth, meanwhile had been looking from her to the paper and from the paper to her, for on the top of the paper he read, in painful capitals: TRAGOS: HERPES ROM. JOST 1. When Louie had finished reciting, he asked in a most puzzled voice, "What is this, Louie?" Louie gravely pointed to the paper, "This means— TRAGEDY: THE SNAKE-MAN. ACT 1. There is only one act," she explained: "I thought we could do it too, this evening when Miss Aiden comes."

The two actors, meanwhile, were swollen with pride and agitation. "Why isn't it in English?" asked Sam angrily. Louie was at a loss to explain this, so she scolded, "Don't put the children off. You follow on the paper." The others meanwhile left their places to crane at the sheet. "There are two actors," said Louie, "The man—*Rom*—whose name is Anteios; and the daughter—*Fill*—whose name is Megara. Evie is Megara, and Ernie is the *Rom*, Anteios."

"Why can't it be in English?" said Sam feebly. Louie smiled vacantly, like a little child, "I don't know—I thought—anyhow, go on, Anteios! Ia deven..."

The boy and Evie then proceeded to recite.

ANTEIOS: Ia deven fecen sigur de ib. A men ocs ib esse crimened de innomen tach. Sid ia lass ib solen por solno or ib grantach.
MEGARA: Men grantach es solentum. (*"Men juc aun,"* said Louie)
Men juc aun. (*"Ben es bizar den ibid asoc solno ia pathen crimenid,"* said Louie, and Evie repeated it with several promptings.)
ANTEIOS: Corso! (*shouted Ernie with enthusiasm*). Ib timer ibid rom.

At this point, Evie, whose memory had failed completely, broke down and burst into tears, much to Louie's discomfiture. With a brusque gesture, she thrust Evie behind her into a seat against the wall (where she sobbed soundlessly for a minute and then looked up, her fat brown face pearled with two tears). Louie announced now, "I will do Megara: Evie forgot it."

MEGARA: Timer este rom y este heinid pe ibid fill.

"I don't understand," said Sam, with a floundering expression, "what is it?" Meanwhile Ernie rushed on,

ANTEIOS: Ke aben ia fecend?

MEGARA: Tada jur vec tarquinid trues ib rapen men solno juc men pacidud. Y hodo men solentum es du. Alienis dovo. Nomen de alienis es hein. Vad por ic vol fecen ibid ocs blog.

ANTEIOS: Ib esse asenen—asanen—men libid fill.

MEGARA: Sid ia pod ia vod chassen ib semba fills re Lear.

ANTEIOS: Roffendo! (*shouted Ernie and again shouted*). Ke tafelis!

At this the children began to giggle and Ernie, repeating with a great shout, "*Roffendo! Ke tafelis!*" all the children cried, "*Roffendo! Ke tafelis!*"

"Do they know what it means?" asked Sam, rousing himself out of a perfect stupor of amazement. Louie explained reproachfully, "Yes: that means, 'Horrible! What a she-devil!'" Sam's eyes popped, but further remarks were prevented by Ernie insisting with his cue "*Ke tafelis! Ke tafelis!*" Louie continued.

MEGARA: Fill in crimen aco ib aben aunto plangid. Cumu mat die ia cada: sol vec incriminenidud. Sid aten atem es grantach ke pos fecem. Ia ocen ib esse volid prin men aten men atem, men jur. Alienis vol mort ib.

ANTEIOS: Ke alienis? Esse ib imnen? Brass im, men fill.

MEGARA: (*Shrieking feebly*) No im! Suppo! Alienis garrots im! Herpes te!

ANTEIOS: Ke alienis? Esse im immen? Ke fecen ib? Brass, brass im! (*Aside*) Ma Herpes? (*At this point Ernie began to writhe and hiss, poking out his tongue instantly at all present, imitating a snake.*)

MEGARA: (*Shrieking feebly*) Ia mort. Ib esse alienis! Ib mort im! Occides! Occides! Mat!

ANTEIOS: Ia solno brass im. Men libid fill (*but in embracing Megara, Anteios hisses again like a snake*).

MEGARA: (*Shrieking hoarsely*) Mat, rom garrots im, Occides! (*And she dies.*)

After this striking scene in double-dutch, Sam, looking with pale annoyance on Louie, asked what the Devil was the use of writing in Choctaw. What language was it? Why couldn't it be in English?

"Did Euripides write in English?" asked Louie with insolence, but at the same time she placed the translation in front of her father, and he was able to follow the *Tragedy of the Snake-Man, or Father.*

Father—Anteios and *Daughter—Megara.*

ANTEIOS: I must make sure of you. In my eyes you are guilty of a nameless smirch. If I leave you alone for only an hour you sin

MEGARA: My sin is solitude. My joy too. Yet it is queer in your company only I feel guilty.

ANTEIOS: Naturally! You fear your father.

MEGARA: Fear to be a father and to be hated by your daughter.

ANTEIOS: What have I done?

MEGARA: Every day with rascally wiles you ravish my only joy, my peace of mind. And now my solitude is two. A stranger is there. The name of the stranger is hate. Go, for he would make your eyes bulge out.

ANTEIOS: You are sick, my beloved daughter.

MEGARA: If I could, I would hunt you out like the daughters of King Lear.

ANTEIOS: Horrible: what a she-devil!

MEGARA: (I am) an innocent girl that you have too much plagued. As mother says, I am rotten: but with innocence. If to breathe the sunlight is a sin, what can I do? I see you are determined to steal my breath, my sun, my daylight. The stranger will kill you.

ANTEIOS: What stranger? Are you mad? Kiss me, my daughter.

MEGARA: (*Choking*) Not me! Help! The stranger strangles me. Thou snake!

ANTEIOS: What stranger? Are you mad? What are you doing? Embrace, kiss me. (*Aside*) The snake? (*He tries to hiss to himself.*)

MEGARA: (*Shrieking*) I am dying. You are the stranger. You are killing me. Murderer! Murderer! Mother!

ANTEIOS: I am only embracing you. My beloved daughter. (*But he hisses.*)

MEGARA: Mother, father is strangling me. Murderer! (*She dies.*)

As soon as Sam had read this, Louie also put beside his plate the vocabulary to prove that her translation and the words were quite correct; and with a cheek of burning pride, full of playwright's defiance, she waited for his verdict. Sam said slowly, "And where is Act II?" Louie was short. "It all happened in Act I." The children, oddly excited, shrieked with laughter, and Louie, after one glare, rushed out of the room. Sam fumbled with the papers, muttering, "I don't understand: is it a silly joke?" He asked the children, "Did Looloo tell you? What is her darnfool idea?"

Ernie explained,

"She said she would have written it in French, but she doesn't know enough grammer, she said. So she made up a language."

"Damn my eyes if I've ever seen anything so stupid and silly," complained Sam, looking at the vocabulary again. He shouted, "Looloo, you come back here: don't stay in there blubbering! Oh, for God's sake, it's my birthday: don't be an idiot." Louie trailed slowly out, while the children, chapfallen, considered her mournfully. Evie, extremely abashed at having forgotten her part, had squeezed herself into her mother's chair with Tommy and put her arm round his neck.

Sam said, "Sit down, Looloo: blow me down, if I know what's the matter with you. Instead of getting better, you are getting more and more silly." He suddenly burst into a shout, "If Euripides or any other Dago playwright makes you as crazy as that, you'd better shut up your books and come home and look after your brothers and sister. I can't understand it with a father like you have. I'm sorry I didn't insist on your learning science, and nothing but science. Whatever your stepmother's influence, you've had my training and love from the earliest days, and I did not expect you above all to be so silly: you were the child of a great love. However, I suppose you'll grow out of it." He sighed, "At least, I hope so: you're growing out of everything else. Well, let's say, some day you'll be better."

Louie began to squirm, and, unconsciously holding out one of her hands to him, she cried, "I am so miserable and poor and rotten and so vile and melodramatic, I don't know what to do. I don't know what to do. I can't bear the daily misery. I can't bear the horror of everyday life." She was bawling brokenly on the tablecloth, her shoulders heaving and her long hair, broken loose, plastered over her red face, "No wonder they all laugh at me," she bellowed. "When I walk along the street, everyone looks at me, and whispers about me, because I'm so messy. My elbows are out and I have no shoes and I'm so big and fat and it'll always be the same. I can't help it, I can't help it," and, still bellowing "I can't help it" with the manner and tone of a half-grown calf, Louie got up and staggered to her room. She stood at the door, halfway open, and beat on it with her soft half-open fists, crying brokenly, "I can't help it!" and weeping endlessly.

Sam said gravely, "Stop working yourself up into hysteria."

"They all laugh at me," cried Louie. "They all laugh at me: I can't stand it any more."

Unexpectedly, Ernie burst out crying, his brown, merry, escutcheon-shaped face bobbing up and down and his wide mouth gone into an oblong. Louie turned round towards them and advanced towards them, her eyes drowned with tears, her hair straying everywhere and darkened with water and her face slobbered over and, coming to the table, as to a jury, she asked in a firmer voice, but still crying, "What will become of me? Will life go on like this? Will I always be like this?" She appealed to Sam, "I have always been like this: I can't live and go on being like this?"

Sam testily cried, "Like what? Like what? What is all this about? I never heard so much idiotic drivel in my born days. Go and put your fat head under the shower. Is it because Miss Aiden is coming that you're making this—excruciating—stupid, oh, I can't find words to describe it. How can you be so stupid?"

Louie turned away again and trudged away, but she cried no more, and merely sat on her unmade bed in the room: while Henny could be heard muttering and cursing in the kitchen.

"A nice beginning to a beautiful day," said Henny. Well, to restore courage to the children, Sam began their invocation to the Free State, "With," said Sam,

"WITH	Susquehanna, Pushmataha, Tuscarora, Octoraro, Cohongoroota,
AND	Assawoman, Mattawoman, Chesapeake, Matapeake, Choptank, Tonytank, Tuckahoe, Piscataway,
AND	Nassawango, Conowingo, Annemessex, Honga,
AND	Wicomico, Rewastico, Chicamacomico, Chaptico,
AND—	Pohick!"

a barbarian chant with which they raised the roof and restored good humor. When this was done, they slid out of their places, and Sam pleasantly went to fit the hinges and watch the sailing of the quite-finished whaleboat and part-finished buckeye in the creek. The children were all excused from school for Sam's fortieth birthday.

"Fer," said Sam, "ef I cain't hev you all around me fer ter skelebrate my forty-years-young, what was the good of hevin you at all? Tell your teacher to put that up his pipe and smoke it. Ef I didn't want ter hev you, he wouldn't hev no job. Tell your teacher to put that up his pipe and smoke it." The children giggled.

Louie refused to stay at home for her father's birthday, but sped off to school as usual, much fretted to know what Clare would do. Yesterday she had avoided Clare, and Clare, with a grin, had kept away from her; and in class she had only sent Louie one note, saying, "Hollow groans from underneath the ground," one of her senseless scribblings which made Louie giggle, however, and relieved her. Today, Louie was sure to find Clare mooding round the gate waiting for her. The play, TRAGOS: ROM HERPES, which had been in rehearsal for a week, Louie now was impatient to show to Clare: before she had been as timid as a convent bride, and now she wanted to show it to the leg of the table itself if it showed signs of animation. Then, she had a bunch of wallflowers for Miss Aiden to keep up her spirits until the birthday dinner in the evening; and, instead of writing a sonnet for Miss Aiden, she had begun a play, called *Fortunatus,* in which a student, sitting alone in his room in the beaming moon, lifts his weary head from his book and begins by saying,

FORTUNATUS: The unforgotten song, the solitary song,
              The song of the young heart in the age-old world,
              Humming on new May's reeds transports me back
              From the vague regions of celestial space—

(to Rosalind, his Marguerite, of course).

Louie's senses reeled with love: it was warm; and yesterday during a lesson out of doors, when Louie, with daring, had recited,

Spirit of Beauty, that dost consecrate
With thine own hues all thou dost shine upon;

(but did not continue this falsely appropriated "Hymn"), Miss Aiden, with a gentle smile remarked, "Love begets love they say!" For a moment, sensation ran through Louie like a sweet summer river, but afterwards she felt a little disappointed in Miss Aiden; it was improper in the goddess to respond. Miss Aiden, in fact, did not understand (having only just come from college) that all the best gods are made of stone and say nothing. At any rate, Louie now felt that the play of *Fortunatus* would celebrate Miss Aiden in a nobler and more austere way than the mere cycle of sonnets. On the way to school, in the bus, she stuffed in quickly the botany lesson. Fortunately, owing to Sam's eternal confidences, botany was second nature to her.

Back at home, Sam was happy as Aeneas in his happy moments, surrounded by his adoring companions and crew, and, occasionally offering up expressions of *love* and gratitude to his goddess, Nature, was circumambulating his estate. He had a happy idea and sent the twins round to all the houses in the neighborhood to ask their friends of junior school age and below school age to come to Spa House at three o'clock in that afternoon, to have ice cream and run round the new Wishing Tree, to celebrate Sam Pollit's birthday.

"And I wish," said Sam; "that dear little Mareta could come and Whitey and Borden, en evvlebody, en even the goat kid."

When Ernie and Louie got back from school, therefore, the Spa House wilderness was piebald with neighbors' children, venturing into desirous nooks and nests, paddling on the beach and climbing the gnarled, neglected fruit trees. By the morning mail, Sam had had a letter from Saul Pilgrim, "It looks like a catch, but I'll have to delay my present for a week or so, but keep your eyes skinned for a whopping big TETRAPTURUS" (marlin), and now he entertained some of the children with a tale of what he would do when he got the whopping big marlin that was promised to him: he would have a tent on the beach and charge one cent admission, but they could all come in free, by special admission, provided they ran round the Wishing Tree once each; and then he would boil that marlin down till it was nothing but oil, when they could each come with a little bottle and get two ounces to rub their arms for muscle strain, or oil their bikes, or give their mothers for dry skins, or even, perhaps, maybe, it might make automobiles go, though Sam could not swear to that yet. But at any rate he intended to oil the universe with the game, and make the luxurious sportsmanlike spearfish work for mankind.

At four o'clock sharp, the children were lined up for the ice cream that Sam had just sent for in pails, ranged from the biggest to smallest and the smallest first. What a pleasure that was for the toddling Doreen Monks, who lived in the cottage at the end of Second Street, and how irritated Red Lomasne was to come last! When they had been round once, Butch Brewer, looking in the pail, asked if he could take some home to his little brother, at which all the girls cried, "Ooh!" and shushed and giggled, themselves looking hungrily at the pails, while the Pollit children stood a little apart, somewhat grim, hoping there would be a bit left over for them after; but Sam at once made them all march round again and gave them all a lick-and-a-half, so that all was fair....

Meanwhile Louie was inside, rubbing up the silver and peeling the vegetables, while Henny went upstairs to change her dress: and Ernie came inside, as soon as "the kids" began to straggle off (some of them disappointed that they hadn't received any presents, for they were confused about whose birthday party it was). Ernie hovered around Louie, much to her delight, asking a hundred questions: where was Miss Aiden now? (At the teashop with another teacher.) Louie began to set the table at sunset with her satellite Ernie. First came the threadbare damask cloth (Henny still thought all colored cloths vulgar and when she could, renewed her Irish damask). The cloth was much darned, yet in holes, and coffee-stained. Over the stains Louie adeptly fixed the cruets (they were not assorted, and one pair was a gift pair got with coupons), and the butter dish. There was one clean napkin for Miss Aiden. The water jug had been broken only the week before and so for water they used a large milk jug. Now Louie noticed, for the first time, that they had only one glass for water. She hunted high and low and found nothing but peanut-butter jars and the like. It dawned upon her that they had had no glasses for a long time; and then she called to mind a slow dwindling in goods, over years. She remembered that once they had had dozens of engraved water glasses, always of the same design, a Greek-key pattern, which had been with them for years, and then had come plain glasses got at the ten-cent stores (Henny despised the florid ones), and then gift glasses got with packets of tea, until now they had only one in the world. But she was enraptured by the dinner that was to come, too rapt to be ashamed, and went on with her work, now noticing that they were really poor, but not caring, for, she thought to herself, "Miss Aiden is above caring whether we have things or not" (but she thought Miss Aiden would observe that they had a wonderful water frontage and would probably think they were "temporarily distressed"). Like Henny, she had too much to do to be able to moon over details.

But Ernie was different. He went to look at the table and count the places, see that all was there, spoons, forks, knives, when he saw the glass, sitting solitary as a lighthouse on an atoll. He poked round, seeking the other glasses, and had to admit there were no more. This caused him to look at the vase, containing Little-Sam's wallflowers, which was an ugly thick tube from the ten-cent store; in a moment he was climbing the stairs, his rosy face most serious, and was in Henny's room (where she was taking an aspirin), asking, "Mother, where's the big silver vase; we had two big silver vases?"

Henny cried, "Stop snooping, will you? It's put away." "But, Mother, can't we have it for dinner tonight?" "Oh, who is she, for the love of Mike," cried Henny, "is it Eleanor Roosevelt that's coming to dinner? I put all the silver away in Aunt Hassie's vault." "But why, Mother, why did you?" "You scoot; I've got a headache."

Ernie was dismayed. He sat down thoughtfully on Henny's old carpet hassock, and as his eye roved round the room, a fearful truth burst on him—there was nothing there, nothing that had been in the old house, nothing that had delighted his babyhood. He jumped up, "Mother, where are all your things from the dressing table?" "What's the matter with you tonight? Surely you're not in love with the wonderful woman, too. You're like a flea." "But, Mother, you had thirty-seven silver things—" He went, quite distracted, to the dressing table, where in the old days the three beveled mirrors had reflected brushes and combs in a silver tray, jewel case and pin trays, scent bottles and every conceivable tool and utensil for a lady's dressing table, all tooled silver. Now, here was a bakelite brush, comb, and mirror and one pinbox. The cut-glass smelling bottles and even the beautiful little self-winding clock had disappeared. "Mother, why did you put them all in the vault?" he asked, coming to her chair. "Did you put your rings there, too?" "Yes," she replied sullenly; "everything."

He turned to the tallboy (which had once held his father's clothes), and searched on it too, for the things that had stood there, but it was bare except for a dusty linen cover and a neglected envelope. Henny watched him grimly, saying nothing. Ernie went impulsively to her wardrobe and pulled open the place where her hats usually were—where were the hats, the three black ostrich plumes got from her cousin, the silk opera cloak, ten years old, that she had once worn? Where was the collection of postcards, with stamps from all over the world, that had been there once—though he could not remember when he last played with them (it was a long time ago). He came back to her chair and looked down at her, while she looked up smiling grimly, into dark eyes like her own. "Mother, why did you put everything away? Did you put the hats and feathers and everything in the vault?" "No," Henny smirked, "they are at Uncle's." "At Uncle Barry's?" "Oh, leave me alone—" Henny broke off and got up. She went to the dressing table and brushed her hair, now almost entirely gray. "Mother, won't you get them back again? Why can't we have them?" She turned round desperately,

"Look, my son, don't pester Mother: I sold them! Now, don't you dare tell anyone, for if you do I'll break your neck. If you want your father howling after me, all you've got to do is to tell him, that's all: the Great I-Am is too damned full of himself to notice what's going on; that's why I don't listen to his raving about margarine and beans and such trash: I'm paying for the dinners, and I'll have what I like. If he knew—" She stopped, listened to the scattered, evening shouts of the children still playing round the place. "He can buy ice cream for all the dirty kids in the neighborhood!" She looked down at her tall twelve-year-old son, who was transfixed on the worn carpet, halfway to her, between the armchair and the table. "Ernie-boy," she continued sharply, "Mother has had to sell everything she ever owned that she could: I've sold the clothes off my back. I only can't sell this furniture and this carpet because they are too big, and he would notice that. Who knows?" she asked Ernie abruptly, "perhaps I'm a Goddamn fool! Perhaps he notices everything and is willing to let me bust my bones over his grocery bills, as long as he has swill to put in his belly; he's more of a child than you are, you poor little wretch. What luck have I? I don't suppose you'll be anything but a cheap little accountant yourself—you haven't any chance to make money with a father like that. And who is going to pay for your education? Listen, Ernie-boy, Mother would have committed suicide a thousand times before now, if it hadn't been for you, because I thought the Big-Mouth would get a job and give you a start and you'd be able to make money for Mother. When I saw you were a boy, I didn't care so much, although I went through hell before I ever saw your face, my boy: because, I thought, my baby boy will be growing up with me and when he's big enough I'll go off with him and perhaps—well, never mind: I don't want to start whining like the Man of Sorrows. Ernie-boy, don't you listen to anything you hear about your mother: you stick to me, baby-boy, or I'll just go and jump in the creek. I haven't any money for you or for anyone. He's taken everything, him and his eternal babies that he's got out of me. I don't know what to do, Ernie. Wait till she sees what I'm going to give her fine schoolmarm tonight. Irish stew and bread pudding. Perhaps she won't notice. She's going about foaming at the mouth with biggity ideas and snobbery such as I never heard, like her beautiful father; they're like as two peas in a pod: she probably won't notice what she's eating. (I wish her stupid crank of a father would notice what a silly stew she's getting into.) Do you hear? What I've got for dinner tonight, with a visitor coming, a fine lady who gets as much in a week as I get in a year, is Irish stew! You—"

"Mother, and there's only one glass."

"Don't I know it? Because we can't pay for a rotten little maid, a kid that's going to trades school, or even Lomasne's little kid, I have to let that great big slummicker wash the dishes and smash every glass and plate in the house; and you kids are no better, with him jigging and singing and you all gaping with your mouths open when you're drying the dishes and dropping everything. Do you wonder I have to scream at you children? Every rag is in shreds, and every dish is smashed to smithereens. What does he care? As long as he can gas and gab and plume himself on his success in life."

Ernie looked at Henny, from his rounded eyes, with his face drooping. He trailed slowly off to the door and, as soon as he was clear, began to search the house from top to bottom; all,

all things valuable had disappeared. Pottering dolefully to the room he shared with the twins, Ernie pried up the loose board (loosened by him) under which he kept his money box and sat down with it in his hand, wondering and occasionally shaking it a little. There were still in it two dollars and seventy-eight cents. Still thinking, he began to shake and poke at it to take out one of the coins, and presently one fell out into his hand. He stared. It was brassy; and then he wondered if it were a dream, for here was no American money, but the one-franc piece that he had often fingered in his mother's collection of foreign coins. In one of the open drawers of her dressing table, she had had, long ago, a heavy collection of old foreign coins. A silver groat, a giant old-fashioned English penny, heavy as four modern ones, a sixpence, some Roman and Chinese coins, a one-franc and a two-franc piece, in all worth very little. (It had been one of Ernie's dreams that here was a treasury worth much in exchange, but Sam had laughed and told him it was "Aunt Tabitha's weeping-willow brooch," which meant that it would bring nothing at all in the market.) Ernie shook again with agitation and this time succeeded in getting a rain of little coins, a few cents, the groat, a three-penny-bit; he shivered, thinking a horrible joke had been practiced on him by fairies or ghosts: and then came yawning into his head the picture of the empty drawer below, and he turned cold with fear—perhaps someone (Henny?) had changed his good money for this trash money. He shook and shook, in a frenzy, but with all the rattling, only the dream money came out, and as he shook out the last coin and heard that the light box made no sound but shook light as a feather, he became pale. He spread the money out before him and looked it over anxiously to see if there was any good money but the few cents, but there was not. He heard a sound, made a quick dart to cover the money, and looking up, with a blush, saw his mother. With great hollow eyes she stood looking at him. Her old red dressing gown, now tattered and dirty, was wrapped round her. Henny's eyes traveled, with a shocked expression, over the coins laid out on the floor. Ernie looked at them again and suddenly his eyes filled with tears; he began to choke, "Mother, someone—" and broke down into miserable sobs. Henny looked at him, with hollow cheeks and desperate eyes, and in a moment sank to her knees, plunged her face into her hands and began to utter cries, "Ugh-ugh." Ernie took no notice but sat amongst the ruin of his money box, scrabbling the coins with his finger, and crying accusingly. Henny took away her hands and, still sobbing windily, crawled over to him and began to collect the money that she put into the palm of her hand. Ernie held out his hand for it without looking, then feeling nothing but air in his hand, stopped in the middle of a hiccough and looked at her. "Ernie-boy," said Henny unctuously, "don't cry: Mother will put all the money back."

"Will you," he insisted, "will you?"

"Yes, dear; yes, dear."

"When?"

"When I get money: next week."

"What did you put that money in my box for, Mother?"

"I didn't want you to be disappointed, darling."

He got up and watched her stumble to her feet, tearing the gown again. She was carrying away the false coins with her. On the floor was the empty red money box. He could not understand what she meant: for to see the empty box there was like the end of his world: the difference between having his "bottom dollar" there and having nothing was the same to him as waking in a dark hour of the night, hearing no clock and no cricket and no sigh, and not knowing whether it was the first or fifth hour of the night. At those times he would break into a sweat and wonder if the sun would rise again, at the appointed hour, ideas that he knew were silly but made him long for the ticking of the clock, which is the whole of life. Mother thought she would trick him with the worthless money, without knowing that she had smashed everything he had. He heard her trailing downstairs. He picked up the money box and put it back again under the board; and then he realized that Mother had found the board, pried it up, stolen his money, put in the bad money, and put the box back, all with the intention of fooling him. He felt sick, but as he did not know what had happened to him, he looked out the window to see the last of the neighbors' children chasing each other round the Wishing Tree and then went downstairs in a vacant mood and, hearing his father's whistle, answered at once, "Yes, Dad!" but all the evening, all through his father's chatter, he was thinking something strange: he did not know what it was.

At five o'clock Sam tied the Stars and Stripes to the Wishing Tree: this was the sign agreed upon, by which Miss Aiden was to know Spa House, when she looked from the end of Eastport Bridge. Louie, looking every minute from the front windows, saw her as soon as she came to the boathouse at the end of Duke of Gloucester Street, and shrieking, "Mother, she's coming." rushed madly round the house down the drive and along the street towards the bridge. At the gas station she slowed down, but too late, for her face was already scarlet. She had left behind her a pandemonium of brotherly laughs, fatherly witticisms, wondering children, staring neighbors and barking dogs, but when she reached the Eastport end of the bridge and looked towards Spa House, for one minute, to see the flag, she saw all her family, except Henny, lined up along the front grass, staring eagerly at the bridge. Very self-consciously she strutted along the bridge, looking everywhere, up, down, at Bancroft Hall, up the creek, at the boathouse, at the ferry, while the fat grin on her face swelled and swelled until she felt as if she must tumble into her own mouth. Miss Aiden was standing at the other end of the bridge, leaning graciously on the rail, taking in the scenery and waiting for her.

"Hello, dear Louie," she said, beaming on the flushed girl. This was the first time she had ever said "dear," and Louie was in ecstasy. She became very quiet and sedate in her great happiness; and then very talkative, pointing out the house, and the points of interest to the family. She even pointed out "Coffin" Lomasne, who was standing on his slipway and looking with interest at the banner attached to the Pollit Wishing Tree; and in long gabble told all about him, his coffins, and how he went, in the family, by the name of "Mud Turtle."

Louie had on the same soiled dress that she had worn to school, Miss Aiden observed, with hurt, for she had expected to be treated with more ceremony. However, she was flattered by the banner and by the family drawn up irregularly there under the trees, and all those eyes searching her from a distance. It was a dear old house, with wonderful old trees, and a sweet little bathing beach, as she told Louie, and they all must be very happy there, especially in summer. "Are there mosquitoes?" she asked. (Yes, there were: but they took measures against them: only Ernie and Tommy suffered badly from the bites.) "You don't need to go away for the holidays," said Miss Aiden. (Oh, but Louie would go, she hoped, to Harpers Ferry. She had a cousin there who had promised to take her down the river in a canoe, if it was not too dry.) "A boy cousin?" said Miss Aiden coquettishly. "Yes, a boy cousin, Dan." Miss Aiden had never been to Eastport before; it was an exceedingly poor part, rundown, with a few broken-down family houses, but splendid old run-to-seed patches that you could do something with, though the soil was poor. The entrance to Spa House was down a short muddy lane bordered with what appeared to be fishermen's cottages, with pails and clothes on the wooden porches. A broad new picket gate, however, with the words "Spa House" painted on it, showed her that she had arrived at Louie's home. The gate was ajar: they pushed it and came quickly up the curving rutty drive, under magnificent trees. The straggling bushes of the bank and somebody's rowboats came right up to the trees on the western side.

A reception committee awaited her, a tall, yellow-haired, red-faced man, with sparkling, self-satisfied eyes, rather heavy cheeks and nose and teeth well met in a kind of religious mouth, a man who would make a good, new-world dissenting minister, thought Miss Aiden. There was a bevy of children, none like Louie, with two blond and two dark boys and one very pretty little dark girl—Miss Aiden did not know if they were all Pollits or not. There was no sign of the mother. Miss Aiden was not experienced enough yet to enjoy meeting the girls' mothers, though she got on well with them afterwards, because of her cheerful good nature.

Louie was evidently very nervous. "Will you come inside and take off your hat?" she kept asking, at every break in the conversation. The conversation did not flag, because Mr. Pollit seemed to be a lively, agreeable, unassuming man with a lot of information that he was anxious to bestow upon her; he was very joky too, and Miss Aiden began to laugh with him in a way which, she noticed, did not seem to please Louie. At length, she went in with the girl. They entered by a wind-broken side porch, over a bit of coconut matting worn through to the boards, and came into a dark, dirty hall laid with defaced oilcloth. In the minute before coming into Louie's bedroom to take off her hat, Miss Aiden revised her visions of the Pollit homestead: they were a raggedy, rackety family, too big for their father's means, and living was hard with them, but no doubt they struggled to put a face on it. The reason Louie was untidy and even dirty was that they were poor and was not merely the slatternliness of adolescence. Miss Aiden was disappointed. She now imagined Mrs. Pollit to herself as a worn blonde slut with soft manners, Louie's predecessor (for she had no idea of the family history), and she was so startled that she hesitated for a moment when she saw come into the room a black-eyed, feverishly rouged hag with pepper-and-salt hair drawn back into a tight knot. Louie said hastily, "This is Miss Aiden. Miss Aiden, my mother."

"Louie," said the apparition, in a voice of sweet admonition, "take

Miss Aiden into my room; it is more pleasant there." Mrs. Pollit had marks of gentility, but at present her graciousness seemed to pester her like an itch—she brought out the kindness irritably, struggling with her worse feelings apparently. Yet, Miss Aiden could tell that she bore her no grudge for coming. "Domestic rift," diagnosed Miss Aiden. She was astonished at the walnut suite in Mrs. Pollit's room: yet, on the bed was a worn and torn cover, and the table covers were not fresh. "Decayed gentility," now thought Miss Aiden, "and in what a state of decay!"

But apart from a couple of pieces of furniture, the Pollits lived in a poverty that to her was actually incredible. They lacked everything. She was shown the bathroom, and found herself in a shanty with wooden walls and a roughly cemented floor. One end of this was filled by a cement tub about five feet long by three deep; but the cement had a surface as rough as a coconut cake; Miss Aiden thought of submitting her soft, sleek, spoiled flesh to its gray rasping ridges and, thinking it impossible, looked about for a rubber sheet—they must use something to cover the cement when bathing. Everything was to match; homemade, rough and ready; instead of toilet paper, they used cut-up newspaper; there was no bathmat but a sodden crisscross of slats. "I had no idea," thought Miss Aiden, "that there was a place as primitive in the whole world"; and she began to wonder how they lived at all.

Greatly disappointed in her visit, she followed the excitable Louie out through the home-cemented back porch and into the orchard wilderness, which was a delightful playground and now in full leaf and dotted with little fruit. There was a stew cooking, and Miss Aiden saw the dark thin woman poking over the stove: she nodded gaily at them as they went past. Miss Aiden could not keep back the question, "Does your mother like cooking?"

"Oh, no! she has too much to do," Louie said with unreflective candor.

Miss Aiden pursued, "You have a lot of brothers and sisters."

"Only one sister," said Louie: "that little fair girl is Mr. Lomasne's little girl. Yes, mother says she has too many," and she laughed.

"But she wanted them," pursued the teacher sentimentally.

"No, she didn't: the doctor said she should only have two—but they came"; Louie laughed.

The teacher looked down sharply, but saw only a fat, fair, laughing face: it's queer to know everything and know nothing at one and the same time, thought Miss Aiden.

Dinner was something Miss Aiden was never to forget; for she had passed what she considered a very rebellious, but what was really a very respectable life within the confines of the agreeably slick. Like Sam (though she was an honors student in English and Higher English), she saw truth, beauty, and progress in terms of the twenty-five-cent story magazines; in fact, she was but a handsome, gracious, and amiable young edition of Auntie Jo. First, from this house of misrule, came the sound of a beautiful gong, like the temple gongs in the movies; then the children came tearing up from all parts of the grassy waste, while two other children (which until this moment she had supposed Pollits) started to run down the avenue and away from Spa House. Mr. Pollit, who had neither washed his hands nor put on his coat, then started to whistle, and as he whistled shouts came from the scampering children, "Yes, Dad; yes, Taddy; yes, Dad, yippo": and so forth. Immediately, Louie, with a pleased confused face, came to fetch her in to the table, and they came into a long, boarded room, with dirty window curtains, a battered dresser, homemade wall shelves, and a long, oak table with fat Victorian legs, on which hung a dirty, worn tablecloth covered with the old silver and stained knives. A thin glass vase, dirty napkins in rings, and one water glass with a Greek-key pattern engraved graced this cloth. On the table besides were cruets, a slab of butter, and a loaf of bread. Miss Aiden found her place to be in front of the one water glass. Mr. Pollit then gave a whistle, and the team sat down, excepting Louie and the wife, who were juggling dishes in the kitchen, which was across the dark passage. Presently, without prelude, Louie began to hurry backwards and forwards with dishes of Irish stew, Miss Aiden getting the first, Mr. Pollit the second, and then in order of age.

"May I have a glass of water?" asked Miss Aiden sweetly, seeing none; but Louie at once seized the milk jug and poured out some for her. No one else got any. After they were all served, Louie and her mother came to sit down. As soon as Mrs. Pollit lifted her knife and fork, all followed suit and fell to in silence. Table talk was apparently considered improper in this family during the first course. As soon as Sam Pollit had finished, however, he began asking Miss Aiden if she liked fishing and if she knew that the Chesapeake was the finest little fishing hole in the world, he himself having fished there from the age of six; and that if she wanted to fish, the boys would take her out any day and not charge her fifteen dollars, the way the party boats did— or at least he didn't know. "Perhaps when Tommy grows up, he'll make us a party boat and then we'll all be rich—for three months a year." Laughter bubbled round the table at this happy prospect.

"Tommo's only six though," said Ernie, "and you have to have a boat, and the tackle costs about two hundred dollars, and there's the oil—"

"Oh, we'll run ours on marlin oil," declared Sam, "and ketch it for nothing! And won't the big boys swim after us when they smell their breruther's oily tang?"

Louie was very indignant at this stupid conversation, which she thought beneath Miss Aiden's level. Ernie did not raise even the ghost of a smile. Mrs. Pollit remained silent throughout, except to say to Tommy, "Tip your plate outwards, Tommy-boy!" and to Evie, under her breath, "Use *both* hands to wipe your mouth!"

Presently, during an awkward lull, while Louie was carrying out the dishes two at a time, Mr. Pollit said in a queer tone, distantly paternal, with a condescending expression, to his wife, "Have we salad, Henrietta?" The wife, flushing angrily, merely lowered her head over her plate and replied nothing. Miss Aiden flashed a look of astonishment from one to the other, then turned to Little-Sam, who sat at her side, "And are you the boatbuilder?" Sam, meanwhile, bit his lip; and in a moment repeated politely, "Have we a salad to come, Henrietta?" At this Henny coolly got up from her seat, smiling to Miss Aiden with an "Excuse me, please, I am the cook too," drew Evie after her, and, when she had stepped into the corridor, said gently to Evie, "Tell your father that the snails ate the lettuce, and I had no money to buy trimmings!" Evie turned back and demurely repeated this message to her father. The children gazed from their father to Miss Aiden, to see what she would make of this. The dessert was brought in by the mother and served by her: it was bread pudding, with some preserved berries from last year. Henny admitted that these were her preserves and carried off the trying situation (Miss Aiden could not help thinking) with aplomb. Yet, she was wondering, "Why did they invite me?" After dessert, Louie went to make the coffee, after asking her mother in a low tone, and her father in a high tone, and Miss Aiden in a languishing tone, what each would take. Mr. Pollit would have prolonged the meal, for he became spirited and garrulous after the coffee, but Mrs. Pollit, fixing her black eyes on his face with a meaningful glare of hate, and slightly rising, forced back the words on his lips, while Louie and Evie rose too slightly and so induced Miss Aiden to get up. The teacher offered to help with the dishes, seeing no help, but Sam said at once, "No, the girls will do it while I show you the lordly acres, Miss Aiden," and with a sort of rustic galloping gallantry, like a sheep dog, he got her out into the yard, and, taking her elbow, began pointing out things to her and talking "nineteen to the dozen," as Henny declared.

"A fat chance you'll have to talk to your beautiful Miss Aiden," she cried. Louie was about to burst into tears. The most beautiful moment of her life had just passed: it had been when she walked with Miss Aiden up and down the aisles of the orchard. But all the time she was rushed, she could not collect her senses, for she knew the time was short: even when Miss Aiden stopped and, looking at her earnestly, begged her to work during the summer, for she would certainly be famous ("be famous," was what she said, though surely it was a hallucination), Louie was fretting that the time was so short; soon Miss Aiden would go away. Louie thus had no time to think about the house, nor how it looked; she was quite satisfied with it—they were poor, but it was spacious, and her expectations were infinite. There was a book called *Great Expectations,* which she had never read: she supposed, though, that it referred to something like her own great expectations, which were that at a certain moment, like a giant Fourth of July rocket, she would rise and obscure all other constellations with hers. She was likewise so used to hearing of her mother's rich family, and of her father's superiority in intellect and feelings to the rest of mankind, that she believed they all occupied an enviable position in the community. They had been brought up in Washington, and if the nation only knew of Sam's capacities, it would clamor for him—what more could be needed by a family? Enviously, she watched Sam, who grabbed everything, to his greater glory, grabbing Miss Aiden too: there he talked, endlessly, by the half hour. What could he be saying to her? Soon he would win her away entirely from Louie: Miss Aiden would think, What a clever, brilliant father Louie has—why Louie is not a patch on him! Louie was racked with disappointment. When she went out to empty the leavings into the garbage can, she went the long way round to overhear their words. Sam was saying, "And my little Looloo—I called her 'Ducky' then—at a very early age showed a most mulish disposition: that's why I'm speaking to you, because she thinks so highly of you—" Looloo! Ducky! Oh, a hell of torment! Louie went back to the kitchen and burst into tears.

"What the dickens is the matter now?" asked Henny, without malice.

"He's talking to her—he's telling her everything—" Henny shrugged her shoulders and went on cleaning the knives. "She's not a bad woman, and if she's not an absolute fool, she'll see the way I'm treated."

Louie flashed up with a smile of gratitude, "Oh, Mother, do you like her?"

"I like her, yes."

"Oh, Mother!"

"Don't faint," said Henny irritably, suppressing a smile. At last, Louie was able to get away, but Sam kept on talking cheerfully until the last moment, when he walked her to the gate. Louie was allowed to walk up to the station with Miss Aiden, a walk of about a mile. When they were on the Eastport Bridge, they heard a faint shout, and looking back, saw the Pollit clan lined up once more in front of the Wishing Tree, waving the flag at them.

"Your father is very amusing," said Miss Aiden, patronizingly. For the first time, Louie found the shadow of a ghost of a fault in Miss Aiden's manner.

3 *Delayed mail.*

Having delivered himself of his heartfelt sentiments once again, Sam was gay and went merrily footling round the place, looking for fresh worlds to conquer. "Tah yez wot I do," he declared, "I'll make Looloo-the-Zulu a new bookcase, now she's learned to read; feelin' fine! Old Aido's a nice old girl! I like Old Aido and if she'd ask me twice, I'd marry her." The children were nodding buttercups of giggles. Some of them departed to other occupations (to pore over the presents they had given Sam that day, for example), but the twins stayed with Sam, who now went into Louie's bedroom, to take down the old bookcase, which was about ten feet high, and measured the wall space for a new one. He began to dust off the top and there found all sorts of things—a forgotten pin box, a pill box with tacks in it, two knitting needles, and an out-of-date diary on which was written in capitals: THE AIDEN CYCLE.

"Sirprise after sirprise," announced Sam shaking his head; "well, blow me down ef it ain't poickry. Say, kids, Looloo's a dang blue blasted better poet then whut I am. Now, what do you know about that, Little-Sam? Say, quick, Sawbones, go get the kids: quick! When Looloo gits back frum a-walkin' out with her beloved, she'll find us all a-joying of her poickry. Quick, quick."

The call went out, and the children straggled back to the house. It was a lovely evening, and the grateful and fascinated children from the party were drifting back to the gate and the fences, poking their heads in and holding wistful conversations with the happy savages of Spa House.

"Oh, Jiminy Jee," sighed Ernie: "if we aren't always at his beck and call."

"You get along," cried Henny, hearing this, "or he'll be whistling and calling, and I can't stand any more today."

She rounded them up. Soon Louie's room was full of them, while Sam, standing on his small stepladder with the book in his hand, declaimed,

All nature is in you, its monsters less;
As nature monsters are, so less are you
Than nature: nature lacks what you have more
Than natural: unnatural, you bless
Our lives too natural—yet world I'd rue
Without this extra-nature I adore.

"Whut in the name of dingbingbusted commen sense," asked Sam, "is this? Hit's a crostword puzzle. Blow me darn, here's another!

> Pearlshell, pearl, and madrepore,
> Purple wampum, rich fish dyes,
> Of gold and silver a great store,
> In megaron, in mattamore;
> But, Rosalind, thou art much more.

Oh, Rosalind; oh, kiss me, Rosalind!"

At this moment, Tommy, who had watched in the falling night for Louie's return, bounded in shouting, "She's coming back now, she's on the bridge."

"Ooh," said Evie, "Daddy, she will be very angry with you."

"You ought to stop, Pad," said Ernie.

"She's in love with Miss Aiden, oh, Rosalind," chanted Sam, squirming. The children imitated him. "She worships Miss Aiden," said Little-Sam shrilly. "Oh, I love you, Miss Aiden."

"Shh!" said Sam leaning over mysteriously, as he was turning over a leaf, "Tommo! Go to the gate and tell me when Looloo is coming: tell Looloo I'm reading her poickry. There were varying tones of assent and dissent, but Tommy galloped off. Louie was coming home slowly, breathing in the soft-smelling, bayside, thickening air; bats flew, mosquitoes sang. She was glad no one was with her, for after all she had nothing to say to anyone, not even to Miss Aiden, since ravishment cannot be spoken.

"Louie, Louie!" It was Tommy calling her from the gate.

"What do you want?"

"Louie, Dad's reading all your poems!

Tommy saw the pale form pelting towards him, "Where?" she called, seizing him by the shoulder. He felt a tremor of fear and anticipation;

"In your room—he wanted to make—" but Tommy was alone, while a large dark shape rounded the corner of the drive. He ducked under the white railing to cut across the lawn, when he saw at his feet two oblong shapes, two letters left lying on the lawn. He picked them up and ran in. The light shone through the two windows of Louie's room, and he could see the mess of children in there, with Sam's laughing face and the book held out as he read; the children lounged round, uninterested. As he passed the open window Sam was saying, "Here's one (where's Looloo-dirl?)—

There is a sick one within these walls,
She is mad I know by the songs she sings—

Louie burst into the room. "Here's Louie, here's Louie," they sang out.

"Give to me," she shouted, "you give it to me!"

"No! Leave me read it," he wheedled. "You ain't got nuffin you don't want your Poor-Sam for to see, hev you?

I must confess I love you,
I love you in my fashion,
'Tis not from lack of passion
I would not say I love—

"Give it to me," shrieked the girl: "I'll make you." The children made way for her and she came up the first step after her father, grabbing for the book, which, of course, he waved away from her. He looked handsome, bewitching, never so handsome as when teasing, "'I love you.'"

She got off the step and stood underneath him, looking up and saying, "Give it to me, give it to me."

The Indian starling, flashing in the shade
Is like your eye, all flecked with gold and blue—

"Here," he said, throwing it to her, so that it fell on the floor, "take it away; and don't write such sickening tommyrot. Write if you want to, but not such silly nauseating stuff. I didn't think you'd be so silly as to fall for calf love for a teacher, I thought you had more in you.

"Looloo," he said turning away to the children, "is trying to practice poickry without a poick's license, and I think she ought to be fined or go to jail. Now, dear old Georgie the Fisherman says to me the other day, he says, with rather a shamefaced look, kids, because of his ignorance, becaze even fisherboys is rayther ashamed of their iggerance, not like Tommy here, and quite evidently with a automobile permit in mind—or whatever fat George Pudding-and-Pie thinks with—'Mr. Pollick,' sezee, 'wy do they give poicks licences to say things wrong?' In conversation that followed, I saw quite clearly that he thought poicks got licences like fishermen, maybe by the traffic department, so these dopey nuts who make schooldays so hard for poor fat boys could get their stuff printed with a licence. So I think we'll get Looloo a licence, maybe a dog licence."

Tommy, who had been listening with his mouth open, now pushed forward waving two letters in his hand, "Mothering says two letters for you, Pad: I found them in the wet grass."

"What," cried Sam, taking them: "that dopey Popeye Banks, again! I'll write to the post office about having a nitwit for a letter carrier: I don't know why boys like him aren't sent to a lethal chamber, or just nipped in the bud at birth. The communication between men ought to be the most sacred of all things: and if we weren't so busy building warships," declared Sam, in a temper, "we would have money for better mail services; and if we weren't despised by people because we live in a mudhole. I'll make a complaint about this and get him removed."

He stopped, looking at what he had drawn out of the envelope. It was a triangle of newsprint dragged from yesterday's paper; round the borders in heavy penciling were insulting words, and part of the message was written across the print.

"What is it, Dad?"

He held it close to the ceiling light and made out words,

"You two faced son of a bitch, would you like to know who was the dad of your last boy take a look in the internal revenue dept and you'll learn lots your wife certainly put one over on you you lowdown bastard while you were getting hot with the chink girlies you sap everyone knows it but you who was away ten months you sap Im glad they threw you out on your can even if your wife owes me an everybody in shoeleather pullenty."

"What is it, Dad?" (They could see enormity in his face.)

"It is one of the foulest things on this earth—" He was still puzzling it, hoping to read something different. His hand began to shake.

"Pad—"

"Get out!"

They ran away, looking back over their shoulders with startled eyes.

"Megalops!" cried Sam. (Megalops, infant crab, was his pet name for Charles-Franklin.) The children hid themselves, with receptive ears, round corners. But after this, Sam was silent. He had sat down on Louie's bed, doing nothing, apparently thinking, while the lights blazed away, running up the electricity bills.

It was a strange night: they were put to bed quickly, and Louie, with red eyes, leaned amongst them to tell them the story of Hawkins, the North Wind.

Evie said, "No, *The Spring House!* Ooh!"

Downstairs a great racket was going on, which was nothing but Henny and Sam going it hammer and tongs, with Henny saying, "You're a sneak and always were," and Sam shouting, "Indiscriminate sexual relations"; but the children paid no attention to it.

Tommy shouted, "No, the Indian ghosts!" while Little-Sam called for *The Invisible Snake*. But Louie, insisting that Hawkins was her new story, because she had just made it up, made it *Hawkins*.

"Chawkins?" queried Tommy with his invented foreign accent.

"One evening in October a black man was working in his potato patch at Jones, over by Rugby Hall; the sun was a flare burning up the trees and smoke and flames came from it. That was because it was cold. Now a withered and warty horse came up through the hill, with a man on its rumpbones; the sun was so low and red, it looked—I don't know what."

"My money box," said Ernie: "it's low and red."

"It looked like Ernie's money box. 'Peaslop,' said the man on the horse, 'I'm hungry and thirsty and I got to get down to the water tonight.' *Down by what water?* 'Down by Severnside.' *Then you better get going.* 'No, my horse's got his night eyes.' *Then stay to supper.* 'Now what you got?' *Got plenty.* The shack was all surrounded with garlic on strings and cobs of corn, beans in packets and black walnuts in bags, salt codfish in dozens and smoked shad in strings and black clove hams and black wild cherries. Then Ambrose, the man on the horse, wiped his hand across his mouth like this—whirrsh! (*Now, Mrs. Peaslop, you cook a dinner for a man with an empty stomach.*) The woman stuck her black head out of the window and yelled,

"'I lack one thing for my fry, Peaslop.'

"'And what's that?'

"'That's my horse's mane, man.'

"The man came up quickly and cut off the horse's mane and threw it in the kitchen window. The frizzling went on and in a minute the woman looked out and sang out, 'I lack only one thing for my fry, Peaslop.'

"'And what's that?'

"'That's horse's tail, man.'

"'I got horse's tail.'

"And the black man came and grabbed the horse's tail, cut off a handful, and threw it in the window. The man on the horse's rump meanwhile had gone right off to sleep, and he nodded, nid-nod, nid-nod, in the slight breeze that was coming up. Then the woman came to the window and yelled (though you couldn't see her, the night had got so black):

"'There's one thing surely I need for my baking, Peaslop.'

"'And what's that?'

"'That's horse's warts.'

"'Now, that's just what I got,' said Peaslop, and he cut them off and threw a handful through the window.

"But the woman yelled, though it was so dark you could see nothing but Peaslop's eyeballs rolling, 'There's one thing would make my stew better, Peaslop.'

"'And what's that?'

"'That's horse's hide; I do need that.'

"So Peaslop took a skinning knife, and he skinned that horse as quick as lightning just as it stood there with its head hanging, asleep in the black night and so quick and smart that the horse didn't know, but it shivered.

"'My horse's catching cold,' said the man on the horse, Ambrose I mean. 'His teeth are chattering to themselves.'

"'Horse's teeth,' said Peaslop, 'why that's just what would flavor my old woman's stew,' and he wrenched out the teeth to stop them from chattering.

"'And my poor nag's knees are just knocking together,' complained Ambrose, 'and every one of his ribs are rattling.'

"'Now horse's rib soup would make good stock for my old woman's stew,' said Peaslop. Without another word, so dark was it, he stole every horse's rib and every horse's shinbone without so much as tipping Ambrose a wink. But he left a hipbone for Ambrose to rest his weary bones upon.

"'Now, friend Peaslop,' said the rider, 'my horse's flesh, it just quivers and quakes like a jelly without ice; and I'm very much afraid it's getting colder.'

"'Then give me that flesh, it certainly will make a good roast for my old woman's table,' said Peaslop; and he snatched all the horse's fine roast from underneath Ambrose, but he still left him a hipbone to sit upon.

"Well, I don't know how fine that cooking must have been, that frying and baking and stewing and roasting and broiling and boiling and basting, nor the feasting and guzzling and gourmandizing that followed. Perhaps they would have put up Ambrose for the night and given him his horse hale and whole again in the morning; only just at that moment was a low sighing moan.

"Ambrose, the horseman, sitting on his hipbone, looked around. He saw the stars and the heads of the woods, he saw the dim shine of water, he saw the track very pale snaking it into the woods, he saw the lamplight falling through the window, and he heard the frizzling and frying, but he didn't see Peaslop.

"'Is that you Peaslop? Is that you boy? Where you gone, boy?' he asked. 'Is that you crying and moaning, boy?'

"'No, sir, indeed, that isn't me,' said Peaslop. But it was so dark Ambrose couldn't see Peaslop, not even his rolling eyes. There came another moan, and it didn't stop. It went on softly, rising and falling, in the depth of the gully but rising more, till it had a high whine like a train under the hill.

"'Why, it's nothing but the train going down to Annapolis,' said Ambrose. Peaslop never said a word. He just breathed hard in the dark and flapped his hands and danced: but the bubbling of the stew in the kitchen went down.

"'I'm getting pretty cold, friend Peaslop,' said the man. All this time the moaning and sighing and wheezing went on. It got louder, and animals began to scuttle through the grass. It wasn't the wind, it was the animals, the groundhog, the weasel, the mouse, the skunk, and perhaps it was Peaslop dancing and flinging his arms. Now the crackling of the oven meat stopped, and it seemed the woman in the house was listening, too. But the moaning and crying went on and it rose always higher till suddenly it ended in a shriek.

"'Hawkins is calling,' cried the woman from the window.

"'Hawkins is calling,' cried the man from the potato patch. Then he took the hipbone in one hand and hurried to the porch and ran in the door and flung it shut, and the window went down with a bang, and the animals ran into the wood, and Ambrose sat there in the dark, in the new cold air that was beginning to blow. His horse was gone, and he had to get down to the river that night. He ran and knocked at the door and listened. But there was no sound at all. Then a voice said, 'What is it?'

"'It's Ambrose,' said he.

"'What do you want?'

"'My horse,' said he.

"'Oh, call next summer,' cried Peaslop; 'we'll give you some pickings.'

"Just then Ambrose thought he heard his horse neighing in the potato patch, and he thought he heard him snorting in the woods, and he thought he heard him trampling on the track, and he thought he heard him galloping down the hill; and when he looked back and felt with his hands, the shack had disappeared.

"'Peaslop,' he said.

"'Hawkins,' cried a voice.

"'Peaslop,' he cried, wringing his hands.

"'Next summer,' said the voice.

"And the keen north wind came up over the sickly yellow woods, shrieking, *Hawkins!*"

Picturing the man on the horse's rump against the stars, the children lay loosely in the warm night; while things just as queer as

Hawkins went on downstairs: Henny, of course, it was not Hawkins shrieking, and Daddy was trying to give away Charles-Franklin, "Megalops."

"He is not mine!"

"He is yours, I've told you a thousand times."

"How long was it going on?"

"Don't be a fool! I can't stand any more of it; I'll kill myself. You're going crazy. No wonder you're a laughingstock, believing every horrible bit of paper."

"There must be some basis for this; is Megalops mine? You haven't answered me direct."

Why was Daddy trying to get rid of Megalops? They couldn't understand it, but after listening for some time, they were too tired to puzzle over the whims of their fantastic father, and one after the other fell happily asleep. It had been a long and glorious day—Daddy's birthday, the neighborhood kids, the chasings round the Wishing Tree, their presents to Daddy for which they had saved up so long, and Miss Aiden coming to see them. Then, soon the holidays would be there, and they would have a glorious time, especially as Sam was still at home; and Sam had promised to take them down to Ocean City one day during the summer to see the people and the fishermen.

"You owe money still in Washington?—Megalops—he came early—who is the man?—" and they were all asleep but Ernie and Louie. Louie stood at her window, listening for a long time to the discussion downstairs (its tone had fallen now), and then she crawled into bed. After a while she lighted the candle she had sneaked upstairs and, pulling her diary out from under the pillow (for she resolved to carry it everywhere with her now), she wrote one line, "Married by misery, seeded by hate, bringing forth screams, feeding in insults." Tired and fully content, she put out the light, when she heard Evie stir in her corner. Evie's bed was hidden by the central chimney piece. Louie slipped out of bed, in the dark, and peered round the masonry. Evie was sitting up in bed. "Why aren't you asleep, Evie?"

Evie said nothing, but started to sniffle. Louie said sharply, "What's the matter?"

"I want to be sick," said Evie, beginning to cry.

"You mean in your stomach?"

"No-ho-ho!"

"Oh, stop it, you silly girl."

Evie began to sob inconsolably, lifting up her head like a little dog about to howl, "Ho-ho-ho!"

Louie got angry with her, "Tell me what's the matter? How can I do anything if you don't tell me?"

"I don't know-ho-ho!"

"I'm going back to bed!"

"I'm too tired! There's too much noise."

Louie instinctively took a quick step and put her arms round Evie and kissed her on the head, "Shh-shh! Go to sleep. You had too much fun. Ssh!"

But Evie had opened the sluice gates, "I can't, I can't."

"Ssh! I'll tell you a story."

This had no effect. Louie continued quickly, "I'll tell you The Gunny-Wolf. 'And the little girl went pit-a-pat, pit-a-pat, pit-a-pat!'" Evie paused in her sobbing to listen, for this had always been her favorite ritual. "Ugh-huh!" she sobbed. " 'And the wolf came galloping pickety-pack, pickety-pack. "Good evening, child!" "Good evening, wolf!"'"

Presently Evie consented to lie down, and though she listened half resentfully, she stopped crying. Louie got back into bed as soon as she could, for she had to think about Miss Aiden.

But the strange couple were still blackguarding each other below.

"I was a goodlooking girl before I met you!"

"Be quiet: perhaps the children are awake!"

"Is there anything they haven't heard? You tell them enough about your women: why can't they hear what you have to say?"

"Because I am an innocent father, and you are a guilty wife."

There was a cackling laugh, and Henny said, "It's a dirty lie; who but a dirty liar writes anonymous letters?"

Sam's voice said, "Henrietta, I admit I despise the anonymous letter and its author—"

"But this time it suits you because you're playing around with one of your childlike souls, one of those innocent girls who go out with other women's husbands."

"Henrietta, I forbid you to talk like that, with your dirty society-woman's mind!"

"You think I don't know about Gillian Roebuck and your secretaries? If you didn't go to bed with them, you're worse still, you see, according to the way I was brought up." Here came Henny's high chromatic artificial laugh.

Louie fell asleep. When she woke much later, there was a strange stillness in the house. She could see, through the open door, that the light was still on downstairs. Had they killed each other? She got up and stole to the head of the stairs; there was, in fact, a sort of scuffling, and Louie listened, in sacred terror, leaning on the stairhead: would they do for each other at last, would she come down and find them in pools of blood? She hoped so. She began to think busily—what would they do for food and shelter if both parents were gone? Aunt Hassie would take Evie and perhaps the little one, Chappy; everyone liked Ernie and he could find a home. Old Ellen would take one— there would be homes for all. (The twins were a problem—who wanted to be saddled with two boys at once?) She would, of course, go to the Bakens, live on the banks of the Jordan (the Shenandoah), and get a job watching the river rise and fall, and she would never have to think about the Pollits or Collyers again in her life.

Henny gave a fretful hysterical laugh, "Oh, leave me alone, you make me sick," and there was again a violent struggle, and then she heard Sam groan. That was it! She began to creep downstairs, expecting to see Henny kneeling in the lighted common room, with Sam's old-fashioned razor in her hand and Sam lying on the floor, with a gaping wound in his neck. But there was nobody in the common room. A broken cloisonné vase lay on the floor. Louie stood at the door of Henny's room for a while with her heart beating fast, and heard Henny weeping, but she did not dare go in and find out if and how murder had been done. She wandered out into the yard, while the breathing, warm, bloody house lay behind her. Presently she came back and crawled back into bed. In the morning she would look: she would be the first to find the bodies; now she was too tired to go through the melodrama of discovery and questions. She went to sleep with visions of herself comforting the children in the morning, running to the neighbors, sending telegrams. So sure was she of her role that when she woke in a sunny morning and heard her father's crisp, gay voice shouting to the boys, and smelled the customary smell of fire, she thought she was still dreaming. She listened while her heart began to throb again! The night before had been a dream then. She got out of bed and looked out the window: yes, there was Sam as large as life, like a great red and yellow apple bounding about.

When Louie came downstairs there was a letter for her from Clare (though she had seen Clare at school yesterday and would see her today) with writing all over the envelope, in her tiny eccentric scribble. In one corner was written, "Haste post haste!"; in the second, "Oh, Louie, the night is long!"; in a third, "Toothache on the right side, knowing you are off at Spa House, that's on the left side!" and round the stamp was written in minute letters, "Oh, little stamp, I have writer's cramp, but I'll put one thing yet there; though they bar, mark and blur you, don't let it deter you, just stick till you get there!" On the stuck-down flap was written,

Pity poor Clare! Her summers are spent
In thinking of mortgages, paying rent:
Not so Louie! With curtain furled
On a stage well set, Lou shook the world!

The children began gathering round like crabs after a piece of bait, to laugh and peer at Clare's well-known comicalities. Sam came peering in, laughing, "She must be a nitwit to write to you in the evening when she'll see you in the morning—why can't it keep? And you must be a nitwit too: the Amorous Nitwits!" At which everyone crowed with laughter, and Louie laughed till the tears ran down her blushing cheeks. She was laughing to prevent further questions and to avoid saying that she had written Clare a letter in school yesterday afternoon and delivered it herself on the way home. In this letter she had mildly said, "Everyone thinks I am sullen, surly, sulky, grim; but I am the two hemispheres of Ptolemaic marvels, I am lost Atlantis risen from the sea, the Western Isles of infinite promise, the apples of the Hesperides and daily make the voyage to Cytherea, island of snaky trees and abundant shade with leaves large and dripping juice, the fruit that is my heart, but I have a thousand hearts hung on every trees, yes, my heart drips along every fence paling. I am mad with my heart which beats too much in the world and falls in love at every instant with every reflection that glimmers in it." And much more of this, which she was accustomed to write to Clare, stuff almost without meaning, but yet which seemed to have the entire meaning of life for her, and which made Clare exclaim a dozen times,

"Oh, Louie, I can't believe it, when I get your letters, you are the same person: when I meet you at school I keep looking at you in surprise!"

Louie would quietly reply, hanging her head, "Oh, I am afraid that I will go from the head down; I think I will go mad," to which

Clare again replied, "I would give the top of my head to have the madness of your little finger."

These answers would fill Louie with melancholy, for she would suddenly see that she had done nothing, and she did not see how she could ever do anything. She would suddenly see a theater large as the world, in which herself, a great coconut shy, was the butt of a hundred thousand shrieks, hoots, and obscene jokes, a great vile blob of a fat girl covered with mud.

Very different from the political girls, the grinds, and the pretty boy-loving girls, Clare and Louie expended themselves in days of mad fervor about nothing at all.

4 *Summer morning scene.*
Louie spent half an hour grinning and moping and mowing over this letter of Clare's, forgot to put on the oatmeal, to take her bath, or do anything else. Even the tea had not been made. Henny remained incommunicable in her room, and when Louie at last came with the tea and knocked at the door, Henny shouted, "Whoever it is, go away!"

"It's your tea, Mother!"

"Put it down outside the door and go away!"

"Don't let it get cold!"

"I'll pour it all over your filthy face, if you don't go away."

Louie retreated, realizing Henny had one of her worst days before her. She made the oatmeal and got ready for school in a pensive mood. Evie sensed storm too, and when Ernie insulted her (as he always did, for there was a grudge from the womb, between them), she began crying quietly. Sam was meanwhile walking about outside, with his head in the air, and evidently cogitating over something very sad. His first hallooing had worn out. He came and stood beside Louie while she was making the oatmeal and, after a while, said in his finest violoncello tones, "You and I can readily understand, Looloo-dirl, the psychological storms and passions which poor Henny goes through, and we can have no feeling of reciprocated or retaliatory hate!"

"Why do we have to go through it?" asked Louie.

"We have a home—you have brothers and a sister! That is the only consideration for me," said Sam gently.

"Why did you have so many children?" Louie turned and faced him.

He shook his head gently, "Looloo, later on you will understand. A month before our marriage, I knew it would be a well-nigh hopeless union, yet so great is a young man's idea of what is honorable and sporting that I could not renege: and so I determined that the union would be fruitful and from misery would come much happiness and splendid men and women; the woman would not count, I thought: I would forget what I could not mend."

"I don't understand," muttered Louie, "why you married her at all, if you felt like that. Mother told me she didn't want to marry you."

Sam's face darkened; but after a moment he said, "And I was thinking of you, Looloo: you were a motherless little girl, and Henny seemed fond of you."

"I don't care, I don't care," suddenly cried Louie.

Sam stared at her, "What do you mean, you don't care? You don't care for my thought for you? You don't care for ray years of torture and what might well have been mental rot and spiritual death for me? You don't care for what I have been through—hell is a very temperate word!"

Louie began to snivel, "I heard it too much, I heard it too much!"

Sam said gravely, "I looked forward to your growing up; I was so happy when you were born—I thought a little girl would be easy to bring up and would have such belief in me."

462 | CHRISTINA STEAD

"Oh, I heard it too often!"

He shrugged away angrily, "Control yourself: you are always so hysterical nowadays. If you didn't get yourself into such darnfool psychological excitements with silly Clare—I thought *she* had more sense!—and silly calf loves for teachers, and even thinking about boys, no better than any man's girl!—I can hardly bear to look at you! Get ready for school!"

"You don't understand, Dad: I am sympathetic, but I heard it too often; I can't stand it any more."

"You only want to think about yourself, that's the truth," Sam said morosely and went out again to walk up and down the grassy orchard. Presently, to show he bore the world no grudge, he began whistling the children round him, and they ran out complaining, in all stages of undress.

Henny suddenly issued out of her room, with her empty cup; and no sooner saw Louie than she pounced on her and scolded her for her appearance, her dirty dress, her cobbled stockings and down-at-heel shoes, her loose straggling hair ("like your disgusting Auntie Jo's") and puffed expression ("you look as if you spent the night in self-abuse, I'll make your father speak to you"). She rushed into the girl's room to look out a clean dress for her, hoping against hope to find something, and suddenly came out screaming that she'd kill that great stinking monster, that white-faced elephant with her green rotting teeth and green rotting clothes, and she'd tear out her dirty filthy hair by the roots rather than let her be seen at school in that state, as if she had never a comb or brush at home to care for her; that Samuel Pollit, who thought all the Pollit breed so fine, had better look at his own stinking daughter who wore the filthy rags that were all he gave her until they were too black to be thrown in "Coffin" Lomasne's black scum. She wanted to know whether Sam knew that his beautiful genius' clothes were smeared with filth and that most of the time the great big overgrown wretch with her great lolloping breasts looked as if she'd rolled in a pigsty or a slaughterhouse, and that she couldn't stand the streams of blood that poured from her fat belly and that he must get someone to look after such an unnatural big beast.

Sam had come into the house when Henny began her screams and stood there goggling, while Louie, going paler, stood petrified with horror and pride, looking reproachfully at her father and expecting him to scold Henny. But Sam goggled like some insignificant wretch crept in secretly on the Eleusinian mysteries, frightened but licking his lips. Henny went on to the worst outrages possible to her vivid imagination; though Louie went upstairs, blubbering so loudly that Sam at last had to go out and call up through the window that if she didn't stop he'd have to come and beat her, big girl as she was, for she could be heard across the bay. Suddenly Sam could stand no more, but went into the kitchen, took a dash of tea in a cup, and began striding off, up the avenue and into the streets, after going softly up to Louie's room and telling her that it would quiet down when he left, for Henny hated him so much that all this came from him. He had put his hand on Louie's shoulder to comfort her, but she shook him off and looked at him with such hate that he shrank back to the door and, with one solemn, reproachful look, went downstairs into the torment that was raging down there, and so away.

Meanwhile, Ernie had come into the common room ready for school, as he thought, in a dirty shirt, and Henny rushed at her son with a slap, which brought out a howl from him. No sooner did she hear the howl caused by herself than Henny felt she could not stand any of this life any longer, nor any of her children, and she rushed at Ernie again and began to beat him across the head, screaming at him, "Die, die, why don't you all die and leave me to die or to hang; fall down, die; what do I care? I beat my son to death: it's no worse than what I have to endure," and beat him still while her eyes started out of her head; her breathing became labored. She could hardly stand but had to clutch at the chair to support herself, screaming still, "I'll kill you children that make me go out of my mind, I'll beat you to death."

Ernie meanwhile, frightened by this and not thinking of defending himself, had fallen to his knees where he cried brokenly, in a warm, pleading voice, "Mother, don't, don't, Mother, Mother, Mother, Mother, Mother, don't, please, please, Mother, Mother!" but the noise of the belting went on until Louie, unable to bear it, rushed downstairs and caught her mother's arm, "Mother! Don't! What are you doing?" Then Henny, suddenly awaking from the horrible murderous delirium, looked at Louie, as if she were about to give an explanation, and fainted. Louie got a cushion and put it under her mother's head, and then pulled Ernie up, from where he lay on the floor sobbing, "Oh, Mother," and said to him, "Come on, get up, get up."

"My head hurts," said Ernie, refusing to get up; but at last Louie managed to drag him from the floor and to get him, still crying, into the boys' room to comb his hair and adjust his clothes. When Henny came to herself, she got up slowly, wiping her wrist across her face, her eyes black and hollow as they had never been, and she, strangely enough, went to the telephone and asked for the cost of a call to Washington, D. C. She telephoned Washington but got no reply, and came away, muttering that she would get him again in the evening—she must see someone who understood her. She then shooed the children off to school, saying that that day she could not bear them round the house, for she might do herself some mischief if she looked at them; and Louie was to give them all their lunches.

Louie at last dragged off to school one hour and a half late, her cheeks scarlet and the whites of her eyes red, and, blubbering still, she walked to school, getting there just before lunch-time, and had been crying to herself all the way, not noticing how everyone looked at her or so much as wondering what she looked like.

She came into the silent playground and went straight to the class that was being held at this hour, which happened to be Miss Aiden's, not observing, still, how the few girls who passed her stared at her. She came slowly into the class, while Miss Aiden and all the pupils stared at her. Her dirty blouse, which lacked buttons, was open and showed a torn slip and foul underwear; her skirt, spotted with food, had a ripped hem at the bottom; she was slipshod, and her stockings had mud on them. Her long hair, usually plaited, hung all round her in wet streaks, and her face was twice its usual size, lobster-red and bloated with tears.

"What is the matter?" asked Miss Aiden faintly, after severely telling the girls to go back to their books.

"Nothing," said Louie.

"I think you have been crying, Louie."

"My mother is sick."

"Go to your place," said the teacher helplessly, with her clean, long fingers quickly fastening and tucking in the broken clothing. In the lunch interval she made the girl come to the empty classroom while with a borrowed needle and thread she sewed up the skirt.

5 *Good-by, Bert Anderson.*

Sam had stayed out all day in Baltimore, and for once did not come home to supper. In the evening, about seven, Henny rang again to Washington, to Bert Anderson's flat where he usually was at this time of night, and made an appointment to see him the next day. To Louie, who happened to be cleaning knives in the kitchen, she came marching in, with her grimmest expression, and said,

"I'm going to Washington to see an old friend: I have to have some legal advice if I'm ever going to get out of this mess; and please don't tell your father, or you'll get me into some more trouble. Do you hear?"

"Yes, Mother."

She than rang Hassie and asked her if she could see her in town (in Baltimore), the next morning early, to talk over something very important. She still had the season ticket to Baltimore, and as for getting to the station, "I'll crawl there on my hands and feet, if necessary," said Henny angrily, "if I can't get the money for a taxi." She left a note on Sam's desk asking for money to go to Baltimore to see her lawyer, and after dining off a four-ounce-curry made for herself from cold meat and raisins, with chutney and tea, she shut herself into her room, determined not to come out again until it was time to leave for Baltimore. "I cannot go through such scenes and won't," said she.

Later, she made herself some tea, and then got into bed, to try and read the saga of upland Georgian gentility, which she had three times abandoned because she, Henny, had "no fancy big buck niggers to wait on her and lick her boots": but once more she threw it away. Where, indeed, was she to find heroes to succor her and how could she succeed in business with her spendthrift ways. "I'm a failure all right," said Henny; "and why don't they write about deadbeats like me—only it wouldn't sell!" Towards five, when the morning came, she fell asleep and when she woke up, Sam had again left the house to go to Washington and had left no money for her nor left her any word.

Thus, she had to set off in a great temper, to walk to the station by the poor cottages, the gas station, the wretched stores and whisky counters, by the boatsheds and over the bridge, by the Market Place, up the stony high street, round the State House and so to the low-set station, where some cars were standing without an engine, in an idle sort of way, apparently asleep and not dreaming of a timetable. But at the proper time they set off, just the same, and racketed through those stray houses, over the Severn and by those woody hills that Henny hated so much, in forty minutes or an hour arriving in Baltimore. As soon as she got outside the station, Henny saw the faithful green car and hobbled towards it. How her legs ached! Honest Hassie, more cushiony than ever, waited till her ant of a sister had got in and then asked,

"Well, my dear, what mess are you in this time? I suppose you want a drink? It's too early for me, but if you want to, we'll go to the Hi-Ho."

"I want money, and I want to go to Washington, and I want never to see that hypocritical gasbag again, if I can help it," Henny explained in her usual succinct way; "and I want you to lend me whatever money you can, Hassie, because I'm in one devil of a hole."

"When were you ever out of the hole?" asked Hassie comfortably. "What's the row?"

"Some son of a bitch wrote to that Forgotten Man that I married, an anonymous letter on a bit of newspaper and told him to wipe his whatyoumaycallit, with it, pardon me! and said Charlie was not Sam's child! I'd like to find the man and send him to Alcatraz; such people should be punished with the worst the law allows." Hassie was silent for a while as she maneuvered the car round a tricky corner and up a stony street, and then she said, mildly, "Well, old girl, not that I care, but what's the story?"

Henny said angrily, "Do you think I'd be such a fool as to let one of those professional bachelors—?"

"I don't know: I think you've been an awful donkey, Henny."

"What would you do in my place, may I ask? Compromise? With what? With the West Wind? Compromise with Mr. Here-There and Everywhere? Am I to spend the next twenty years in the high-minded company of a smug Philistine who doesn't so much as make me a decent husband? Have you any recipe for that? Don't be so tiresome! You don't know what you're talking about."

"Gosh," said Hassie, sighing, "I didn't say anything; don't get mad. You and Sam should never have married, that's all."

"Any marriage I made would have gone smash," cried Henny, scoffing and throwing back her head: "I was born for excitement."

Hassie brought the car to a stop, "Well, let's drown our sorrows in drink. I really ought to be at the store, old girl, but now you can tell me what happened. What did the beast say in the anonymous letter? Oh, it really is too foul just the same, isn't it?"

"I'd bet my bottom dollar that it's old Middenway, dirty old leering goat," said Henny, angrily staring at the bare table in the little booth. "I never could stand him, and I had to kowtow to him and ladida with his servant girl of a wife because I never could get enough to foot his dirty bills; and I left owing him ninety-four dollars if you want to know. I need that at once, but if I had a gun I'd go and shoot the rat. I wish I had. a man and not a dishrag printed over with big words like 'constitutional rights' and 'progress'! Did you ever know me to do anything right in my life? I should have been drowned when a pup."

"You look so feverish," said Hassie. "What have you been doing? Have you been drinking? Your eyes are so bright! Are you well?"

Henny tossed her head, "Where the dickens would I get the money for drink? I'm just boiling mad, I'm going out of my mind: I may look cool and calm to you, but inside I'm one blaze, I'm insane."

"No, you're not, you're cool enough," said Hassie; "you're always pretty collected when you're not in a tantrum. Now, don't work yourself up."

Henny pointed to her cheeks, "I've been up all night, trying to think what to do. I realized where I was the other week, with June week—we used to flounce along and think we were the pick of the bunch; I should have married a mud rat or one of the boatmen then and there and saved myself a lot of hard work and worry and travel. I would have had the same kids and ended up in the same slops."

"Don't you think everyone has troubles?"

"A lot of people have a million dollars."

"How much do you owe?"

"Never mind; I want to have one friend left in the world."

"I don't like you going to see this man, Pet; it's disastrous; I know it, I feel sure of it: I can see you're being terribly reckless. You might ruin yourself; you know how those things turn out. What good can he do you? I don't see it."

Henny laughed scornfully, "I've got to try everything. If he won't give me money, he'll put me up in his room for a night till I collect my senses!"

Hassie said tartly, "Of course, that's all Sam wants, to get the children forever. Have you gone mad?"

"He's my only friend," said Henny obstinately, wiping a tear from her eye. "Or was."

"There's a sale on at the Palais Royal," said Hassie at this; "I'll drive you over for it, you can see this fellow, and I'll meet you again wherever you like; but I won't leave you in Washington with him: that's beyond the limit. I'll wait for you. I still don't know what good it is, but I don't want you to go streeling off there making a spectacle of yourself, and I know you'd stop at nothing."

"All right," said Henny, "come along: don't let's sit here. I'll buy myself a new hat before I meet anyone: I look like a hundred-year-old hag in this. I'm a bag of bones, he probably won't know me. No one will recognize me now."

They got into Washington in about fifty minutes, but Henny spent a good deal of time feverishly turning over the remnant counters at the Palais Royal and other stores, Henny saying that a spot of shopping would pep her up and give her a bit of color in her cheeks, and "When I feel downright low, I can always get out of it by buying something." Hassie bought her a cheap new blouse and a hat, so that by lunchtime, when she was to meet Bert Anderson in Maynard's Ship Bar in Eye Street, she wore a new spotted veil to mask her thinness, and through this her large burning eyes glowed sickly.

Bert came prancing in exactly as in the old days, at one moment holding out his hands and looking for a place for his hat. "Henny, Henny, hullo! Where have you been?"

She said, "Hullo, Bert," thinkingly vaguely that he had the best of all bargains, being still young, strong, and fresh-colored and free.

They had the bar special, twice, but it did Henny little good. She could see Bert stealing glances at her both inquisitive and surmising.

"You didn't spend the winter in Florida at any rate, that's one good thing, not with the idle sons of riches," said Bert, rather low. "Are you eating? I got to snatch a quicky, Henny old girl. You're not staying in Washington with the Great Man? I say, I never sent you a word, it certainly was too bad about—"

"It must have been painful for you," she said.

He looked up quickly to catch her laugh. "Yes, yes, I had to go to the ILGWU to have my stitches taken out with laughin'. But you, poor thing; it came hard on you, eh? Been shopping?"

She muttered feverishly, "Someone sent him a dirty anonymous letter about me and you."

Bert's fork stopped halfway to his mouth, and his great brown eyes opened wide in his face, "Gee," he said, "Gee, Henny, that ain't so good! Who could ha' been the son of a bitch who—gee! You see, Henny, be sure your sin will find you out, as my old schoolteacher used to say when I wrote on the lavatory wall. What did he say?" He dropped his voice.

"I told him I had thought he prided himself on being above such things; he got hot and holy, and I got so mad I told him to blow his nose in it." She shrugged, "I'm through with him."

"Oh, you can't do that, you mustn't do that. The children, dear?"

"I thought I'd poison him myself, but I thought I might get some money somehow and get away. Why couldn't I go to the Pryors at Frederick and stay? Why do I have to be chained to him?"

"Gosh," said Bert, "I didn't mean to get you into trouble, Henny.

He wasn't mean to you, didn't beat you up?" He grinned palely and wiped the smile quickly off his face as he saw her black look. "Poor old Henny, no luck!"

"Listen," she said nervously, rushing ahead, "you remember one time, you said you wished I were free; I could use a little friendship now. If I see that man again tonight I'll go mad, I think: I'm sure to do something desperate."

He lifted his eyes slowly from his plate and gave her a long searching look, "Dearest, what do you want me to do?" he asked softly. He slapped his pockets, pretended to pull them inside out, "Money—I haven't it! A home—I haven't it! Someone to help you—how can I ask for you, Henny? Gosh, you used to be so rich!" He shook his head slowly, "And I really can't afford to let anything get about. It's not you, but it's my job and Mother—you know what old-fashioned old ladies are?" He nodded sympathetically. "Some-one's got to get you out of this mess, though. I think you'd better go away to Frederick for a bit, don't you? And not see me—that's very important; never see me. Jesus, I hope no one—" he looked cautiously around. "Of course, I thought of this a long time ago, Henrietta, long before—" he nodded. "I was afraid, I told you I was afraid. We were too conspicuous. You see, if you were nobody and I wasn't a Government employee—but placed as we are, we can't hide under a doormat, can we?" He forced a laugh and looked up from his plate. "The principal thing is, don't lose your head. You shouldn't have come here, old girl. Jesus, it might be a trap. Perhaps he followed you."

"Oh!" She raised her eyes too from her cup, "Oh! What a life! What a man! Oh, you make me sick! Bert, you're big as an elephant with the soul of a mouse."

He frowned, "Look at it my way! Oh, gee, Henny darling, don't go on that way; you know how I'm fixed. My mother's sick, and I've been going home straight from work for weeks. Really, I haven't been making whoopee; I've been a good boy, and if Sam started a suit, wouldn't it finish everything? What good would it do you? You see? You must go right away to Frederick, that's my advice to you, old girl: let it blow over. If he don't see you with me, he can't prove anything. It's just chitchat. He'll probably get over it. Have you got any dividends yet?"

"What about that?"

"If you do get them, old girl, you can still hold out on him."

She laughed, "Let's have a Scotch and soda, Bert! I haven't had a good time for so long; and I don't think you have, either: you're getting positively moldy."

He laughed, rounded his chest, "Well, I suppose I am that: I suppose being the good little boy does settle over me like a sort of mildew. Well, there are plenty of good times to come. I don't regret treading the straight and narrow for a change. It's amusing. I get new emotions!"

"You'll be whoring when I'm dead," Henny said bitterly, stirring her glass. "Do you want to take the afternoon off and give me a good time on what might be my last day on earth? Will you do that?" She begged him with her glowing eyes.

He was embarrassed, "Well, Henny, love, Jesus, I would, you know that—you and me have been really good friends; we got along all right. You understand things; you're the right cut. But I must go back to work; you don't want Bert to get demoted or promoted to the Civil Service Commission's carpet strip, or anything like that?"

"Bert," she begged.

"I wish there was a way out, I wish there was, believe me, Henny," he said uneasily.

"Will you meet me this evening then?" she asked, nervously.

"Well, I oughtn't to, you know the old girl expects me. No, I don't think I can, Henny old girl; sorry, really, I'm sorry."

She fastened a peculiar look on him, "You do take me for a two-dollar pickup, don't you? I always suspected there was no difference between me and the street trotters."

"Now, Henny," he said reproachfully.

"Because I've lost my money," she said to herself: "you know I half thought that this morning. Aren't you a bit ashamed!"

"Of what?" he cried.

"Of not coming with me on my last day on earth," she cried triumphantly.

"I don't understand you; what are you trying to fasten a scene on me for? Is this a setup?"

She began to light a cigarette, very carefully, with trembling hand, so that he leaned across the table and held it for her, "Poor Henny, poor old girl! Don't lose control, Henny."

"Advice is cheap. You are a bounder, aren't you?"

"Jesus, if you knew how I'd like to help you, Henny!"

"That's a wonderful end to my love affair," said Henny, her face blazing yellow; she turned her head aside and hid her eyes in her hand. He heard her whispering, "Oh, God, Oh, God, this is terrible!"

"Henny darling, you had me, and I had you, and this is no good, it's over. We can't go back. I can't help you. Why, I got you into this mess! See what good I am to you? Be sensible, old girl."

"That's smug."

He shrugged, "I am smug, I suppose: I come from the lower bourgeoisie, my dear."

Her breast was heaving with her painful breaths. He looked at her quizzically, "What exactly did you come for, Henrietta? Why did you do such a foolhardy thing? Are you really feeling desperate?"

"I'm being torn to pieces inside," she said in a rare contralto voice, looking sternly at him. "I don't know why I came, I knew you. You're not bad, but you're not good either. You're a loathsome thing! But I knew it. I don't blame you. At the beginning, that winter day— I nearly fainted when I saw you in your great jumbo BVD's and now

I see you in your moral BVD's; it all hangs together. Don't think you're hurting me. You can't. I'm beyond all your yellow cowardly tricks. You never saw me again when you heard I was pregnant: when I rang up, even though we had a regular appointment, you threw it in my face that you had another girl to supper; not a letter all that time. You knew my money troubles—did I ask you for a cent?"

"Steady, there, steady: yes, you did, if the truth must be told. But we were going steady—"

She bit her lip. Then, after thinking a bit, looking down into her clasped hands, she said quietly, "I used to wait for the telephone to ring: the door wasn't a door but a living leather thing that might bang to and fro, to let you in. I used to dream at night I heard you coming to see me."

"Gee, old girl," he said collectedly.

"I wasn't in love with you, but I wasn't out of love with you, and I wanted your help. And you weren't there. I used to look down at all those lights and think, Somewhere under one of those lights Bert is singing some girl his old sweet song; why can't he take one night off to come and see me? That winter!"

"Jolly good thing I didn't! It's bad enough—"

She looked at him with hate, "I know where it came from: you were boasting round the place that you were sleeping with the wife of a departmental head and putting on his horns while he was away: everyone knew, I could tell by the way they looked at me."

"Why didn't you stop me—or stop yourself?"

"I can't go on, Bert; I'll scream."

"No, you won't," he said, alertly, getting up and picking up her wrap: "you're not hysterical. Now, will you go to the movies, and I'll see you again after work?"

"I wouldn't see anything in the movies, but what can I do? I'd rather go shopping, but I have no money."

"Well, I haven't any," he said rather sharply. Then, sweet again at once, he continued, "You ring me, old dear—or better, you wait for me in the old joint. 'Say baby, that ain't a joint, it's a dump.' Ha-ha-ha. Say, can you pay for a movie or are you flat, stony broke?"

She said sullenly, "You're not going to hand me a dollar on the sidewalk, are you? Go to hell, Bert! I'll be at the bar maybe."

"You'll be there, old girl, you'll be there," he said, apparently in high feather. He kissed her, "There, be a good girl."

She wandered round all the afternoon, sitting on public seats and looking in secondhand shops, wandering through the shops disconsolately. She met Hassie at last at the appointed hour and told her she was to meet "her friend" in a certain bar; but at last she told her which bar and Hassie gave her some more money, because she had bought a dress for Evie, enough to pay for a cocktail while she waited. She waited over an hour, with her one cocktail before her, but the door did not swing in that unique breezy way which was Bert. At last it did swing for her, though. In came Hassie, with a set expression, and after sitting beside her five minutes and talking vigorously, she persuaded her to come away. Henny had dark circles under her eyes.

"I rang too," she said. "I need another nickel to ring his home to see if an accident happened."

"Henny, don't be a fool."

"I can't believe he would do that, even so."

"Come and get a bite to eat at home with me: I'll ring up Sam and keep you overnight. Then you simply have to go back and face the music. And on Saturday I'll come down and talk to Sam. You ought to go away. You look done up."

She led her out. The broad, middle-aged lady leading the thin, wrecked, rakish one were studied by all the wildly gay Washington couples there, and a very audible ripple of laughter followed them, three girls near the door going into fits of laughter.

Chapter Ten

1 Baby's bedroom.

Henny stayed two days at Hassie's, not paying much attention to her troubles but reading and sitting round with Hassie or Cathy or the servant, in the dark back room, furnished in oilcloth and dark-smeared pine, reading, tatting, and taking tea or coffee. She sewed up some seams in Cathy's doll collection and looked into the old trunk of silver from Monocacy which Hassie had taken as her portion. There were two Dresden figures, two shepherdesses, one in black lace and one in white, which Louie had adored from babyhood; and Henny took these in a duster to Hassie, asking if she could have them for the poor kid, who always liked them so much.

"It is a rotten shame, when I think that the poor kid is dragged into all our rotten messes," said Henny.

"I'm sure I don't want them," Hassie consented, bustling about in a great blue-striped apron. The saline and slimy smell of the wet cement floor of the fish store came through the back screen door. Henny hated fish and complained about it good-humoredly all the day. Fish was in the curtains, on the oilcloth, in the cooking, said Henny, while Cathy made a face. There was practically nothing the wasp-waisted Cathy would eat because of her delicacy; her father had made a living out of foods made from entrails and offscourings, sausages and the like, and loved tripes and stuffed neck and the parson's nose; her mother was a sturdy fishwife, slapping down fish, stacking them in salt, plunging her hand in barrels. Cathy had seen her mother screw a chicken's neck and could eat no more; she could not eat a rabbit because she had seen it skinned; she could eat nothing but baby lamb chops and was doing her best to move into an esthetic vegetarianism, but the poor thing was too young to have any rights and still had to dive into the family messes. She sat round gratefully with her Auntie Henny who said "fwee" and "pooh" to everything, and listened owlishly to pungent tales of loathsome folk, scabby with leprosy, spineless with caries, both moral and medical, whom Henny and Hassie knew intimately, or met in the street.

Henny rang up every few hours to ask about Charles-Franklin and find out what the "children's father" was doing today, and what Louie was giving them for lunch, and whether they stayed up late singing and jigging with the children's father, or whether they went to bed, and how was Little-Sam's earache. At night she tossed, and would put on her bedside lamp at all hours of the night while she tried to read popular novels which she called, universally, silly rot, muck, and a lot of hooey. She was really waiting for Sam to come to get her, or for him to send a letter saying he had started divorce proceedings. She did not much care. Her life was such a ruin that she preferred not to think about it at all. But on the third day, she took the train back to Annapolis. It was Saturday. She saw the little ones on the lawn jumping up and down and for all she had to face, her heart beat faster: how odd that this tumble-down windy mansion in which she had to live with a despised man was home! But her heart sank as she came up the drive. The children, seeing that unusual sight, a taxi, serpentining into the drive, ran to it with screams and halloos and started tumbling all over her. She brushed them off, paid the taxi driver, and went in, saying, "Where's your father?"

"Oh, the marlin's coming: Mr. Pilgrim is sending Dad the marlin—they caught a marlin," Henny heard. "Why did you stay away, Moth? Why did you stay at Aunt Hassie's, Moth? It's coming by the ferry: they're sending it in a car to Matapeake, ooh, we're going to boil it!" Henny took no notice of this, but with a grim expression on her face went into her room. There she had a great shock: the little fairy daughter of "Coffin" Lomasne was standing at the dressing table prinking before the glass. Henny sank down on the bed, putting her hand over her heart. The little girl turned round guiltily and flushed.

"Who let you in?"

She said shyly that Mr. Pollit had let her come in to breakfast to play with Tommy. Henny sneered and laughed. For weeks, Tommy the boatbuilder had done little but think about Lomasne's baby girl, and could not understand why she could not come and live with them. Now, thought Henny, no sooner do I turn my back than even Tommy gets in another woman; what a pack men are! And of all little girls it has to be Sam's "Little-Fairy" Lomasne.

Sam came up from the tool shed where he had been arranging Ernie's bottles in a row, preparatory to washing them and stalking into the hall outside Henny's room said, "I see you've come back."

Henny was silent, but in a minute walked out of her room softly as a ghost, and passing him with a black look, but a distant pasty one not like her old recriminatory ones, went into the baby's room. Here she sat down, and Sam, having nothing to say, went outside again and began singing, "Dare to be a Daniel, dare to stand alone, dare to have a purpose true and dare to make it known."

Baby Chappy was on the front veranda, playing with his blocks without saying a word. Henny sat in the room he shared with Tommy in the front of the house and looked round. Louie had not yet made the beds: the twisted week-old sheets and battered pillows, the faded flannel pajama suits and ragged bedside mats with sand and loam ground into them, lay about in mild disorder, while the single finger of sun in the far corner sought for them and moved delicately towards the center of the oilcloth. Flies buzzed inside the wire screens on the windows. On Monday all that would have to go into the wash, and Henny had not paid Mrs. Lewis for the last

Monday's wash. Louie came into her with a cup of tea. The room smelled of babies' dirt and babies' effluvia. Over Tommy's bed a great sun-tanned girl with wild curly hair grinned down from a grove of oranges—a poster that Tommy had fallen in love with at the age of one year. Over Charles-Franklin's bed was the picture that someone had given Henny on her wedding day, a brown man and a white-skinned girl kissing in a field of poppies at sunset, in a gilt rococo frame. Pollit art had never gone beyond this. On each side of the door was a sketch in water colors, one a sunken garden with trees by the Monocacy as it winds through Frederick, and one of the old Chesapeake and Ohio bridge which crosses the Monocacy River, with the low bushy landscape and the stones spouting water. Henny had only learned three things in her school life—water-color-painting, embroidery, and the playing of Chopin, and her children could not do one of these things. Instead, they were carving boats, painting outhouses, putting in rubble for cement floors. But she did not think about her futile, anemic youth now. Instead, she looked vaguely about, sniffing that familiar smell of fresh dirtiness which belongs to mankind's extreme youth, a pleasant smell to mothers. Henny had spent twelve years in that atmosphere.

"Poor Chappy," she thought mildly, "of course, he's just a Pollit like the rest: only Ernie is a Collyer, and he doesn't like me so much since the red money-box business—I don't blame him! Well, Tommy—but I don't want to see a son of mine to grow up getting women into messes; I'm not sorry for the stupid girls, but it's not sugarplum for either side. How tired I feel!" She was surprised to feel tired after a holiday. She thought, "I can't bear to get old, lose all my energy, not be able to sleep because I'm too weak to sleep, and snivel along after life. Oh, why shouldn't I live with Sam?—he's as good to me as any man would be: men are all the same. To beat them, you have to have so much energy—I haven't got it."

For a long time she thought of nothing but found it sweet to sit there and think of her boys' future: strange to say, Evie never entered her mind. She had never bothered about Evie, or tried to dress her well, or taught her household matters or manners, for she regarded such a nice, obedient, pretty girl as cursed from birth: "Some man will break her or bend her," she always said to Hassie bitterly; while about Louie she always said, "I'm sorry for the man she marries!" About the girls she only thought of marriage, and about marriage she thought as an ignorant, dissatisfied, but helpless slave did of slavery. She thought the boys would get on by the brutal methods of men, Pollit or Collyer. She fingered the little, dirty, glazed-chintz cover, the thin summer blanket with matted spots, the cotton sheet. Before she was married she had made up her mind never to have anything but linen sheets, but it was four years since she had had one, and the present sheets were of the shoddiest cotton, and Mrs. Lewis, who turned them yellow, with her conceit, kept saying, "I'm sure you never had whiter sheets, Miss!"

Henny thought, "I like a baby's room best: there are no books, no lead, no nonsense," and she thought of evenings when she had come in to see the usual sight, a baby's head lying sideways, the eyes closed, the fine dark hair growing thicker over the thin-skinned oval skull, the little nightgown frill, the eyes closed, and one fist clenched on the pillow. She pulled the edge of the blanket straight thoughtfully, "A mother! What are we worth really? They all grow up whether you look after them or not. That poor miserable brat of his is growing up, and I certainly licked the hide off her; and she's seen marriage at its worst, and now she's dreaming about 'supermen' and 'great men.' What is the good of doing anything for them? Anyhow, He always wins! Well, that girl has been cooking for them for three days: I suppose I'd better see about some lunch."

She looked out of the kitchen window and saw Louie lying on her back in the orchard, waving her arms in the air, with Sam and Saul sitting on her belly jigging up and down while she shrieked and laughed. The screen door swung, and Evie's pattering came down the hall, "Mother! Mother! You came home! Oh, Mother, we had such fun last night—we all had dinner in our bathing suits and after we had a water party; and the people over on the houseboat had a party too, in bathing suits, and Louie and Ernie swam over and looked in."

"Very nice. Did Louie tell you what she got for lunch?"

"Sausages and apple fritters; and last night we had 'cah-nah-pay.'" Evie giggled, "It was raw bacon and almonds out of your drawer, and Saul spat it out."

"I see you're living on Pollit distinction," said Henny. Sam's voice on the heavy, electric summer air sang out, "Megalops, Megalops! What are you donin?" Henny heard him going past the back veranda with the three boys, saying, "See what Megalops donin: he don't say nuffin, maybe he thinkin; wook [look], Little-Sam, Megalops drornin [drawing] designs in the dirt."

"He's eating dirt, Pad," shrieked Saul appreciatively. Louie, who had been trying to swing on a branch of a peach tree, desisted and looked soulfully after the three boys and their father.

"The baby's eating dirt, Looloo," shouted Ernie.

"Well, stop him," she shouted back, at the same time walking after them nonchalantly.

"Of course he's eating dirt," said Henny. "Who is looking after him? I'd give a lot to know what he's eaten the last three days."

There fell round the corner of the house a scatter of guffawing children, turning up the corners of their eyes and holding their hands over their mourns, "Moth! Oh-ho-ho! Mothering! The baby's eating—shh!—well he is!—shh!—Megalops is eating—she doesn't like you to call him that!—Daddy says to come and see, Mother: the baby's eating his own crap—shh!—excrement, Mother."

"Don't be silly, that's not a joke," Evie told Saul severely.

"He is, he is, go and see!"

"Didn't your silly fool of a father stop him?" cried Henny.

"Yes, Mother, but Daddy says its natural, it's no harm, only he stopped him too."

"And yesterday he ate a caterpillar," said Ernie gravely. The boys burst out laughing, again holding their sides and each other. "Ooh," cried Evie, "it's so dirty, it squidged out...." They shrieked with laughter. "And Louie ate a snail to show it wouldn't make you sick," Ernie said, "and Daddy said it didn't matter." Little-Sam dropped suddenly to the ground and began rolling about holding his belly, in a paroxysm of laughter. "We had a good time, Moth, we had such a good time," Saul said hopping about, trying to convince her she should have been there. "But Louie made some nasty things, and I got sick."

"I firmly believe that," Henny said grimly. "It is quite a pity I came home: Mr. Lomasne could have done a nice business in a few days. Evie, why haven't you emptied the slops? The little boys' room hasn't been touched. Has any work been done since I left? You'll all have cholera or typhoid yet."

"We have a schedule," Ernie cried, "and we're going to make a new bartenoom [bathroom], Moth: and I'm making the frun television." (The twins chanted, "Front elevation, frun television, from Tilly Buzzum!") "And next summer, Ermo is going away with his sissy Mervyn for a walking tour," cried Little-Sam. "Oh, Mervyn the Pervyn sat under a tree, and Ernie the Mernie said, 'What do I see?'"

"You shut up," said Henny, "before I go mad. I don't know why I came home. Why isn't someone doing the potatoes? So you have a schedule? Get out of here before I scream."

A great shout blew round the house, and they heard the sound of pelting footsteps. Sam was calling, "Kids! Kids and goats! Whistletime! Worktime! Gotta make da layout for da new bartenoom. Whar you got to, fellers?"

"Comin'! I'm a-comin'! O.K., Pad!" shouted the boys, running out and leaving Henny and Evie to get the dinner. Tommy burst in through the other door calling, "Molly! Molly!" looking wildly for the little blonde Lomasne girl; and at the same moment Ernie rushed in through the western door shouting, "I see Auntie Jo's car! She's coming to lunch! Auntie Jo's coming!"

"Go and stop her at the gate and ask her if she got any choc?" shouted Sam. The children rushed off to meet her. Henny worried, "I wonder what the silly old upholstered frump wants at this hour in the day? Does she expect lunch? Did you expect your Auntie Jo? What can she expect coming without notice?" Henny sliced away at the apples anxiously.

"I wish I could go and see her car," poor Evie pouted. "Look, Moth, I cut my finger."

"Oh, then go and don't drive me mad," cried Henny, more vexed than ever. "God knows what the Man of Sorrows has been up to! What the deuce is his big slummicking sister down here for before lunch?" She went impatiently to the baby's room to look out and saw Jo in great excitement walking about with Samuel, who seemed depressed; Jo expostulated, was bright with indignation; Sam put his hand to his eyes and brushed them. They turned and came towards the house.

"That's it," thought Henny, with indignation, "she pried and poked, and she found out—let the old maid go home, she knows nothing."

But when the yellow-haired couple came towards her, she saw they were both crying; and Sam said, "We found Bonnie, or rather—she came to Jo."

"I didn't recognize her," said Jo. "I opened the door and there was a terrible-looking woman, thin, with hair in a knot and looking—"

"She got a taxi to bring her to Jo's house because she knew she was going to be ill." Sam looked humbly at Henny, with a face tortured by shame and distress. "Bonniferous is there now, in Jo's flat: she had a baby there. I am going up to see the man."

"Where is the baby?" asked Henny.

"I don't know," Jo said.

"It's dead!"

"I don't know!"

"What are you talking about?"

"Someone came and took it away: I don't know. It wasn't I that arranged it. I won't keep her there, either. What am I to say? What can I tell them? She hasn't even a wedding ring."

"Where is the baby, Samuel?" Henny asked angrily. "What is it, a girl? A boy?"

"I didn't look and I didn't ask. Someone came last night and took it away and it may as well be dead: she will never see it again. I had to pay to have it taken away, and I don't wish to hear any more about it. I've never seen anything like it: she tried to kill herself, and she asked me to kill her. I didn't know what to do. She kept shrieking so loud you could have heard it a block away, and I tried to keep her quiet by putting a pillow over her mouth, but she was so strong I couldn't hold her down. They came at the door knocking, too. She got there at four and she kept it up till eleven-thirty, and there was I in jail with this horrible thing going on and people knocking at my door. At last the woman on the floor underneath got her husband to break in the door. She said she would go and get a woman, but I said, 'I would never allow my sister to be seen like that'; but she went anyhow. Think of my horrible position! She came back with a woman who did something—I don't know what; I never looked towards her. Then she asked me if she would send the baby away and told me what it would cost. I told her I would never pay for it, I knew nothing about it; but she insisted—I would have to pay for its keep, if there was no father, as it seemed—" Jo's voice broke in a sob.

She began to walk up and down the room, not looking at any of them, avoiding their glances, delivering a manifesto, "She isn't my sister: to come there at the last moment without giving me any warning, after being silent all that time and in that state—why didn't she die? I thought she was sure to. What am I to do? Everyone must know. She wouldn't be quiet; I kept trying to stop her. I had to give the woman ten dollars to take the horrible thing away, the baby, early this morning, and she's coming back on Monday. Don't you see it's blackmail? I'm ruined. I won't have her; I'm finished with her. Sam can do what he likes. She'll never see my face again. And this morning I had a telegram from Miss Atkinson—she was one of those who knocked at my door yesterday afternoon! What am I to say? I rang her up and told her someone was taken very ill with accidental poisoning, and we had to have the stomach-pump. But will she believe it? I've got to get that thing out of my rooms. What will I do, Henny?"

"Is she alive? What do you mean?"

"She's ill," said Jo solemnly.

"It would have been better if she'd died," said Henny.

"Will you come and get her, Henny? Down here no one comes: she could stay here until she can get up. Then she must go away. I'm sorry I have to talk about her."

Sam looked angry, "I'm going up at once to see the man."

"What can he do? He's married, isn't he? The rotten coward took a young girl, knowing he couldn't be stuck with her. Don't be wasting your valuable time."

"To think of the way I've lived and fought for every penny," said Jo, stopping and standing in front of Henny. "Now I must sell the house. I can't face the disgrace. I can't go back while she's there when I think of what she's done to me. A sister of mine!—oh, I don't know how I can bear it! How can this happen to me, when I've worked so hard. Miss Atkinson came with two of the teachers—

we were going to have a cup of tea and go to the cinema. What can I say to them on Monday? I can't face it. I must get temporary leave. Oh, it's dreadful, it might ruin me, a thing like that."

"What about Bonnie, Jo?" Sam asked gently.

Jo shouted rudely, "Do you think I care about a thing like that, a prostitute trailing around with married men and having babies in the street? Oh, it's awful. It's awful, Henny. I don't know what to do. In our family—I didn't know such things happened."

"You big brass-mouthed old-maid cow," said Henny, "I hope a thousand worse things happen to you to teach you to be a bit human, instead of always prancing about with your head in the air."

"Henny! I thought that you at least—Henny! Don't, don't say that! You don't understand. You have your father's money and estate: I had to build up every cent of this with my own hands; don't you see? It might ruin me. You don't know what it means to have to be your own father and mother the way I had to, and look out for your old age. You have a husband, little ones for your old age; but who is there for me? I'm darned if I'll stand such a thing," cried Jo, suddenly getting angry again. "I should have strangled her with my own hands, yesterday: I had the chance; I was too cursed weak. What difference would it make?"

"You ought to have had a man to make you wash floors and kick you in the belly when you didn't hurry up for him," said Henny with all the hate of a dozen years. "I'm as rotten as she is—I've had men too—I've gone trailing my draggletail in all sorts of low dives—I've taken money from a man to keep his children—I'm a cheat and a liar and a dupe and a weak idiot and there's nothing too low for me, but I'm still 'mountains high' above you and your sickly fawning brother who never grew up—I'm better than you who go to church and than him who is too good to go to church, because I've done everything. I've been dirty and low and done things you're both too stupid and too cowardly to do, but however low I am, I'm not so filthy crawling in the stench of the gutter, I haven't got a heart of stone, I don't sniff, sniff, sniff when I see a streetwalker with a ragged blouse, too good to know what she is: I hate her but I hate myself. I'm sick of the good ones; I'm sick of that stupid staring idiot standing goggling at me who's going to be as good as you are; nothing's too good for you, nothing's too bad for me; I'll go and walk the streets with that poor miserable brat sister of yours—we'll both get something to eat and some men to be decent to us, instead of loudmouthed husbands and sisters who want to strangle us—that's what you said, that's what you said, you can never go back on that, and in that your whole black cruel cold heart came out of you and you tried to strike her down with it, like a stone as he'd like to strike me down when he gets all he can out of me—and I know you both, I know you all—she's the only decent one and that's because she's like me—no good—good because she's no good—take your eyes off me, you staring idiot, get out of here, you filthy child—tell your daughter to get out of here—I can't stand it—" Henny could say no more but began to scream and then fell to the floor, bumping her head hard. Her eyes were closed; she seemed cold as stone.

Louie, with streaming eyes, went slowly to get her a cushion as so often before, while Jo said, "Well, in all my life!"

"Shut up, Jo: the trouble with you is you don't understand anything and you don't try to learn," Sam said, in a voice low and mortified. "Let us go outside and leave her alone. Louie, leave your mother to come to herself. Jo, I can't go on. You don't know what I have to put up with, so don't give me advice. I will go up with you, and you and I will get Bonnie out of your place. I'll bring her down here. Jo, you must try to be kinder. You are beyond human life."

"I've never done any wrong," said Jo, stony with pride and passion; "I've never done wrong to a single human being: no one can say that."

"Get your hat, Jo: we'll go and see Bonnie."

Henny groaned and stirred slowly. Louie, who had been watching, snuffling and sobbing in the corner of the room, came forward, "Will I help you up, Mother?"

"Yes, take me into the baby's room."

But when she got up she withdrew her hand quickly from the hated child's touch, and, going into the baby's room, slammed the door. Louie went round outside and peered in the window. Henny was lying on Tommy's bed, under the picture of the girl with oranges, and large tears were rolling from under her dry, tanned lids.

The boys, who had been playing down on the beach, now rushed up shrieking, "Auntie Jo; can we take your car to the ferry to get the marlin? It's coming now." So it happened that, as they couldn't let the marlin lie corrupting on the street end where the Matapeake ferry comes in, they went and brought home the marlin before Jo and Sam went to see Bonnie. The boys staggered down to the beach with the weighty spikefish. Its great eyes were sunken; it looked exhausted from its battle for life; there was a gaping wound in its deepest part. They attached it by a cord to a stake and immersed it in the creek, to keep it as fresh as possible till Sam came home. The children began to run towards Spa House from all over Eastport, and people started to look at them from the bridge and Shipwright's Street. The children were proud and happy and would not stir from the beach all the morning. The air was crisp, electric, nervous, but the children only flickered, leaped, and played like fish.

But Evie, up in the house, grunted under the tables and round the chairs, removing old dust and musing in a delirium of contentment: Louie had just told her that Auntie Bonnie had a little baby and that they were both coming to stay. Evie was already arranging in her mind that the baby should sleep in her room, so that she could mind it.

2 *Gold mare's tail.*

Sam did not come till the sky was green and a cloud hung above Bancroft Hall and the lost horizon. He was alone. Bonnie had been neglected all day except for little visits of consolation from the neighbor from below and was ill, angry, and feverish when her brother got there. Where was the baby? The neighbor had told her that it was being looked after by a nurse, but she wanted to see it. Was it a boy or a girl? It was a boy with faint white hair. She must feed it. No, not for forty-eight hours. She whined, went to sleep, and woke up again, worrying about the baby, and said she must get up, and asked where the nurse was. The neighbor said, and believed, that Jo had gone to make arrangements for her to go to a nursing home with the baby. But Bonnie knew about Jo what no one else knew, having seen her in her agonized fury during the previous twenty-four hours. She would have stolen out if she could have moved, because she felt so weak that she was sure she was going to die. Very little had been done in the room: the flies buzzed, and it was sultry, thunderstorm weather. Bonnie cried and in her new helplessness and anxiety thought over the secrets of the past few months. She would never in her life admit her humiliations: she had been and would again be a gay, buzzing girl with the disease of optimism. When she woke once she found her loved brother Sam in her room and wept bitterly in his arms, saying how weak she felt and that she thought she was going to die.

Jo wanted to move Bonnie away at once, to avoid explanations, but Sam explained to her that Bonnie could not be moved ("Don't tell me—please tell me when you came from the maternity ward!—ridiculous!—I understand as well as you!—nonsense!" ejaculated Jo meanwhile); and he suggested that it would be better to keep Bonnie close and quiet till she could move, say a week or ten days, and then let her go out at nightfall. Bonnie could then go to him at Spa House, and he would come to fetch her.

Jo became very tormented at the idea that she would have to live in the same two-room apartment with Bonnie for a whole week or more, wrung her hands, and said she could not face the school—she must get sick leave, she could not face her tenants with rent day nearly due, and what would she do about the decorator who was coming to paint her walls Nile green? But Sam became stern and forbade her to move Bonnie; and as soon as she was so ordered the domineering, unruly Jo became meek at once, if not acquiescent. Sam told her to get food and clothing for Bonnie, saying bitterly that after such a few days the burden would fall on him, Jo need not fret. He was very thoughtful coming home, but the thickset woods and the broad, fish-silver Severn made his heart lighter. He had not been to see "the man, the card-trick horror," whom Jo asserted was the cause of Bonnie's downfall, because Bonnie had said so often and positively that the man was a bachelor, an actor now on tour (withholding his name), that Sam dared not interfere at present. He was grave and deeply ashamed, offended with Fate, not with Bonnie; he muttered his favorite saying over and over as the train racketed along,

> Good name—in man—and woman—good my Lord,
> Is—the Immediate—Jewel—of their—souls!
> Who steals—my purse, steals trash—'tis something—nothing!
> Good name—in man—and woman—good my Lord,
> Steals trash—'tis something, nothing—good my Lord—
> 'Tis something, nothing, 'tis something, nothing—good name—

He stopped at the boat basin as always and chatted with the captain of the *Mary III* and then walked to the bridge. Birds were flying in funnels and purse seines in the steep air, dragging, trawling the air for insects, getting ready to settle in trees and already in tree shapes. In the air was the strange cloud, bright gold, in the shape of an ostrich feather or the tail of a sculptured horse. It was late; the dark was closing globularly round, and little was left but the green top and the strangely lighted west. Many people stopped to look at the ominous cloud, which, after remaining for some time with its pure, glittering, fimbriate forms, began to dissolve; the light retired behind it where it burned still. Gradually the texture of the rest of the sky became apparent; the sky was covered with short mares' tails of cloud which were now lengthening, anastomosing, knitting. Sam heard a chattering on the other side and in the dusk saw a small group of children, with "Coffin" Lomasne and old Bill the fisherman, standing on his own beachlet, discussing the marlin which lay in the water.

"Gee Whittaker!" said Sam, "she will pooh if I don't hurry," and he widened his stride.

The children had seen him though and came hallooing towards him. "Pad, you're so late; Pad, it's too late to cook the spikefish; Dad, can we build the fire now under the copper?" while Ernie came towards him chanting, while he pointed to the flimsy sky, "Mares' tails and mackerel scales make heavy ships carry light sails," the old saw.

As soon as dinner was finished, they went down with their own railway storm lantern (which was named "Old Man Hat") and with lamps borrowed from the boatmen, and with the ax saw and skinning knives, to dissect the fish. Soon Little-Sam came leaping down the dark earthy cliff to say the fire was hot and the water singing to the boil. They were going to boil the fish through the night. There were basins alongside, on boards on top of the washtubs, into which the oil was to be ladled as it floated to the top; and all the washed bottles, with some gallon jars, stood along the wall of the washhouse. Sam had made up his mind to show them an item of his economy and to provide for as many household oils as he could from this single fish. Henny sent a message out to ask how on earth she was to do the washing on Monday, but Sam sent back a message to say that the boys would get inside and scrub it out with sand and washing soda. They then cut the fish up fairly small into pieces six to nine inches in length and threw them into the copper in which was a little water (it should have been done in a double boiler, said Sam, but "necessity was the mother of invention"). They kept the head separate to boil in a caldron in the yard the next day, because Sam wanted to see how much oil was in the head alone, out of mere curiosity.

In about twenty minutes, at about nine-forty-five in the evening, a strong smell of fish stew arose, which increased as the boiling went on. They banked the fire, as the fish began to stick, and threw in more water. It was a to-and-fro all the time, with the children simmering and carrying messages to each other and to their father, and Henny coming out to find out what was that horrible smell and was it going on all night. The boiling water was now covered with large oil spots and scum, which they occasionally ladled off into the available enamel hand basins and the kitchen pail; long tubes of steam went off, and the air in the washhouse was palpable. Henny was walking through the house now, wringing her hands on her skirts and saying she would never get the smell out of the house.

"Hassie's place smells like fish, and I come home to this: my life has been one blessed fish chowder!"

Then when she had gone upstairs "away from the stink"—though, heavy as it was, almost leaden in the heavy air, it was rising slowly, and flowing round the house, to reach the second story and the roofs and chimney pots and float sluggishly away to other parts—the fun really began. It was a night of jamboree with Sam, the boys and girls, the fire on the lower part of their faces, taking turns at watching the fire under the boiler and telling long anecdotes, joking, reminiscing, Sam reciting, "Good name in man and woman, good my Lord," and Louie, "When Moloch in

Jewry munched children with fury, 'twas thou Devil dining with pure intent." Presently the house was ready for the night, and they expostulated with Sam about the smell, one at a time, but ended by settling down with the others and dreamily taking it in.

"*Superbus,*" cried Sam, "*superbus,* it is a good whiff; when you fellers snuff my mortal remains, it won't be half what this is!"

"Stop it!" cried Louie.

"They is stinx en stinx," Sam said, beginning to caper on his haunches; "they is good sniffs and bad whiffs; they is snot smells and pot smells; they is green-grown wells and hell's bells; they is dogs what prowls and cats what howls, and showers what lowers for hours and hours, and they's dead fish and dirty dish, en dead gulfweed what's dead indeed, en clams en corpses en barnacles en all of the salt sea's miracles; what is dead, what is dead en tho hit is dead, it floats en it bloats, en it gloats en—ef you stick a knife in it, whew!"

And he held his nose, while all around him they held their noses and said, "Phew!"

"Phew!" he continued, "say, kids, ain't you en me havin' a good time? Now, we got to take turns watchin' this yere fire all the livelong night; we cain't afford to let it get away from us: we live in a wooden house, though it don't look wooden. Now, who is game for a fishing expedish?"

"I think it's going to rain, Pad," said Little-Sam, wrinkling his nose; "it sure smells like rain."

As if in answer to him came a low growl, perhaps from the northwest, and the air trembled like a curtain.

"The fish will be there," said Sam, "but maybe we are too late. So we'll go to bed, and Little-Womey will take first watch till eight bells; then she will wake Looloo, who will take the dog watch becaze she is dogged, and then we will have two shifts, Little-Sam for two hours and Saul for two hours becaze they cain't do nothin' by halves."

"When will you watch, Pad?" asked Ernie.

"Now, I am doing the superintendin'," said Sam, "and I cain't watch, it stands to reason de boss cain't do everything." He grinned wickedly at them. However, when Henny heard the watches the children were to keep, she sent down an angry message from her room, and presently they drew up a new roster, in which each was to watch two hours, including Sam, to watch and keep the fire, skim the scum, stir the stew, and make a cup of tea for the watch to follow.

The night was with them. Mutterings ran through the sky, and the land began to moan, and the trees heaved as if the whole earth was a timbered ship trying to make headway on a threatening sea. The thundering increased, coming nearer, and brilliant lightning began, splitting the entire sky, in which balls of fire seemed to bounce in an instant from the close doorstep of heaven to earth; then the sky and earth began to shudder and dissolve into one another like one corrugated sheet along which the lightning spilled. The children ran about pallid and tremulous through all this, long trained to be afraid of none of the effects of nature, and yet surprised at this bizarre electric storm.

Upstairs, Henny could not sleep and went downstairs to get the baby, which she took back upstairs with her. She got into bed, holding the heavy body of the unconscious child as long as she could, and then placed it in the bed alongside her. Meanwhile, she could see what she was accustomed to see from her bedroom window—the ghastly tilted roofs, a bit of stony street, the clumsy wooden bridge, the colorless lashing water with shells of boats tossing. Somewhere beyond the world, an enormous voice shouted, whips cracked, and sheet-iron clanged through space, while every few minutes the flares of an open hearth, distant and beneath, lighted the entire sky. Sometimes it was as the seven candlesticks seized at the horizon and carried by a rushing wing flickering to the other verge. Surge after surge in spouts and cataracts roared the rain.

Henny once wrapped her dressing gown round her and rushed down the stairs furiously, to knock at Sam's door and ask if the children were not even to be allowed to have their night's sleep on account of the cursed great fish and if they were to be allowed to drown down there in the brimming yard.

"Go back to bed," called Sam's voice from behind the door.

"If the miserable fish has to be watched, I'll watch it, much as I hate it, rather than see the poor kids kept up all night for your idiot whims!"

"Go away," called Sam, "now you've wakened me, and I'll watch it."

Henny went upstairs grumbling and whimpering to herself, but when she saw him come out dressed, she went back to bed. She began to play cards, determined to take the next two-hour watch after Sam, instead of Saul, who had to be waked then according to the roster.

Darkness poured from the sky with the hissing as of falling ashes, trickles of fire, and sudden explosion. Henny got out her cards and started to play her famous double patience (with two packs of cards). The first layout was all hearts and diamonds, yet impossible to make a move, the second all clubs and spades and again impossible to make a move; the third time, the layout, mixed, looked unpromising, but the game started to come out with the greatest rapidity, and yet by accident not by bad shuffling, and Henny, used to cheating herself, this time was tempted to cheat the other way, blocking the solution. In five minutes the game was out! Henny forgot the storm and the fish in the copper and looked helplessly at the eight stacks of cards before her, each with a king on top. The game that she had played all her life was finished; she had no more to do: she had no game. She was angry and, picking up the cards again, shuffled them carefully and started to lay them out in the same old pattern, but she had only laid down nine cards when she was seized with such a violent nausea, such a feeling of the emptiness and aimlessness of the game—thinking that she might have to go through another fifteen or twenty years before it came out again!—that she gathered them quickly and threw them into her drawer loosely. She got up and looked out at the window and the surging, swelling, yellowed creek.

When Ernie, who was wakened by the storm, got up to see the change of watch, his mother said, "Tell your father to let Saul sleep: I will go and sort the clothes and do my knitting out there," and the message was delivered.

Sam, who merely regarded this as a feeble, shamefaced concession on Henny's part, an admission that she was interested in the marlin boiling and his planned economy, said mischievously, "All right, tell your mother that she can watch the fish from two to four A.M. if she wants to—but only if she wants to—and Saul can come at four."

Ernie said, "No, Tadpole, don't let her: you know Mother doesn't like the smell of fish."

Sam laughed, "There are more things in heaven and earth, Horatio, than are dreamed of in your philosophy. Never mind, son: what the eye doesn't see the mouth gapes at; the quickness of the intellect deceives the crooked; watch my patter, and I'll hear you picking my pocket: Mothering, my dear boy, has a sneaking interest in our little proceedings, and this is her queer, obstinate, mulish, womanish way of showing it—she pretends to sacrifice herself, when she really wants to be one of us!—don't you see that, Ermy? You must get to know women, Ermy! Women is trouble; women is cussed; you have got to learn to run women, boy, yes, sir. If Mother offers to watch the marlin, let her watch, says I."

Ernie, laughing uncertainly backed down. Louie, waked by the commotion and the storm, came walking through the house and out to the washhouse too, and was most indignant when she heard that Henny was to watch, but Sam only laughed joyously, poked her in the ribs, and told her not to interfere, "Poor Old Mother Interference, someone ruined her appearance!"

Through the wet air, in the intervals of the storm, pockets of marlin fumes blew around them. Louie went storming upstairs, "Mother, I'm awake, I'll watch the boiling."

"You go to bed: you'll look like the usual boiled owl in the morning!"

"I'll watch!"

"I'll watch! I can't stand argument, go to bed. I hope I catch my death of cold!"

Louie, looking from their window, saw Sam and Ernie walking down to the bluff to look in the risen creek and plodding round the sodden grounds, squelching, laughing, dashing wet sprays in each other's face.

"Race you to the washus," cried Sam.

"All right," said Ernie.

Neither was a good runner, and the boy soon got a stitch in his side, so that Sam got there first.

"Beatcha," said Sam cheerfully, throwing down the stick he was carrying and darting into the washhouse to lift the lid and look into his stew. "My cooking," said Sam, "my cooking—worth something! What Sam-the-Bold cooks up ain't a angry stew like womenfolks. Sam-the-Bold cooks what air useful to man en horse en motorbike: the essential oil!"

Henny, with sunk angry eyes, got up and brushed past him suddenly. She said to the boy, "Ernie-dear, since your clever father is here, perhaps the stupid people can go and get something to eat: come, and I'll give you some milk and put you to bed."

Sam gave a comical jeering snarl, "Ermy-boy, you c'mere! Boy, you're on sentry-go: you're up, you may as well stick along o' Sam. Go tell your mother to make some corf for all hands."

"I'm so sleepy, Pad," said the boy.

"You do what the Old Man says," Sam smiled.

Henny said outside, to the white night, "I wish he'd stop playing his silly monkey tricks with the children and let them grow up," and she went into the house to make the fresh coffee. When it was made, she put it steaming on the table with fruit and sandwiches and, going to the door of the porch, called, "Ernie, tell your father his coffee's on the table."

"Is it on the table, is it on the table?" Sam shouted. "Can't come unless it's on the table."

"Oh, shut up," Henny said to herself. The boy looked at his father.

"Get me corf," said Sam; "then you get a drop of suthin good what slides down quick, and you go to bed. Meanwhile, you unravel them grapevines you got in the line, Ermy: you'll never make a proper fisherman with the instincts of a fisherman if you let grape-vines stay in."

The boy took up the wet mess of tangled line and began to pick it over. As Sam continued to give him advice, Ernie sulkily moved across the yard to the kitchen to do his picking.

Sam felt lonely suddenly in the washhouse, with only the bubbling of the fish stew to keep him company. It was a glorious, rich smell certainly, and Sam counted on getting a gallon of oil at the least, probably nearer two gallons, but what was the purpose of it all? Wasn't his life empty, always amusing the kids, thinking up projects for them, teaching them to be good men and women when they ran off upon their own bents and a woman was always twisting them, snatching them away from him? I mustn't think that, thought Sam, shaking himself and beginning to hammer out bent nails that he had saved from old packing cases: waste not, want not, same applies to energy. Mustn't waste emotion, want it for a great job in the future, maybe: I may be called to a great position later on—never can tell, preparedness is everything; you work for years and the opportunity comes—meanwhile, here I work with my little community, leading it, creating a feeling in Eastport, a civic feeling, speaking to the Parents' Association about peace and progress, and soon I'll be helping to watch our waters and foreshores and increasing their fertility. Man is the symbol of fertility, and increase is his job. Yes, mustn't despair: everything comes to him who waits—waits with preparedness. Overcome all enemies, including spiritual enemies, weariness, disappointment. I carry the torch, I will pass it to one, two, three, of my spawn; in the meantime, I must watch, wait, pray—not pray, no, but learn to lead my fellow man, for the spirit was given to me. Where is Looloo? These are thoughts which she should understand. Poor, lost, worrying Looloo! I bet she's awake now; because my spirit is awake and between her and me is immediate communication, mental radio....

Sam walked round the house. As he reached the front lawn, Henny's light went out. The effluvia of the fish, all that could be conveyed by air, were seeping again round the house, for the storm was passing away at last, and all that remained of it was the flickering of the sky, fringes of rainy cloud, and the pools of water underfoot. The water in the creek was lapping high too. It seemed to Sam that nature was licking at his feet like a slave, like a woman, that he had read of somewhere, that washed the feet of the man she loved and dried them with her hair.

The light went on in Louie's room. "Just as I thought," said Sam to himself, "I knew it." He saw Louie come to the veranda and look out, look down on him, and then go back. He thought, "It's early, nearly light, and she's awake: we'll go for a little walk since she's awake." He went back into the house and crept up the stairs, thinking about Jenny Maxim, the little girl in Baltimore, that he met at Mrs. Pilgrim's house and who was so in love with Nature. Henny's door was shut. Louie was muttering in her room, but the door stood open. The light was on, and through the crack of the door Sam perceived Louie lying on her bed with her hands crossed behind her head (she was twisting her hair round and round on her fingers), and he heard her say, "'Bear me out in this, thou great democratic God! who didst not refuse to the swart convict Bunyan the pale poetic pearl: Thou who didst clothe with doubly hammered leaves of finest gold, the stumped and paupered arm of old Cervantes....'" (Melville: *Moby Dick*.) Sam, who was ignorant of all literature and thought Louie had invented this herself (but said to himself that it was no more than might be expected of a child of Samuel Clemens Pollit), leaned against the crack, peering still and smiling to himself.

After a silence, during which he breathed quietly, he heard her begin to mutter again, "'Enmity calls for death and I am longing for life'" (Nijinsky's letter to Diaghilev), but at this Sam merely smiled again, thinking with joy, yes, she loves love and hates hate even as I do. Nothing could be better for a lead-in to his heart-to-heart talk with her that he planned in this dawn (it could be her watch with the fish, for example, and they could let Little-Sam sleep).

"There is love in the city, lust in the country," said Louie to herself; "the storm suffocates the land, the creek ravishes the beach, the hilltop violates the sky—"

At this, Sam came into the room and said sternly, "I hear a lot of darn nonsense, but I don't hear much sense: what sort of an author are you quoting, Looloo-girl?"

Louie frowned menacingly, "Nobody: I made it up."

"A nice sort of thing to make up," said Sam. "You are too much alone: I hear so much stupidity, I can't understand it. Get up and get dressed, I want to talk to you."

"It isn't morning," said Louie, burning red and angry.

"It is your watch at the marlin boiling, and anyhow, I am up and I see I have to say many things to you."

Louie curled her lip, "You don't know anything."

"Get dressed, you dogged wretch."

"Well, you go out."

Sam withdrew, pulling the door violently after him and shouting through it, "Now hurry, hurry: Samulam want to talk," being pleasant again so that she would be friendly when she came downstairs. The fire was now low, and Sam said, "Let us watch the dawn rise, we will just walk about over to the cove and back, and peek in at the fire all the time," and after they had looked in at the stew on which the oil was now in some spots two inches thick, they began their walk down the heavy-headed avenue, dark with rain. Banks of loose cloud covered the sky, floating higher and away. The east seemed distant, a glum blue, but the waves and trees seemed still of one element.

"Looloo," said Sam solemnly, "I perhaps should have spoken to you as a woman before. We should like relations between men and women to be ideal, but, as you are apparently coming to realize, they are not. Your own bringing-up, whatever its apparent defects, has helped you to realize that we must not blame either side: it is all a question of adjustment and patience. I hope you will be happy, Looloo. The great question is self-control, Looloo, and to fix the mind on the many many problems of science, both solved and unsolved. In the arcanum of the unsolved of nature is much for busy brains to do: I hope you will be of the number of the searchers and finders. What do you want to do, Looloo?" She was silent. "You can tell your father."

"I don't know."

"Now, for women there is a greater freedom. I am hoping that you will choose to remain with me and work with me for the greater freedom of all men; but you must understand in your own life that liberty isn't libertinism, not that that is yet a problem for you, though men and women alike today, as they go out in the world, face temptations. Now, you must know without my telling you, Looloo-girl, that temptation in sex, which comes to some early and some late and to some happy ones not at all, can betray us into being not ourselves. I heard you mention something which, I might say, had a venereal implication—symbols, examples, words, which—of the meaning of which you are doubtless not quite cognizant as yet—whatever you feel like, Looloo, and I leave that all to you. Remember that self-control is our only safeguard and that the abuses of the instinct lead to—either waste of energy and emotion and the finer feelings, or indiscriminate recourse to members of the other sex, upon which follows venereal disease, a thing too dreadful to contemplate or to talk about and which I would not have to speak about if you had a decent mother—but you have not: this duty is left in the hands of a father. I feel as embarrassed about it as you. Promise me, Looloo (this is a strange thing to be talking about in such a wild, pure dawn, between night and day, between sea and sky), that if you are thinking of a man or boy, you will not think seriously of him without marriage; or if you must, if you must ever go with man or boy, Looloo—I leave it to you, it seems inadvisable to me, understanding these things so much better than you—that you will first demand a medical certificate from him."

Louie laughed, "I will never do that."

"Never promise?"

"Never do it. It's so silly."

"You know not whereof you speak," said Sam huskily.

"I love, I love, I only know about love," cried Louie madly, bursting into tears. "What has that to do with it? You keep out of it."

"Hush, Looloo: I was speaking to Ernie too tonight, and I told him when he begins to think about girls he must tell me."

Louie said bitterly, "There is one thing I am quite sure of: he never will. Not one of the children will ever confide in you."

He looked at her, shocked, "Looloo! But I confide in you! I tell you all I can, suited to your understanding of life and human nature! My dear girl, naturally, you look upon me as a father, someone above ordinary temptations, but that is not so: I have been tempted.

The worst thing about temptation is," he smiled coaxingly at her, "Looloo, is that you want to yield to it. You even like it!" He smiled to himself and looked at the ground. "There is a wonderful young woman, Looloo, who seems to me to be—is—my perfect mate: it would be for me one of those marriages made in heaven. I cannot think of it because of your mother. Naturally. But she too feels this way about me, and she would sacrifice everything for me, if it were possible. I said to her, 'I know you, my girl, I know you would give up everything for me: all I would ask out of life now—for my pride has fallen—is to have you be my constant companion, to be by my side, in my utmost need to go by my side. I know' (I told her only yesterday, Looloo) 'that life means little to you either, without me. I know you are prepared to live in a little flat waiting for me when I can come, that you will live in the back street of life, without children, but the two of us facing the future wide-eyed and full of its promise, that is even better than children, perhaps—and besides I have children'—and she said, 'Yes,' Looloo," his voice broke: "she said, 'Yes,' she would do so.

"But I cannot ask her to do it! It is dishonorable in the eyes of the world. And the little old world is not always wrong. Good name is something too. Without good name, Looloo, what good could I do? Most people are simple good folk: they believe in the plain, honest ways of living, the old-fashioned ways that my mother believed in. No, we cannot contravene the ways of the honest, humble poor, the ways of innocence and the integrity of family life. The home, the hearth, the family and fatherhood, the only ideals the old Romans ever had that were any good, little as they lived up to them."

Louie burst out crying.

Sam said tenderly, "Always blubbering, Looloo, what a big mass of blubber yet!"

"You must let me leave you," said Louie, "you must give me some freedom."

He became stern, "Looloo, you will never leave me, you must never leave me: you and I must cleave together through the storms to come. The house is cold and full of bitter hate. I told my darling girl that, too. I want you, Looloo, as a bulwark between me and her hate, a bulwark of living love. I cannot live in such an atmosphere of hate. It is not for me. And I know it is hard on you, too, Looloo—now don't tell me that again; but if you could know what you meant to me when I first saw you come from your mother's womb. Women have meant so much in my life, believing in me (as they believe in men, for they are born to do that, Looloo, and that's why I don't want you cynical), listening to me, loving me too, I verily believe, though I was always too modest and bashful perhaps, to rightly see love when it came, and always helping me and wanting to love Nature, as I loved it. Women are the blessing of men. Oh, Looloo, if I could have had the right wife, what a great man I would have been! Certainly a good one, better than I am now. And our children, happy in the love of father and mother, playing round my feet, growing from innocent, lusty, laughing babyhood to strong forthright boyhood and to wide-eyed, idealistic youth, and to vigorous loving manhood! But I am satisfied with what I have: do not think I am criticizing your brothers and dear Little-Womey. They may not be all exactly as I would have wished, but they are dear to me: they will go the right path and follow the light; they will come through, Looloo. I want you to know I am optimistic for you all."

He waited for a response, then added, "What have you to say to me about your own little affairs, Looloo?"

"I want to leave home."

"After all I have said to you?"

"I must leave home. You must give me some money to go to Harpers Ferry."

"I must, I must! I won't! You're still in tutelage, thank God, and

I hope still to make you more amenable! I won't have this cussed obstinacy. I'll break that miserable dogged spirit of yours: it will get you nowhere. What man will look at you with your piggish, sulky, thick face always gloomy? Do you think any man is going after a face like that? Thank God, now women can get jobs anyhow, if they have sufficient education; when I was a boy some looks were necessary: you had to charm men. You can get your living, but I want to see you happy. You have got to cheer up; you have got to smile. Don't you notice when we walk down the street together that the women and men too look after me with a smile; and that they look at you surprised at your glum, stupid, sullen air?"

"I notice," said Louie. "You must let me go. I will have to go, anyhow."

"What can a girl do by herself?"

"Clare and I are going on a walking trip this summer by ourselves."

"With boys, I suppose."

"Oh, no!—we are going to walk."

"What fools, what stupid puppies!" He flung himself off to the distance of two yards in advance. "Stupid little spoiled conceited puppies. What can two girls do on the road? Don't you know that you are helpless? What will you do at night? Where will you sleep? In the fields?"

"At Auntie Jo's and at Harpers Ferry and at Hazel's in Charlestown, West Virginia," said Louie. "We thought it all out, and Clare has friends too, and there are the Pryors, Mother's relatives in Frederick. It is not stupid at all."

"Where will you get the money? To live, to eat?"

"Why—" she faltered, "I suppose, they will give us something to eat."

He said savagely, "If you want to know, your aunt at Harpers Ferry has just refused to take you for the summer; she cannot afford it any more—no sooner does the Collyer money fade than all my resources go: the servility of men is humiliating. That's something you don't happen to know about. You are going to stay here, and be a good daughter to me, and look after your brothers and sister; and I am going to send Henny away, if you are so obstinate as to force me to tell you. Your stepmother has deceived me often—" he ceased speaking and held his hands before his face, squeezing them together, "with another, with another man. I never thought such a thing would come into my family life. I have been the best of husbands, never deceived her, whatever the temptations, and they are many. And now I know what has been going on for years. Why, in the very first years—my own very best friend—a man called Mark Colefax, hard as it is for me to pronounce his name— after him I never thought I could believe in friendship again—your stepmother went out with him: I trust, she said it was no more. But all men lie in those situations through a mistaken idea of gallantry, and I never found out the truth. Now, however, thanks, I regret to say, to a horrible anonymous letter, filthy but true, I know that your mother was going out with a man when I was away in the Pacific, and I hardly know—Looloo, Looloo!—" he began to sob, and Looloo stood still, frightened, "Looloo!—I hardly know whether Chappy, my little big-eyed Megalops, is mine or not. A human life—and perhaps it were better he had never been born. Outside the pale, perhaps; perhaps it will come to light. What will I do then?"

"What will Mother do?"

"She has made her bed: let her lie on it. I cannot worry about a woman who never worried for a moment about my name. Yet," he said, with regret, "I have to, Looloo: we have had children together—that is the infernal tie, the bond of carnality. I don't know what to do."

After a silence, during which they turned towards the fateful Spa House, he said, in a low voice, "You see, you see, Looloo? You see why you must stay by me forever? I have had too many burdens."

She was silent until they reached the house. The dawn broke clear, with light yellow wisps of cloud scattered over a wide, wind-swept sky. Sam took her silence as submission and, brushing away his sorrows, went cheerfully back to poke the fire under the copper.

3 *The offal heap.*

At breakfast time, the children, tired and excited, beat time on tin plates and chanted, while porridge was being brought in, "Am marlin, is marlin, was marlin, be marlin, marlin along of me!"

Sam shouted, "Who for the washus, kids! Who wants to take up the stand?"

"No one," said Little-Sam: "we wanna rest, Big Chief."

Sam told them that "arter brekker" (after breakfast) he was going to photograph the marlin's head, and then put it on to boil in the yard, for "serpently bad weather was a-blowin' up." He told them that during the night he had had a good idea—he would take down the chimneys before the gale came, because he reckoned that gale was going to be a humdinger. He was afraid of falling from roofs, with his vertigo (which fear the twins and Ernie shared), and yet he loved the altitude and great sweep of landscape. He told them that as soon as he got into the Conservation Department he was going to agitate for a plane for his own use in observation, and that they would soon see their own beloved Dad circling over Spa House, and that they must arrange bags of coffee (in a thermos) and bananas and choc, so that he could come over with a big hook and pick them up while he was on his job. He could also get letters that way and telephone messages, and Mothering could send up her fifty-foot bills.

Sam had now rigged up the developing room in one corner of the boys' bedroom and after breakfast, while the girls fixed up the house, with many yawns and flagging, stumbling steps, the boys rushed between the washhouse, the photographic room, and the caldron in the yard, which had just been put on a tripod, over a bricked-in fire, all put up for the occasion. Presently they had a picture of the twins holding the marlin's head and Tommy holding his nose, in a group, Sam all the time expatiating on light and sun's angle, lenses and how he could get a better photograph with an old kodak than most people could with a Zeiss-Tessar, papers, chemicals. "Scenes that are brightest, te-te-te-te-TE!" sang Sam; "All chime in! Ain't home nice? Te-te-te-te-te! Da-da-da-da! Fathead, you're tipping the bottle of KCN," he continued to Little-Sam, "Da-da-da. KCN kills customers neatly, kindly, cunningly noxious; kids, cyanide nullifies! One bit of that, my lads, in a glass of water and you ain't, maybe twa draps for Little-Sam because he's mean. What is KCN, my boyos?"

They told him.

"Ah-ha," said Sam, going on with his work, "it looks like salt or sugar to you, but you know what it am? It am death, complete— total annihilation: yes, rabbits take a whiff of that, and they don't even wait for the Angel of Death. Light doesn't go as fast as KCN. In that little bottle, see, is death for one and death for all, you take that, kids, for your alevena, and—

Looloo doesn't want to leave home,
Ermy doesn't collect lead,
Evie doesn't pipe her eye,
Gemini don't insult their poor little dad,
Tommy doesn't run after Fairy,
Megalops doesn't eat crap!

You all just get awful tired and you lie down and you don't get up no mo'; so be careful, oh, be keerful, for the results of that are fearful! See, kids, quick, quick! It's coming and it's not so bad, but it ain't good either, bad light today. And now, who's for the washus watch?"

Little-Sam hastened to claim the washhouse watch; then it was Ernie and Saul for the taking down of the chimney, Tommy to watch the marlin head, Evie to cover up the furniture in the house with cloths to keep off the dust, Louie to get alevena, and Mother to get the lunch.

Sam, on the roof, began to sing. The cries came, "Under below!" and the bricks came flying down into the grass. The sun began to heat the roof, and Sam called out that his head was swimming, but he was staying up just the same: "where there's a will there's a way." In the house, dust crept down the chimney, or shot down in handfuls, with soot and bits of brick. Henny grumbled; the "three women," in fact, were crabby and saw no beauty or generosity in Sam's liveliness. Sam had taken the bricks out of the south chimney as far as he could reach and now went cautiously over the roof to the north. The sky was getting cottony again. Suddenly Louie shouted, "Alevena," and Sam and Saul came off the roof, sliding hastily down the ladder, hungry, red-faced, inclined to squabble. They crowded into the common room and sat round the table like a crowd of parrots. Sam sent for the raccoon, Procyon, and Procyon paraded up and down the table, nosing at them, shaking hands with them, sniffing at things. While Louie was pouring out the tea in the kitchen, Sam started hallooing for bananas, his favorite "alevena food." On the table were the bread and margarine but no bananas. Sam beat on his plate with his knife, shouting,

"Mothering, Mothering, bananas, bananas! Go and tell Mothering bananas," he told Evie, who slid off her seat. Tommy, apple-cheeked, gay and square-set, rushed to the kitchen and shouted, "Mothering, bananas!"

They all shouted this. Henny muttered. Louie, with cups of tea, stalked in, saying severely, "There are no bananas. Don't make such a noise."

"Mothering, bananas," cried Sam.

"Tell the children's father, there are none," Henny said bitterly. "Have we a banana tree? Have we a money tree?"

"Our father, we have none. Have we a bamoney tree?" inquired Tommy, meanwhile imitating an express train.

"Dad, Mother says there aren't any," Evie said.

Sam flushed with anger. "Why aren't there any bananas? I don't ask for much. I work to make the Home Beautiful for one and all, and I don't even get bananas. Everyone knows I like bananas. If your mother won't get them, why don't some of you? Why doesn't anyone think of poor little Dad?" He continued, looking in a most pathetic way round the table, at the abashed children, "It isn't much. I give you kids a house and a wonderful playground of nature and fish and marlin and everything, and I can't even get a little banana. And bananas are very healthy. Who here likes bananas?"

"We all do, Pad," said Saul cheerfully.

"Then we should all think of them. Now, I'll detail someone each week who must get the bananas."

"With what?" said a voice from the kitchen. "Bananas don't grow in the sea. Tell your father I had no money for them."

"It's all I ask for," Sam lowered his voice and with a plaintive voice continued his banana song. "All I esks for is a pore wittoo [little] bandana: I works a-takin' deown de chimbleys so that the heouse won't be knocked to smithereens in the next gale en yore little mushheads with it, en so that Mothering kin sleep peaceful like— though why she should with what she's been a-doin' to your poor dad, I don't know—en all I esks is a pore wittoo bandana sangwidge en I don't get whut I esks. You cain't blame me for a-grumblin', I ain't a grumblin' man; I'm a goldurn cheerful man considerin' whut I hev to put up with—"

"Oh, dry up," said Henny's voice.

"Shh," said Louie.

"Don't shush me," complained Sam, "I got a right to utter a few improving words in my own home, I hope." He went on droning dolefully, "All I wants is a pore little bandana en I don't get nuffin I esk fower: who's a-goin' deown to the cornder to get their pore wittoo dad a coupla bandanas."

The twins said they would go.

"Orright," Sam whined. "The Gemini kin go en get their pore little dad the bandanas wot ought to hev bin here afore, en the heouse weren't full to bustin' of lazy womenfolk which some of them is traipsin' eout and spendin' money in bargin basements not to say wuss and which some of them is got their heads full of boys and which some of them don't come to their pore little dad's bedroom no mo' in da fornin," he said, fixing a watery eye on Evie, who squirmed and dropped her eyes. "Womenfolk ain't no good, en yore pore little Dad wot was brought up to worship women as sweet pure beings. He's hed to learn a lot these last few days."

"I could wring his neck with pleasure," said Henny in the kitchen, to Louie.

"En I mout fall off de roof," said Sam to the children, "en whut would you do, Ermy? Whut would you do ef your father broke his neck?"

"Nothing," Ernie said coolly.

"Nuffin!" Sam shook his head, looked round the table tragically. "Ermy wouldn't do nuffin?"

"What could I do?" inquired Ernie. "You would be dead."

"Too logical," said Sam, laughing into his hand, meanwhile, "Well, here are the bananas. Hooray! Now get busy. Now, why did we have to wait? You see, no foresight, no order, no preparation! Everyone thinking of their own mean business. A woman who eats away the foundations of the house like a mean little termite, it's soft, it's little, it doesn't seem to count, but it's got uncles, aunts, cousins, children that it teaches to eat away at the house, and soon, down comes the house. Now, did you notice, kids, that the termites have got into the piano? Now, I want you to take a lesson from that. Dad is carpentering away, while the white ant eats at the house: but we will carpenter faster than Mothering eats away. Some day I will tell you kids what is the termite that's trying to eat away your father's loving heart and his peace of mind, but not now, but she—it's your own mother, kids—but she can hear me, and she knows what I'm talking about. Now, kids, some day you'll know what I'm doing for you. And whut I mean is, that this yere bandana business is only another example of whut I mean."

Suddenly Henny appeared between the drapes and said loudly, "You and the children ate all the bananas last night, and I've had too much to do cleaning up after your filth to think of bananas. Another thing is, I want some money. And I'm damned if I'll put up with your insults day and night. I'll take poison. Do you think I'm going to hang round here and let the children hear their mother insulted?"

Sam did not even look at her, but said, looking down at the table,

"'The one thet fust gits mad's most oilers wrong,' es Mr. Lowell up and said. De fack is, kids, there warn't no bandanas: a hegskuze is a hegskuze; a bandana is a bandana; I cain't eat no hegskuzes en I got a nawful big hole in my stumjack."

The children laughed; Henny muttered. Louie came in, red as a turkey cock, "You should be ashamed, Dad!"

"When she walks she wobbles," said Sam.

"I despise you," said Louie.

"Now, Louie, now Looloo! Looloo always sich a hothead: Louie a pighead cause she got a bighead! I always had a lot of trouble with my head, kiddos—nedakes [headaches] en sich, becaze I got a bighead. Now Sausam, they have big heads and they was meant to do a lot wiv em; en Louie would do a lot wiv her big head if she wasn't sich a lame duck en sich a goose en sich a turkey cock, now—With a gobble-gobble here and a gobble-gobble there!" (The children repeated this.) Sam continued, "With a hwonk-hwonk here and hwonk-hwonk there, and where are you going my pretty maid? For to mind my father's barnyard! For to mind my father's barnyard. En if Looloo weren't sich a wet hen, she'd do all right."

"I'm the ugly duckling, you'll see," shrieked Louie.

"You're ugly all right and when you walk you wobble, and you're all wet, I swan, en you've got a long neck and a big beak so maybe you're a swan—" Little-Sam said. "And she has a sweet voice like a swan," and Evie said, "And Louie does a dance, *The Dying Swan*."

They shrieked with laughter. Louie burst out into loud, raucous sobs and rushed from the house, while Sam said, in some surprise, "The great big galoot: why, girls are no better than boys at that age," and he laughed heartily.

Tommy ran after Louie to see where she had gone and found her crouching by the copper fire and poking it into a bright flame.

"What are you crying for, Louie?" he said patting her on the arm. "Don't cry, Louie, don't cry! He's only fooling."

"'What is fun to you is death to me,'" said Louie. "That is what the frog said to the boys, you know?"

"Yes, I know that story."

"Well, go and tell him that."

Tommy ran back to the common room where alevena was in progress and, grinning somewhat, planted himself on his two legs while he recited, "Pad, I have a message for you from Looloo. 'What is fun to you is death to me.'"

"Did she tell you to tell me that?"

"Yes."

Sam shook his head, "Looloo always was very tragic."

"Ooh," shouted Little-Sam, "ooh, Pad! Ooh, whew! It's getting me, Pad."

"Whappills?" inquired Sam, in delight.

"Ow, wow," said Saul instantly, holding his belly, and writhing,

"It's got me, chilluns. Farewell, my bluebell, farewell to you. I'm dying, Pad."

"Whippills?" inquired Sam again, enchanted.

"It's nawful," cried Ernie and let out a shout of joy.

"The marlin," explained Evie, with disgust. "They're fooling. They're doing it all the morning. Mother is angry with them."

"Go on," said Sam, "go on? What is it?"

"Oh, it's a-follerin' of me," cried Little-Sam, looking behind, craning his neck over both shoulders. He slid off the homemade wooden bench, "I can smell it here—look, there it is, oh, look out the window, oh, the crick is yaller, oh, the oil."

"Tell Mother I died bravely," said Sam, pleased with their skit.

"Why don't you take it off now, Deddy?" asked Tommy.

Sam began to chant, "We're a-goin' to rav marlin erl, marlin erl, marlin erl; we're gona rav marlin balm, marlin salve, marlin butter, marlin oingming; we're gona eat marlin, be marlin, think marlin, sleep marlin; it's marlin for our bikes and marlin for kikes. Say, let's go, while we're having a bit of a rest and put the oil into bottles."

"No sooner said than done," said Saul.

The stuff had been boiling for over twelve hours, and Sam now told them to rake the fire out. The cleaning-up was a great satisfaction to him. The entire crew of children (except Louie) was around him, grunting as they carted the gluey soup out in all the large household utensils, buckets, basins, watering cans, and pots. The liquid they dumped on the children's gardens, along the fences, near the dead end near Lomasne's shed and in front along the lawn, round the Wishing Tree. The tatters of fish, mostly jellied skin and bones, they were to take and put in a heap at the bottom of the orchard. Over these remains they sprinkled loam to keep off the flies. Sam said that at "one fell swoop" they had two sorts of manures—fish offal and ashes, and if this was not a wonderful example of planned economy, they had only to tell him what might be. Meanwhile, in the washhouse now stood nine large and five small bottles of unrefined marlin oil, which would be refined at an early date, said Sam. Sam at first had meant to boil the marlin down to glue, but too many exclamations by Henny had let him know that she expected the copper to be ready for the weekly wash bright before tomorrow morning, and Sam's work gang was pretty tired already. He knew he would have to clean up before nightfall. Little-Sam, who hadn't much stomach, was just staggering out with a bucketful of marlin remains, when he dropped it at his feet and looked frightened.

"Little feels sick," declared Saul.

"What, with marlin? Not with marlin!" said Sam, laughing, and ordered the boy to take it to the offal heap, which, after a moment, he did.

"Triumph of mind over matter," said Sam, nodding to the others, and when Little-Sam came back, to illustrate this, ordered Little-Sam to take out another shovelful. Little-Sam sulkily did so, but in a minute dropped it and looked mutinously up at his father.

"Take dat offal marlin to dat offal heap, Little-Sam," said Sam gently.

The boy bent down, then gave his father an appalled look, turned from the family, and disgraced himself.

"Little-Sam frowin' up da marlin," said Sam.

Suddenly Henny was before them, black and angry as a witch, her loose hair flying out, "You ought to be ashamed, a man your size tormenting the children," she cried. "If I were to tell the neighbors what you do, you wouldn't be so high and mighty."

Sam ignored her but addressed himself to Tommy, her favorite,

"Tommy, my boy, one of my great handicaps in life was my weak stomach; now, many a great man has had a weak stomach:

Julius Caesar had one, though I don't want any of you to go round with an army. Now, you kids have got to have strong stomachs. Little-Sam here is the dead spit of his old man, and he got to have a strong stomach: he got to stomach anything. I made myself stronger, when a lad, because I recognized my weakness, by boiling the flesh off carcasses for their skeletons and articulating the skeletons—also taught myself anatomy. And I had no father interested in me. Now, Little-Sam, and you have. Now, Little-Sam," he continued very gravely, "you get some more," and he picked up the shovel and handed it to Little-Sam.

"Are you insane?" cried Henny.

"Get out of my way," Sam growled. "You get to the kitchen and mind your business—don't you put your spoke in here, or I'll get rid of you, mind that; I'll have no more interfering with my children and putting them against me; now, get out of here."

Little-Sam, expecting his mother to intervene, sullenly stooped and picked up another shovelful of the mess. He took two steps away, bent over it, but when he passed Sam suddenly threw it down and put both hands on his belly.

"Sam," cried his father, "stop that belching. No hysteria, come along! Look," he said, turning angrily to his wife, "this is your doing! He would have been on his way in perfect calm but for you: don't I know there's no kindness in this, but sabotage? Do you think I don't see through your miserable tricks? You pretend to defend them in order to make me seem harsh and cruel. I'll have no more of it. Get back to the kitchen, you miserable wretch. Little-Sam, you come back here before I whale you: look sharp."

"Ai, ai," cried Henny, beginning to cry like a little girl, and putting the fold of her dressing gown to her face, "ai, ai!"

"Daddy," said Evie. "Little is sick, what do you do it for?"

"You stop imitating your mother and looking at me with that sneaking Collyer grimace, ready to burst into tears," said Sam. Evie turned pale but dared not cry.

"Little-Sam is sick," said Saul severely to his father. Sam gave him an admonitory kick in the shins, shaking his head meaningly.

"No," Little-Sam bellowed surprisingly, "no, it makes me sick."

"There," said Sam, throwing out his hands and getting up, "there, she's done it—and you've done it, Pollux [to Saul], stirring up rebellion! There's one thing you don't understand about Little-Sam: I understand him because he is myself. Now, I suffered in life from a certain diffidence, which in Little-Sam is sullenness and morbidity: I'll conquer it. Castor [Little-Sam], you come here!"

The eight-year-old boy suspiciously and slowly drew near, eying his father with all the hate of his wide blue eyes.

"I'll finish this," Sam said.

He picked up the dipper that Henny used for the washing, sunk it in the bottom of the copper, and drew it out half full. He took Little-Sam by the neck, drew him out of the wash-house, and, when he stood on the newly cemented yard outside the door, suddenly flung the liquid over him, drenching him. Little-Sam and the children were petrified with surprise. Sam did not even laugh but considered his son triumphantly. Not a tremor passed over the boy's face. He stood dripping with the juice, fish tatters on his head, one long shred of skin hanging down over one eye, making him look like the offspring of a mermaid and a beachcomber. He looked funny. Suddenly, Ernie began to grin, his face widened, and he began to laugh; the laugh spread, and the children stood round the queer little Neptune laughing, Sam joining in, and only Saul, the twin, standing by as quiet as Little-Sam himself. Henny, standing with evil face inside the glassed-in porch, gabbled furiously to Louie, and in a minute, it was Louie dashing forth, crying to her father not to be "so horrible, so disgusting," that broke up the circle. It was cooler than the season that day, and Little-Sam had begun to pick the wet shirt off his arms, saying, "Ooh, it's nasty!"

"Good," said Sam, "good! Now Little-Sam, you take another shovelful down to the manure heap, and you can go and get washed. Kids, read, mark, learn, and inwardly digest! Little-Sam could and did get over his abhorrence, you see! And if I didn't have a lot of interfering, miserable beasts," he gave a kind of malicious smile at the two little girls, "I'd have you all right in no time. I'm sorry," he continued to Evie, "I'm sorry I didn't take a dipperful of that and sling it at your Motherings: it would have taught her a thing or two; it would have given her something to think about, instead of always filling that empty, worthless head with the wrongs done to her. I'm the one that's suffered, I'm the one that's had things to think about, but do you see me go about sniveling and calling names? Women is the devil! The tyranny of tears, Little-Womey, and don't you never make no man suffer that." He began to laugh, as he saw Little-Sam trotting off with the fish offal to the manure heap. "Yes, Ermy," he said confidentially, putting his arm round his eldest son's neck and drawing him closer, "you know I should have done the same to Looloo too: I'll bet she would have kicked up a riot, oh, boy! Why didn't I think of that? Will I do it, eh, will I do it?"

"Not now, it's all over," Ernie said.

Sam laughed, "All right: whatever you say."

Now the twins came back and Saul said, "Pad, can Little go and have a shower now?"

Louie came to the back door and shouted indignantly, "Now Mother fainted! It's your fault."

"Good heavens, you mean wretch!" said Sam. "You'd think she enjoyed it! Can't Little-Sam use his own tongue to ask his little father for a shower?"

Little-Sam said nothing.

"Eh?" inquired Sam, "did he cough up his tongue, too?"

"He's got fish in his mouth," said Saul.

At this the children burst out laughing excitedly again, and Sam had the sense to send Little-Sam away, for he saw that he was working up to a roar of misery. The old shower room opened on to the new cement yard. They could see the two butter-yellow boys standing under the shower, both scrubbing away at Little-Sam's body and hair. Meanwhile Sam sat down to wait for lunch.

"Too much trubsy, love," he said to Little-Womey, "do myed, love." While she stroked his head, he watched the twins with pleasure and directed their operations.

"Drop your clobber [clothes] in the cornder, it's washday tomorrow: rub yourself down. Twins is queer cattle," he continued in a low tone to Evie, "there's no hegsplaining twins. (Little-Sam, don't make yourself too clean, you can get inside the copper and clean it after lunch: it's very convenient.) Twins are not two children, but one, you see, love: one egg that has split and become two of the same. Twins have always known each other from the same moment, from the day they were jellies: yiss, love, Castor and Pollux were jellies and sardincs and lizards and funny monsters all the time together; they had to fight for their life at the same time and came into the world at the same time, only twenty minutes' difference."

Ernie came up inquisitively, "And if one twin has a pain in his leg, the other feels it too: a boy at school got hit in the leg with a ball, and his brother had a pain," he laughed.

"Wery inconwenient," said Sam, "but wery mysterioso. But they mustn't be sissies, just the same, neither one nor the other."

Although they scrubbed the copper out with soft sand and kitchen powder, they could not get out the fish smell. It was in all the cracks of the old cement floor, in the hairy timbers of the walls and shelves, in the chimney, the washtubs, the mangle, wringer, clothes boxes, and the dirty clothes. The fourteen bottles were greasy with it; and Sam, at last giving up the job of cleaning, decided to try a few experiments with the oil first drawn off, from which a sediment was now drifting down. He oiled the bike with it, wiping off the excess on various bits of rag, oiled his old brown tramping shoes, cracked and stiff with spring mud, rubbed down a few bits of old iron going rusty, massaged Tommy's legs to see if it would keep off the blains he usually got in spring, and sent in a bottle of the best to Henny to tell her to try cooking with it. After this, he suddenly felt very tired and said he must have a snooze before he went up on the roof again.

The sun had come out hot again; and the house settled down to a needed siesta, by which time the heavy reek of fish oil rose up, swirled quietly round, and invaded the timbers of the house. One marlin had been enough, with their kneading, manuring, trotting about, plastering, oiling, and dripping, to give Spa House a scent of its own for many years to come. When they were all resting, prior to the four o'clock snack, Henny came downstairs in one of her silk dressing gowns, to look round. At least they had cleaned the copper, and perhaps it was imagination when she thought she smelled it in everything. On the shelf in the washhouse were bottles neatly labeled in Sam's capitals: FISH-FRY, BIKE-OIL, MARLIN-BALM, MACHINE-OIL, HAIR-OIL, LEATHER-GREASE; OIL, OIL, OIL on the rest. When she went back upstairs, she was conscious of the rich rotten smell and the softness of it in her hair; there was a faint mark already on the pillow where she had lain and a greasy finger mark on the library book. She lifted her old slippers and smelled it on their sodden soles; there was a dark mark on the light gray silk hem. Just when she had reached this point in her examination, Evie came panting up the stairs, holding a little medicine bottle in her hand.

"Daddy says, you can use this instead of cold cream: he says please try it, because whale oil is very good for the skin."

Henny took it without a word and stood in the doorway while Evie deprecatingly climbed downstairs again. Then she marched into Louie's room to show the girl how impossible her father was. Louie was stretched out on her unmade bed, dead asleep, with her legs resting high up on the back of the bed, and a book open on her chest.

4 *A headache.*

Henny frowned at the streaky creek through the window and turned back to her room, pulling the door after her. She began going through bundles of papers and old letters that she pulled out from long-closed drawers.

A telephone ringing without answer presently woke the house. Ernie came panting upstairs, excited, "Moth, it's Miss Wilson, Tommy's teacher."

"Tell her I'm out."

"She says to say can she see you for a minute if she comes over?"

"Tell her I'm out."

"O.K."

At the same time she heard Sam shouting outside, "Hey, Tommo! Your teacher is coming to pay us a visit."

"Oh, keep your sticky beak out," muttered Henny miserably. Louie, who had awakened, wanted to know if Miss Wilson was coming: "No, no, no, no," Henny said.

Then there was Sam questioning Ernie in the hall and, "Your mother told you to tell a lie and you told it, despite what I've told you?"

Then some muttering. "More trouble," said Henny to Louie. "Why doesn't he drop down dead? Was he sent by God to worry women?"

Then Ernie coming upstairs and saying, "Mother, Daddy says you are not to make us tell lies," with a very frightened face; and Henny screaming at Sam over the balustrade, and Sam shouting, "Shut up."

Ernie was stuck on the stairs between them but Louie withdrew backwards into her room.

"You wanted to see the old maid so you could pour your woes into her ears," Henny cried; while Sam, pushing Ernie aside, started to come upstairs, saying in a deep voice that she must close her trap.

But Henny went on laughing, "You can't shut me up now. You want the truth, let it be the truth: he only wants the truth, but he wants my mouth shut. Why don't you leave me alone? This is my house. Go and sit on the beach with your clothes. I'm sick and tired of washing the fish out and your dirty papers full of big talk."

"Henny," said Sam sullenly, "you be quiet or leave my house. I have the whiphand now, owing to your own deed; if you do not get out, I will put you out by the force of law."

She screamed hoarsely, "You get out of here, get out, I'll kill you, I'll kill you; you've only been waiting for this like a great foul monster waiting, sneaking, lying in wait to take my children away. If you touch them I'll kill you: if you try to put me out, I'll kill you."

She turned quickly to Louie, who was standing thoughtfully in the doorway, and shouted, panting, "Louie, don't you ever let a man do that; don't you ever do what his women are doing—a woman's children are all she has of her body and breath, don't let him do that, Louie, don't let him do that. He has been waiting for years to snatch them from me; now the dirty wretch has been watching me and thinks he has an excuse. Don't let him."

She picked up a slipper which had stood on the washstand since she had smelled the fish oil on the sole and rushed at him to strike him in the eyes with the heel. He seized her arm and tried to bend it down. "Put that down, you fool, you madwoman," he bellowed. "You'll push me downstairs, Henny—look out!"

"I'll kill you," she panted, "I'll push you downstairs, I don't care if I go too. I'll break your neck."

She suffocated, struggled as he put his large hand over her mouth, bit it.

"Henny, Henny," he cried in desperation himself, "shut up. Don't let our children hear."

She tore the hand away in a violent spasm. "You rotten flesh," she screamed, insane, "you rotten, rotten thing, you dirty sweaty pig-pig, pig."

She vomited insults in which the word "rotten" rose and fell, beating time with it.

"Henny, shut your foul mouth." He let go of her and flung away to the doorway of Louie's room, himself revolted by her and the terrible struggle.

The children who had crept into the hall below stood rooted to the floor, listening to this tempest, trembling. Louie sank down on her bed in a stupor, her heart beating hard. It was not the quarrel, nor even the threats of murder, but the intensity of the passions this time that stifled them all. And why, out of a clear sky? They never asked any reasons for their parents' fights, thinking all adults unreasonable, violent beings, the toys of their own monstrous tempers and egotisms, but this time it seemed different.

Henny was shrieking, "Ernest, Ernest, Louie, your father's struck me; come and save me, Ernest, your father's killing me, he's trying to kill me, help—"

Louie started up and rushed out into the hall, "Leave her alone."

"Henny, Henny, be quiet, or I'll knock you down," shouted the desperate man.

She rushed to her window, which was at the back nearest a neighbor (though that was still a hundred and fifty yards distant), and cried, "I'll call Mrs. Paine: I'll tell everyone in the street, and you won't get away with this, you rotten foul murderer. You think you're so fine with your bragging and science and human understanding—oh, I've heard all about it till I could scream myself insane with the words; and you can run everything, and world problems, when all the time it's other women, you hypocrite, you dirty, bloodless hypocrite, too good, other women, scientific women, young girls, and your own wife—I'll write to all your scientific societies, I'll write to the Conservation Department, I'll tell them what my life has been—

beat me, knock me down, I can't stand it. You threaten but do nothing, nothing to give me a chance, to get out, not till you've got something on me to steal my children: you won't—you won't—I'm going to kill them all, I'll kill them all tonight, I'll pour that stinking oil on fire down your throat and kill my children, you won't get them—there'll be a sight tomorrow for the people to see: try to explain that away, try to explain it to God or in hell, wherever you go—"

"Louie," said Sam sternly, "go and throw cold water over your mother; go and force her to be quiet. If she sees you—" But Louie had only entered the room, in her confused, embarrassed way, when Henny turned to her and began to vociferate abominable insults, and pushed her out of the room after which she locked the door, and shouted through the door, "I'm going to kill myself; tell your dirty father to go downstairs. I'll kill myself, I'll do it: I can't stand it any longer."

"Mother, Mother," called Louie.

Ernie had come upstairs and now rushed to the door and beat on it, crying out, "Mother, don't, don't, please."

Henny was silent. Louie sobbed brokenheartedly against the door, and Ernie seemed to have lost his wits. He sank to her feet and blubbered there.

"She won't do it," said Sam nervously.

They heard the children whimpering downstairs, and Sam with a gesture sent Louie down to them, but she clung to the door, "No, no, Mother, don't!"

Suddenly, they heard the bolt being drawn: Henny stood there with chalk-white face, her great eyeholes, coal-black, "Get out of here, you lot of howlers, leave me alone."

"Henny," said Sam; but at that she screamed in such a fury, "If you speak another word to me in your life, I'll slit my throat the same minute," that they all retreated, leaving her again behind the bolted door.

There she stayed for hours. Louie, creeping breathlessly up the stairs, avoiding the creaking boards as well as she could, heard the tearing of papers stop and Henny call out, "Who's that spying on me now?" and then would ask feebly, "Can I get you a cup of tea, Mother?" until Henny at last answered, "Yes, I'll take a phenacetin: this headache is killing me."

Louie saw her mother at last. Henny was dressed, as if to go to town, but only snarled when Louie showed her surprise. There was a smell of fire at which Sam bolted upstairs to thunder on the door and ask (without response) what Henny was doing; and at last, Henny came downstairs with her hat on, an old red hat, left over from the previous summer. At once Sam barred her way, asked her where she was going, if she was coming back to her home again, and particularly ordered her not to show herself in the streets, looking like a hag of eighty in that skittish little hat. Then he snatched it from her head. At once Louie ran up, full of indignation, calling upon Ernie to defend his mother, but Ernie was too overwhelmed to know how or when to defend her. As she at last ran jerkily down the avenue, in a black hat, sobbing and trying to fix the collar of her blouse, Ernie ran after her with a very pale, working face, to ask if she was going to come home again.

"I don't know," she replied stonily.

"Won't I ever see you again?"

"I don't know."

"Where are you going?"

"I don't know."

"Mother," he burst out crying, buried his face in her waist, "are you going to kill the children?"

"Don't be a fool; I'll leave that to your father."

"You won't give me my money back, Mother?"

"Do you think I have any money, you poor wretch? I don't know if I have any. Perhaps I'll have to beg on the streets to get my train fare;

perhaps I'll have to go on my knees to Jim Lomasne to get a dollar; perhaps I'll have to scrub a floor first for his wife. Where do you think money comes from? I'll never be able to pay you any money in your life, Ernie, and you may as well get used to the idea now. I'm broke, so dead broke that I don't know where to turn; I'm out of my mind, Ernie, and don't pay any attention to what Mother says."

"You won't pay me," he said, hanging on to the stuff of her dress, "Mother, you owe me so much, five dollars and eighty-nine cents. I can't save it up any more, we're so poor."

"You poor wretch," she said, bursting into tears, "you poor sniveling little kid: why do you have to get into my messes? Well, it makes me feel so rotten—go on, go away, go back."

"Are you going to beg for money, Mother?"

"Yes," she cried impatiently, "yes, yes, I am: I'm going down in the dirt. Now, leave me alone. Go back and tell Louie to give you something to eat."

She forced him away at last and in great trembling herself made her way along the street. Ernie and Louie watched for a long time but did not see her cross the bridge. Louie was afraid she had gone to drown herself.

However, late that night, Henny did return, and no sooner was she in the house than Sam, fresh and angry, began a great scene asking where she had been; but to this he got no response. The children were asleep, but not so Louie. She was afraid that the man and woman would kill each other: yet the quarrel dragged on, with its long tedious conversations and spurts of drama, all through the night. She would hear Henny drinking tea, or Sam drinking coffee; each would retire to a separate room, but would come out again, to rage again, first one, then the second, as if they could never have enough of this rage.

"I look awful," thought Louie, "and it is because I have no decent home; and the children are all getting sulky-looking too, except

Evie, and she's going to be browbeaten for life. They're too cowardly
to separate. If I killed them both we would be free. The only thing
is, I don't want to go to jail, I must get through school and go on the
stage, so I have to go to dramatic school. All this quarreling and
crying is just ruining my face for the stage too. I'm pretty stupid
though, clumsy that is, and I'd be sure to make a mess of things, if I
killed them with a knife. There would be the fingerprints and blood
marks; I know myself, I'd never get rid of them, and I'd be sure to
give myself away after. The thing to do is to do something that is
sure but looks like an accident. Poison! Permanganate, the thing
that girl killed herself with when Uncle Barry left her with a baby,
that's no good; carbolic acid neither, because of the pain and the
length of time. There is that cyanide, but it's so quick—"

She paused for a while to wonder about the cyanide, frightened
of it because it seemed too simple and quick. She went on to think
that if the cyanide worked she would then have a houseful of
children on her hands, have to explain things: "How did it happen?"
"I don't know; I wasn't there!" "Where were you?" "In bed: Mother
was making the morning tea." (Absurd! How could she slip down
unobserved, and slip upstairs into bed again, and yet be sure that
none of the children got the cyanide?) No, "How did it happen?" "I
was making the tea, and saw Mother slip something into the cup
but thought it was; for her headache." (Absurd! The children would
recognize the cyanide bottle, and she certainly would.) No.

Louie puzzled about this until her head ached. Then she began to
worry about the children. First: Ernie would go to the grandmother,
Evie and the twins, for a short time to Aunt Hassie, Tommy to Aunt
Eleanor, and Hazel Grey in Charles-town would take the baby. She
would go to Harpers Ferry, or Auntie Jo's, or Miss Aiden's, preferably
the last, to finish her education. She must be very careful about
her attitude—let it be sullen, stupid, she had better say she had
been badly beaten the night before and did not remember much:

"They were always quarreling." Louie saw herself in court and began to sweat, for surely the lawyers smart as foxes would see through her transparent lies, her miserable devices. "But then," thought Louie, "I am still a schoolgirl—my confusion will be put down to trouble: who will suspect me?" Then she thought that perhaps a lot of people thought she was a very wicked, lying child, believing Henny's tales (what she believed to be Henny's tales), and that the finger of suspicion would veer to her in no time. She could not sleep but, after tossing for a long time in her bed, got up and sat by the window, thinking this thing over. Only one thing was certain: it must be done, to save the children. "Who cares for them but me?" she thought coldly. "Those two selfish, passionate people, terrible as gods in their eternal married hate, do not care for them; Mother herself threatened to kill them. Perhaps she would: at any rate, their life will be a ruin even if they are allowed to go on living. There is no question of it: I have the will, I must have the firmness to get rid of the two parents." She no longer thought of Sam as her father: she had not thought of him as anything but a mouthy jailer for months; as for Henny, she did not see how her fate would be better if she went on living. Louie had doubts of herself that made her sweat cold again. She had brought so little to fruit in her life: she sometimes thought she had dementia praecox, and at other times thought she was a terrifying genius, and at other times again thought she was one of those pitiful sham-talents which glitter in youth and dance in maturity and are malicious apes, sometimes suicides later on in the dread arctic of age, around forty.

Now she thought of these three possibilities and turned from one to the other like a weathercock; but it was only because she doubted her ability to do the deed and fool people afterwards. She never once doubted that the right thing to do was to use cyanide tomorrow morning, or that she must liberate the children: it fell to her, no one else would do it or understand the causes as she did. Then she would at once be free herself. She made up her mind to do it at last. She planned the few simple motions necessary to get the cyanide, take out a little (with gloves on), put it in a small pillbox that she had in her drawer (no, false move—in a pillbox she would take from Henny's drawer tomorrow morning or next time Henny went down in this infernal night), and so on. Let the rest take care of itself, thought Louie: "I am sure to cry, that will help me out a lot: they won't question a child deprived of its parents in a morning, and there will be the children to get breakfast for." She saw, with free lungs and a regularly beating heart, that this was the right thing to do: she should have done it before but had not had the insight nor the will. Everything was will: "The world stands aside to let the man pass who knows whither he is going!" Louie fell into a light refreshing sleep but woke up soon after, and was able to steal into Henny's room to get the pillbox, during one of Henny's trips downstairs. The quarrel raged again. This she did with perfect ease, and even pushed her self-assurance so far as to go downstairs where the unhappy pair were and noticed that her mother was eating one of her nervous meals—tea, almost black, with toast and mustard pickles.

"What are you wandering about for, looking like a boiled owl?" Henny demanded harshly. Louie looked at her for a while calmly, thinking, "Perhaps I won't see her alive again"; and then she turned, humping her shoulders as she passed her father, not even looking at him, her flesh revolting at his nearness. He said nothing to her, but when she was on the stairs, she heard Henny snarl, "Why don't you go to bed: you see the children can't sleep? Are you going to stay up all night to pick on me?" Louie heard her father creak heavily into a chair. "Yes," thought Louie, "I won't have any peace with their squabbles."

5 *Monday morning.*

Henny slept very little, in a restless rage, and got up at five to sort the washing. The fish smell had by this time seeped into everything in the lower house, it seemed: and Henny hung over the basket, cursing like a fishwife indeed. An electric storm threatened again. Henny always hated them and felt ready for a fight before them; but this was the sort of weather that suited Louie best—she always felt lithe, vigorous, and calm before a storm. The weather had been electric for some time, the skies unusual, and the winds various. They all felt certain by their own animal symptoms of the approach of big weather. The sky was barred with cloud, and the trees were uneasy. Sam felt qualmish, with a slight fever this morning, and lay late in bed, calling to the children to get up, and to Evie to come and stroke his head. It reminded him of Singapore. He kept the Venetian blind down and in a weak, sick voice kept making his little jokes, calling his syce, wishing, with all its faults, that for a moment he were back in dear old Singapura. "A man should travel," he told Evie suddenly: "home deadens a man's wits: I'm a better man away from home"—but scarcely were these words out of his mouth than he regretted them, dark treachery to his home, his native land, and his loved ones!

"Looloo," he called, feebly. "Dotta det up, Loogoobrious: maka da tea."

She woke up and thought at once, "This is the morning, and I slept late!" She put on her dressing gown, took the little box, and with a stern strut went downstairs, not replying to the few remarks addressed to her on the way. She thought, "This is the hour: soon it will be all over." She put on the kettle, began to arrange the cups fussily, making a noise about it, when there were yet some cups to get down, slipped into the boys' room, which opened on to the kitchen, and into the darkroom. The boys were both up. Ernie had left a pile of clothes, his pajamas, perhaps, ready for the wash, through the bars of the bottom of his bed, but there was no one in the room. But her hand trembled, and she was only just putting some grains of cyanide into the box when she heard a noise and saw Henny in the kitchen.

"What are you messing in there for at this time of the morning when we're all so late?" called Henny. "Give me a cup of tea before I pass out. Every rotten thing in the place is alive with his fish oil; I'm nearly going mad with headache."

With a scarlet blush that covered her entire body, Louie came out of the darkroom, but Henny did not see her—she was already bustling back to the washhouse with a pile of kitchen towels. "God," thought Louie (the first time she ever used that word), "Oh, God, I nearly was caught." Her heart began to beat so heavily that she could hardly stand. She was now afraid that she would never have the strength to do it, with her blood beating so madly. She made the tea in a convulsion of trembling, and when it was made, a nausea of fear and doubt came over her—was she doing the right thing? To settle it, she slid the grains of cyanide all into one large breakfast cup, holding the box through her apron meanwhile, blew the grains off her apron into the cup, and threw the box into the garbage pail. At this moment she heard her father thumping cheerfully downstairs and talking to Evie. "I can never do it," thought Louie and turned round, to back up against the table on which the cup stood. There stood Henny.

"My womb is tearing," said Henny, holding her body, "with the weight of the great lolloping sheets. I am in such agonies that I don't know how to bear it. How can this go on another week? He takes no notice; I know my insides are torn to pieces—" She stopped and examined Louie, "What are you staring at me like that for? What is the matter with me? Don't stare at me!" Louie had lost all power of speech. Henny now recollected something, "What did you do? I saw you doing something!" Louie opened her mouth but only like a fish taking in air: she was struck dumb. She pointed to her mouth, the cup, shook her head. At this moment, Sam came into the kitchen, bringing with him the little carved wooden chest in which were the six tiny cups made from carved wood and lined with soft silver.

"Daforno," said Sam, gently ignoring Henny, "daforno, we is going to hev our tea in poor Lai Wan Hoe's beautiful little gift to his god-master—no, he had too much brains to think I was a god." He planted the little chest tenderly on the pine table and, pointing to the big cups, said "Frow dat out, Looloo, we goin to hev Chinese tea daforno: it's so hot I reckon we ought always to have it, anyhow."

Louie looked from one to the other, waiting for what she could not imagine to open before her; but she was unable to speak a word: she just shook her head to them, to herself. Henny, with blazing black eyes, was looking wildly at the child; she raised her hand and pointed at her but said nothing. Then she said slowly, "You beast, you pair of beasts, my womb is torn to pieces with you—the oil is everywhere and your dirty sheets falling on to me to suffocate me with the sweat, I can't stand it any more—she's not to blame, she's got guts, she was going to do it—she's not to blame, if she were to go stark staring mad—your daughter is out of her mind—" Sam looked at Henny with hatred. "All right," said Henny, "damn you all!"

She snatched the cup and drank it off quickly, a look of horror filling her as if she would have stopped herself but could not arrest the motion. She made a few steps with the cup, while Sam said, very puzzled, "What is this? What is going on?" Louie tried to explain but could only shake her head: even in her mind she could not think of any words. At the outer door of the kitchen leading to the glassed-in porch, Henny stopped, turned round, and then fell straight towards them, to her full length along the new cement floor.

This time Sam was shocked, for Henny had fallen face forwards and met the pavement with a heavy crack. The cup smashed. Louie still stood staring, with rather an amiable expression (for she was trying to say something), at her father, mother, and Evie. Evie had already run for the cushions and was trying to stick them under her mother's head; and, for once, Sam helped her. He said anxiously, "I think Mothering is rather badly hurt, we must get her to bed."

Louie came forward, and Sam, taking her quietness for disobedience, frowned at her but said nothing. He called Ernie but couldn't get any of the boys. They staggered with her to the boys' room and laid her on Ernie's bed. Sam kept whistling for the boys, and now they heard the cries coming running, "Yippo! Yippills! Yes, Pad!"

Henny's forehead and nose were bruised and cut. "Get some water and peroxide," said Sam irritably, "you ought to know what to do."

Louie gave a deep sigh and said slowly, with a clogged tongue, "Whatever is this?" She tried to pull the bundle of Ernie's clothes off the bottom of the bedstead. He had stuffed two dirty pillowcases inside his pajamas; two corners of one protruded from the top like ears. The funny little shawl that Louie had knitted for Tommy, yellow wool with a face in red wool, and that Tommy took to bed for a comforter, had been fixed over this end of the pillow slips to make a face. A piece of string round "the neck" attached this manikin to the bed. She pulled at the knot.

"Get the water and a sponge," said Sam irritably.

Louie left the manikin and started to the door, but there she stopped and said, "I think she's dead."

"Don't be a goat."

"I think she's dead, Dad."

"'Dead, Dad, Dead Dad,'" he said: "go and do what you're told."

Louie turned round, saying in a deep rebellious tone, "What's the use? You'd better call a doctor, or you'll be in trouble."

Sam was astonished at this, and, pulling Henny's sleeve, said gently, "Henny? Henny? Pet?" He said to Evie, who looked worried, "I think Mothering's got concussion."

Louie returned with the little basin of water, which she put down beside the bed on a chair littered with boys' clothes. The children, who had stayed outside, to hear from her about their mother's accident, now came peeping, tiptoeing round the door, like birds creeping back to spy on a motionless man in a clearing. Tommy laughed suddenly, a laugh clear as summer river babble, "Look, there's Ermy!" Ernie frowned. Tommy giggled, "Ermy hanged himself: he jacked himself up." He pointed to the thing hanging on the bottom of the bed. "Look, he-he, he took my shawl for his face." Sam's face browned with its flush, "What are you talking about, you dope?" Tommy suppressed his laugh, "That's Ermy. He said he hanged himself!" Sam's eyes wandered back anxiously to Henny. Louie was bending over her listening; she got up, with unmoving face, "You see, you listen! Her heart isn't beating." Sam started with an expression of terror, and bent over. He jumped back, "First aid, kids, clear out! Get the doctor, Louie." Louie half smiled, "I told you she was dead."

Ernie rushed past the knot of children and threw himself on his mother, pulling at the bosom of her dressing gown, disarranging it wildly, screaming, "Mother, Mother, you aren't dead? Is she dead? Is she dead? She isn't dead!" He began to moan, saying, "Mother" and a moan. The children stood stricken in the doorway. Sam, after a queer movement of his chin, looking round as it were for help on all sides, strode through and over the huddled children and rushed to the telephone. Louie patiently came up and began sponging the forehead. "Let me do it," said Ernie excitedly, and he began pasting away at the forehead, thinking that was a way to cure her. The children began to break down, each in his own way, and Chappy, sitting on the porch, who had just been bitten by an ant, began to yell for assistance. They heard Sam talking into the telephone, and then his quick tread. He began to question them, "What was Mother doing?" And the scene he had witnessed came to his mind: "What were you and Mother quarreling about?"

"Nothing," said Louie, "only the dirty clothes; then Mother said she would take poison, and she drank a cup of tea full of cyanide."

Sam thundered, "What?"

"She had it in a little pillbox," faltered Louie; "she threw it in the garbage can!"

Sam rushed to the photographic chamber. They heard him running out verifying, saying aloud, "This is terrible! Oh, God, what a terrible thing! I never thought she meant it. God above, Louie, Louie!"

Tommy came out with great round black eyes, Henny's eyes, and, tiptoeing up to his raging father, whispered, "Pad, will we go to school today?"

At this moment, the front-door bell rang. Louie, thinking it was the doctor, ran to open the door and saw standing there a middle-aged woman, with streaky black hair, a puffy, good-natured face, and brown eyes, in a go-to-meeting straw hat and a speckled silk dress. She looked at her for a minute without recognition and then saw it was Tommy's teacher, Miss Wilson. Miss Wilson seemed embarrassed but said stiffly, "Is your mother in?"

"No," said Louie, "that is—she's sick."

"I'm sorry," said the woman stiffly, "I tried to get her yesterday on the phone and Saturday too, but either she wasn't in all the week end, or she wouldn't answer me. It's very important."

"What is it? What is it?" cried Sam testily, "What is it? You must go away. There has been a dreadful accident."

"I'm Miss Wilson, Tommy's teacher," said the woman. "I'm at the school; I wanted to see Mrs. Pollit about the money."

Sam looked confused, and the woman had to keep on explaining to him how important it was, that it was urgent about the money.

"Money, what money?" Sam asked confusedly again.

"It's the money: the piano's no good to me," said the woman, anxiously. "What can I do with a grand piano? I let her give me that security. I'm sorry if she's sick. I really am. I know she's a good woman. I like Mrs. Pollit. I respect her. But it's just now, I've got to pay some things, my taxes were so high—"

Sam said, "Mrs. Wilson, will you come back? Mrs. Pollit has had a bad accident. I don't know if she will live," and he sobbed.

"Oh," cried the woman, "Oh! Oh, no! Oh, I didn't mean—oh, about the money. I'll manage somehow—but when can I come to see you? I wouldn't trouble her for the world, only—" Suddenly she began to cry too and asked for a glass of water, so that they had to take her into the common room while the children began to gather slowly round her; and, between crying and drinking her water, and wiping her eyes, she gabbled some story about lending Henny one hundred dollars at six per cent, against the grand piano, though she knew you could hardly sell such things nowadays when the rage was for little pianos: but that as Henny was the sister-in-law of Miss Josephine Pollit, such a splendid woman, and Mr. Pollit too, everyone knew him, but now she found out that Mrs. Pollit had borrowed too from the teacher of the twins and from Ernie's teacher, and she had been to the high school and taken fifteen dollars for clothing from Louie's teacher, and now she heard that Mr. Lomasne, that horrible man, a dreadful usurer who lent fifty dollars and then you owed him money for the rest of your life, and she didn't know what else, and she was afraid she would never see her money again. She was a poor woman. She didn't grudge Mrs. Pollit the money—she was a good woman, a wife and mother, but she had to have it: she had a mother to keep herself and an old father—she sobbed and sobbed till she became inarticulate.

At this moment, the doctor arrived. Miss Wilson waited passionately to hear what was the matter with Mrs. Pollit and when she heard that she was dead, she let out a dreadful cry and threw her arms round Tommy, calling him her "poor dear little darling, how dreadful for the baby!" At last she went, but at the door she stopped and asked Louie, very low and ashamed, if she thought she would get her money. "I'm so ashamed, dear, but I'm a poor woman myself, and I'm getting on," she said. Then she nodded and walked away with a tottering gait, till she got to the avenue and was lost to view.

Louie turned back to give the children some breakfast.

6 *Truth never believed.*

It was three weeks since what remained of Henrietta Pollit, after the disgrace of a coroner's inquest, had gone into the earth; that earth was the Collyer plot in Greenmount Cemetery. A strange company of jackals, smelling each other, had slunk, or strutted before the coroner—Jim Lomasne and a busy, neat little downtown usurer, the manager of an auto loan company, and good-looking, respectable little Archie Lessinum, and even Henny's sisters, Auntie Jo, Louie, Sam, Miss Wilson, and Miss Aiden, and it had come out that the meek, sweet-smiling, unassertive Henrietta had been a bundle of sordid secrets, from life's end to life's end, had not only stripped herself naked to pay the household bills and the usurious interests which had mounted and mounted from the time she had had Ernie, but had begged and cadged from every member of her family, from domestic suppliers, the children's teachers, and all sorts of strangers, to all telling her story of the children's needs.

Where had it all gone? people asked: but Archie Lessinum found that no mystery—where had the Collyer estate gone? he asked. With twelve children to rear and of those, some to marry and many incapacitated sons (incapacitated by temperament) to keep, and their families after them, the good-natured, self-made merchant David Collyer had had no difficulty in dissipating a great estate. What was left was held in spendthrift trust for his sons and daughters, all but Hassie (a trustee) financial ne'er-do-weels. The estate needed repairs, had second mortgages to pay off; old Ellen Collyer had to be kept; and only after her death, and at the time when the estate became self-supporting again, would it begin to pay out dividends to the many sons and daughters or their heirs. Now, each of them had numerous heirs, Henny being no different from any other Collyer in this, Hassie and Eleanor alone being exceptions. The money due to Ernie and the other children of Henrietta, when the dividends began to come in, would be very little: but as they were young minors, this money, for the time being, would be applied to paying off Henny's large debts. But Henny had begun owing money from the time she was married. She had contracted debts before many times, but these had always been paid by her indulgent father. These debts had been kept secret from her husband, whose puritan wrath she feared, though not from her money-wise family; and, lacking his firm hand, she had run on and on, until at the last she had come into the hands of despicable, predatory usurers like James Lomasne, who lent without papers and collected through blackmail.

All one could say of Lomasne was that he had a peculiar reputation for an honest man: Lomasne, on the other hand, said, with great assurance and an appearance of charitable respectability, that he had lent money indeed to his neighbor Mrs. Pollit, but only because he liked the children and he knew she was in need—and he ventured to make some remarks upon the character of Samuel C. Pollit which revolted everyone. His honesty was shown by his having signed no papers with Mrs. Pollit and having never demanded any interest. She paid him back when she could—but so little had she paid him back that there was still owing to him a sum of five hundred fifty dollars. He had lent this money, too, he said, because Mr. Pollit had told him he would go into his boat-and-coffin business: and he regarded this money lent to Mrs. Pollit more in the light of an investment, and then, they were friends and neighbors, and Mr. Pollit took an exceeding interest in his little girl, "Fairy," as in all other little girls of the neighborhood.

True, the world was all ears and eyes for Sam's misfortune, but Sam bore it with noble dignity, for now at least people knew what he had borne all these years. But as to where the money had gone, he was as innocent as a babe, he told the creditors later on: it was like lightning opening the ground at his feet, and now, to a certain extent, he could understand some of the rages of the unfortunate, guilty, but miserable woman. She had been harassed by the bloodhounds of debt; their tongues had been belling in her brain, their maws opening at her shins, their hell-breath mixing with her breath all these years. Yes, if she had only confided in him, he would have been able to deny publicly his responsibility and so take possibility of credit away from her, or he would have been able to rein her in, save her from this criminal recklessness. For she knew, he said sadly, to Jo, alas! she knew only too well what money waste was: it was in the blood. She knew better than he, but she was a foolish, weak, silly woman with a taste for extravagance and no means of gratifying it. Where did the money go? They must not ask him. His salary would have been ample for a sensible woman, and he should have known better than to marry a rich girl with no idea of a planned economy.

Now, he proposed a five-year-plan for his creditors: he refused to let one borrowed cent go round the world in ragged trousers with his name to it—he would pay back everything. He had no money. They saw in him a penniless man, whose good name had been torn from his back by the wickedness of the world, but he would win his way back, make a new world for his children, and pay back all the money that the wretched creature had borrowed. There was not even any sense to all this waste: it was mere pointless ruin, for the money had gone to buy clothes and food that would have been paid for out of his salary if his salary had not been eaten up secretly by the loan sharks and bloodsucking usurers against whom he had no recourse, since their procedures were illegal. He walked back to Spa House a beaten man, with his pockets out and his name mud-spattered, true, said he; but what did he care for slander and name-slinging? In five years he would have paid off all, and his children would be prouder than ever of their father's honor; his truth crushed to earth would rise again, fresher from her mud bath.

For a few weeks they remembered Henny. They would hear her footsteps in the hall, in her bedroom upstairs; Louie would hear her in the kitchen making tea or poking the fire on a few Mondays, out in the washhouse. Streams of visitors came, mostly women, to look after the motherless children, so horribly orphaned, and to help out the fourteen-year-old girl who now would be "a little mother to them all" (as no one failed to remark): they helped with the cooking, put the children to bed, even scrubbed and washed, neighbors, aunts, cousins alike, and Sam's men friends, who had secreted themselves for years in their dugouts in Baltimore and Washington, began to roll down in cars or on shanks' ponies and hold long commiserating confabs with him. The world had changed entirely. Aunt Hassie had a quarrel with Aunt Eleanor about who should take Chappy for a few weeks, until Sam got a housekeeper. Aunt Hassie won, and the anemic Cathy, who up till now had played with her platoon of dolls, now had a human doll to take care of. She got some color in her cheeks and even put on a little flesh round the waist, and Hassie began to think that it would be a good idea if she, Hassie, adopted Chappy and let Cathy get married to some good man who could bring her up firmly.

The friendly folk who came down gave the children small pieces of money and one day, after quite a party of them had gone, Ernie found a five-dollar bill in the grass. He could hardly believe his good luck, but went round in silence for several hours, at the end of which he took the money to his father and said glumly, that he supposed one of the visitors had dropped it. Sam, however, who had in the meantime inquired into Ernie's finances (needing money himself), told Ernie rather gruffly that he could keep it until its claimant turned up. Its claimant never turned up, and this led Ernie into several heartening thoughts about the possibility of money's dropping from heaven upon the place beneath. He made up his mind to leave school as soon as possible and go out into that world in which five-dollar bills nested in double-lined pockets, and yet where so little care was taken of such charming nestlings that no one noticed them when they flapped off clumsily on their own account.

When the guests went each day, then was the time that the image of Henny started to roam, and also in the early mornings, before Sam started to whistle them up and also just after. The window curtains flapped, the boards creaked, a mouse ran, and Henny was there, muttering softly to herself, tapping a saucepan, turning on the gas. The children were not frightened. They would say, laughing, somewhat curious, "I thought I heard Mothering," and only Evie or Tommy ("that little kissing-bug who is always mugging me," as Henny had said) would look a bit downcast; and perhaps Chappy missed her, that queer, gypsy-like, thin, tanned, pointed face with big black eyes rolling above him which, with its regular white teeth, had looked for, begged for his smiles, had tickled him into smiles, and hugged him just under its chin, when he smiled. But Chappy was away learning to punch playfully the large bosom of Hassie, and already his ideas of faces were confused.

For days Louie would not think of her, having too much to do. It was the summer vacation, and the entire work of the house, outside washing day, fell on Louie and Evie, with occasional help from the boys. Sometimes women came and helped, sometimes Sam would do the dishes; and not only was there so much to do, but the boys and Sam grumbled bitterly about the food, their beds, and so on. Not all would grumble at once. Ernie would come sweetly to them with that touching dependence on them that women laugh at but cultivate in their husbands, and ask, with melancholy, about his buttons or his socks; or Tommy would come, rather timidly, to show a large hole just "come somehow" in his shirt, or bathing trunks would have to be mended before they were "arrested by the society for indecency." This period was hard for them, but it was in many ways sweet, too. Sam told them that soon they would have someone to help them. He thought that someone might be Bonniferous.

Yes, Bonniferous had run away from Auntie Jo's in rebellion, hate, and anger, saying dreadful things, saying she was going to get her baby somehow, find it wherever they had stuck it, even if it was underground, and bury it herself, or if it was living, make a living for it herself, "any way, any way at all" (and when they repeated this, the women would lower their voices and look at each other). But Sam had already been several times to the police to ask them to look for Bonnie and to look for her baby too, for perhaps one was with the other. He liked the police: they were good, decent fellows, helping people in misery, keeping order, punishing only crime, and friendly enough if one approached them in the right spirit as man to man, not calling them names (for they were only workers like him and his friends), but jollying them, being kind to them. And these kind men liked him, too. The Commissioner himself had put himself out to help Sam; so that now Sam had every hope of soon seeing his favorite sister again. He had spoken very severely, in the midst of his sorrow, to the frightened and contrite Jo. Jo showed her contrition in the usual way, by gobbling, quarreling, and blaming everyone but herself; but she was contrite, said Sam, and she would show it: she would be kind to Bonnie, she had promised it. She would make clothes for the lost little baby born beyond the pale.

So the little girl struggled on from day to day, hoping to hear about Bonniferous and, in the meantime, getting the house into a mess much worse than ever poor Henny had got it in. Sam was puzzled by all this, and was heard, at least once a day, to wonder how on earth he had got into "sich a passel of uncompetent shemailes": when Bonniferous came back to them, with her little baby, he would have to "organize them shemailes, and all would run like clockwork under scientific management." Life was noisy, busy, and full of speculations, and so Louie had little time to think about the strange day when Henny died.

But sometimes, when she least expected it, she would think about it: the terror of it, and her secret complicity would seem so naked to the sky that she would break out into an icy sweat and wonder that no one could hear what was going on in her brain. She would never tell anyone, and this was as a corpse sealed up in the house which she alone knew of and which would eventually molder and leave little trace, until the mindless years, with the vague gesture of an idiot, brought it unaccusingly to light. This was a terror she could live with. But she lived a queer life, and the noises, cries, philosophies of others seemed like silly games that kindergarten children play. She was on the other side of a fence; there was a garden through the chinks that she had once been in, but could never be in again. Yet she did not care. She still believed that she had done the only right thing, the only firm thing, and that Fate itself had not only justified her but saved her from consequences. It annoyed her only to hear Sam talking about Henny's rash act, dreadful deed, and shameful self-ruin, folly next to wickedness and mindless self-destruction, and the long, long talks he had with one and another about the whole thing. "What do you know?" she would think. She soon reached a point when she could not sit at the table with him and listen to his misbegotten notions and morality with its mistaken examples. When they were served, she would take her own plate and go with it to sit on the front lawn, or down the orchard, and no matter how many messages were sent to her to come in and join the family, she would obstinately and even mutely sit there, self-righteous, proud, and contemptuous.

The tempests of July and the swamped earth and flooded rivers had come to wash away the sorrows of Henny: headstones sank in the graveyard, and the new earth piled over her fell in. Towards the end of July it was as if Henny too had stormed, but in another room in the universe, which was now under lock and key.

On Monday the twenty-fifth, the heavy rain having at last stopped, Sam went into Baltimore to talk about a favorite project of his. Many friends had urged him to try to get on to a radio program, and they thought either foreign affairs or the children's hour would suit him, but he himself thought of himself as "Uncle Sam," and for some time had discussed his "Uncle Sam" with friends, journalists (whom he highly respected as a communicating medium between recondite truth and the truth-hungry mob), and "responsible" people with whom he was intimate. Sam was no bootlicker of people in high place: he so honestly admired them, and so wholeheartedly believed that capacity is always rewarded by "the people" in the shape of high place that his love for them was a pure thing. Sam had been doing the rounds of the elect of the people, for some time, and saw "Uncle Sam" as "an eventuality of the immediate future." On his Uncle Sam Hour, he would tell not only folk tales that had been handed down from our forefathers, things devised in their frontier nights after hand-to-hand battles with hardship, and distorted stories brought over from crooked old Europe, but also tales of our revolutionary past, high deeds of stern men and brave women whereby we won the freedom we have, such freedom that, thank Heaven, there is no need to go through again the turmoil that now confronts poor bonded Europe. He would lead them by the hand down the highways of the world and the bypaths of Nature and teach them all her secrets, even as Hiawatha learned them.

Sam had no difficulty in interesting advertisers, and these were days of great hope for him: at last he had found his function. He had told his children and friends for many years that the radio was the great new medium of spreading enlightenment—radio and the movies. He wished that he knew the directors of M.G.M. and

Warner Brothers, for they must be good men, since they catered to the people, and he had the same dear wish about Franklin D. Roosevelt and Stephen S. Wise. They made mistakes, he felt, but after a short talk with them, they would become his friends, and he could give them ideas, put them more intimately in touch with the people, a thing for which they lived. He had always said that though, no doubt, Jesus Christ never existed, the idea of "the second coming" was a touching illustration of mankind's wish for uplift and regeneration; and that if a real savior ever came, he would come over the radio. Perhaps, he, Samuel Clemens Pollit, was a forerunner of the truly great man. At any rate he would begin by touching the heart of the little world, the Lilliputians. Far from despising the advertisers of radio programs, he liked them, he thought them wonderfully humane people because, instead of merely broadcasting crude publicity, they wished to entertain and educate the people.

After a most satisfactory talk with a sponsor, Sam took a walk this Monday down South Eutaw Street, between Lexington and Mulberry Streets, to look in the pet shops, and then turned up Mulberry Street to go to the library. Coming towards him was a touching young mother, with long silver-gilt hair, and a baby in her arms. Sam's heart jumped, his eyes misgave him, and then he saw that it really was Bonnie. He rushed to her and took her into his arms.

"Oh, Bonniferous! Bonniferous! Why didn't you come to your poor brother? Bonniferous! Where are you? Everyone has been looking for you. Did you know Henny died? I am all alone, Bonniferous."

Sam wept openly, and Bonnie wept openly, and then the baby (which was a boy and which Bonnie was quite sure was her baby) wept openly, and as he had the great lust for weeping in him, he outdid them, and insisted upon attention to himself alone. Sam was for taking Bonnie home at once, but Bonnie had to get her things and give notice at the place where she worked and—

"And see the man?" inquired Sam, in a sad voice.

"Oh!" cried Bonnie, "I'll never look at him again if I live to be a hundred."

Then Sam wanted to know if the boy was to be without a father, and Bonnie said better no father than such a wretch; and Sam said, in that case, he would be its father—what difference would another little fellow make in his great phalanstery of sons down at Spa House? He was getting two jobs, both in the public service (later on he would be a biologist)—his own children were growing up, and Bonnie could look after the house for him and save him the expense of a housekeeper: and he would protect her. Perhaps later on, she would find a good man—Mr. Right, this time, not Mr. Wrong. He saw Bonnie to her room, kissed his new nephew (whom she had called "Samuel-Charles"), and went galloping home, singing to himself. He could hardly wait to get home, burst into the house, and tell them all the wonderful news: they had a new brother, Samuel-Charles (yes, another Sam, Little-Sam), and he would soon be Uncle Sam on his own Hour, he thought. "All things work together for the good of him that loves the Truth," said the train to him as it rattled down towards the Severn, "all things—work—together—for the good—of him—that loves—the TRUTH!" Even Henny's death had worked for him: even Henny's debts, for now he had got a new sphere of influence, and friends had rallied round him in an altogether unexpected way. "It is—lovely—to be loved!" said the train to him. "It is splendid—to be—loved! If we only—can—live up—to the thoughts—of us—by them—that love us!"

When he got home, there were jobs to do. The house could never run without him. The icebox had broken down; and he rejoiced in his handyman's skill as he showed them the wherefore and how easy it was to fix it with a little *knowledge*. At dinnertime, he showed them how to fry the fish in a new oil he had brought from town—it made an exceeding stench, but who cared?—now that querulous poor Mothering was not here to smell it. Then gently he chid the girls for this and that, a floor not washed, a dirty window, and over the dinner table (he insisted on Louie's being present this time and ignored the sullen, brutish face she put on, as she sat there mute in Henny's place) he told them the details of his new home economy. There would be three shemailes for the interior—Bonnie, Louie, and Evie, and all the horsework, the donkeywork, would be done by his great tribe of men. Charles-Franklin, Chappy (little Megalops was coming home, he said, with a faint droop of the eyes that they did not comprehend), and the new Charles, Samuel-Charles, a wonderful little boy with a great blond head full of brains and bright salty eyes, very observant, although only five weeks old, sure to be something exceptional; and he told them there was a superstition about boys born like Samuel-Charles, though he could not tell it to them till they grew up. Now, he said, nothing lacked, nothing at all: it only remained for Louie to cheer up, bear a hand, and stand there as his lieutenant when he piped all hands on deck.

After dinner, he took Louie for a long walk, round by the great house in its seedy grounds, by the unspeakable ruin of the Negro village, which had suffered so much in these storms, and by the slimy, rotting cove where the carcasses of old boats were, and spoke out all his heart to her—what the future would mean for him and her, if only she would stick to him and be happy.

"The same old story," muttered Louie at last.

Sam shot her a troubled glance. "Looloo, now that poor Henny has left us, so awfully, so mistakenly, but gone, I thought a weight would be lifted off your shoulders. A young girl should bloom like a peach tree, but you are sullen, like a tree that will not bloom."

They were both silent for a while. At last, out of her terrible gloom, Louie said quietly, "One night you were quarreling all night:

I was standing up there next to the box I had from my mother, that redwood box full of pieces and patches."

"I know," said Sam, sympathetically, "with the little bit of blue dress she wore the day I proposed, and the little blue dress you wore when she died, and your baby shawl."

"It was a very oppressive night," said Louie, "and I saw a tree wave, like a shoal of fish that suddenly darts aside after they have been drifting in the water. Then I thought I saw an eagle dash itself against my window. Then I thought I would kill both of you."

"Looloo!"

She took no notice of him, except that a very tiny smile crept round her mouth, the first, in his company, in many weeks. "I am telling the truth: I never lie. Why should I lie? Those who lie are afraid of something."

"Pull yourself together: what is the matter with you? I don't understand you."

She smiled more, "You never will." She chuckled, "You never will either. Thank goodness. But it is true—I got some cyanide out of your darkroom and put it in a pillbox, you know that pillbox—I got it out of Mother's room the night before, and I meant to put it in both cups, but I lost my nerve, I suppose; I didn't quite know what I was doing, I only put it in one cup. I got frightened." She became sober, depressed.

"Looloo! Be quiet! I won't allow this incredible absurdity to go on."

"Then you came in with the cups—but before that, Mother came in, and I think she saw me. Anyhow, she seemed to know: then she didn't say anything except what she said then, 'I don't blame her, you can't blame her, she's not to blame if she were to go stark staring mad'—she meant, it was just the same, that anyone would have. Then she took it: she couldn't stand it any more."

"Looloo! 'Couldn't stand it any more!' You don't know that I had to stand everything. The tyranny of tears: one person bears, and the other person cries and shrieks, and everyone—even you, even you—sympathize with her. And you make up this incredible, insane, neurotic story. For it is neurotic. I thought you had self-control. And you make up the damnedest, stupidest, most melodramatic lie I ever heard in all my born days. You talk about the truth. You don't know what truth is. The truth isn't in you, only some horrible stupid mess of fantasies mixed up with things I can't even think about. What happened to you? Henny ruined you. I have got to take you away from school and keep you at home with me until you recover. You are not yourself."

"You don't notice anything. Everything has to be what you say," said Louie. "For instance, Ernie was so unhappy at that time, right on that morning, that he tried to hang himself."

"What do you mean?"

"You remember—we took mother in, to his bed?"

"I know."

"On the bottom of the bed was that doll he had rigged up. It was himself. The children told us, don't you remember: it was Ernie. Ernie hung himself. He made a doll. How do you know he mightn't have done it really?"

"Child's play, horseplay," he said roughly. "That only goes to show how far out of your senses you are, Looloo, that in a little joke like that you see melodrama. I am going to take you away from all this foolery, this drama and poetry and nonsense they are putting into your head. You haven't a good brain at all—you are just crammed with the most idiotic nonsense I ever heard of in my life. It has got to end. You are coming home to me, and I am going to watch every book you read, every thought you have."

"All right! All right! You remember when you used to take me to see the Lincoln Memorial, walking along the Reflecting Pool from your office on Saturdays. I learned from him, not from you. You used to say your heart always beat when you were going towards it; my heart used to beat, but you always thought about yourself. When I was at Harpers Ferry, I only thought about John Brown. I always thought Israel Baken was just like him—my grandfather. Not a Pollit, thank goodness, not one of you."

"That mean old vicious superstitious man!" Sam ejaculated. "Yes, you are like him, I am sorry to say. Your mother had none of that."

"What do you know about my mother? She was a woman. I found a letter from her in the old redwood box. Someone who died sent it back to her when they knew they were dying. It was just after you were married. She said, 'Samuel is a very young man. I am very sick or I would not be writing such foolish things, I am sure. But he does not understand women or children. He is such a good young man, he is too good to understand people at all.'"

Sam said dreamily, "Yes, I was a very good young man. I never allowed a breath of scandal or of foolish small talk to be spoken in my presence; and your mother understood me. She was ready to sacrifice everything for me. Perhaps she loved me even better than I loved her. But I was very young: I did not see things as I see them now. She loved you too dearly, 'little Ducky,' as she called you. It is a pity you never had a mother."

"Well, I'm my own mother," Louie said, without emotion. "And I can look after myself. I want you to let me go away. You can't want me to live in the house with you after what I was going to do."

"If you think I believe that cock-and-bull nonsense you made up out of your soft, addled melodramatic bean," he said with rough good humor, "you have another thunk coming, my girl. You are going to stay here with me until you get out of this stupid adolescent crisis, and that's all there is to it."

"Then you don't believe me?"

"Of course not. Do you think I'm going to be taken in by a silly girl's fancies? You must think me a nitwit, Looloo, after all." He laughed and put his arm on her shoulder, "Foolish, poor little Looloo."

She shook him off and said nothing. Sam went on talking to her gently, chidingly, lovingly. When they reached home, she made him another cup of coffee and went upstairs. Out of the old redwood box she took an old-fashioned bag made of grass and raffia, and embroidered in beads by her mother, at one time. Into this she put a few clothes and a dollar bill that one of the visitors had given her after Henny's death. She hardly slept at all, but when she heard Sam begin his whistling early the next morning, she got up and dressed quickly and quietly. She heard the warm, old, jolly, pulsating home life beginning its round: "Little-Womey, *Philohela minor!* Git up, git up!" It was only six o'clock, and the boys were still drowsily groaning and rubbing their heads on their pillows. She heard Evie grumbling in her bed and dragging herself out of it and Sam thumping on the wall: "You, Gemini, hey, you Navel Academy, what's about your early-morning swim?" She expertly got downstairs and to the kitchen with her satchel. Once there, she banged the kettle about to sound as if she were making the tea, and heard Evie's grumble, "Looloo's making it," and, taking some food out of the icebox (she was always hungry), she ran out of the house and in no time was screened by the trees and bushes of the avenue. She smiled, felt light as a dolphin undulating through the waves, one of those beautiful, large, sleek marine mammals that plunged and wallowed, with their clever eyes. As she crossed the bridge (looking back and seeing none of the Navel Academy as yet on their little beach, or scrambling down the sodden bluff), she heaved a great breath. How different everything looked, like the morning of the world, that hour before all other hours which Thoreau speaks of, that most matinal hour. "Why didn't I run away before?" she wondered. She wondered why everyone didn't run away. Things certainly looked different: they were no longer part of herself but objects that she could freely consider without prejudice.

In a few minutes, she reached Clare's little cottage and saw Clare walking about in her nightdress, down the passage. Clare came to the door, seeing her, with big eyes, and half whispered, "I say, where are you going?"

"I'm going to Harpers Ferry. I'm going to my Auntie Jo's to get some money, and then I'm going out there; won't you come along?" Clare stared at her longingly, but Louie could tell from her hesitation that she was going to refuse. "You won't come, too?"

"Oh, Louie! Oh, Louie! Oh, Louie!"

"You won't come?"

"I can't."

"Why not?"

"I just can't. I don't know why not. I have my little sister."

"I suppose, if I had any decency," said Louie slowly, "I'd think of my little sister and brothers, but there's Auntie Bonnie. No, there are plenty of them. Well—good-by."

"Are you really going?"

"Yes, of course."

"You're all right," said Clare.

"Why don't you come, Clare? What is the good of staying here?"

"I can't, Louie, I can't."

"All right." Louie turned about and went down the path till she got to the gate, then she looked back. Clare had come to the front door. A milkman was coming down the street. Louie lingered, "I'll write you a letter when I get there."

"You send me your address, and I'll write to you."

It was this that was final: Louie's last hope went then. "Well," said Louie, going out of the gate, "I won't see Miss Aiden any more, will I?"

"What will she say?" asked Clare. "Well, anyhow, I suppose, you'll come back for school."

"Will I?" cried Louie, awaking from a doleful mood, "will I? No, I won't. I'll never come back."

Clare sniffed, and Louie saw that she was crying. Louie looked at her stupidly and, humping one shoulder, began to walk away.

"Good-by, Louie!"

"Good-by!" She walked away without looking back, feeling cheated and dull. Clare did not really think she should go. She walked across the market space and into Main Street, looking into a little coffee shop and wondering if she would have a cup of coffee. She had never been in there, because it was like a fishermen's hangout, dingy and dubious. But no, she walked on. Everyone looked strange. Everyone had an outline, and brilliant, solid colors. Louie was surprised and realized that when you run away, everything is at once very different. Perhaps she would get on well enough. She imagined the hubbub now at Spa House, as they discovered that she was not bursting up the stairs with their morning tea. They would look everywhere and conclude that she had gone for a walk. "So I have," she thought, smiling secretly, "I have gone for a walk round the world." She pictured Ernie, Evie, the twins, darling Tommy, who loved the girls already and loved her, too; but as for going back towards Spa House, she never even thought of it. Spa House was on the other side of the bridge.

About the author

CHRISTINA STEAD (1902–1983) was born in Sydney but lived for most of her life outside Australia. She wrote fifteen novels and several volumes of short stories. Her most praised fiction, *The Man Who Loved Children*, was first published in 1940. In it, she transposed the experiences of her childhood in Australia to Depression-era America. The book has been hailed as a masterpiece by Randall Jarrell, Jonathan Franzen, Jane Smiley and many other writers.

More from Apollo

THE LOST EUROPEANS
Emanuel Litvinoff

> *Coming back was worse, much worse, than Martin Stone had anticipated.*
> *When he got into the boat train at Liverpool Street, with English newspa-*
> *pers and periodicals stuffed under his arm, the usual drizzle falling from*
> *the grimy London sky, he'd told himself this was just a business trip...*

When Martin Stone returns to Berlin after the war, he knows his
homecoming will be a painful one. For he is a Jew, and he is back
to seek restitution of his family's fortunes. First published in 1958
after Litvinoff's own visit to the city, *The Lost Europeans* portrays
a vibrant, flourishing Berlin, underlaid with an ever-present sense
of sin and rot.

BOSNIAN CHRONICLE
Ivo Andrić

> *For as long as anyone could remember, the little café known as 'Lutvo's'*
> *has stood at the far end of the Travnik bazaar, below the shady, clamorous*
> *source of the 'Rushing Brook'.*

First published in 1945, this sweeping saga from the Nobel prize-
winning Ivo Andrić looks at life in Bosnia under Napoleonic rule.
Set in the remote town of Travnik, two rival consuls are caught
up in the ceaseless game of diplomacy. This Tolstoyan epic tells us
more about the Balkans than a dozen history books.

NOW IN NOVEMBER
Josephine Johnson

*Now in November I can see our years as a whole. This autumn is like both
an end and a beginning to our lives, and those days which seemed confused
with the blur of all things too near and too familiar are clear and strange
now.*

This Pulitzer Prize-winning first novel tells the story of a ruined city
family who take on the lease of a farm somewhere in the American
Midwest. The work is backbreaking and the isolation punishing. In
the tenth year, a young man from a neighbouring farm comes to
work with them, upsetting the fragile balance of their lives. And in
the summer of that year, the rains fail to come.

MY SON, MY SON
Howard Spring

*I liked fetching the washing from the Moscrops', and my mother liked wash-
ing for Mrs. Moscrop better than for anybody else. That was because Mrs.
Moscrop always wrapped a bar of yellow soap in with the washing. There
wasn't anyone else who thought of a thing like that.*

First published in 1937, Spring's powerful novel tells the story of two
hard-driven, determined men, one a celebrated English novelist
and the other a successful Irish entrepreneur, and their sons, in
whom are invested all the love, ambition and hope that fathers can
imagine. Oliver Essex and Rory O'Riordan grow up as friends, but
their father's lofty plans threaten to have disastrous consequences
as events in Ireland spiral out of control.

DELTA WEDDING
Eudora Welty

The nickname of the train was the Yellow Dog. Its real name was the Yazoo-Delta. It was a mixed train. The day was the 10th of September, 1923–afternoon. Laura McRaven, who was nine years old, was on her first journey alone.

A vivid portrait of a large Southern family, set in the Mississippi Delta in 1923, from one of the twentieth century's greatest American writers. The story is exquisitely woven from the ordinary events of family life, centred around the visit of a young relative, Laura McRaven, to the family plantation as they prepare for her cousin Dabney's wedding.

THE AUTHENTIC DEATH OF HENDRY JONES
Charles Neider

Nowadays, I understand, the tourists come for miles to see Hendry Jones' grave out on the Punta del Diablo and to debate whether his bones are there or not; and some of them claim his trigger finger is not there, and others his skull; and some insist the spot is no grave, that it's just a little mound of abalone shells.

This stark and violent depiction of one of America's most alluring folk heroes, Billy the Kid, is set on the coast of California. Doc Baker, the Kid's former sidekick, narrates his tale of a gunslinging youngster's capture, trial, escape and eventual murder. Written in spare and subtle prose, this is one of the great literary treatments of America's obsession with the rule of the gun and of murderous vengeance.

THE DAY OF JUDGMENT
Salvatore Satta

> *At precisely nine o'clock, as he did every evening, Don Sebastiano Sanna*
> *Carboni pushed back his armchair, carefully folded the newspaper which*
> *he had read through to the very last line, tidied up the little things on his*
> *desk, and prepared to go down to the ground floor...*

Immediately hailed on publication as a classic of Italian and world literature, *The Day of Judgment* is a beautiful meditation on what a life really means. Around the turn of the twentieth century, in the isolated Sardinian town of Nuoro, the aristocratic notary Don Sebastiano Sanna reflects on his life, his family's history and the fortunes of this provincial backwater where he has lived out his days.